The Underwood and Flinch Chronicles

Volume I

- RESURRECTION -

Volume II
- BONDED IN BLOOD -

CW01499195

MIKE BENNETT

Underwood and Flinch

I would like to thank the following friends and cohorts: Pauline McGrath, Jason Andrews, M.J. Hahn, Kerry Heron, Rachel Sinnamon, the podcast listeners of Planet U&F, and especially ...

The Patrons of Underwood and Flinch

This book was made possible by the generous contributions of the following wonderful people to the 2012 Underwood and Flinch fundraising campaign at Indiegogo.com.

This book is dedicated to them with my deepest thanks.

The Black Circle

Pons and Melissa Matal, Joel Palmer, Daniel Price, Dale Bennett, Brandon Foster, Benjamin Tovar, Mitchel Bynum, Matthew Bushong, John R. Orr, Steve Bown, Michael Bowers, Florence Wall, Paco Marquez.

The Sect Members

Alan Lee, Robert Pinter, Jeffrey C. Claytor, Dan Shaurette, David Rogers,Laura Faichney, Chess Griffin, David Goodwin, Seth Wolfson, Kcith Hunt, Rocheen Maclean, Martin Heron, Kate Matthews, Monday Matlock, Lord Revell, Ben Wright, Terry Bailey, Michael Graham, Elizabeth Mast, Dave A. Alcock, Chris Hurst, John Mcleish, Rick L . Abbott, Craig Large, Ieva Klava, Steve, Nick Robinson, Mark "Woof" Brown, Luke Race, Marcella Tapp, Jason Vion, Cathi Iuliano.

The Fang-Tastic!

Ann Smith, Jon Cape, Stephanie Price, Jeffrey Crane, Mark Bailey, John Noonan, Steve Hyland, Darren Ledgerwood, Tara and David Haroon, Linda Mendes, Kym Durham, David Heyes, Scott Thompson, Martin Reindl, William Campsey, Jake Kozak, Stephanie Crosskey, Thomas Reed, Maryanne Torgerson, Mandy Lancaster, Jude Cuddy, Stefan Moody, Michael Micklethwaite, Justin Elsdon, Nanna Bjerre Larsen, Magnus Lonberg Carlsen, Maia Olsen, Richard Wodehouse, Nima Aleagha, Michael Metz, Suzanne Holt, Gonzalo Gonzalez, Tom Lytle, Larry Horne, John & Mindy Milfelt, Kameron Dodson, Dawn Wancura, Elliot Gould, Nancy Stevenson.

The Stake Holders

Alison Benowitz, Heather Brady, Keith Burnage, David Fisk, Dave Wangrow, Dr Jon Durrant, Andrew Rothman, Mick Everett, Karl Jones, Mark Wiard, Brendon King, David Dean, Dave Mallon, John Lingard, Shane Alonso, Gavin Armit, Craig Bristol, Nelline Henning, Daryl Miller, Patrick Jones, Kerry Heron, Paul Bull, Adam and Jo Roxby, Dillard Hayes, Mr S.R.Hart, Eric Neff, Tracy Smith, Karen Lind, David Campbell, Paul Warren, Sandra Allan, Shaun Curry, Mark Dales, Roy Murphy, Stephen Ormsby, Stephanie Gagnon, Amanda B. Larssen, Tony Robinson, Denise Romero, Garry Ogle, Mika Eloranta, Angela Sorrey, Katharine Parke, Richard Hart, Natasha Webb, Nick Nilsen, Rebecca Stacey & Darren Jarvis, Tracey Storer, Adam Carter, Paul Hurst, M Domanko, Sophie Barwick, Jason Andrews, Uli Scheuss, Alexander Dietrich, Colin Lawton, Steve Loxdale, Alan Smith, Lisa Burke, Jeremy Opsahl, Yuhri Miller, Eric Husen, Tena Kolakowski, Rich Girardi, Mike Dunham, Melissa Mosier, Joseph Carson, Ryan Caesar-Brown, Gerard Griesbaum III, Mike Sandidge, Wan Park, Andrew Hunter, Pamela Culpepper, Nancy Paris.

The Jolly Rogers

Teri Humphries, William Hill, Amy Olshever, Jeremy Avery, Robbie Keene, Brent Boyd.

The Blood Donors

Steve Bickle, Daniel Perdue, Emma Hastings, Chris Pragman, Joshua Arnold Durham, William Berry, Dan Johnson, Karen Walters, Ryan Waldon, Andrew Richardson, KT Smith, Dean Baratta, Matthew Lunde, Mark L Berry, Mark Horrocks, Veronii Giguere, Shevaun O'Neill, Stephen Pountney, Leonardo, Schlongasaurus, Stephanie Newland, Andrea Dixon, Jerry DeMario, Jamie Bennett, Simon Rishton, Elizabeth Johnson, Steve, Christina Nelson, Alison Kilgour, Hilary Jones, Gerard McCann, Nathaniel Kajumba, Neil Hutchings, Erica Turner, C2012, John Pitchford, Paul Anderson, Si UrenSibongo, Joe Schweinzger, Rudy Toledo, Brad Bucholtz, J. Alexander Greenwood, Jennifer Marzetta, David Haupt, Kelly Stouffer, Jeff Turro.

The Candle Bearers

Ken Wieland, Damien Smith, Debbie Neff, Simon, Dennis C. Nolasco, Simon Cowlard, Nicole McGarrigle, Quinn Kurenda.

My profound thanks to you all. This book is for you.

Mike Bennett, Sussex. January 2014.

Prologue I: Night Crossing

ON A CHILL NIGHT in the spring of 1958, the cargo ship *Glenmalloch* sounded its foghorn as it had done every ten minutes for the last twelve hours and edged slowly onward through mist towards Spain. The ship had left the Algerian port of Oran the previous morning carrying a cargo of fresh fruit, dates and tobacco; it also carried seven passengers, the majority of whom were in their cabins getting ready for dinner. However, two passengers stood alone at the stern. The men were dressed in formal black suits. The taller man appeared to be in his late thirties, while the shorter, who also wore a black overcoat, looked about ten years older. There was an attitude of stoical regret about both men, as if misfortune had recently come to visit and was now reluctant to leave.

'I'm so sorry, Lord Underwood,' said the shorter man as he extended his hands to take the body of the cat.

Underwood handed him the corpse and sighed. 'Never mind, Flinch. I know you did all you could. Let's just forget about it, shall we?'

'I know you're not fond of – '

'Really Flinch, forget it,' Underwood drew his watch from his waistcoat pocket and flipped it open. The second hand wasn't moving and he tapped gently at the scratched face. The hand began to move. He smiled. 'What time do you have, Flinch?'

Flinch dropped the cat over the side of the ship and checked his wristwatch. 'It's just after eight-thirty, sir.'

'Hmm,' Underwood adjusted his watch, wound it and put it back in his pocket. 'And what's our current speed? Any idea?'

'Five knots, sir.'

'Five knots?'

Underwood looked over the side and down at the sea. The ship's slow-churning wake confirmed Flinch's report.

'It's the fog, sir. A necessary precaution, I'm told.'

Underwood ran a finger along the hand rail and looked up at the single red and black funnel as the fog horn again sounded its low, two-note warning. 'I see. So what does that make our estimated time of arrival?'

1

'We should reach Malaga in about two hours, sir.'

'Oh damn. I'd hoped we'd be there by now.'

'Yes, sir. It is regrettable.'

'Oh well, never mind, eh?' Underwood began to reach for his cigarette case when he noticed the blood on his hands. 'Oh, dear. Do you have a hanky or something, Flinch?'

Flinch pulled a white handkerchief from the breast pocket of his jacket and passed it to his master without a word.

'Thank you.' Underwood wiped the blood from his hands and then inspected the soiled handkerchief. 'Sorry, Flinch,' he handed it back. 'I'll get you a replacement when we reach port.'

'Very kind, sir,' said Flinch, folding the handkerchief in such a way as to conceal the bloodstains before popping it back into his pocket.

Underwood reached into the inside pocket of his jacket and took out his silver cigarette case. 'Fag?'

'Oh, don't mind if I do, sir.' Flinch accepted one of the proffered cigarettes and took out his lighter. He extended the flame to Underwood, who leaned forward to meet it.

For a moment, the flame illuminated a pale, handsome face, though one with an impression of being somewhat undernourished; the cheeks were sunken beneath high, sharp cheekbones. His hair was dark, parted from the left and fashionably slick with Brylcreem that shone in the light from Flinch's flame.

His cigarette lit, Underwood stepped back. Flinch lit his own cigarette and slipped the lighter back into his pocket. 'Everything go all right with the car?' Underwood asked. 'I didn't really notice earlier on.'

'Everything's fine, sir. It's lashed securely to the cargo hatch. Not that there's much chance of it rolling around the deck in this weather.'

'No indeed. What about the other things? How's the move going?'

'All very well, sir. Most of it is, as you know, coming by sea in the next few months. Until then, we'll have to make do with what's already in the house.'

'You mean *you'll* have to make do, such things are hardly my concern.'

'No, sir.' There was a note of regret in Flinch's voice and he looked down at his shoes. He noticed a spot of blood on his left toecap and he took out the already-stained handkerchief and bent to wipe it off. He gave the shoe a brief, cursory polish before rising again with an air of complete composure.

'Don't worry, Arthur,' said Underwood, smiling. 'It's got everything you could possibly need. You've been in touch with señor Hernandez?'

'Yes, sir. His handwriting is a little cryptic, or perhaps just his turn of phrase, but he reports everything is ready and awaiting your arrival. Other members of the Sect are making themselves very useful in the area. Besides Hernandez in Ronda, we have señor Lago, a notary in Almacena itself, and a retired couple who are going to be helping out around the house and estate.'

'Good show.' Underwood took a drag on his cigarette. Then his eyes narrowed as, over Flinch's shoulder, he noticed a figure in the shadows further down deck. 'I say, have you noticed anything queer about any of the other passengers?'

Flinch frowned. 'No sir.'

'No one asking any questions?'

'No. Might I ask why, sir?'

Underwood watched as the figure, perhaps sensing he had been seen, receded into the mist. 'Don't look now, Arthur, but I think we're being watched.'

'Watched, sir?'

'Yes. Chap about twenty yards behind you, wearing a bowler hat.'

Flinch nodded slowly. 'I think I know the fellow, sir. I caught his eye once or twice this afternoon.'

'No contact though?'

'No, sir. Not a sausage.'

'Hmmm, I see.'

'Is he still there, sir?'

'No, he's gone.'

Flinch turned to look but there was nothing other than the mist. He reached into his pocket and a second later the blade of his flick-knife snapped open. 'Shall I ask to see his ticket, my Lord? Perhaps punch it?'

'That won't be necessary, Flinch. They'll be serving dinner soon and I'm sure you'd rather murder a nice steamed steak pudding, hmm?'

'I'm not overly hungry, sir. I ate a most satisfying luncheon.'

'Did you, indeed? Well, I'm famished. So, why don't you toddle off now and get yourself ready for dinner, okay?'

'But what about the snooper, sir?'

Underwood smiled. 'Oh, don't concern yourself with him. I think I might seek him out myself. Perhaps he'd like to join me for dinner?'

Flinch nodded and closed the blade of his knife. 'Right you are then, sir.' He bowed slightly before turning and walking off in the direction of his cabin.

Underwood watched him go, and then rubbed his hands briskly together. The mist was chill and damp and he wished he'd had Flinch bring him along a warm coat. Still, he'd soon warm up. He slipped his hands into his trouser pockets and struck out in the direction in which he'd seen their observer skulk off a few minutes earlier.

His search was brief; as he turned the corner, he almost ran straight into him. The man started and Underwood held up his hands in apology. 'Oh. I do beg your pardon. I was just out for a vigorous stroll around the deck. I didn't expect anyone else to be about; it's such a dismal evening.'

The man in the bowler hat laughed nervously. 'Oh well, no harm done.' He made as if to continue, but Underwood laid a hand on his arm.

'I say, pardon me, but have we met before somewhere?'

The man frowned. 'I don't think so.'

'You're English, aren't you?'

'Well, yes, but, er ...'

Underwood smiled. 'I know, England's not exactly a goldfish bowl, is it? But I was just thinking perhaps we'd met in Algeria. You know, ex-pats, small communities?'

'I'm sorry, I'm not an ex-pat.'

'Oh, really?'

'Yes, I'm afraid you're mistaken. Good evening.' The man again attempted to walk away.

'So, are you here on business or pleasure?'

The man stopped and turned back. 'If you must know, I'm travelling on business.'

'Ahhh, I thought as much,' Underwood chuckled. 'I do hope you don't mind me being so forward, but as soon as I saw the bowler I thought, ah, there's a fellow Englishman.'

'Really? Well, congratulations.'

'Thank you. May I ask what business you're in?'

'Carpets.'

'Oh? How interesting.'

'Not really. Now if you'll excuse me, I'm late for dinner.' The man turned and walked on.

'I mean,' Underwood persisted, walking after him. 'It's interesting because I thought you may be something else. A detective perhaps.'

The man stopped. He answered without turning. 'Oh?'

'Yes. I wondered if perhaps you might be following my companion and I?'

The man turned and looked back. He frowned. 'Whatever gave you that idea?'

'Oh, I don't know, just the way you were watching us earlier on. I thought perhaps you might be a sleuth of some sort, perhaps from Scotland Yard.'

The man smiled uncertainly. 'You have a vivid imagination, sir.'

'Yes, I do.' Underwood strolled up to the man and extended his hand. 'My name's Underwood.'

The man looked at the hand for a moment before taking it. 'Jenkins. Harry Jenkins.'

'Of the Yard?'

'No, nothing so grand, Mr Underwood.'

'It's Lord Underwood, actually. Sorry, I should have mentioned that earlier. I keep forgetting; you've no idea who I am.'

Jenkins raised his eyebrows. 'Oh, a Lord, eh? I didn't notice a Lord on the passenger manifest.'

'Really, Mr Jenkins? Why were you looking at the passenger manifest?'

'I, er, I always like to know who I'm travelling with. It pays to know.'

'Oh yes, always on the lookout for a potential carpet sale eh?' Underwood took out his cigarettes and opened the case to Jenkins. 'Fag?'

'Thank you.' Jenkins took one and reached into his coat pocket for a box of matches. 'So, er, as I was saying, your Lordship. It's strange, you not being on the passenger manifest. I'd have thought you'd have been at the top of the list, being a member of the aristocracy and all.' He struck a match and cupped it for Underwood.

'I like to keep a low profile when I'm travelling, Mr Jenkins,' Underwood lit his cigarette. 'I asked for my name to be kept off the list and the shipping company obliged. The captain and crew are well aware of my being here.'

'I see. So, no red carpet treatment for you when you came aboard then?'

'No.'

'But they must have given you some kind of a welcome, surely?'

'Of course.'

'They did? Oh. It's just that I didn't see you come aboard, sir. I saw your friend alright, the undertaker chap, and I watched as they winched that hearse of his aboard. But I didn't see you anywhere.'

'Ah, so you are watching us, then, Mr Jenkins.'

Jenkins chuckled. 'Well, a hearse swinging in a net isn't exactly everyday cargo, your Lordship. A number of us were watching it, not just me.'

'Yes. Yes, I suppose it is a little unusual.'

Jenkins nodded. For a few moments the two men stood silently smoking; regarding each other like chess players with cool aplomb. Then Jenkins dropped his cigarette and ground it out underfoot. 'Well, I think I'd better be getting along, your Lordship. I don't want to be late for dinner. Nice to meet you and er, thank you for the cigarette.' Jenkins touched the brim of his hat and turned.

'Yes. Nice to meet you too, Mr Jenkins.' Underwood watched the other man walk for a moment before flicking his cigarette away and calling out. 'Oh, Mr Jenkins?'

With an air of annoyance, Jenkins stopped and turned back. 'Yes?'

Underwood took a step towards him, moving into a pool of light from an overhead bulb. His sunken face fell into the shadow of his brow, yet his eyes shone, reflecting light from some unseen source. 'Come here.' His tone was casual, but firm.

Jenkins swayed slightly with the gentle motion of the ship, his eyes held by Underwood's. Then he walked slowly back to where he was bidden. When he stood face to face with Underwood, he stopped.

'What is your business?' asked Underwood.

'I'm a detective.' Jenkins' tone was flat, devoid of emotion.

'A police detective?'

'No. I'm self-employed.'

'Who hired you?'

'Mr and Mrs Haverlay, of Knightsbridge, London.'

'Why?'

'Their daughter was murdered in Oran by an Englishman, believed to be a gentleman or perhaps a confidence trickster posing as a member of the aristocracy.'

'And you believe me to be this man?'

'Yes.'

'Do you have any evidence to support your belief?'

'Some people have described you, named you as being a likely suspect.'

'But nothing more concrete?'

'No. Not relating to Miss Haverlay. But I have since linked you to other murders in Algeria and Tunisia.'

'Have you now?'

'Yes.'

'And you suspect me of being – what? A homicidal maniac, is that it?'

'Yes.'

'And have you shared your suspicions with anyone else?'

'No. I'm waiting to catch you in the act.'

'Are you, indeed? And then what, you'll come to the rescue I suppose?'

'Yes. I'll arrest you.'

Underwood smiled. 'Really? Are you armed? You'd better be.'

'I have a pistol.'

'Show me.'

Jenkins opened his raincoat and revealed a revolver in a shoulder holster.

'Well, well, you're quite the man of action, aren't you Jenkins?'

'Yes. I was a commando in the war.'

'It was a rhetorical question, Jenkins, I don't want to hear your life story. Tell me – and this is a real question – which is your cabin?'

'Cabin 14.'

'Sharing?'

'No.'

'Very good. Why don't you take me there and offer me a little something to drink before dinner?'

'I don't have anything to offer you. I don't drink alcohol.'

'Really, Jenkins,' said Underwood taking the detective lightly by the arm, 'who said anything about alcohol?'

Underwood opened Jenkins' cabin door and flicked on the light. He looked around then beckoned Jenkins to follow him inside. Once the detective was in, Underwood closed the door and locked it. It was a small room with two bunk beds fixed to the wall. The top one was undisturbed but the one beneath had been slept in. There was also a chair and a table. On the table was a briefcase, an ashtray and various papers. A single porthole looked out over the sea. To the right was a door. Underwood opened it and found a tiny shower room with a washbasin, a toilet and a shower stall. He turned back to Jenkins. 'Take off your hat, coat and shoulder holster and gun and put them on the bed there.'

Jenkins did as he was instructed.

'Now roll up your sleeves.'

Jenkins obeyed.

Underwood turned on the light in the shower room. He motioned for Jenkins to enter. 'In here, please.'

Jenkins stepped past Underwood and into the room. There was only enough space for one person to stand at a time.

'Get into the shower stall.'

Jenkins did as he was told.

Underwood inspected the items around the washbasin. He saw what he was looking for. The safety razor was slippery with soap scum and Underwood grimaced. 'Oh dear, you really ought to rinse this out more thoroughly, Jenkins. You know you could get an infection if you were to cut yourself with this?' He turned on the hot tap and rinsed the razor under the slow gurgle of water, washing away the soap and beard detritus before carefully unscrewing the head and removing the blade. He held the razor blade up between his finger and thumb. 'Hmm, looks a bit old. Obviously detective work isn't paying too well, eh Jenkins?'

'I – ' Jenkins began slowly.

Underwood cut him off. 'Oh, it's alright old chap, just another of those silly rhetorical questions of mine.' He looked to where Jenkins was standing facing the wall of the shower. 'Turn around, will you?'

Jenkins turned around.

'Now, sit down.'

The detective sat in the shower tray, his legs protruding out onto the floor and his trousers riding up his ankles to expose gartered black socks.

'Are you right or left handed?'

'Right-handed,' said Jenkins.

'Okay,' Underwood handed him the razor blade. 'Take this and open the veins across your left wrist.'

Jenkins took the blade, pressed it against the pale underside of his left wrist and then, without hesitation, drew it slowly across, slicing down, deep into the flesh. Blood erupted around his fingers. Jenkins, his face impassive, continued to draw the blade until it fell away from the wound. Then he looked back to Underwood for further instruction.

Underwood reached out and took the bleeding arm. He held it so blood sprayed over the shower walls for a moment, then pushed the hand inwards against the wrist joint to staunch the spurting arteries. He then positioned himself on top of Jenkins' legs, leaned into the stall, and brought the wound to his mouth. He hesitated for a moment to smile at the detective, then, opening his mouth, he eased the man's hand back. Blood gushed into Underwood's mouth. He closed his lips about the wound and let the blood surge around his tongue. He parted his lips and let it spill over them as he savoured its taste, its heat, its richness before finally closing his eyes and beginning to drink.

He was hungrier than he had realised; the cat had done little more than appease the gnawing hunger within. And now, as the blood began to fill his stomach, he felt his strength returning. His dull headache began to disperse and clarity returned to his thoughts. He held Jenkins' arm a little more tightly around the wrist, lessening the flow for a moment before letting the flow again and then relaxed his grip, giving himself a second rush of blood.

Tempting as it was to play with his food until his victim was dead, Underwood knew there was still work to be done. He gasped as he tore the wound from his lips. Blood continued to pour and he again staunched the flow by pressing the hand in against the wrist. He looked at Jenkins, who was watching him with mild interest.

Underwood licked his lips. 'Now, Mr Jenkins, dip your finger into the blood and write, "Forgive Me", just there, on the shower wall.'

Jenkins, his movements weak and trembling, rubbed his finger in the blood that seeped down his arm, and began to write.

Underwood waited patiently. When Jenkins had written the *M* in "Me", he could wait no longer: he opened the wound and resumed drinking. He watched as Jenkins unsteadily continued to write, determined, it seemed, to complete his message before finally relaxing and letting his hand slide down the wall.

Underwood continued to drink until Jenkins' pulse was so weak as to signal the imminence of his death. Then, he relinquished his meal and lay the arm down beside the body so that the remaining blood would flow down into the drain. Then, feeling suitably sated, he stood up to examine the scene of the poor detective's apparent suicide. He smiled. If he did say so himself, it was a work of art. With an air of satisfaction, he wiped his chin on the back of his hand. 'Well, thank you for dinner, old boy. But now, I'm afraid I have to go. The ship docks presently and I have to be in my coffin and ready for the off.'

Whistling fragments of a Bing Crosby tune that had recently been haunting him, Underwood went to the basin and washed his hands and face with a small cake of soap. Afterwards, he had to clean the blood from both basin and soap as well. Once the area met with his satisfaction, he dried himself with the hand towel and neatly hung it back on the rail. Then, as he stepped over Jenkins, making sure that he wasn't trailing bloody footprints behind him, he said, 'As you so rightly observed, Mr Jenkins, I'm not on the passenger manifest. But, had you checked further, you would have noticed I am listed among the cargo... as deceased.'

Thirty minutes later, Flinch found his master at the bow of the ship, gazing towards the distant horizon. Without turning, Underwood said, 'Hullo, Flinch. How was dinner?'

'Very nice sir. Steamed steak pudding with peas and slightly lumpy mashed potato. And you?'

'Oh, a chap called Jenkins. Turns out he was a detective. But yes, very tasty.'

'A detective, sir? Should I be concerned?'

'No. Anything he had on us I bunged out of his porthole, along with his gun.'

'What about the body, sir? Do I need to do any cleaning up?'

'No, poor fellow made his own quietus.' Underwood smiled. 'At least, that's what it looks like.'

'Oh. Very good, sir.'

Flinch joined his master at the rail. Ahead of them the fog was thinning. A full moon shone like a smudged thumb print on the sky, its light reflecting on the surface of sea as if painting a silver path to their destination. Underwood pointed to a distant lighthouse that winked at them from the blackness. 'Look: land. It won't be long now. You must be quite excited, eh?'

Flinch tried to smile. 'I, er, I daresay life in Almacena will be very interesting, milord.'

Underwood looked at him. 'Is that all? I thought you'd be thrilled.'

'Well, yes, but,' Flinch looked down at his shoes, 'I just wish you'd reconsider, sir. I mean, it's not as though you'd be in any danger, not in Spain of all places.'

'It has nothing to do with danger, Arthur. It's more a matter of,' Underwood sighed. 'Exhaustion. What with the last war, that business in New York, the Suez affair. I need a rest, old man. Surely you can understand that?'

With a tight smile, Flinch nodded. 'Yes, sir.'

'I mean, it's a pity we couldn't be going to the United States, California perhaps, but we both know that's quite out of the question. And you say you've no desire to go to England, even if we could?'

'No, sir. The weather's so bloody grim. I'd like to see a bit of sunshine, you know?'

'Er, actually no, not really. But you're right, yes, you could do with a spot of sun; you look positively ghastly.'

Flinch chuckled. 'Well, it comes with the job, I'm afraid, sir.'

'Well, you'll soon be able to remedy that, eh?'

'Yes, sir.'

For a few moments they stood in silence. Then Underwood said. 'Shame about the ship's cat.'

'Yes sir.'

'Still, never mind, eh? I'm sure they'll find another one.'

'Oh, yes, sir. No shortage of cats in the world. Especially in ports. It's the rats that attract 'em.'

'Yes. Wherever there's a plentiful source of prey there's usually a predator.' Underwood took out his watch. It had stopped. He tapped the glass and the second hand began to move again. 'I say, Flinch. Do you have the right time?'

Flinch looked at his watch. 'Ten past ten, sir. Time we were getting ready, perhaps.'

'Yes,' Underwood looked to where the lights of Malaga now glittered on the horizon, 'though I think I'll have one last fag before I get back in the coffin.' He reached for his case.

'Oh no, sir,' said Flinch, 'My flash.' Flinch took out his packet of cigarettes and offered them to Underwood.

'Thank you, Flinch. What would I do without you?'

'You never need to worry about that, sir,' said Flinch, flicking on his lighter. 'Of that you can rest assured.'

Underwood accepted the light and both men turned to face the dark, oncoming land on the horizon. The first breaths of a warm wind drifted to them across the sea and Flinch sniffed. 'Do you fancy you can smell oranges on the breeze, sir?'

Underwood smiled. 'Sorry Flinch. But all I can smell is blood.'

Flinch chuckled. 'Oh, very good sir. Very droll.'

Prologue II: Spain

FLINCH LOOKED IN THE REAR VIEW MIRROR and saw headlights, their distant beams shimmering over the surface of the coffin behind him like moonlight on water. Then a third light, a blue one, began pulsing above the headlights, and the trill ringing of a siren started.

'We seem to have attracted the attention of the authorities, sir.'

For a moment there was no answer. Then a low, muffled voice came from the back of the hearse. 'Drive on, Flinch.'

'Very good, Your Lordship. Should I attempt evasive action?'

For a moment, besides the noise of the siren, the hearse was silent, then the lid of the coffin slid aside, and Underwood sat up and looked out of the back window. 'Where are we?'

'About thirty miles inland from Malaga, sir.'

Underwood looked around, out into the night. 'Not much chance of losing them in this countryside. What's all that, out there?'

'Olive groves.'

'Oh, how nice.'

'Perhaps I could attempt to outrun them?'

'No, don't bother, Flinch.' Underwood looked back at the pursuing vehicle then turned to address Flinch in the rear view mirror. 'Actually, I'm feeling rather peckish, and it's been so long since I had a drop of Spanish. What say we stop and see what they want? Do you have your gun?'

Flinch opened the glove compartment and took out his Luger. He slipped it under the black top hat beside him on the passenger seat. 'I do, sir.'

'Right,' Underwood lay back down in the coffin and settled himself. 'Pull over, Flinch. Tell them you're British; even Franco's fascist coppers should respect that and let you go about your business. And if they don't, well, they'll jolly well regret it, won't they?' He reached up and pulled the coffin lid closed on top of him.

'Yes, sir.' Flinch slowed the car and pulled over on the side of the road. He waited, watching as the lights of the pursuing car drew nearer. The siren fell silent and the car rolled to a halt behind them. Two figures got out. In the glow from his rear lights, Flinch recognised the distinctive tricorn hats of the Civil Guard. The men unbuttoned their holsters and drew their guns.

Flinch took his passport and travel documents from the glove compartment and wound down the driver's window. '*Hola, señor.*'

The guards paced around the hearse, eyeing it suspiciously. Then one of them barked a command in Spanish. '*Salga del coche!*'

'Sorry, *señor. No comprendo mucho Español.*'

From the coffin, Underwood spoke, his voice muffled by the lid. 'He wants you to get out, Flinch. Don't disappoint him. He sounds awfully miffed.'

Flinch opened the door and got out, his hands raised. 'Pardon me, *señors.*'

The guards looked at him as if he were something someone had carelessly trodden into their carpet. One of them – the taller of the two – reached out and gestured for Flinch to hand over his documents. Flinch did so. The guard inspected his passport. '*Inglés?* You no speak Spanish?'

'No, sir. I'm, er, here on business.'

'Oh? What is your business?'

Flinch cocked a thumb at the black Rolls Royce hearse beside him. 'I'm an undertaker. I've been hired to deliver the body of a Spanish gentleman to his family estate.'

'Undertaker?'

'Yes, dead people. My business, is, er … dead people.'

The guard smiled. 'My business too, sometimes.' He liked the joke and repeated it in Spanish for his friend.

The other guard chuckled and tried the handle of the hearse's rear door; it was locked. He spoke to Flinch in rapid Spanish. Flinch's face was a picture of bewilderment.

The tall guard translated the order. 'Open the car and take out the box.'

'But, *señor, por favor,* the casket is – ' Finch's protest was cut off by a backhanded blow across his face.

'Open the car, now!'

Flinch wiped his mouth. It came away dark with blood. He looked at the guard evenly for a moment before bowing his head. Then he reached in through the driver's door and took the keys from the ignition. He held up the keys to show them he wasn't holding a weapon then walked around to the back of the hearse and unlocked the single, heavy door. He pulled it open then stood back.

The guards looked in at what to them was an incredibly expensive coffin. 'Okay. Take out the box,' said the tall guard.

Flinch hesitated for a second then replied, 'Well, you'll have to help me, *señors*. It's very heavy.'

The guards exchanged a few words in Spanish then the shorter of the two went around to the opposite side of the coffin to Flinch and took one of the coffin handles. He motioned at Flinch to do likewise. Flinch obeyed. The tall guard took a few steps back and aimed his gun at Flinch's head.

The shorter guard looked at Flinch and nodded. '*Uno, dos, tres.*' They pulled and the coffin slid out, foot end first. When it was half way clear of the hearse, the shorter guard grunted an incomprehensible command and began to lower the coffin down to the ground. Flinch followed suit.

'Now, open it,' said the tall guard.

The moon found a break in the cloud and spilled silver-grey light over the scene. 'Really, *señors*, I can't imagine what you think I might be hiding in here, there's only a body – '

'Open the box!' the guard shouted, and pointed his pistol into Flinch's face.

Flinch bowed and then came around so his back was to the guards, both of whom were now aiming their guns at him. Flinch smiled, and then lifted the lid from the coffin.

The tall guard grimaced. Inside the coffin was the body of a man whom he estimated could have been aged anything between thirty and forty, it was difficult to tell when they had been dead for a while. The cheeks were sunken, as were the closed eyes, which were barely visible under the shadow of the man's brow, and the skin – typical of a cadaver – was the colour of white ash; it seemed almost to glow in the light of the moon. The guard admired the corpse's suit. It was expensive, black, and more or less his size.

Flinch cleared his throat. 'Gentlemen, may I present the late señor Underwood.'

The shorter guard stepped forward, aimed his pistol at the corpse's chest, and fired. The body rocked with the bullet's impact.

'Gentlemen! Please,' Flinch began to protest.

'You want to go into the box also?' snapped the tall guard.

Flinch raised his hands and lowered his head.

The short guard walked up to the coffin and began to feel the lapel of Underwood's suit. He said something in Spanish.

'*Si*,' the tall guard chuckled. He was about to add something when suddenly, the body in the coffin opened its eyes.

'Well, it *was* a nice suit,' said Underwood, grabbing the short guard by the shoulders. 'Until you went and put a bullet hole in it.'

The guard managed to utter a syllable of disbelief before Underwood yanked him forwards as if to embrace him. The guard struggled, hands flailing, trying to fight but unable to get a blow to connect due to the sides of the coffin.

'Stop!' shouted the tall guard, trying to get a clear shot. 'Stop, or – ' The order froze on his lips as Underwood suddenly sank his teeth into the short guard's neck.

The tall guard stepped back, away from his partner's screams. '*Dios mio!*' He fired a shot without thinking, and cried out when he saw it had hit his partner in the left shoulder blade. The bullet passed through the short guard and hit Underwood in the chest. Underwood's eyes flashed up to see the tall guard trying to aim at him with wildly trembling hands. Underwood fixed the guard with a stare, savouring his terror for a few moments before releasing him with a friendly wink. '*El diablo!*' The tall guard fired again, repeatedly, no longer caring whether he hit his partner or not, which was just as well, because he did. '*Lo siento, Carlos! Lo siento!*' He was about to fire again when Underwood raised his face from the still-pumping wound and shouted:

'Flinch! For God's sake, man! What am I paying you for?'

The tall guard had a clear shot at Underwood's head. He held his breath, aimed …

But then another gun fired. The tall guard's head snapped back as a bullet from Flinch's Luger hit him just above the right eye. He toppled over backwards, dead. 'Sorry sir,' said Flinch. 'I had to go around the front of the car to get my gun.'

'Yes, yes. Well, never mind.' Underwood resumed drinking.

'Shall I get you a cloth, sir?' said Flinch, walking around to the passenger door. 'We've no napkins of course, but I believe I may have a clean chamois somewhere.' He listened for a reply, but there was none, save the gurgle of blood in the throat of the dying guard. Flinch sighed and looked at his watch. He sat down in the passenger seat and took out his cigarettes. He lit one and pushed the door open wider so as to get a better view of the moonlit landscape. It was a lovely night, cloudy but warm. From behind him came the sound of a body falling to the road.

'Flinch?'

'Yes, sir?'

'Where's that cloth? I've got this bastard all over me.'

'Sorry, sir, I was just enjoying the night.'

Underwood came around the side of the hearse, the blood that covered his chin and clothes glistened black in the moonlight. 'Oh yes. Yes it is nice, isn't it? Still, time waits for no man, old chap. You've got to get going.'

Flinch got up and handed Underwood a cloth.

Underwood grimaced. 'That's dirty. Don't you have a clean one?'

'I'm sorry, sir, I haven't had a chance to do any washing these past few days.'

'Oh you *are* a clod, Flinch.' Underwood took the cloth and wiped his face and hands.

'Yes, sir. Very sorry, sir. Will you be getting back in the casket or driving up front with me?'

'Neither. I mean, look at me, Flinch; this suit's utterly ruined.' He ripped his shirt and waistcoat open and pointed to the bullet wounds on his chest. The black holes had stopped bleeding and already begun to heal. 'Look where that bloody fascist shot me.'

'Not a very nice welcome, sir.'

'No, indeed,' said Underwood, kicking off his shoes. He picked them up and inspected them. 'These are all right, though; nothing a spot of spit and polish won't take care of.' He handed them to Flinch.

'Yes sir, I'll have them looking as good as new before tomorrow evening.'

'Not that I'll be needing them tomorrow evening, but still, good show, Flinch.'

'Would you like me to take the suit, sir?'

'No, it's had it I'm afraid. It's soaked up more claret than your grandfather used to at Christmas.'

'Oh dear.'

Underwood removed his cufflinks, took out his cigarette case and lighter, and unhooked his watch from his waistcoat. He handed them all to Flinch. 'Here, take these, would you?'

'Of course, sir.' Flinch took them and put them in his jacket pocket.

'Now, are sure you know the way?'

'Yes, sir, I have a map and directions. '

'Good, I'm going to have to go on ahead. It'll be light soon and I want to get in and smarten up before the sun rises.'

'Very good, sir. Lago and his friends have been there tonight and made the place all ready for us, so there should be a fire burning in the hearth, and something for you to eat in the kitchen.'

'Jolly good. I'll see you in a bit then.' Underwood shooed him back. 'You'd better get back, I know the suit's wet but it'll still go up.'

Flinch nodded and took a few steps back. Even though he had seen Underwood's transformation process perhaps a thousand times, the sight still filled him with awe, and he felt a thrill of anticipation run through him.

Underwood grinned. 'Right-ho then, Flinch. Carry on.'

Flinch watched as Underwood dropped into a crouch and then sprang upwards, launching himself into the night as the miracle that always made Flinch want to simultaneously weep and applaud, happened again. Underwood's body lost its corporeal form, disintegrating into what the superstitious peasants of Eastern Europe had once believed to be smoke; a dense cloud of blood-red molecules – Underwood's molecules – swirled up and away from the road. The intense heat generated by the molecular destabilisation caused Underwood's clothes to burst into flames and fall away from him in blazing ruins as, still rising, the vampire began to take his new form.

Flinch raised a hand to shield his eyes as tatters of burning clothing fell around him. Then he looked up into the sky to where Underwood – phoenix-like, with smoke and burning embers still trailing in his wake – spread his black wings against the cloud-shrouded moon. The bat beat its wings, and even though it was perhaps twenty feet overhead, there came a strong down-rush of air that fanned the flames below and caused Flinch to stagger amidst the whirling eddies of ashes and embers. When he looked up again, his Master had gone.

He laughed. 'There goes another Saville Row suit. Some people have got money to burn, all right.' He shook his head and walked over to kick around the burning scraps. As always, there was nothing left to identify the clothes or their owner.

He walked around to the back of the hearse and looked down at the guard that Underwood had been feeding upon. He bent to feel for a pulse. The guard was alive, his pulse was faint but it was there. Flinch straightened up, drew the Luger from the waistband of his trousers and shot the man twice in the neck where Underwood had bitten him, and once – for certainty's sake – in the head. Then he replaced the lid on the coffin before easing it back into the hearse and slamming the door. He turned to the dead guards that lay sprawled in the light from the headlights of their car. *'Adios amigos.'* He gave them a friendly salute before getting back into the hearse and leaving them under a fine cloud of dust and exhaust.

Flinch saw the distant light of the farmhouse from miles away. At first he thought it was a star, low in the sky. But as he drew nearer, the light grew larger, becoming a small cluster, then distinct, individual lights. Now he could see the shape of the building against the hills and trees that surrounded it.

He felt a mingled sense of sadness and trepidation as he approached the gates. He was forty-seven years old and had been Underwood's guardian for twenty years, succeeding to the role after his father retired back in 1938. What a time for the old man to retire, the eve of the Second World War. The war had been a ferocious and terrible time, but what adventures he and his Master had had together. And now here he was, rolling towards his own retirement; much earlier than his father had done, and much earlier than he himself had ever expected to. He'd never thought of himself as being a farmer, not least an olive farmer. But when His Lordship had made the decision to lay himself to rest, they'd had to decide where that resting place should be. All the allied Western countries were becoming increasingly difficult to keep a low profile in. It really came down to Africa, Spain, or possibly Italy. However, His Lordship was uncomfortable with Italy's proximity to the Eastern Bloc countries, and since it had a thriving Communist Party of its own, he had felt it best to steer clear of it for now. Underwood didn't want to wake up under communism, so of the remaining two, Flinch by far preferred Spain. Underwood had accepted his decision and they'd made the necessary arrangements to procure this remote farmhouse deep in the countryside of Europe's only remaining fascist dictatorship. As much as Flinch disliked the idea of being in a fascist state, the Sect were strong here and he had no fear of being interfered with – though obviously their earlier run-in with the law suggested that word had yet to filter down to the lower ranks of the Civil Guard, but these things took time.

The Spanish house had seemed perfect. It was surrounded by olive groves for miles around. The groves had come with the land, and Flinch had arranged for a farmer and his family to move in to a smaller house on the land in order to manage the crop. The farmer would teach him the tricks of the trade, though whether or not he would actually become a farmer himself or just be a wise overseer, he hadn't yet decided.

Members of the Sect had been making the place ready for weeks now, receiving items belonging to both Underwood and himself and installing them in readiness for their arrival. Flinch had been consulted on every stage of the preparations; he'd wanted to get it just right. After all, it was to be his home for what might turn out to be the rest of his life.

He drove through the open gates and up the winding path to the house. Lights burned in most of the windows. Obviously, His Lordship was making himself comfortable. Flinch parked the car in front of the house and got out.

The front door was ajar and he entered the candlelit hallway. The tiled interior was cool and Bing Crosby's, *Aren't You Glad You're You?* drifted from deeper inside the house. Flinch smiled; evidently the phonographic records had arrived intact. He walked towards the sound of the music and entered the lounge. The phonograph was playing, but there was no one in the room.

He wandered through the house to the kitchen. A girl of about eighteen years sat slumped in a chair at the table. Her head hung forward so her chin rested on her collarbone, and her dark hair was tied back in a pony tail. Blood had trickled down her neck but stopped short of the collar of her white cotton blouse. Flinch went over and felt her pulse. She was alive; the Civil Guardsman had evidently taken the edge of Underwood's appetite. Flinch took his handkerchief and wiped the blood from her throat. He'd put her to bed and she could be on her way tomorrow. She'd have no memory of what had happened to her.

There was a note on the table from señor Hernandez saying he had arranged things to the letter of Flinch's instructions and that he hoped His Lordship enjoyed the meal. Flinch smiled and went through to a small room, along the far wall of which hung an arras. A breeze played around the bottom of the curtain. Flinch drew it aside to reveal a small flight of stairs that led to the roof patio. He ascended and emerged to find Underwood dressed in a fresh black suit and staring out across the dark expanse of countryside.

'Hello, Flinch,' he said without turning.

'Hello, sir. Is everything alright?'

'Everything's fine, Flinch. I'm just savouring the night for the last time. Listen to the crickets: must be millions of them out there.'

Flinch joined him. 'Well, not exactly the last time, sir. Just the last time for a while.'

Underwood smiled. 'A very long while, Arthur. Fifty years is a lifetime for many people.'

'It is, sir. Certainly it's the rest of my days. I sometimes wonder what kind of a world you'll be awakening to.'

'Yes, so do I. The way the world's going these days, mankind will either be flying rocket ships to Venus or ... well, it won't *be* at all, eh?'

Flinch nodded. 'Yes, sir. Nuclear war is indeed a frightening thing.'

'Insane, isn't it?' Underwood sighed. 'I'm tired, Arthur. These last two wars have been so bloody awful. Don't get me wrong, I enjoy a good war. In war, vampires are the last thing on anybody's mind, and the feeding is out of this world, as you know. But things just seem to be getting out of hand, you know? And now, with the bomb and this bloody race to build ever bigger, ever nastier versions of it. I mean, well, that's not war, is it? War's a rotten business, certainly, but it's not all bad. Besides bringing out the worst in men, it can often bring out the best in them too: courage, honour, camaraderie. But nuclear war?' He shook his head. 'That'll be the end of everything, I fear.'

'Yes, sir. We do seem to be heading into a very dark time.'

'Yes, and I don't want to be here when it happens. The human race isn't just my favourite tipple, you know. It's very dear to my heart in many ways. I mean, I used to be part of it.'

Flinch nodded. He reached into his jacket pocket and took out his cigarettes. 'Perhaps a fag would cheer you up, sir?'

Underwood took one and accepted a light. 'Thanks.' He exhaled the smoke in a sigh. 'I've grown tired of death as well. I used to be able to respect what I did, you know? I saw myself as part of nature's design: a leveller, a harvester of a crop that needed to be contained lest it grow out of control, you know?'

'Well, one could argue that it has grown out of control, sir. The population of the world isn't exactly dwindling.'

'No, I realise that. But the A-bomb, the H-bomb and whatever other lettered bomb they might be working on at the moment, they'll take care of the population in an instant – do the work of a billion vampires overnight.'

'Yes, sir. You're not wrong there.'

'Unfortunately.'

'I think all of us question the meaning of our existence from time to time, sir. "What am I here for?" we ask ourselves. "What does it all mean?"'

'Any ideas, Flinch?'

'Not really, sir. Life is just being here and trying to make the best of it before they finally do drop the bomb.'

Underwood smiled. 'Yes. Yes, of course it is.'

'Still, I do know what *I'm* here for. And my reason – as I see it, *my purpose* – is about to lie down and, as you say, die for fifty years.'

'I'm leaving you at sixes-and-sevens with your *raison d'etre* am I, Arthur?'

Flinch looked away over the balcony. 'No sir. I, I shall continue to serve you. My duties may be about to change, but you'll still need me, even if it's just to polish the silverware.'

Underwood smiled. 'Thank you, Arthur.' He laid a hand on Flinch's shoulder and looked to the east, where the night was beginning to pale at the horizon. 'Ah look, the morn in russet mantle clad walks upon the eastern thingy-me-bob.' He dropped his cigarette and ground it out underfoot. 'Come, old chap. We have work to do. I've already been down to check the crypt and everything's been done to order. All we need do,' he smiled wanly, 'is get on with it.'

They went downstairs and through the house until they came to a room that had been designated as the library. Packing crates filled with books were piled up everywhere and the walls were lined with bookcases waiting to be filled.

'Do you plan on spending much time in here, Arthur?'

'I imagine I'll spend a good deal of time here sir. Books will probably be my primary source of entertainment.'

'Did you speak with señor Lago about getting a television?'

'I did sir, but decided against it. No doubt it will only show what General Franco and his chums want us to see, and I've no interest in any of that nonsense.'

'Not that you could understand it anyway, eh?' Underwood walked to one of the bookcases. It was the only one with a book in it. Underwood picked up the book. It was a paperback copy of *Dracula*. He handed it to Flinch. 'A cunning marker, by the way.'

Flinch smiled. 'I had Lago and his people mark the spot with what I felt was an apt title.'

'Yes, I must say it made me chuckle. But not as much as this.' The book had being lying against a concealed switch. Underwood pressed it and there was a click. He stepped back and took hold of the edge of the bookcase. It was hinged and he swung it slowly open to reveal a staircase that led down to dim candlelight. 'Bravo, Flinch.'

'Merely following your instructions, sir.'

'Yes, but still. It's terrific fun, isn't it? Shall we close it up again and then you can have a go?'

Flinch looked at his watch. 'I really think we should be getting on, sir. I can have plenty of goes in the future.'

'Yes,' said Underwood with a note of regret in his voice. 'Yes, I'm sure you shall. Oh well, let's be getting on then.' He stepped into the secret passage and started down the stairs. Flinch followed. The stairs ran down the side of the wall into the cellar. Candelabras had been set into the walls at regular intervals and all now blazed with light as Underwood and Flinch walked to the oak coffin that sat on a low stone plinth in the centre of the floor.

'Lovely job down here too, Arthur. Still a bit musty, though. You'll need to air it fairly regularly.'

'Yes sir.'

Underwood laid a hand on the coffin lid, feeling its smooth, waxed surface. Then he turned to Flinch. 'So, about the resurrection procedure; you're all clear on what to do?'

'Absolutely, sir. Everything will be done according to your specifications.'

'I don't want a big fuss. None of that Dennis Wheatley nonsense.'

'No, sir. I shall pass on your instructions in this, and in all things, to the letter.' Flinch's voice trembled slightly. He cleared his throat and smiled.

Underwood patted his shoulder. 'Don't worry, old friend. I'll be fine. I've done this many times before.'

'It's not that, sir, I know that. It's just – well, this is goodbye, isn't it?' A tear ran down his cheek.

Underwood smiled. 'Yes, Arthur. I suppose it is.' He extended his hand. 'Thank you, for everything. You're a credit to your family name, and when I look in your eyes I see your father, his father, and all of their fathers going back over the centuries to dear old Matthias. You have all been my friends and most trusted servants, and I shall always be thankful for that. You have done them proud, Arthur.'

'Thank you, sir,' Flinch took out his handkerchief and dabbed at his tears. 'Thank you very much.' He took Underwood's hand and shook it.

'All right then,' Underwood tapped the coffin lid. 'It's that time, I'm afraid.'

'Oh, just one thing, sir.' Flinch reached into his pocket and took out Underwood's watch. 'Will you be wanting this with you in your, er, repose?'

Underwood smiled. 'No. I think it's best if you hang on to that. Keep it wound for me, would you?'

'Of course, sir. I shall wind it every evening at sundown, just as I always do.'

'Capital.' Underwood turned and opened the coffin, lifting off the heavy lid as if were made of cardboard and not fine Spanish oak. 'Mmm, nothing like the smell of a new coffin, eh, Flinch?' He set the lid down against a nearby pillar.

Flinch smiled. 'No, sir.'

Underwood got inside and settled himself down. 'Very nice. Just my size.'

Flinch wrung his hands. 'Are you absolutely sure about this, sir?'

'Yes, Flinch. Everything needs to die once in a while, even if it isn't a real death.'

'Just hibernation, sir.'

'Precisely; just hibernation, Flinch.'

Flinch nodded sadly and picked up the coffin lid. He laid it carefully onto the coffin and slid it into position, stopping short of Underwood's face. 'May I just say, sir, just how much of a pleasure it's been to serve you?'

'Thank you, Flinch. And may I say that the pleasure has been entirely mutual.'

Flinch laughed and wiped a tear from his eye. 'Goodbye, Master.'

'Goodbye, Arthur. Enjoy your retirement.'

'Thank you, sir. I shall, sir.'

Underwood crossed his hands over his chest and closed his eyes. Then Flinch slid the coffin lid over the face of his Master and let it fall into place with a dry, heavy sound of finality. He drew his palm slowly and silently over the smooth surface of the coffin. 'Rest well, sir.' He turned and walked to the nearest candelabra where he blew out the candles, one by one. He continued slowly around the cellar until he came to the stairs leading back up to the library. There, he snuffed out the last light, and slowly ascended the stairs towards the dim glow of a new dawn.

1

'HELLO, MY NAME'S DAVID and I'm an alcoholic.' David Smith nodded once in general greeting to everyone who sat with him in the small circle.

'Hello David,' came the collective response with varying degrees of interest. They were gathered in a small, fluorescent-lit room in Hove Community Centre.

David ran a hand through his short dark hair, and scratched his head. 'Er, not a lot really going on with me right now. I've been sober for over two years and, well, as you know, it's not always easy but, I'm getting there one day at a time.' He shrugged. 'Thanks.' He looked at the group leader, Mary, to indicate he had finished.

'Really, David?' said Mary. 'Nothing at all to share?'

'No, not really. My girlfriend is going back to Germany this week, which is a bit of a bummer, but, you know, that's life.'

'Well, how do you think you'll cope with that?'

'Fine.' David took a sip from his machine-vended cup of coffee.

'Really?'

'Yeah, I mean, it happens doesn't it? People come, people go.'

'Doesn't happen to me,' said a slightly chubby man opposite David. 'My wife cleared off three years ago and I haven't had a woman since. "People go" about sums it up for me.'

'Please, Steve,' said Mary. 'You'll get your turn to speak.' She turned back to David. 'Sorry David.'

'No really, you go, Steve. I've got nothing to say. Honest.'

'Are you sure?' said Mary. 'You know, if you think this situation with your girlfriend could be a problem ... ?'

'No, I don't, really. I don't mean to sound shallow or anything but, it's not a big deal for me. I'll be fine.'

'Be another one along in a minute eh, Dave?' said Steve. 'Like a number seven bus?'

David smiled and shook his head. 'No, mate.'

'I don't know how you do it,' said Steve. 'I really don't. I mean, it's not like you're much to look at, now is it?'

'Oh, hark at Brad Pitt,' said a woman to David's left.

There were a few chuckles around the circle before Mary brought things to order again. 'Thank you, Carol. Can we just let David speak please?'

David shrugged. 'I've spoken, Mary. That's it. I'm fine, no worries. Ask him if you don't believe me,' he pointed to Steve. 'He's my sponsor.'

'Oh yeah,' said Steve. 'He's fine all right. Have you seen that German bird of his? Bloody hell, anyone'd be fine who had that to come home to. And when she goes, seriously, there'll be another one along before you can say "trousers". There must be something in the chalk dust at that school he teaches at; them foreign birds throw themselves at him.'

Mary raised an eyebrow at David. 'Do they?'

David smiled and shook his head. 'No. I do meet the odd girl there, sure. But it's never anything serious.'

'And ain't that just the way you like it, eh?' said Steve with a wink.

David turned to the man next to him. 'Peter. I think it's your turn.'

Peter sat back and folded his arms. 'No, no. I'm enjoying hearing about this school of yours. What do you teach that has such an aphrodisiac effect?'

'English,' said Steve. 'He gets all these young girls over here wanting to learn English, and he takes them home for some extra-curricular lessons, don't you Smithy?'

'Oh that is *so* not true,' said David. 'You're making me out to be some Casanova type, which is just bollocks. I'm a thirty-five year old man living in a rented one-bedroom flat; I ride a bicycle and I teach English, part time. I'm not exactly what you'd consider a catch, am I?'

'Not me, no. I think you're a minger. But them foreign birds, they must go for bike-riding mingers coz you always seem to have one on the go, duncha?'

'Bollocks do I.'

'Are there any jobs going there then?' asked Peter. 'I've got a bike.'

'Yeah,' said Steve. 'And I speak English.'

'And you're a minger an' all,' said Carol. 'If you borrowed Peter's bike, you'd be well in.'

'Thank you, Carol,' said Steve with a sarcastic smile.

'Yeah, why not?' said David. 'I'm sure they'd be all over you like bees round a honey pot, Steve.'

'Bloody right mate, I *am* a honey pot.'

'Chamber pot, more like,' said Carol.

This got a laugh from everyone but Steve.

'All right, all right, settle down,' said Mary. 'Well, if you've really nothing to say, David, let's move on to Peter.'

Peter sighed and sat on his hands. 'Hello everyone, my name is Peter and I'm an alcoholic.'

'Hi Peter,' everyone replied.

Steve made a clandestine "wanker" hand gesture at David. David poked his tongue twice into his cheek in response. Then they both settled back to listen to Peter, whose anecdotal updates on his wife's snoring were always highly entertaining.

An hour later, as they were stacking away their chairs, Steve spoke again to David. 'So, seriously mate. You all right about this bird leaving, are you?'

'Yeah. Like I said, it's not a big deal.'

'But I thought you really liked her.'

'I do.'

'So, you must be feeling *a bit* pissed off then, surely?'

David pushed the stack of plastic chairs against the wall and shrugged. 'What can I do? That's life, mate.'

'Well, you could ask her to stay?'

'She can't stay. She's got a family and a job and all the rest of it.'

'So? Have you asked her?'

'What?'

'If she'd stay?'

'We've talked about it. She says I can go over there and – you know – teach English, but,' he made a face. 'I don't really fancy it.'

'Don't fancy what?'

'Germany.'

'Well that's all right, you ain't gonna be shagging Germany are you? I mean, it's her what you fancy, innit?'

David smiled. 'Are you trying to get rid of me, Steve?'

'No, I just don't want to see you chucking a good thing away. She's a lovely girl that one. You'll kick yourself if you let her go.'

David shook his head. 'You don't get it, mate. I don't mind not being in a committed relationship, you know? Since Sarah died, I just, I dunno, I like to keep it simple.'

'You can't go on keeping it simple forever, Dave. One day, whatever magic chalk dust it is you sprinkle over them girl students' eyes is gonna stop working. Oh yeah – you'll wind up old and alone, smelling of piss, and wearing a kettle for an army helmet as you re-live that war you was in. I can see you now, shouting out "surrender" at the milkman in Czechoslovakian.'

'Serbo-Croat,' David corrected.

'Eh? What's that? The Czechoslovakian for "surrender"?'

'No it's the language I'll be shouting "surrender" in; I was in Bosnia.'

'Yeah, well it all sounds the same when you've got a kettle on your head, dunnit? Point is, your life's slipping away from you. You ain't getting any younger.' They walked out into the corridor. 'Take me,' Steve continued. 'I used to be like you, I could have had any woman in town. But I had Brenda didn't I? I was faithful to that woman. And then,' his lips tightened, 'and then she went and bloody left me, didn't she?'

'Well, yeah, not be funny or anything Steve, but that was because you were always pissed.'

'That's beside the point.'

'Is it? I thought that *was* the point.'

'No, I mean it's not the point I'm trying to make to you, is it?'

'I don't know. What is your point then?'

'My point is, I had it, but I let it slip away: I fucked it up. And now, you've got it too, and you're gonna let it slip it away an' all. And you ain't even gonna have the consolation – not that it is much of a consolation – of being able to say it was coz you was pissed all the time. No, you're fucking it up, and you're stone cold sober.'

David pushed the front door open, grateful of the damp evening air after two hours of central heating. Steve took out his cigarettes and offered David the packet. David shook his head. 'No, thanks.'

'What? You're not giving up the fags an' all are you? You'll go mental!'

'No, I just want to breathe for a bit, that's all.'

'Fair enough. So anyway, you see what I'm saying about this bird?' David nodded.

Steve exhaled smoke. 'So do me a favour will you? Just think about it, okay?'

'About what, going to Germany?'

'About doing whatever it takes, mate. If she's the one for you – and I know Sarah was, but you know, sometimes fate deals you more than one chance – you should do whatever it takes to keep her.'

David looked at his friend and nodded. 'All right Steve, I'll think about it.'

'Good lad. So, what you doing now?'

'Going home, making dinner.'

'What you having? Pizza?'

'No. Lisa's coming over. I'm making a chicken korma.'

'Ooh, very exotic. They say a bloke that cooks knows the quickest way to a bird's heart.'

David frowned. 'Who does?'

'Well, no-one actually, I made it up. But it sounds right, dunnit? If you can cook, you're half way there. They'll understand that you won't be expecting them to do all the cooking. It's metrosexual, innit?'

'Is it?'

'Oh yeah. I'm totally metrosexual, me. I can do beef and spuds, spagbol, sausage and mash, you name it,' He pointed at David with his cigarette. 'And I always put the toilet seat down after I have a piss, which to some women is a more important thing about a bloke than him having a big dick.'

'Is that so?'

'Oh yeah.'

'Where did you read that?'

'I didn't read it; a bird told me herself.'

'Was this after you slept with her?'

'Yeah. I'm going back years, mind you, but it's as true today as it was then.'

David smiled. 'Of course it is.' He looked at his watch. 'Listen, I have to go. I'll see you soon, yeah?' He trotted down the steps to the street.

'Yeah. Next week – if not before. And you stay dry, yeah?'

David turned and waved. 'You too.'

'And don't forget,' Steve called after him. 'It's her you're shagging, not Germany.'

Peter came out and stood beside Steve. 'Alright, Steve?'

'Alright Pete?'

'What's wrong with shagging Germany?'

'Eh?'

'What's wrong with shagging Germany? I'd shag Germany.'

'Yeah, you'd shag anything, Pete.'

'No I wouldn't,' said Peter, mildly affronted. 'I wouldn't shag France. Would you?'

'Course not. I couldn't, it ain't possible.'

'Ah. So, I'm not the only one, then.' Peter accepted one of Steve's cigarettes.

'Oh, I'd say you probably are, Pete,' said Steve, giving Peter a light. 'I'd say you probably are.'

An hour later, David was in his kitchen reading the instructions on a jar of chicken korma sauce when the phone rang. He wandered through into the lounge and picked up the receiver. 'Hello?'

'Hi, it's me.'

'Lisa? Where are you?'

'I'm in a cafe with Claudia and Maria. I just wanted to check; you're cooking tonight, right?'

'That's right. Chicken korma.'

'Have you started it?'

'Well, I've opened a jar of *Chicken Tonight*. Why?'

'Claudia and Maria have invited us to a party tonight at Marco and Giuseppe's apartment. People are meeting in The Cricketer's at ten. Do you want to go?'

David sat down on the sofa. 'Uh, I dunno, Lese. It's just gonna be a load of students getting pissed up, isn't it. I mean, *you* go by all means, but I think I'll give it a miss. Students never really understand when you say you don't want a pint, they take it as a rejection.'

'You can just tell them you don't drink.'

'Yeah, and then they start asking you, "Why not? Why you no drink?". But you go, it'll be a laugh. You should make the most of your last few days in Brighton.'

'I intend to, Mister Teacher. What time is dinner? I don't want to be late.'

David smiled. 'Whenever suits you.'

'Okay, I can be there in about thirty minutes.'

'Okay.'

'Should I get anything on the way?'

'Get yourself some wine if you like, but I don't need anything.'

'Okay. I'll see you soon.' She made a kiss sound at the receiver. 'Bye.'
He returned the kiss. 'Bye.'

She hung up. He looked at himself in the large mirror that hung over the fireplace: he was blushing. He shook his head. 'You sap.'

As promised, she arrived at his flat thirty minutes later. She held up a bottle of expensive mineral water. 'Do you like this? I asked the supermarket assistant for a non-alcoholic drink to have with dinner and he suggested this.'

David kissed her and took the bottle. 'Sure. Thanks.'

She came in after him and closed the front door. 'The food smells lovely. Chicken korma is a curry?'

'Yeah.' He entered the lounge and turned down the stereo.

'*Mmm*, how long will it be?'

'We can have it any time. Why are you hungry?'

'No, I'm horny.' She came up to him, put her arms around his neck and kissed him.

David tasted the wine on her breath. He kissed her back. Then he said, 'Wait a second, just let me go and turn the cooker off.' He went out. When he came back she had gone through into the bedroom. He went in. She was sitting on the bed in her underwear.

She held out her hand. 'Come on please, teacher. It's time for my private lesson.'

It was shortly after nine when they finally ate. The meal was a success. Afterwards, they sat talking at the table, David in his boxer shorts and Lisa in one of his t-shirts. Then Lisa got up to clear the plates. David held up a hand. 'Leave them, I'll wash them up later.'

'But you cooked.'

'That doesn't matter.'

She sat down again, smiling. 'Well, if you insist.'

'I do.' He picked up his cigarettes.

Her smile faded. 'Oh David, do you have to smoke now?'

David put the packet down. 'No, I can leave it if it bothers you.'

'I wish you'd just give it up altogether.'

'I can't give it up, it's my hobby, Lese. Everyone needs a hobby. Drinking used to be my hobby and I had to give that up, so this is all I've got left.'

'Don't you have any real hobbies?'

He shrugged. 'Does Playstation count?'

'No, I mean *real* hobbies.'

He shook his head. 'No. Not anymore.'

'You know, I thought you'd be more of a book person.'

'I like books.'

'But you have hardly any. In fact, you don't have much of anything.'

He topped up her glass. 'Well, I don't like clutter. It's good Feng Shui.'

'What's that?'

'It's Chinese for throwing out your crap.'

'You see? This Feng Shui thing. I didn't know this about you, yet we've been seeing each other for months now. You're really quite a private person, aren't you?'

He raised an eyebrow. 'Am I?'

'Yes. I sometimes think I hardly know anything about you.'

'Well, there isn't much to know.'

'I don't believe that. I think you have – I don't know how you say it English – hidden deepness?'

David smiled. 'Hidden depths.'

'Yes. You have the hidden depths. But I think some things in there are not good. You know, at night you have bad dreams, you moan and wrestle with yourself.'

He laughed. 'Sounds like I'm dreaming of you.'

'No, I have to soothe you sometimes to help you relax.'

'*Really?* I didn't know that.'

'You don't remember your dreams?'

'No,' he lied. 'Not usually.'

'You twitch and fidget, you cry out sometimes also.'

'Do I?' he was beginning to feel embarrassed. 'Sorry.'

'It's not something to be sorry about, David, but I think that it is something you need to talk about, these … things, whatever they are that disturb you.'

He smiled. 'I'm probably just dreaming of chasing rabbits or something.'

'I don't think so.' She sipped her drink, then asked, 'What is "Underwood"?'

David's smile faded. 'Underwood?'

'Yes, you say it sometimes when you are dreaming. Is it a place?'

He shrugged. 'I've no idea.'

'In your dreams you sound frightened of it, like it's a bad thing.'

'Do I?'

'Yes. You know if we ever got serious, we may have to have sleep in separate rooms. I'd never get any sleep otherwise.'

He topped up his own glass. 'But we aren't going to get serious, are we Lisa? You're going to go back to Germany at the weekend.'

She shrugged. 'Maybe I could come back again, I've been thinking about it. I could get a job here. My English is good enough.'

'Your English is excellent.'

'So, maybe I could stay with you here – at least until I found a place of my own.'

'Stay here?' he failed to keep the surprise from his voice. 'In this flat, you mean?'

'Yes.'

'But, but you have a career in Germany. What would you do for work here?'

'David, I'm only talking about the possibility.'

'And then there's your friends and your family? What about them?'

'They are only a plane ride away.'

'Yeah, but, you'd miss them, wouldn't you?'

'Perhaps not as much as I will miss you.'

'Oh me,' he waved a hand, avoiding her eyes. 'I'm sure you'll forget me soon enough.'

'As you will forget me?' There was a note of sadness in her voice.

David looked up, meeting her eyes. 'No.'

She nodded. 'I think perhaps, yes.'

'No. I won't forget you, Lisa.'

'So, would you like me to stay?'

David shifted on his seat. 'I – well, yes, of course. But you can't, can you?'

'Why? It wouldn't be so difficult.'

David smiled, but his smile had difficulty reaching his eyes. 'Well, that'd be great, if you did. I mean, if you didn't mind giving up your career and … everything else.'

'I wouldn't mind. Not if we were together.'

David reached for his cigarettes. 'So, you mean, *in this flat* together, or just *going out* together?'

'Would it be a problem if I were in this flat with you?'

He lit a cigarette, drawing out the action to steal a few seconds in which to think, then he exhaled his reply in smoke, 'Er, I, I'm not sure. This is a pretty small space, Lisa.'

She dropped her eyes and nodded. 'Of course. That's okay.'

'I mean, I'd *like* you to move in, but, as you can see,' he waved a hand around the room. 'It's tiny. And my dreaming, my fidgeting and stuff – '.

She got up. 'It's alright, David. I understand, don't worry. I go back to Germany.' She walked into the bedroom and closed the door.

'Lisa?'

'I'm getting dressed,' she called.

He looked at their plates; her unfinished drink; the closed bedroom door. 'You're not angry, are you?'

'No,' she laughed, though he heard no amusement in it. 'I'm just getting dressed, that's all.'

He sighed and looked at the ceiling. He took another drag on his cigarette then dropped it into the remains of his drink. He got up and started stacking plates.

'Actually,' she called. 'I am thinking I might go to the party tonight after all.'

'Okay.'

She walked out of the bedroom fully dressed, and there was a business-like air about her. 'You were right earlier; I should make the most of my last days here.'

He put down the plates and nodded. 'Sure.'

'And so, I'd better go now.'

'Lisa – '

She turned and walked out to the hall. 'I'll see you, I don't know, before I go, I suppose.'

He went after her. 'Look, I didn't mean to say we couldn't share *somewhere* together, Lese, just – '

'Really, David, it's okay,' She opened his front door and started down the stairs. 'I know you like to keep your life free of the clutter.'

'Oh come on, Lisa. You *know* that's not what I meant.' He went out after her. 'Lisa?' He watched as she turned the corner on the lower landing before descending the next flight of stairs. 'Shit!' He looked down at his boxer shorts and bare feet, swore again, then ran after her. He lived on the third floor, and as he reached the last flight of stairs he was rewarded with the sight of the front door closing. 'Bollocks!' He hurried down and pulled open the door. He stepped outside into the cold April night to see she was already halfway down the street. He stood for a moment watching her go, hoping she might turn back, but she didn't.

The sound of sudden laughter made him look round to where two teenage girls were approaching from behind him. 'Nice pants,' said one of the girls.

'Thanks,' said David flatly.

'Not really!' said the other girl, and they both laughed behind their hands. David nodded. 'Thanks again.' He turned and went slowly back into the house. As he closed the door he saw the mail in the basket that hung beneath the letter box. He hadn't checked it that day so he reached inside and pulled out the assorted letters and junk circulars, quickly riffling through for anything addressed to him. There were two things: a bill, and a plain white envelope with his name and address typed on it.

Back in his flat, he sat down on the sofa and opened the white envelope. It contained a single sheet of paper. He opened it out, and the first thing he noticed was the name at the top of the headed paper: *Daventry and West Solicitors.*

Solicitors? What had he done to merit a letter from solicitors? Anxious, he read on. It was short, only three paragraphs in length. But when he had finished, the letter trembled in his hands. 'Oh my God,' he whispered, his eyes filling with tears. 'How did they find me? How did they fucking find me?'

2

LISA LEFT THE CRICKETERS' PUB at just after eleven to return to David's flat. She didn't want to leave things they way they had done earlier, she hadn't been able to relax and enjoy herself all night. As she walked, she wondered if he might have gone to bed already. He usually went to bed at about twelve, provided the students in the flat beneath him weren't having one of their spontaneous parties, but that hadn't happened for a while now.

She smiled as she remembered how David had gone down to put a stop to it the last time it had woken them up. It had been two in the morning; he'd wanted her to stay behind in the flat but she'd insisted on accompanying him. David had gone down and knocked, repeatedly but patiently, on their door. A short time later, a drunken man in his early twenties opened the door. He was immediately on the defensive; the music flowing out from behind him at an unmitigated level while he stood there in the doorway, with his chin out and his arms folded across his chest. David had smiled and begun to chat to him about the situation. Five minutes later they were back in David's flat, the music had been reduced to an acceptable level, and David was pinning a piece of paper with the man's telephone number on it to the kitchen notice board. The man, whose name was Nathan, had given it to David in the event he might need it in the future to call to complain about noise or anything else.

She'd been impressed and had told him so. He told her that disarming an enemy with diplomacy was something he'd learned in the army. Surprised, she'd asked him to tell her more, but he hadn't. He told her he was tired and that he'd tell her later. She didn't press him in on it. She figured he'd tell her whenever he was ready, though of course, he never had. She bristled as the feeling of rejection she'd felt earlier began to stir again: the unwelcome, though insistent thought that reminded her that while David may be fond of her, he apparently had no room in his life for her. Then her anger returned: Jesus, if he didn't want to see her again, why couldn't he just come out and say it instead of blaming it on his apartment?

'Stop it!' she said out loud. There was no use going over it again and again in her head, she needed to discuss it with him, not herself.

As she turned onto Lansdowne Place she was met with the sound of distant music; someone must be having a party. She looked up along the row of terraced town houses to David's building. The music seemed to be coming from there. The lights were on in all the apartments. Perhaps the effects of David's diplomacy had worn off and the students in the flat below had gone back to their old ways. She stopped outside the house: this was definitely the source of the music, the sound of drums and guitars radiated from the house like heat from a blaze.

She went up the steps and pressed David's door buzzer. There was no response. She pushed it again, but still nothing happened. Maybe he'd gone down to try to reason with the guys downstairs and was involved in doorstep negotiations right now. She decided to check; she pushed the buzzer of flat two. A moment later, an irate voice came back through the intercom.

'Yeah?'

'Hello? I'm sorry to bother you. My boyfriend lives in the flat upstairs from you. I wondered if – '

The intercom crackled and went dead. A moment later a buzz came from the door and she pushed it open. Inside, the very air of the hallway seemed to resonate with the beat of the music. She hurried up the stairs. When she got to the first landing, the door of the flat beneath David's was already open and Nathan was waiting for her.

'Thank fuck you're here. Have a word with him will you, love? He's gone completely fucking mental up there. It's been like this for over an hour now.'

'Yeah,' said another guy, emerging from the flat. 'And when we knock on his door, he threatens to kill us.'

'Seriously,' said Nathan. 'We went upstairs, yeah? Knocked on the door, and your boyfriend flings it open – all mad in the eyeballs – and tells us we're going to bloody die. Then he laughs and slams the door in our faces. Mad as a walnut whip, eh, Josh?'

'Yeah.'

Lisa didn't know what to say. 'You mean, David? David said that?'

'Yeah, him,' said Nathan. 'Your bloody loony boyfriend. We called the police, but they said it was a domestic matter and they couldn't do anything about it. Fat lot of fucking good they are. I mean, listen to that.'

He cupped an ear in the direction of the stairs. 'If that's not a breach of the peace I don't know what is, yeah?' He looked to Josh for agreement, and found it.

Lisa looked up the staircase. 'Okay, I, I don't know what to say. I'm really sorry for the disturbance. I'll speak to him now.'

'I should bloody think so,' said Josh. 'Some of us have to get up in the morning, you know?'

Lisa hurried up the stairs. When she got to the landing she saw a woman outside David's front door that she'd never seen before. She was barefoot and wore a pink velour tracksuit. The woman was knocking on David's door with her fist in slow, rhythmic blows that were barely audible above the music coming from within. Lisa came up beside her and smiled. The woman turned to face her, her features knotted with rage.

'Do you live here?' the woman demanded.

'No,' said Lisa. 'Not exactly. But my boyfriend does.'

The woman's eyes narrowed and she pointed at the door. 'This fucking wanker has been driving me out of my fucking mind for hours. And he hasn't even the guts to come out here and face me.' She pounded and shouted at the door. 'Have you? You selfish bastard!'

Lisa opened her bag and fished out a single Yale key. 'It's okay, I have a key. I'll go in now and turn it off.'

The lines that tortured the woman's forehead softened and she closed her eyes with relief. 'Oh thank God,' she sighed. 'Thank you so much.'

'I'm so sorry – ' Lisa began, but the woman raised her hands.

'No, it's not your fault. Don't apologise.' She pointed at the door. 'It's him in there, Mr Total Arsehole that should be fucking apologising.' The woman touched Lisa on the arm. 'Sorry love, but what the fuck is wrong with people these days?'

Lisa put the key into the door and felt the bass line of the song resonating under her fingers. 'I know, I'm sorry. He's never usually like this, you know?' The woman nodded and walked wearily to the staircase. She managed a weak smile and then went upstairs. Lisa took a breath, and opened the door.

The air was thick with cigarette smoke. Lisa went in and walked down towards the lounge. 'David?' she called out, trying to be heard over the music. The lounge was empty, and so was the whiskey bottle on the coffee table.

'Oh shit, *David?*

She moved quickly to the stereo and shut it off. Silence fell almost palpably against her ears. 'David?' There was no reply. She looked around. The whiskey bottle stood in the centre of the coffee table beside an overflowing ash tray and a single glass tumbler that lay on its side. Scattered on and all around the sofa were papers and documents, his passport among them. 'David?'

She turned and went down the hall to the bedroom. His drawers were all open and in disarray, his clothes lay strewn over the bed and for a moment it crossed her mind that perhaps David had been burgled. Then, she heard a familiar sound coming from the bathroom: a low moan punctuated by yelping noises. She went to the bathroom and pushed open the door.

David sat on the toilet with his trousers and underpants around his ankles. On the sink beside him a cigarette had burned down to the filter leaving a sticky brown burn on the porcelain. David yelped again and his legs twitched. 'No,' he moaned. His head was slumped forward with his chin resting on his collarbone; drool ran from the corner of his mouth and soaked into his shirt.

'Oh my God, David.' Was this her fault? Had her walking out on him earlier pushed him to this? She knelt down before him and took his face in her hands. She lifted his head up, 'David?'

He made no response.

'David!' she said more sternly, patting his cheek.

His eyes flickered.

'David, wake up!'

He woke suddenly, as if he'd been hit by a cattle prod, his legs scissoring her and causing her to fall sideways. 'No!' he cried. 'I won't do it!'

Lisa regained her balance and took his hand. 'David? It's okay, it's okay. You don't have to do anything.'

He looked at her, confused, as if expecting someone else. 'Lisa?' His voice was slurry and his breath thick with alcohol.

'Yes. You're drunk. You fell asleep on the toilet.'

'I,' he looked down at himself, 'I'm not shitting ... I, I just didn't want to miss ... you know – the toilet ... I miss when I'm pissed, see.'

'It's okay,' she pushed his hair back from his forehead. 'You didn't miss.' She glanced down at the linoleum around the toilet and realised she was mistaken. She looked back to his face. He was deathly pale and a dew of sweat had broken out across his forehead. 'Are you alright? You don't look too good.'

'I'm fine,' he said, reaching down and trying to untangle his trousers. 'Really I, I just didn't want to miss, you know? See, when I'm pissed, I miss, and Sarah gets all angry with me. She makes me clean it up.'

'Who is Sarah?'

'She,' he stopped his struggling with his trousers. 'She's dead.'

Lisa drew her hand away from his face. 'Oh. I see.'

He looked up at her. 'She was ... we, we were ... ' He had tears in his eyes. 'She died.'

Lisa moved forward and held him as he started to cry. His arms moved around her and he embraced her tightly.

'I'm sorry, Lisa. I'm so sorry.'

'Shhh,' she soothed him, stroking his hair. 'There is nothing to be sorry for.'

'Yes there is. There's everything to be sorry for.'

'But you haven't done anything wrong, David. You just got drunk. It's not the end of the world.'

At that he seemed to change, his sobs became more erratic and she realised he was laughing. He looked up, but he wasn't smiling – not properly anyway. It was if she had made a sick joke and he was laughing despite his moral revulsion at what she had said.

'*Isn't it?* I'm not so sure about that.' His silent laughter was abruptly cut off as he turned and vomited into the sink.

'Are you sure you don't want a coffee?' said Lisa, handing David a glass of water. They had moved into the lounge and he sat at the end of the sofa looking generally ghastly.

'No, thanks,' he took a sip. 'This is the best thing,' then he chuckled, 'apart from more whiskey, of course.' He managed a slack-mouthed smile. 'Jus' kidding.'

'I hope so. I can't believe you were drinking. What made you do that?'

He closed his eyes and slowly rubbed his face. 'I got – I got a letter. I got some bad news.'

Lisa sat down beside him. 'Oh my God,' she lay a hand on his shoulder. 'Do you want to talk about it?'

'Oh, I'd love to. I'd love to talk all fuggin' night about it. But,' he shrugged, 'it wouldn't do any good.'

She smoothed back a lock of hair that was stuck to his forehead. 'Of course it would do good. People need to talk about their problems, David. Maybe if I had been here when you got the letter, you wouldn't have got drunk.'

'Hmm. Yeah, maybe.'

'Why didn't you call your sponsor friend, Steve?'

'Because he would've have stopped me, and I didn't want to be stopped.'

'David, what was in this letter? Please, talk to me.'

He set the glass on the coffee table and looked down at his hands. Then he met her eyes. 'My brother has cancer, and he's going to die.'

'Oh no, David. That's terrible. Are you – are you sure there's no chance?'

'Yeah. Apparently he's had it for a while now. It's too far gone, you know?'

'How come you only just learned about this?'

He looked back down to his hands, they trembled slightly, and he clasped them together. 'I don't ... I don't really talk to my family. As a matter of fact, I hide from them. They didn't know where I was.'

Lisa said nothing for a moment. She stroked his hand, trying to read his expression in profile. 'You *hide* from them?'

He nodded and a tear spilled from his eye.

'And so, how did they find you?'

He smiled. 'Oh, they have eyes everywhere. The letter came from their – I mean *my* – family's solicitor.'

She waited but he said nothing. She asked, 'And, so what are you going to do now?'

He shrugged. 'I'm going to go to them. I have to, I haven't got a choice.'

'Of course you should go, if that's what you want. Is that what all this is?' She indicated the general chaos of bag packing and disordered paperwork that lay around them.

'Yeah. I fly out tomorrow.'

'Fly? You're flying? Where does your brother live?'

'Spain.'

She seemed surprised. 'You told me your family left Spain when you were a child.' It had been one of his few biographical disclosures to her.

42

He shook his head. 'Yeah, my mum and me, we left, but my dad stayed.'

'And your brother stayed with your father?'

'No, he left with his mum an' all. We grew up in England.'

'With different mothers?'

He nodded. 'Yeah. Cool, huh?'

'But then he went back to Spain? Your brother?'

'He did, yeah.'

'I see. And so you fly tomorrow. At what time?'

'Nine.'

'In the evening?'

'Nah, in the morning.'

'In the morning? Jesus, David, you'll never be able to get up and catch a plane that early. You're too drunk!'

He laughed. 'Drunk? *This?* Baby, this is nothing. Five a.m. start? Piece of cake.'

'Don't be stupid. It's not funny.'

'No,' he shook his head. 'It's not fuckin' funny.'

'I can't believe you can joke about your drinking. What if you had choked on your own vomit or something? What good would you be to your brother then? He needs you.'

David turned on her, and there was a sudden look of contempt in his eyes. 'He doesn't need me!' Lisa drew back, startled. 'He doesn't want me in some kind of *Waltons* death-bed-drama-type way. See, he *has* to summon me, and I *have* to answer that summons. It's nothing personal.'

'But, I don't understand. Don't you like your brother?'

'Like him? I hardly fucking know him, Lisa. He's someone I've met from time to time, just like all of my family,' he laughed. 'We're not what you might call close. We're more like associates rather than brothers and sister.'

'You have a sister?'

'Oh yeah. She's great, she is. A real fuckin' pearl. I bet she's the bastard that found out where I was.' David picked up his cigarettes and fumbled one out of the packet. 'The fucking bitch.'

Lisa watched as he searched among the litter on the coffee table for his lighter. She had never seen him like this; not just drunk, but angry, spiteful. The things he'd kept hidden inside were now spilling from him like some time-fermented acid. 'David, perhaps you shouldn't go; at least not tomorrow. Give yourself some time to think this over. You know you don't have to go at all if you feel this badly about them.'

He lit his cigarette and shook his head. 'You don't get it, darlin'; of course you don't. I mean, why would you? You think I come from a normal family, and all this, this is just normal family shit. Like I say – you know – some *Waltons* episode, or maybe *Dallas* – which is closer, but still way off. See, this isn't like those things; this is more like something out of *Hammer House of Horror*. You see we're not a family, my family, we're a disease.' He took a drag on his cigarette. 'See, when I say I got no choice, Lisa, I mean I *really* have no choice. My destiny was carved out for me long before I was even conceived.' He laughed. 'Fuck, I wasn't even conceived, me. I was bred, like a horse or a pedigree fucking dog.'

Lisa frowned. 'I don't understand.'

David's lips drew back from his teeth in a smile that bordered on a snarl. 'Of course you don't, Lisa. How could you possibly understand?' He got to his feet and walked into the centre of the room where he turned back to her with a certain theatrical flair. 'You see, I am the fruit of a poisonous vine. A family line, that's old, and pure, and cruel in heart. And as much as I wish, I dearly, dearly, wish that I was plain old David Smith, I can't be. For Smith, you see, was my mother's name. I took it as part of my brilliant disguise.'

'What are you talking about? You *are* David Smith. Who else do you think you are?'

He inclined his head forward and his eyes seemed to darken. 'My name is David Christopher Flinch. And I am damned.'

3

IN A REMOTE, RATHER SHABBY, COUNTRY VILLA on the Spanish island of Ibiza, Anton Marashov was trying to relax and keep cool in the heat of the afternoon. There was no air conditioning in the villa so a free-standing fan was all Anton and his colleague, Ivan Trushko, had to circulate the air between them. Both men had packed inadequately for their brief stay. As a result, they both now sat in their underwear. Anton rolled the cold can of *Cruzcampo* beer over his forehead. 'Shit, it's hot. Give me Moscow winter any day.'

Ivan took a large toke on the joint they were smoking and handed it to Anton. 'You hate climate wherever you go; it's always too hot or too cold. If we were in Moscow winter now you'd be saying exact opposite.'

'I would not,' Anton reached for the joint. As he did so, he noticed Ivan's big hand pressing down on the armrest of the white sofa. 'Ivan, you idiot! You've got blood on the sofa.'

Ivan's heavy brows knitted. 'Where?'

'There,' Anton pointed to the armrest.

Ivan saw the red stain. Then he looked at his hands; there was still blood all over his knuckles. He showed it to Anton. 'Oops. It is the English. I forgot to wash hands.'

Anton groaned. He dropped the joint in the ashtray and stood up. 'That's because the sight of blood on your hands is so fucking normal you don't see it anymore. You have to get into habit of washing in-between beatings.' He dragged the coffee table aside, wincing as it screeched on the tiled floor. Ivan rubbed his bloody knuckles on his thighs and Anton slapped his shoulder. 'Come on, don't just sit there, we have to get it cleaned up before it stains.'

Ivan waved Anton back to his chair. 'Relax, you act like woman. Sergei doesn't care about this place.'

'Of course he cares about it. He owns it; it's part of his investment. You don't believe me, you can ask him yourself later. When he gets here, he's going to want answers. If there are bloodstains on your answers, that's okay. But bloodstains on his sofa? That's bad.'

Ivan grunted dismissively. 'He didn't even pay for it. That fat little German gave it to him.'

'No. Sergei took it as debt payment because the German couldn't pay what he owed.'

'He was lucky Sergei didn't kill him.'

'Yeah, well maybe *you* won't be so lucky if you get blood all over his sofa. Now get up.'

'What for?'

'So I can take the cover off, you fucking blockhead.'

Ivan's smile faded. 'Don't call me blockhead, Anton. It's not nice to call people names. Names like Rat Boy, huh? You remember how regiment used to call you that in Chechnya?' Ivan was a big man and a natural baritone, but Anton knew well the deeper note of menace in his voice; he had heard it often enough.

'Okay, I'm sorry. I'm just worried – for you, that's all.'

Ivan's expression softened. 'You are like my brother, Anton. You look out for me, no?'

'Yeah, that's right. Now, will you get up and go and wash your hands? I need to get this cover off. Hopefully the blood hasn't soaked through to sofa underneath.'

Ivan got up. At six-foot-four he towered over Anton like a tree. He laughed and sauntered off in the direction of the kitchen. Anton pulled off the sofa cover and checked the arm rest. Thank God, the blood hadn't penetrated. He gathered up the cover and looked at the stain. It wasn't too bad. If he got some soap onto it and ran it under a cold tap, he should be able to get it out. If not, fuck it, they'd just have to go to Ikea and get a new cover. The German had liked Ikea; it was everywhere. The villa was like an Ikea show home. Anton took the joint from the ashtray and took a toke. He looked out into the kitchen to where Ivan now shook his wet hands into the sink.

'Hey, Anton. Where is towel?'

Holding a lungful of smoke, Anton pointed to where the towel lay on the kitchen table. He let the smoke go in a long sigh. 'Behind you. On the kitchen table there.'

Ivan saw it and grinned. 'Thanks. How is sofa, okay?'

'It will live,' Anton walked into the kitchen and held up the sofa cover. 'But this is going to need to be scrubbed with soap or detergent.'

'Seriously, you want me to do it? It's my mess.'

'No. I can manage. Why don't you go out and see how the English is doing?'

Ivan made a face like a disgruntled teenager. 'What? I just washed my hands.'

'I didn't say get your hands dirty, did I? Just go out and see how he's doing. Maybe he's had enough of being in the pool.' Anton went to the washing machine and picked up the box of detergent beside it.

Ivan smiled. 'I think for sure he's had enough of being in pool.'

'Well maybe then he is finally prepared to do what it takes to get out, eh? Go and check on him.' He reached into the detergent box for the small plastic scoop and scooped a measure of the soap powder onto the stain.

Ivan watched, interested. 'You think that will do any good?'

'How the fuck do I know? I figure it's what my mother would do if she were here.'

'My mother would have made me lick it clean.'

'She sounds like a smart woman. But I don't think Sergei would appreciate you sucking on his furniture.'

The sound of dogs barking erupted from outside. Ivan turned to the sound and grinned. 'It sounds like English isn't making any new friends out there.'

'Yeah, so go, will you. Make sure they aren't eating his fucking face off.'

'Okay. I leave you to woman's work while I go out and do man's.'

Anton smiled thinly and began rubbing the powder into the stain. 'Yeah, you do that. And remember, Sergei wants him alive. Try and keep your hands clean.' Ivan waved and stepped outside and into the brilliant sunshine. Anton looked down to where his hands were now grinding a gooey pink paste. 'Big idiot,' he murmured. 'Next time we do it *your* mother's way.'

In the centre of the drained swimming pool, Mark Coleman, the man to whom Anton and Ivan referred as *the English*, sat naked and bound to a wooden chair. On his head was a dusty cowboy hat fronted with the phrase, 'I love Ibiza' (the word *love* being represented by a once-shiny heart motif). The hat was red, though not as red as Mark's body, which – after over a day in the pool – had burned to the colour of raw steak. His mouth worked against the strip of cloth that gagged him, sucking at it for moisture, even though it tasted of blood and vomit.

Sweat stung his eyes; it trickled into them almost constantly. He blinked and shifted on his seat. The chair scraped on the broken tiled floor, and the three Rottweilers that had been dozing in the shadow of the deep end, looked up at him. One of them growled; a low, ominous reminder of the impossibility of his getting anywhere near the shade they occupied. The dog's fellows joined in and Mark lowered his gaze – a deferential gesture that he had learned which could sometimes keep the dogs from becoming aggressive. The growling simmered a moment longer, before dying down to be replaced by disinterested panting.

Mark listened as paws padded off to the right, the swaying chink of the dog's chain dragging across the tiles behind it. Then the sound of water as the dog lapped in the steel water pail that had been left for them. The sound was maddening. He looked at the hateful, vicious animal as it drank, water splattering around the pail to where it would slowly evaporate on the tiles. A fresh trickle of sweat ran into Mark's eyes and he blinked, angry now despite his fear of the dogs. His blinking only increased the flow and sting of sweat and, momentarily lost to exhausted rage, Mark shook his head. His hat flew away and landed about a metre to his left. He cried out; a muffled howl of sudden panic as he felt the sun on his head and neck. The dogs began to growl again, getting to their feet and baring their teeth. Mark looked down, but this time it didn't placate the animals. They began to bark. He looked up to see the dogs moving out of the shade, ropes of saliva splattering from their jaws. He instinctively tried to move away from them; twisting and shifting his weight on the chair, when suddenly, he felt himself toppling over backwards. He screamed as the world spun head over heels and he crashed down. The dogs charged, running to the length of their chains, snapping and snarling, almost choking themselves in their frenzied efforts to be free and to be able to tear him to pieces.

Then a voice roared something in Russian from over the rim of the deep end. Mark raised his face as best he could, terrified that he would see the owner of the voice and yet at the same time hopeful, knowing that the man was the only way he was ever going to get out of the pool. Slowly, the shape of Ivan rose into view as he sauntered to the edge of the deep end and looked down at the dogs. Again he shouted in Russian and the dogs fell silent, padding back to the shade. Ivan looked up from the dogs and smiled at Mark. 'You see, they are Spanish dogs, but they speak Russian.' He laughed. 'Perhaps because their dinner gets served in

Russian, no?' Then his expression changed to one of mock compassion. 'Oh, look at you, stupid man. You've fallen over and lost your hat.' He dropped down into the deep end and walked over to Mark. He reached down, took the back of the chair in one of his hands and dragged both it and Mark back to a sitting position. 'There. That is better, no?' He patted Mark's cheek. 'You want your hat?' He walked over and picked up the hat, dusting it down before setting it firmly back on Mark's head. 'You don't want to lose that, my friend. You lose hat and your brain will roast like the English beef, and we don't want that, do we? You're no good to us dead.'

Mark moaned through his gag.

'What,' said Ivan. 'You want to tell me something now?'

Mark nodded.

'So now I have to take that pukey gag out of your mouth after I just washed my hands?' He frowned. 'This'd better be worth it, English.' He put his fingers into Mark's mouth and pulled the gag out. 'There. Now, talk to me.'

'Water,' Mark croaked, 'please, water. I'm dying.'

'Oh, you're thirsty are you?'

Mark nodded.

Ivan smiled and patted the non-existent pockets of his boxer shorts. 'Unfortunately I didn't bring beer with me, but if you don't mind dog water?'

'Please,' Mark's voice was little more than a rasp.

Ivan smiled. 'Okay.' He reached out and grabbed the top of the chair's backrest, then began dragging Mark and it backwards towards the dogs. Immediately, the animals began to growl.

'No,' Mark cried. 'What are you doing?'

'Taking you for drink. You think I'm going to take dog's bucket?' He laughed. 'Oh no, that would be rude to dogs. But if I bring you over and introduce you, I'm sure they will be happy to share.' The dogs began to bark and pace uncertainly as Ivan brought Mark within the reach of their chains.

'No, please, don't! They'll kill me.'

'What, you don't want drink now?' Ivan set Mark and the chair upright next to the bucket. 'After I dragged you all the way over here?'

Mark's eyes darted back and forth between the dogs and the water in the bucket. 'Please.'

'Oh, now you want drink again?' He sighed. 'Make up your mind, English.' Ivan took the back rest of the chair and leaned Mark forwards so his face was just above the rim of the bucket. The front legs of the chair scraped the ground as the rear legs rose up. The cowboy hat fell off and rolled away.

'Please!' Mark begged as the rim of the metal bucket struck his forehead.

'Oh,' said Ivan, 'you can't reach water.' He gripped the ropes that bound Mark's waist to the chair and hoisted him from the ground. He suspended him in mid-air for a moment before taking the back of his head and tipping it forwards so the top of his head entered the bucket. 'Here we go, better now?'

Mark screamed as his head was pushed as far into the bucket as it could go before the sides stopped its progress, he could feel the warm water touching his scalp.

'Oh, your big head is too big for bucket, uh?' Ivan pulled the chair back and Mark came up again, the bucket still on his head. Water poured over him before the bucket fell and clattered onto the tiles. The dogs continued to bark and snap. Mark gasped, his tongue groping at his lips for water.

'Oh look, clumsy man. You spilled dogs' water. I don't think they be very happy now.'

'I've told you all I know,' Mark gasped. 'Portugal. They're in Portugal. I can't tell you any more because I don't know any more. I haven't seen them since it happened. Oh please – please let me go.'

Anton called down to them. 'Ivan, what the fuck are you doing with him? Shut those fucking dogs up, will you?' He was carrying the dripping sofa cover over to a clothesline that was strung between two trees.

'I'm trying to give our friend nice drink,' said Ivan. 'But he spilled it.'

Anton stopped. He was looking away into the distance to the dirt road that led to the villa, to a white cloud of dust that was rising behind a shimmering black car. 'Oh shit.' He turned back to Ivan. 'Sergei's here. Quick, get the English away from the dogs before they fucking eat him. And shut them up for Christ's sake!'

Ivan again took hold of the back of the chair and dragged Mark out of range of the dogs. He shouted at the dogs in Russian and their barking died down.

Anton pegged the sofa cover to the washing line, all the time watching the car as it rippled towards them through the heat haze. He turned and hurried back to the pool. 'Did he talk?' He jumped in at the shallow end and walked over to Ivan.

Ivan shook his head. 'Nothing new.'

'Fuck!' Anton grabbed Mark's hair and pulled his head back. 'Listen asshole, you'd better stop fucking around and tell us about your murdering English friends right now, because any minute our boss will be here, and if he doesn't hear what he wants to hear, he's going to kick our asses. And that means when he's gone, we're going to pour a bottle of olive oil over you and leave you here to fry like the fish and chips. You understand?'

Nearby, car doors slammed.

'Three men,' said Mark. 'Mullins, Hodgekiss, Sullivan. They set me up. I had no idea what they were planning.'

Ivan spat onto the dusty tiles. 'Of course you didn't. Even you couldn't be that stupid.'

'I didn't know. I swear I didn't know!'

A voice came from the poolside. 'Your friend looks like he could use some calamine lotion, Anton Marashov.' Anton and Ivan turned to see the silhouettes of three suited men in sunglasses. The man in the centre continued, 'I take it he hasn't told you anything more. '

Anton shielded his eyes from the sun. 'He does not know any more, Captain. If he did, he would have told us.'

The man addressed as Captain, whom Anton and Ivan privately referred to by his first name of Sergei, came down the steps into the pool. 'You're sure of that?' He walked over to them, his hand-stitched Italian loafers crunching on the tiny stones and cracked tiles. He was about six feet tall, his short, silver-grey hair thinning at the temples over a face that looked about fifty years old. The other men came down and followed him.

Ivan nodded. 'He told us all he knows yesterday, Captain. I don't believe he has anything else. He is weak, a coward. He would give me his mother if I asked him.'

'And so this,' Sergei waved a hand to where the dogs panted and lapped at the water around the upturned bucket. 'What? You've just been playing around with him?'

Ivan shrugged, unsure of his position. 'He was thirsty. I gave him drink.'

Sergei's face remained inscrutable. He looked at Mark and took off his sunglasses. 'You are thirsty, Mr Coleman?'

Mark looked up and nodded. 'Y-yes, sir.'

Sergei held out a hand to one of the men behind him. 'Water.' A small bottle of mineral water was handed to him. Sergei unscrewed the cap. 'Here.' He slowly poured the water over Mark's cracked lips and into his mouth. 'Easy,' he stopped pouring. 'Swallow it slowly.' Mark did so. Sergei poured a little more into his mouth. 'Mr Coleman, as I'm sure you know all too well, your friends murdered my nephew and two of my men, yes?' He stopped pouring to allow Mark to respond.

'I didn't know they were going to do that, I swear to you,' said Mark, water spilling over his lips. 'They said they wanted me to get some pills for them, so they could sell them on in Portugal. They said they couldn't deal with you themselves because you and Mullins were enemies or something. I trusted them and the bastards set me up.'

'But that did not stop you taking the pills from my nephew after his death and selling them for your own gain.'

Mark's face contorted with despair.

'Did you really think I would not hear about you selling those pills, Mr Coleman? Yes, Ibiza is a long way from Benidorm, but since I am the controlling source of these pills in Spain, it was really only a matter of time before word of their … unauthorised circulation here reached me.'

Tears spilled from Mark's eyes. 'I – I would've brought them back to you, I swear, but – but I was scared. Oh God, please, please don't kill me.'

Sergei squatted down in front of Mark. 'I believe you, English. You are a coward; and a coward like you would never have had the courage to be involved in an act of violence against me.'

Mark nodded. 'Yes, I am. I'm a coward.'

'And I also believe – for that same reason – that you don't know any more than you have already told my men here.'

Mark nodded again. 'Yes. That's right; I don't owe those bastards anything. If I could, I'd kill them myself.'

Sergei smiled. 'Then I must thank you for telling us what you *do* know. I apologize for what you have had to suffer: our mistreatment of you here is, how you say, making us even?'

Mark wasn't sure if he understood correctly. 'Please, I'll do anything you say. I won't say a word to the police.'

Sergei nodded. 'Yes, I know.' He stood up.

Mark squinted up at him. 'Does that mean you're gonna let me go?'

'Of course,' said Sergei. He handed the bottle back to the men behind him.

Anton and Ivan looked anxious. Ivan asked in Russian, 'You really want us to let him go?'

Sergei smiled. In Russian he replied, 'Always the comedian, Ivan Trushko. Cut off his head. Feed the rest to the dogs.'

4

WHEN LISA WOKE UP, David's side of the bed was cold. The luminous digits of the clock told her it was four forty-seven. She listened: she could hear the bathroom extractor fan. She turned on the bedside lamp and called, 'David?'

He walked in. He was already dressed in black jeans, a grey suit jacket and a faded Motörhead t-shirt. His hair was damp and he had shaved, but he looked rough: his face was puffy and his eyes red and bleary. His toothbrush was sticking out of his mouth. He took it out. 'Hiya.' His voice sounded like he had a head cold. He looked down, embarrassed. 'Sorry about last night.' He came over and sat down on the bed. 'I must have been ... pretty ugly.'

'Yes, and you don't look so good this morning either.'

He smiled. 'Did I do anything, sort of ... stupid?'

'You mean besides drink a bottle of whisky on your own?'

'Yeah, well, besides that – like chucking a TV out of the window or anything like that? I know the TV's okay, but I'm worried in case I damaged anything else.'

'Like us?' She smiled. 'No. But you're going to have to apologise to your neighbours. You upset a lot of them. Apparently you are a big asshole.'

'Oh. What was it? Music?'

'Yes. And you told the guys in the flat downstairs that you were going to murder them.'

He put a hand over his face and sighed. 'Oh shit. Still, at least I didn't actually murder them.'

'Yes, thankfully, but don't worry. I apologised for you.'

'Thanks. I should really go down and say something myself, but ...'

'You aren't going to be here.'

'No.' He scratched his head. 'Not for a while anyway.'

She took his hand. 'When do you think you will be coming back?'

'I don't know, it's impossible to say. Listen, can I ask: how much did I tell you about what's going on?'

'Last night?'

He nodded.

'Well, you told me your brother was dying, that your family was evil and that you were bred – like a cow. You said your name was Flinch and that you had a terrible job to do that you couldn't escape from. I tried to get you to tell me more, but you said that for me to know more would be dangerous.'

'Hmm, Not exactly a date with David Niven then? Sorry if I freaked you out.'

'Never mind that; is it true?'

'What part?'

'All of it?'

He sighed. 'Well, my brother *is* dying, yes, and my name – my father's name – is Flinch. As for the family being evil and the terrible job; it sounds as if I was being a bit hysterical. There *is* a job to do, it's a family thing. But it isn't anything for you to worry about; you're not in any danger.'

'But what about you? Will you be in any danger?'

He rubbed his temples and she thought for a moment that she saw his hand tremble slightly. 'Damn it. Why did I have to drink? That's two years of sobriety down the drain.'

'I know. I still can't believe it. Why didn't you call your friend, Steve?'

He smiled weakly. 'Because I wanted to get fucking blotto. I wanted to just let go of the steering wheel; put my foot down hard and shut out the ... '

'The what?'

He thumbed the bristles of his toothbrush. 'I don't know. The news about John I guess.'

She stroked his back. 'It's okay.'

He met her eyes for a second before looking away to his suitcase. 'You remember that word you were saying I call out in my sleep sometimes, "Underwood"?'

'Yes?'

He got up and dropped his toothbrush into the suitcase. 'I don't know why I didn't tell you when you mentioned it yesterday, but I suppose I was just ... embarrassed about it.'

'About what?'

He turned back to her. 'It's a business. My family's business in Spain.'

'This is the job you have to do?'

'Yeah.'

55

'The terrible job? The one that you couldn't speak about last night?'

'Yeah, but I was just drunk, talking shit, you know? It's not a big deal. John was running the business, and since he's going to die, now it falls to me to become the head of the family firm.'

'Is that so terrible?'

David knew she deserved some kind of a logical explanation for all this. In the shower earlier he had been thinking about how to broach the subject and he'd remembered the old family cover story. It was, of course, perfect. He cleared his throat and said, 'It's an undertakers.'

She raised her eyebrows. 'Underwood the undertaker?'

He smiled. 'It's Underwood and Flinch, actually. At least that's what we call it.'

'Oh.' She lay back, supporting herself on her elbow. 'I can't imagine you dealing with dead people.'

'Neither can I,' he sat down again. 'And I don't intend to either. See, I've been thinking. My sister, Lydia – she's been out in Spain for ages, fluent Spanish speaker, and completely devoted to the family in ways I could never be – well, she'd be perfect for the job.'

'And so she can do it instead of you?'

'Yeah. Well, hopefully.' His expression was doubtful.

'But there is a problem?'

'Yeah. The problem is, she's a woman.'

'What? Why is that a problem?'

'Well, Underwood and Flinch is a father-to-son type business, you know? Eldest boy gets to run the company? It's old-fashioned I know, but that's the way it's always been.'

'But that's sexist. Surely it won't be a problem in this day and age?'

He scratched his head. 'Yeah, well I hope not. What I want to do is go out there; be there – you know, for John – until after he's gone, and then just sign everything over to Lydia and get myself out of it.'

'So you want no role in the business at all?'

David was thoughtful for a moment. Then he said, 'Their business is death, Lisa. I want no part of it.'

She squeezed his hand. 'Yes, I think you are more suited to teaching than the disposal of bodies.'

'My feelings exactly. More than you could know.'

'But tell me, what are you going to do about this flat while you are away? And your job?'

'Well, I'm sure I can get some kind of compassionate leave from my job. As for the flat, my rent will keep going out by standing order, and, well, if you like, you can stay here – till you go back to Germany, or as long as you like. You have a key, after all.'

'What? I? Live here?'

'Sure.'

'And when you get back?'

He lifted her hand to his lips and kissed her fingers. 'Stay. If you still want to, that is.'

She smiled. 'You don't have to say that.'

'I know, but mean it. I was an arsehole yesterday – not just when I was pissed, but before as well. That solicitor's letter made me think about a lot of things: not just John and me and the family, but about mortality, you know? We only have so much time on Earth, and we need to hang on to the things – the people – that matter to us. And you matter to me.'

She leaned forward and kissed him on the cheek. 'Thank you. You matter to me too. Though I don't know if I will stay or not. You weren't a complete arsehole yesterday; you were right in some things: I do have commitments in Germany, but soon, maybe, I can come back.'

He took her in his arms. She was warm and sleepy and he held her close, his senses awakening to the delicate fragrance of her hair and skin. Then he realised how he must smell to her and he moved away, embarrassed. 'Sorry, Lese. I must reek of alcohol.'

She smiled. 'That's okay, just as long as you don't make a habit of it.'

He raised his hand as if swearing an oath. 'No way. I'm back on the wagon, and this time I'm staying on it.'

'Good. I'm happy to hear that. But, there is just one thing with your plan, David: if you are going to be the Flinch half of the company, what about the other man, Mr Underwood?'

David's smile faded. 'Underwood? Well, I don't know. I'm sure he'll be reasonable enough; a traditionalist probably and set in his ways, but I don't doubt he'll see the practical advantages of having Lydia in the driving seat. Mind you, I haven't seen Lydia in years, but she always struck me as being very committed, both to the family and to Mr Underwood.'

'But what if Lydia doesn't want the job?'

'Oh, she'll want it,' he said, his face unsmiling. 'She'll be thrilled.'

'Well then, it sounds hopeful.'

'Yeah.'

In the hallway, the front door buzzer sounded.

'That'll be my taxi.' He got up, zipped up his bag and turned back to her with a mildly anxious expression on his face.

'Don't worry,' she said, 'everything will be fine.'

He nodded.

'And I'll be back in a few months.'

He nodded again.

'You look worried.'

'I am.'

She smiled. 'I know. It's not going to be an easy time.'

'I know.'

The door buzzer sounded again.

He bent to kiss her 'I have to go.'

'Take care, David.'

'Yeah. You too.' He picked up his bag, and without turning back, he left for Spain.

Lydia Flinch screamed. Her back arched up away from the bed, and for a moment she was rigid, breathless, trembling on the edge of some inner abyss. Then she gasped, collapsed back against her pillows, and sighed contentedly.

Beltran Morales' face rose smiling from her lap. 'That was good, no?'

Lydia looked down at him. 'It was alright.'

Beltran frowned. 'Alright? It sounded better than alright to me – you came like a porn star!'

'Well of course I did: one does. Would you prefer it if I just lay here like an anaesthetised patient? Actually don't answer that *Doctor* Morales, I don't think I care to know.'

Beltran climbed up her body so he lay face to face with her. He raised his hips and reached between his thighs to grasp his erection. 'No. I like it when you come like the porn star.'

'I know, Belly,' she pushed him off and sat up. 'And I'd love to help you do the same, but unfortunately I have to go. My brother's arriving this morning, remember?'

Beltran looked crestfallen. He shook his erection, 'But you can't go now. Look at me!'

She looked. 'Yes, poor thing. But don't worry, it'll go down eventually.'

'Jesus, Lydia! Come on. You know you want me.'

'Actually, I want a quick dip in the pool and a cup of coffee.' She got up and went to the bedroom door. 'What about you?'

'What about me?' said Beltran, reclining in a pose that was intended to be alluring.

'Do you want coffee?'

He gripped his penis. 'I want you, you little *puta*.'

'Yes, well,' she glanced at his lap, 'I'll just leave you two alone.' She left the bedroom, smiling at the string of Spanish obscenities that followed her down the hall.

Three minutes later, Beltran strolled out of the bedroom wearing a towelling bathrobe and a hangdog expression. The white marble floor tiles were cool underfoot as he walked down the corridor towards the lounge. The sun streamed in through the open balcony windows, through which he saw Lydia sitting on a sun lounger beside the pool. He went out to join her. Apart from her sunglasses, she was naked. She had no immediate neighbours, her villa being situated as it was in the wooded hills on the outskirts of Malaga, overlooking the Mediterranean. She was brushing the tangles from her wet hair when Beltran walked up to her, his face still sulky. She looked up at him. 'Hello Belly. How was the wank?'

He ignored the question. 'Did you make me a coffee?'

'Not yet. I've just got out of the pool. Be a love and put it on, will you?'

Beltran shook his head, disgusted, and sat down. 'No fuck, no coffee, what's *not* next?'

'Oh, Belly, stop acting like a baby. You know my brother's arriving today. We can have sex any time.'

'Yes. But my trouser friend, he does not understand that. He only thinks about now; he lives for the moment.'

'Well, you tell your trouser friend I'll make it up to him later, okay?'

'When?'

'Well, hopefully tonight if everything goes according to plan.'

Beltran grinned. 'Don't worry, baby. Everything is going to go according to plan.'

'Well I *do* worry, Belly,' Lydia pouted. 'You know how much it means to me. I hate having to leave such an important ingredient of our big ceremony to chance. It's not like we can just put an ad in the paper for a human sacrifice, is it?'

Beltran took her foot and kissed her toes. 'Don't worry. I have the perfect candidate.'

'But what if you can't get him?'

'I can get him, don't worry. Okay?'

She smiled. 'Okay.'

'So, tell me about your brother.'

Lydia picked up her cigarette from the ashtray and took a drag. 'I've told you everything I know, darling.'

'Those were just the fundamentals you got from some private investigator; what do you know of him personally?'

'Not a lot, I haven't seen him since we were teenagers. He's spent most of his life trying to avoid us.'

'Why?'

She laughed. 'Why? Because he's scared of us, that's why.'

'But surely he is one of you, no? A Flinch.'

'In name only. *I* blame his mother.'

'Why?'

'Because she was a fucking hippy; a part-time Satanist who stumbled into the family along with her boyfriend. She probably thought it was going to be all one big hedonistic love-in with free booze, marijuana and endless Hawkwind records.'

Beltran smiled. 'She sounds like a fun girl.'

'That's beside the point. There's a selection criteria for Flinch mothers, Belly: breeding, money, status, and above all a deep commitment to Underwood and the Sect. David's mother had none of these things.'

'Maybe she had the nice booty, no?'

Lydia gave him a contemptuous look. 'My father was above such things as women's arses, Beltran.'

He grinned. 'That is the best place to be!'

She dismissed the comment with a wave of her hand and sat back. 'Anyway, the upshot of this ill-advised *bonk* was David; a nice boy – but that's not a compliment. Flinch boys shouldn't be nice. And if they are, the problem should be caught at an early age and nipped in the bud.'

'What does that mean?'

'It means they should be drowned at birth, darling. Like an unwanted kitten, David should have been put in a sack and chucked into the nearest canal.'

'So, I er, I take it you don't get on with your brother?'

Lydia shrugged and looked out to sea.

'Lydia?'

She stubbed out her cigarette. 'Like I said, I hardly know him.'

'Since you were teenagers you say, huh?'

'Yes. We used to spend summers with Dad at the house in Cadiz. Then one year ...' She resumed brushing her long dark hair. 'Well, he just left. We never saw him again.'

Beltran sensed she was keeping something back. 'Did he hurt you?'

'What?' She sounded genuinely surprised.

'You look like he hurt you, like maybe you had a big fight or something?'

'Don't be ridiculous.' She got up suddenly and put on her towelling robe. 'Time's getting on, I have to get dressed.'

'Lydia,' he reached out to her. 'You can tell me.'

She looked at him. 'Okay, yes, we argued. We had a fight. But we were young, stupid; I can't remember how old I was – seventeen, eighteen?'

'That's a long time to have bad feelings in your heart for someone.'

'Yes,' she tied the robe at the waist. 'I know.'

'But you are both different now, no? You are adults.'

'Yes.'

'And now he is coming home to fulfil his duty to his family.'

A cruel smile played at the corners of Lydia's mouth. 'Yes, the un-drowned kitten returns, emerging from its sack as a fully grown – and no doubt soggy – cat.'

'You think he is going to be a problem?'

'No. His weakness is our strength: he lacks the necessary bollocks to be a Flinch.'

'Good,' He took hold of her belt and drew her gently to him. 'I think it will be fine. You will become good friends. And assuming you are right and he lacks the – what did you say?'

'The bollocks.'

'Yes,' he smiled. 'The bollocks. I must remember that word. If your brother is lacking the necessary bollocks for the job, then everything is just so much easier; he will go home to England like the good boy and leave everything here to us – to the true servants of the Lord Underwood.' He slid his hands up her thighs and under her gown.

'Mmm,' Lydia closed her eyes. 'Yes.'

'But if he turns out to be a problem, and you still hate him ...' He pulled her gown open and kissed her tummy.

Lydia giggled. 'Then killing him will be a pleasure.'

5

KEITH MULLINS SAT ON HIS SUN TERRACE reading the online edition of *The Sun* newspaper. The terrace was situated at the rear of the two-floor apartment above the pub he and his wife, Michelle, had bought last year in the little town of Almacena, Cadiz.

A fly buzzed around and landed on Keith's face. He slapped his face, but missed the fly. It flew away. Keith picked up the plastic fly swatter that lay next to his laptop and waited. A few seconds passed and the fly returned. Keith grinned, watching it as it crawled around on his empty breakfast plate. Then he struck – the swatter mashing the fly into bacon grease and egg yolk. 'Yesss!' Keith put down the swatter and returned to the newspaper.

He had wanted to call their new pub, *The Queen of Hearts*, in memory of the late Princess of Wales; he'd had a vision of Diana's face on the pub sign, smiling angelically down at the punters as they supped their pints on the front terrace. A beautiful image perhaps, but Michelle had reminded him that if he wanted to keep their presence discreet, perhaps it wasn't the best choice. She was right of course – though Keith at least got part of his wish after they translated *The Queen of Hearts* into Spanish and christened the pub *La Reina de Corazones*. He'd had to give up the pub sign idea too. The sign they finally agreed on wasn't the saintly visage of the dead princess, but the Queen of Hearts from the playing card pack. Keith hadn't been happy, but he'd been able to see the logic.

It was eight-thirty in the morning, and from the kitchen he could hear the voices of Michelle and their daughter Melanie as they went through their usual morning mixture of instructions and rebuttals. Then came the sound of a chair being abruptly pushed back; Michelle shouting; a slammed door, and then Michelle emerging onto the terrace looking flustered. 'Little madam,' she said, 'she gets it from you, you know.'

'Gets what? Good looks, animal magnetism?' Keith looked up over the screen of his laptop computer and grinned. 'Balls?'

'Yes, balls. She's got your balls. I don't know where they are exactly, but they got into the ingredients somehow.'

Keith chuckled. 'That's a good thing, girl. A woman needs balls in this world.'

'Not when she's talking to her mother, she doesn't.' Michelle pulled out one of the plastic chairs opposite him and sat down.

'Aw, leave it, Chelle. She's just at that age. It's a phase. She'll grow out of it.'

'That's easy for you to say, you don't have to feed her. Now she's saying she doesn't want milk anymore. She wants soy milk. She not eating her bloody corn flakes.'

'What's that then?' said Keith, returning his interest to the screen, the back of which was facing Michelle. He clicked to see the day's Page Three girl.

'She says it's from a bean or something, a soy bean.'

Keith's brow furrowed. He looked up from admiring Amii from Birmingham. 'A bean that's got milk in it? What? Like a coconut?'

'Well, I don't know, do I? She says Teresa drinks it and it's better for you than what milk is. Apparently you can make shepherd's pie and everything out of it.'

'What? Bean milk?'

'No, not the milk, the bean; it's a meat alternative. Vegetarians eat them.'

'Don't tell me she wants to become a bloody veggie.'

'Well if she does, I'm not cooking for her. Bloody bean pies; she can do it herself. Either that or you can. After all,' she smiled sarcastically, 'It's just a phase, isn't it? You won't have to do it for long.'

Keith laughed and returned to admiring Amii from Birmingham.

'Anyway,' said Michelle. 'What're you looking at? Page three?'

Keith closed Amii's window and returned to the newspaper. 'No,' he said, feigning offence. 'Actually, I'm reading about women's problems. I'm reading about the G-spot in *Dear Deirdre*.' He nodded to the screen. 'It says here that some women feel it's the greatest turn-on ever while others hate it. Some feel it's a pleasurable variation, while others find it irritating.' He looked up. 'How's your G-spot then, Chelle?'

'How should I know?'

'Well, who else is gonna know if you don't?'

'That's your job, that is. Does it say where it is?'

Keith read on then looked up with a smile. 'Yeah.'

She smiled and opened her dressing gown a little at the chest. 'Fancy having a look for it then do you?'

Melanie's voice came from inside the apartment, 'I'm going to school.'

Michelle pulled her gown closed. Keith leaned sideways and called, 'Not without kissing your old man goodbye you ain't, young lady.'

Footsteps approached through the kitchen, and then Melanie, clutching the mobile phone they had bought her for her fourteenth birthday, stepped out into the sunshine. She said nothing, moving quickly to her father and planting a kiss on his cheek before turning and heading back the way she had come.

'Oi!' said Keith. Melanie stopped in the doorway, her back to him. 'What was that?'

Melanie turned. 'A goodbye kiss. That's what you asked for isn't it?'

'A goodbye kiss without saying goodbye is only half the deal, girl. And what about your mother?'

'What about her?'

'Don't she get a kiss?'

Melanie looked at her mother. 'She didn't ask for one.'

'She doesn't have to,' said Keith, 'she's your mother; she gets one anyway.'

Melanie sighed and walked back to Keith, kissing him again on the cheek and saying, pointedly, 'Bye Dad.'

'Much better.'

Melanie looked at Michelle. Michelle met her eyes and raised her finely-plucked eyebrows. Melanie bent and pecked her on the cheek. 'Bye Mum.'

'Good girl,' said Keith to Melanie's back as she disappeared back into the shadows of the apartment.

'I'll get your bean milk later, love,' Michelle called after her.

'Thanks, Mum.'

A moment later, they heard the front door bang shut.

'There, you see?' said Keith serenely. 'All it takes is a bit of fatherly guidance.'

Michelle smiled and stroked her neck suggestively. 'Hmm. I think I might need a bit of fatherly guidance an' all.'

'Oh? How can I help you, then?'

'I can't seem to find my G-spot.'

Keith grinned and looked back to the computer screen, quickly reading and memorizing the directions. 'Fortunately for you girl, I happen to know the way to that particular pleasurable variation.' He got up, his arousal already conspicuous from the front of his shorts.

Michelle pulled her gown open. There was no need for modesty; they were not overlooked by any of their neighbours. 'I hope I'm not one of them women that reckon it's all just an irritation.'

'Don't worry, girl,' said Keith tugging his shorts down. 'It won't be.'

Candlelight flickered on the white stucco ceiling, the black beams with their nails and hooks, the small boy kept his eyes diverted upwards, not wanting to look at the black-robed figures that were focused on him, staring, their faces shadowed by the hoods they wore. His mother's hand squeezed his and encouraged him to take a step forward. Afraid to do so, but even more fearful of being left behind should she choose to let go, the boy followed. The man he had been told to call "father" stood beside the coffin. At his left hand stood a robed figure holding a silver bowl that contained the blood of the cockerel they had just killed. His father beckoned to him then turned to dip his fingers in the blood.

The boy faltered at the sight of the blood. His mother pulled at his hand but he refused to budge. He began to cry. Then he felt himself lifted up, he turned and saw the face of Martin, the man he had been told to call "brother".

Martin whispered in his ear, 'Shhh, David, it's all right. It won't hurt you; it'll make you strong.'

The boy, David, cried and twisted but he felt himself carried forwards to the dripping red fingers of his father. The old man smiled and spoke in a language he didn't understand, words that made no sense. The other people in the room began to repeat the words. David struggled as the fingers reached for his forehead. He turned his face away. And then he saw the lid of the coffin beginning to tremble, rising slowly as if it were being lifted from within.

Then Martin was trying to turn his face back to the old man's fingers that were reaching for him, dripping with blood. David was struggling now, fighting to get away, because he could see other fingers, long-nailed, yellow fingers curling around the edge of the coffin lid.

David screamed –

The Ryanair 737 hit the tarmac with a bump that jolted David from his dream. The youth in the aisle seat next to him was already texting someone. He looked at David and smiled. 'Alright mate?'

'Sorry?'

'You alright? Sounded like you were having a bit of a nightmare, there.'

'Yes,' David rubbed his face. 'Yes, I was.'

'Still,' said the youth. 'We're here now, eh?'

'Yeah,' David nodded. He looked out of the window as the aircraft taxied into its resting place. He squinted at the brightness outside; under a sky of brilliant blue, the world was drenched in dazzling sunshine. David sat and waited for the seatbelt light to go out. When it did, the usual chaos ensued: the sound of hundreds of buckles clattering open and being flung aside was followed by the wriggling stampede of passengers into the aisle, all of them struggling to pull bags from overhead lockers and turn mobile phones on at the same time. David looked out of the window at the ground crews in their short-sleeved shirts and sunglasses. Despite everything, in that moment he felt strangely happy to be here. He turned back to where the mass of his fellow passengers had now coagulated in the aisle; cramped and entangled, waiting for the cabin door to open. Then it did open and a warm breeze drifted through the cabin. Then the passengers began to slowly shuffle and nudge their way forwards to freedom.

David yawned and looked out of the window. The bags were being off-loaded and those passengers that had already disembarked were now being herded towards the bus that had been sent to pick them up to transport them to the terminal building. He turned to see that the aisle was now almost empty. He got to his feet, pulled his bag from the overhead locker and strolled towards the exit. Someone had left a newspaper on a seat; he picked it up and slipped it under his arm, then with a parting smile at the stewardess, he stepped out into the heat.

On the tarmac, the first bus was already pulling away and a second was now filling up. He trotted down the steps and made his way over to join the struggling crowd, glancing as he did to where the first bus now pulled up about a hundred yards away at the terminal building. He resisted the urge to walk the short distance and risk the wrath of the ground crews, and instead stepped onto the bus and turned to the back pages of the newspaper to see how Arsenal had got on the night before.

Fifteen minutes later, having reclaimed his bags, David pushed a luggage trolley into the arrivals lounge where an array of expectant faces waited for persons other than him. Dozens of pairs of eyes simultaneously noticed and dismissed him, but one pair of eyes remained fixed on him: they belonged to an attractive woman in her late thirties wearing a white blouse and beige skirt. At first glance, her tanned skin and long dark hair gave her a Latin appearance, but he recognised her – just as she evidently recognised him. In her hands she held a sign with one word written in black marker: "Flinch". A pair of young men just ahead of David obeyed the sign and flinched comically from her. She scowled at them and David read the words 'fuck off' on her lips. The young men swaggered away, and David rolled his trolley up and stopped before her.

'Hello Lydia.'

She smiled. 'David.' They embraced and she kissed him, first on one cheek, then the other.

'It's been a while.'

'Yes, it has,' she looked him up and down. 'You're looking very well.'

'So are you. I wasn't sure if I'd recognise you. How long have you been here now?'

'Since I was twenty-one, I moved out for good after I finished university.'

'Well it certainly seems to suit you.'

'Thank you.' She ran her hand through his hair. 'I see you've lost the long hair. I like it.'

He smiled, slightly embarrassed. 'It's been that way since the army.'

'Yes, so you joined in the end then?' She stepped aside and indicated the corridor behind her. 'Come, my car's this way.'

David pushed his luggage trolley forwards and they began to walk. 'Yeah. I did it to keep my mum happy. She felt it would be best – for everyone – if I followed the family tradition.'

'I always knew you were a good boy deep down. I was sorry to hear about your mother.'

He looked at her. 'Oh? You know about that?'

She nodded. 'Yes.'

'Of course you do. You found me, didn't you? It stands to reason you'd have found out about my mother's suicide. Tell me, how did you find me?'

'John hired a detective.'

'A member of the Sect, I suppose?'

'Naturally. A retired police detective.'

He nodded, searching his memory for the thousands of faces that blurred in his background for one who he might have noticed again and again looking at him from the shadows. But no suspicious characters arose: he'd never seen nor suspected anyone. 'Well, he did a good job.'

'Within reason. Of course he couldn't tell us why you chose to ... distance yourself.'

David smiled. 'Oh come on, Lydia. I think you know why.'

She shook her head. 'No, I don't. Tell me.'

He glanced around the arrivals lounge, looking for a distraction. He fixed on a queue of people at a car rental place. There were signs by the sales window announcing the disappearance of a young man. 'Let's just say it was a combination of factors.'

'Like?'

David saw another sign for the missing young man at the next car rental place. He turned back to Lydia. She was waiting patiently for an answer. 'You really don't know?'

'If I knew I wouldn't be asking.'

David shook his head in disbelief. 'Well, there was you for one thing.'

'Me?'

'Yes, you. Don't sound so surprised. I felt it best if we didn't spend so much time around each other.'

'Oh? Why?'

'Oh don't come the innocent, Lydia. You know why.'

For a moment they walked on in silence, neither looking at the other. Then Lydia said. 'I see. I always thought it might have had something to do with Lord Underwood.'

'Well yes, there was him too. But mostly it was you.'

'Oh. Well, I'm sorry to hear that.'

'Yeah, well, anyway, it's all ancient history now. Let's just put it behind us and get on with the present, shall we?'

'Yes. I suppose that would be the sensible thing to do.'

'So tell me about John, how bad is he?'

'About as bad as it gets I'm afraid. He's not expected to last much longer.'

'I see. Was it him or you who decided to contact me?'

'Him.'

'How long did it take to find me?'

'Oh we found you years ago. John hired Feltham – that's the detective – to track you down about five years ago. He's been keeping tabs on you ever since, sending John little updates, you know.'

David stopped. 'Really?'

Lydia nodded. 'Of course. Why? Does that surprise you?'

He resumed pushing his trolley, 'No, I suppose not. I suppose now that I think of it I'm surprised he left it so long. Why five years ago?'

'For a long time John was happy to just let you do your thing. He had hoped that you'd make your own way back to us, but I suppose he eventually came to realise that you weren't going to and so he contracted Feltham. He wanted to know where you were, if you were happy, if you were okay. Just normal family stuff.'

'Yeah, like we're a normal family.'

'We're the only family you've got, David. Normal or otherwise.'

'Oh I'd say it's definitely a case of "otherwise", Lydia.'

She smiled. 'So how does it feel, coming home to your *"otherwise"* family after so long?'

He gave a short dismissive laugh. 'Weird. I mean, I'm happy on some levels but obviously very sad – and terrified – on others.'

She laughed. 'Terrified?'

'Yes. Why's that so funny? Although it wasn't stated in the letter, I presume that now John is going to die the role of Underwood's Guardian is going to fall to me?'

'Yes, but surely you're not afraid of Underwood? He's our family's great benefactor, you've nothing to fear from him.'

'Well, that's easy for you to say, you're not the one in line for the job, are you?'

'No, more's the pity. As soon as the midwife saw I lacked a penis I was out of the running.'

'Count yourself lucky.'

'Lucky? To be prejudiced against because of my gender?'

'In this case, yes, I would say so.'

'Well you'd say wrongly. You've been given an amazing opportunity that I can never have, and frankly it makes me sick. I'd give anything to be in your shoes.'

'Well as far as I'm concerned you can have my shoes. I don't want this bloody job.'

She smiled. 'Yes, I suspected as much. But you forget David, what we want is irrelevant. Tradition dictates that this is a boy's job: only male Flinches need apply for it.'

'Bollocks to tradition, Lydia: if you want the job, you can have it. We'll work it out between us.'

She put her hand on his, stopping the trolley. 'Really?'

He turned to her. Suddenly her face was very serious. He nodded. 'Sure. Like I said, I don't want the job. I've got my own life, you know?

It's not much, but I'm happy. This Guardian thing is ...', he sought for the right word; he didn't want to offend her.

'What?'

'I dunno ... horrific?'

She laughed. 'Yes, it is rather. But surely John – and Underwood himself – they'd never accept me, a woman, in the role.'

'Well, they might, times have changed, haven't they?' He felt lighter, relieved that Lydia was willing to take the job off his hands. He chuckled. 'Hey, maybe we should threaten to report Underwood to the Spanish board of equal opportunities? They'd soon sort him out.'

Lydia smiled but she wasn't amused. 'I'm serious David, and so should you be. This isn't a subject I see as having a particularly funny side.'

They approached the glass doors that opened onto the road outside. Warm air, rich with exhaust fumes and the cigarette smoke from a group of taxi drivers in highly animated discussion rolled over them. 'Yeah,' said David, reaching into his breast pocket and taking out his sunglasses. 'I have a feeling you may be right about that.'

About thirty minutes after embarking on what turned out to be a fruitless but enjoyable quest for Michelle's G-spot, Keith returned to his daily perusal of the online British press. Michelle was in the shower and he had made himself another mug of coffee. He was just about to take a sip when somewhere in the apartment his mobile phone started ringing.

'Oh bollocks,' he muttered.

'Your phone's ringing!' Michelle shouted from the bathroom.

'I know, I'm not deaf!' he shouted back as he got up and followed the sound of the ringtone, a tinny version of *The Final Countdown* by Europe.

'I'm only saying,' said Michelle defensively, a towel wrapped around her body as she passed him on her way to the kitchen.

Keith ignored her and picked up the phone from the dining room table. He looked at the caller display: it was Hodge, his best friend and member of his team for five years. Keith answered the call. 'Hodge! Alright mate?'

'Alright Keith. Are you okay to talk?'

Keith looked back to the kitchen. Michelle had put the kettle on and was now returning through the apartment. He smiled at her.

'Who is it?' she asked.

'It's Hodge.'

'Oh,' she said brightly. 'Say hello for me.' She went off to the bedroom. A moment later, Keith heard the sound of her hairdryer.

'Yeah, it's okay. Chelle says hello.'

'Oh right, say hello back,' said Hodge. 'Listen, have you heard about that pill-head Mark Coleman?'

'No. What about him?'

'It's in all the papers, mate. And it's flipping gruesome stuff, an' all.'

'What is? Whatchoo on about?'

'He's been decapitated.'

'Decapsitated? What? You mean someone's cut his head off?'

'Yeah. They found it on a bench on an Ibiza seafront.'

Keith's legs felt weak. He sat down. 'Fucking hell. Who do they think done it?'

'They're not saying, but I don't reckon it was bloody Al-Qaeda, do you?'

'Well, you never know. Maybe he was selling pills in the wrong neighbourhood.'

'He was in Ibiza, not Baghdad.'

'Well maybe they were on holiday.'

'I don't think so, mate.'

'You never know.'

'Yeah. I think we do though, don't we?'

'What?'

'Know.'

Keith's jaw tensed. 'Know what? What are you tryin' to say, Hodge?'

There was a moment of hesitation from Hodge's end, then he said, 'I reckon it's Sergei. I reckon it's like ... some sort of warning.'

'Warning? Who to?'

'Who to? To us, mate. I reckon Sergei caught up with Mark and got all medieval on his arse. And most likely he tried to get him to say where we are an' all.'

Keith was silent.

'Keith?'

'Yeah.'

'What do you think?'

'I dunno. I bloody hope not, but it could be, couldn't it. Did he know anything?'

'Mark? No, he only knew the lies what we told him about us going to Portugal to play golf for the rest of our days.'

'Nothing more?'

'No chance. That's the story we told him, the same story we told everyone down in Benidorm. You can't be too careful, can you.'

'Yeah, well tell me about it, H. That's why I put this pub in Chelle's name, innit? In case they ever started looking for me in the Yellow Pages.'

'I know, mate. Smart move, that.'

'Yeah, still, cost me a nice pub sign though, giving her all that clout.'

'Well if I'm right about Coleman and Sergei, maybe it's just as well eh?'

Keith nodded thoughtfully. 'Yeah. 'Ere, but hang on, what about Damo?'

'What about him?'

'He wouldn't have said nothing to no-one, would he?'

'Course not! He knows the score.'

'Yeah, course he does.'

'Anyway, check it out, it's front page news on *El Pais* online.'

'I can't read that, it's in Spanish.'

'Well you can look at the pictures can't you? Either that or get your kid to translate it.'

'Oh yeah, good idea: draw her attention to it – an article which might make daddy shit his pants. Oh, I know, I can get her to read it to me through the bathroom door, that way I can be ready on the bog when it gets to the bit about how the bad men are going to come and cut daddy's fuckin' head off.'

'All right Keith, no need to be sarcastic.'

'I'm sorry, mate, but you've gone and got me all nervous now,' Keith heard the hairdryer cut out in the bedroom. 'Listen, I have to go, I'll have a butcher's at it meself in a minute.' He lowered his voice as he heard Michelle approaching.

'Have a butcher's at what?' she asked as she walked past.

Keith ignored her. 'I'll see you later, mate,' he said to Hodge before disconnecting the call and putting the phone back on the table. With a long sigh he sat down and lowered his face into his hands. His mind went back to the night of the shooting…

The dark interior of the van as it pulls out and speeds across the car park. Through the partly-open rear door he can see again the ground blurring; he's holding the shotgun in both hands, ready to fire; his footing unsteady, he staggers against Hodge.

Then Damo is shouting in the driver's seat followed by a massive thump as the van hits one of the Russians. Keith falls to one knee, a shooting pain, forgotten immediately as guns open fire outside, the thin panels of the van afford no protection at all; bullets rip through the walls, whizzing through the air behind him. Then Damo brakes hard and again, Keith staggers against Hodge, swearing, trying to keep the shotgun steady.

Damo screams from the cab: 'For fuck's sake shoot the bastards!'

Hodge's boot rises and kicks open the door, his gun goes up: two men outside, bringing their guns to bear on them. Then the flash and boom as Hodge fires. Keith raises the shotgun, feels his fingers tightening on the triggers, then both barrels, one after the other belch fire and smoke. He sees one of the Russians falling backwards, his pistol falling from his hand. Then Hodge's second barrel booms and the other Russian, the only one still standing, flies back in a red mist.

Michelle stepped into the kitchen doorway. 'Have a butcher's at what?'

Keith blinked and the dining room returned. 'What?'

'What is it you're going to have a look at?'

'Oh, something in *El Pais* online. Hodge said he saw something interesting.'

'What was that then?'

'Some ... druggie geezer's been murdered.'

'Oh. No great loss there then,' said Michelle as the toaster popped behind her. 'I'll tell you what that is. It's them bloody East European mafias that's what that is, same as in Benidorm.'

'It wasn't in Benidorm, Chelle. It was in Ibiza.'

'Oh right?' said Michelle, surprised. 'I thought that was supposed to be Love Island.'

'Yeah. Well, not any more it ain't.'

'No, not by the sound of it.' She went back into the kitchen to butter the toast. 'Thank God we moved away from the coast, eh?'

'Yeah,' said Keith quietly. 'Thank God.'

David sat in the passenger seat of Lydia's white Land Rover Discovery and looked out of the windows at the scenery as they drove up into the high country. He listened with interest as Lydia told him about how, after finishing studying Spanish and German at University, she'd returned to Spain in the early 90's. Initially she'd stayed with John at Casa Underwood – which is what they'd called the family's house since they were teenagers – but she soon moved out and got a job and an apartment down in Malaga.

Her job had been with a firm of estate agents that specialised in selling property to foreigners, mostly British, Irish, German and Dutch. She learned fast. Four years later, with a loan from John, she went into business for herself. By the end of the 90's, she was rich. She had two offices on the Costa del Sol and in recent years had begun to move into the inland property market. She'd opened an office in Almacena, four kilometres from Casa Underwood, and business had been booming.

'Inland is the new coast, David. Lots of cheap property and lots of Brits keen to buy it all up.'

'Why?' He asked, turning back to her. 'I mean, what do they see in it?'

She smiled. 'Oh, pretty much the opposite to England, I suppose: good weather, safe streets, happy children.' She looked at him over her the rims of her sunglasses. 'England's not a happy country any more David, or hadn't you noticed?'

'I like it,' he said without enthusiasm.

'Oh come on! You can't tell me you don't miss it here. We always had so much fun.'

'Did we?'

'Of course we did. I hated having to leave when our school holidays were over. Leaving Dad and all my brothers and going back to rainy old England. Yeuch. I couldn't wait until I was old enough to get back here permanently.'

'Well, that's good for you then. You got what you wanted.'

'Yes,' she turned to him. 'Mostly. Still, it's not for you, eh?'

'No.'

'So, why are you back here if you don't want the job?'

'Because I have to be.'

'For John?'

'Yeah. He's my brother. He's always been good to me.'

'Yet you turned your back on him all these years?'

David took out his cigarettes. 'Do you mind?'

'No, actually can I have one?'

He lit two and handed her one. 'Look, I didn't turn my back on John personally.'

'No, you turned your back on all of us, the whole family.'

'Yes, because, frankly Lydia, the family is evil.'

'Oh rubbish! John's not evil. Martin wasn't evil.'

'Dad was evil.'

'Dad was eccentric.'

David turned to her, his face unbelieving. 'Black mass rituals aren't eccentricities, Lydia. Daubing inverted crucifixes on your own kids' foreheads with chicken's blood, getting them to kneel before coffins with fucking vampires in them, these aren't fucking eccentricities.'

'Oh, it was all just part of the normalisation process, to prepare us for what we had to do in later life.'

'Namely?'

She shrugged. 'To serve the Lord Underwood.'

'By serve you mean what? Ring the bell at four o'clock to say tea is ready?'

She chuckled. 'I don't think His Lordship drinks tea.'

'You know that whoever "serves the Lord Underwood" as you put it, is going to have to kill people, don't you Lydia? Are you capable, seriously capable, of murder?'

'Are you?'

'No.'

She laughed. 'So what did they teach you in the army? Flower arranging?'

'I trained as a medic. I saved lives, Lydia, I didn't take them.'

'Ah, but I read Feltham's files on you, David. You didn't start as a medic, you were in Bosnia. Surely you killed a few people there?'

'Obviously you didn't read very closely. If you had you'd know I was there as part of a United Nations peacekeeping force. Our job was to protect people.'

'Oh, I see,' she nodded with mock gravity. 'And then you went on to more life-saving larks when you became an ambulance man; a paramedic, isn't that what they call it these days?'

'Yes.'

'But you then you left that and became a drunkard. Interesting career choice.'

David said nothing.

'So why did you leave the ambulance service?'

'Didn't your Mr Feltham tell you?'

'He told us about your girlfriend's accident.'

'She was more than my girlfriend; we were going to be married.'

'Oh,' Lydia was surprised. 'I'm sorry, I didn't know that.'

'Yeah, well, now you do. So let's leave it at that, shall we?'

They drove in silence for a while. Then, David turned to her. 'Lydia, about this Guardian business.'

'Yes, what about it?'

'I'm not going to do it.'

'I know, you said that.'

'Yes, but, neither should you.'

'What?'

'Be Guardian.'

She laughed. 'Oh David, don't be ridiculous. If you don't do it and I don't do it, who will?'

'No one does.'

She frowned. 'No one?'

'Yes. Listen, I've been thinking about it, about the role of Guardian. Not just since yesterday, but for years.'

She smiled wistfully. 'Yes, haven't we all?'

'No Lydia, not in a good way, because it's not a good thing. It's diabolical. Though to hear you talking about it now, talking about Dad as if he were just some loveable old eccentric ...'

'He was.'

'He wasn't! Jesus, Lydia. Arthur Flinch, our father, was a murderer in the service of a vampire.'

'And?'

'*And?* Underwood is vampire. A real one! Not like something off the television but a real creature that rises every night and kills people for food.'

Lydia flicked her cigarette out of the window. 'Why don't you finish your cigarette so we can close the windows and put the air conditioning on?'

'Lydia, when Underwood wakes up, he's going to start killing people again.'

'Unless of course you prefer the windows open.'

'Fuck the windows! Listen to me! Whoever becomes Guardian will become an accomplice to murder. Not to one, but hundreds, maybe thousands of murders.'

'Oh, so what?' she shouted. 'I know that! You know that! We've always known that!'

'And you can do that, can you? You can kill innocent people?'

'If necessary.'

'But don't you see?' David appealed with open hands. 'It's not necessary. We don't *have* to resurrect him. We can just kill him; you and me. This whole resurrection thing just doesn't need to happen.' He laughed. 'Underwood's been rotting in his coffin for fifty bloody years. All we need to do is bang a stake in his heart and then it's all over. We can both get to go back to our lives and live happily ever after.'

Lydia was silent, her eyes on the winding road ahead.

'Lydia?'

'Oh, I heard you, David.'

'So? What do you think?'

'You know, I said to John you weren't up to the role of Guardian, but he said you were. I said you were a wimp, but he said you had guts. I said you'd let him down – and I was right. But even I had no idea just how far away from us you'd gone. And what a complete fucking coward you are.'

She pulled off to the side of the road and braked in a cloud of dust.

'Lydia, for Christ's sake.'

'Don't talk to me about Christ, David. There is no Christ! There is only Underwood. He is our God. He is our sole purpose and always has been. That you don't want to be Guardian comes as no surprise. Fine. Fuck off! Run away and hide under your bed with a bottle of Jack Daniels. But if you think you're going to stop the resurrection of *my* Messiah, you've got another think coming, because in my heart, I accepted the role of Guardian long ago. And I can, and will, kill anyone who would do him harm. And trust me, David: that includes you.'

David looked at her and suddenly knew beyond any doubt that she was deadly serious. He smiled, his mouth was dry. He nodded, slowly. 'Good. That's good. I was just checking, see, 'cause you'd have to be, you know? Prepared to kill. I wasn't really serious.'

Lydia's face remained grave for a few moments then she began to laugh. 'Oh, you should see your face. I really had you going there, didn't I?'

David blinked. He tried to laugh but a strange sound came out instead. 'Uh, oh yeah. Yeah. Nice one.'

'Still the same old David.' She put her hand on his thigh and gave it a squeeze. 'Still afraid of your own sister.' She laughed as she eased the car back out onto the road. 'Oh, that was priceless.'

6

'OH GOOD, our favourite table's free,' said Gerald Benson with a smile as he and his wife, Cynthia, approached *La Reina de Corazones*. 'What'll it be for you this morning, Cyn?'

'Oh, I think I'll have one of those little coffees to get me started.'

'Ah yes, the same for me I think. Just the ticket. Is it a *cortado* or *cortada*? I can never remember.'

'*Cortado*, Gerald,' said Cynthia. 'Coffee is masculine.'

'Yes, of course. I'll try and think of it in masculine terms. I know – I'll mentally draw on a penis in the milky head of the coffee.'

'Oh, really, Gerald, I do wish you'd keep your technique for remembering masculine and feminine nouns to yourself. Now, I too shall be seeing willies in my coffee.'

Gerald chuckled. 'Sorry.'

The Bensons had come out to Spain six months before to enjoy early retirement. Gerald was fifty-five years old. A yellow cotton shirt flowed over his ample belly and a white Panama hat protected his bald patch from the sun. Cynthia was fifty-two; plump, but not overweight. She wore a white cotton dress and a pair of expensive sunglasses. They stepped onto the front terrace of the pub just as the barman, Luis, was wiping down their usual table in the corner.

'Morning, Luis,' said Gerald, dropping his edition of yesterday's *Daily Mail* onto the table.

'*Buenas días*, Luis,' said Cynthia. '*Que tal?*'

'*Muy bien, gracias*,' said Luis cheerfully. 'Your Spanish is very good, Cynthia.'

'Oh, Luis, you're too kind,' said Cynthia, pulling out a plastic chair. 'I can barely say my own name in Spanish.'

Gerald sat down. 'It's still Cynthia, surely?'

Cynthia ignored him and focused her smile on Luis, who was as handsome as he was charming.

Luis laughed. 'Gerald is right, there is no Spanish equivalent of Cynthia.'

'Oh. How unfortunate,' said Cynthia.

'What's "Gerald", Luis?' asked Gerald.

'Geraldo,' said Luis. 'We pronounce the G as a H.'

'Geraldo!' said Gerald.

'I could have told you that, darling,' said Cynthia.

Luis took out his notebook and pencil. 'What would you like this morning?'

'*Dos cortados, por favor,*' said Gerald.

Luis's smile was dazzling. 'Very good, Gerald.'

Gerald laughed. 'Who's Gerald, eh? Call me Geraldo, Luis.'

'Okay, Geraldo,' Luis gave a nod and went into the shadowy interior of the pub.

'Well done, Geraldo,' said Cynthia.

Michelle, who had seen the Bensons arrive, walked out from inside the pub shading her eyes with her hand. 'Who's Geraldo?'

'I am,' said Gerald, delighted with himself.

Michelle pulled out a chair and joined them. 'That's nice, isn't it? Of course you know who I am, don't you?'

'You're Michelle; Keith's girl,' said Gerald. 'You live here.'

'No, I mean in Spanish,' said Michelle, giving his arm a little pat. 'Tell me.'

'I'm Miguela.'

'Oh, that's lovely isn't it, Cyn?'

'Yes, charming. But I have no Spanish equivalent, apparently,' said Cynthia. 'Cynthia is uniquely English.'

'Aw,' said Michelle with a sympathetic look. 'Never mind, eh?'

'Ahhh,' said Luis, returning with the coffees. 'But in Portuguese of course, there is Cintia.'

'There you are,' said Michelle. 'We can call you Cintia.'

Cynthia smiled. 'Thank you, Michelle, but I prefer Cynthia. Where's Keith?'

'He's still upstairs trying to read a Spanish newspaper online,' Michelle's rings clicked against each other as she pushed her straightened blonde hair back over her ears. 'Apparently some bloke got his head chopped off in Ibiza.'

Cynthia grimaced. 'Oh dear, how careless of him. Anyone important?'

'No, just some druggie bloke. His head turned up on a bench, apparently.'

'I say,' said Gerald, 'I had no idea Ibiza was such a perilous island.'

'It's probably them East European Mafias, innit?' said Michelle. 'They're everywhere these days.'

'Hmm,' Cynthia murmured. 'It was on a bench you say?'

'Yeah, by the seaside.'

'Do you suppose somebody forgot it?'

'Eh?'

'Well, perhaps they were going somewhere and they stopped at the bench for a rest – '

Gerald frowned. 'And what? Left their head behind? I doubt it, Cynthia, chap couldn't have got too far without his head.'

Cynthia sighed. 'No, Geraldo, perhaps the *murderer* forgot it.' She turned to Michelle. 'Was it in a bag or something?'

'I dunno, I'll ask Keith later. He knows the Spanish word for "bag", so if that's in the article at least he'll be able to read that.'

'Perhaps there's something about it in the *Daily Mail*.' Gerald picked up his newspaper and began to scan the front page.

'I don't think you'll find anything in there, Gerald. It's yesterday's edition, remember? You're not in Hayward's Heath anymore.'

'Oh, yes, of course.' Gerald abandoned his search. 'Perhaps tomorrow then.'

Cynthia spoke to Michelle. 'Didn't you used to live on the coast, in Benidorm?'

Michelle nodded. 'Yeah, that's right.'

'I hear there's a lot of gangland activity down along the Costas. Is that true?'

Michelle smiled 'Oh, I wouldn't know, Cyn. I suppose there's probably a bit here and there.'

'It's just that you said it was probably a mafia thing. Are the East European mafias known for cutting off heads?'

Michelle shrugged. 'I dunno to be honest. But it wouldn't surprise me.'

'Very popular with the terrorists in Iraq for a while, wasn't it,' said Gerald. 'And other places too, I believe.'

Michelle grimaced. 'It's bloody disgusting, isn't it?'

'Yes, but frightening though,' said Gerald. 'Puts the willies up the enemy. That's what it's all about, Michelle – fear. Mark my words, whoever did this is trying to put the willies up some enemy.'

'Oh really, Gerald,' said Cynthia. 'Do you think we might change the subject? All this talk of heads and willies is making me feel quite ill.'

'Sorry, Cyn,' said Gerald. He turned to Michelle. 'Anyway, how's young Melanie?'

'Oh, fine,' said Michelle. 'Her friend's allergic to milk at the moment so she thinks *she* is. She wants to drink soy milk now.'

Cynthia's lip curled slightly. 'Oh no, Michelle, that's like flour and water paste, it's disgusting. You'll have to talk her out of it.'

'Ah,' said Gerald raising a finger. 'I know what to do here. The best thing is to sit her down and make her drink a couple of pints of the stuff. That'll turn her off it. When I was a teenager, my father sat me down and made me drink whiskey 'til I puked all over myself.'

Cynthia smiled. 'Yes, but your father was mad, Gerald.'

'Didn't do me any harm,' said Gerald. 'Taught me a lesson, I can tell you.'

'And what lesson was that, dear?'

Gerald's brows knitted as he tried to remember. 'Well, er, don't drink alcohol, I suppose.'

Michelle slapped his arm affectionately. 'What are you going on about, Gerald. You drink like a bloody fish, you do. You're one of my best customers.'

Gerald chuckled. 'Oh, I don't know – Cyn's probably right. Father was a little odd. Obviously it's a somewhat flawed strategy. Still, you could try it.'

Michelle shook her head. 'I don't think so, Gerald. Thanks all the same.'

Cynthia sipped her coffee. She had no interest in the eating fads of Melanie Mullins and so she changed the subject. 'I hear Lydia Flinch's brother is arriving from England today.'

'Is it today?' said Michelle, surprised.

'Yes, flew in this morning. She's gone to pick him up from the airport and then they're going back to her brother John's place.'

'Oh my God, that poor man,' said Michelle. 'Still, nice for him to have his family all around him. I think if I was gonna die like that, I'd want my family around me; awful to die alone.'

'Yes,' said Gerald. 'Apparently this younger brother chap hasn't seen John or Lydia for about twenty years.'

'Yeah, Lydia was saying the other day,' said Michelle. 'He's the baby of the family, by all accounts.'

'How old is he?' asked Gerald.

'Oh, I can't remember. About two years younger than Lydia. So that'd make him ...'

'Thirty-six,' said Cynthia.

'Yeah, that sounds about right. Be nice for them to be all together again though, won't it? Even if one of them *is* going to die?'

'Yes,' said Cynthia.

'You two are really good mates with Lydia, aren't you?' said Michelle.

'Yes, she helped us move out here.'

'Yeah, I remember. Everyone says she's a really good estate agent, but we bought through a company in Benidorm.'

'Oh, yes, she's marvellous. But Lydia's been so much more to us than just an estate agent, Michelle. Hasn't she Gerald?'

Gerald smiled. 'Oh yes, much more.'

'Without her, life here for us would have been quite impossible. She's taught us so much and introduced us to so many wonderful people.'

'Yes indeed,' said Gerald. 'It's fair to say that she's shown us a whole new way of life.' He chuckled. Cynthia shot him a look, and he fell silent.

Michelle smiled. 'Oh, that's nice. So have you met the brother, John, then?'

'Yes,' said Cynthia. 'Lydia's taken us out to the family home once or twice. '

'It's quite a big place isn't it? A farm?'

'Yes, a *cortijo*.'

'What's that, the Spanish word for farm?'

'Farm house, yes.'

'Is it a nice place?'

'Oh yes, it's lovely,' said Cynthia. 'Been in the family for yonks.'

'When did they buy it?'

'They acquired it in the 50's, I believe.'

'Wow,' said Michelle. 'I bet they paid fuck all for it, back then.'

Cynthia smiled. 'Yes. As you say, fuck all.'

'I wonder what it's worth now, eh? Must be millions.'

'Yes, very probably. But they'd never dream of selling it, it's so much more to them than just a home.'

'Ahh, that's lovely,' said Michelle. 'So what time's the brother's flight getting in?'

Cynthia looked at her watch. 'Oh it should have landed a while ago. In fact, I'd say they must be arriving home about now.'

For the remainder of the car journey, David had tried to steer the conversation away from the topic of Underwood. Despite her subsequent joking about the whole guardian business, something in Lydia's eyes when she had said that she would kill anyone to protect her "messiah" had profoundly unsettled him. Since then, he'd managed to keep the conversation focused on neutral things they might have in common, like TV and movies, and they were mulling over the old chestnut of which band was better – Oasis or Blur – when Lydia suddenly pointed.

'There it is!' She was pointing to a spot ahead of them in the gently undulating landscape of hills and valleys. For a moment David had to squint. Then he saw it; amid the endless ranks of olive trees, a spot of white on top of a low hill. It was still far away, but even from this distance it was possible for him to see that the house had been extended.

'It looks bigger.'

'Oh yes, it is. John's done wonders with the place. You'll hardly recognise it.'

David nodded thoughtfully and watched as the house grew nearer; the white walls and terracotta-tiled roofs becoming slowly more distinct as the distance closed.

Lydia turned off the main road and through the open gates of the property. They drove along a long gravel track through the olive tree groves up to the house. 'Blimey,' said David as they approached the house. 'John's certainly been busy, hasn't he?' The main building was as he remembered it – a large, traditional Andalucian farmhouse, but next to it was now a high, white wall with an archway set half-way along it that opened into a paved courtyard.

'Yes,' said Lydia. She turned off the engine. 'John's quite the handyman.'

David opened the door and got out. After the air-conditioned comfort of the car, the heat was intense. He adjusted his sunglasses and looked out across the sun-baked landscape. 'Phew, it's been a while since I've seen weather like this.'

Lydia smiled. 'You've been under grey skies too long, David. This is only Spring, wait until the summer kicks in.'

David followed her as she walked towards the archway into the courtyard. From the other side of the wall he could hear the sound of splashing water. They entered the courtyard and he laughed with unexpected delight to see the source of the sound: a large fountain was set in the middle of the yard. Water danced and sparkled in the air above it and momentary rainbows flashed in the fine spray. 'Oh my God! How cool is that?' He walked over to the fountain and trailed his fingers through the churning water in the pool.

'Very cool actually,' said Lydia. 'It helps to keep the air fresh.' She was waiting for him by the kitchen door. He flicked the excess water from his fingers and walked over to join her.

Lydia looked at him over the rims of her sunglasses. 'Now David, about John – you should be prepared.'

He nodded. 'Okay.'

'He's in his bedroom. He has nurses who attend him around the clock. Conchi is with him during the daytime.'

'Conchi, right.'

'Now, he's pretty far gone. I mean, he looks different, you know?'

David nodded.

'He's heavily sedated against the pain and he's – ' Lydia broke off. She looked as if she were about to cry.

'Hey, come on.' David put his arm around her shoulders and held her. 'Are you okay?'

'Yeah,' she sniffed. 'I'm all right.' She moved away from him and he withdrew his arm. 'Here I am worrying about you, and I'm the one getting all upset.'

'Well, that's okay.'

She smiled. 'Yeah,' she turned and led the way into the kitchen. It was just as he remembered it: a large farmhouse kitchen with a big wooden table at its centre. A thought occurred to him and he looked over to a work surface along one wall. He smiled. Just as there had always been, a leg of cured ham was set upon a slicing rack and covered with a tea towel. He went over and lifted the cloth, picked up a tiny sliver of meat, and popped it into his mouth. Lydia had moved on into the hallway and he followed her.

In the hall he could hear quiet Spanish guitar music coming from somewhere ahead. He stopped as he was passing the lounge and looked in. The old phonograph record player still sat in the corner; an antique now, like so many other things in the house. Behind it, he saw a modern hi-fi system set into the wall, all black glass and tiny glowing lights.

'Ana likes to have the radio on while she's working,' said Lydia.

David nodded and walked into the room. It hadn't changed in size, only in decor. Large sofas were arranged around an open fireplace and a big plasma screen TV. Above the fireplace, an antique cutlass was mounted against the white wall. David frowned. Didn't there use to be another one crossing it? He stepped closer and saw the empty mounting fixtures for the other sword. He turned back to Lydia. 'Wasn't there was another sword here?'

'Yes, but don't worry about that now.' Lydia gestured for him to follow.

She led the way further down to where the hall opened out into the reception area and staircase. Opposite the front door was a large, full length portrait of Lord Underwood. He had a voluminous moustache and heavy sideburns and was wearing gentleman's Victorian evening dress, replete with a top hat and black evening cape. One of his white gloved hands rested easily on a cane, and a serene smile played upon his lips as he looked out into the room. David felt a cold sensation in his bowels.

'It was painted over a hundred years ago,' said Lydia from the stairs. 'Impressive, isn't it?'

'Yeah, I suppose. I always tried not to look at it when I was a kid. I was afraid of the eyes following me around the room.'

Lydia smiled. 'Yes. They do have that effect, don't they?'

David looked up into the eyes. They seemed to look straight back at him: cheerful, cool, confident to the point of arrogance. David looked away. 'Let's go.' He followed her up the staircase to the upper floor.

She stopped outside the room that had been his during summer holidays when he was a boy. 'Your room.' She opened the door. 'John added an en-suite bathroom to this and all the other bedrooms, but otherwise I think you'll find it's just as you left it.'

It was. The room was exactly as he remembered it, right down to the picture of the 1978 Arsenal squad pinned to the wall above the single bed. He walked over to the window and looked out at the hills to the east. Then, he noticed the swimming pool outside. 'There's a new pool?'

'Yes. Nice, isn't it?'

'When did he put that in?'

'Oh, ages ago. About ten years now.'

David was impressed. 'Well, he's certainly made the most of it out here, hasn't he?'

'Yes, he has. Shall we continue?'

He nodded and they returned to the hall. 'Why did he leave my room the same as it was?'

'Because it's your room.'

'Yeah but ...' he found he couldn't finish the sentence.

Lydia smiled. 'This house has been waiting for you, David. Just as it's been waiting for our Master. Come.' She led the way down the hall and David followed, becoming aware of a chemical smell that grew heavier the closer they got to John's room. When she got to the door, Lydia stopped.

'Okay. Are you ready?'

David nodded. 'Yeah.'

She opened the door for him and he stepped inside. David's breath caught in his chest as he saw his brother for the first time in twenty years. When last he had seen John, he had been a young man – younger than David was now; he had been fit, strong, and almost annoyingly energetic. The man sleeping in the bed before him now was barely recognisable as the same person. Under the white cotton sheets, his body was wasted and brittle-looking; all of the thick blonde hair had gone from his head, and his face was gaunt, his eyes were dark and sunken, and his cheeks concave.

Lydia took David's hand and he was grateful for it. He looked at the photo frames around the room: Martin and John with their father, Arthur; himself at about age eight with Lydia and Arthur; Lydia in a graduation gown; John in his army uniform; a woman he knew to be John's mother, and another picture of a young man he had never seen before. He was relieved to see that there wasn't a picture of Underwood. The balcony windows were open and a light breeze stirred the smell of disinfectant.

Next to the bed a nurse put aside the book she was reading. 'Señorita Flinch.' She stood up.

'Conchita, this is my brother, David.'

Conchita smiled and shook David's hand. 'John has been asking for you for so long, señor Flinch. He will be so happy to see when he wakes up.'

'Please, call me David.'

'How is he today, Conchi?' asked Lydia.

'He is comfortable, señorita Flinch. He has been asleep for a few hours now.'

David moved John's bedside. 'Oh John, dear God.'

John's eyes flickered open. For a moment he stared at David as if he were dreaming him, then he smiled. 'David?'

'Hello mate.'

John reached out and David took his hand gently. 'Oh, David, I'm so glad, so very glad to see you. I, I was beginning to think you weren't going to make it.'

David frowned. 'Make it?'

'Yes, for the resurrection.' John chuckled weakly. 'What else has there been on the Flinch calendar these last fifty years?'

'But, that's not for a while yet, surely?' He turned to Lydia for confirmation but her expression told him nothing.

John looked concerned. 'Lydia? You haven't told him?'

'Not yet, no. I thought you'd want to give him the good news yourself.'

'I see.' John turned to David. 'Well, it's tomorrow night, David. At long last: after fifty years of deathly slumber, Lord Underwood, our family's sole reason and purpose, shall rise again. And you, David, you will be there to welcome him; his loyal guardian and trusted servant.'

David grew pale and sat down on the bed. 'Tomorrow?' He turned to Lydia as if to say, *you knew this?*

Lydia shrugged.

John squeezed David's hand. 'Your return to us on this eve of resurrection is a blessing from Hell, David. For while I may soon be dead, in you, the Flinch line shall survive.' He laughed and his voice was dry and raspy. 'Rejoice! Underwood and Flinch are born again!'

7

KEITH REMOVED HIS WEST HAM BASEBALL cap and wiped a dew of sweat from his brow. He stopped a moment to adjust the tightness of the hat so it wasn't quite so snug, then slipped it back on and continued towards Hodge's apartment. As he walked beneath the orange trees that lined the road, his mind continued to gnaw at the news of the discovery of Mark Coleman's head. It had to have been the Russians – Coleman had been a dickhead, but he wouldn't have been on anyone's hit list. Anyone, that is, other than Sergei Alexandrov's. And his presence on that list had been entirely Keith's fault.

He stopped to step aside for a young woman and her elderly mother. He smiled and both women greeted him with a "*hola*".

Keith touched the brim of his cap. '*Hola.*' He liked the way people here said hello to you even when they didn't know who you were. He knew from old movies that it had once been like that in England, but that would have been before his time.

He and Michelle had come out to Spain in 2003. Before the move, they had owned a pub in Slough, but they'd sold up and moved out to Benidorm looking for a better life in the sun. They'd bought an already established British pub near the seafront called John Bull's Tavern. It was a popular spot and they were soon making a good living, mainly from the tourist trade but also from regulars in the ex-pat community, some of whom did little other than hang around in the bar from opening through to closing time every day.

Among the younger ex-pats the demand for the dodgy little extras soon became apparent, and Keith quickly learned to spot the purveyors of those dodgy little extras: the dealers who used to hang around the bar with the same lazy persistence as vinegar flies.

It had been Damo who'd suggested that instead of simply putting these dealers out of the pub, he should be putting them out of business – and then making their business his own. Damo, Hodge and Pete Sweeney had been initially hired as bar staff. Keith hired them because he liked them; he saw something in each of them that mirrored aspects of his own personality. For that reason perhaps, all four had quickly became firm friends.

Keith had warmed to the drug dealing idea and sat down with the Damo and the lads to talk it over. They were all men of the world and each of them had, at some stage, dabbled in narcotic distractions. Damo and Pete had especially enjoyed being distracted – though, of course, never when they were on duty – and their source of drugs had been Mark Coleman.

Once Coleman was established as pub's supplier, they had begun dealing – nothing serious, and never beyond the door of John Bull's, but that wasn't necessary: their regulars were the only custom that Keith was interested in. He'd thought of it as an extra service to give him the one-up on the competition; all the seafront pubs had Sky Sports and a full English breakfast advertised on the placard outside, but Keith had two unique selling points his competitors didn't have: a jar of pickled eggs on the counter and, for regulars, easy access to marijuana, ecstasy and cocaine.

The police may or may not have known about it, either way they had never hassled them. It was just a bit of *guiri* business – "guiri" being a Spanish word used to identify obvious North European tourists of the fair-skinned, socks-and-sandals variety.

For a few years things had ticked over very nicely, but then the Russian problem began. Sergei had bars and clubs in Malaga and Alicante but then he had started moving into Benidorm, buying up British and Irish pubs. Keith didn't know why, though he had read somewhere that one of the mob's key activities was money laundering. He assumed it was that, rather than a love of Sky Sports and pickled eggs, that had been on Sergei's mind when he approached Keith to make an offer for the John Bull Tavern. The offer had been a generous one and despite Keith's conviction not to sell, he'd been tempted, though ultimately he declined. The visit had ended amicably, with Sergei handing him his business card and telling him that if ever he changed his mind, to give him a call.

A few days later, the problems began. His staff started to report being hassled on their way to work by burly East European guys. These big skinheads would approach in twos and offer the staff member better rates of pay to work at one of Sergei's bars – the recently acquired King's Head and O' Driscoll's Irish Pub. One lad had unwisely told them to fuck off and had wound up in hospital.

Sergei came in again to make another offer. Keith had declined. After that, groups of big Russian skinheads had started coming in to drink in

John Bull's. They'd start trouble with the punters, kicking off fights in which they'd do as much damage as possible before Damo, Hodge and Pete managed to get them out.

Keith had had to call the police on more than one occasion, but the Russians had always seemed to run off by the time the cops arrived. The same thugs never came in twice, so short of barring anyone with an East European accent, there was little Keith could do. Then one night, things came to a head when a brawl kicked off and Pete waded in to sort it out. Keith could still see the face of the Russian skinhead as Pete fell away from him, dropping to his knees. The Russian had looked Keith straight in the eye and smiled as he held up his blood-stained knife for Keith to see. The people the guy had been fighting with backed away and panic had moved through the bar like an electric current. As punters ran for the exits, Damo and Hodge rushed to Pete and the Russians fled out through the fire escape. A moment later, Hodge had ran after them only to see a car driving away at speed. By the time he got back, Pete was dead.

Descriptions were given to the police, but no-one was ever caught. Keith had always suspected that Sergei had certain key police officers in his pocket; bribery and corruption weren't exactly unknown in this part of the world and Sergei had no shortage of cash.

Pete's death had been the end of it for Keith; afraid for his family, he'd given in and sold out to Sergei. He'd told him he was going to move to Portugal, that he was getting out of the pub trade for good, retiring early and putting in some work on his golf swing. They'd shaken hands, and that had been that. Michelle had been relieved to be getting away from it all, though Melanie, being too young to have really understood what was going on, had been predictably pissed off.

They'd moved not to Portugal, but here, to Almacena, some one hundred and fifty kilometres inland, north of the Costa del Sol. Melanie soon settled in and made new friends, the best of whom was Teresa. The two of them would often wander in to *La Reina*, nattering away in Spanish and come up to the bar where Melanie would switch to English long enough to get a couple of cokes, then they'd drift off into the shadows to continue their mysterious conversations. It never ceased to amaze Keith how quickly Mel had picked up Spanish, but her teachers had told him it was natural; that children were able to absorb language far more readily than adults.

Mark Coleman's head bobbed to the surface of his thoughts again, breaking through images of Melanie and Teresa, and rolling round to face him with its dead eyes as if to pose the question: *What if Sergei finds you, Keith? Will he be content with taking it out on you and the lads, or would he hurt Melanie and Michelle as well?*

Keith suddenly felt a queasiness in his stomach. Jesus, why hadn't he just done like Chelle wanted when they moved away from the coast? Just move on and put it all behind them? He shook his head. No, neither he nor Damo and Hodge had ever been able to forgive and forget Pete's murder. It had poisoned their peace of mind, coming up in conversation any time they got drunk or stoned together. They'd always vowed to take some kind of revenge. They'd agreed to wait, to bide their time until there was enough water under the bridge, wait till Sergei had made even more enemies down on the coast so there'd be a well-populated list of suspects – the last of which would be them – then they'd go back down and get the bastard. And so, just over a year after they'd all moved out to Almacena, they'd begun to make their plans.

Sergei had become the principal player in the Benidorm drug trade, and Damo and Hodge got in contact with Mark Coleman again. The plan was to use him to arrange a meeting with Sergei, ostensibly in order to buy fifty grand's worth of ecstasy, but in fact, to blow his head off. They'd told Mark they were going to go into business in Portugal and wanted him to be their connection, just like old times. They told him they wanted Sergei's drugs as they were reputedly the best. They'd also told him to keep their names out of the arrangement, as their relationship with Sergei after Pete's murder was sour, to say the least. Mark had agreed and had set up the meeting. He'd been assured that Sergei would be present in person at the meeting, which was arranged to take place in an underground car park not far from the Benidorm sea front.

Before the meeting, Damo and Hodge had given Mark a sports bag containing what they claimed to be fifty grand in used bills. In fact, it was about five thousand euros carefully arranged so high denomination bills were piled on top of blank pieces of paper. The wads on top had been authentic in order to pass Mark's cursory examination. The bag wasn't expected to get any further than Mark's possession, so a more thorough, Russian examination of the bag's contents was not a consideration. When it was all over, the money in the bag would be given to Mark as payment.

They'd then followed Mark to the underground car park, where they parked the van so they had a clear, all-round view, and direct sightlines on the meeting place. They'd watched through the front window as the Russians arrived in a black four-wheel drive with tinted windows. When the three men inside got out, Sergei wasn't among them. Keith and the lads had had a panicked conversation about what to do, but there was no choice; Sergei or no Sergei, Coleman had a bagful of nothing, and when that became apparent, he'd point to the van, and they were fucked. Keith and Hodge had picked up their guns and Damo had floored the accelerator.

When it was over, the Russians were dead and Mark was freaking out. Keith gave him a slap and pushed the sports bag into his hands. He'd told him to keep the money and to keep his mouth shut or he'd get the same as the Ruskies. There hadn't been time for debate and they fled the scene after telling Coleman to do the same. Afterwards, he'd heard that Coleman had gone back to England.

The shooting had made the national papers. Police had no leads but it was believed to be a gangland hit. It was also through the papers that they learned they'd killed Nicolai Alexandrov, nephew of "Russian bar and club entrepreneur", Sergei Alexandrov. The papers mentioned that Sergei had alleged connections with the Russian mob, but stopped short of saying that he was a gangster. Keith had followed the story every day, watching as it occupied increasingly smaller space until it finally fizzled out.

Keith had been able to relax. They'd settled the score and they'd got away with it. Sergei had too many enemies active in the area to ever suspect them, so the only loose end was Coleman, and he was out of the picture. Or at least he had been, until now.

Keith turned into the street where Hodge lived. 'We shoulda shot the plonker ourselves,' he murmured. It would've been cleaner: four dead bodies and no loose ends. He shook his head. No. No way they could have done that. Coleman was all right, and they'd thanked him by ruining his life and getting him executed. He stopped outside Hodge's building and pushed the buzzer.

'Si,' Hodge's voice crackled through the intercom.

'Hola,' said Keith. 'Soy Keith, innit.' The door buzzed as the lock was released. Keith pushed it open and entered the cool interior. The floor was tiled with large slabs of smooth, flecked marble and Keith's flip-flops slapped noisily as he walked to the stairs. He heard a door open above, and then Hodge's voice echoing down from the second floor. 'Alright, mate?'

Keith looked up at the big bald head peering over the rail. 'Not particularly, no.'

'No. Not exactly champagne-popping news, is it?'

'Fucking tell me about it, mate,' said Keith, slowly ascending the stairs. 'I mean, how's this come about, eh?' The front door to the building opened again and Spanish voices filled the hallway. Keith looked up to Hodge and put his finger to his lips. Hodge nodded. Keith walked up the remainder of the stairs in silence. When they were both behind the closed door of Hodge's apartment Keith asked, 'Louisa around, is she?'

'Naah. She's round at her place. Probably gone shopping with her mum.'

'Oh yeah,' said Keith going into the lounge, 'Harvey Nick's?'

Hodge chuckled. 'No, Harrods.' He walked across the tiled floor to the kitchenette. 'Drink?'

'Whatcha got?' Keith sat on the couch, took off his cap and wiped his brow.

'What would you like?'

'I dunno. Bit early for beer, innit. You got any ice tea?'

Hodge opened the fridge and took out two cans of ice tea. He came back and sat down in an armchair. The seat sighed as he sank into it. He was a big man; once his bulk had been all muscle but over the last year or so it had softened. ''Orrible business, eh?'

'Barbaric,' said Keith. 'It's like we were saying on the blower earlier – it's like that bloody Al Queda lot had a go at him, innit.'

'Yeah, I did some reading up about that on the Internet. Apparently they did it in Chechnya too.'

'Who did?'

'The Chechens.'

'Whatchoo going on about? Who are they?'

'They're people what live in Chechnya. They're always having wars with the Russians.'

'Oh yeah,' Keith nodded. 'Them Chetchnyen ... nz.'

'It started out with the Chechens decapitating Russians, but then the Russians started doing it back.'

'Sounds fair enough.'

Hodge waited for the penny to drop. Keith slurped his ice tea. Hodge said, 'So you see what I'm getting at?'

Keith's brow furrowed. 'What? That decapsitation's a popular sport in Russia?'

'No.'

Keith clicked his fingers and pointed at Hodge's nose. 'I know. You think Sergei might have read about it in the Russian newspapers and thought to himself, "Aye, aye, that's a good idea. I'll do that an' all."'

'Yeah, more or less.'

'Yeah,' Keith nodded, 'and of course he'd have seen the Iraqi crowd doing it on Sky News an' all, wouldn't he?'

'Yeah, well, it's terror tactics, mate. He's telling us that he's on to us and we're gonna get the same thing.'

'Fuckin' hell! Calm down, Hodge. Even if it was Sergei, how's he gonna do that to us? He can't hurt us if he don't know where we are.'

'Yeah, but what if Mark Coleman told him where we were?'

'How could he? As far as he knew, we were in Portugal.'

'Ah, but what if he knew we were here?'

'How's he gonna have known that? And anyway, if he had, he probably would've come and killed us himself. After all, we stitched him pretty bad, didn't we?'

Hodge shrugged. 'Maybe he didn't have the bottle, or maybe he just forgave us.'

'Forgave us for making him a fugitive from the Russian mafia? I doubt it, mate.'

'He might have done.'

'Would you?'

'No. Probably not.'

Keith slurped his drink. 'So, have you seen Damo today?'

'No. I haven't been able to reach him.'

Keith grinned. 'He's probably lost in the folds of Carol's arse, eh?'

'Maybe we should call round to Carol's? See if we can prise him out.'

'Nah, he'll find his own way out eventually. But I'll tell you one thing – after all this Coleman business, he's gonna have to stop going clubbing down the coast. It's too bloody risky.'

'He goes to Marbella though, Keith. Sergei's not in Marbella.'

'How do you know? I mean, he's not going to advertise himself, is he? He's not like Planet fuckin' Hollywood.'

'No, I suppose not.'

'Even if Sergei ain't there, Damo still might get seen by someone, mightn't he? He might get talkin' to someone, say the wrong thing, you know what I'm saying? I've told him before but he don't listen.'

'Well, I reckon he'll listen now.'

'Yeah, well I should bloody hope so. He'll have to do his dancing locally from now on.'

'What at *your* place?'

'Nothing wrong with our discos mate – proper music: 70's and 80's – none of that bollocks he listens to. And no fuckin' pills neither. We run a clean ship these days. He'll have to give all that lark up for good.'

'He has done.'

'Has he? You sure?'

'Yeah. He still smokes a bit of weed from time to time, but who doesn't? Carol grows it in her garden. She's got some lovely plants. She fertilizes them with her own pee.'

Keith made a face. 'Urgh, charming. Remind me never to smoke any of that shit.'

'Works wonders she reckons. Nitrates I think it is. She washes in it too.'

Keith looked horrified. 'Do what?'

'Oh yeah,' Hodge chuckled. 'She says it keeps her young-looking.'

'Well, maybe she should start using it to clean her bleedin' mirror. She's about as young looking as Mother Teresa.'

'Mother Teresa's dead mate.'

'Yeah, exactly,' Keith finished his drink.

Hodge pointed at the empty can. 'You want another one?'

'No mate, I'd better be off. Things to do, people to see.'

'Who've you got to see?'

'No one. It's an expression busy people use, innit.'

'What? You busy, are you?'

'Well, no, not particularly. But I like to create the air of a busy man, you know what I mean?'

'Busy men don't wear flip-flops, Keith.'

'Tell that to Ghandi,' said Keith, rising. 'He wore flip-flops and he was *well* busy.'

Hodge tried to think of a comeback but couldn't.

Keith grinned. 'Ahh, gotcha there, didn't I?'

Hodge laughed and they went to the front door of the apartment. Opening the door, Hodge said, 'So how's Chelle feel about all this? You told her anything yet?'

'What? About how we popped Sergei's nephew?'

'Yeah.'

'No mate. She'd go fucking mental. You know that.'

'Yeah, but what if she starts talking to people? What with all this Coleman business in the paper. I mean, she might say about how Sergei was hassling you two, and how you had to sell up and all that?'

Keith suddenly seemed to sag. 'Oh, Jesus Christ.' He closed the door and put his face in his hands.

'You all right, Keith?'

Keith slid his hands from his face and nodded. 'Yeah. I'm sorry. It's just ... ' He shook his head slowly. 'This is a fucking nightmare, innit? Having to make sure our friends and families are suitably gagged.'

Hodge laid a hand on Keith's shoulder. 'I know, mate. But it's worth making sure. You gotta remember, Michelle thinks this whole business ended when you sold up and moved on. Why wouldn't she talk about it? I mean, it's gossip, innit? Women are always gossiping – and juicy titbits like knowing a bloke who lost his head go around like wildfire.'

Keith rubbed his chin. 'Yeah, but, me and Chelle, we agreed when we first moved here to keep quiet about all that Russian shit. I told her – the last thing we need is Sergei finding us and moving into this neighbourhood and pushing us out of business again. And she's always accepted that and kept her trap shut.'

'Yeah? What about Mel?'

'What about her? She's a kid, she don't know nothing.'

'Well, you don't think she does, but maybe seeing these pictures in the papers will jog her memory, you know what I mean?'

'Bloody hell, Hodge.'

'You'd just be playing it safe, mate. You could have a word with the pair of them at the same time.'

Keith sighed. 'Chelle don't need reminding, she knows well enough.'

'People forget, Keith. Urgency fades with the sense of danger.'

Keith frowned. 'Who are you? Yoda all of a sudden?'

'You know what I mean, Keith. Either of them could let something slip unintentionally.'

'Yeah, well, I suppose I could use Coleman's head to freshen up the old sense of urgency, eh?'

Hodge smiled. 'Sounds like a smart move, mate.'

'Yeah, well,' he took Hodge's hand from his shoulder and shook it briefly. 'I've got myself some very smart advisors, haven't I?' He opened the door. 'Thanks, mate. I'll catch you later.'

'Alright mate. Do you want me to get Damo to call you when he turns up?'

Keith thought a moment then shook his head. 'Nah. Just give him the news and make sure he's fully mentus on the matter.'

'Mentus? What's that, Spanish?'

Keith frowned. 'I dunno. Compus mentus, innit. It means knowing stuff or something like that.'

'Oh right. Yeah. Mentus.'

'Nice one,' said Keith starting down the stairs.

'Alright mate. I'll make sure he's ... fully mentus.'

'Lovely. Cheers then,' Keith waved as he disappeared from view.

Hodge smiled and went back into his flat and closed the door. 'Mentus? I should bloody co-co.'

Meanwhile, in the Flinch family home at Casa Underwood, John Flinch turned from David and Lydia and spoke to his nurse. 'Conchita, could you leave us alone, please?'

'But, John, you – ' Conchita began to protest.

'Please, Conchi, I want to speak with my family alone.'

Conchita reluctantly picked up her book. 'Okay. I will go to the kitchen for coffee, but if you need me ... '

'Don't worry Conchi,' said Lydia. 'We'll call.'

Conchita looked doubtful.

'I'll be fine, Conchita, really. Now that David is here, everything is going to be just fine.'

Conchita left. David drew her seat to John's bedside and sat down. 'I had no idea the resurrection was going to be so soon. I came because ... well ... I came to see you.'

'Of course you did,' said John, 'and I'm so happy to see you. You've changed so much. You've become a man.'

David suddenly felt the years they had lost. He bowed his head for a moment then said, 'I'm sorry, John. I'm sorry I ... I lost touch.'

'It doesn't matter, David. You're here now. At least I get to see you again before I leave this world.'

'I – I didn't know,' said David.

'You couldn't have done anything even if you had known. It started in the prostate; I had no idea, by the time I was displaying symptoms it had gone pretty much around the houses. But I've accepted my fate. It's the way of things for us mortals.'

A tear spilled onto David's cheek and he wiped it away.

John smiled. 'Don't cry, David, this isn't a time for sadness. We should be celebrating: tomorrow night, Lord Underwood will rise and walk among us once more.'

David nodded. 'Yes ... That's ... that's great news.'

John laughed. 'You mustn't fear him, David. I don't. I've come to know Lord Underwood well over the years I've lived here.'

'How? He's lying in a coffin.'

'Oh, initially from our father, I had a few good years with him before he died.' John's eyes focused for a moment on his memories. 'My God. He told me such stories.' He blinked and his attention returned to David. 'Also from reading and studying the old diaries of our ancestors – they were all educated men and quite a few were very good diarists. Their works are down in the study. You can read them yourself.'

'I will.'

'But also, I came to know him by just *being* with him, down in the crypt, in silent communion.' John smiled. 'He's alive, you know? Oh, he looks dead, but he's still very much with us.'

David felt a wave of dread pass through him. He reached for his cigarettes. His hand skittered over his packet for a moment before he managed to overcome the urge.

John continued. 'You can't imagine how I've looked forward to meeting him: this man that I've devoted my life to all these years. I *have* been the guardian, David, even though my tenure has been spent in overseeing his slumber. I have protected and served him faithfully.'

'I know, John. And I'm sure he knows it too.'

'Yes, he does,' John's expression became bitter. 'Damn this fucking disease. I was so close.'

'You shouldn't talk like that, John. You don't know you aren't going to be here tomorrow night. Sure, you mightn't be able to get down to the cellar, but, well, he could come up and see you, couldn't he?'

Lydia's phone rang. 'Oh, shit, sorry.' She rummaged in her bag as she turned and headed to the door. She pulled out her phone, opened the door and stepped outside. 'Hello?'

John waited until she had closed the door behind her, then he turned back to David. He spoke in a low voice. 'Good, she's gone. I didn't want to have to dismiss her, but I would have if necessary. David, listen to me. You mustn't let Lydia persuade you to hand over the role of guardian to her.'

'What?' David leaned closer. 'What do you mean?'

'Ahh. She's already spoken to you, hasn't she?'

'Well, yes, she did mention it in the car. But – '

'You mustn't listen to her, David, no matter how much you may not want to do this job. It's not about you – your needs, your wants – they don't matter.'

'They matter to me.'

'*Listen to me!*' John seized David's hand with surprising strength. 'I can't debate this with you, David. I don't have time. You have to listen and do as I say.' He pulled at David's hand, urging him to come closer. 'Lydia is a bad seed.'

David frowned. 'Well, yeah, she can be a cow at times but – '

'No, forget the past! The cow you knew has grown into – I don't know, a monster.'

'A monster cow?'

'Don't joke, David. I'm serious. She's evil.'

'Well, so what if she is? It's not like she'd be Guardian to the Dali Llama, is it? Surely being evil's an advantage in this job?'

'No, you don't understand!'

'No, you're right, I don't. She's a Flinch, isn't she? I thought that was all that mattered. Or is it because she's a woman?'

'No, although that plays a part. We, the Flinch brothers, we were raised for this – boarding school, the army, discipline, they were all part of our preparation for the role, part of Dad's plan for us and for this time. But Lydia was never intended for this.'

'That doesn't mean she can't do a good job. What about women's rights and all that?'

'Forget women's rights. They may be relevant now but they weren't when all this was put into motion. Tradition demanded a male heir to continue the line; a man who could fight, and kill if necessary, physical strength, stamina, discipline. That's why our father bred with so many women; why we were born of different mothers – a male heir had to be found, David. Dad couldn't just have had a wife and hope he got lucky with a boy eventually.'

The door opened and Lydia entered. They fell silent and looked at her. She smiled uncertainly. 'Sorry, boys, I didn't mean to interrupt – I can see you're in the middle of something. I just wanted to let you know, I have to go out. It's business, I'm afraid. Can't be helped.'

'Oh, right,' said David. 'Yeah. Okay.'

Lydia came over to the other side of John's bed and stroked his head. 'Now, don't you go getting all excited, okay? You've got plenty of time to speak to David, now. He isn't going anywhere. You should rest.'

'Thank you, Lydia. I shall, soon.'

'Okay.' She kissed his forehead. 'See you tomorrow.' She waved as she went out the door. 'Bye both.'

They waited a moment then David got up to check the corridor to see if she had gone. She had. He closed the door.

John looked at him gravely. 'Aside from sexual politics David, Lydia mustn't ascend to the position of guardian. She has … another agenda. She could never be content merely to serve. She's greedy, ruthless, and ambitious. These are not the qualities of Underwood's servant.'

David sat down again. 'So Lydia is a bit ambitious, so what? I'm sure Underwood will be able to keep her in line – discipline her himself if necessary. I can't imagine he's got to this stage without slapping a few wrists here and there.'

John shook his head. 'David, *please.*'

'No, John. That's not good enough. As far as I'm concerned, she'd be perfect for the job. Give it to her, because I want out.'

'Don't you understand? There is no "out".'

'Oh yes there is. It's called ta-ta, *adios* – I'm off.'

John's expression darkened. 'You must stay. You *must* serve him. It is your destiny.'

'No, John, it's not. I say, fuck him. Do you really think he gives a rat's arse who polishes his coffin while he's out and about slaying innocent people? Of course he doesn't! This is just a domestic position with a bit of body-guarding and murder chucked in. It doesn't even have to be a Flinch. Let him put an ad in the paper, I'm sure someone suitable will turn up. But remember, he can't say, "women need not apply", not these days.'

'No! You must, you – ' John's voice was cut off by a gasp of pain and he fell back against his pillows.

'John?'

John reached out for David's hand. He gripped it hard. 'Listen to me. You must educate yourself. I've prepared a guide for you; it's on a disc – a computer disc.'

'John, for God's sake, calm down, try and relax.'

'It's too late, David. My time has come. The disc ... it's in the safe ... in the study. The codes, I changed it to your birthday so you won't forget.'

'Please, John – '

John let go of David's hand and began fumbling behind some of the wires and tubes that flowed over the nightstand.

'Please, John, stop,' David turned in the direction of the door and shouted. 'Conchi!' When he looked back, John was lifting something metallic from behind the nightstand. It was the sword from the lounge. 'John! Jesus, be careful!'

'Take it,' said John, holding the sword out to him with both hands. 'Take up the sword.'

'*What?* Do you mean?'

'This is the sword of Matthias Flinch, handed down from him to his son, and so on and on through the ages. Our father gave it to me, now I pass it on to you.' He winced as if the weight of the sword was suddenly unbearable.

'Conchita!' David shouted.

'Take it!'

'*Okay!* For Christ's sake, John, don't excite yourself,' David took the sword.

John relaxed back against the pillows. He smiled. 'You'll be wonderful, David. I know now that it was always meant to be you. It is your destiny.'

The door opened and Conchita, cursing in Spanish, ran to John's side. She gestured impatiently at David to get out of the way. David got up, his chair falling over behind him. 'He needs morphine.'

John reached out to David. 'Remember ... the disc ... in the study ... he needs you. Promise me.'

'Fuck!'

'Promise me, David. Promise you will serve him.'

David knelt, taking John's hand in his. 'All right. I will. I promise.'

At his words, John smiled. 'Good boy, Davey. Good boy.' His grip relaxed.

'John?'

Conchita took John's wrist and felt for a pulse. She looked at David. 'He is gone.' David sank back on his haunches. She gently closed John's eyes. 'He was a brave man.'

David nodded. 'Yes. He was.'

'But now it is your turn to be brave, no?'

David settled his brother's hand on the bed and looked at Conchita. 'Sorry?'

She indicated the sword. 'You are now the guardian of Lord Underwood.'

'You know about that?'

Conchita smiled. 'Of course.'

'So you're ... you're part of the Sect?'

'We are all part of the Sect, David.'

'Yes. I suppose you would be.'

'It is an honoured place you fill,' said Conchita, her eyes wide with passion. 'When the sun goes down tomorrow night a new age of evil shall be born unto the world, and you shall be at the very heart of it.'

'Yeah,' David picked up the sword and got slowly to his feet. 'And don't I know it?'

8

JOSÉ ALMONTE LEFT HIS MALAGA OFFICE and decided he would treat himself to a celebratory drink. That afternoon, he'd gone to the clinic to learn the results of a HIV test that he'd taken following a drunken indiscretion with a prostitute a month earlier. He'd gone to the clinic in a state of darkest anxiety, as he'd managed to convince himself that he had contracted AIDS and was surely going to die. So the news that he was all clear came as an almost overwhelming relief. He'd gone through the afternoon like a man reborn, with joy bubbling in his heart like champagne, and now he decided that if you had champagne in your heart, the best thing to do was to have another glass in your hand to keep it company – or even better, a gin and tonic.

As he rode the elevator down, he thought back to the night of madness that had started it all. He'd gone out for a drink with some of the other guys from the office to celebrate his fifty-third birthday. By ten o' clock, most of the older men had started to drift away, pointing to their watches and explaining that their wives would be expecting them. But José had felt no such obligation because he and Luisa had had a furious row that morning, and he was in no mood for a re-match. His conscience had been nagging him to get her some flowers and make it up, but after the second drink, another part of him – the part that wanted a third drink and possibly a fourth or even a fifth – won; and when the younger lads had decided that they were going to go on to a strip club, José had gone along too.

It was after midnight when he'd left the club, and no sooner had he done so than she had approached him. He hadn't understood her at first; she was an immigrant and her Spanish wasn't very good; but her intention was clear, and that was all he needed to understand. He had accompanied her back to a nearby apartment. When the sex was over, he'd wanted to stay and sleep off the booze, but a man with a much less amiable disposition than the prostitute had entered the apartment to tell him that an overnight stay wasn't an option.

He'd managed to find a taxi and had woken up the next morning in the guest room of his own house. Luisa had already left for work. He called in sick before rushing off to the bathroom to vomit. Afterwards, as he lay hanging onto the toilet like it was a life belt in a stormy sea, he thought about his encounter with the prostitute. What had possessed him? He'd never done anything like that before in his life. Had he used a condom? He must have done – she would have made him, surely. Wouldn't she?

He'd tried to remember putting one on – stopping sex to sheath his penis was usually quite a memorable event, if only because it was an awkward halt to the proceedings – but no fiddly condom fumblings bobbed among his memories of the night before. Cold sweat had broken out all over his body, and a fresh vomit reflex sent his face back into the toilet.

Now, José clicked his tongue at the shameful memory. Thank God it was all going to be okay now. The nightmare of not knowing was ended. He could finally stop cringing away from Luisa's touch in the bedroom, lying to her about feeling tired or having a headache. She had been patient and understanding, and on more than one occasion he had wept with shame. But tonight, he would return home, guilt free and hard as a fine chorizo sausage.

He left the elevator and walked across the lobby to the exit. Yes, he thought, just a couple of drinks and then home – and no strip clubs. He chuckled as he went through the front doors of the building and out into a beautiful late spring evening.

A man touched him lightly on the arm. 'señor Almonte?'

José frowned, startled. 'Yes?'

'You don't recognise me perhaps. I am Doctor Morales, from the clinic?'

José hadn't recognised the doctor without his white coat. 'Oh yes, doctor. Er, how are you?'

'Fine, thank you, señor Almonte, but I'm afraid I need to talk to you. It's about ... well, perhaps we should speak in my car?'

José suddenly felt weak. 'What? Why? I'm fine, you told me yourself not four hours ago!'

'Please, señor Almonte. Could we step into my car?' He indicated a white Mercedes parked beside him. A man got out from the driver's seat and opened the back door for him.

'But I'm fine,' said José.

'Please, señor Almonte, if you would just get into the car. There's something I need to show you.'

José's legs felt numb. He walked slowly to the car. He hesitated, then got inside. The doctor got in after him and pulled the door closed. The driver got back into his seat and started the car. 'Where are we going?' José asked.

'To the clinic, *señor*,' Dr Morales nodded to the driver and the car moved off.

'But my test ... my test was clear.'

'I'm sorry *señor*, but there's been a little confusion.'

'What do you mean, "confusion"? Oh my God! Are you telling me there's something wrong?'

Dr Morales smiled. 'Oh, no, your test results are exactly what were hoping for: you're all clear.'

José covered his face with his hands and sighed with relief, 'Oh, thank you.'

'But, unfortunately,' Dr Morales continued. 'You *are* going to die.'

José lowered his hands, his expression confused. 'Sorry?' He suddenly became aware of a strange smell in the car. He hadn't registered it earlier as he had been consumed by dread and anxiety, but now it tingled in his nose, a chemical smell redolent of hospitals. He was about to ask what it was just as Doctor Morales provided the answer by pressing the chloroform-soaked handkerchief over José's nose and mouth. José lashed out, but there was no room for leverage – the doctor was upon him, pushing him down with all his body weight. José tried to call for help, but already he was falling away, as if Doctor Morales were pushing him through the upholstery and down into a soft black oblivion beyond.

David sat on a patio chair on the balcony of John's bedroom, smoking a cigarette and watching a tiny grey lizard. The lizard lay absolutely still in the shadow of one of a group of pot plants. David leaned closer; it looked dead. He reached out tentatively and touched it lightly with his finger. It was smooth and dry and cool to the touch. Then quite suddenly, it woke up and scurried off, disappearing into the shadows between the other pots.

David dropped the butt of his cigarette and ground it out underfoot. He felt exhausted. He closed his eyes and rubbed his face.

John's words came back to him, saying that Lydia had an agenda of her own. What had he meant by that? He'd said she was evil, a bad seed. But that didn't make sense either: evil was the family business. It was like the head of a family of jockeys complaining that a kid was a bad seed because they were great on horseback. Surely a Flinch that *lacked* evil would be a bad seed.

Conchita stepped out onto the balcony behind him. She laid a hand lightly on his shoulder. 'You don't have to worry about anything now, David. It will all be taken care of.'

He looked up, confused. 'What? What do you mean?'

'The funeral: arrangements were made weeks ago. John will be taken away and cremated. Afterwards, his ashes will be stored with your father's and Martin's alongside the Master.'

David sat back and frowned. 'You mean in the cellar? In Underwood's crypt?'

'Yes.'

'Really?'

'Yes. There is a special alcove for the Flinches.'

David thought for a moment, then looked away to the mountains. 'Oh well, if that's what he wanted.'

'It is. It's what they all wanted – to be near their Master in death, as they were in life.'

'Fine. But for the record, if I die, don't go putting my remains down there, will you? That's the last place I want to be ... or rather it isn't, if you see what I mean.'

Conchita raised her eyebrows. 'You don't want to be with your family and Master?'

David turned to her. 'No. I want to be free in death, as I haven't been in life.'

'Whatever do you mean?'

'I mean, I – ' he shook his head slowly. 'I'm not ready for this, Conchi. It's come very suddenly and – well, I just don't know if I can handle it.'

'But of course, it's a lot to have to absorb.'

He laughed. 'Oh yeah, you're not kidding. Twenty-four hours ago I was opening a jar of chicken korma sauce, getting ready for a nice romantic dinner with my girlfriend, and now look at me: my brother's dying wish was for me to swear on the sword of our ancestors that I'd raise a vampire from the grave and guard him for the rest of my life. I've got to play Jeeves to Underwood's Wooster. Only instead of just being an upper-class twit, my Master's a serial murderer of gargantuan proportions. Oh, yeah – it's a lot to absorb all right.'

'You sound like you don't want the job, David.'

'Would *you?*'

'Of course, I would be honoured.'

He laughed bitterly. 'Now you're starting to sound like Lydia.' He took out his cigarettes and lit one. He offered her the pack. She shook her head. He took a long drag then said, 'I dunno. Maybe it's because it's just so much more normal for you here. You guys are all involved in the Sect, you're near this – near *him,*' he pointed to the floor and to Underwood's crypt below. 'This is what you are, but it's not what I am. I've got a life far away from all this and it's one I don't want to leave, you know?'

Conchita sat down beside him. 'You are scared?'

'Yes. You bet I'm scared.'

'I understand. It is for you to decide David, for you are guardian now. Lydia will do it if you don't want to. But you know ... that is not what John wanted.'

He nodded. 'Yeah, he said that before he died.'

'And I think he was right. It is good that you have fear of Underwood; fear is what keeps us alive in dangerous situations; it tells us to protect ourselves and the things we care for.'

'Yeah, but Underwood is the thing I fear – not the thing I care for, not the thing I want to protect.'

'But you will protect him. It is in your nature. John knew this. He told me so.'

'Oh? Did he tell you why he didn't want Lydia to the job, by any chance?'

'No,' she looked away. 'He only told me that it must be you. You are a man, after all.'

David felt she was holding something back, but he didn't push the issue. Instead he said 'Oh yeah, the old *man's work* business. He gave me that speech as well.'

The sword John had given him now lay across the small patio table in its scabbard. Conchita made to pick it up. 'May I?'

'Sure. Mind your fingers.'

She picked it up and raised it before her. 'Can you imagine the battles – the fights to the death – this sword has seen?' She gazed at the sword in wonder.

'You want it?' said David. 'Only a hundred or so previous owners.'

She smiled. 'It was the sword of Matthias Flinch.'

'Yeah. John told me. I didn't know that.'

'Really?'

'Yes. I haven't been here for twenty years, Conchita. Last time I was here, Rick Astley was number one. I wasn't interested in swords and ancestors, I was interested in ...' He shrugged. 'Well, things that sixteen-year-old boys are interested in.'

'Like this Rick Astley? Who is he?'

David smiled. 'Never mind.' For a moment they were silent then David said, 'So, if this is the sword of Matthias Flinch, then whose is the other sword downstairs, the one that crosses this one over the fireplace?'

She looked at him and raised an eyebrow.

David frowned. 'Is that – ?'

'The sword of Lord Underwood?' She nodded. 'Yes.'

'Jesus Christ. All this time and I never knew!'

'I think there are many things that you do not know, David. And much you need to learn if you are going to take this sword as your own.'

'Yeah, I know.'

'So, are you going to take it?' She inclined the handle towards him.

He reached out for it and she passed it to him. He took it, curling his fingers around the worn handgrip. With his other hand he gripped the scabbard and slowly drew the oiled blade out.

'It's magnificent, isn't it?'

David nodded, an unconscious gesture as he looked along the length of the blade. The aged steel, nicked and scratched and scored with battle, gleamed in the late afternoon sunlight.

'You know I don't want to influence your decision,' said Conchita, 'but I have to say, it suits you.'

David swung the sword lazily from left to right. 'Really? You know it *does* feel weirdly ... comfortable.'

Conchita smiled. 'I think perhaps you were made for each other.'

David lowered the blade. 'Yeah, and that's what scares me most of all.'

José Almonte returned to consciousness like a man rising slowly through cold black water, his dreams of pain dissolving into a reality of the same: a hangover? His head pounded, which was to be expected after a night out drinking, but more than that, he ached in other places too – unusual places. Jesus, he must have really gone to town last night. But why? What had been the occasion?

Not having HIV of course.

Suddenly, the memory of his last waking moments returned to him: the doctor from the clinic, the car, the handkerchief, sodden with chemicals. He opened his eyes to darkness – but not complete darkness, there was light moving on the surface in front of him, the surface he hung over. *Hung over?* José's eyes came fully open. He was tied to something, but his weight wasn't on the thing he was tied to. He was suspended from it, his body hung horizontally, as if the thing he had been lying on had been flipped over in space and he had remained attached to it. Panic seized him. He tried to move and found he couldn't. He turned his head to the right and saw his arm lashed by duct tape, beyond that his wrist was manacled by handcuffs. He snapped his head left to see his other arm fastened the same way. He raised his head suddenly and it struck whatever it was he hung from. He cried out and discovered that his mouth had been sealed shut with tape. He struggled, writhing against his restraints which he could now feel at various points the length of his whole body, chafing against his bare skin, tearing at the hair of his naked body.

Oh God! What was going on? As he struggled, José felt himself swaying slightly. Above him, he heard the sound of chains clinking gently against each other.

What was this? *What the hell was this?* His mind raced for reason, for sanity. Could this be the prostitute's work? Was this her revenge for ... for what? No, that was insane. But there was something sexual – sexually perverse happening here. There had to be. Why else would someone kidnap a middle-aged man, strip him naked and suspend him from ... from what? Where the fuck was he? A dark room. The air was cool, almost cold. A cellar? His eyes were now accustomed to the gloom and he focussed on the floor beneath him. He had to be about six or seven feet up from it. It was black, its surface rippled and shone dully like oil, then he realised it was just a sheet of clear plastic spread out over a large black square. But why? Why spread plastic over the floor? To keep it clean? What did that mean? Ejaculations? Whose? The doctor's and the other man in the car who had kidnapped him? Oh Jesus, what sick game did they have planned? Panic returned and he fought, contorting helplessly against his bonds, his howls of anger and desperation loud only in his head as he gently swayed along with whatever it was he was lashed to. After a few moments, he realised it was hopeless. He gave up the struggle and allowed himself to hang, breathing hard through his nose and watching the dim light flicker on the surface of the plastic beneath him. But where was that light coming from?

As best he could, he looked up. The light got brighter as he did so. It was coming from a point ahead that he couldn't raise his head high enough to see. It was candlelight, he was sure of that. He pushed his head back as far as he could, the skin of his bald patch scraping against the irregular metal surface of whatever it was he hung from. Then, he saw the source of the light and his breath stopped suddenly in his chest. Two candelabra, each with three candles burning, stood at either end of a long table that was covered with a deep red cloth.

Hanging on the wall behind the table was a painting. Red eyes stared back at him from the canvas. José recognised the subject of the painting immediately. He screamed, though against the gag his scream was a pitiful muted whine. The face before him was that of the horned beast. With the head of long-horned goat and the body of a man, it sat cross legged, a pentagram in the centre of its forehead, its wings furled behind it, and its malevolent eyes alive in the flickering candlelight. José suddenly understood that the doctor had meant it when he said he was going to die. He wasn't going to be used as part of a kinky sex game; he was going to be sacrificed.

David walked down the stairs carrying the sword and trying not to look at the painting of Underwood that hung on the wall opposite. He knew the sensation had to be just his imagination, but he could feel the portrait's eyes on him as he descended, commanding him to look up and meet them.

He stopped on the bottom stair and raised his head to look into the eyes of his Master. The face in the portrait smiled at him.

David drew the sword from its scabbard. 'What are you looking so smug about?'

He pointed the sword at Underwood's face, the tip of its blade aiming right between the mocking green eyes. 'You should fear me, you know? I'm the one with the weapon here, and you – you're nothing but a dusty old corpse.'

Underwood smiled back at him from the canvas.

'Oh, but you don't see it that way, do you? You think I'm just like all the other Flinch boys, don't you? Someone to fetch and carry your bags and mop up the blood after your murderous mealtimes. But I'm not like them, y'see? Just because I told John I'd serve you, that doesn't mean I actually *will*, you know. I'm my own man!' The sword wavered slightly in David's grip and he lowered it. He looked down to where the tip rested against the marble stair. In his imagination, Underwood's portrait was on the verge of breaking out into guffaws. Then, David was suddenly struck by the simple truth of what he just said: rather than he being afraid of Underwood, it was Underwood who should be afraid of him.

Lydia had gone out, John was dead, and Conchita was busy upstairs. David tapped the sword against the stair. How fitting it would be to use it on Underwood, to just open the coffin, pull up his rotten old corpse, and chop his head off with a single slash of Matthias's steel?

A smile, which almost exactly mirrored Underwood's, rose to his lips. He looked up, his eyes bright with purpose. 'You know, Milord, we may never get another chance to be alone like this again. Just you, me,' he raised the sword. 'And this.' He slashed the blade through the air between himself and Underwood's throat. He glanced quickly around, then, assured he was alone, turned and hurried down the corridor towards the library.

As he was passing the lounge, from the corner of his eye, he noticed something different. He stopped and looked into the room. Above the fireplace, the other sword had gone. That was odd. He went into the room and glanced around to see if the housekeeper was polishing it, but she was nowhere to be seen. Maybe she had taken it away somewhere to polish it with some special antiques-only polish. It didn't matter. He turned from the room and hurried on down the corridor.

He knew the library door from childhood; it was a door he had always avoided whenever possible. As he approached it, he suddenly remembered why, and stopped.

When he was nine years old, Lydia had rewarded his confession that he'd almost peed his pants at his baptism the year before by daring him to go down to touch Underwood's coffin. Determined to prove that he was no longer a silly little kid, he'd taken the dare. Immediately, Lydia had grabbed him by the hand and hurried with him straight to the library. She dragged a chair over to the bookcase against the far wall and climbed up, pulling books out until she found the concealed release switch. A few moments later, the doorway yawned open onto the stairs that led down into the darkness of Underwood's crypt. She'd turned to him, grinning, pointing down the stairs with one hand while holding tightly to the door with the other.

He heard her voice again, taunting him from his memory. 'Come on, Scaredy-Cat. What's the matter? Afraid you're going to pee your pants again?'

'You'll shut me in!'

'Course I won't, Davey. I wouldn't do a thing like that.'

He'd taken a step closer to the door, then another. Then, he stopped. The darkness beyond the doorway seemed almost a breathing thing. He shook his head, 'No.'

Suddenly, Lydia had lunged for him. He'd lashed out, terrified she'd manage to get a hold of him and pitch him into that terrible darkness. His fist connected with her face and she screeched in pain. He'd turned and ran as fast away as he could.

David blinked, returning to the present. He forced a little laugh. 'Gave you a shiner didn't I, Lyddie? And you deserved it too.' He turned the handle and entered the library. All the walls were lined with books, but David's attention was fixed on the panels directly opposite, against the far wall. He closed the door and walked over to them. What shelf was it? He couldn't remember. Then an idea occurred to him: there was bound to be some dust. He stepped up close to the shelves and looked along each one towards the light from the window. There was a fine layer of unbroken dust in front of the all books – except one; a spot where the dust had been disturbed. He checked the books at that point and saw a very old paperback copy of *Dracula*. He smiled, and pulled it and its immediate neighbours from the shelf.

Behind them was a small wooden switch. He pushed it, and with a low click, felt the panel in front of him come loose from the wall. He stood back and took hold of the bookcase. It swung open easily on well-oiled hinges, and there before him, just as he remembered it in his nightmares, was the staircase to the cellar. A coldness crept up the stairs and poured around his ankles, the musty air causing his skin to prickle and crawl away from it. But this time, there could be no running away. David gripped the handle of the sword and drew it from its scabbard. He took a deep breath, and stepped through the cellar door.

9

THE RED SUN WAS SINKING behind the house as Lydia turned the
Land Rover onto the drive of her Malaga home. As she approached the
house she saw the cars of her guests were already parked outside.
Everyone was here on time. She thumbed the remote control for the
garage door and sang along absently with Oasis's *Live Forever* as she waited
for the door to roll open. She then drove inside and turned off the engine.
She reached down and popped the boot open before taking her handbag
from the passenger seat and getting out. As the garage door rolled closed
she went around to the back of the car and opened up the boot. Inside
was a loosely bundled blanket which she flipped open to reveal the sword
she had taken earlier from the wall over the fireplace at Casa Underwood.
Underwood's sword was different to Matthias's; its blade was shorter and
heavier than the elegant weapon of her ancestor. As a young girl she had
asked her father why the two swords were not of the same design.

'Well, they aren't some fancy display swords like you might get in some
stately home, Lyddie,' Arthur had replied. 'They're real swords, owned by
real men.' He'd pointed at the longer of the two. 'This is your ancestor,
Matthias Flinch's, sword. It's what they call a sabre.'

'And what's that one?' said Lydia, pointing at the other.

'That one is Lord Underwood's, our Master's sword.'

'Why is it smaller than the other one? Why doesn't the Master have the
biggest sword?'

'Well, he chose this sword himself, dear. Of all the swords that he
could have had – and there were many – Lord Underwood chose this
one.'

'Why?'

Arthur tapped the blade of Underwood's sword lightly with his finger.
'Because this, Lyddie,' he turned to her with an expression of comic
wickedness on his face, 'this does a man more damage.'

Lydia laughed and reached out her hands. 'Can I have a go?'

Arthur chuckled. 'No, my dear,' he reached down and picked her up.
'You might chop your toe off or something like that.'

'I won't, honest,' she pleaded. 'Please, Daddy.'

'One day, Lyddie, when you're bigger, maybe Lord Underwood himself will let you have a go on it – maybe even let you use it on a bad man who wants to hurt His Lordship. Would you do that for him?'

Lydia nodded fervently as if she were being asked if she'd like another scoop of ice cream. 'Yes, I'd chop up anyone who tried to hurt the Master.'

Arthur laughed and nuzzled her hair. 'Good girl, Lydia. Oh, you're going to do us proud.'

The sound of laughter from inside the house brought Lydia back to the present. From beyond the door that led directly into to the house's entrance hall, she could hear Gerald Benson guffawing at something.

She picked up the sword. It wasn't in a scabbard. She checked the blade with her thumb: it was so sharp it felt almost hungry against her flesh. She slammed the boot shut. Then, with the sword in one hand and her handbag in the other, she went into the house.

Flamenco music was drifting from the lounge.

'*Hello?*' Lydia called.

Various voices came back in reply before Miguel, her personal assistant, came out into the hall to meet her. He was twenty-four years old and had lived with his parents in Malaga until Lydia had re-located him to a small house near the office in Almacena. His face lit up when he saw her. 'Lydia, you are here.' Then he saw the sword. 'Oh my God, you got it! Can I see?'

'Of course,' she exchanged kisses with him on either cheek and let him take the sword.

Miguel admired the gleaming, battle-scarred blade. 'It's amazing.'

'I wouldn't go that far, Miguel. It's an old cutlass, not a light sabre.'

'But still, it is Lord Underwood's cutlass, no?'

'Yes,' Lydia said with a smile. 'It is.'

'Lydia?' called Cynthia Benson from the lounge. 'Where are you? Come on in before Gerald eats all the finger food.'

Lydia entered the lounge. The Bensons were sitting on the sofa, each with a glass of wine and Gerald with a tiny bread stick daubed with Russian salad heading for his mouth. Lydia wagged a finger at him. 'Gerald? Don't you go spoiling your appetite, now will you?'

'No fear, Lydia,' said Gerald. 'Cynthia's exaggerating, I've only had a tiny bit, though she's been carping at me like I'm Billy Bunter.'

'Oh you big fibber, Gerald,' said Cynthia. 'You've been positively hoovering that stuff up.'

Gerald looked at the nearly empty dish of Russian salad on the coffee table. 'Well, I, I like it,' he pouted. 'Damn it all, it's Beltran's fault for making such lovely nibbles.'

'Where is Belly?' asked Lydia.

'In the kitchen,' said Cynthia, 'mixing up a jug of his one of his exotic pharmaceutical cocktails.'

'I see.'

Miguel began parrying invisible assailants with the sword. Lydia rolled her eyes. 'Put that down Miguel, it's not a toy.'

'Sorry.' Miguel put the sword on the table. 'How is your brother?'

'Dull. I left him with John.' Lydia turned in the direction of the kitchen. '*Belly?*'

Beltran entered carrying a tray adorned with five glasses and a jug of red liquid. Pieces of fruit and ice bobbed and tinkled in the jug as he crossed the room. '*Hola guapa*, how was your day?'

'Oh, never mind my day, how was yours? Did everything go according to plan?'

Beltran set the tray upon the coffee table. '*Perfecto*. No, Miguel?'

'*Sí, perfecto.*'

'Excellent,' said Lydia. 'But don't say anything now; I want it to be a surprise.'

'As you wish,' said Beltran.

Cynthia leaned towards the tray and picked up one of the already-filled glasses. 'What is this, Beltran?'

'It's sangria a-la Beltran: brandy, Cointreau, red wine, fresh orange juice, and of course, my secret ingredients.'

'Tell us, Beltran?' said Gerald, sucking Russian salad from his fingertips. 'What is it you put in it? Ecstasy, that sort of thing? Hmm?'

'I cannot say, Gerald,' said Beltran. 'If I tell you, it will not be my secret anymore.'

Cynthia sipped her drink. 'Mmm, lovely.'

'Thank you,' Beltran picked up a glass and handed it to Lydia. 'And your brother? Is he going to be a problem?'

'Oh, I don't think so,' said Lydia, accepting the drink. 'He has no taste for the … necessary bloodshed.'

Beltran smiled. 'It is an acquired taste, no?'

'Yes,' she raised her glass. 'It certainly is.'

'I propose a toast,' Beltran announced. 'To Lydia, resurrector of the Black Circle, and soon, also its Master – the Lord Underwood.'

Glasses were raised by all. 'To Lydia.' They drank.

'Thank you, Belly, you're too kind. But all I did was revive an old family tradition – and by that I don't mean His Lordship.'

'Ah,' Gerald chuckled. 'But a terribly important one if I'm any judge of these things. How old is the Black Circle, Lydia?'

'It was established by Lady Vanessa Crichton in 1736 as the inner circle of the Sect. By that time, the Sect was growing and she wanted to reward its original members with special status.'

'And special powers too, eh?' said Gerald.

Lydia smiled. 'Such things weren't hers to bestow, Gerald.'

'But she was one of your family, no?' said Beltran. 'You have noble blood in you.'

'Yes, she bore Matthias's son, at the command of her – and our – Master.'

'I say, it's fascinating stuff, isn't it?' said Gerald. 'I wish I could get my hands on those old diaries of your ancestors. I mean, the scrapes they must have got themselves into, eh? The things they must have seen!'

'Alas, Gerald, the diaries are locked up in John's study for the eyes of the guardian only, so even *I* wasn't supposed to see them – though of course, being the clever little thing I am, I managed to copy his key several years ago. I read oodles of stuff before John cottoned on to me and put that dratted code lock on the door.'

'Oh, what a rotter,' said Gerald, 'I, of course, mean that in the nicest way possible.'

Lydia waved the matter away. 'He was only doing his job as he saw it. In the time I had access to the study, I learned all I needed to know.'

'And so, the Black Circle was re-born,' said Miguel. 'And now we stand on the brink of a new age of the vampires.'

'Hear, hear!' said Cynthia, raising her glass. 'To a new age of vampires.'

They toasted and drank again. Then Lydia said, 'Anyway, enough of all this toasting and arsing about. I want to get into something more comfortable, these shoes are absolutely killing me.'

'Splendid,' said Gerald. 'Then onto the main course, eh? It's been ages since we all got together like this.'

'Yes,' said Cynthia. 'It's been so long, poor Gerald's dry skin rash has come back. Hasn't it, darling?'

'It has, yes,' said Gerald, holding out his arm and pointing to a patch of white, scaly skin.

Beltran inspected it with interest. 'Mmm, yes, I have just the thing for this problem, señor Benson.' He gave Gerald a knowing wink that set both the Bensons off into a fit of giggles. Evidently the cocktail was beginning to take effect.

Cynthia ran her fingers up Gerald's arm and onto Beltran's hand. 'Oh, Dr Morales, I do believe you've got the perfect thing for all ailments.'

Lydia knocked back the last of her drink and set the glass down on the table with a flourish. 'Alright then, what are we waiting for?' She slipped her jacket off and dropped it to the floor.

The others began to unbutton their clothes.

'I say, Beltran,' said Gerald, fiddling with his shirt buttons. 'I think that mixture of yours is already starting to kick in. My fingertips feel wonderfully odd. I think I'm starting to come up.'

Cynthia looked at his lap. 'Yes. Aren't you just? You know, Beltran, I simply must get that recipe off you.'

David felt to the left of the cellar door and found the light switch. He pushed it and a light came on below to his right. He knew that if he looked down in that direction, that among the whitewashed stone pillars he'd see Underwood's coffin lying on its plinth; but instead, he averted his eyes and focused on the stairs ahead of him. They too were of whitewashed stone but were scuffed black from the comings and goings of countless feet over the years. Whose feet? He wondered. All those hooded men and women of the Sect that had come down here to take part in the weird and twisted rituals of his father? Who were they? Some were, no doubt, rich and powerful; others merely useful, like his mother or Conchita.

John had said that he used to come down here to *commune* with Underwood, but was that all he used to do? Had he too conducted the strange rituals?

David took a step down. As he did so, in his mind he saw again the robed figures that had been gathered in the candlelit cellar for his baptism into the Sect on his eighth birthday. Their faces had been shadowed by their hoods, but he'd been able to see their expressions. Some had smiled at him encouragingly, while some others had regarded him with colder eyes.

He took another step down, the musty, dank smell of the cellar rising around him as he recalled how he'd felt sick, giddy, his skin prickling with dread – as it prickled now as he took another step down. He could sense the coffin now, a dark shape in his peripheral vision, but still he didn't turn to look at it; he didn't want to see it, not yet, just as he hadn't wanted to see it on that night of his baptism either; the candlelight reflecting in its dark, polished wood; the man inside, alive, waiting for him.

David stopped and put a hand to his brow. It was cold, yet damp with perspiration. He looked at his hands: they were shaking. Jesus Christ, stop thinking about the past, you're freaking yourself out. He gripped the sword handle tighter to try to stop the blade from trembling. 'Fuck it!' he hissed. 'What's wrong with me? Underwood's about as dangerous right now as someone in cryogenic suspension. That makes him about as dangerous as Walt Disney, doesn't it?' *But he's not Walt Disney, is he? Walt Disney's a dead man in a fancy fridge; Underwood is a vampire and he's not dead. Technically speaking, he's alive, and he's within spitting distance of you. You want to get your nerves under control? Forget all this shit and go upstairs and have a drink. That'll work wonders!*

'Oh yeah, that's a fucking great idea,' he said aloud. He shook his head and determinedly took the last few steps to the cellar floor. Then, without giving either his fear or his reason a chance to debate the decision, he turned to face the coffin.

His breath caught in his chest at the sight of it. It was exactly as he remembered it, though now there were no robed figures around it; no Arthur Flinch crooking his bloody finger at him, beckoning forward like he had a pile of Christmas presents lying in the coffin by his side. Now there was just the coffin and the stone plinth it lay upon. Above it hung a single naked light bulb.

'Hello, Your Lordship, long time no see.' David's throat was dry, his voice little more than a whisper. He stood a moment, staring at the coffin, as if waiting for a reply. He raised the sword, looking along the length of it to Underwood's resting place in the centre of the room; and in that instant, the enormity of what he was about to do came home to him. He suddenly felt nauseated, dizzy, like he was going to faint. *Jesus Christ – come on! Pull yourself together!* He noticed he was breathing in short, shallow gasps and forced a deep breath to enter his lungs. Immediately his dizziness dispersed. He forced himself to take a step forward towards the coffin. The sword handle felt slippery in his grip, despite its rough material. He transferred the weapon to his other hand and wiped his damp palm on his jeans.

Don't do this. You can just turn around and go. John must have had a car. Take it. Drive to a hotel. Fly home tomorrow. Surprise Lisa. Ask her to marry you. Have kids. Have a life. Have a fucking gin and tonic if you want one but just get the fuck out of here!

David shook his head. *I can't do that. This is the best chance – the only chance that me, or anyone else, is ever going to get to kill this bastard. If I don't do it now, people will die. I might die! Shit, if I don't do it now and I try and run out on him later, then he'll track me down and kill me for sure!*

He transferred the sword back to his right hand and raised it again. The blade still trembled, so he gripped his right wrist with his left hand to try to steady it. He took another step towards the coffin, focusing his eyes on it and trying to ignore the shadows of the pillars that felt as if they were blotting into a single darkness at the edges of the room. The temperature seemed to be dropping the nearer he got to the coffin, like moving through water towards a body of ice. But he knew these things were just illusions, his fears playing tricks upon him; that even now, as he took another step forward and the shadows seemed to begin to move. That couldn't be, not unless the source of light itself were moving and – he glanced up from the coffin to the bulb that hung above it – and froze.

The bulb *was* moving.

It was covered in thick dust, toasted brown over the years and it threw a nicotine yellow light that hardly seemed to reach the edges of the room. And it was moving – barely, but it was moving.

David held up a hand to feel for a draught, but there was none. And still, the bulb moved, more noticeably now, in the weird manner of a magnet when dangled over another, their poles repelling each other. Around him, the shadows swayed with the movement of the bulb, heaving and yawing left and right as if they were rolling on a swelling tide.

This is bad, this is all wrong; this is unnatural shit in here now! Leave, leave now and forget killing him; he can't be killed by the likes of you, so just leave. Get the fuck out of here!

But he was frozen, transfixed by the swaying bulb, its movements slow, like a pendulum under water. Was Underwood doing this?

Manipulating the light from inside the coffin? How? He was dead – or at least half-dead.

Wasn't he?

Then the bulb made a fizzing sound. It flickered. Whatever mesmerising effect it had had upon David was suddenly broken, and a small cry escaped from him.

The bulb flickered again.

'Oh shit,' David's voice trembled. He took a step back. The bulb, still swaying, hissed and popped as if it were somehow overheating.

Get out! Get out now!

No, be rational, it's a bad circuit. It has to be. Just an electrical fault.

Then, with a rising buzzing sound, the light bulb flared into brilliance before exploding, its shattered fragments flying in all directions.

David cried out. He staggered back, his free hand shielding his eyes. When he opened them again, the room was almost pitch black. Almost. He turned and looked up to the light coming in from the library door at the top of the stairs.

The door was closing.

'*No!*' David screamed. 'No! It's me, David! I'm down here!' The door closed, clicking quietly into place, and plunging the cellar into absolute darkness. Panic seized him, and he ran in what he believed to be the direction of the stairs – only to crash blindly into a pillar. He screamed, staggering back, feeling at his head for the wetness of blood. His fingers came away warm and sticky.

'Oh Jesus.'

Then from behind him came a low sound. He froze, listening. There it was again. It sounded like wood, like the scrape of a heavy oak coffin lid unsettling from an age of stillness.

'No,' David whispered. 'Oh no. That can't be. Y-you're supposed to be as good as dead.' The scraping came again, this time long and protracted, as if the coffin lid were slowly being slid aside. David, his heart pounding, raised the sword unsteadily before him against the darkness, because now he knew that dead or otherwise, whatever was in the coffin was rising.

10

AT THE SOUND OF THE DOOR OPENING, José Almonte stopped praying. He turned his head as best as he could towards the direction of the sound: a door had opened at the top of a staircase, a rectangle of light, broken now by the shadowy shapes passing through it. José made a sound of despair against the tape that covered his mouth, while in his head he resumed begging the forgiveness of the Blessed Virgin.

The door closed. José could hear the footfalls of people descending the stairs. Then, one by one, they came into view before the sacrilegious altar. They wore robes similar to those worn by monks, but these robes were black and the hoods hid the faces of the wearers. In rage and terror, José screamed at the figure that seemed to be leading them.

They ignored him. The leader went to the altar, momentarily blocking the light from the candles. There was a sound, like steel on stone. Then, the leader began to light other candles from the ones already burning. The other hooded figures took the candles and began to place them on the floor at different points around the room. José began to panic, his breath coming in short gasps. He strained against his bonds, sending ripples through his body fat. The chains above him clinked gently against each other. Then, at the altar, the leader picked up a candelabrum and turned around. José's breathing got faster and louder as the figure approached him, stopping at a point just before his face. Then, the hooded head rose and José found himself looking into the face of a beautiful woman. She smiled at him. José whimpered against the tape across his mouth, his eyes were wet with tears.

'I say,' said the woman. 'Well done, Belly. He's so big and fleshy. Better than those skinny crack whores and homeless types you usually get.'

The other hooded figures now moved in closer and raised their faces to look up at their prisoner. José immediately recognised the doctor from the clinic, the one who had kidnapped him – and there was the driver of the car, the younger man.

The doctor smiled and replied to the woman in Spanish, so José would understand. 'Thank you, Lydia. He's an adulterer. And of course, being a married man who has been to a prostitute, he has told no-one about his little visit to the sexual health clinic.'

José roared against his gag, shaking his head so hard his whole body shook. He wanted to tell them that he'd told everyone he knew about his visit: Luisa, his boss, the chief of fucking police. But all he managed to communicate was stifled, impotent rage.

'Don't worry, señor Almonte,' said Beltran in Spanish. 'All records of your visit have been destroyed. It's as if you were never there, so there's no need to worry about your wife ever finding out about your little ... indiscretion.'

'Can I touch him, Lydia?' said Cynthia.

'Of course,' said Lydia. 'Help yourself.'

Cynthia came forward and reached up to run her hands over José's chest and stomach. 'Oh, he's lovely, isn't he? I *do* like a well-fed man.'

'Well, that's just as well, eh?' said Gerald. A ripple of amusement ran around the group and he smiled, delighted with himself.

'Enough,' said Lydia. 'The time has come. Take your places, brothers and sisters.'

José couldn't speak English and understood none of their conversation. As the older woman stroked his face, he appealed to her desperately with his eyes. She smiled at him, then turned away to join the others as they formed a circle beneath him. He watched as the leader set the candelabrum down on the floor, the candlelight illuminating all of their faces in its soft, flickering glow. The leader then turned and went back to the altar. Again, there came the sound of steel on stone, then she returned to the circle.

At the sight of the sword in her hands, José screamed, his gag forcing the sound to bubble through his nose.

Lydia held the blade out above the light of the candle. 'Brothers and sisters of the Black Circle, on this night, this eve of resurrection, we give thanks and rejoice that after fifty long years, Hell is set to open its gates and return to us our eternal Master, Lord Underwood.'

The others replied in unison. 'Hail the Lord Underwood!'

'In return, we offer unto Satan this man, strong and ripe with sin. We ask that his blood shall strengthen and nourish us, just as his soul shall strengthen and nourish the fires of Hell, to whence he is bound.' She looked along the sword into José's tear-filled eyes. He howled in anguish. She continued. 'We praise the name of Lord Underwood; rejoice in his

123

resurrection, and humbly beg that in his rising, we too shall find life eternal.'

'Hail the Lord Underwood,' the others responded as one.

'This noble weapon,' said Lydia, twisting the sword so the candlelight flashed along its blade, 'that has felled so many of our Master's enemies, has been dry and wanting the taste of human blood for at least half a century. But tonight, brothers and sisters, on the eve of our Master's rising, let us slake both its and our thirst so we all may be nourished and strong, and ready to serve our Master.' Lydia raised the edge of the blade so it pressed against José's forearm. She looked into his eyes and smiled.

'Hail!'

She drew the blade across his arm and sliced into his flesh. José screamed in shock and pain, watching as his blood began to spill from the wound.

The other members of the Black Circle watched as Lydia stepped across to raise the sword to José's other arm. José turned his head at the touch of the blade, screaming continuously against the tape. Lydia drew the blade smartly back and watched as José's arm opened in its wake.

'Hail!'

José shook his head in denial at the sight of his blood splattering down onto the plastic sheeting below.

Lydia opened her robe and let it fall from her shoulders. She nodded to the others and they too began to disrobe. Naked, she walked around the spreading pool of blood until she was in line with José's feet. Then, she raised the sword again and sliced open each of his ankles in turn. José screamed, snot and tears flowing over the tape that covered his mouth. Lydia threw her arms back and let the sword fall behind her. 'Now,' she cried, 'you mortals who would taste eternity ... ' She stepped forward so the blood that poured from José's ankles rained down upon her body. She gasped as if at the touch of a lover, then moved forward, raising her face to one of the wounds and opening her mouth to the blood. And she drank, reaching up to José's legs and caressing them as his blood spilled over her lips and down her cheeks and neck. Then, she turned to her friends with outstretched arms. 'Come and get it! Feed like the beautiful, eternal creatures you shall soon become.'

The others came forward, their faces excited and their bodies aroused. They each moved to stand beneath a wound and raised their open mouths to catch the falling blood. Beneath José's ankles, Beltran embraced Lydia;

caressing her, the blood on her body slick beneath his fingers. He turned his face to a wound and filled his mouth; he drank, then turned back to Lydia. She curled her fingers through his wet hair and pulled his mouth to hers.

Cynthia and Gerald lapped together at the blood from one of José's arms, kissing each other and lowering themselves to the slippery floor. Miguel looked from them to Lydia and Beltran. Lydia smiled and extended a hand to him. He came to her and she ran her hand over his stomach and chest and up to his face. Miguel looked uncertainly to Beltran, as if seeking permission. Beltran chuckled. He smoothed Miguel's wet hair back from his forehead, and moved away to join the Bensons. Lydia drew Miguel to her, running her hands down his blood-slicked back and buttocks before throwing her head back so blood poured down onto her face. Miguel brought his face close to hers and together they drank.

Then, Lydia became aware that the strength of the blood flow was lessening. She broke from Miguel's arms and went to pick up the sword.

She skirted around the glistening, writhing, bodies of Beltran and the Bensons, and went to stand beneath José's face. Too weak now to raise his head, he looked down at her, his expression strangely calm. She looked up at him, a look of genuine compassion and sympathy in her eyes. She knew he was now beyond pain and near death. She reached up and caressed his cheek for a moment before standing on tip-toe to kiss him once on the forehead and whisper close to his ear in Spanish. 'Go now, I release you.'

She raised the sword so its blade pressed against his throat and, with one swift movement, drew it cleanly across. Then, she lowered the sword to the floor and held out a hand to Miguel as she stepped through the spilling blood to join the Bensons and Beltran.

They reached for her. 'Lydia. Darling,' said Cynthia. 'Join us.'

'In the name of Underwood,' said Gerald.

'In the name of Underwood,' said Miguel.

'In the name of – ' Beltran started, but Lydia pressed her fingers to his lips.

'No. I think he's had his share of hails and hallelujahs.' Lydia took Beltran's hand and licked the blood from his fingers. 'I think it's time you venerated me for a bit.'

Beltran smiled. 'Yes, my lady.'

Lydia sank back, reclining in the still-spreading pool of blood and gestured for her followers to come to her. 'Come, come and worship me, sinners.'

Gerald licked his lips and chuckled. 'I'll drink to that.'

Conchita was coming down the stairs, wondering how she would break the news of John's death to Ana, the housekeeper, when she heard a distant scream. She stopped and turned in the direction of the sound. It was the corridor that led to the east wing of the house. Could it be Ana?

Another scream echoed down the hall. It wasn't a woman's voice.

'David?'

Conchita ran down the remaining steps and into the corridor. A cry came from the farthest end.

'Get away from me!'

It was definitely David, and he sounded terrified.

'David!' Conchita ran to the closed library door at the end of the corridor. She knocked, loudly.

'David?'

'No!'

David's voice sounded as though it came from somewhere from far beyond the door. Conchita turned the handle and entered. Directly opposite her, a section of the book panel against the far wall yawned open onto the stairs that led down to Underwood's crypt. She had been down there only once, for her baptism into the Sect when she was a child.

'David?'

'What?' David's voice echoed up from beyond the door in the bookcase. *'Who's there?'*

Conchita ran across the room and through the bookcase door. She started down the stairs, 'It's me, Conchita. I heard you screaming. Are you all right?'

'Conchita! Oh Jesus, be careful – he's here!'

Conchita reached the bottom of the stairs and looked around. In the centre of the cellar floor stood the coffin on its stone plinth. Above it, glowed a single, naked light bulb. Her breath caught in her throat and she genuflected instinctively. She had grown up in Almacena, where Catholic school had been inescapable, but her father had been doctor to Arthur Flinch and she had grown up a child of the Sect. She had genuflected to Christ because she had had to, but now she did so with genuine awe.

'Over here!' a voice hissed behind her. She turned and saw David on the floor, pressed against the wall in the shadows beneath the stairs. He was holding the sword John had given him, swinging it this way and that, as if to ward off an invisible attacker. His face was covered in blood.

'Be careful – he's here! He knows!' His voice was tight with fear.

Conchita looked around, confused. 'Who? Who is here?'

'Underwood!'

Warily, Conchita walked around the coffin, looking behind pillars and into alcoves as she went, but there was no-one else in the cellar. She came back to where David cowered under the stairs, taking care to keep clear of the sword which he slashed erratically before him.

'David, there is no-one here, only us.'

'No,' David shook his head vehemently, 'he's here, in the dark! We can't see him, but he can see us.'

She craned her head slightly. David's eyes were darting in all directions, staring madly yet seemingly registering nothing. When his eyes skittered across her, it was as if she weren't there.

'David, please, put down the sword. I'm not going to hurt you.'

'No – not you, *him* – Underwood!'

'But Lord Underwood is … in his coffin.'

'No, he got out. He's toying with me, like a cat with a mouse!'

'Please, David, give me the sword.'

David turned his face to the sound of her voice, his expression flickering between fear and confusion. 'Wait a minute   you   how did you get down here?'

'Why, I came down the stairs of course.'

His face contorted with disbelief. 'But – the door! How did you get through the door? The secret panel?'

'Well, the door was open.'

'No – he shut it! He shut me in! He broke the light and then shut the door – I saw it shut! And then, he-he got out of his coffin.'

'David, the coffin is closed, and the light,' she stepped aside so he could see, 'it is not broken.'

'Of course it's fucking broken! Why's it so fucking dark in here if the light's not broken?'

Conchita frowned and came around so her shadow didn't fall over his face. As closely as she could, she looked at his eyes. They were almost completely black, the pupils fully dilated as if he were staring into deepest darkness.

'He smashed it! I don't know how he did it! Maybe he used the fucking Force or something but he made it go all ... weird and then it shattered. I saw it!'

'David, can you see me?'

'Of course I can't see you, its pitch fucking black!'

He's gone blind, Conchita thought, but how? She considered the blood on his face; it came from a cut on his forehead. Concussion? Loss of sight or hearing was unusual but not unknown.

'Okay, David. First of all, lower the sword. I promise you, you are in no danger. I want to look at your eyes.'

'But you can't look at my eyes any more than I can look at yours!'

'Put down the sword, please.'

'No – he's still here!'

'Yes, he *is* here, in his coffin.'

'No, he's watching us, he's listening!'

'He is not, David, trust me.' Her tone was reassuring but firm. 'You have hit your head and you are confused. Please, do as I ask.'

David recognised the authority in her voice. It was the same tone that he himself had used to take when he was a paramedic dealing with patients who were distressed beyond reason. Cautiously, he lowered the sword and laid it on the floor.

'You – you speak like you can see. How? How come you can see but I can't?'

She took the sword and put it out of his reach. 'David, you may be suffering from some kind of temporary blindness.'

'*Blindness?*'

She reached out. 'Give me your hand.'

David held out his hand.

Conchita took it and came to him. 'Don't worry, it's going to be okay.' She reached into her breast pocket and took out a penlight which she shone onto his head wound. It was fairly superficial and had stopped bleeding.

David clung to her. 'I'm blind. Oh Jesus, the bastard's blinded me!'

'David, it's okay, it can happen after a head injury. I'm sure it's only temporary.'

'No, no he's blinded me! This is punishment.'

'Why would Lord Underwood want to punish you?' As she said this, she felt him suddenly grow tense.

He shook his head. 'I ... I don't know,' he lied. 'Maybe he doesn't like me.'

'But that's crazy! How can he not like you? He is in his hibernation, he hasn't even met you.'

'No, not physically he hasn't, but John said he came down here to commune with Underwood and that's how he got to know him. Underwood must have some psychic power or something. I've heard of that, you know, in vampires? And he must have used it to reach into my mind and take away my sight!'

'Is that why you came down here, to commune with Lord Underwood?'

He nodded. 'Yeah, yeah that's right, to commune.'

'And so, what happened to your head? How did you cut yourself?'

'I ran! I ran when the light exploded. I hit a pillar or something, but he was coming for me, you see? Getting out of his coffin!'

'You saw him?'

'I *heard* him!'

'You're sure?'

'Of course I'm sure!'

'Perhaps it was a rat that you heard.'

'No, Conchita, I heard the coffin opening. It would take some muscle-bound rat to lift that up, now wouldn't it?'

'I'm sorry but that couldn't be. Lord Underwood has not the strength to open this coffin. He has been asleep without food – without blood – for fifty years.'

'You think I don't know that? That's why I came down here!'

Conchita frowned. 'What do you mean?'

David stammered, 'I ... I mean, I thought it would be safe, you know? For a first meeting, sort of.'

Conchita considered, uncertain, then said, 'I see.'

'But – but he didn't want to talk to me, he wanted to kill me.'

'No, David, you are his friend. If he has this psychic ability you speak of, then he must know that.'

David found her hands and closed them in his. 'I swear to you, Conchi, I heard him just as surely as I hear you now. I didn't imagine it.'

She took his hands and squeezed them reassuringly. 'I believe you, David.'

'Y-you do?'

'Yes.' She tilted his face so she could look directly into his eyes. 'I believe you experienced what you *believe* you experienced; but I'm afraid that what you believe you experienced is not what happened.' She raised the penlight and shone it into his eyes. Immediately, his pupils shrunk away and he gave a small cry of surprise. 'Do you see anything?'

'Yes,' he nodded, 'a light – dark, blurry. You know, like its shining through the bottom of a beer bottle or something.'

'But you can see it?'

'Yeah. Is it a penlight?'

'Mmm hmm.'

'So, what – are my pupils equal? Did you get a brisk reaction?'

'Yes. Now, close your eyes for me.'

He did so. 'So, what? Do you think it's concussion?'

She was relieved to see he was becoming calmer, more logical. 'You are a doctor?'

'Well, not exactly, no. I was a field medic in the army, and a paramedic, too. Until a few years back anyway.'

'Well, then I think maybe, yes – you gave your head quite a knock, you know? Did you lose consciousness at all?'

'No.'

'Are you sure?'

'Sure I'm sure! I'd know if I passed out, wouldn't I?'

'Not necessarily. You may have lost consciousness immediately and all this talk of opening coffins and shattering light bulbs is just … '

'Just a dream?'

'Maybe, yes. Or a hallucination – both auditory and visual. The bulb is, after all, intact.'

'Oh no, the bulb broke *before* I hit my head. I didn't dream that.'

'I'm sorry, David, but the bulb isn't broken. Open your eyes again.'

David opened his eyes, and the world appeared as if it were under water. He blinked repeatedly.

Conchita moved in front of him. 'Can you see me now?'

'Yes,' he nodded. 'You're blurry, but I can see you.'

She moved aside and pointed to the light over the coffin. 'Then you can see the light too, no?'

David hesitated. Then, in a low voice, he replied. 'Yes.'

Conchita patted him on his shoulder. 'So, tell me – and please, think like an army medic – what do you think happened down here?'

David sagged. 'I don't know. I can't forget what I saw, what I heard. He *was* getting out of his coffin.'

'To hurt you?'

David shrugged. 'Well, either that or to change the bloody light bulb.'

She looked confused. 'You are joking?'

'Yes,' he managed a weak smile. 'Yes, I'm joking.'

'Oh. Well, that is good, then.' She held up three fingers. 'How many fingers do you see?'

'Three.'

'Good. I think you will live.' She stood up and held out a hand to him. He took it, and she helped him to his feet. 'But you need to get some sleep. I'm sure you must be exhausted. You have experienced a lot today: grief at the loss of your brother, and the sudden weight of responsibility on your shoulders; a responsibility which you admit you are afraid of. This is stressful, no? I am not a psychiatrist, David, but I think perhaps your mind has been playing tricks on you.'

David looked beyond her at the coffin. *No,* he thought, *not my mind. But him. He – Underwood – has been playing tricks on me. I don't know how, but somehow he made me experience those things. I didn't imagine them; he did. And he put them in my head to drive me fucking mad!*

'David?'

He turned to her. She was looking at him, concerned; waiting for a reply that would confirm for her that he was okay, that he wasn't going crazy – and perhaps, more importantly – a reply that would assure her that he wasn't a threat to Underwood. He knew he had to give her the response she desired. He put his hands over his face and slowly drew them down. 'Oh, I don't know,' he sighed. 'I suppose so. Yeah, I guess you're right; I *am* exhausted. I ... I was very drunk last night, and I didn't get any sleep – not proper sleep, anyway. And yes, this has all been a massive shock, to say the least. Throw in the stress, the fear and ... yes, I suppose I must have imagined the whole thing.'

She smiled and took him by the elbow.

'Come on. Let's get you cleaned up, and into bed. I have some Ibuprofen upstairs – you must have quite a headache, no?'

He realised, for the first time, that he did. 'Yeah. A real bastard, actually.'

She led him to the stairs. 'Well, we'll soon take care of that, and then in the morning I'm sure all of this will make a lot more sense to you.'

David nodded. 'Yeah, of course you're ... you're absolutely right.'

'Oh, one moment.' Conchita stopped and went back under the stairs. A second later she emerged, carrying the sword. 'Your sword. Why did you bring it down here, anyway?'

He licked his lips and tasted dried blood. 'I ... just had it with me, you know?'

'Well, you don't want to leave it down here.' She handed him the weapon. 'You are the guardian now.'

'Yeah.' David took the sword. 'How could I forget that?'

Conchita came alongside him and put a hand lightly on his back, and together they walked up the stairs. Conchita urged David to go through first into the library. As he did so, she turned back to look at the coffin.

'Goodnight, My Lord, until tomorrow night.' She switched off the light and followed David back into the house.

11

THE CALM, ALMOST FLAT MEDITERRANEAN shimmered in the heat haze, its surface glittering in the sunlight as its small waves rolled quietly against the beach. Keith started, realising he was in danger of dozing off. He wasn't wearing his cap or any sun block; if he fell asleep in this heat, he'd probably wake up in accident and emergency.

Where was everybody? On a day like today, Benidorm's beaches should be heaving with people, yet there was no one to be seen or heard anywhere. He had the beach to himself. If it wasn't so eerie, it would be great. But it was eerie. A bead of sweat rolled down his forehead and into his eyes. He blinked, but the salt still stung and he tried to wipe his eye but … he couldn't.

'Bummer, isn't it?' said a voice beside him.

Keith tried to turn his head, but again, he couldn't. He looked from the corner of his right eye and saw Mark Coleman's face next to his. A couple of flies crawled on Mark's lips but he didn't seem concerned.

'Mark? You're dead!'

'You don't look so good yourself, you stupid cockney wanker.'

'What? Who you calling a wanker?'

'Look around, Keith – oh, I forgot, you can't – but take my word for it: there's just us. So I must be calling you a wanker, mustn't I?'

Keith made to grab Mark but found he couldn't. It was as if his arms had gone to sleep.

'See where your stupid, macho revenge crap has got us, Keith?'

'Fuck off, Coleman. Your dying was your own fault. You should've hid yerself better.'

'Oh? Hark whose talking.'

Keith gritted his teeth and strained to do something – anything that might result in Coleman crying out in pain, but all he could do was strain.

'*Hello,*' said Mark. 'Here comes your mate.'

Keith's eyes looked forward and immediately bulged in fear. Sergei was walking towards them along the beach. However, besides his sunglasses, he wasn't dressed for the beach; he wore an expensive suit and black shoes, and in his hand he carried a sports bag. Keith recognised it as the one that he, Damo and Hodge had used to carry the money when they'd done the hit on Sergei's boys. Sergei saw Keith and waved.

'Who do you reckon he's bringing this time?' asked Mark.

'Eh?'

'In the bag: I reckon it'll be that bastard Damo. Or maybe your other mate, Hodgekiss.'

'What are you on about? You can't fit Hodge in a sports bag.'

'No? He brought you here in it.'

'What?' From the corner of his eye, Keith could see that Mark was grinning.

Sergei walked up to them and Keith found himself unable to look up beyond Sergei's knees. Sergei laughed. 'Well, look who is awake. Hello, Mr Mullins.'

'Sergei! You bastard! Come here so I can – '

'So you can what, Keith? Give me the hard stare?' Sergei hunkered down in front of Keith and peered at him over the top of his sunglasses. 'You don't have nobody to help you this time, Mullins.' He started laughing and Coleman joined in.

As best as he could, Keith looked down. Instead of seeing his body, he saw the seat of a bench, sticky with congealed blood. A fly landed on his nose, then another. A whimper of fear escaped him.

'Oh, don't be sad, Keith Mullins,' said Sergei. 'I have brought you some company.' He began to unzip the sports bag. Inside, Keith saw smooth blonde hair streaked and clotted with black blood. Keith whimpered again, a long, keening sound.

'Keith?' Michelle's voice, muffled and frightened.

'Michelle!' cried Keith. 'Oh God, no! Please God, no!'

Sergei reached into the bag and gathered the locks of hair in his fist.

'Noooooo!' Keith's head shook from side to side, but it wasn't him shaking it.

'Keith!'

Keith opened his eyes to find himself in bed. Michelle stopped shaking him. He sighed with relief to see her head still firmly attached to her shoulders. 'Oh God. Nightmare. It was only a nightmare.'

'I could see that. Blimey, I thought you were going to start screaming any minute.'

'Yeah. Yeah, I probably was,' Keith pushed himself up onto his elbows. 'I couldn't move or nothing. I was like a headless corpse ... but, I was the head bit, if you know what I mean.' Michelle put her arms around him and he moved into her embrace. 'My head was cut off and sitting on a bench, next to that druggy geezer's.'

'Oh, that's awful, Keith. No wonder you're so upset,' she stroked his head, its shorn stubble rasping beneath her touch.

Keith closed his eyes. Hodge was right: he had to tell her. Not everything, but at least some of it – she was in danger if he didn't. That was what the dream had been about: a warning from his subconscious of what would happen to him – and her – if they weren't careful. He sat up and took her gently by the shoulders. 'Chelle, I have to tell you something.'

'Oh? Tell me what, darlin'?'

He looked into her eyes. What could he tell her? Should he tell her that he was a murderer? That he'd murdered three men in cold blood, and that their murders had led to the decapitation of another, completely innocent, man? No, bad idea. He swallowed. 'You remember that Russian bloke we sold the old pub to?'

Michelle's expression soured and she nodded. 'Yeah, old Sergei whatsisname.'

'Yeah, that's the fella. Well, I think he might have had something to do with that decapsitation on Ibiza.'

Michelle frowned. 'What makes you think that?'

'Because,' Keith began nervously. 'Because, the bloke who got decapsitated, was Mark Coleman.'

'Eh? Who's he when he's at home?'

'He's – he was – a bloke I knew and, well, he was involved with Sergei.'

'What do you mean? He worked with him?'

'Not exactly, no. Coleman was *involved* with Sergei, and I was *involved* with Coleman.'

'What do you mean, "involved"? You make it sound like you were in some kind of gay love triangle.'

'I mean we was all involved ... in drugs, Chelle. I used to buy drugs from Coleman back in Benidorm. Back when, you know, me and the lads were making a bit on the side dealing to the locals.'

Michelle pushed a lock of hair over her ear and looked away. 'Well, you know I never approved of any of that business.'

'I know, love, I know, but listen, hear me out. We used to get our stuff off of Coleman. I didn't know where he was getting it from at the time, but I know that later on at least, he was getting drugs off of Sergei.'

'And so you think Sergei cut his head off?'

'Well, I don't know. Maybe.'

'Why'd he do a thing like that?'

'I dunno. Maybe Coleman tried to cheat him or something. Remember, Sergei's boys killed Pete.'

'Yeah, but the police never caught anyone for Pete's murder.'

'That don't mean nothing – I saw the knife in that bloke's hand.'

'Yeah, *you* did, but no one else. The picture you drew of him for the police looked like Mr Potato Head – and their artist didn't come up with much better.'

'It's not my fault if he looked like a spud. *I* look like a spud, Hodge looks like a spud, spud-headed blokes are everywhere these days.'

'Well, whatever about that, no one ever saw that particular spud again.'

'That's probably coz Sergei sent him back to Russia.'

Michelle was silent for a moment, then she said, 'So what does this all mean then, why are you telling me this in the middle of the night?'

'Coz I'm worried, Chelle. I'm worried for us.'

'Why? We've left all that behind us now. Even if Sergei did cut that Coleman bloke's head off, it's got nothing to do with us.' Then her expression darkened as a thought occurred to her, '*Has it?* Don't you tell me you've been messing around with drugs again, Keith, or so help me, I'll call the bloody police myself. I'm not having you – '

'No, love,' Keith interrupted her. 'It's nothing like that. I'm done with all that business, cross me heart and hope to die.'

'So, what then? What are you worried about?'

'I'm worried about Sergei, you know .... in general.'

'*Why?*'

'Because he might come after us, here, in Almacena.'

Michelle frowned. 'Eh? What on Earth for?'

'I dunno!' Keith said, distressed now. 'It's unfinished business, innit? He knows we know that his boys killed Pete. Stands to reason he might come after us. He wants to silence me and the lads forever, don't he!'

Michelle's expression softened and she put her arms around him. 'Oh Keith, don't be silly. All that's finished and in the past now, darlin'.'

Keith allowed her to bring his head to her chest. He cupped her breast – an automatic response. 'I know, girl. But, I worry, don't I?'

'You just had a nightmare, that's all. If Sergei was going to hurt us, he would've done it long ago.'

'Yeah, I suppose you're right, Chelle, but I just want us to be careful, y'know? That we don't say nothing to nobody about how we sold the pub to Sergei, or had anything to do with him whatsoever – ever, like.'

'Of course, darlin'. Let's just try and forget about it now, eh?'

Keith raised his head to meet her eyes. 'Really, Chelle, say nothing to anyone about Sergei, or Coleman, or any of it. You know, play it safe.'

Michelle smiled. 'Why would I want to tell anyone about how my husband was a part-time dodgy geezer?'

Keith smiled, relieved. 'I was just worried, babe. I can't help it. I'm a family man, aren't I?'

'I know.' She kissed him. 'And that's why I love you.'

Keith kissed her back. 'And I love you too, girl.' He smiled and sank down against her chest again, though this time he eased himself a little lower so his face was against her breasts.

'Hello,' said Michelle, recognising his apparent arousal. 'Someone's feeling better all of a sudden.'

Keith enfolded her in his arms before rolling onto his back and pulling her on top of him. 'Yeah,' he said, smoothing her hair back from her face, 'and if you play your cards right girl, I won't be the only one.'

David opened his eyes. The bedroom window framed a square of cloudless blue. From outside drifted the sound of birdsong and the distant staccato of Spanish voices in animated discussion. His Spanish was rusty, but he concentrated and gradually began to distinguish coherent words, then a flow of meaning. It was a radio news programme, and the speakers were discussing football results. He looked at the bedside clock: it was just after midday. He frowned. Why had he slept so late? For a moment, he wondered if he had been drunk the night before; then the memory of the cellar came back to him. He closed his eyes and his mind replayed the events exactly as he had experienced them. As it did so, he felt again the terror, the certainty that he was going to die at Underwood's hands. Then he remembered Conchita's voice close to him in the darkness. She had found him – blind, apparently, and raving like a lunatic at nothing. Nothing? No, it had been real, even though all tangible evidence plainly stated otherwise. She'd cleaned him up and put him to bed. She said she'd check on him during the night. David suddenly raised his head and looked around, half-expecting her to be sitting in a chair, watching him. But he was alone. He sighed and dropped his head back onto the pillow.

So what *had* happened? Was Conchi right? Had he imagined it all? No, that wasn't possible; it had all been too real. In which case, the only options remaining were either he was going crazy, or Underwood had manipulated his mind. Much as he preferred the idea of his being a candidate for a nice safe padded cell somewhere far away from all this, he knew for sure it was the latter: Underwood had made him see and hear things that weren't real. But more than that, he'd managed to induce temporary blindness in him. Or was that somehow part of the whole illusion? What if he hadn't really experienced blindness, only a further manipulation of his senses, an illusion of total darkness? If Underwood had made him see the light bulb move and shatter, making him see nothing at all would be easy in comparison.

David sat up. He set his pillow against the headboard of the bed, then sat back against it. He took his cigarettes from the night table and lit one. Jesus Christ, he thought. What kind of mental power must Underwood possess to be able to do that? It wasn't even as if he was up and walking around yet, he was still in hibernation. Or was he? Could he be awake already? No, we've dismissed that possibility: he's unconscious and needs to be resurrected, that's what all this is about. So what if it happened as part of Underwood's dream – if Underwood's dreaming had reached out and somehow affected reality? No, that was insane. What he needed were facts. He took a long draw on his cigarette, and then suddenly remembered that John had said something about notes he'd made for him; files he'd left for him on a computer that explained everything. Facts. Everything John had known about Underwood, perhaps everything Arthur had known too. David stubbed out the cigarette and sprang out of bed. He glanced again at the clock: how long did he have before the resurrection ceremony began? And Lydia? When was she getting back? He had to hurry, there was a lot to learn before now and sundown. As he entered the bathroom, he stopped at the sight of himself in the mirror.

'You could still run,' he said to his reflection. 'You don't have to stay here. Lydia can do everything.' He saw the cut on his forehead and lightly touched the area around the scab; it ached dully. He walked up to the wash basin and looked deep into the mirror. 'No. One way or another, he's my responsibility now. You can't run; you can't hide; you have to stay and see this through to wherever it takes you. Okay?' For a few moments he was silent. Then his reflection nodded slowly back at him. 'Okay.' He turned and got into the shower.

Twenty minutes later, David walked into the kitchen. The radio was playing flamenco music and a plump woman, who looked like she might be in her early fifties, sat at the kitchen table weeping steadily into a wad of kitchen towels.

David cleared his throat. '*Buenas Dias, señora. Soy* David. David Flinch.'

The woman looked up. She wiped her eyes and got to her feet. 'Oh, señor Flinch. Pardon me. I am so sorry about your brother. He was a wonderful man.'

'Thank you. Please, don't get up, er ...?'

'Ana, I am Ana, the housekeeper.'

'*Hola*, Ana,' he extended his hand. 'Very nice to meet you.'

Ana shook his hand and sniffed. A heavy tear rolled down her face and she wiped at it with her tissues. 'The same, *señor*.'

'Oh, please, I'm no *señor*, just call me David.'

'Thank you, *señor*.'

David smiled and looked around. 'Do you mind if I make myself some coffee and toast?'

Ana started to get up. 'Please, this is my job. You sit.'

David held out a hand to stay her. 'No, really. You're upset. In fact, can I get you anything? Coffee, tea?'

Ana sat down again. 'No, thank you, señor David. I am not thirsty.'

'Are you sure?' said David, opening the cupboards and peering among the contents.

'Yes, I am sure.' She pointed to a cupboard in the corner above the coffee percolator. 'The coffee is in there, and the bread is in the fridge. It keeps better in the fridge.'

'Thank you.' David took out the coffee and put a pot on. He got two slices of bread and dropped them into the toaster, then sat down opposite the weeping housekeeper.

'So, er, have you worked here long, Ana?'

'I have worked here most of my life. My mother was housekeeper before me.'

'Carmella?' David asked, remembering the housekeeper who had been around when he was a child. 'You're Carmella's daughter?'

'*Sí*, yes. She was my mother.'

'Really?'

'*Sí, señor*. She died four years ago.'

'I'm sorry to hear that. She was a lovely person.'

'Thank you.' Ana smiled. 'I remember you, you know? When you were a boy? I used to help my mother sometimes in the kitchen with the cooking and the cleaning, and I remember when you used to come and visit. You have grown into a fine young man.'

David's eyebrows bobbed with interest. Yes, he remembered Carmella's daughter. She had been a lot older than him, dark-eyed, raven-haired, and when he entered puberty, capable of making him blush from head to toe with even a suggestion of a glance in his direction. Was this her? He looked closely. Yes, the skin around the eyes was fleshier, but they were the same. As if on cue, he felt a blush rising to his cheeks. 'Oh my. Ana, yes, I remember you now. How are you? I mean, in general, aside from ... the current situation?'

'I am very well, thank you *señor*.'

'Please, call me David.'

She smiled. 'David.'

'Is there a Mr Ana?'

'No. I am married to my work. Taking care of Mister John and this house leaves me no time for anything else.'

David wondered for a moment if John and Ana had ever been lovers. Behind him, the toast popped. He got up and went to butter it.

'Ah, Poor John. It's so sad for him to have held on for so long, and then to die on the eve of his life's expectation.'

David poured his coffee. 'Yes. He ... he was looking forward to it.'

'As are we all,' said Ana, as David came back to the table. 'Lord Underwood is also my life's expectation.'

'I see. So you're a part of the ... ' he gestured vaguely, hoping she'd finish the sentence for him.

'The Sect?'

'Yes.'

'*Sí, claro*, of course!'

'Right,' David nodded. 'I suppose that makes sense – you, Conchita. By the way, have you seen Conchita?'

'*Sí*, she went into Almacena to get some things for tonight.'

'Oh, yes, tonight. The big night, eh? How are you feeling? Excited?'

Ana's face lit up. 'Oh, very excited. Both John and Miss Lydia said I can attend the resurrection ceremony.' Then a doubt clouded her expression. 'Is okay with you too, no?'

'Me? Oh God yeah, sure. What do I know? The more the merrier, eh?'

'And so now you are the guardian, no?'

He took a bite of his toast and nodded.

'It is a great honour. You too must be very excited.'

He shrugged. 'Well, "excited" isn't exactly the word I'd use.'

Ana frowned. 'No? What then?'

David scratched his chin trying to remember an adjective that Lydia had used to throw at him when they were kids, meaning scared shitless. 'Er, how do you say? *Estoy Acojonado?*

Ana laughed. '*Sí*. I suppose it is understandable. You are unprepared?'

'You could say that.'

'Do not worry, señor David. You will do well. John had much faith in you.'

David smiled. 'Well, thanks. I hope it was justified. Tell me, Ana, what do you know about the ceremony tonight?'

'I know only that which is permitted for me to know.'

'Which is?'

'The arrangements for the catering, the food. This is my task.'

'The catering arrangements?'

'*Sí*, for the Sect members who are attending.'

'You mean it's going to be like a *soirée* or a party? For how many people?'

Ana sighed. 'Things have been difficult these last few months, *señor*. There have been many arguments between your brother and sister. Miss Lydia has said me one thing, John, he says me another. I suppose now John has passed on, Miss Lydia wins, no?'

'What, so how many people does she want?'

'Thirty people.'

'*Thirty?* What, in that cellar? It'll be packed!'

Ana shrugged. 'Of course, the final decision rests with the guardian. So maybe you will change things?'

'Why does Lydia want so many guests?'

'It is not what *she* wants, it is what *they* want. The Sect is worldwide and has many powerful people; all of them want to come tonight. Lydia has been making the decisions since John has been sick.'

'So, John wanted less people?'

'*Sí*, he says it is the wish of the Lord Underwood.'

David nodded. 'I see. That's quite a pickle.'

'What is "pickle"?'

'Never mind.' He popped the last of the toast into his mouth. 'If you'll excuse me, Ana. I think I need to learn more about these wishes of Lord Underwood.'

'*Perdón, señor*, but how much *do* you know about the resurrection ceremony?'

'Er, well, pretty much nothing, actually.'

'*Nothing?* Ana sat up straight in surprise. '*Nada?*'

'Nada.'

'What do you know about the role of guardian?'

'Not a lot.'

'About the rules of the etiquette and domestic service?'

David shrugged. 'Well, I can boil an egg.'

'What about the resurrection ritual? Surely you know how that is to be performed, no?'

'Er … no.'

Ana looked at the wall clock then back to David. 'You are going to need another coffee, I think.'

'Yes, I think you're right,' David got to his feet. 'Could you bring one along to me in the study in about ten minutes?'

'*Sí, señor.*'

'*Muchas gracias*, Anna. I'll, er, be in the study.' David downed the dregs of his first cup of coffee and then left the kitchen.

Ana smiled, then shook her head resignedly. '*Joder.*'

12

MICHELLE STEPPED OUT ONTO THE FRONT PATIO of *La Reina de Corazones* and shielded her eyes from the sun. Over at their usual table in the corner sat two rather dishevelled-looking Bensons. She smiled and sauntered over. 'Oh, hello. Looks like you two could do with the hair of the dog. Late night, was it?'

Cynthia, who had not long ago showered off the coagulating blood of José Almonte, turned her sunglasses in Michelle's direction. 'Yes,' she murmured. Whatever benefits Cynthia might have derived from ingesting human blood, hangover relief wasn't one of them.

'What was the occasion? And why wasn't I invited?'

'Oh, no occasion,' said Cynthia. 'Just mid-life ... exuberance.'

'Mid-life?' said Gerald. 'Huh! I wish. We're a bit past that benchmark, Cyn.'

'You may be, Gerald. I, however, remain forever 40, and damn the calendar's contradictions.'

It was mid-morning and the bar was still quiet before the swell of lunchtime trade. Michelle pulled out a chair and sat down. 'Good for you, Cynthia. You don't look a day over 39. I don't know how you do it.'

'Flatterer,' said Cynthia.

'Seriously though, you do look young for your age – what with all those fags you smoke and the sunshine; what's your secret?'

'Early to bed, early to rise, and a daily facial in my own urine.'

Michelle grimaced. 'Ugh! You're kidding?'

A smile played at the corners of Cynthia's mouth. 'All right, the early-to-bed thing is something of a fib.'

'No,' Michele patted Cynthia's arm. 'I'm talking about the urine. You're having me on, aren't you? You don't really wash in your own wee?'

'I wish I could, it's supposed to work wonders. I read an interview once with an octogenarian actress who had the face of a wood nymph, and she swore by it. So, in a moment of madness – or stupidity – I did once give it a go, but just the once.'

Michelle looked mildly appalled. 'Oooh, what was it like?'

'*Pungent* is a word that springs to mind.'

'Did it work?'

'At making me smell like a urinal, yes; at making me look younger, sadly, no.'

Gerald chuckled and squeezed Cynthia's knee. 'No. Now it's back to bathing in the blood of virgins, eh, Cyn?'

Cynthia shot Gerald a look. 'I think you mean *Radox*, Gerald.' She swatted his hand from her knee.

'Oh, yes. Sorry, that was er, Ingrid Pitt wasn't it? Countess Dracula.'

Cynthia turned to Michelle. 'Gerald has an Ingrid Pitt fetish, dear. He squandered his youth foaming at the mouth – amongst other places – gawping at her from the back row of the cinema.'

'I've never heard of her,' said Michelle. 'Who's she when she's at home?'

'She's an actress. She popped up – or *out* might be a better word – in certain horror films in the 60's,' said Cynthia. 'You know the sort of thing: *Heaving Cleavage, Heaving Cleavage Rises Again, Taste the Blood of Heaving Cleavage*, and so on.'

Michelle gave Gerald's shoulder an affectionate shove. 'Ooh, did you have a crush on her then Gerald?'

Gerald's cheeks flushed pink. 'Er, perhaps I did, yes – just a small crush.'

'Did?' said Cynthia. '*Do* is more like it. You know, Michelle, if they made Ingrid Pitt masks, I'd be spending most of my nights lying on my back, gasping through a rubber-fanged mouth hole with Mr Small Crush here putting a big crush on my pelvis.'

'Oh, nonsense,' Gerald chortled. 'I'd never ask you to wear a mask, Cyn. Not unless it was a mask of your own lovely face ... which, of course, would be rather pointless.'

'Ah, aren't you sweet, Gerald?' said Michelle.

'Yes, isn't he?' said Cynthia. 'Weird, but sweet.'

'Oh!' said Gerald, opening his newspaper. 'Speaking of masks – or heads anyway – there's a bit in today's – or rather yesterday's – *Mail* about that chap that lost his in Ibiza.'

Michelle felt a sudden knot of anxiety in her stomach. Keith's horror following his nightmare of this morning was still fresh in her mind. She looked away to where Luis was tending the bar. Did he need any help, she wondered.

'Oh, must we, Gerald?' said Cynthia, stoking her brow wearily. 'Can't it wait until we've each had at least one bloody Mary?'

Michelle brightened. 'What was that? Two bloody Marys?' She got up.

'Yes, please Michelle,' said Cynthia. 'Two, and some pain killers if you have any.'

'Here it is,' said Gerald, opening out the pages on the table. 'Look!' He tapped a photograph beneath the headline: BRITON DECAPITATED IN SPANISH GANGLAND SLAYING. 'Says here his name was Mark Coleman.'

Michelle saw the picture and her hand went involuntarily to her mouth. The picture wasn't recent, it was a family snapshot that looked like it had been taken some years ago, but Michelle recognised the face immediately. He'd been a regular at their pub in Benidorm. She'd known he'd been a part of Keith's little drug clique, but she'd always thought that Keith had been dealing to him. However, after Keith's confession this morning, she now knew the opposite to be true.

'Michelle? Are you all right?' asked Gerald.

'Yeah,' Michelle looked up, smiling. 'Yeah, it's just, a bit ... shocking, innit?'

'Says here that he may have been involved in the murder of this fellow,' Gerald tapped one of two other faces further down the article.

Michelle looked; she couldn't help herself. Gerald was pointing to the picture of a man she'd never seen before, but next to it was a face she knew all too well: Sergei Alexandrov. Keith was right, Sergei *was* involved. She suddenly felt weak. 'I,' her voice sounded unsteady. She cleared her throat and continued in a cheerier tone. 'I'll get those drinks then, shall I?'

Cynthia peered over the rims of her sunglasses at Michelle's suddenly ashen face. 'Michelle?'

'Two bloody Marys and some painkillers, wasn't it?'

'What is it dear? Do you recognise these men?'

'Recognise? Who? Them? Oh God, no. No, I just, I thought,' she laughed nervously. 'I'm sorry, I try not to read the papers, you know? It just depresses me, all this violence and war and talk about recession. I'll just go and get those drinks.' She turned and went into the pub.

Cynthia and Gerald watched her go to the bar and speak to Luis for a moment before she disappeared into the deeper shadows within. 'I say,' said Gerald. 'That seemed to give her a queer turn.'

'Yes.' Cynthia looked at the two pictures. 'Nicolai Alexandrov, nephew of this chap, Sergei Alexandrov, owner of a number of bars and clubs along the Costa Del Sol and Costa Blanca.'

'Sounds like Russian mafia shenanigans to me, hmm?'

'I really wouldn't know, dear. I'm more concerned with Michelle; she looked as if she'd seen a ghost.'

'Well, Costa Blanca, that's Benidorm isn't it? Her old neighbourhood.'

'Yes, but she said she didn't recognise any of the men in the pictures.'

'Ah well, you don't have to recognise a bad egg by sight to have your stomach turned over by one, do you? Sometimes the general whiff is enough and maybe Michelle caught the whiff of local villainy from these chaps.'

'Yes, Gerald,' said Cynthia, evidently no longer listening as she looked to where Michelle's daughter, Melanie, was now emerging from the pub. Cynthia raised a hand. 'Hello, Melanie.'

'Hiya,' said Melanie, stopping beside them. 'How are you?'

'Fine thank you, dear. And you? How's school?'

'Oh, it's alright. Same as usual.'

'I imagine you're the best in the class at English, eh?' said Gerald.

Melanie smiled. 'Yeah, I do alright in that. It's maths I have trouble with.'

'Ah, maths,' said Gerald knowingly. 'Never my cup of tea either. History was my subject.'

'Yeah, history's alright,' said Melanie. 'I quite like that.'

'Do you want to be a historian when you leave school?' asked Cynthia.

'No. I don't know what I want to be, really.' She noticed the newspaper headline and craned her head to read more. 'What's that?'

'Oh, chap got his head cut off.' Gerald turned the paper so she could see it. 'Says here he spent a few years in your old home town.'

'Urgh,' Melanie's nose crinkled. 'That's horrible, innit?'

'Yes,' said Cynthia, suddenly interested. She pointed casually at Coleman. 'Do you recognise him?'

Melanie shook her head. Then she pointed at the picture of Sergei. 'But I know that bloke.'

'Oh, really?'

'Yeah, he's the one my mum and dad sold our pub to. He came around a few times, but I don't think Mum and Dad liked him very much. Especially Dad.'

'Mmm, yes, of course,' Cynthia nodded sympathetically. 'It's always hard, the emotional wrench of selling a home.'

'Yeah, I suppose. I know I didn't want to leave.'

'But you like it here now, though, don't you?' asked Gerald.

'Oh yeah, I love it. Except, well, it's nice to be near the sea, and to have cinemas and stuff nearby so you don't have to depend on your parents for lifts everywhere, you know?'

Gerald laughed. 'You're becoming quite the independent young lady, aren't you?'

'Yeah, I suppose,' said Melanie. 'Anyway, I gotta go. Nice to speak to you.' She waved and stepped out onto the street.

'Lovely girl,' said Gerald, watching her go. 'So nice to see good manners in the young, especially these days.'

'Yes,' said Cynthia, easing a mentholated cigarette into her slim, black cigarette holder. 'Charming.'

'I say. It's rather queer how she recognised that Russian chap in the paper and Michelle didn't, don't you think?' He picked up Cynthia's lighter and sparked a flame for her.

'Yes,' Cynthia took a light and sat back, the cigarette holder clamped thoughtfully between her teeth. 'Very queer indeed.'

David sat back from the computer monitor and rubbed his eyes. He looked at his watch. It was two-thirty. He'd been reading through John's various guides, instructions and history manuals for an hour and a half. He should have kept his studies to the subject of the resurrection, but his reading had turned out to be much wider than he'd originally intended.

Earlier, when he'd first keyed his birth date into the code lock on the study door, his uppermost intention had been getting to the safe and the computer disc that held all of John's notes on Underwood. However, upon entering the room, his attention had been seized by the glass cabinet that held row upon row of old books of varying size, condition and age. He knew immediately that he must be looking at the Flinch diaries. He'd tried the cabinet doors but they were locked. He'd felt around the cabinet and gone through the drawers of the desk, but found no key. It too must be in the safe, he reasoned.

He looked around, but there was no sign of any safe. A small portrait of Underwood regarded him from the study wall. This time the vampire wore a white wig and a high collar, typical of the Georgian era. The picture was perhaps a hundred years older than the Victorian portrait in the hall, but the face of its subject was unchanged; as far as Underwood's age was concerned, this picture could have been painted just a day before the other one. David looked closer. The ravages of time were only evident in the paint itself; hundreds of tiny cracks spread across Underwood's face in a way that nature herself never could. David took hold of the gold-leaf frame and tried to lift it. It didn't move. Underwood continued to regard him with cool amusement.

'Fucking wanker,' David murmured. He felt around the picture frame and his fingers fell upon a tiny button. He pushed it and the picture shifted with a light click. The picture was hinged and David eased it away from the wall. Behind it was a safe with a digital keypad. He keyed in his birth date as he had done with the study door and the safe clicked open. Inside, he saw the computer disc on top of various papers and envelopes. He took the disc and put it on the desk. Then he took out the papers and riffled through them with mild curiosity before tossing them onto the sofa to his right. Where was the key? He reached into the safe and felt around and his fingers touched the links of a small chain. He gathered it and lifted the thing it was attached to; not a key as he had hoped, but an old, full hunter fob watch. He popped a button at the top and the front face opened. On the inside of the case, in letters almost faded with ages of polishing, was inscribed, "To Daniel. Forever yours. Lilly."

David held the watch to his ear. It was silent. Carefully, he wound it up. Nothing happened. He tapped the scratched face with his fingernail and the second hand suddenly began to move. David swung the portrait back so he was again face to face with Underwood. 'Who's Lilly, then, eh?' The picture made no reply, and David knew that it was just his imagination, but he fancied that Underwood now seemed a tad less sure of himself than he had done earlier, perhaps because David now knew something about him that the vampire mightn't care for him to know.

'Was she your girlfriend, then? Or your wife?' Despite the fact that he was only talking to a picture, the question seemed somehow inappropriate. Feeling suddenly uncomfortable, David dropped his eyes back to the watch. He lifted it to his ear and listened to its ticking. 'It's a good watch you've got here, Milord. They don't make 'em like this anymore.' He held up his cheap Casio digital for the portrait to see. 'I doubt this'll still be keeping time in ten years, let alone, what – two hundred, three hundred years? More?'

Cautiously, David reached out to touch the painting, but his fingers stopped a few millimetres from the surface. 'Just how old are you?' He whispered. He stood for perhaps a minute, lost in thought, adding decades to his own natural time on Earth, going on into the future and imagining himself just as he was now, never aging, never changing with the advancing years: 2008, 2108, 2208, 2308 ... David blinked and re-focussed his eyes. In the portrait, Underwood seemed to have regained his air of confidence. David shook his head and swung the picture so it was again facing the wall. He reached into the safe and felt around for the key to the bookcase, but there was nothing more inside.

He returned the watch and the papers to the safe and closed it, but he decided to leave Underwood facing the wall; he liked him better that way.

Now, gazing at the ceiling in reflection, he felt that it was probably just as well he hadn't been able to find the key to the diaries after all; if he had, he might have wasted precious time browsing the adventures of his father, grandfather, great-grandfather and Heaven knew how many others. Instead, he'd sat down, turned on the computer, and slipped the disc into the drive. Then, opening up the contents of the disc, he'd clicked on the file simply labelled, "Underwood".

Immediately he found himself looking at files that held the answers to every question he'd ever had since childhood. He'd begun clicking on all of them, reading snatches of one thing and whole pages of another. One of his main concerns had been his question of this morning about Underwood's ability to influence things from within his coffin. He'd found something germane in a document entitled "Communion" which he'd printed off and now he leaned forward, took the sheet of paper from the printer and drew a circle around the key area of text with a red biro:

"The blood of the sacrifice should be uncontaminated. No sedatives or any other drugs should be used. Secure the sacrifice and extend a limb over the Master's mouth. Make a small cut across a minor vein so that blood will drip – but not jet – from the wound. This flow of blood should be directed to the Master's mouth. It may be necessary to part the Master's lips so that the blood can flow into his mouth, but only a little at a time. If nothing happens, withdraw the limb and wait. Do not allow the Master's mouth to become filled with blood in case he inhales it and chokes. About a tablespoon's worth should suffice."

David raised his eyebrows. It sounded like something out of a cookery book. What the hell did John mean by *the sacrifice*? A goat? A chicken? David hadn't seen any animals around the place. Could they be intending to use a volunteer human being; someone from the Sect who was willing to give their blood? No, that would be a donor, not a sacrifice. So did that mean that there was perhaps someone who was willing to die? Scenes from Hammer movies flashed across his mind: girls dressed in flimsy white robes, trembling on stone altars, getting turned on by the sight of the curved dagger that was about to be plunged into their heart. Would a Sect member, someone like Conchita or Ana, allow themselves to be in that position? They were devoted, yes, but were they *that* devoted? David lit a cigarette and read on.

"*When the Master begins to revive and drink the blood, bleed the sacrifice some more, repeating the process until the Master is able to feed for himself.*"

David sat back. Feed for himself? And so, what? Drink from the sacrifice? Perhaps unto their death? Surely no one would go willingly to that end? How into something do you have to be to die for it? Was anyone into *anything* that much? He immediately thought about himself and the other junkies and addicts of the world: was their relationship – *his* relationship – with alcohol really that different? Whiskey may be a slower route to the grave than a vampire's teeth, but it would get you there in the end. Then there were the suicide bombers, of course – they all see their deaths as a necessary sacrifice to the desired long-term end. So was Underwood's resurrection a cause worth dying for? For him, no, but then he was sane. He read on:

"*After feeding, the Master may wish to rest, or alternatively may wish to rise and engage with you and the small gathering of the faithful present at the Ceremony. This cannot be predicted, however, as we have no record of the effects of such a long period of hibernation.*

One thing I should stress is the importance of avoiding what the Master refers to as "Denis Wheatley" type ceremonial activity. The numbers of those attending should be kept to a minimum. Many in the Sect will seek to attend the resurrection, but I urge you to keep numbers to the absolute minimum. I know that many members of the Sect are important to both our family's interests and the Master's, but he expressly requested that things be discreet. I personally would not exceed ten people, including the guardian. David, if you have returned, then heed this well. Do not let Lydia convince you otherwise."

As if on cue, David heard the sound of Lydia's voice in the kitchen talking to Ana. 'Finally,' he said. He got up and started for the door just as Lydia stepped through it.

'David,' she said brightly. 'Ana said you wanted to see me.' She grinned. 'I'm almost surprised to see you here; I'd half expected you to be on a flight back to London.'

'No, I'm still here.' He sat down again. 'Where have you been? Didn't you get any of our messages about John?'

'Yes. He's dead.'

'Oh, you got the messages then? Conchita and I, we tried to contact you but your phone was switched off.'

Lydia slipped off her suit jacket and draped it over the back of David's chair. 'I had a meeting with clients. I never have my phone switched on during meetings, David. It rings too often. I'm sorry, but I only found out about John this morning when I reached the office.'

David nodded. 'I see. Well, you'll be consoled to know that he went peacefully.'

'Yes, of course. Has the undertaker been?'

'Yeah. He came about an hour ago.'

'Good. So, tell me, what are your plans?'

'How do you mean?'

'Well, you know, about the things we were talking about yesterday. John's dead, so you don't need to be here anymore, so … when are you off?'

David drew on his cigarette. 'You're assuming I'm still going?'

The look of excited expectation on Lydia's face slipped slightly. 'Well, that's what we agreed yesterday.'

'A lot's happened since yesterday, Lydia.'

Lydia hesitated a second, as if she were not hearing things correctly, then she said: 'Look, if you're feeling guilty, David, forget about it. Your family duty is done. If you go now, you could be back in your own life tomorrow morning: back with your students and your girlfriend and your AA meetings. It'll be just like none of this ever happened.'

David closed the Resurrection Protocols document on the computer screen. 'Yeah, well thanks, I appreciate that, but like I say, a lot's happened since yesterday.'

'What do you mean?'

'I've accepted the job as guardian, Lydia. I promised John just before he died that I'd do it and – '

'David, any promises you made to John can be cremated along with him as far as I'm concerned. No one's going to hold you to your word now.'

'Yes, but, he really wanted me to do this, Lydia. I mean, *me* – me specifically.'

Lydia sat on the edge of the desk. 'Oh. I see. That's what he told you, is it?'

'Yes.'

'Are you sure that what he really didn't want was a woman in the job? Remember I told you he had a lot of antiquated notions about all that sort of thing?'

'Well, yes, he did mention that.'

'What did he say?'

'It doesn't matter.'

'Yes, it does. What reasons did he give? Did he slag me off? I bet he did, didn't he?'

'No, Lydia, he didn't slag you off, he just said you were ... ' he gestured vaguely, trying to think of a euphemism for "evil". 'Not quite ... cut out for the job.'

'*What?*' Lydia shook her head in astonishment. 'Is that all the appreciation I get? My God, do you have any idea how hard I've worked for this family?'

'I'm sure you've worked very hard, Lydia, and of course John must've known that too, but – '

'I've built up connections, David,' Lydia continued. 'Connections that frankly, John was jealous of. The Sect is a powerful organisation now, thanks to me. We have people with real power in the world. And I don't mean like those silly little burgomeisters and bicycle-riding coppers of Dad's day. Oh no, I have major industrialists, millionaires, commissioners of police and, and I even have a member of the British Parliament, for God's sake!'

David raised his eyebrows. 'Really? Who?'

'Oh, wouldn't you like to know?' Lydia tapped the side of her nose.

'I *should* know, Lydia; I'm the guardian now. I need to know this stuff.'

Lydia laughed contemptuously. 'Ha! Do you seriously imagine for a moment that you could run an organisation of this complexity?'

'Why not? I can do anything you can do.'

'Oh, don't talk rot, David. Until a couple of days ago you didn't give a shit about the family or its business. I bet you wished we'd all just die and never trouble you again, didn't you?'

David ground out his cigarette. 'That's ... that's not true.'

'Isn't it?'

'No, it's not,' David immediately lit another cigarette.

'Oh, yes it is. You hate Underwood; you hate your family; and deep down, you hate yourself too. That's the reason you drink, isn't it?'

David looked into her eyes, angry now. 'How dare you!'

'Ahh,' Lydia smiled and helped herself to one of his cigarettes. 'I've hit a nerve, haven't I?'

'Of course you have, you fucking idiot; you're being outrageously offensive! You don't know me at all – other than from what you've read in some private dick's book of times, dates and half-arsed speculations.'

'Oh no?' She lit her cigarette and eyed him knowingly. 'I seem to remember I once knew you rather ... intimately.'

David pushed the chair back from the desk and got up. 'That was a long time ago, Lydia.'

'Oh, I see. All water under the bridge now, I suppose?'

'Yes,' he walked to the window and looked out. 'We've got enough on our hands raising one member of the dead as it is. I don't see any point in digging up any other skeletons. So let's just work together and focus on the business at hand. There's a lot to do before sundown.'

'Oh, I know only too well what needs to be done.'

'Really?' David turned to her. 'So how come your plans go directly against Underwood's express wishes as passed on from him to our dad?'

She frowned. 'What are you talking about?'

'How many people are coming tonight?'

'Oh, this old chestnut. I see. Five minutes poking around in John's computer and you think you're suddenly the big expert, the high priest of the Sect?'

'Well, actually, I think I may be, now that you come to mention it. But that's neither here nor there. How many guests?'

'A few.'

'Thirty?'

'More or less.'

'It's too many, Lydia. Even if you discount Underwood's wishes, there's no way we can fit thirty people down in that cellar.'

'Oh, of course we can, at least thirty. Oh, it'll be a bit of a squeeze, granted, but that's no matter. David, I had this out with John a million times: if we want the Sect to work for us then we have to work for it. We need to strengthen our powerful connections.'

'We don't need powerful connections.'

'Oh, you may not, perhaps. But *he* does,' she pointed to the floor. 'There are going to be times, many times in the future, when he's going to need help from the highest echelons of society. Underwood can't just go running around killing people willy-nilly anymore. We no longer live in a world where you can stick a picture on a passport with a piece of chewing gum and then go anywhere you please. Oh no, it's all digital now isn't it? Photos, fingerprints, shared information between security services and governments alike. It's not enough to have a few bureaucrats in his pocket or police officials to turn blind eyes anymore; the world has changed in the last fifty years, especially since 9/11. So believe me, David, Underwood needs powerful friends – and I've got them.'

David hadn't thought of this. He paced back and forth across the room a few times before nodding reluctantly. 'Okay, I agree, you have a point.'

'You mean, I'm right.'

'Yes, you're right, but nevertheless, Underwood supposedly stipulated that only a small crowd be present at the resurrection. John reckoned no more than ten.'

'Oh, John! John was an idiot! He was simply parroting what dad told him without taking into any account society's evolution. Underwood can't expect to wake up in the 1958 he dozed off in. Things have changed. He's waking up to the Internet and mobile phones, global warming and, and,' she waved her hand trying to think of another example. 'Coldplay.'

David nodded. 'Yeah. What a wonderful world. Maybe he'll just roll over and go back to sleep.'

'Oh, I don't know,' Lydia shrugged. 'I quite liked their early stuff.'

'Yeah, all right, forget about that. Just tell me, straight up. How many people are coming?'

'I've invited forty-three.'

'*Forty-three?* Ana said up to thirty!'

'Well, she was quoting my last figure, but I've just updated her – we need to make sure there are enough *canapés*.'

'No way! I agree, you have a point with the whole "changed world" argument, but John was right too: we have to respect Underwood's wishes. Thirty people is too many; forty-three is just plain madness. I mean, it's not a bloody Tardis down there.'

'So what, you're telling me I have to cancel people?'

'Yes. You have to cancel people.'

'Jesus Christ, David. I can't, it's humiliating.'

'You don't need to take the blame. You can tell them it was my decision.'

'You?' She scoffed. 'They don't even know who you are. Who are you?'

'I'm the guardian, Lydia. In case you haven't noticed, I'm not sipping a diet Pepsi on the plane back to England. I'm here and I'm running this show from now on.'

Lydia's face was turbulent with stifled rage.

David squared up to her, eye to eye. 'So, please, cancel people.'

She folded her arms tightly across her chest. 'How many?'

'Well, I'm happy to compromise. How about we whittle things down to about … twenty guests. That includes us and house staff like Ana – '

'Twenty? I've got twenty people from Spain alone who want to come!'

'Well, that's just too bad, Lydia! Twenty. No more.'

'Christ, you're worse than fucking John.'

'Lydia, please don't speak that way about John, he was our brother and he's just died.'

'Oh, so what? His death should have been my ascension! Oh, but he didn't want me, did he? Oh no, balls only in the guardian's trousers – even when the ascendant guardian has none. It's just not bloody fair!'

'Life isn't fair, is it, Lydia? I mean, I didn't ask for this any more than you did.'

Lydia clenched her fists and let go a part stifled scream. 'So don't take it! Pack your horse and cart and *leave*. I'll take responsibility with Underwood. Believe me, I know what I'm doing, and Underwood will understand – even applaud it when he's fully restored to us.'

David wanted to put his hands over his ears. More than that, he wanted a drink. He took a deep breath and spoke slowly, as if he were addressing a child. 'Lydia, I promised John that I'd take this job, and for reasons of my own, I'm taking it. So can we stop this bickering and get on with what needs to be done?'

Lydia glowered at him.

David ignored her and went on. 'As guardian, I'll be overseeing all matters regarding tonight's ceremony, and that includes conducting the resurrection ritual itself.'

'Are you sure? He bites, you know.'

'Yeah, well, he won't bite me, will he? No Flinch shall bleed – it says that there,' he tapped the computer monitor.

'Oh, you know about that, do you?'

'Of course,' said David. 'The founding promise between Underwood and Matthew Flinch.'

'You mean, "Matthias".'

'Yeah – yeah, him. Underwood won't bite me, or you. We're both safe.'

'Unless he decides to choke you to death, of course.'

'He won't. You see, I've thought about it: that's more than a promise not to bite us, Lydia; it's a promise never to do any harm to members of the Flinch line.'

Lydia smiled. 'Oh, is it?'

'Isn't it?'

She exhaled smoke in his direction. 'Stick around: maybe you'll find out.'

'Yeah, well, I *will* stick around, don't you worry. Which reminds me, in his notes, John goes on about a "sacrifice". So, what are you planning on using?'

Lydia inclined her head slightly. 'Sorry?'

'What are you planning to use as a sacrifice? An animal? A volunteer donor?'

'Er ...,' Lydia's expression was a mixture of amusement and disbelief. 'What do you mean, "an animal"?'

'Well, you know – a chicken, something like that? Like Dad used to kill in his nutty rituals when we were kids?'

'You seriously think we're going to raise the Lord of the Undead with *a chicken?*'

David shrugged. 'Well, I don't know, that's why I'm asking you.' As he spoke, something in her mocking smile sent a chill through him.

Lydia shook her head and laughed. 'You see? This is what I mean: are you wilfully trying not to understand, or are you just genuinely stupid?'

David didn't know what to say. He considered a moment then he said: 'So, you mean you intend to use a person?'

Lydia gawped at him sarcastically. 'Er ... yeah?'

'So you've got, like, a donor? Someone who's prepared to give some of their blood?'

'No, but you're getting warmer.'

David felt the skin on his back prickle. 'You have someone who's ... willing to die?'

Lydia tilted her hand in a so-so gesture. 'Warmer.'

David was having difficulty reconciling the smile on Lydia's face with the conclusion she was driving him to. 'You mean ... you're going to kill someone who isn't willing to die?'

'Bingo!'

'But... that's murder!'

'*Hello?* Murder is the family business, David – in case you've forgotten. These last fifty years have been an aberration, a vacation from the norm. But now the holidays are over and the Flinches are back in business. Or, should I say, *you're* back in business? Since it now seems that I can go back to my little estate agent life and just leave you to take care of all the murder and skulduggery.'

David sank down onto the sofa.

Lydia continued. 'Unless, as I say, you don't quite have the balls for it. In which case, no problem ... because I do.'

David stared at her in disbelief. 'How? Lydia, how can you be so casual about something so horrifying?'

'How can you not? I mean, it's not like it's some big surprise. You've always known about it.'

'I guess ...' He looked down at the back of his hands. 'I guess I thought it would never actually fall to me to have to deal with it. I was the third in line.'

'Well, fourth if we count me, but of course we don't.'

'I never thought I'd actually be in this position. I thought I could just go on and ... forget about it.'

'With a little help from your friends, Jack Daniels and Johnny Walker?'

David nodded.

'Do you miss them?'

'Sometimes, yeah. They make the forgetting easier, at least in the short term.'

Lydia came over and sat down beside him. She laid a hand on his knee. 'David, please. I'm offering you the opportunity to carry on forgetting, with or without alcohol. Underwood doesn't have to be in your future – not as long as he's in mine.'

'Thanks. I appreciate that, Lydia. But tell me,' he turned to her, his expression grave, 'where is this *sacrifice* of yours?'

Lydia frowned. 'Why?'

'Where are you keeping them?'

'You don't need to know. I think it best if you just leave all that to me, don't you?'

He got up. 'Take me to the sacrifice.'

She stood up and blocked his way to the door. 'David, for fuck's sake, just go! You're not cut out for this.'

'I'm the guardian, Lydia, and I'm ordering you to tell me where the sacrifice is.'

'No, I won't! You're going to spoil everything.' She pushed him. 'Why don't you just go back to fucking England!'

David staggered a little. He realised his fists were clenched. He took a deep breath and relaxed his hands. Then, after correcting his posture, he walked past Lydia and out into the hall.

Lydia ran after him. 'David? Just wait a minute! Maybe you're right; maybe we could just drain him a little bit.'

David stopped with his back to her. 'Oh, it's a "him" is it? So where is *he*?'

'He's not here,' said Lydia, unconvincingly. 'He's somewhere safe, where he can't be found.'

He turned on her. 'Don't lie to me, Lydia. He's here somewhere, in an outhouse maybe, or somewhere down in the cellarage?'

Her eyes shifted from him for a second.

He smiled. 'Ah, so he's down in the cellarage, is he?' He turned and headed in the direction of the east wing of the house and a passage down to a part of the cellar that was separate from Underwood's crypt, a storehouse where they had always kept logs and hung Serrano ham.

'David!' Lydia hurried after him. 'You can't just do this! We need that boy. He's young and strong and full of good A Rhesus Positive.'

He strode on ahead of her. 'He's a person, Lydia.'

'Oh, for God's sake, stop being such a prig!'

He reached the cellar door. It was locked. He turned back to Lydia. 'Unlock it.'

'I don't have a key.'

He reached up on top of the doorframe and found the key. 'Oh, here it is.' He unlocked the door and pulled it open. Coolness rose to meet him, and something else: the bitter smell of excrement. He looked at her, anger etched deep into his brow.

Lydia shrugged. 'Oh, for Heaven's sake, what did you expect, The Ritz?'

David flicked on the cellar light and from below a voice cried out in surprise. David pushed past Lydia and descended the stairs. There was a shuffling sound and David saw a shape stumbling in the shadows along the far wall. The layout was similar to Underwood's crypt with a single bulb hanging over the centre of the floor.

David approached the figure slowly. 'Hey, it's okay now. You're going to be alright.'

The young man reached towards a wooden table. He picked up a sack and pulled it over his head, but in the seconds before he managed to hide his face, David recognised him. He turned to Lydia.

'Jesus Christ, Lydia!' he hissed. 'That's the kid in the posters at the airport!'

Lydia put her hand over his mouth. 'Shhh, keep your voice down. He's English, he'll understand you.'

'Have you gone completely mad? There's a fucking manhunt going on for this guy!'

'Oh, it's no big deal, a couple of posters in an airport or bus terminal here and there. He's a middle-class junkie, a rent boy. Those posters were put there by his family. The police themselves couldn't care less.'

David stared at his sister aghast. 'Oh, and that's all right, is it?'

'Well, it's not a problem if that's what you're asking – though I suspect it's not.'

'You're bloody right it's not.' He looked at the young man who now stood with his back turned to them. 'What's the bag for?'

'So he can't see our faces. That way, when we let him go, he won't be able to identify us.'

'But you're not going to let him go!'

'Well, I know that, but he doesn't. It just makes the whole situation easier to deal with, for him as well as us.'

David's horror deepened. 'Jesus, Lydia, this is monstrous!'

'No, David, this is business. Underwood needs fresh blood; I got it for him.'

'But you just said he's a junkie! His blood's got all kinds of shit in it, maybe even disease.'

'No, we screened his blood for disease early on, he's clean. After that, it was just a case of weaning him off the smack, which was a piece of cake actually. All this stuff you hear about heroin withdrawal being tough is nonsense. The trick is not to pamper them. All I needed was this cellar and a gun, and look at the results. I ought to start a clinic.'

'You think this is funny, Lydia?'

'Funny? God no, you should have seen the mess he made when – '

'Stop it!' David raised his hand before her face. 'Just don't, you're making me feel sick.'

Lydia rolled her eyes and placed her hands on her hips. 'Fine.'

David looked back at the young man. 'Where did you take him from?'

'One of my people found him in Torremolinos.'

'Does he have a name?'

'Who, him?'

'Yes, him.'

'Gavin.'

David looked around the room. On the table next to Gavin were a couple of books, a dirty bowl, and a spoon. Against the opposite wall was a rusty single bed, and in the far corner, covered by a towel, was a plastic bucket. A roll of toilet paper lay on the floor beside it. David went over to the bucket and lifted it. He felt the weight and brought it back to Lydia. 'It needs emptying.'

Lydia took it and set it back down on the floor. 'I'll tell Ana.'

David picked it up again and held it out to her. 'Lydia, this is your mess, not Ana's. Now you can either leave here carrying it in the bucket or wearing it all over that expensive suit of yours. But one way or the other, it's leaving with you.'

She sighed and took the bucket. 'You know, one day you're going to regret this, David.'

'Perhaps.' He went over to Gavin and gently called him by his name. Gavin tensed. 'It's okay, my name's David. I'm a friend.'

'Please ... d-don't hurt me,' said Gavin.

'I'm not going to hurt you. I'm going to get you out of here.'

Beneath the sack, Gavin's head turned towards the sound of David's voice. 'Y- you are? Has my family paid the ransom?'

David looked at Lydia. She shrugged nonchalantly. He turned back to Gavin. 'Yes, they've paid.'

'Oh, thank God!'

'But, listen, I can't get you out right away, because there are some things I need to do first. Things I need to organise, like transport. Do you understand?'

'No!' Gavin stepped away from David, his hands outstretched behind him, groping for the wall. 'No, you're going to kill me, aren't you?'

'No, no, Gavin. I promise. You haven't seen us, and we have the money, so we can let you go. All I need you to do is cooperate with me for just a little longer, okay?'

'Do, do you really mean it?' There was hope in Gavin's voice.

'Yes, I really mean it.' From inside the sack came the sound of sobbing as Gavin began to cry, thanking him now, over and over again. David felt his own tears pricking at his eyes and he took a second to suppress them. Then, he took Gavin gently by the shoulders and led him to the bed. 'It's okay. Here. Just rest now and I'll be back soon.' He turned to Lydia and his face darkened with rage. 'Upstairs. We need to talk.'

Lydia sighed with exaggerated boredom as he took her by the arm and lead her up the stairs. 'All right, take it easy, Jesus. I don't want to spill any slops from the bucket on your sandals.'

Once they were back in the corridor, David closed the door and said, 'Last night, Lydia, John told me you were evil. Now I know cancer victims can get bitter and angry, and I thought maybe it was just the disease talking. But I can see now that it wasn't. You really are evil, aren't you?'

She smiled. 'David. What kind of a thing is that to say to your only sister?'

'How could you do a thing like this to another human being?'

Lydia folded her arms. 'How could *I* do this?' She laughed. 'You seem to think that this was all my idea and that dear brother John was completely unaware of it all.'

David said nothing, but his jaw tightened.

'Oh yes, that's right. I don't know whether John lost his evil marbles in his last moments in this world, but if you think he wanted me to pop down to the nearest farmyard and grab a couple of chickens for the resurrection, then you need to think again.' Lydia leaned in close to David, letting the bucket knock against his knees. 'All of this, this sacrifice procedure, was done following John's explicit instructions. Instructions given to him by our father, who in turn got them from Lord Underwood.' She smiled. 'And we must adhere to Lord Underwood's instructions, mustn't we, David?'

David turned and walked away down the corridor.

Lydia chuckled and called after him, 'You know, you could always try to round up a few rabbits to sacrifice, David, there's always plenty of those hopping around.'

'Just empty the bucket, Lydia,' David called without turning. 'Empty the fucking bucket.'

13

DAVID WALKED THROUGH THE KITCHEN. There was no sign of Ana; maybe she was off polishing the family knuckledusters or something. It was hard to believe that the nice little woman he'd been chatting over toast that morning was complicit in the imprisonment of Gavin. But at the same time, it followed – she was in the Sect, she was a servant of Underwood. He was angry with himself for not suspecting the worst from the outset: Lydia, Ana, Conchi, they were all a band of cut-throats, and he'd been a fool to ever think they were anything less. He looked at his watch: it was two-fifteen, siesta time. That explained Ana's absence. She was probably off dreaming sweet and bloody dreams of her fanged Prince Charming, which was just as well; David was going to get Gavin out of there, and the fewer objectors there were to that, the better.

He stepped outside into the afternoon heat and hurried across the courtyard past the fountain to the front of the house. There on the drive was Lydia's Land Rover and beside it, in prime parking position under the trees, was Ana's red hatchback. He glanced around, there had to be another car somewhere, John must have had one; it was impossible to live this far out in the country without a car. Then he remembered the garage. Quickly, he walked around to the side of the house, his feet crunching on the hot gravel which grew thinner underfoot the farther he went around the house. As he rounded the back of the building, he saw the garage ahead. It was an old white building that had originally had been a farm machinery storehouse. The old corrugated tin roof had been replaced with terracotta tiles and the two front doors looked as though they had recently received a new coat of green paint, but otherwise it looked much the same as he remembered it. One thing that was definitely the same was the padlock and chain that held the doors closed. David tried the lock. It was well-oiled and shut tight.

'Fuck it!'

The garage had always been out of bounds, and as a boy, he'd always accepted that; never before had he tried to get inside, and as he reached up and felt along the door frame, he got the vaguest sense of doing something naughty. Then his fingers touched a small, sun-heated key. He smiled, took it down and slipped it into the padlock. The lock sprang

open and he removed it before pulling the chain through the door
handles. He gathered the lock and chain together, flung them aside and
pulled on the right-hand door. It swung open easily and warm air, heavy
with the scent of engine oil, spilled over him. He looked inside. As his
eyes were accustomed to the glare of the sun, the interior of the garage
seemed at first to be almost a solid blackness. Then he made out the
silver-rimmed headlights, which for a moment appeared like the eyes of a
night predator watching him from the darkness. David smiled as the
shape of the car before him slowly revealed itself; its sleek lines reflecting
the sunlight like the surface of a black liquid. How could he have
forgotten the Citroën, the DS that Arthur had used to take them out for
drives in when they were kids? Apparently it had been Arthur's retirement
gift to himself. He had once told David that Underwood didn't much care
for the shark-nosed design of the car and so he'd had to wait until after
Underwood had been interred before he could treat himself to one.

David walked over and touched its warm body. His fingers traced lines
through a fine coat of dust to reveal an immaculately wax-polished finish
beneath. No doubt John had inherited ownership of the car when Arthur
died. So whose did that make it now? Was it his?

'If you think that's impressive,' said Lydia from behind him. 'Take a
look over there.' He turned back to her. She stood silhouetted in the
doorway pointing into the deeper shadows to the left of the garage. He
followed her finger to the shape of another car. It too was black and
almost hidden in the darkness.

'Here,' said Lydia. 'Let's shed some light on the old girl.' She swung
the left door of the garage open and the sun drove the shadows back to
reveal a large, vintage hearse. But not just any hearse, David observed: it
was a Roller. The silver lady ornament and double-R Rolls Royce logo
shone in the sunlight above the radiator grille and the old-fashioned, bug-
eyed headlights.

David stared at the car. 'Is that ... ?'

'Underwood's?' Lydia walked in and stood beside him. 'Yes. It's a 1947
Rolls Royce Wraith. They used to travel around in it, and during the
daylight hours, Underwood would ride in the back; in repose, as it were.'

David walked over and ran his hands reverently along the bodywork.
'I'm guessing it's still roadworthy.'

'Oh yes. It's roadworthy alright. The maintenance of these cars was
another of John's little hobbies. As you know, the Citroën was Dad's car

after Underwood was laid to rest, all Dad needed it for was his retirement. But this,' she tapped the silver lady on her head. 'This was in service.'

'Oh? What do you mean by that?'

Lydia smiled and walked around to the back of the hearse. 'Our father was a practical man. He made some little adjustments here and there that made this car better suited to his and Underwood's needs. Then John, who was also a practical man, ensured that Dad's adjustments were always as well-maintained as any other part of the car.' She opened the back door and stepped aside for David to see.

David looked in and saw only an empty hearse. 'What? This is the bit where the coffin goes, right?'

'Yes. Nothing unusual?'

'I don't know. I haven't looked inside that many hearses.'

'But it looks as you'd expect it to look?'

David looked again. The area where the coffin went appeared to be made of smooth polished chrome. Beneath it was a solid supporting structure upholstered in black velvet. He shrugged. 'Yeah.'

'Good. That's precisely what Dad always intended.' Lydia bent forward and placed her hands flat and about two feet apart on the black velvet section. She moved her thumbs around slightly for a moment then she smiled. 'Here, and here,' she pushed with her thumbs. There was a click, and the black velvet section sprang forward about a centimetre. Lydia reached beneath it and pulled.

David stood back as the drawer rolled silently out on smooth runners. When he saw what was inside, his mouth fell open. 'Oh – my.'

Lydia looked up at him. 'It's dead cool, isn't it?'

In stark contrast to the exterior covering, the interior of the drawer was lined with red velvet. It had been divided into compartments. In one compartment were clothes held down by black elastic fastenings: a pressed black suit, a white shirt, a tie and a pair of new black socks. Above them in another compartment was a pair of polished black shoes – not new, but worn. David looked at Lydia and pointed at the shoes. She simply nodded in reply.

David looked back to the drawer. On either side of the clothes, nestled in shapes especially cut to hold them snugly, were two Thompson submachine guns. David lifted one out and admired it. Its black metal surface shone dully in the shadows of the garage and it smelled of warm oil. 'Oh, man. I used to have a toy one of these when I was a kid.'

'It's good isn't it? Have you ever fired one before?'

'In the army I fired plenty of guns. But never a Thompson,' he felt the weight. The area around the circular magazine felt heavy. 'It's loaded?'

'Naturally. It wouldn't be much good in an emergency if it weren't, would it?'

'No, no I suppose not.' David raised the gun to his eye and looked along the barrel to the gun sights. 'It's a real antique isn't it? What is it, 1930's, 1940's?'

'How should I know? Maybe John has a little section on them in his notes. Search under "armoury".'

'Armoury? You mean there's more weapons?'

'Oh yes. All sorts. If you like killing people then this is the job for you. It comes with a wide range of death-dealing tools and accessories.'

David put the Tommy gun back into its place in the drawer. 'Yeah, well, I don't like killing people.'

Lydia smiled. 'I know. What conflict you must be feeling right now.'

David ignored her. He pointed at the only remaining object in the drawer: a briefcase. 'What's in the case?'

'Why don't you open it and see?'

He knelt and popped open the case. It was full of cash: bundles of euros, British pounds, American dollars and Russian roubles each in separate sections. David was impressed to see that all the money was current; John had obviously kept an eye on how notes – especially British ones – changed from time to time.

Then he noticed the passports, two of them, both UK issue. He took one out and opened it at the picture page. Underwood smiled back at him. The passport was current, though it had to be a forgery; a colour photograph that looked as if it had been cleaned up and colourised from an original black and white version, had been digitised and sealed under a skin of plastic. Underwood's face, as always, was unchanged. He wore a shirt and tie, and his hair was short and shone with hair oil. David read the name next to the picture: Underwood, Daniel William. Born: 1970. He smiled and held it up for Lydia to see. 'Talk about lying about your age.'

'Yes. The other one's John's,' said Lydia. 'I suppose you'd better remove it and replace it with yours now.'

David said nothing. He closed Underwood's passport and put it back beside John's: the two together, Underwood and Flinch. Now the other passport would be his. He felt a momentary wave of dizziness and closed his eyes.

'What's the matter?' asked Lydia. 'Overcome with emotion? Or did someone just walk over your grave?'

David ignored the question and pointed to the clothes. 'Why the clothes?'

'What, John didn't mention the clothes situation in his manual?'

'I don't know. I haven't been researching how to *dress him*, have I? So, please, what is the "clothes situation"?'

'Oh, don't worry,' Lydia said as she slid the drawer closed. 'You'll be able to ask the Master in person soon enough.' She got up and slammed the back door of the hearse.

David smiled thinly. 'Fine. Well, I won't be taking this motor into town anyway. The last thing I need is to get pulled over with a kidnapped kid *and* a couple of Tommy guns on board.' He went over to the Citroën. 'This will do me nicely.'

Lydia sighed and followed him. 'David, look. I know you're angry and you think you're doing the right thing, but you really haven't thought this through, have you?'

'There's nothing to think through, Lydia. I'm not going to let you murder that boy and that's all there is to it.'

'And so what are you going to do? Take away our only tested and guaranteed-clean source of blood; spend half the remainder of the day driving him to Torremolinos or wherever, and then the other half driving back again? Assuming you even come back at all.'

'I'll come back, you don't need to worry about that.'

'Oh sure, no doubt followed by an armada of police. What do you think he's going to do when you drop him off? Leave the sack on his head like the Elephant Man, counting slowly to a hundred to give you time enough to get away?'

'I'll be careful. I'll drop him somewhere remote ... ish.'

'He'll still take your license plate number, you stupid hippy! Jesus, David, you're living in a dream world! You simply can't do this. Don't you understand? There is no Plan B.'

'There has to be.'

'There isn't.'

'Damn it, Lydia!' David slammed his hand on the roof of the Citroën. 'You're talking about murder.'

'Oh, David, come on. You have to get past that notion. Do you think the men who work in slaughterhouses burden their consciences with words like "murder"? They probably think of the animals they kill as just things on a production line – which is what they are, really, isn't it? Just things on a food production line? And that's all the boy in the cellar is.'

'Lydia.' David pressed his fists against his head. 'It's not the same thing. We can't just murder him!'

'We have to! What else do you suggest we revive Underwood with? Smelling salts? A vampire lives on blood – human blood. And that boy is a source of, what? Eight or nine pints? Where else are we going to find that much fresh human blood on a Saturday afternoon, hmm?'

David shook his head. 'I don't know.'

Lydia laid a hand on his shoulder then said in a gentler tone, 'Maybe it would help if you tried to think of it as taking one life to save another.'

David shrugged her away and walked out into the sunshine. He looked out across the miles and miles of olive groves that shimmered in the heat, as if the answer to the dilemma might suddenly appear, mirage-like, somewhere among them.

Lydia came out and stood beside him. 'As I said, we don't have a Plan B, David.'

'Then we have to come up with one.'

Lydia sighed. 'So what do you propose? We bleed Ana to death? There's no one else around.'

David frowned. He turned to her. 'Bleed Ana?'

'Well, no, I'm joking, obviously.'

'No. No, you might have something there! I thought about it earlier but dismissed it because I didn't think it was what John was getting at, but now I know what John actually was getting at, I'm suddenly thinking, why not?'

'Bleed Ana to death?'

'No, not to death, just a little. We take a pint – no more than they'd take in a blood donor clinic.'

'And then what? Sit her down with a cup of tea and a biscuit? Are you mad?'

'No,' David was suddenly excited. 'Think about it: it doesn't even have to be Ana, it can be any of us, you, me – '

'No Flinch shall bleed.'

'Alright, so not one of us, but what about all these Sect people you've got coming? Surely they'd be happy to sacrifice a pint of their blood in order to raise their Master?'

Lydia's top lip curled in contempt. 'You can't be serious? You want to bleed our guests? It's not exactly good manners, is it?'

'Not all of them. We won't need to. We'd only need one or two pints to do the job – if that, even. See, the stomach is a sensitive thing; after a long period of disuse, it can't take too much of anything – and fifty years is a very long period of disuse. So my guess is, all Underwood will actually be able to digest is a couple of mouthfuls.'

Lydia waved a hand. 'Oh, pooh! Why are we told to bleed a whole person's worth of blood if all he needs is a couple of mouthfuls?'

'Because that's probably what they always used to do. They'd grab a victim, Underwood would take what he needed in terms of blood, and then they'd just kill 'em – regardless of the amount needed, or taken.'

Lydia shook her head. 'I don't like the sound of this. It's not what Underwood wants at all.'

'Well, he has to adapt, Lydia. You said so yourself – he's not waking up in 1958, is he?'

'No, but – '

'But nothing! Work with me on this, will you? Who could we use to start with?'

'You're serious?'

He nodded.

'You're seriously suggesting we bleed our guests? The Sect members?'

'Well, it may not even come to that, we can probably get by with staff and trusted friends. Ana is one, Conchi's another. Who else? Humour me. Who'd be up for it, in theory?'

Lydia shrugged. 'Well, there's Beltran of course – Doctor Morales – he's a masochist, amongst other things. He'd do it at the drop of a hat.'

'A doctor?'

'Yes, he runs a sexual health clinic in Malaga. He's the one who screened Gavin's blood for us.'

'Can he get medical supplies?'

'Get them? The man's apartment is positively awash with them. It's a fetish of his. He's quite incorrigible.'

'Oh yes, yes. Lydia, this is it! This is our Plan B!'

'Oh dear.'

David touched his temples, as if trying to further coax Plan B by stimulating them. 'This doctor friend of yours, could he bring us the stuff we'd need for a blood transfusion?'

Lydia shook her head. 'David, this isn't a plan, it's an arse on a stick.'

'No, this will work! We raise Underwood and no-one gets hurt. There'll be no corpses, no cops, no trail of death and destruction. It's brilliant!'

'It's deranged.'

'Answer me! Can Doctor Morales get blood transfusion equipment?'

'I imagine so.'

'Okay, call him now and ask him to bring it out here along with anything else he thinks we could use.'

'David – '

'Oh, and don't forget to ask if he'd be willing to donate a pint personally.'

'Underwood won't like this.'

'I'll take that risk, Lydia. I'm the guardian and it's my call. If he doesn't like it, don't worry, I'll take full responsibility.'

'And so what are we going to do about the boy, Gavin?'

'Uhh,' David's mind was racing. 'I don't know. He'll be okay for now, I mean, we can leave him here for another night. You're right: dropping him in broad daylight – especially today – well, it just isn't practical. I can take him tomorrow morning.'

'Well, that's something at least. He can be on standby in the event that you finally come to your senses.'

David turned to her, his eyes bright. 'Oh, I've come to my senses, Lydia. Don't you see? You were right when you said that society had evolved and Underwood has to evolve with it. And this – this is a key part of that evolution.'

'What is? You've lost me.'

David took her by the arms. 'It's this: no one has to die – not tonight, not ever. The vampire is going to evolve, and we shall be the architects of his evolution, Lydia. Using science and practical methods of blood transference, we can ensure that Underwood need never kill anyone ever again.'

Lydia was silent for a moment. Then she said, 'You know, that's possibly the weirdest idea I've ever heard.'

'But it's possible, isn't it?'

'Well, yes, I suppose it's possible, but – '

'No buts. It's possible, and that's enough.'

'David, can you hear yourself? You sound like Victor Frankenstein.'

David smiled. 'Ahh, but Frankenstein was a genius.'

'Frankenstein was a nut.'

'Come on. We have to get cracking.' He turned and strode off towards the house.

Lydia watched him go. To herself, she murmured, '*Get* cracking?' She shook her head and started slowly after him. 'Brother dear, you've already cracked.'

Nigel 'Hodge' Hodgekiss sat at a table in Bar Pepe Mendes with a glass of Cruzcampo beer and a tapas portion of green olives. He was reading a novel written in basic Spanish intended for learners of the language. On a previous reading of the book, he'd made copious notes in the page margins explaining what – for him at the time – had been new words. Many of these words were now in his active Spanish vocabulary, but not all. Hodge popped another olive into his mouth and stared in utter bewilderment at a phrase he'd evidently once been quite familiar with – since he hadn't made any notes about it – but had now completely forgotten.

'*Estoy agotada,*' he murmured, hoping that maybe the sound of the words might jump-start his memory. It didn't. He looked over to the bar. A couple of local men were engaged in lively discussion about something mysterious; Hodge couldn't follow a word of it. For a second he considered going over and asking them what *estoy agotada* meant, but even if they explained it to him, Hodge wouldn't be able to understand their explanations. It was for this reason that Hodge sat at a table rather than at the bar; people always spoke to him when he sat at the bar, and try as he might, he could never understand a word they were saying.

He'd come out to Spain in 2002 with his then girlfriend Sharon and they'd rented an apartment in Benidorm together. He'd got a job at Keith's pub and Sharon had tried to find work as a beauty technician. Nails were her speciality. Unfortunately, none of the English-speaking salons needed a nail technician, and Sharon couldn't speak a word of Spanish – not even "nails". So she'd abandoned her job quest and – specialist professional that she was – sat around on the beach waiting for a suitable position to become available. They'd split up three months later.

Sharon returned to England, and Hodge stayed on at The John Bull Tavern.

Hodge loved Spain. He loved everything about it. But the one thing that had always proved an insurmountable obstacle for him was the language, or more specifically, the Andalucian pronunciation of it. He'd been studying Spanish for years; the bookshelves of his apartment were bowing with the weight of dictionaries and textbooks, CDs and cassettes. But these recordings were all invariably made by speakers of Castilian Spanish from the north of the country. On the cassettes they always spoke very clearly, and Hodge could always rewind anything he didn't catch the first time. However, here in Andalucia, the pronunciation sounded completely different. Andalucian Spanish was famously hard to grasp, even for northern Spaniards, who had told Hodge that in Andalucia, people "eat" the endings of their words. He'd found that to be true, especially inland here in Almacena. Here they ate not only the ending of a word, but as much of the remainder as they could swallow with it – or at least that's how it sounded to Hodge.

He closed his eyes and strained to understand the flow of the conversation at the bar trying to glean a flash of meaning from a word or phrase.

'How's it going?'

He understood that phrase well enough, and the voice spoke with a Dublin accent. Hodge opened his eyes as Damo Sullivan pulled out the chair opposite him and sat down.

'Alright mate,' said Hodge. ''Ere, what does, "*estoy agotada*" mean?'

'I'm knackered,' said Damo.

'Yeah, sure you are. But what does, "*estoy agotada*" mean?'

'It means, "I'm knackered".'

'Oh, bugger,' Hodge rolled his eyes at his own stupidity. 'Of course it is. *Agotar* – to exhaust. How could I forget that?'

'Maybe because you're never knackered enough to need to use it.'

'I get knackered often enough.'

'How? What do you do that's knackering?'

'I go running sometimes. That's knackering. Especially in this heat.'

'Yeah, but you're not gonna go up to a Spanish person, all puffing and panting with a face like a wet turnip and say, "*estoy agotada*", now are you?'

'Well, no.'

'Well, that's why you've forgotten it then, isn't it? If you don't use it – you lose it. So, what's the story? What do you wanna see me about that can't wait until tonight?'

'It's about Mark Coleman.'

'What about him?'

'Haven't you heard?'

'No. Heard what?'

'He's dead.'

'Dead? Oh no, the fucking eejit. What was it, smack? I knew he'd get into that one day.'

'No, he was bloomin' murdered.'

Damo's mouth was open, ready to receive an olive. He dropped the olive but his mouth stayed open. 'Fuck off!'

'It's true, and do you have to say "fuck off" when you mean "I don't believe it"? It's not very nice.'

'Alright, well I don't fucking believe it.'

'Well, like I said, it's true.'

Damo picked up another olive and popped it into his mouth. 'How?'

'Someone cut his head off.'

'Get away! You're fucking shitting me.'

Hodge shook his head. 'I wish I was, mate.'

'*They cut his head off?* What with?'

'I dunno, the paper didn't say.'

'Fucking hell!'

'Do you want a beer?'

'Yeah.'

Hodge raised his hand and gestured to the barman. '*Dos cervazas por favor.*' The barman nodded and Hodge turned back to Damo.

'Do they know why?' Damo asked.

'Why he was murdered? No, not that they're saying anyway, but I reckon it was them Russians.'

'What, the Russians in Benidorm?'

'Yeah, of course the Russians in Benidorm, how many other Russians was Coleman involved with?'

'How do I know? He was a dealer, he might have known loads of Russians.'

'Alright, well, let me re-phrase that: how many Russian mafia type's nephews was Coleman involved in murdering?'

Damo shrank down in his seat. 'Shut the fuck up, H,' he whispered urgently. 'You never know who can speak English in these places.'

'Oh, yes I bloody do. You and me and no bugger else – more's the pity.'

'You don't know that. The barman speaks a bit.'

'Yeah, he knows "hello" and "Manchester United", but I don't reckon he knows "murdering" somehow.'

'He might do, it's on the telly a lot.'

'Well let's find out shall we?' Hodge turned to barman who was approaching with their drinks. The barman set the drinks down. '*Gracias* and murder,' said Hodge.

'*De nada*,' said the barman with a smile. He turned and walked away.

'See? We could be discussing plans to put a bomb under King Juan Carlos's bed and no-one would be any the wiser.'

Damo shook his head. 'Bollocks, mate. You got to be careful at all times, because you never know who can understand you. It's that fucking simple.'

'Oh, good. So can I take it then that you've been careful at all times?'

Damo took a sip of his beer. 'What do you mean?'

'I mean, you haven't told any of our old associates where we are?'

'Wha-! Why the fuck would I do that?'

'Not intentionally, sure, but – you know – maybe by accident, like when you're out clubbing or something down on the coast.'

'Wha-! Are you fucking mental? Here's me telling you to be careful with your gob – because you're not – and now you're asking me if I am? *Me?* I'm the fucking soul of discretion, I am. Not like you with your big flapping cake hole.'

'Well, what about when you're all loved up?'

Damo was aghast. 'Do I look fucking stupid or something? Have I got a track record of being a fucking eejit that I'm unaware of?'

'No, but, you know, you've got a track record for taking the kind of chemicals that loosen lips and sphincters.'

'What are you going on about sphincters for? Are you saying I take it up the arse?'

The men at the bar looked over. Damo grinned at them amicably. '*El futbul es la vida.*' The men chuckled and went back to their conversation.

'Look mate,' said Hodge in a lower tone. 'I'm not accusing you of being a canary or a queen, I'm just asking if you might have said anything to anyone. We need to be sure.'

'It fucking sounds like your accusing, Hodge. But for the record, no – I've said bugger-all. Jesus. I gotta say, I'm a bit fucking hurt.'

'Aw, come on, mate. You know I don't actually think you'd say anything stupid. I just wanted to check is all.'

'Well now you know. So, you can apologise.'

Hodge sighed. 'Aw, come on.'

'Apologise, please. First you tell me that a dear friend of ours is dead, and then when I'm all in shock, you accuse me of being an idle gossip with a slack arsehole. Seriously, I am – I'm hurt.'

'Alright, I'm sorry.'

'I should fucking think so.'

Hodge looked into his drink a moment. 'So, what do you reckon then? You think it was Sergei's mob what's done him in?'

'Oh yeah,' Damo nodded and finished his drink. 'Deffo. We're in big fucking trouble.'

The men at the bar laughed. Damo and Hodge looked over at the men and then back at each other. 'See?' said Damo, tapping the side of his nose, 'I reckon they understood that alright.'

14

LYDIA ENTERED THE STUDY to find David staring deep into the glow from John's computer monitor. 'Hallo, still swotting up on all things vamp?'

David ignored the question. 'Have you cancelled the excess guests?'

'Yes, but they weren't very happy I can tell you. Naturally, I told them it was your fault – I mean, your *orders*. And seeing as how you're the new guardian, they've agreed – reluctantly – to abide by your demands.'

'Good. Did you take those chairs downstairs?'

'Anna did.'

'But I asked you to do it.'

'Anna's your servant, David, not me. Anyway, why couldn't you do it yourself? Don't tell me you're still afraid of the cellar after all these years.'

'No,' David answered, perhaps a little too defensively. He checked his tone. 'I mean, er, I'm just ... busy, researching.'

Lydia smiled. 'Of course you are.'

'So how many can we expect?'

'What, guests? You said twenty, remember?'

'Yes. I just wanted to check that you did.'

'How could I possibly forget?'

'So who are they?'

'Oh, no-one you'd know. In fact they're mostly locals: our lawyer, señor Hernández and his father; our notary, señor Lago – both family firms, been with us for yonks. Then there's Miguel – my personal assistant, Conchita, the Bensons, and your sacrificial donors of course – Beltran and Ana. I can't believe they're actually going to let you do this to them. They're nattering about it now in the kitchen.'

'Who? Beltran the doctor? He's here now?'

'Yes. He's just arrived.'

David pushed his seat back. 'Did he bring the blood transfusion equipment?'

'I believe so, but you'd better ask him yourself. I'm afraid I don't speak *medicalese.*'

David looked at his watch and got up. 'Right then, let's go.'

Lydia smiled, amused. 'You're very determined, aren't you?'

'I find it helps when you need to get things done.' He left the room.

Lydia strolled after him. 'You know, when I was speaking to you yesterday, I thought you lacked the balls for all of this. No offence, but I honestly thought you'd have legged it by now.'

'Don't think I wouldn't have preferred to.'

She smiled. 'It's not too late.'

He stopped and turned back to her. His face was resolute. 'Yes, it is.'

'Oh, of course it's not. There are planes flying out all the time these days, and so many airports – '

'Look, Lydia,' he walked back and stopped when they were face to face. 'Fair or unfair, I'm the guardian, you're not. That's it, the end. Are we clear?'

She traced the line of one of his biceps with her fingernail. 'There's that determination again. You know your eyes seem to darken to a deeper shade of blue when you're like this; it's very attractive.'

He turned and walked away. 'And don't say stuff like that either. It's fucked up.' He entered the kitchen. Ana was making all manner of buffet foods for the evening and talking to Beltran in Spanish. Beltran was sitting at the table with his back to David and didn't hear him enter.

'Doctor Morales?'

Beltran turned. 'Yes,' he smiled. 'And you must be David.' He got up and extended his hand.

'Oh, señor David!' said Ana. 'I have to thank you for making the guest list more manageable for this kitchen. Your sister, she wanted to feed the five thousand.'

David shook Beltran's hand. 'Did you bring the medical equipment?'

'Yes. It's in my car.'

'Excellent. Shall we go?' He held out a hand to the door.

Beltran nodded and led the way out. 'It's quite a radical step you're taking, if you don't mind my saying so.'

'I know. But surely one that's preferable to taking a human life, Doctor?' said David with a subtle emphasis on the word "doctor".

Beltran smiled. 'Of course.'

They stepped out into the late afternoon sun. The droning of crickets filled the air as they walked across the courtyard towards the cars.

'You are a doctor yourself?' asked Beltran.

'I was a paramedic.'

'Was?'

'Yes, I teach English now – or should I say, I *taught* English.'

Beltran chuckled. 'Ah, you have accepted your new position as guardian, no?'

'Reluctantly, yes.'

'You know Lydia will do the job if – '

'Yes, thank you she's made me well aware of her career aspirations.'

'You think because she is a woman – ?'

'No, I think because she is a nutter – not to put too fine a point on it.' They stopped at the rear of Beltran's white Mercedes and Beltran opened the boot.

'She is a passionate woman, David. She always gets what she wants.'

'Yeah, well not this time.' David looked into the boot. In addition to general boot clutter there were a number of telescopic metal stands and a couple of bulky-looking travel holdalls. He nodded. 'Is this everything?'

'*Sí*, I think it's sufficient for the purpose.'

David gestured to a holdall. 'May I?'

'Of course.'

David unzipped the bag and looked inside. It was full of clear plastic tubes and assorted electrical equipment. 'Looks good, but then I'm sure you know better than I do what's needed for a job like this. Lydia says blood is your speciality.'

'Yes,' Beltran's smile widened. 'I've always been drawn to the sight of blood.'

'Er, I see,' said David. He looked away, suddenly uncomfortable. 'Well, thanks very much for bringing the gear.'

'*De nada.*'

'I'll take the bags and, well, if you could bring in the stands?'

Beltran inclined his head in the smallest of bows. David picked up the bags and started back for the house. Beltran took out the stands, slammed the boot closed, and followed him. 'Lydia tells me you've severely restricted the guest list.'

'That's right.'

'For, er, safety reasons, eh?'

'Partly. Lydia's plan to invite a trainload of people was ... ' He hesitated a moment, then continued using a phrase he knew would provoke the least disagreement. 'Contrary to the wishes of the Master.' It had the desired effect.

'Of course,' Beltran's tone was deferential. 'We must obey the Master's wishes. But he also wishes to be resurrected by human sacrifice, no? And this, you feel, is *optional*?'

'Well, it's a question of semantics really, isn't it? He wishes to be resurrected, yes,' said David walking back into the kitchen, 'and to that end he needs fresh human blood, straight from a living source.' He put the bags down and turned to face Beltran. 'But I believe the term "sacrifice" can be replaced with "donor". If we do this, we can achieve exactly the same results but without anybody dying – which,' he arched his eyebrows, questioningly, 'as a medical man, I'm sure you'd agree is preferable?'

Beltran smiled. 'My becoming a doctor was my parents' idea, David. I did not hear any medical calling, as perhaps you did.'

'But still, you must surely value human life?'

'Of course, but, er, perhaps not in the same way as you do.'

Ana intervened. 'Me, I think it's a magnificent idea. I was speaking with Doctor Morales a moment ago and we are both deeply honoured to be giving our blood to resurrect Lord Underwood, no Beltran?'

'*Sí*, of course, it is unquestionably a magnificent honour.'

'I only wish my mother could be there to see it,' said Ana, beating eggs in a large bowl. 'What she would have given to be part of this ceremony.'

'Well, I'm glad you both approve,' said David, picking up the bags again. 'Doctor, whenever you're ready?'

'Could I use the bathroom first? I need to freshen up.'

'Sure,' David nodded, glad to have the chance to go on ahead. 'Ana will show you the way when you're ready to join me.' He turned and left the room.

In the library he opened the cellar door and took a deep breath. The lights were already on below. 'Happy thoughts,' he murmured. 'Negative, fearful thoughts will be turned against you.' He tried to whistle and a dry note rasped tunelessly from between his lips. He puckered up but just couldn't whistle, so instead he started humming and stepped into Underwood's crypt doing as cheery a version of *Happy Talk* as he could manage. He went down the stairs like he owned them – briskly, without any hesitation, as if he were back in the army and following orders to just get down there and get the job done. But he didn't look at the coffin, so he didn't notice Lydia already downstairs and waiting for him.

'David! There you are'.

David started. 'Jesus!' he turned to see her sitting on one of two dining chairs that Ana had positioned either side of the coffin. 'You made me jump.'

'Feeling nervous?'

David ignored the question. 'What are you doing down here anyway?'

'Oh, I just wondered how things were coming along. I have to say, I'm a little disappointed: it's not exactly what I've been dreaming of all these years.'

'Oh?' said David setting the bags down beside the coffin. 'And what have you been dreaming of all these years?'

'Oh you know, tethered virgins, jewelled daggers, screaming, bleeding , the usual stuff.'

'You like that kind of thing, do you?'

Lydia's reply was sensual. 'Mmm, I love it.'

'Well sorry to piss on your firework, Lydia, but tonight is going to look more like an episode of *General Hospital.*'

'*General Hospital* meets *Dracula*,' said Beltran walking down the stairs to join them.

'Yes,' said Lydia. 'Belly, did you ever see that old Hammer movie, *Dracula, Prince of Darkness?*'

Beltran shrugged. 'I don't know the titles in English. Which one was that?'

'It was one of the Christopher Lee ones, the second I think. I always remember there was a resurrection scene in it at the start.'

David started unpacking the bags.

Lydia continued. 'Dracula was just ash, you see, and his human servant – the David of the piece, I suppose – poured Dracula's ashes into a sort of man-shaped stone mould. Then he hoisted his sacrifice up over the ashes and slit his throat and the blood all splattered down into the mould and Dracula rose up out of the smoke. It was very good.'

Beltran shook his head 'No, I didn't see that one.'

David sniffed dismissively. He spoke without looking up from his work. 'So, Dracula was like a blancmange-mould man, was he?'

Lydia frowned. 'What do you mean?'

'Well, it sounds like he was the powdered blancmange mixture that you add milk to, you know?' He glanced at Lydia whose frown was undiminished. He smiled. 'It's a good thing the servant got Dracula's ashes arranged in the right order, isn't it? I mean, imagine if he'd got the ashes of Dracula's arse where his head should have been.

'Don't be silly,' said Lydia.

'And if he did, would that arse have fangs? Just think, he'd rise up from the smoke with a fanged arse on his shoulders. Now *that* would be scary.'

'Oh, for god's sake, David!' Lydia snapped. 'It was just a film.'

'Exactly.' David stood up. 'But tonight isn't, which I think is something you keep forgetting, Lydia. The creature in this box isn't Christopher Lee, or Bela Lugosi, or any of the rest of them. That lot are all actors with pointy dentures in. But the creature in this box – ' he was about to slap the lid of the coffin, but then thought better of it. 'God help us, the creature in this box is real. And yes, while we are going to revive him, we are at least going to do it using sane and humane techniques, not B-movie butchery.'

Lydia rolled her eyes. 'Really? How quaint.' She got up and peered down at this work. 'So what's that then?'

David swatted her away impatiently. 'Look, why don't you just clear off, Lydia? I don't even know what you're doing down here. You're about as much use right now as a chocolate teapot, so why don't you go upstairs and give Ana a hand with the food or those robes you were going on about earlier?'

'Oh, I see,' said Lydia. 'Of course, all the women can go and make the tea while the men...' She waved a hand at the apparatus David was assembling. 'Play with their sane, humane Meccano sets.'

'Oh, no, no, you don't have to feed your guests, Lydia. You don't need to feed them, and you don't need to dress them up like a bunch of Jawas either. In fact, you don't even need them here at all.'

'They're not *my guests*, David, they're his.' Lydia pointed at the coffin. 'And as for the robes – are you seriously suggesting we all stand around looking like we just rolled in off the street? This is the most important Sect event in over 50 years!'

'Fine, so go and attend to it.'

'I will,' said Lydia. She walked to the foot of the stairs. 'Oh, and while we're on the subject, what size robe do you take?'

'How the hell should I know? I'm normal – I've never been measured for Satanic evening wear.'

'Well going by the clothes you wear, I'd say you've never been measured for anything.' She looked him over. 'Well, you look about the same size as Beltran, wouldn't you say, Belly?'

Beltran considered David's physique a moment, then nodded.

'Oh, no,' said David. 'I'm not wearing one of your stupid robes.'

'Sorry?'

'I said, I'm not wearing a robe.'

Lydia looked aghast. 'But – you'll look ridiculous! You can't be serious?'

'Lydia, I need to be able to supervise things tonight, not just the resurrection of Underwood but also a delicate medical procedure, and I can't very well do that flapping about the place dressed like Friar Tuck, now can I?'

'But you must, you're the head of the ceremony.'

'So what? I can wear what I'm wearing now.'

'Jeans and a t-shirt?' Lydia was scandalised. 'You most certainly will not! You're the guardian. You can't turn up looking like a scruff. Have you lost all sense of decorum?'

David looked at Beltran for support.

Beltran shrugged and nodded gravely. 'I'm afraid she is right. It would be – how do you say? Unbecoming?'

David sighed. 'Oh, all right. Okay, I'll wear a robe – but I'm not putting the hood up.'

Lydia smiled. 'Fine.'

'And I'll need to have the sleeves fixed back somehow. I don't know – have you got any bicycle clips?'

'*Bicycle clips?* Oh David, don't be ridiculous. I suppose we might have some elastic bands somewhere, but you'll have to take them off as soon as His Lordship revives.'

David nodded. 'Okay. Robe, elastic bands. Could you sort that out for me?'

'Of course,' Lydia started up the stairs. 'I'm a woman, aren't I? Would you like me to iron your robe for you while I'm at it?'

David looked up. 'Would you?'

With a sweet smile, Lydia raised her middle finger and left the cellar.

An hour later, David stood in front of the full-length mirror in his bedroom wearing just his boxer shorts and trainers. He held the robe Lydia had given him awkwardly in front of himself, as if it might have been contaminated with the Ebola virus. Apparently, it was a spare of Beltran's that he'd had in the boot of his car. It was black and made of light cotton, which had come as a surprise to David; he'd been expecting something similar to what a monk might wear, something brown and heavy. He looked inside for a label but found none. Hardly surprising, who the hell would manufacture these? Evidently Beltran had had it made specially, as had Lydia with hers. David opened the robe and put it on. His nose wrinkled as he caught a whiff of B.O. from the armpits of the gown. Strange, he thought; what could Beltran have been doing in this to work up a sweat? It was hardly the sort of thing you'd wear in the gym. Then he noticed the Velcro fastenings. Not exactly gothic, but practical. He fastened the front and tied the black cord at his waist. Then he looked at himself in the mirror. He pulled up the hood, tugging it forward so it hung slightly over his brow and cast a shadow over his face.

'Oh, very cool,' he said, turning to check his profile. 'This season's must-have Satanic hoodie from Lydia and Beltran of Malaga.' He turned and walked over to the window. Outside, the sky was darkening as the sun sank into its fiery bed at the edge of the world. This was it: the sun was setting on Underwood's rest. When the sun rises again, the vampire will have been resurrected, and he, David Flinch, will have done it. He will have suckled it, fed it, and nurtured it back into the world of the living. He will have unleashed the monster.

He threw off the hood, sat down and lit a cigarette. God, he wanted a drink. Maybe he could allow himself just one – just one to calm his nerves. He smiled at his reflection in the mirror and spoke aloud. 'No way, José, not tonight or any other night.' The guests had started arriving about an hour ago and he could hear them below, laughing and chatting, English and Spanish voices drifting up along with a truly dreadful 80's music mix that Lydia had put together. Right now Wham's *Wake Me Up Before You Go-Go* was playing. David smiled bitterly, it was if Underwood were channelling messages to him through George Michael.

Then he caught sight of a stain on his robe, difficult to see because it appeared almost black on the black fabric, but the red light of the setting sun gave it a rusty coloured tinge. He scratched it with his fingernail. What could that be? He wondered. What does Beltran do in this thing? Maybe he watches TV in it – maybe it's wine or tomato sauce. He remembered what Lydia said about Beltran and his fetishes and the thought crossed his mind that perhaps it was some sexual secretion. He wiped his fingernail on an unstained area of the robe and looked back to his reflection.

'Great. Here I am, sitting in Beltran's funky, muck-stained robe waiting to raise the Lord of the Undead. Could things get any weirder?'

Lydia called up to him from downstairs. 'David, *canapés* are served.'

In the mirror, he raised his eyebrows. 'Well, that's a "yes" then.'

Lydia called again. 'Come on down and meet people.'

David stood up and straightened his robe in the mirror. 'Well, if I'm going to be damned, it may as well be on a full stomach.'

It was a warm, sultry evening as David stepped out into the courtyard. The fountain was illuminated by white lights set in its pool, while all around coloured floodlights threw a warm fiery glow against the white stucco walls. Various tables of food and drink had been laid out against the walls. No-one paid any attention to David as he was dressed exactly the same as everyone else. All the guests were robed and were wearing their hoods down – eating, drinking and chatting in groups around the courtyard.

'David!'

He turned at the sound of his name to see Lydia sweep from the crowd to thrust a plate of *canapés* under his nose.

'Have a *canapé*.'

He suddenly realised he wasn't hungry, but took one anyway. 'Thanks.'

'I see the robe fits. You look superly sinister. Aren't you glad you dressed for the occasion? Imagine what a sore thumb you'd be if you'd worn jeans and a t-shirt.'

'Mmm,' he said, taking a bite of *canapé*. 'A real freak.'

Lydia wore her robe open at the chest revealing the top of her cleavage and a small inverted silver crucifix. David nodded to it. 'Nice crucifix. Did you get it from the same Satanic costume shop as the robes?'

She looked down at the crucifix then back up to him with a smile. 'Do you like it? I think it goes rather well with the occasion. Come on,' she set the tray aside and linked his arm, 'I want to introduce you to the few members of the Sect that survived the whittling-down process.'

'Lydia, I don't really feel very sociable right now. I'm kind of distracted.'

'Oh don't be silly,' said Lydia, leading him forwards despite his resistance. 'You'll soon warm up.'

David was about to pull away when he saw a little old man in the group she was heading towards. 'Jesus, Lydia,' he whispered. 'There's an old man here.'

'Yes, that's señor Hernández Senior. He was dad's original lawyer back in the 50's.'

David was aghast. 'Oh, please tell me he's not going downstairs!'

'Of course he is. Don't be obtuse, David – he's almost one of the family.'

David looked at señor Hernández Senior; he had to be at least eighty. David was about to object to his attendance when the old man's thick spectacles found Lydia and his face lit up.

'Lydia,' he croaked.

Lydia steered David into the heart of the throng. 'Señor Hernández, may I present my brother, David Flinch, Lord Underwood's new guardian.'

The old man reached for David's hand. '*Hola y beinvenidos*, señor Flinch. I am your humble servant, as I was to your brother and his father before him.'

'Er, *gracias, señor*.' David shook señor Hernández Senior's hand briefly before allowing the old man to kiss it.

'And this,' said Lydia, indicating a handsome bald man in his fifties, 'is señor Hernández junior, our lawyer here.'

'An honour,' said señor Hernández Junior, shaking David's hand.

'Yes, for me too, *señor*. Very pleased to meet you.'

'If I can be of any assistance in facilitating your move to our country, please, don't hesitate to contact me, day or night.'

'Thank you, señor Hernández.'

'Please, call me Ildefonso.'

'Ildefonso, yes and – well, call me David.'

Ildefonso pumped David's hand with renewed enthusiasm. '*Gracias*, David. This is a blessed night in Hell.'

'Yes, er, I'm sure it is.'

'And on Earth,' added the old man.

'Praise Satan. Praise Lord Underwood,' said Lydia.

A murmur of consent went around the group. David suddenly felt mildly nauseated. With a polite smile, he took a step away from the group. 'Excuse me, *señors* and *señoras*, I, I think I need a glass of water.'

'Well, I'll get you one,' said Lydia. 'Here,' she indicated the woman next to Ildefonso, 'this is Eugenia, Ildefonso's wife.'

David smiled and exchanged kisses with Eugenia. '*Encantado, señora.*' Then he caught Lydia by the robe as she made to leave and said: 'No, really, Lydia, I think I need to sit down for a moment.'

'Are you okay?' asked Eugenia. Everyone in the group regarded David with concerned expressions.

'Yes,' David smiled. 'Just a combination of heat and nerves, I think.'

Señor Hernández Senior nodded. '*Sí, claro.* Tonight is a very important occasion. You should rest and prepare yourself, señor Flinch.'

'*Muchas Gracias, señor,*' said David. He turned to Lydia. 'You see? I need to rest and prepare myself.'

She smiled. 'Of course you do.' Then to the rest of the group, she added, 'We can always socialise later, perhaps in the company of His Lordship?'

This was greeted with a murmur of awed approval by the group and David took the opportunity to head back to the kitchen. He bowed slightly and left. He hadn't gone more than a few feet before Lydia came up alongside him again.

'What do you think you're you doing?' She hissed. 'You need to meet these people!'

'Look, I just want to chill somewhere, okay?'

'David, these people are the members of the Sect. As guardian you need to know every one of them personally and this is the perfect occasion to meet and greet.'

'Fuck meet and greet! I feel sick. These people make my skin crawl, they're evil.'

'Oh stop being such a wet blanket! Everyone is evil at heart, it's part of human nature; it's what made us the dominant species, for God's sake. And the dominators of the dominant species – every really successful person on Earth, from CEOs to presidents – well, they're all in touch with their inner evil, aren't they? And so should you be; it makes ruthless decision making so much easier – it even makes it fun.'

'Oh, bollocks. The only reason man is still around today, Lydia is because we've evolved beyond evil and barbarity.'

Lydia laughed. 'Oh, you're such a wally. I bet you like *Star Trek*, don't you?'

'Eh?' David sounded hurt. 'What's that got to do with anything?'

Then Lydia noticed the Bensons approaching. 'Oh, never mind. These people are my best friends so be nice.'

'Yeah, in a minute. Tell me, what's wrong with *Star Trek*?'

'Shut up and smile!' She pinched his arm.

'Ow!'

'Lydia brightened as the Bensons drifted alongside. 'Why, Cynthia, Gerald, I don't believe you've met my brother, David.'

'Ah, the guardian himself,' said Gerald. 'Should we bow, or just shake hands?'

'Bow,' said David.

'Really?' said Gerald, surprised.

David smiled. 'No, I'm just kidding,' he extended his hand. 'Nice to meet you.'

'Ah, jolly good,' said Gerald, shaking David's hand. 'Benson. Gerald Benson. And this is my wife, Cynthia.'

'Lovely to finally meet you, David,' said Cynthia. She moved in and kissed him on both cheeks. 'Lydia has been going on about you for positively ages. David this, and David that. I'm only sorry this wonderful occasion comes so hard upon poor John's passing. I'm *so* sorry for your loss.'

'Thank you,' said David.

'Yes,' Gerald nodded, 'Deepest sympathies. A good man, John. Like his brother before him, by all accounts. Never knew him, of course, but Lydia said he was a sterling chap. Like all you Flinch boys, eh? Must be in the genes.'

David smiled. 'Thank you.'

Ana came over with a drinks tray. 'Would you like a drink, señor David?'

'Thank you, Ana.' He looked at the drinks. 'Do you have anything non-alcoholic?'

She pointed to a glass at the edge of the tray. 'Still water, especially for you.'

He took it. '*Muchas gracias.*'

'Ah,' Gerald chuckled. 'Keeping a clear head eh? Very wise.'

'Actually, I don't drink.'

'Oh, no of course not,' said Gerald, taking a glass of champagne. 'Lydia mentioned that. Spot of trouble with the sauce in the past, eh?'

'Yes,' David gave Lydia a cold smile. 'In the past.'

'Well, you're obviously a man of character, David,' said Cynthia. 'It takes character to beat an addiction. I'm afraid I've no willpower whatsoever. What was it Wilde said? "The only way to get rid of temptation is to yield to it." That's me all over.' She looked David straight in the eyes. 'Always yielding to temptation.'

David smiled politely. 'Well, you have to take life one day at a time, Cynthia, that's what they say. But now, if you'll excuse me, I have to make final preparations downstairs.'

'Oh yes, of course,' said Gerald. 'Nearly time, eh? The great moment approaches.'

'Oh, surely not yet, David?' said Lydia.

'Well, I just want everything go smoothly, Lydia, as I'm sure we all do.'

'Lydia tells us you're going to make radical changes to the resurrection ceremony,' said Cynthia.

'Yes,' said David. 'I'm not going to murder anyone.'

'Capital idea,' said Gerald. 'Weird of course, but I'm always up for a spot of the weird.' He chuckled and added with a wink, 'it's what keeps me so young-looking. Ha!'

Cynthia gave Gerald a tolerant smile then said to David, 'Yes, murder is, of course, undesirable, but surely murder – or should we say, the taking of life – is fundamentally part of what a vampire *does*, isn't it?'

'Exactly,' said Lydia. 'That's what I keep telling him.'

Cynthia continued. 'Surely after fifty years in the grave Lord Underwood is bound to be rather … parched? I honestly can't imagine how you're going to raise him without just the teensiest spot of homicide?'

'Well, I don't doubt that he's going to be thirsty, Cynthia, but thirsty creatures – really dehydrated creatures, can't drink fast and they certainly can't drink much. The body just won't take it. The re-hydration process needs to be gradual, and I'm betting that the same is going to be true for Lord Underwood.'

Gerald nodded. 'Hmm. Makes sense.'

'Yes,' said Cynthia. 'But it's not what we've come to expect, is it?'

'What have we come to expect?' said David. '*Dracula*? *Salem's Lot*? The gospel according to *Buffy the Vampire Slayer*?' He shook his head. 'These are all fictions. The only facts we have are those which my family's ancestors have recorded in their diaries and notebooks. John was familiar with these, and he left me notes on my role as guardian and how to deal with tonight's ceremony – and there's nothing that I've read in there that convinces me that that creature in the cellar has to kill in order to live. Yes – it has to feed on warm, living blood – but murder as a necessary objective in its day to day function? No. Murder is an occupational hazard, not a physiological need. I mean, think about it: a domestic dog doesn't have to hunt and kill in order to eat, now does it?'

'You see?' Lydia moved alongside David and took his arm. 'David's planning on domesticating our Master like a common Chihuahua.'

'*No*,' said David, moving away from her. 'I'm planning on teaching him how to survive in the twenty-first century. You were right when you said he needed to adapt to our world, and one thing's for sure, in the modern world, you can't go around murdering people willy-nilly for very long before you wind up getting nicked.' A few other people began to drift over to listen more closely.

'Yes, but not a vampire, surely?' said Gerald. 'They'd never catch him, would they?'

'Why not?' said David. 'Because he'll turn into a bat and fly away?'

'Well, er, yes, I imagine that would help.'

'Hammer movies, Gerald. He can't turn into a bat any more than I can.'

Lydia frowned. 'I seem to recall Dad told us on more than one occasion that he could.'

'Stories for children, Lydia, that's all. John mentions that Underwood can turn into a bat too, but that has to be based on myth – maybe one propagated by Underwood himself to inspire awe in his followers. The bottom line is, one creature can't turn into another creature. It's just not possible.'

'Tell that to the caterpillar,' said Cynthia.

'Or the tadpole,' added Lydia.

'Or even the ugly duckling,' said Gerald. 'Oh, but then, of course it wasn't a duckling at all, was it? – because if it became a swan then it'd have to have been a signet in the first place. Hmmm. I'm sorry, ignore me.'

'No,' said David, 'Essentially, you're right, Gerald, these are all examples of creatures maturing. But tell me this, can the butterfly return to being a caterpillar?'

They were silent.

'No,' said David, 'Exactly.'

'Alright then, so even if he can't turn into a bat,' said Gerald, 'he can't have existed for hundreds of years without giving the coppers the slip from time to time, now can he?'

'Yes, sure, the coppers of old, Gerald, the coppers that couldn't catch Jack the Ripper. But how long do you think Jack the Ripper could evade detection these days with all the advances of modern forensic science?'

Gerald pouted thoughtfully. 'Hmm, not long perhaps.'

'Just imagine the scenario for a minute: bodies turning up, bites on the neck, drained of blood, same thing night after night; first based in this area, then moving south, then west – a pattern emerges both in M.O. and in the direction of flight. Oh, it might take them a while, but they'd catch him for sure.'

'So supposing you're right, David?' said Cynthia. 'What would they do with him if they did catch him – put him in prison? Surely he'd escape.'

'More likely they'd put him in some sort of lab,' said David. 'Study him, probe him, run tests on him. He'd be treated like what he is: an aberration of nature, a freak species that needs to be experimented on, catalogued and understood.'

'I say,' said Gerald. 'An aberration of nature? That's almost blasphemy, David.'

'Only if you see Underwood as a god, Gerald, and I don't.'

'So what do you see him as?' asked Lydia. 'A freak?'

David turned to her. 'I see him for what he is Lydia: just another creature, the same as we humans or any other living thing.'

'I thought he wasn't living,' said Gerald. 'You know, undead and all that.'

'That's just more nonsense,' said David. 'Dead things don't need sustenance, Gerald. They don't need to rest every night and they certainly don't need to rest in a box for fifty-odd years. No, he's a living thing in a state of hibernation, a state that will soon change to one of wakefulness – or at least it will if I could be excused in order to make my final preparations.' He looked at his watch. 'Time really is getting away from us, ladies and gentlemen.'

'Oh, yes, of course,' said Gerald. He stepped aside slightly and the small crowd that had gathered behind him parted to let David through. David walked to the kitchen door where he stopped beside the stereo to silence Duran Duran in the middle of *Hungry Like the Wolf.* Everyone stopped talking and looked over.

'Doctor Morales and Ana,' David announced. 'Would you come with me, please? It's time.'

Five minutes later, David, Beltran and Ana stood gazing at the coffin where it stood on its low stone plinth. The rich, dark oak had been recently polished and it gleamed dully in the light of the candles that burned all around the room.

'We're going to need more light,' said David. 'Let's get this turned on.' Warily, he indicated the single bulb that hung directly over the coffin.

'Lydia will not like that,' said Beltran. 'It will spoil the ambience.'

David turned to him. 'Bollocks to the ambience, Doctor. These candles are barely enough to see by as it is. How bright do you think it's going to be later with that Sect mob all gathered around? I could play *pin the tail on the donkey* with your veins if you like, but I think it would be a lot better for all of us – His Lordship included – if I could see where I was sticking the needles.'

'He is right, Doctor,' said Ana.

'But this,' Beltran tapped the bulb. 'It's so unforgiving!'

David raised his eyebrows. 'Well I'm open to suggestions, Doctor. Maybe we could all wear head lights?'

'No,' Beltran shook his head. 'I don't have any of those and anyway, they would not go with the robes.'

A voice came from behind them. 'Maybe someone could simply hold one of those candlesticks over you while you work?' They turned to see Conchita coming down the stairs to join them. 'Forgive me, David. I know you want to prepare, but you forget – I am a trained nurse. I could assist, no?

Beltran nodded. 'It's a good idea.'

'Okay,' David agreed. 'I suppose since you're going to be here anyway, you might as well lend a hand. Thanks – I mean, if you're sure you want to be, you know, up close.'

Conchita smiled. 'You think I would rather be at the back?'

'I know I would,' said David. 'The back of bloody beyond. But let's not get into that right now.' He turned to Beltran. 'Well then, Doctor, I suppose we'd better get this coffin open.'

Beltran laughed nervously. 'It's funny, I feel kind of apprehensive. I don't know if it's fear, excitement, or both. How about you?'

David looked at the coffin. 'Frankly? My balls have shrivelled to the size of a walnut and I feel like I'm going to throw up.'

Beltran grinned. 'Yes, that's it exactly.'

'Well, just keep telling yourself it's excitement, Doctor, and try to think happy thoughts.' He glanced at Ana and Conchita. 'Same to all of you: don't be afraid. Just try to think of Underwood as a friend that we're returning to health.'

'I have no fear, David,' said Ana, 'I would give my life for the Lord Underwood!'

'Yeah, I'm sure you would, Ana, but for now all we need is a smile.'

Ana smiled broadly, as if she were posing for a photograph.

'That's beautiful.' David turned to Beltran and nodded. 'Ready?'

'*Sí.*'

'Okay. Let's get this lid off then.'

The men moved forward and took up positions at either end of the coffin, David at the foot end and Beltran at the head. Ana and Conchita moved in close behind Beltran, ready to get a first look at the vampire when the lid came off. The men took hold of the lid.

'Ready?' said David.

Beltran nodded.

'Okay, we lift on three and you step to your left. Okay?'

'Okay.'

'One, two, three.' They lifted the lid and immediately a sickly stench filled the air. David winced and turned his face away.

Ana gasped. '*Madre de Dios!*'

David and Beltran carried the lid over to the far wall. Once they had stood the lid up against the wall they turned back to Ana and Conchita. Ana stood staring into the coffin with her hands over her mouth and Conchita put her arm around the older woman. Beltran and David exchanged a glance, then Beltran walked over to the coffin. When he saw the body he took a step back.

'What is it?' David asked.

Beltran turned back to him. 'I think he is dead.'

David picked up a candelabrum with three candles burning and walked cautiously forwards. The thing that awaited him for so long in the coffin rose slowly into his view. The body was dressed in a black suit. The once-white shirt was now an irregular off-yellow, and all the clothes were loose and crumpled on the cadaver-like form. David looked at the hands that lay crossed at the chest. The parchment-yellow skin was drawn tight across the bones and the fingernails had grown long and yellow, perhaps four inches in length. David pointed them out to Beltran. 'Look at his nails.'

He nodded. 'I know.'

'It's normal, no?' said Ana. 'When the body dies, the hair and nails continue to grow.'

'No,' David replied. 'That's a misconception. When the body dies it desiccates, like this one seems to have done. It's not that the hair and nails grow; rather it's the body that shrinks away from them.'

'He *is* desiccated,' said Beltran. 'But this nail growth is considerable; it's *real* growth, not retraction of the flesh.'

David nodded. Much as he wished that Underwood had miraculously died in his sleep, he knew from his recent foray into the cellar that the thing in the coffin was far from deceased. He took a few steps closer to the head end of the coffin and held the candelabrum over Underwood's face. Despite the black beard that flowed to the shirt collar, the face was still recognisable as the one he had come to know from portraits and passport photos. David leaned in closer. Unlike a dead man's, Underwood's eyes hadn't sunk deep into their sockets; instead, they bulged like a pair of ping-pong balls beneath the waxy skin. Veins that appeared black and bloodless scrawled across the face and hands, like the cracks in the oil painting in the study. David resisted the urge to touch them, and shifted his gaze to Underwood's hairline. It was strange to see live hair growing from what appeared to be a dead scalp. He estimated it had to be about a foot and a half in length.

'He looks like *The Mummy*,' said Beltran.

'Yeah,' David murmured.

'But why is his hair not longer?' asked Ana. 'If I don't cut my hair for fifty years, I need a wheelbarrow to carry it round in.'

David shrugged. 'Massively reduced heartbeat leading to massively reduced growth metabolism? His hair and nails have grown about as long as ours would in maybe six or eight months.'

Beltran nodded. 'It makes sense. Either that or the growth ended 49 years ago and he's as dead as a door knob.'

'That's er, door nail,' said David, leaning closer over the face. He considered feeling for a pulse but found he couldn't bring himself to touch the body.

'Oh, thank you. As dead as a door nail – it sounds better.'

'And yet if the stories are true,' said Conchita, 'he's neither alive nor dead, but something in-between.'

'He is undead!' said Ana, dramatically, 'The Lord of the Undead!'

'Alright, Ana, calm down,' said David. 'Let's not get hysterical.'

'I am not hysterical. I am right! You know it in your heart.'

'I will check for a pulse,' Beltran picked up one of Underwood's wrists and felt carefully, as if he were afraid that he might accidentally break off the hand.

David waited, nervously. 'Well?'

Beltran shook his head. '*Nada.*'

'Did you bring a stethoscope?'

'Yes,' Beltran lowered Underwood's hand and went over to the equipment in the corner. He opened his doctor's bag and took out a stethoscope. He put the earpieces into his ears and returned to the coffin. He pressed the stethoscope to Underwood's chest and listened. After a moment he moved it around a little, as if the heart may have drifted. Then, he looked at David and shook his head. 'By all common definitions, this man is dead.'

'But this is not a man, is it?' said Conchita.

'He is a vampire,' said Ana. 'The Lord of the Undead!'

'Yes, thank you, Ana, you did mention that,' said David.

'What's going on down there?' called Lydia from the stairs. She walked into view, behind her the Bensons were craning to see what was going on.

'Nothing,' said David. 'We're just ... getting things ready. Come back in ten minutes.'

'Ooh, you've got the lid off. Can I have a look?'

'Not yet, Lydia!'

'I say,' said Gerald from his high vantage position. 'He looks a bit on the dead side.'

'He is dead Gerald, you clod,' said Cynthia. 'Undead.'

'The Lord of the Undead,' added Ana, sombrely.

'Can you see his fangs?' asked Lydia.

'No!' David walked to the foot of the stairs and pointed to the door at the top. 'Now go away. I'll call you when we're ready.'

Lydia trotted down a few stairs and held out her hand. 'Here,' Two thick elastic bands dangled from her fingers, 'for your sleeves.'

David took them. 'Thank you. Now please, clear off.'

Lydia turned and ushered the Bensons up the stairs. 'Go on, Cynthia, get that arse of yours up those stairs and out of my face.'

'Oh shut up, Lydia,' said Cynthia, giving her bottom a wiggle. 'You like it.'

Lydia slapped Cynthia's bottom and Cynthia gave a little cry of delighted alarm as they went through the door and back to the party.

David turned back to the group around the coffin. 'Well then, despite the fact that the patient has neither pulse nor heartbeat, we have a job to do. So, Ana, Beltran, take your places and I'll get you prepped for sacrifice.'

Both Ana and Beltran started.

'Oh, sorry.' David grinned. 'I mean, prepped for transfusion.' He pulled the elastic bands up over his sleeves and snapped them into position. 'Right then, *señores* and *señoras*, the hour is finally upon us. If there's any life left in that body in the coffin then we shall soon revive it, and after fifty years, Lord Underwood will rise again. If anyone needs to use the bathroom, now is your last chance.'

No-one expressed any need.

'Okay then, let's resurrect this bastard … and may God have mercy on our souls.'

15

BELTRAN AND ANA SAT on the dining chairs on either side of Underwood's coffin. David had completed the setting up of the apparatus that now extended between them and over the coffin. It consisted of two metal stands with a cross-section; along this, two transparent I.V. tubes had been threaded that ran from each of the donors to the centre of the cross-section where they dangled down directly over Underwood's face.

David held up an I.V. needle in a sterile wrap so Beltran could see it. 'Eighteen gauge canula: my, that's a big one.'

Beltran tapped the ash from his cigarette onto the floor. 'You want the blood to pump along this tube? You're going to need a big needle, and a big vein.'

'So where do you want me to stick you? Crook of the arm?'

'An anti-cubital? Hmm, a pretty good flow, but if you want to get a really good rush, we should go for the jugular, no?'

David shook his head. 'Oh no way, Beltran. That's too risky. I'm not happy tapping into that gusher.'

'David, remember – my blood is not thinned because we are not permitted to use any drugs. Consequently, we are going to need the strongest flow possible to get the blood through the tube while it is still warm.'

'He is right, David,' said Conchita. 'It would be an advantage to have a strong flow, even if only to get things started. And then, when Beltran has almost given his fill, we can begin to bleed Ana.'

David considered for a moment, then nodded. 'Okay, but I don't like it.' He turned to Ana. 'So, where do you want the needle, Ana? Please say your arm.'

Ana shrugged. 'Arm, neck, I don't mind. I would give every drop of blood in my body for the Master. My life for the Lord Underwood.'

'Yeah, well, let's not get too generous, eh? We'll get to you in a minute, dear. First we'll prep the good doctor. Conchita, could you tape the canula down after I stick him?'

'I'd be delighted.'

David nodded and went to the Hostess drinks trolley that they were using as a wheel-able table. He opened a bottle of surgical spirit and drizzled a little of it over some wads of cotton wool in a steel dish. 'Very well, Beltran,' said David, pulling on a pair of surgical gloves. 'The jugular it is.' He walked over to Beltran and felt for the jugular in his neck. Then he swabbed the area with the moistened cotton wool. 'So, tell me, doctor. To volunteer for a needle in the neck like this you either have to be very brave or – I don't know, very weird. Which are you?'

'We already admitted that neither of us was feeling particularly brave, David,' said Beltran with a smile. 'So I suppose it must be the latter.'

David ripped open the packaging and took out the I.V. canula. The needle was one-and-a-half inches long and surrounded by a clear plastic catheter. 'Well, this is going to hurt, but it sounds like you won't mind that too much anyway.'

'No, I don't mind,' Beltran turned his head to one side so David had easier access to his neck. 'The blood sings in my veins, calling out to the needle.'

David exchanged a doubtful look with Conchita. She smiled and pulled out a strip of surgical tape in preparation. David turned back to Beltran. 'Righty-ho then. Well, let's answer that call.' He pressed the needle against Beltran's skin and gently eased the point into the vein. Blood immediately filled the safety flow chamber and a trickle ran from the wound. David swabbed the blood with cotton wool and then withdrew the needle, leaving the catheter in place in the vein. 'Conchi, do you have some tape there?' Conchita moved in beside him and he made way for her to tape the canula against Beltran's skin. Then David connected the hub of the canula to the I.V. tubing that ran over Underwood's coffin. He then tightened the small roller clamp on the tube, pinching it and so halting the flow of Beltran's blood.

'There we are, then, said David. 'Lovely job. How do you feel?'

Beltran grimaced. 'Like an aperitif.'

David smiled. 'Not too uncomfortable?'

'David, please. I have a tube in my jugular. Yes, I'm uncomfortable, but I'm also very ... aroused.'

'You mean excited?' asked David.

Beltran took a last draw on his cigarette and dropped it to the floor. 'That too.'

'Does it hurt?' asked Ana, who was looking intently at the tube attached to Beltran's neck.

'Sí.'

'Maybe I don't want that, then.'

David raised his eyebrows. 'I thought you said didn't care where we put the needle, Ana?'

'That was before I saw the look on the doctor's face. I don't want a face like that when the Lord Underwood wakes up.'

'Oh, right,' said David. 'Fancy your chances with His Lordship, do you?'

Ana shrugged. 'A girl likes to look her best.'

David felt a sudden need for a cigarette. He looked at Conchita. 'Could you prep Ana please, Conchi?'

'Of course,' Conchita wheeled the Hostess trolley around to Ana's side of the coffin while David went to where his cigarettes were, on a small table beside the cellar stairs, and lit up.

'How much blood will you need from me?' Ana asked David.

'Hopefully none, but if we do, we won't take more than a pint.'

Conchita swabbed a vein at the crook of Ana's arm then inserted the I.V. as David had done with Beltran.

'And after Ana has donated her blood?' asked Beltran. 'What if Underwood still thirsts?'

David shrugged. 'Well, if he still needs more after that, we'll just have to use other Sect members.'

Conchita raised a hand. 'I volunteer.'

'There we are then, there's the answer to your question, Doctor: Conchita will go next if necessary. And I daresay everyone else upstairs will be just as keen to bleed for the cause.'

Beltran grinned. 'For sure, it is an incredible honour.' He looked across the coffin at Ana. 'Ours will be the blood that revives the Master, Ana. Maybe he will remember us, and one day, he will make us immortals like himself.'

David frowned. 'Oh? How do you work that one out?'

Beltran looked admiringly at Underwood. 'He will be drawn again to our blood, that first sweet blood that revived him from his deathly slumber. He will come for me in the night and drain me. And then I shall be born again, a vampire like him.'

David snorted. 'Sorry, mate. But I don't think so.'

'Oh, but I do,' said Beltran. 'I feel it in my heart; he will take me, and I will rise from the dead to stalk the night at his side.'

'It is my wish also,' said Ana. 'To live forever as a vampire. A true servant of the Lord Underwood.'

'Oh, come on,' said David, walking to the foot of the coffin so he could face them both. 'You think he's actually going to make the pair of you into vampires?'

Ana and Beltran glanced at each other for confirmation then back to David. She nodded, 'If he wills it.'

David raised his hands in a gesture of surrender. 'All right, whatever gets you through the night is fine with me.' He looked at his watch: it was half-past eleven. The resurrection was set to take place at midnight. 'Okay, in a minute now I'm going to go up and get the others. Do either of you two donors have any last requests? Let me re-phrase that: is there anything I can get you before everyone else comes down?'

'For me, no,' said Beltran. 'I have all I need: a tube in my neck and a song in my heart.'

David looked at Ana. 'Ana?'

Ana considered a moment then turned to Conchi and said in Spanish. 'How is my make-up?'

Conchi smiled. 'You look beautiful, Ana.'

Ana was delighted. She turned back to David. 'I need nothing, señor David. As they say in the United States, bring it up!'

David chuckled and gave her the thumbs up. 'Okay, Ana. I'll do that.'

Fifteen minutes later, with slow and stately steps, the hooded members of the Sect descended the stairs to the cellar. They proceeded in single file to where David gathered them against a wall towards the back of the cellar. No sooner had they taken their positions than many of them, realising they had a poor view of the coffin, began to shuffle about, pushing each other and vying for a better view. David told them to settle down. Then he noticed that Lydia was missing. He turned to see her and the Bensons chatting to Beltran beside the coffin. He called to them. 'Er, Lydia and Mr and Mrs Benson.' They looked over. 'Could you come here, please?'

Lydia rolled her eyes, muttered something to Beltran, and she and the Bensons walked over to David. 'Yes, your guardianship. What is it?'

David held out a hand to the hooded assembly. 'If you could just join the other Sect members here, please.'

The Bensons did as they were asked, but Lydia's face darkened. She grabbed David by the sleeve and pulled him aside. 'What are you talking about, David?' she hissed. 'I'm a Flinch. You can't shove me in with the rank and file. I demand to be at the foot of the coffin. It's my birthright!'

David closed his eyes and massaged his temples. 'Lydia, if I make allowances for you, everyone else will want to come forward. They've all got some claim to a better view, you know?'

'I don't give a shit about everyone else! I'm your sister, a Flinch – and a proper Flinch at that.'

'What do you mean by that?'

'What was it you changed you name to? David Smith?' she poked him in the chest. 'Unlike you, I've never been ashamed of who *I* am, David. So stop being a git and let me stand at the foot of the coffin.'

David ran a hand through his hair. 'Alright, alright, but just you.'

Lydia went back to the coffin and took up position at the foot end. Seeing this, the Bensons immediately broke rank and started forward to join her.

'Whoa! Stop right there,' David held up a hand to the Bensons. 'I'm sorry, but this is a delicate medical procedure, not a dinner party. So please, get back with the rest of the spectators.'

'But we're ...' Cynthia wanted to say Black Circle, but knew she was forbidden to do so. 'Close friends of the family.'

'Me too!' said Miguel, holding up his hand and waving from the group. 'I am a close family friend also.'

Making the most of the distraction, various Sect members started to drift away behind the stone pillars trying to improve their view of the coffin.

'Oh, for fuck's sake!' David shouted. 'All of you, get back – get back against that wall!'

'Except me,' Lydia called.

David spotted a hooded figure skulking in the shadows behind Lydia. 'Oi!' The hooded figure froze. David pointed at him. 'You there! Yes, I can see you!'

The hooded figure pointed at himself doubtfully. 'Who? Me?'

'Yes, you!' David cocked his head to the rest of the Sect members. 'Get over there with your mates.' The hooded figure walked back sulkily. 'And from now on,' David said, addressing all the Sect members. 'There'll be no more going walkabout around the cellar. The next person who goes creeping around looking for a better view will be sent upstairs. Do I make myself clear?'

No-one responded.

'I said, do I make myself clear? *Comprende, amigos?*'

Begrudgingly, the twenty or so hooded heads nodded and mumbled in the affirmative.

'Good.' David looked at his watch: it was 11:45. He went over to the coffin and beckoned to Conchita who was holding a candelabrum with three candles burning. 'Could you bring those candles over here, please, Conchi? I could use a bit more light seeing as how we have to work in these ...' he waved a hand at the candles that lit the walls around them. '... dungeonesque conditions.'

'Oh, stop moaning,' said Lydia. 'It's atmospheric.'

'It's bloody dark, is what it is,' said David.

Lydia turned and went to where another candelabrum flickered in an alcove. She picked it up and returned to the coffin. 'There. Better?'

'Yes, thank you.' David took a fresh pair of surgical gloves from the Hostess trolley and pulled them on. 'Okay.' He looked at the candlelit faces gathered around the coffin. 'Are we set?' They nodded. 'Right then,' David reached out over Underwood's face and took the end of the tube that ran along the apparatus from Beltran. 'Time to insert the feed tube.'

Carefully, he pulled down on the tube and drew out the slack. Then he found Underwood's chin through his beard and eased it down. The lower jaw moved down and the withered lips parted soundlessly. The mouth was dry, like the inside of an old leather purse. David used both hands to open the jaws wider, and as he did so, he noted with interest that the canine teeth were not the pointy fangs of fiction but were the same as those of any normal man. He felt a small sense of relief; perhaps the creature he was working on was more human than monster, after all. He took the end of the tube and fed it into Underwood's mouth. He inwardly recoiled at the touch of the thin, leathery tongue, pushing it down so as to allow the tube to pass over it and into the throat – the last thing he wanted was blood flowing into Underwood's windpipe and choking him. He continued to feed the tube in until the remaining inches of slack had been taken up, then he stood back and gave Conchita a nod. She withdrew the candles.

'Do you need to do the same with my tube?' asked Ana.

'No,' said David. 'By the time we need to use yours – if we need to use yours at all – he should be able to suck by himself. We can just take Beltran's tube out and slip yours in.'

'Just like feeding a baby,' said Lydia.

'Yes,' said David. 'Sort of.'

'Well, let's just hope you don't have to burp him, eh?'

David ignored the comment and looked at this watch: it was 11:55. He took a deep breath and turned to address the Sect. 'Ladies and gentlemen, I know that this,' he gestured to the arrangement behind him, 'isn't quite what you were expecting. Indeed, some of you may be a little, er, disappointed to see that no-one is being murdered here tonight. I can't say that I regret that, and so I shan't apologise for it. But the thing is – as some of you know, and I'm sure by now most of you have heard – I don't believe murder is necessary to sustain the life of – '

'It's almost midnight,' said Lydia tapping her watch.

David waited a moment then continued. 'As I was about to say ... it may be necessary for some of you to act as blood donors tonight, to give a small amount of blood in the unlikely event that Lord Underwood requires more than Beltran and Ana and possibly Conchi here can safely provide. I see this as an infinitely preferable way to feeding His Lordship than murdering innocent people. In fact, I believe Underwood's nights of murder are over. We stand, ladies and gentlemen, at a new beginning – not only for Underwood, but also – '

'Please, David,' said Beltran. 'Lydia is right. It is too late for speeches. We must proceed!'

David's lips tightened. He sighed and looked at his watch. 'Yes. Well, as my lovely assistants here insist on reminding me, the hour is at hand. So, with no further ado, let's proceed.'

'About time too,' said Lydia.

David turned and spoke to Beltran. 'If you start to feel faint or anything, tell me, okay?'

Beltran nodded.

'Okay. Here we go.' David loosened the roller clamp on the I.V. tube, and Beltran's blood started to flow. A gasp of awe went up from the Sect members when they saw the red line moving. They pointed, nudging each other and muttering in various languages.

David watched as the blood crept along the tube, moving out now over the coffin, and approaching Underwood's face.

'Oh, my God,' said Beltran. 'It's so exciting!'

'I wish I could say the same,' said David.

'You are not excited?'

'No, I'm shitting myself.'

'*Really?*' asked Ana.

'No,' said David. 'It's just an expression. It means I'm scared.'

'Will you two shut up?' said Lydia. 'This is a sacred moment, not a smutty English class.' She turned to the Sect. 'All hail, Lord Underwood!'

The Sect members took up the chant in low voices. 'Hail, Lord Underwood. Hail, Lord Underwood.'

David gripped the edge of the coffin and watched as the blood reached the point where the tube twisted downwards. As the blood started to descend it seemed to flow faster, as if it were eager to get to its destination.

Lydia stopped chanting and came to David's side. She laid her hand over his on the coffin's edge, but David barely noticed her as the blood in the tube passed between Underwood's lips.

'How long is the tube?' asked Lydia.

'Not long,' said David. 'Maybe twenty centimetres.'

'So the blood should run into his throat about – '

The tube feeding into Underwood's mouth gave a minute twitch.

'Now.' David felt Lydia's hand tighten on his. He looked at Conchita. 'Did you see that?'

'Yes,' said Beltran.

'He's alive,' said Lydia. 'Praise Satan, he's really alive!'

The chanting behind them stopped and certain bolder Sect members shuffled forwards.

The tube twitched again, stronger than before.

'Oh bloody hell,' David's voice trembled.

Underwood's lips closed on the tube.

'He's sucking!' cried Lydia. 'Isn't it amazing? He's sucking!'

Underwood's chest began to rise and fall.

Lydia gripped David's hand. 'You've done it, David! You've done it!'

David was unable to tear his eyes away from the vampire's hands and the black veins that slowly rippled as they filled with blood. 'This is ... this is incredible.'

'Yes,' said Lydia. 'Isn't it?'

'No – I mean incredible in a bad way, Lydia. Look at his veins!'

She looked, her eyes excited. 'Yes, isn't it brilliant?'

'No, it's *impossible!* Beltran's blood can only just have entered Underwood's stomach, and yet already, somehow his body is processing it – turning it from food into fresh arterial blood!'

'Well, that's good then, isn't it?'

'No, this isn't supposed to happen! He's not supposed to be able to digest more than a pint or two at most. At this rate ... ' David looked at the I.V. running from Beltran's neck, then at Beltran. 'Everyone! We have to stop this! It's happening too fast!' He reached for the roller clamp.

Beltran pushed him back. 'No, David!'

David fell into Lydia, causing her to drop the candelabrum to the floor. She cried out, 'What the hell are you doing, you bloody lunatic?'

David regained his balance and again went for the roller clamp. 'Beltran, we have to shut it off, it's too dangerous!' Beltran held out a hand to stop him and Lydia called to the Sect members who had crept in closer.

'Seize him! Hold him back!'

The hooded figures ran forward, grabbed David by the arms and dragged him back. 'No!' David cried. 'Let me go! Lydia! Stop it, before it's too late!'

'Oh, shut up, you wimp!' said Lydia. 'It is too late – for you.' She turned back to the coffin – and froze.

Underwood's hands were moving. Slowly they crept up his body, his talon-like nails brushing through his long black beard until they came to his mouth and touched the plastic tubing.

'Conchita,' said Lydia. 'Bring those candles closer.' Conchita came closer and the candlelight fell over Underwood's face. Immediately, Underwood turned towards the light.

'Master?' Lydia whispered.

Underwood's hands moved away from the tube at his mouth and found the sides of the coffin. His fingers spread out and gripped the edges. Then slowly, he began to rise.

'He's getting up!' cried Lydia. 'Isn't it amazing? So strong, so quickly.'

'Lydia,' said Beltran, his voice thick and slurry. 'I think perhaps, I have given my pint now.'

'Shhh, Belly,' said Lydia. 'Can't you see, he's rising?'

'Lydia!' shouted David. 'Listen to him! Underwood's taking too much!'

'Shut up, David!'

Underwood sat upright. He opened his mouth and inhaled – a slow hiss that caused the blood in his throat to bubble noisily. With his eyes still closed, he slowly turned his head from side to side, as if making an assessment of the room with his other senses.

'Lydia,' said Beltran weakly. 'I'm sorry, but I have to stop my blood.' With trembling hands he reached for the roller clamp and closed it.

'Oh, damn it, Belly,' said Lydia. 'Must you be so bloody selfish?' She turned to Conchita. 'Conchita, get Ana's blood going – quickly!'

Conchita put the candelabrum aside and opened the roller clamp on Ana's arm.

As Ana's blood began to creep into the second I.V. tube, Beltran's blood in the first tube now stopped flowing. Underwood sucked but nothing happened. His fingers moved to his mouth and drew out the tube. Blood drizzled out and ran over his fingers. He sniffed at the tube, then his tongue emerged to lick at the sticky discharge.

'Hurry up, Conchi!' said Lydia.

'The blood cannot come any faster, Lydia,' said Conchi. 'It is not thinned and it comes from a weaker vein.'

Underwood's fingers now began to explore the tube, feeling the warm blood inside and how the temperature of the blood grew warmer beneath his touch the further along the tube his fingers went; the closer they got to Beltran's neck.

'Beltran!' David shouted. 'Get away from there!'

Beltran watched the hands reaching for him along the tube and a woozy smile rose to his lips. 'Master ... '.

Underwood's eyes opened.

'*Bienbenidos* ... Welcome. Welcome back to life.'

Underwood's lips drew back, and David noticed that the vampire's canine teeth had grown long and sharp. 'Oh my God.'

Underwood grasped the I.V. tube and yanked it savagely towards him. Beltran screamed as the catheter tore from his jugular in a spray of blood that splashed across Underwood's face.

'No!' cried David.

Underwood seized Beltran by the head and pulled the spurting wound to his mouth.

Suddenly, the hands that held David became limp and he shook them off. Behind him the Sect group was breaking apart, many of them were now making for the stairs. Somebody screamed, 'Papa!' but David barely registered it as he ran forwards and grabbed Beltran by the shoulders. 'Stop it!'

'David!' Lydia shouted. 'For God's sake, stop interfering!'

'No!' David pulled, but Underwood's grip was surprisingly strong. David put his arms around Beltran's chest and put a foot up against the stone plinth. 'Let him go!' He pushed back from the plinth with all his strength and tore Beltran from Underwood's grip. Then he was falling backwards; unable to turn or brace himself, he landed on his back, his head bouncing off the flagstone tiles in the seconds before Beltran's unconscious body fell on top of him.

For a moment David lay stunned, tiny points of light exploding before his eyes and voices sounding as if he were hearing them from underwater. Then, he became aware of the warm liquid that was spreading around him; he raised his hand up before his eyes and blood dripped onto his face. It shocked him into alertness. He tried to get up but Beltran was like a dead weight on top of him. He raised his head as much as he could and saw Lydia backing slowly away from the coffin. David struggled, his shoulders slipping in the blood that pooled beneath him. Then, he saw why Lydia was backing away: Underwood was climbing out of the coffin. His body, which had been cadaverous only minutes before, was now almost fully restored. His skin was the watery-grey colour of slush and his eyes – which had sunk back to a normal set – were fierce above his blood-saturated beard.

'My Lord,' said Lydia. 'I-I am Lydia.'

Underwood ignored her and walked unsteadily towards David. David redoubled his efforts to get out from underneath Beltran; he pushed and tried to roll him off but found himself slipping and sliding in the blood. Underwood reached for him.

He knows, thought David. He knows I came down to cut his head off. He's going to kill me. 'No!' cried David. 'No!'

Underwood now stood directly above him, his taloned fingers descending. David closed his eyes and turned away. A moment passed, another, and then he felt Beltran's weight lifted from him. He opened his eyes to see Underwood hauling Beltran into an upright position. Underwood took a moment to adjust the angle of Beltran's head, then brought the now weakly-pumping wound back to his lips. David turned his face away. He was about to drag himself clear when Underwood, evidently anticipating his move, brought a foot down hard upon his neck, pinning him to the floor. David grabbed at the blood-slicked sole of Underwood's shoe and tried to push it away, but he could barely lift it enough to breathe. Helplessly, he watched as Beltran raised a hand, as if in meek protest. It fluttered for a moment, then fell twitching at his side.

Lydia cleared her throat. 'My Lord, I am your servant.' Underwood gave no indication that he had heard her as he continued to drink, noisily now, like he might be sucking at the dregs. In the candlelight, Lydia's facial expressions flickered between awe, horror, and something that might have been pity for Beltran. But as Underwood dropped Beltran's lifeless body to the floor, her features settled into a smile of most reverent obedience. 'My name is Lydia Flinch, daughter of Arthur.'

Underwood wiped his mouth with the back of his hand. 'Are you indeed?' His voice was hoarse.

'I am, My Lord,' Lydia curtseyed.

'Hmm.' Underwood looked down at David, who was still clawing at his foot. 'And who,' he said, lifting his foot from David's throat '... might *you* be?'

David choked and gasped for breath.

'He is David, My Lord,' said Lydia. 'The youngest son of Arthur, and, regrettably perhaps ... your new guardian.'

Underwood squinted at David. 'Regrettably?'

Lydia smiled. 'Yes, My Lord. I'm afraid all this,' she indicated the blood transfusion apparatus, 'was his idea.'

'Lydia,' David coughed. 'You fucking bitch.'

'And these?' Underwood nodded to the remaining members of the Sect who now cringing against the far wall. 'Who are these ... sorry-looking wretches?'

'They are of the Sect, My Lord,' said Lydia. 'Your faithful servants.'

Underwood used one of his long fingernails to pick a morsel of Beltran from between his teeth. 'I see. Didn't your father give you my instructions? I specifically stated I should have a quiet resurrection: just a victim to be bled and nothing more. Instead, I awaken to this ... pantomime.'

'He did, My Lord, but I thought – ' Lydia began.

'You thought you'd disobey me?'

Lydia bowed her head. 'Forgive me, My Lord, I can explain.'

Underwood took her by the chin and raised her face to his. 'Look at me when I'm talking to you.' His nails pressed into her flesh as he spoke.

'Mark this well, Miss Flinch, I don't look kindly upon disobedient servants. With me you get one chance and then you're out, and when people leave my service, they do so in a pine box.'

'I'm sorry, Master.'

'Yes, I've no doubt you are,' Underwood let her go; at the same moment, he stepped on David's fingers. David gasped and gritted his teeth, but didn't cry out. 'The same goes for you, Flinch: don't think because you come from a noble line, I won't put you down like a dog if you displease me.' He lifted his foot and staggered slightly before regaining his balance.

Lydia took a step towards him. 'Are you all right, My Lord?'

Underwood raised a hand. 'No, I've been dead for fifty years. Suffice it to say I'm feeling a little … off-colour.' He pointed at the Sect members. 'You lot.' He cocked a thumb to the stairs. 'Get out!' The hooded figures hurried out, all except three, one of whom lay on the floor while the other two tried in vain to lift him. 'Didn't you hear me?'

David rolled over and looked behind him to see Ildefonso Hernandez pull his hood down and look appealingly to Underwood. 'Forgive me, Lord Underwood. It is my father; I think he has had the heart attack!'

'Ildefonso?' David got to his feet and hurried over to them. señor Hernandez Senior was lying on the floor. His face was ashen and his breathing thin and raspy. 'You're right; we need to get him to a hospital.'

'Ticker packed up, has it, Flinch?' asked Underwood, picking up Beltran's overturned seat and dropping down onto it.

'Yes, My Lord.'

'Pity. He's no use to me then. My meals need a pulse.'

'It is my fault!' said Ildefonso. 'I should never have let him come, but he insisted.'

'Don't blame yourself, Ildefonso,' said David. 'I shouldn't have let you bring him down here.' He called to Conchita where she stood on the other side of the coffin. 'Conchi! Can you help us?' He turned and shouted up to the last retreating members of the Sect on the stairs. 'Hey, you three on the stairs.' They stopped and crouched down on the stairs to look at him. He waved them back. 'Come back here and give us a hand.'

Conchita came around the coffin, genuflecting to Underwood as she passed him. Underwood nodded to her, amused. She joined David at the same time as the three Sect men.

'We have to get señor Hernandez here to a hospital immediately. Conchi, will you go with him?'

'Of course. I will do whatever I can,' she knelt to help señor Hernandez.

'Oh, and Conchi?' said David.

She looked up at him.

'Stay away from here, okay?'

She nodded.

A few minutes later, Conchi and the others were gone, and David and Lydia stood facing Underwood across the empty cellar.

'So,' Underwood sat with his legs crossed and an arm draped over the back of the seat. 'This is it. You two are all that remains of dear old Arthur Flinch.'

'I'm sorry, My Lord,' said David. 'This is – this is all my fault.'

'Yes, so I understand.'

'I thought we could bring you back without,' David shook his head helplessly, 'without murdering anyone.'

Underwood inclined his head as if he hadn't heard correctly. 'Come again?'

'I thought we could you resurrect you ... humanely.'

'Humanely?' Underwood looked around the cellar at the blood that seemed to have sprayed onto practically every surface. 'Well, it looks like I'm not the only one who's had something of a rude awakening tonight.'

'No, sir.' David hung his head.

'Of course, I expect all this bloody mess to be cleaned up by sunrise.'

'Yes, My Lord,' said Lydia.

Underwood considered her for a moment. He smiled. 'Good. Well, carry on then. You're dismissed.'

Lydia curtseyed, 'Yes, My Lord.' She turned to leave. David followed.

A chair scraped on the far side of the coffin and Ana stood up. She had been so still and quiet in all the chaos that David had forgotten all about her. He noticed that her IV line was now closed, but that blood had nonetheless reached the end of the tube and dripped into the coffin.

'Not you, dear,' said Underwood.

'Master,' said Ana. 'I am your humble servant.'

'No madam. You are my humble breakfast. Kindly remain seated.'

'My Lord,' said David. 'Please – '

'Run along, Flinch. This doesn't concern you.'

'But – '

Underwood turned on him. 'I said run along! Before I cut your worthless throat.'

'Well, why don't you!' David shouted. 'Let her go! Take me. I'm the one that's failed you. And God knows, I've got nothing to live for now.'

'Oh no, Flinch, not so,' Underwood's lips drew back from his bloody teeth in a smile. 'You've got me.'

Lydia moved to David's side and took him by the arm. 'Come on, David. Let's just go.'

Reluctantly, David allowed her to lead him away. He looked back to Ana. 'Ana,' a tear spilled onto his cheek. 'I'm so sorry.'

Ana shook her head. 'Don't be sorry, señor David. It's alright. My life for the Lord Underwood.'

'That's the spirit, Ana,' said Underwood as he walked around the coffin to her.

Lydia pulled David to the stairs. 'David, let's go. This is what he does. You were a fool to ever think otherwise.'

David went up the stairs. At the top he turned back.

Ana stood with her back to him, her face raised to Underwood's. Underwood brushed her long hair back from one of her shoulders then looked up at David. He raised his eyebrows, as if to enquire what David were still doing there.

'For God's sake, David,' said Lydia. She looked back to Underwood and Ana. 'Can't you see? They want to be alone.' She pushed him through the doorway into the library. Then she stepped in after him before pulling the door quietly closed behind her.

16

DAVID AND LYDIA ENTERED the kitchen to find Miguel sitting at the table smoking a cigarette and clutching a large glass of red wine. His hands trembled as he drew on the cigarette. When he saw Lydia he stood up and tried to smile. 'He is risen. All hail the – '

'Oh, fuck all that wank, Miguel!' snapped Lydia, glancing about. 'Where are all the others?'

'Gone. They left.'

Lydia took his glass of wine. 'What, even the Bensons?' She drained the glass at a swallow and handed it back to him.

Miguel nodded and refilled the glass. 'Yes. They said they didn't want to be in the way.'

'Didn't want to be on the menu, more like. Give me a cigarette, will you?'

Miguel handed her the pack and spoke to David. 'Conchita and señor Hernandez took the old man to hospital, but he didn't look too good.'

'Well, that's heart attacks for you, Miguel. They're so fucking unflattering, aren't they?' David went to the back door and walked outside.

'Where are you going?' called Lydia. She took Miguel's glass and drank again. Miguel got himself another glass and filled it.

David returned carrying a bottle of Scotch from one of the party tables. 'Same place as you by the looks of things, only faster.'

Lydia put her glass down. 'You can't start drinking now, David. For Christ's sake!'

'Why not? You are.'

'*I'm* not an alcoholic.'

'So what difference does that make?' He picked up a coffee mug and filled it with Scotch. 'Cheers.' He took a mouthful and swallowed it at a gulp then clenched his teeth at the burning sensation in his throat 'Oh, yeah! That hits the spot.'

'You can't go crawling inside a bottle now, you selfish prick,' said Lydia. 'In case you hadn't noticed, Underwood just had my boyfriend for a main course, and now he's polishing off our housekeeper for dessert!'

'What do you want me to do about it?' David took another drink. 'This is what you wanted, isn't it? What did you think it was going to be like? Woodstock?'

Lydia slapped the mug out of his hand and it shattered against the wall. 'How dare you, you fucking shit! This is *your* mess, David, not mine. You're the one who had to fuck everything up with your stupid no-one-needs-to-get-hurt crap. If we'd just sacrificed that boy in the cellar, then none of this would have happened. Beltran and Ana would still be alive; the guests would all still be here; and Underwood would be happy as a pig in shit. He'd be mingling and getting to know his new social circle. Instead, he's down in the cellar tucking into it!' She turned to Miguel. 'Speaking of which, you should go, Miguel; God knows how many more necks he's going to be opening before the night is over.'

'Oh, that's very convenient isn't it, Lydia?' said David, wiping his mouth after taking a slug straight from the bottle. 'It's all my fault now, is it? Do you really believe Count fucking Underwood would be swanning about your party like some fanged Prince fucking Charles, going up to people and asking them what they do for a living?' He laughed contemptuously. 'He's a monster, not someone out of *Hello* magazine.'

Lydia slapped him. 'My friends are dead because of you, David. And now you stand there, denying all responsibility and taking the bloody piss.'

David rubbed his cheek. 'Look, I'm sorry about Beltran and Ana, all right. But for Christ's sake Lydia, they're just the first of hundreds, maybe thousands! And all of the dead-to-be are gonna leave behind family and friends, grieving just as you are now – no, more so – you see, because you know what's happened and why it's happened, but for everybody else, there's just gonna be a corpse; no fucking explanations, just a – '. He stopped; Lydia was staring at the door behind him. He looked at Miguel and saw his eyes also fixed in the same direction.

'Oh, do go on, Flinch,' said Underwood. 'I'm enjoying your insights.'

David turned around. Underwood stood in the hall doorway, his beard glistening and his shirt saturated with blood. David took a step back. Half an hour ago, this man had been barely more than a mummified corpse – now he stood in the doorway, breathing, smiling, fully restored. His skin was smooth, and his complexion pale with spots of pink high on his cheekbones. He looked like he might be in his mid-thirties, just as he did in the portraits that hung throughout the house; portraits painted hundreds of years ago.

'I,' David stammered. 'I was just saying that you're gonna be ... killing a lot of people.'

'Yes. I daresay I shall,' Underwood's voice was no longer hoarse, but smooth; his tone, easy and relaxed. 'I take it you disapprove?'

'Er ... well, yes, I do ... for what it's worth.'

'How interesting,' Underwood entered and walked over to one of the kitchen work surfaces. He pulled out the top drawer and rummaged inside before taking out a large pair of scissors. 'Are these the only scissors we have?'

At the sight of the long blades, David instinctively took a step away from Underwood and looked at Lydia.

'What is it you want them for, My Lord?' asked Lydia.

'Well first of all I want to get rid of this hideous beard. These should suffice for that purpose. But then I want to cut my nails, and, well, I was hoping for something a little more ... elegant.'

'I'd say a pair of secateurs is what you need for that job,' said David. Underwood's eyes darkened. David, who hadn't intended to be facetious, attempted to clarify: 'Seriously, I mean, they're very thick, aren't they? No scissors, not even those big ones, could really cut through those.'

'Their thickness isn't a problem, Flinch,' said Underwood. He put down the scissors and held up his hands. 'I can deal with that quite easily.' He smiled as his talon-like nails began to glow red, their edges blurring and becoming indistinct.

David squinted, unable to comprehend what he was seeing. 'Wha – ?' Underwood grinned and the smouldering talons suddenly vanished into his fingertips as if they had been inhaled. David frowned. 'H-how did you do that?'

'Let's just call it mind over matter.'

'You ... *absorbed* them?'

'Yes, something like that.'

'So ... what do you need to cut them for?'

'Because they still exist, dear boy. I'm merely withholding them.'

Under her breath, Lydia said to Miguel, 'What wouldn't I give to be able to do with my thighs after a visit to the pizzeria?'

Underwood chuckled. 'Yes. It is rather handy. But as I say, I do need to remove them permanently.'

'I have a manicure set upstairs,' said Lydia.

'That would be perfect,' said Underwood. 'Would you mind getting it for me?'

Lydia nodded and went out. Underwood pulled out a chair and sat down. He picked up Miguel's cigarettes. 'Yours?' he asked.

Miguel nodded. 'Please, take them, My Lord.'

'Thanks. I'm simply gasping.'

Underwood took one and leaned to accept a light from Miguel. He drew on the cigarette and immediately coughed on the smoke. 'I say!'

Miguel tensed. 'I'm sorry, My Lord.'

Underwood waved a hand and patted him on the arm. 'Don't be. My fault.' He looked at the pack. 'Ah. French, eh?'

'Yes, My Lord,' said Miguel. '*Gauloises*.'

'*Êtes-vous français?*'

Miguel shook his head. 'No My Lord, I am Spanish.'

'Oh, how nice,' Underwood looked at the cigarette packet. 'Ah, the French, they'll be the death of me yet.' He grinned at Miguel. 'You know, if I had a penny for every French bullet I've taken over the years, I'd be a rich man – or, should I say, richer than I actually am. Oh, of course, I've had the lead of practically all nations under my skin at some stage or other, but overall I'd say the French have been the most zealous when it comes to shooting me.'

'So, you don't like the French, My Lord?' asked Miguel.

'*Au contraire, mon ami*, I love the French. Perhaps it's the quality of the cuisine they enjoy, but something certainly gives their blood that delicious … *je ne sais quoi.*'

Miguel laughed.

Underwood turned to David. 'So, this must be 2008 then, Flinch? From what you've said so far, I presume Arthur is no longer with us?'

David shook his head. 'No. He died in 1984.'

Underwood nodded, his eyes fixed on David, but seeming for a moment to lose focus as he digested the news. 'Hmm. And you – you're his youngest son?'

'That's right,' David took another swig from the bottle.

Underwood frowned. 'I say, do you always drink like that?'

'Lydia broke my cup.'

'Well why don't you get yourself another one? Really, you have the manners of a baboon.' Underwood watched with growing distaste as

214

David took a dirty glass from the sink and poured whisky into it. 'So, tell me, are the fascists still in power in this country?'

'No. Franco died in the 70's. Spain's now a democracy within the European Union.'

'European Union?'

'Yeah,' David took a drink from the glass. 'It's a political union of European countries. The fascists are all long gone.'

'What about the communists?'

'They're dying out, at least in Europe. Though there are still a few communist countries: China, North Korea, Cuba.'

Underwood seemed surprised. 'I see. So, was there a war? Did they use the Bomb?'

'Which bomb?'

'*The* bomb.'

'Oh, no, there wasn't a war – thanks, perhaps, *to* the bomb. Gradually communism broke down and global capitalism won the day. Now we're all friends, more or less.'

Underwood laughed. 'Well, fancy that. So now there's this European Union?'

Miguel reached into his pocket and pulled out some euro notes. 'Yes, look, My Lord. There is even European money now!' He handed the notes to Underwood who took them and held them up to inspect.

'Well, I never. And what about the Space Race? Who's winning?'

'Oh, that's over too,' said David. 'America got to the Moon first and then Russia just sort of … lost interest.'

'I see, and so are there American colonies on the Moon? Or Mars perhaps?'

'No. The Americans pretty much lost interest as well.'

Underwood's face fell slightly. 'Oh, what a pity. I'd rather hoped we might be able to go to Mars. Never mind, I can wait.'

Lydia returned with a small patent leather pouch. 'Here we are,' she said, taking out a small pair of nail scissors. 'Would you like me to do them for you?'

'That's very kind of you, Lydia. Would you mind?'

'Not at all, I'd be honoured.' She knelt down before him.

Underwood raised his hands so his fingers were pointing at the ceiling. Then, ten tendrils of red smoke rose from his fingertips to solidify once more into his talon-like nails. He lowered his right hand to Lydia and she took it in hers. She closed the scissors on the nail of his index finger but nothing happened. 'They're a bit strong, My Lord. David might be right about the secateurs.'

Underwood smiled. 'Oh, sorry, I meant to soften them for you.'

Lydia felt his hand grow warm and watched as his nails glowed at the point closest to his fingertips.

'Try them now.'

Lydia did as he asked and the scissors cut through the nails as if they were made of warm wax. She laughed and looked at him. 'Oh, how weird!'

'Yes. Isn't it? You should see me when I really flex my metamorphic muscles. I'm really quite the contortionist.'

Lydia suddenly felt herself blushing and she turned her attention back to his nails. David muttered something under his breath and he lowered his face, wary that his expression might betray him.

'Did you say something, Flinch?'

David looked up, startled that he had been heard. 'No! I, I'm sorry, Your Lordship, I was just ... thinking aloud.'

'Oh? Sounded like, "wanker" to me. Why were you thinking that?'

Lydia turned around to look at David. He looked frightened. She smiled.

'Oh, no, no, My Lord,' David stammered. 'I was saying ... er, "hanky", I was looking for my hanky,' he slapped his sides and clutched at the robe. 'But there's no pockets in this thing, you know? I, I was feeling a bit ... sad, you see, and tearful – about Ana and Beltran.'

'Oh,' Underwood nodded. 'I see.' His eyes continued to scrutinise David for a moment, then he said, 'I do hope you're not a bold one, Flinch. I mean, bold not in the sense of courageous – for that, I welcome – but rather in that other sense of the word, the boldness one associates with the undisciplined child.'

'Oh, no, sir, I, I'm not bold – not in that sense, anyway.'

'Good. I dislike undisciplined children, Flinch, and I don't spare them the rod, you understand?'

David nodded. 'Er, yes, sir. I understand.'

'Good. Next time you feel the need for ... a "hanky", best you keep it to yourself.'

'Yes, sir. I will, sir.'

Underwood continued to hold David's eyes for a moment longer then he turned back to Lydia's manicuring of his nails. 'Oh, they're coming along very well, aren't they?'

Lydia looked up at Underwood and smiled. 'Thank you, My Lord.'

Without looking up, Underwood resumed his conversation with David. 'I suspect you weren't the first in line for this job, Flinch. Am I right?'

'Yes, sir.'

'Yes. You seem a tad ... ill prepared.'

'Yeah. You could say that.'

'David was the third in line, My Lord,' said Lydia. 'Fourth, if you count me – but no-one does, but anyway – we had two older brothers, Martin and John. Martin was killed in a helicopter crash in Germany. He was stationed there with the army.'

'Oh, I'm sorry to hear that.'

'Thank you,' said Lydia, cutting off another nail.

David noticed his whiskey was trembling and he tightened his grip on the glass.

'When did he die, David? 1980, wasn't it?'

''81. Could I have a cigarette, Lydia? I left mine downstairs.'

'Please,' said Underwood, taking the pack given to him by Miguel. 'Have one of mine.'

David walked over and reached for the proffered pack. As he drew a cigarette his trembling fingers caused the pack to rustle. Underwood noticed this and met his eye.

'Don't worry, Flinch. They're French, but they won't kill you.'

David took the cigarette and stepped back. Miguel sparked a light for him. David accepted it and nodded his thanks before going back to the sink and refilling his glass.

Lydia, having finished cutting the nails on Underwood's right hand, now accepted his left, and went to work. 'So then our other brother, John, died just the other night.'

'Oh, how tragic,' said Underwood. 'What was it?'

'Cancer.'

'Oh dear, I am sorry. Such an awful disease. Before I went to sleep, I wondered if maybe that would be a thing of the past by the time I woke up.'

'No, not yet, sadly. John spent the last twenty-odd years here, waiting and preparing for this night. Our father educated him personally in how to be your guardian.'

'Did he?' Underwood pointed David to a chair. 'Sit down, Flinch, for God's sake. All your fidgeting and pacing is starting to get on my nerves.' David sat down. 'Did you know Arthur well?' The question was for Lydia.

'Oh, quite well. I didn't grow up here though, I grew up in Windsor.'

'Oh, how nice. Near the castle?'

'Yes.' Lydia went on, 'So, yes, we lived in Windsor, but my mother and I would always come out here for our holidays. Although saying that, Mum would sort of leave me with Dad and John, and then go off to Malaga with my stepfather until it was time for us all to go home. She and Dad didn't really get on.'

'Hmm. Yes, that sounds like Arthur; he was a man's man.'

Lydia smiled. 'Yes, I suppose he was. Anyway, *I* liked him and when I was twenty-one, I came out here to live, and I got to know him – Dad – quite well.'

Underwood turned to David. 'And what about you, Flinch? Did you know your father?'

David shrugged. 'Not really. He used to scare me.'

Underwood laughed. 'Yes, I can see that he might. Lovely chap, Arthur, though a tad ... how should I put it ... evil?'

'Yeah, that just about hits the nail on the head.'

'But he never hurt either of you, did he?' Underwood asked, concerned.

'Oh no,' said Lydia. 'He never hurt us. He loved us. He loved to tell us tales about you and our ancestors, and the responsibilities we inherited by being young Flinches.'

'Mmm,' said Underwood. 'Responsibilities of which you seem to disapprove, Flinch.'

David looked down at his glass, nursing it in both hands like it needed him as much he needed it. 'I respect life, sir, I don't take it.'

'No, of course you don't. But of course you realise I take life by necessity; it's a matter of personal survival.'

'Yeah, well, I call it murder.'

Underwood exhaled a stream of smoke and sang, 'You say murder, and I say survival, you like potato, and I like pot-ahto.'

David shook his head in disbelief. 'With respect, My Lord, how can you be so flippant?'

Anger suddenly flashed in Underwood's eyes, 'Flippant? You dare to call *me* flippant, when all this time I've been nothing but patient and gracious with you – *you*, a plaguey little sot who deserves to be dragged outside and horse-whipped?'

David opened his mouth to reply but no words came out.

Underwood saw this and smiled. 'But there you are; I have manners, which is more than I can say for you. I could see the younger generation's manners going to pot back in the 1950's. Obviously, you're something of a contemporary teddy boy, hmm?'

'No, sir,' said David. 'I, I'm just ... '

'A conscientious objector?'

'Yes, I suppose that's about right.'

'Ah, and a vegetarian too, I'll wager?'

'Er, no,' said David, puzzled. 'No I'm not a veggie.'

'You mean, you eat meat?'

'Yeah.'

'I say, it's rather hypocritical of you to call my carnivorous behaviour *murder,* while you yourself are, in all probability, currently digesting flesh.'

David frowned. 'Well … respectfully, sir, I don't think your murdering a human being is quite the same as me having a cheeseburger.'

'Oh no, there is a big difference, Flinch: I kill my own meals, while you prefer to have yours killed for you, hacked up by some butcher who gets the poor beast's blood all over his apron, so you don't have to get it all over your conscience.'

Lydia grunted. Since his momentary anger, Underwood's nails had hardened again and she found herself struggling with the remains of a straggler.

David shook his head. 'Look, I know the whole meat-is-murder argument, and I agree that from a certain point of view – maybe a Buddhist's – that I might seem a bit of a hypocrite.'

'Hear, hear,' said Underwood.

'But you aren't exactly a Buddhist.'

'Nor am I a hypocrite.'

Lydia managed to sever the straggler. It flew across the room, pinged against the rim of David's glass and rebounded into his drink. David looked at the remains of the nail in the bottom of his glass. He put the drink aside, took another glass from the sink, and filled it. 'I'm just saying, Your Lordship, man is more than … an animal.'

'Tell that to Darwin, Flinch. He'd tell you man is nothing *but* an animal: a "long pig", as the cannibals used to say.'

David took a drink. 'Yeah, well, try telling that to a judge and jury.' He was beginning to slur his words. 'Tell them that man is just a long pig, an animal that you've got every right to dine on as you see fit. You tell them that, and see what they say back.'

Underwood rolled his eyes. 'Oh do shut up, Flinch, your tedious platitudes are beginning to give me indigestion. I hope this is just the drink talking; if you turn out to be a bore I may have to terminate your employment. And I believe I did mention the terms of dismissal?'

David shut his mouth and a silence ensued.

Lydia, who had been filing the rough edges of Underwood's nails, suddenly became aware that the noise of her filing was now the only sound in the room. She stopped and lay down her file. 'There, that's better. All done.'

Underwood looked at his nails and his dark expression brightened. 'Oh, that's lovely, Lydia. You have a talent.'

'Thank you, My Lord,' said Lydia. 'Would you like me to do your toenails as well? I imagine they could be a bit in-grown, seeing as you've had your shoes on all this time.'

Underwood nodded. 'Yes, I daresay you could be right there. I'm holding them back right now, and that's where they'll stay until I'm in the bath where I can tackle them myself. I don't think it would be quite gentlemanly to inflict such a potentially unpleasant sight on a young lady.'

'Oh, I don't mind.'

'Ah, but I do, Lydia. I have my vanity, hard to believe though it may be in my present condition.' He got up. 'So now, if you'll permit me, I've been more than sufficiently hideous for one evening already – for which, incidentally, I must apologise. I behaved terribly earlier on. My only defence is that I was … unwell.' He held out a hand for the manicure set. 'However, presenting you with my feet is one grotesque display I can, and will, avoid. So if I may?' Lydia handed him the manicure set. 'Thank you. Now, I have to get cleaned up. I've been in the grave for fifty years and frankly, I smell like it.' He walked to the door.

'My Lord?' said Lydia.

Underwood stopped in the doorway and turned back.

'Beltran and Ana: they believed they would be coming back – as vampires, like you.'

'Yes. I know.'

'Will they?'

Underwood shook his head. 'No. I'm sorry.'

'Oh,' Lydia looked down to her feet.

Underwood scratched his beard. 'The, er, resurrection was a bit of a disaster all round, wasn't it? But, for what it's worth, I know you were both doing what you thought was best, and I'm willing to move on; make a clean slate of it, as it were, if you are?' He raised his eyebrows expectantly.

Lydia looked at David, who picked up the bottle of whiskey and poured a generous measure into his glass. She looked back to Underwood and smiled. 'Of course, My Lord, and we apologise to you as well.'

David's jaw tightened, but he said nothing.

'Oh, no, really,' said Underwood. 'There's no need for apologies. You are, after all, only human.'

Lydia broke into a peal of girlish laughter. 'Oh, very good, sir. We are, aren't we, David? Only human?'

David's mouth contorted into a smile. 'Yeah. Some of us, anyway.'

Underwood was about to leave when he turned to David. 'Oh, and Flinch, lay out one of my suits, would you? Nothing too sombre and I think we can forget the tie as well, since you're all dressed rather ... ' he gestured to their robes, '... informally. Hmm?'

David's expression smudged with bewilderment. 'But, I don't know... er ... '

'Don't know what, Flinch?'

'I don't know where your clothes are, sir.'

Underwood frowned. 'Oh. Come to think of it, neither do I.' He looked at Lydia. 'I don't suppose you know where my rooms are?'

'I do, My Lord. John has had everything prepared for you for months.' She got up and went to join him. 'I'll take you there and give you the tour.'

'Thank you so much.'

Lydia extended her hand to the hallway. 'After you, My Lord.'

'Oh no, ladies first.'

Lydia bowed slightly before leading the way. Underwood turned back to David. 'Looks like you've got some competition here, Flinch.' He turned and followed Lydia out into the hall.

David raised his glass and said in a low voice, 'Cheers, Milord. I'll drink to that.'

17

WHILE LYDIA WAS SHOWING UNDERWOOD around upstairs and Miguel was tidying up the kitchen, David took his drink and sauntered off to the lounge. The TV in the corner was on with the sound turned down. On-screen, a naked couple were entangled in a sweaty, gyrating knot. David raised his eyebrows; evidently, one or two of the party guests had been in here seeking amusement prior to the ceremony. He sat down on the sofa and took a sip from his drink. As he watched the buttocks rise and fall on the screen, he wondered how he was going to get Gavin, their sacrificial guest, back to Malaga. He looked at the glass he held loosely between finger and thumb, listening to the ice clink as he swirled it slowly around.

'I should call Steve,' he said, slurring the words. 'Tell him I've fallen off the wagon and ask his advice.' Then he sniggered as the absurdity of the scenario played out in his mind. 'Hello, Steve? It's Dave. Listen, I'm pissed, but I've got a really good excuse ... '

'Who are you talking to?' asked Lydia. She stood in the doorway with Miguel behind her.

'That arse,' said David, pointing at the screen. 'It's a good listener, but it's not so hot on advice.'

'Why are you watching this, you pervert?'

'Because it's a distraction. Look at it, see how distracting it is? Look at her, how can she do that?'

'Yes. It is pretty amazing,' said Miguel.

'David,' Lydia walked in and stood between him and the television. 'You're drunk.'

'I know. Get out of the way, will you?'

'You know the Master will be down soon, don't you? He'll want to talk to you.'

'Bollocks to him.'

'David!'

'Your friends are still in the cellar, Lydia. Shouldn't you be cleaning them up?'

'Hey, David, come on, man,' said Miguel. 'Have some respect.'

'Who asked you, *man*?' David sneered. 'She has to get used to this nightly chore if she wants to be his guardian. Ha! Guardian? Glorified corpse disposal operative, that's what that job is. Under normal circumstances we might be able to leave the mess for Ana, but unfortunately tonight she *is* the mess.'

'Hallo everyone,' said Underwood. He had showered and shaved and his damp hair was tied back into a pony tail. He wore a white shirt, open at the neck; a perfectly pressed pair of black trousers, and a new pair of black shoes. 'Having another ding-dong are we? Seems every time I join you two you're in the middle of a row.' He saw the entanglement of naked limbs on the television. 'I say, that doesn't look too comfortable.'

'I'm sorry, sir. David's taking things rather badly. He's – '

'Pissed,' said David.

'Yes, I can see that. Perhaps you ought to have a coffee or something, Flinch.'

'Yes,' David said without looking up. 'I should. I don't like drinking.'

'Why do you do it then?' asked Underwood.

'It's a hobby,' David got slowly to his feet and handed his glass to Lydia. 'Everyone needs a hobby, that's what I say, and drinking is mine. I tried to give it up recently but, events have sort of ... overtaken me this evening. It won't ... happen again... probably.' He looked Underwood up and down. 'You look a lot better.'

'And you look a lot worse. Why don't you go and change out of that ridiculous gown? Take a shower. And, er, better make it a cold one, eh?'

'Yes. I'd like that, actually,' said David. 'I've been wanting to get out of this stupid get-up since before I even put it on.'

'Well, go on then. We'll see you when you come down.'

David nodded. 'Alright.' He walked past them, staggered a little, lined himself up with the doorway, then went out into the hall and off in the direction of his room.

'I'm so sorry about David, Your Lordship,' said Lydia. 'He's ... well, he's an alcoholic. He has a disease.'

Underwood was taken aback. 'A disease? Really? What?'

'Alcoholism.'

'Alcoholism's a disease?'

'Yes.'

'Well, I never,' said Underwood. 'Have they found a cure?'

'No, sir.'

'Oh, that's a pity. So, I suppose the old remedy still applies, eh? Keep the rum beyond reach of the rummy.'

Lydia nodded sombrely. 'Yes, ideally, though as you can see, David is rather a chronic case.'

'Yes, poor chap. I'll have to see if I can do something about that. Anyway, I'm glad he's gone since it's actually you that I wanted to talk to.' He held a hand out to the door. Miguel stepped aside from where he stood in the doorway. Underwood smiled at him. 'Would you excuse us, old chap? I have some delicate matters to discuss with Miss Flinch.'

'Of course, My Lord,' Miguel gave a little bow as Underwood and Lydia passed into the hall.

'Let's go to the kitchen,' said Underwood. 'I always think of the kitchen as the heart of the home, don't you?'

A moment later they were sitting at the kitchen table. Underwood folded his hands before him and smiled. 'So, you're older than your brother, yes? Not by much, though – am I right?'

'I'm thirty-eight, sir.'

'Ah, I didn't ask your age, Lydia. A gentleman never asks a lady her age. But thank you. May I say that you don't look it – you could be ten years younger.'

Lydia blushed. 'Thank you, sir.'

'Now, how old would you say I am, hmm?' He turned his face from side to side so she could inspect his profile.

She laughed. 'I've no idea, My Lord. But I'm sure you look a lot younger than you are.'

He smiled. 'I was thirty-two when I became a vampire. Mind you, we aged a lot faster back in my day – my *human* day, that is. A man was lucky if he reached his mid-fifties, so by that reckoning I was middle-aged. And I've aged since I was changed too. Not much, but I've put on a couple of years.'

'Well, you look very good for any age, sir. Perhaps it's your diet?'

He laughed. 'Oh, very good, Lydia. I do like a woman with a sense of humour.' Then his expression became a little more serious. 'Your brother, he doesn't seem too keen on the idea of becoming my guardian, does he?'

'No sir. He's only doing it because he thinks I'm evil.'

'Are you?'

'Evil?'

Underwood nodded.

'Yes, sir.'

Underwood smiled. 'I see. And your brother?'

'Well, you can see for yourself: he's a complete disaster.'

'I mean is he evil?'

'No, sir. He's a wimp.'

'The resurrection blood transfusion business – that was his idea, you say?'

'Oh, totally. John and I were all set to stick to the sacrificial tradition.'

'So what happened?'

'David did. John sent for him. He wanted David to get the job over me because, as he so often said, David was the next in line – next *brother* in line, of course. David turned up just before John died, which gave John just enough time to pass the sword.' She shook her head, slightly drunk and not a little disgusted. 'If you ask me, the whole ascension thing's got nothing to do with birthdays, and everything to do with willies.'

Underwood raised his eyebrows. 'What?'

'Sorry, My Lord. I mean, gender: David's a man, apparently.'

Underwood smiled. 'Oh, well yes, traditionally the position of guardian is a man's job. But it hasn't always been practical, or even possible to have a male Flinch as guardian.'

'Really? I never knew that.'

'Oh yes, Catherine Flinch was the first woman to become my Guardian, she was one of three daughters – their father couldn't seem to seed a boy. Catherine became my guardian while her sisters went on to bear sons, and so the line went on.'

'What happened to Catherine?'

Underwood looked down at the table, as if seeking for his memories in the whorls of the knotholes in the woodgrain. 'She ... she served me well.'

'I'm sorry, My Lord, I didn't mean to pry.'

'No, no,' said Underwood, brightening. 'I was just remembering her, that's all. Anyway, tell me, you say you were going to stick to the sacrificial tradition; did you have anyone in particular in mind?'

Lydia leaned forward confidentially. 'Oh yes, I've got a young man in the cellar, all ripe and ready for the slaughter. John and I discussed the procedure and I knew exactly what to do.'

'I see. Well, I think had you been able to stick to tradition, your friends would still be alive. Again, my sincere apologies for their deaths. It was most unfortunate.'

'Really, sir, there's nothing to be sorry for, you were only doing what comes naturally. And like you said, they wanted it, didn't they? But can I ask you? How come they aren't coming back as vampires?'

Underwood smiled. 'If everyone I killed came back as a vampire, and then in turn, everyone they killed became a vampire too, just how many humans do you think would be walking the Earth right now?'

Lydia thought for a moment then said, 'Not many, actually.'

Underwood nodded. 'Quite so. Vampirism isn't spread like a cold sore; it's something I bestow, and I do so rarely. So rarely in fact, that I can't remember the last time I did.' He seemed to lose focus for a moment then said, 'Oh, that's a lie, actually. I remember perfectly well – but it's neither here nor there.' He picked up Miguel's cigarettes and offered her the pack. 'Fag? I'm sure Miguel won't mind.'

She took one. 'Thank you.'

Underwood gave her a light. 'So, do you feel that you're more suited to the role of guardian than your brother?'

Lydia smiled. 'Oh yes, sir.'

'And so, I take it you think the masculine privilege to be somewhat unfair?'

'I do, sir.'

Underwood lit his cigarette. 'Well, the system exists, Lydia, not because women are kinder and gentler than men – experience has certainly taught me otherwise – but simply because it's never been the *done thing* in society. You see, from a public point of view you would be my valet, my man, as it were. And it's quite unthinkable, generally speaking, that my man should be a woman.'

'So how did Catherine get away with it?'

'She played the role of a man: wore her hair short and a selection of specially tailored corsets.'

'Well, that can't have been much fun.'

'On the contrary, we had a great deal of fun. Nothing like pulling the wool over the eyes of the establishment, eh? And in our case, it was a double deception: me as a human, she as a man. And if anyone found out, then they didn't live long enough to make it public knowledge.' He chuckled.

'Well, these days, My Lord, no deception is necessary; women are considered equal to men in every respect.'

'Are they, indeed?'

'Yes sir. Why, there have even been women Prime Ministers in Britain, India ... and some other places too.'

'Really? How interesting.'

'Oh yes. Times have changed while you've been sleeping, sir.'

'Haven't they, just? I half-expected to wake up to a nuclear wasteland. Instead I find women Prime Ministers and ... you.'

Lydia smiled. 'Welcome to the 21st Century, Lord Underwood.'

David stood under the cold water of the shower with his eyes closed and scenes from the resurrection ceremony flickering over and over on the silver screen of his memory. He saw again the desiccated Underwood pulling Beltran towards him; saw again the fanged mouth closing over Beltran's horrific wound; and then Beltran's death, shaking as the life was literally sucked out of him. David began to tremble, though it was nothing to do with water temperature.

'Oh God, what have we done?'

He felt tears in his eyes and for a moment, he let them come, mixing with the water that flowed over him as in memory he looked down again from the top of the cellar stairs, terrified and powerless, as Underwood embraced Ana. He saw again the face of the monster as it looked up at him, dismissing him with contempt before Lydia pushed him away from the scene of the crime. He wondered if Ana had tried to fight; if at some point she had realised that all she was, was food.

'Oh, what have we done, Lydia? John? Dad? Dad, you fucker! Why didn't you just bang a stake through his fucking heart back in '58 and free all of us from this fucking curse!' He slammed a hand against the tiled wall of the shower stall and it slipped on the wet surface, causing him to stagger and almost fall. 'Shit!' He righted his balance and shut off the water. 'Fuck! FUCK!' he struck the wall again, defying it and drunken gravity to knock him down. But he stood steady.

He got out of the shower and looked at his face in the misted mirror, wiping it so he could meet his own eyes. 'And so,' he whispered, 'it falls to me to be either his guardian or executioner.' He pointed at his refection, as if telling himself how it was going to happen. 'If I can get him to do things my way – and that's looking pretty bloody unlikely right now – then I will guard him. But if he won't, I can't just allow him to go on murdering people. Potato or fucking *potahto*, it all boils down to the same thing, which means that I'll have to be his executioner. I don't know how, but I can find out from the diaries. I don't know when or where, but I do know that one day the moment is going to present itself, and when it does I *will* kill the bastard. I swear it.'

'Ah, Flinch,' Underwood said as David walked into the kitchen fifteen minutes later. 'Feeling better?'

'Yes, thanks.' David had shaved and put on Levis and a fresh t-shirt. He walked over to the coffee pot, averting his eyes from the vampire and trying to appear as nonchalant as possible. 'Would anyone like a coffee?'

'Not for me,' said Underwood. 'I never touch the stuff.'

David sneered, his back turned to Underwood and Lydia as he tapped a couple of spoonfuls of coffee into the percolator. 'Of course not, My Lord. Lydia?'

'Why not?' said Lydia. 'I don't think I'll be getting much sleep tonight, anyway.'

'I shouldn't think so,' said David. 'After all, we've got corpses to dispose of, haven't we?'

'Oh God, David, not tonight, for Heaven's sake!'

David turned to face them. 'Well what else are we going to do? Leave them down there to stink up the Master's chamber?' He smiled. 'That wouldn't do, would it, Milord?'

Underwood watched David through the unravelling smoke of his cigarette. 'Have a care, Flinch. You're obviously still rather tipsy.'

'Yes, sir. Sorry sir, I am. But still, I think you'll agree, I do have point about the bodies in the cellar.'

Underwood raised an eyebrow. 'Oh, you think I'll agree, do you?'

'Was, was I wrong to think that?'

'Yes, you were. Really, Flinch, you seem to have absolutely no sense of your position. You act like we're a couple of chums, when in fact I am your master, and you are my servant.'

'I apologise, sir. I don't wish to speak out of turn,' David's tone was sincere, albeit with a slight whiskey inflection. 'But, if I may just say ... ?'

Underwood nodded. 'Please, do.'

'I never actually wanted to be your servant, sir.'

Underwood smiled. 'Well, that's rather your hard cheese, isn't it?'

David's jaw tightened. 'Yes, sir, I suppose it is.'

'You are, by right of birth, the next in line for the job. Why, if you didn't do it, then the role would fall automatically to Lydia here.'

'Actually,' said David, 'I don't know if that would be a very good idea either.'

'Oh? Why?'

'Let's just say I don't think you'd be good for each other.'

Underwood turned to Lydia. 'Is that so, Lydia?'

'David thinks I'd be a bad influence, My Lord.'

Underwood chuckled. 'Yes.' He turned back to David. 'Perhaps her bad influence is just the thing I need, Flinch. She's just been telling me about this young man you have down in the basement; that you knew all about him, and yet refused to use him as a sacrifice.'

David shot a look at Lydia. 'As I told you before, sir, I wanted to resurrect you humanely. I felt we could restore you without necessarily killing anybody.'

'And as I told you before, in that, you were entirely mistaken.'

'Yes sir, but I felt we had to try, didn't I? To try to turn over a new leaf – for your own sake.'

'Oh? Explain.'

'Well, I have explained my reasons to Lydia, My Lord, but she's obviously omitted to explain them to you. To be brief, forensic technology has come a long way in the past fifty years; if you think you go around killing people as you've done in the past then you're seriously mistaken. The days of draining a corpse and just tossing into a ditch by the side of the road are over.'

'By "modern forensic technology", you mean, the constabulary?'

'Yes, the constabulary, the law, the fuzz, the coppers – they'll track you down, sir, and they will bang you up in no time.'

'Will they? I hardly think that likely. Lydia has been telling me that we have a number of senior police officials in the Sect.'

David looked at Lydia. She beamed at him like the cat that got the cream. He shook his head and turned to Underwood. 'That's as maybe, sir, but it's not enough. A bent copper on one force or another isn't gonna be able to save you from the modern Spanish equivalent of Scotland Yard. I mean, already there are corpses piling up: we've got two downstairs that will soon be attracting the flies. What are we gonna do with them?'

'Bury them?' Lydia suggested.

'Okay. So we bury them, and then tomorrow night we'll have one, maybe two more. And what're we going to do with those?'

Lydia narrowed her eyes at him. '*Bury* them.'

'So how long will it be before half the town is buried around the back of our house? There'll be a trail of blood leading to our door so red you'd be able to see it from outer space!'

Underwood nodded. 'Of course, you have a point Flinch, which is why in the past I've always tended to move around a lot.'

'In the past, sir, that might have been a solution. A body here, a body there, different police forces with no lines of communication. I'm sure you could evade detection for a good long while. But you see, it's not like that anymore. Police forces work together, even on an international level, and they *will* find you – and quickly too. And then what? To them, you're a new species, a thing of myth and folklore made flesh. They'll have you locked up in a lab in no time and be running tests on you for … well, forever.'

'The cell hasn't been built that can hold me, Flinch.'

'I've no doubt that was the case, sir, but they could build one now, trust me.'

Underwood thought for a moment then turned to Lydia. 'What do you think, Lydia?'

Lydia looked uncomfortable, she shrugged. 'He may have a point, My Lord, but I feel sure that with the right Flinch at your side you could evade capture as easily as you always did with our forefathers.'

Underwood smiled and turned back to David. 'Yes, perhaps. But it is true, I am, shall we say, "acquainted" with MI5, MI6 and a number of other of the world's secret service departments. Actually, I remember your father and I had a spot of bother with the FBI in New York shortly after the last war. Dashed clever chaps, I have to say.'

'Exactly,' said David, 'and however smart they were like then, they're a lot smarter now. Which is why if you want to remain free, My Lord, then using donors as I … *tried* to do earlier, is the only way forward. You could use Sect people, they'd all be more than willing.'

'Yes,' said Lydia, 'but that doesn't mean – '

Underwood held up a hand. 'Enough, please. Clearly there is much to consider in what you're both telling me.' Without saying another word he stood up, walked to the kitchen door and went outside.

For a moment, both David and Lydia waited for him to return. When he didn't, David turned to the coffee percolator and pulled out the pot of freshly brewed coffee. 'How do you take it, Lyd? Cream, sugar?'

'Just what are you playing at, David?' hissed Lydia. 'One minute you say you don't want this job, next minute you say you do. And now, not only are you saying you don't want it, but you're trying to fuck up my chances of getting it as well, filling the Master's head with – '

'With the truth, Lydia. Like it or not, what I said is true. You'd be caught. He'd wind up in a lab and you'd go to prison for the rest of your life, if you were lucky.'

'Oh don't be so bloody practical! You've no romance in you, David Flinch, you never did have. You should have been a fucking accountant.'

David held up her coffee mug and pointed at it enquiringly.

'Black!' she snapped. 'No sugar.'

'Here you are, then.' He set the mug before her and sat down on the opposite side of the table. 'We'll drink this then we'll get Miguel and go down to the cellar and start bringing the bodies up. It'll be hard work, and messy too, but with a bit of luck we might get them into the ground before sun-up.'

'Oh, fucking wonderful,' Lydia snatched up Miguel's cigarettes. 'Why couldn't he have killed them outside?'

'Yeah,' David shook his head. 'So thoughtless of him, wasn't it? Still, at least we haven't got white carpeting down in the cellar, eh? That's something at least.'

Despite herself, she smiled at him. 'Have a care, Flinch.' She laughed a little.

'Yeah, and have a care yourself. And give me one of those fags, will you?'

Underwood strode in from outside. 'My word, it's a lovely night. I'm going out.'

'Out, My Lord?' said Lydia.

'Yes, but don't concern yourselves,' he said as he crossed the kitchen. 'You just carry on and enjoy your coffee.' He disappeared into the hallway.

David looked at Lydia. 'He's, er, he's going out.'

Lydia nodded, her face suddenly pale. 'Yes.'

'Still, don't worry yourself.' He raised his coffee mug. 'Let's just enjoy our coffee.'

Underwood returned, carrying one of the sports bags that Beltran had brought the medical equipment in earlier. 'I say, I saw this beneath the stairs in the cellar. Could I possibly have it?'

Lydia did her best to smile. 'Yes. It's ... just a bag.'

'Smashing,' Underwood looked at David. 'Follow me, Flinch. I need to talk to you, man to man, as it were.' He smiled at Lydia. 'I hope you don't mind.'

'Oh ... of course not, sir,' said Lydia. 'Why would I mind?'

David got up and followed Underwood out of the kitchen door.

Lydia watched them go. She thought about Underwood's new bag, and then about Beltran – who had no further use for it or anything else – lying dead downstairs, waiting for her to drag him up and bury him. She felt her eyes filling with tears and she quickly wiped them away. Then, she picked up David's whisky bottle and poured a generous measure into her coffee.

David followed Underwood across the courtyard. They passed the fountain and went out under the archway onto the front drive. When they were a short distance from the house, Underwood stopped, turned to him, and held out the bag.

David was unsure how to respond. 'Sir?'

'Well, take it Flinch, it's a bag, it won't bite.'

David took it.

'You know Flinch, there are several reasons why the position of guardian is best suited to a man, and I'm going to show you one of them.' Underwood began unbuttoning his shirt.

David's brow furrowed. Suddenly uncomfortable, he looked down to the bag. He opened it and checked inside: it was empty. He looked back to Underwood, whose shirt was now fully unbuttoned and fluttering in the breeze. Underwood bent forwards and started to remove his shoes. David wished he weren't so drunk so that he might be able to make better sense of what was happening.

'I was just saying to your sister,' said Underwood, 'that traditionally, a gentleman's gentleman had to be, well, a gentleman. You see, there were places that only men could go. I'm not just talking about clubs and societies, but institutions and things – you know, like Parliament for example. You follow me?' Underwood handed David his shoes.

'Er, yes, sir,' David took the shoes and held them.

'Put them in the bag, Flinch, soles first if you please.'

David did as he was told.

'But that's not the only reason it's a man's job,' said Underwood, taking off his socks and handing them to David.

David put them in the bag also.

'There are the physical reasons too. Men are stronger and more aggressive than women, which always comes in handy in a scrap, eh?'

'I ... suppose.'

'And then there's this,' he indicated his current semi-dressed state. 'You see, sometimes I have to fly out of a place in a hurry.' Underwood handed David his shirt. 'And when I do, it's necessary for me to take off all my clothes – lest I lose them.' He began unfastening his trousers.

'Er, I'm sorry sir, I don't think I understand.'

Underwood dropped his trousers and stepped out of them. 'Well, it's obvious isn't it, Flinch? I can't go stripping down to my birthday suit in front of a woman, now can I?'

'You can't?'

'Oh good heavens, no, of course not. It'd be embarrassing for both of us, and of course, it's not unthinkable that she might have inappropriate desires,' he held out his trousers, adding with a smile, 'I mean, considering my age, I like to think I'm still in pretty good shape, eh?'

David took the trousers and put them in the bag. 'Er – yes sir, but, what I don't understand is why you need to get undressed in the first place.'

Underwood stopped. 'You mean you don't know?'

'Know what?'

'About the whole transformation thing?'

'Well, I read something about it in John's notes but I thought ... '

Underwood took off his boxer shorts and handed them to David. 'Thought what?'

'I thought he was ... parroting myth.'

'*Myth?*'

'Yes.'

'I see. Well, you need to read that chapter again I'm afraid, Flinch, because there's nothing mythical about me, I can assure you.'

'Oh. I see.'

Underwood smiled. 'No, you don't. But you will in a minute. Zip up that bag and stand back, will you?'

'Sir?'

'Stand back. I haven't done this in a long time, you know, so I'll probably be a bit rusty. When I'm in tip-top shape I can do it in the wink of an eye, but needless to say, I'm not. Anyway, get back.'

David took a couple of steps back.

'Good. Now, I want you to start counting down slowly from five to zero, that should be plenty of time. On zero, throw that bag up in the air as high as you can. Okay?'

David frowned. 'Er, could I ask why, sir?'

'So I can catch it, of course.'

'But why catch it when I can just pass it to you now?'

Underwood clucked his tongue. 'Just do as I say, Flinch. I'm going into town and I may be some time, so don't wait up for me, take the rest of the night off – after you've taken care of the … household chores, that is.'

David doubted whether his "chores" would be over before sunrise but he felt little good would come of saying so. He nodded. 'Okay.'

'Good. Start the count.'

David took a step back and started counting out loud. 'Five.' Almost immediately he felt a heat begin to radiate from Underwood's direction.

'Four.' Red smoke began to seep from Underwood's skin. David stared in disbelief. Was it smoke, or something else? It certainly appeared to be the same as whatever Underwood had turned his nails into earlier, but now it was surging from his whole body.

'Three.'

The smoke poured, thicker, hotter, not rising as smoke should, but funnelling around the core of Underwood's form like a small tornado. 'What?' David cried. 'What are you doing?'

'*Count!*' Underwood's voice was almost unrecognisable: distorted, inhuman.

'Two!' David watched as Underwood's arms rose and the crimson smoke began to stream straight upwards into the night. David cried out as he realised what was happening: right before his eyes, Underwood was disintegrating, coming apart at a molecular level and pouring himself into the sky. David looked up, but there was nothing above but a cloudless canopy of moon and stars. And when he looked down again, all that had been of Underwood, was gone. He blinked, looking at the gently-smoking spot on the driveway.

Numbly, he whispered the last of his count down, 'One.'

Suddenly, from overhead, there came a whooshing sound. David's head snapped up, searching the sky, but there was no sign of the thing that had made the noise. He staggered back, looking this way and that as the sound came again and again, but never from the same place twice. Then, from directly above him, a rush of warm night air buffeted him. David spun and cried out. He felt the weight of the bag in his hand and remembered that he had to throw it up at the end of the countdown.

'Wh-where are you?' he shouted up at the stars. Suddenly, from out of the darkness, a black shape flashed overhead in the moonlight, and again David felt the powerful downdraft from its wings. 'Jesus Christ! You're a bat! It's true, you're a *fucking bat!*' He drew his arm back and flung the sports bag upwards, watching it as it sailed up perhaps twenty feet into the night. Then, just as it was about to fall back to Earth, the thing that was now Underwood swooped out of the darkness and snatched it. David gasped as, for a split second, he saw the creature against the moon; it was indeed a bat, but it was huge. David watched as it now moved rapidly away, a patch of living darkness gliding between the earth and the glittering stars above, soaring over the miles and miles of olive groves towards the distant splash of light in the hills that David knew was the town of Almacena.

'David? Lord Underwood?' Lydia called from somewhere behind him.

He turned around to see her coming out from the courtyard. 'O-over here.'

She saw him and walked over. 'What's going on? Where's Lord Underwood? Did he speak to you?'

'Yeah.'

Lydia looked around. 'Well, where is he?'

David looked away in the direction of Almacena. 'He's gone.'

'Gone? Where?'

David turned back to her. 'My God, Lydia. He really is a monster.'

'Yes, so you keep saying. But where has he gone?' Her face was all impatient irritation. David pointed a finger at it, amused. He laughed out loud, then fell away into a dead faint.

18

IT WAS SHORTLY AFTER OPENING TIME on Friday morning at
La Reina de Corazones. Keith sat reading *The Sun* in the cool gloom of the
pub. At a fluttering sound, he looked up towards the bright glow of
sunshine that flooded the front terrace where Damo and Luis were
putting out plastic tables and chairs. A sparrow hopped in through the
front doors and flew onto a nearby table. It looked around for a few
moments, then, having assessed that it was too early for any pickings, it
turned and flew outside again. Keith smiled and returned to his perusal of
the sports pages.

'Keith! How's it going?'

Keith looked up again to see a lanky silhouette ambling through the
doorway. Gangly limbs dangled from a loose t-shirt and knee shorts as the
silhouette headed to the bar.

'Alright, Giles,' said Keith, without enthusiasm. 'How are you today?'

'Yeah, I'm cool,' said Giles, taking off his baseball cap and sweeping
back a lock of long hair from his face.

Keith returned his attention to his newspaper, hoping that perhaps
Giles might be happy to simply sit at the bar and wait until Damo
returned before asking for his first pint of the day. Giles was a musician
and had made a lot of money in the 90's after one of his band's songs was
picked up by an advertising agency. The song went on to reach the
number one spot in many countries. The band had split up soon after but,
since he was the song writer, Giles had made a lot of money and was now
living off a continuing stream of cash from royalties. Three years ago, he
had moved out to an old farm house on the edge of Almacena, apparently
to find peace and inspiration away from what he called the bullshit of the
London music scene. He'd built a studio with a plan to work on the songs
that would make up his eventual comeback album. However, he seemed
to spend most of his time looking for his inspiration in *La Reina*.

Giles pulled his cap back on and planted himself down on a bar stool.
'Pint of the usual, whenever you're ready, landlord.'

Keith looked to the front of the pub: Damo and Luis were still putting
out tables. He sighed, and got up.

'How's Michelle?' asked Giles as Keith came around behind the bar.
'All right, is she?'

'Yeah, she's fine. Same as yesterday.'

'Cool. What about young Mel?'

'Yeah, yeah, she's fine.' Keith set a pint of Cruzcampo down in front of Giles.

'What's she listening to these days?'

'Eh?'

'Mel. What's her favourite band?'

Keith shrugged. 'I dunno, mate. You know what kids are like, it's always changing, innit.'

'Yeah,' Giles took a sip from his pint. 'Don't I know it? By the time I get a fucking song written, it's already starting to sound out-of-date.'

Keith nodded, not really listening. 'Yeah. I know she was into some crowd called Second.'

'Second what?'

'No, just Second.'

'Oh, right. I'll have to check 'em out.'

Damo and Luis walked back into the pub.

'How's it going, Giles?' said Damo. 'How's that new album of yours coming along? Still stuck on the opening track?'

'If you mean am I still having trouble coming up with something commercial enough to pay the bills then yeah, yeah I'm having a right old time. I mean, it's not like I've dried up or nothing, 'cause I mean every night I play some fuckin' *amazing* stuff – like you wouldn't believe it. But, in the morning, like, when I play it back, I think, there's no way the record company are gonna dig this, you know, it's just too out-there. That's my problem, I'm just too "out-there".'

Damo nodded. 'Yeah I know exactly what you mean. I write a lot of genius stuff myself when I'm shit-faced.'

'If you ask me,' said Keith. 'Ninety percent of what's in the charts these days sounds like it was written by people who were shit-faced. Your stuff'd probably sell like hot cakes, Giles.'

'Ah, not like the old days, eh Keith?' said Damo, pointing to a poster at the end of the bar with Adam Ant in his *Stand and Deliver* attire.

'Yeah, proper music, those days,' said Keith. 'You coming to the 80's disco tomorrow night, Giles?'

Giles shrugged. 'Yeah, but all that commercial stuff you lot play is like, so non-representative of the decade as a whole. You know, you should be playing some Smiths, or Echo and The Bunnymen, some Bauhaus or some Killing Joke. That's the sound of real 80s music.'

'Yeah it's a disco, Giles, not a fucking mass-suicide,' said Keith. 'And anyway, you're always first up on the floor when *Rio* comes on.'

'Yeah, well, *Rio*'s a classic, innit?'

'And then you stay on the floor all night.'

'Yeah, well, they're all classic songs really, in't they? But what I'm saying is, 80s discos and the compilations you get in the shops these days, they're not really representative of the era as a whole, are they? I mean, there was a *darker* side.'

'There was a shite-er side, you mean,' said Damo. 'People want a laugh, that's why you don't get the likes of Joy Division on your 80's compilations, and that's why we don't play them at the disco. They'd clear the dancefloor faster than a turd clears a swimming pool.'

Michelle came down from the upstairs apartment and entered the pub. She saw the group at the bar and was about to join them when she noticed some customers sitting on the terrace. She stopped and squinted, leaning sideways to get a better view.

'You alright, Chelle?' said Keith.

Without taking her eyes from the customers, Michelle moved quickly to the bar. 'Look out there, on the terrace.'

Everybody looked. 'What?' said Keith.

'Isn't that the newsreader from the local TV station?' asked Michelle.

'Where? Which one?' said Keith.

'*There*,' said Michelle, pointing at one of the men. 'The one with the slick-back hair do.' 'Oh, *sí*,' said Luis. 'Alfredo Salinas. He is the newsreader on Almacena TV.'

'Who?' said Keith.

'That guy!' said Michelle, jabbing her finger in Alfredo's direction. 'You know, the bloke you say looks like your Uncle Jim used to?'

Keith's eyes widened. 'Oh yeah, it *is* him, innit? Quick, Chelle, go out and serve him.'

'What do you mean, me? I'm not even supposed to be working this morning.' She slapped Damo lightly on the arm. 'You go. Go on.'

'No,' said Keith. 'You should go, you're a woman, ain'tcha – he'll respond better to you. And you're a representative of management, ain'tcha? It looks better, and of course *you* look better than Damo – no offence, like, mate.'

'None taken,' said Damo. 'I'm glad you feel that way. I'd hate to think things might be the other way round.'

'Me too,' said Michelle. 'Alright, I'll do just this one, then I'm clearing off back upstairs.'

As she picked a menu, Keith suddenly had an idea. ''Ere, hang on.' He turned and took down the jar of pickled eggs from behind the bar. 'We'll give him some eggs.'

'Do what?' said Michelle.

'Eggs,' said Keith, unscrewing the jar and wincing as the smell hit his nose. 'It's a friendly gesture, innit. Complimentary tapas.'

Damo watched in undisguised horror as Keith fished four eggs out of the vinegar with his bare fingers and placed them on a small plate. 'Eh, you don't think they'd prefer a dish of nuts, Keith? You know, the same as everybody else?'

'Ah, but he's not everybody else, is he?' said Keith handing Michelle the plate of eggs. 'He's a celebrity, isn't he?'

'And so for this you're gonna give him a plate of stinking eggs?'

'You don't understand, mate. The Spanish love eggs! They have them on everything, don't they – *huevos* this, *huevos* that. Isn't that right, Luis? You Spanish love eggs, don'tcha?'

Luis looked doubtful. 'Er, well not everyone likes the same thing, Keith.'

'Bollocks,' said Keith. He gave Michelle a wink. 'Trust me. I've seen pickled eggs in action before. Tell him they're traditional British tapas, Chelle.'

Michelle took the eggs and the menus and went outside.

'British tapas?' said Damo. 'Jeez. I suppose it could be worse. It could be jellied eels.'

Keith considered the idea of a jar of jellied eels behind the bar for a moment before shaking his head, deciding against them on aesthetic grounds. 'No, you don't get it, do you, mate? Them eggs, they're a U.S.P.'

'And what's that?' asked Damo, 'A Useless, Smelly Product?'

'No. A Unique Selling Point. You may scoff, sunshine,' said Keith pointing at the newsreader and his friends, who were now all engaged in lively conversation with Michelle. 'But just look at that: that's the power of pickled eggs in action, that is.'

'No, I'd say that's the power of your missus, Keith. The real power of pickled eggs'll be unleashed in that fella's trousers in about half an hour's time.'

Giles drained his pint and set down the empty glass. 'Another pint, please Keith. And I'll have one of them eggs as well.'

'See?' said Keith to Damo. 'Giles likes them.'

'Like that's a recommendation. Giles has probably got the fuckin' munchies, don't ya?' Damo patted Giles on the back.

Giles smiled as Keith handed him his second pint, 'Yeah. This is my bloody breakfast, innit.'

Hodge entered, smiling as all eyes shifted from Michelle and the newsreader's party to him. 'Alright, lads? What's going on?'

Damo nodded to the front terrace. 'Keith just sent Michelle out to poison a local celebrity.'

'Oh aye. Pickled eggs is it?'

'Yeah,' said Keith, handing Giles an egg. 'You want a napkin with that?'

'No thanks, man.'

Everyone watched as Giles bit into the egg.

'How is it?' asked Damo.

Giles shrugged. 'Hmm, I've had better.'

Hodge cocked his head to the table where Keith's newspaper lay. 'Can I have a quick word, Keith? It's about … security.'

Keith's eyebrows knitted, but he nodded. 'Sure.' He came over and joined Hodge at the table.

'So,' said Hodge. 'Did you have a word with Michelle yet?'

Keith's smile quivered uncertainly. 'About what?'

'About keeping mum, you know, about the Russian thing.'

'Bloody hell, Hodge,' said Keith, with a covert glance at Giles. 'Keep your voice down.'

'He can't hear me – look, he's talking to Luis.'

'Yeah, but he could still be listening.'

Damo pulled out a chair and joined them. 'Ah sure, he's not listening, lads. He's talking about himself.'

'Yeah. So, anyway,' said Hodge in a lower voice. 'Have you had a word with her?'

'Yeah ... sort of.'

'*Sort of?*' said Damo.

'Yeah. Yeah, I had a word with her and she knows the score.'

'Sort of.'

'No. She knows, there isn't any sort of. She knows she needs to keep her mouth shut, all right?'

'You're sure?' said Hodge.

'Yes, I'm fucking sure.'

'So why did you say *sort of*?' said Damo. 'I'm sorry to go on about it, but that phrase always sounds like, "I'm not fuckin' sure", to me. I mean, if you were buying a used car from a bloke and he turned round and said the brakes were *sort of* safe, would you buy it?'

'I'd buy it for you, you cheeky – '

'Alright, lads,' said Hodge. 'If Keith says Chelle knows the score, then she knows the score, alright?' He looked pointedly at Damo.

Damo nodded. 'Yeah, alright.'

'Oh no, no, I mean, if you're not satisfied, Damo, I could go out there now and have a word with her while out there chatting to the town newsreader. How does that sound?'

'It sounds a bit fucking daft, mate.'

'Oh, for God's sake,' said Hodge, intervening. 'Would the pair of you stop being so flipping stupid.'

At the sound of laughter from the terrace, everyone turned. Michelle gave Alfredo and his friends a wave as she came back into the pub. She came up to Keith's table with a huge smile. 'Well, what a nice man. Guess what?'

'What?' said Keith.

'Alfredo is only going to be sending along a camera crew to do a piece on us. You know, *Los Ingleses en Almacena*? What do you think about that then?'

Keith's smile fell. 'What, a camera crew? Here? On us?'

Michelle nodded. 'Yeah, how about that?'

Damo and Hodge exchanged a look.

'That'd be the power of the eggs,' said Giles. 'I take it he liked them?'

'Well he said he did,' said Michelle. 'He ate one. So did his mates.'

'Yeah, I bet it was like that Russian roulette scene in *The Deer Hunter*, only with pickled eggs instead of the old gun, and you shouting out, "*Huevos! Huevos!*" Giles cackled with laughter.

Michelle's nose wrinkled as if someone had placed a particularly pungent cheese beneath it. 'What *are* you going on about, Giles?'

'You know,' said Giles. '*The Deer Hunter*? It's a classic.'

'The only classic round here is you, mate – a classic wally. Unlike Alfredo, who was charming, as were all of his friends.'

Damo and Hodge looked expectantly at Keith. Keith saw this and tightened his lips. He gave a little nod of understanding then stood up and put an arm around Michelle's shoulders. 'Well done, Chelle.' He kissed her on the cheek.

'What's that for?' asked Michelle.

'For, er, for being the best wife in the world.'

Michelle pushed him playfully. 'What are you after, Keith?'

'Nothing, love. I just wanted to take you upstairs and make you a nice cup of tea to thank you for ... bringing us to the attention of the media, like.'

Michelle indicated the people strolling onto the front terrace. 'But it's just getting busy, Keith. You can't go off upstairs making me cups of tea.'

'Don't worry about that, girl, the lads've got it covered, ain'tcha lads?'

'Yeah, no worries here, Chelle,' said Hodge. 'You two go and have a nice cuppa.'

'Yeah, have a nice cuppa, and a nice chat,' said Damo.

Keith gave him a stern look.

'And take your time, why don't you,' Damo grinned. 'Don't worry, we've got it covered – at our end.'

Michelle chattered on about how nice Alfredo was all the way up to the apartment and into the kitchen. 'Have you ever noticed,' she said as Keith went about preparing the tea. 'What lovely brown eyes he has?'

Keith said nothing. He set two mugs beside the kettle and stared into their white emptiness.

'Keith?'

'Mmm?' Keith turned to face her. 'Sorry love, I was ... thinking.'

'I said have you ever noticed what lovely brown eyes Alfredo has?'

'Who?'

'The newsreader bloke I was just talking to!'

'Oh, yeah. Yeah, I'm sure they're very nice.'

'Keith, have you been listening to a word I've been saying?'

'Yeah, yeah of course I have. He's got lovely eyes and he's going to be doing a TV piece on us.'

'Well, isn't that great? Imagine the trade we'll get as a result; not just ex-pats, but Spanish people as well. They'll want to come and try something different, won't they? They'll all be clamouring for a bottle of Bishop's Finger and a pickled egg. It's your dream come true, isn't it?'

'Chelle – ,' Keith started.

'We might even have to go down to Gibraltar to stock up on stuff from Morrisons.'

'Chelle, please,' Keith said more insistently. She stopped and looked at him. 'We can't be on the telly. You're gonna have to tell your mate Alfredo, thanks, but no thanks.'

Michelle was stunned. 'What?'

'We can't be on the telly, can we? Jesus, love, have you forgotten already?'

'Forgotten what?'

'What we was talking about yesterday morning? About Sergei?'

'Sergei? Oh Keith, come on, he isn't going to be watching Almacena TV, is he? It's only available locally. He's bloody miles away!'

'But he could have eyes and ears around here, couldn't he? Especially if he's looking for us.'

'But he's not looking for us, Keith. I saw that thing you were talking about – about that Mark Coleman – in yesterday's newspaper. Gerald was saying – '

Keith suddenly held up his hand. 'Whoa! Hang on! You were talking to the Bensons about this?'

'Eh?'

'Chelle, I told you, for fuck's sake, don't tell no-one about that business with the Russians, didn't I? And what do you go and do? First chance you get, you're piping it into Radio fucking Benson!' He slammed his hand on the table. 'Jesus Christ, Michelle!'

'Now hold on a minute! I didn't say anything to the Bensons about Russians or anything else, it was in the bloody newspaper, you idiot! Gerald's the one who was doing the talking about it, not me!'

'It doesn't matter, you shouldn't have said nothing!'

'I didn't say nothing, you paranoid arsehole! What's wrong with you, Keith? You're acting like a man on the run, like a bloody fugitive!'

'I am a fugitive, Michelle, don't you see that? He's out to get me, just like he got Coleman.'

'*What?* Michelle was dismayed. 'Why? That's mad, Keith!'

'It's not mad, Chelle: it's a warning. Coleman's head is a warning!'

'A warning of what?'

Keith sat down. 'A warning to us, or to anyone who … might have crossed him in some way.'

'Crossed who?'

'Sergei!'

Michelle's sense of dismay deepened. 'Keith, we sold him a pub, that's all. That's not *crossing* someone, that's just business.'

'But he might not see it that way, might he? It's like I said, yesterday: his people murdered Pete Sweeny, didn't they, and we were witnesses.'

'And like I said yesterday,' she reached across the table and took his hand. 'If he was going to kill you for that, he'd have done it long ago. He's not looking for you, love.'

'Isn't he?' Keith held her hand tightly.

'Of course not. I mean, you haven't actually done anything to hurt him, have you? If you'd have let me finish earlier, I was going to say the newspaper said that that Coleman might have been involved in the murder of Sergei's nephew.' She closed her other hand over Keith's. 'So that makes sense, doesn't it? Coleman's killing the bloke's nephew is one thing, but your selling him a pub is – ' she laughed. Then Keith turned suddenly away from her, taking back his hand and wiping at his eyes. 'Keith?'

'No,' he said, his voice strained. 'It's alright, girl.'

She got up and came to his side. 'Keith, what's wrong, love?'

He twisted away from her. 'It's nothing, Chelle. Please.'

She crouched down and put her arms around him. 'Oh, Keith, stop it. We're going to be fine. It's not like *you* murdered Sergei's nephew or anything, is it?' She felt his shoulders suddenly tense. She frowned. 'Keith?' Keith said nothing. A thought crossed her mind, one that made sense of his behaviour and yet was so dreadful it was almost unthinkable. She made a joke about it. 'You couldn't do a thing like that could you? Eh? Not a big teddy bear like you?'

Keith, sniffed loudly and wiped at his eyes.

Michelle's embrace relaxed and doubt crept into her voice. 'Keith? Keith, tell me you didn't have nothing to do with this ... this nephew business.'

Keith sniffed. 'I, I was only trying to protect us, Chelle.'

His words had a strange effect on her. She would later recall it was how she imagined someone might feel if they had been shot by a silenced pistol. Her strength left her quite suddenly, replaced by a sense of numbness. Her crouching knees gave way her legs folded beneath her.

Keith turned to her, his face wet with tears. 'We were supposed to get *him*, you see? Get Sergei.'

'Oh my God,' her voice was barely a whisper.

Keith slid from his chair to drop down in front of her and he placed his hands on her shoulders. 'We didn't know the nephew was gonna be there, Chelle. He shouldn't have been. The arrangement was for Sergei to come and then – and then – '

She pushed his hands away. 'And then *what*? You were going to murder him?'

'It wasn't murder, Chelle! It was self-defence. He killed Pete didn't he? He might have come after us!'

'Keith, that is fucking insane! You can't have really believed that. We were done with him! He wouldn't have come after us, you fucking madman!'

'He might have done!' Keith reached for her again, but she struck his hands away and crawled to her feet.

'Oh my God, oh my God,' she whispered over and over again as she moved around the kitchen, clutching at the work surfaces for support. Then she spun to face him. 'Do you have any idea what you've done, Keith?'

He nodded, his face crumpling with emotion. 'I'm so sorry, Chelle. I did it for us.'

'For us?' She grabbed the first solid thing that came to hand – one of the mugs he'd readied earlier – and threw it at him. 'You fucking lunatic! You're as bad as he is! You're a murderer, Keith! You're a fucking murderer!'

Keith managed to get his arms in front of his face in time to deflect the mug. 'I know, I know! I'm sorry, Chelle, please! We did it to protect ourselves.'

'*We*? Who's "we"?'

Keith said nothing.

She snatched up the other mug and flung it at him, this time he ducked and it shattered against the far wall. 'Who's "we", you fucking moron?'

'Damo and Hodge.'

'Oh my God!' Michelle reeled as if from a blow. 'You murdered a man and you took those two with you as accomplices?'

'Who else was I gonna take? *You?*'

'Don't you – !' she ran at him, raining blows on the arms that shielded his head. 'Do you know what you've done, Keith? Do you know what you've done?'

'Please, Chelle! I'm sorry!'

'You've killed us, that's what you've done. You've killed yourself, you've killed me, and you've killed our daughter, just as sure as if you'd pulled the fucking trigger yourself.'

'I'm sorry. Please, please, forgive me.'

Michelle stopped hitting him and dropped onto a chair. Her own tears began rolling slowly from her eyes. 'How can I forgive you, Keith? How can I ever forgive you? I'm dead. And the dead can't forgive.'

19

DAVID AWOKE to the sound of birdsong. He opened his eyes and squinted; the room was filled with brilliant sunshine. His window was open and a warm breeze stirred the curtains which he hadn't closed the night before. He lifted a hand to shield his eyes and saw the mud that caked his nails and the creases on the backs of his finger joints. He grimaced at the acrid smell of dried sweat that rose from under his arm. Then he noticed he was still wearing the clothes he had been wearing the night before. They were filthy with dirt, and something else – dark, rust-coloured stains. Blood – but not his.

Everything came back to him in a sudden flood of memory: the resurrection; Underwood's murder of Ana and Beltran; the way Underwood had turned into a bat and flown away into the night; and how finally he, Lydia, and Miguel had laboured into the small hours of the morning trying to bury the vampire's victims.

David rolled over, turning his face away from the sunlight. As he did so, his fragile memories cracked and broke apart and pain exploded in his head. The broken images swirled like shards of glass in the gelatinous sludge that his brain seemed to have been reduced to overnight, scraping against the inside of his skull before slowly settling into scenes of partial recall. He remembered the whiskey, and he remembered why he'd started drinking it, but it was no excuse. A feeling of self-loathing enveloped him; he pulled a pillow onto his face and groaned into it. After Underwood had flown away, he remembered he'd passed out. Lydia had kicked him back to wakefulness and together they'd gone with Miguel to drag the corpses up from out of the cellar. By the time they'd got them onto a plastic sheet in the back of Lydia's Land Rover, his hangover had started to kick in. To stave it off, he'd gone back into the courtyard and fetched a water-filled ice bucket containing an unopened bottle of champagne. He also grabbed three mugs from the kitchen.

Lydia had driven them out for about half a mile into the olive groves of Underwood's estate, to a ruined farmer's hut that John had prepared for just such an occasion as this. He'd equipped it with shovels, pick-axes, a coil of rope and a couple of kerosene lamps. They'd then set to work digging a large hole. The soil was riddled with tough, spidery olive roots that made progress slow and difficult. He'd drunk the champagne on his own; Lydia and Miguel said they weren't in the mood for bubbly, but thirst had made them grateful for the bucket of water. They'd got back just as daylight was beginning to blot the horizon like a litmus stain. He'd come straight up to bed, leaving Lydia and Miguel in the kitchen to no doubt plot his downfall. He laughed. Downfall indeed – as if he could he fall down any further than he already had.

His tongue was sticky and the roof of his mouth felt corrugated with dehydration. What was the time? He pulled the pillow from his face and looked at the bedside clock. The LED told him it was five twenty-two.

'Shit.' He sat up and the shards of glass in his head swirled again and embedded themselves in the soft flesh behind his eyes. He groaned and clambered from white sheets filthy with grave dirt, noticing as he did that he'd remembered to kick his shoes off the night before. He was impressed. He staggered off in the direction of the en-suite bathroom, struggling out of his clothes on the way and almost falling over as he tried to kick his jeans from his ankles. He got into the bathroom and took a packet of paracetamol from the cabinet. He popped two pills from the pack and dry-swallowed them before turning on the shower and climbing in underneath it. He switched the water temperature to cold, turned his face up to the shower-head and opened his mouth. He drank, the water filling his mouth faster than he could swallow it. He drank for perhaps a full minute before he reached for the soap and began to lather away the stains of last night's horror. Something was gnawing at his memory. Something he needed to remember, not to do with Underwood, nor with Lydia, but somehow connected with both of them and himself. Something, or someone ...

The prisoner.

Shit. Gavin, the prisoner – the guy Lydia had kidnapped with the intention of sacrificing at Underwood's resurrection. He had to get him out, and fast. He shut off the water and snatched up a towel. He ran into the bedroom and looked out of the window. The sun was still fairly high in the sky, but it was in its descent.

'Shit!' he hissed. He dried himself as quickly as he could then hurriedly dressed in a pair of shorts, a t-shirt and baseball boots. As he struggled with the laces, he recalled the details of the deal he had made with Lydia concerning Gavin the night before as they were digging the grave. Lydia had been bitching about the spade work and how her hands were getting blistered. He'd told her she'd have to get used to it. She looked at her hands and showed them to him: in the lamplight they looked raw.

'Look at my hands,' she said. 'I'm in agony! I can't do this for the rest of my life. I feel like a fucking slave.'

'No, you're a *servant*,' he replied, 'not a slave. Slaves don't get paid, do they?'

'Are we getting paid?'

He stopped and leaned on his shovel. 'You know, in all the excitement earlier on, I completely forgot to ask about terms and conditions. I *presume* we get some kind of wages. We should ask His Lordship tomorrow. And of course, we'll need to ask about holiday pay, sick pay ... maybe there's even a union we could join.'

'Oh shut up, David. Stop taking the bloody piss! This is serious. My hands feel like they've been blowtorched.'

'Don't worry, Lydia,' said David, going back to his digging. 'They'll toughen up in no time.'

'I don't want them to toughen up! What do you think I am, a docker? A navvy?'

'Oh, no, but from now on, you *are* a gravedigger. It's yet another glamorous ingredient of our wonderful new life with Underwood.' He grinned, but she wasn't amused. 'That is, of course, unless we can get His Lordship to stop killing people and start using blood donors instead. That way, there'll be no more corpses, and so no more grave-digging.'

Without looking up at him, she nodded. 'Yes, yes. I suppose you're right.'

He stopped digging. 'Thank you.' He took a swig of the champagne and wiped his mouth on the back of his hand. 'So, does this mean you're gonna back me up on the transfusion idea with His Lordship tomorrow night?'

She looked at her hands, then at the bodies of Ana and Beltran where they lay beside the hole, ready to be rolled in. She nodded. 'Yes. All right.'

'And what about the kid in the cellar? Will you help me get him away?'

She snorted. 'Now hang on, David. His Lordship knows all about our guest. He'll be expecting him for breakfast.'

'Yeah, but what if we made it a *fait accompli*? Got Gavin out of there; set up a couple of donors; and just offered him a transfusion breakfast instead?'

'He'd go bloody mental on us again, that's what. Have you already forgotten how we came to be standing in this hole?'

''Course I haven't, but don't worry, I'll take the blame for it. All you need to do is get the donors. All right?'

Lydia looked unconvinced. 'But what if he kills the donors again? We can't afford to lose any more Sect members.'

'No, he won't kill any more Sect members,' he nodded to Ana and Beltran. 'He killed these two because he was starved, he was ravenous. But he won't be like that again. We'll be all right.'

'We'll be all right? I don't know how you can stand there, pretending to be such a bloody expert – you got it really rather wrong last time.'

'Yes, all right, I was wrong, I admit that. But you know yourself, he's rational now, he regrets what he did, and he'll be reasonable when it comes to letting the kid go. I'm sure of it. Oh, he might be a bit pissed off with me, but I can deal with that.'

She made a lazy strike at the dirt with her spade. The impact sent a fresh shock of pain to her hands and she shrieked and flung the spade aside. 'Oh, fuck this! I've had enough.' She clambered out of the grave. 'Yes! I'll back you up, all right? Just get me away from this fucking hole.' She went to the car, got in and slammed the door. Without looking back at David and Miguel, she slid down in her seat and out of their view.

'You hear that?' asked Miguel. 'I think she's crying.'

The sound of Lydia's weeping was low, like she was trying to muffle it. David pushed his spade into the earth and resumed digging. 'She'll live, Miguel. Just leave her alone for a bit. She'll be all right.'

Now, David stood up and went to his bedroom door. He went out and hurried down the hall to Lydia's room. He knocked, but there was no reply. 'Lydia?' he called, opening the door a crack. 'Lydia? Are you up yet?' He looked inside. The bed had been slept in, but was empty. Her bathroom door was open. 'Lydia?' There was no reply.

He turned back to the hall and shouted down its length, 'Lydia?' The house was silent. 'Fuck it.' He ran to the staircase and hurried downstairs. Careful to ignore Underwood's ever-amused portrait on the wall, he ran on through to the kitchen. 'Lydia?' Two coffee mugs stood on the kitchen table. He picked one up: it was cold, but the ring of liquid in the bottom was still wet. It was a hot day; in this temperature the liquid would have dried in only a few hours. So she must have left fairly recently. He put the mug down and noticed the note propped against the salt and pepper mills. He picked it up and read:

Flinch.

I need a haircut. Kindly pop into town and arrange for a barber to come out to the house this evening. Oh, and get him to bring along a jar of Brilliantine or Brylcreem, or whatever chaps are using on their hair these days.

Pip pip

U.

The signature letter "U" was signed with a flourish. Beneath it, in the same ink but by a different hand, was written:

David,

I'll sort this out. Get the blood transfusion equipment ready. Back before sundown.

L.

David considered Underwood's note for a moment. Had it been on the table last night when he came in? He hadn't seen it. But then there could have been a sheep in a blonde wig and a bikini on the table last night and he wouldn't have seen that either. He put the note down and went to the fridge. He was starving. Inside were various party leftovers that Miguel had cleared away the night before. He took out a plate of thick Spanish omelette that had been cut into segments. He took a piece and pushed it into his mouth. As he chewed, he took out a plate of cold sliced meats and a carton of UHT milk. He drank from the milk carton and helped himself to another piece of omelette. Then he picked up both plates and the milk carton and set off in the direction of the storage cellar where Gavin was being held prisoner. When he got to the cellar door, he set the food down on the floor and reached up along the door frame for the key.

It wasn't there.

He tried the door.

It was unlocked.

David froze, momentarily paralyzed by the wrongness of the situation. What was going on here? Warily, he pushed the door open. 'Gavin?'

Silence and cool air, tainted with the acrid smell of the toilet bucket, drifted back to him. David entered and went down. Everything was as it had been when he was last here: the bed, the table and chair, the bucket, but no prisoner, no Gavin.

'Gavin?' he shouted. 'Are you here? It's me. I'm, I'm going to take you home.' He had hoped Gavin might be hiding somewhere, that he might have come out of the shadows, frightened but relieved to see it wasn't Lydia or Ana. But he didn't come. David dropped to the floor to look under the bed. His hand landed in something wet. He checked his palm. It was blood.

'Oh no,' he whispered. 'Oh, God, no.' He knelt and looked more closely at the filthy floor. Here and there beside the bed were small, dark splashes of blood.

'Underwood!' David got to his feet. 'You bastard! You came here last night, didn't you? What? Tired from all the flapping around, were you? Fancied a snack before turning in? And so you came down here and killed him – but – ?' He looked around. 'But where's the body? What did you do with the body?'

It didn't fit Underwood's *modus operandi*, or at least what David knew of his *modus operandi* so far. Underwood discarded the dead, tossed them aside to be cleaned up by his servants. He didn't dirty his hands with such domestic drudgery as tidying up. So then, where was the body? Unless Underwood hadn't been here at all, which meant ... David's expression darkened. 'Lydia.'

He ran up the stairs and out into the corridor. He almost stumbled over the food he'd left by the door before righting himself and running on down to the kitchen and out the back door into the courtyard. Heat and light struck him, and he ran, half-blinded by the glare, out onto the front drive. Amid the droning of the crickets, Ana's red Fiat sat alone beneath the trees. Lydia's Land Rover and Beltran's Mercedes were both gone. David's mind raced.

'Damn it, Lydia!' he shouted. 'What the fuck is going on?' He turned back to the house. Underwood. All right – what if he *does* have Gavin? What if he started snacking on him last night, then took him down to his crypt, half-dead, to be finished off for breakfast. Would he do that? David began clenching and unclenching his fists. He might.

Slowly, he started towards the house. He was a few steps from the front door when, above the sound of his footsteps crunching on the gravel, he became aware of another sound: the sound of distant engines approaching. He turned to see Lydia's Land Rover coming up the drive in a cloud of dust. There was another car behind it, but he couldn't make out if it was Beltran's Mercedes or something else. He walked back and positioned himself in the centre of the drive. As the Land Rover drew closer, David recognised Cynthia Benson sitting in the passenger seat. She and Lydia were laughing at something. Probably me, he thought.

The car rolled to a halt and Lydia waved at him. She got out. 'What's that face for? You look like bigger boys stole your ice cream.'

'Where's Gavin?'

'What?'

'The guy in the cellar: your prisoner.'

Lydia frowned. 'What do you mean, where is he? He's in the cellar, isn't he?'

David shook his head. 'No.'

As Cynthia got out from the passenger side, the back doors opened and Gerald and Miguel got out as well.

Lydia pushed her sunglasses up onto her head. 'You mean he's escaped?'

'I very much doubt it.'

'Sorry, what's going on?' asked Cynthia.

'The prisoner's escaped or something,' Lydia replied.

'I say,' said Gerald. 'Clever chap! Any idea how?'

'He didn't escape,' said David. 'There's blood on the floor.'

'Oh dear,' said Lydia. 'Well, I wonder what's happened to him?'

'That's what I'm asking you.'

'*Me?* How should I know?'

'You took him out of there, didn't you?'

Lydia laughed. 'Why would I do that? He doesn't matter to *me*. He's a scrap for you and Underwood to fight over.'

'Lydia, please, don't fuck about. If you know where he is, you've got to tell me.'

Another car door opened and David turned to see a small, portly bald man getting out of a VW hatchback. The man then reached back into the car and took out an old leather briefcase.

Lydia turned and extended a hand to the new arrival. 'David, this is señor Alberto Ramales, the town barber.'

'*Hola*,' said Alberto with a smile.

'*Hola*,' said David. '*Habla Ingles, señor?*'

'No, no.' Albert smiled and patted his briefcase. 'Cut, cut.'

Gerald laughed. 'I taught him that, eh, Alberto?' He indicated his own hair to David. 'He does me, you see? And all I ever need to say is "*recorte, por favor*, Alberto," and he's off like a whirling dervish.'

Alberto joined in Gerald's laughter.

David turned his attention back to Lydia. 'All right. So where's Gavin?'

'I told you, I don't know. As soon as I got up, I went in to town to get rid of the Mercedes and pick up the Bensons.'

'What do you mean, get rid of the Mercedes?'

'Well, we have to get rid of it, don't we? After all, the owner's gone missing. What would happen if a police helicopter should chance to spot it on our drive? A search warrant? I need hardly tell you that that's the last thing we need around here.'

'So what did you do with it?'

'Well, fortunately I have a mechanic friend in town who doesn't mind turning his hand to some dodgy work now and again. I paid him to take it off my hands – change the plates, give it a re-spray, whatever these people do – and he'll sell it on, and that'll be the end of that.'

'And then she came to get us,' said Cynthia. 'I understand you need a couple of blood donors.'

Lydia smiled. 'Like we said last night, David, it's the best thing for everyone.'

'So, what, have you seen Gavin at all? Did you take him any breakfast this morning?'

'No, sorry. I've got so used to Ana taking care of him he just, sort of, slipped my mind.'

'So, that must mean Underwood's had him, then,' said David. 'Last night, when he came home from his trip into town.'

Lydia shrugged. 'Well, I suppose he might have done. He knew about him, after all.'

'Yeah, thanks to you.'

'Oh, David, it was inevitable he'd find out. He'd probably have smelt him or something.'

'That doesn't mean handing him Gavin on a plate was the right thing to do.'

'Oh, bollocks to the right thing! It felt right enough to me at the time. And anyway, the whole matter is neither here nor there since the poor boy's almost certainly dead. Right now, we need to focus on the living and how to serve them this evening.'

'Ah yes, David,' said Gerald, his chuckle barely masking the anxiety that was suddenly in his voice. 'Lydia says there's no chance of a repeat of last night's little ... er ... *mess* happening again, but are you quite sure about that? I mean, I'm always game to help out a chum, of course, but not to the extent that I – well, you know, die, as it were.'

'You'll be fine, Gerald,' said David. 'Underwood's been fully restored last night, and it's looking like he had a little supper before bedtime as well. He's not going to need more than a few pints.'

'Yes,' said Cynthia. 'Of course, while I have no doubt that you know what you're talking about, David, what if it should turn out that His Lordship *does* need more than a few pints? I mean, we're still in rather … uncharted waters here, aren't we?'

David's headache throbbed. He closed his eyes and massaged his temples. 'If he needs more, he won't hurt you. You're Sect. If he's unsatisfied, I guess he'll just hunt some poor bastard down and kill them.'

'I say,' said Gerald. 'Maybe we should keep old Alberto around as a standby meal, you know, just in case His Lordship does go a bit potty.'

'Oh, that's an excellent idea,' said Lydia. 'I mean, obviously we don't want to have another burial on our hands, but I'd rather dig a dozen graves than have another tongue-lashing from the Master.' She smiled at Alberto. *'Quieres algo para comer*, Alberto? Mmm? A little something to eat? We need to keep your strength up, don't we?'

'Oh Jesus,' said David in a low voice. 'And so begins another night on the murder-go-round of Underwood and Flinch.'

Gerald overheard him and laughed. 'Yes, rather. Round and round and round it goes, where it stops, nobody knows.'

Oh, I know, thought David. He turned and walked away towards the house, he was suddenly feeling nauseated and felt sure it had little, if anything, to do with his hangover.

'Where are you going?' Lydia called after him. 'I hope you aren't planning on getting drunk again.'

'I'm going to get the transfusion gear set up,' he called back. 'I may be some time.'

'Okay. We'll be in the kitchen if you need us.'

David raised a hand without turning and entered the house through the front door. Once inside he slumped against the wall. The stone felt cool on his back and helped him to focus.

Okay, he thought. Either Gavin is dead, or lying in the cellar half-dead and waiting for Underwood to rise and finish him off. Either way, Underwood seems to have decided that murder is still the preferred way of satisfying his hunger. And that means this barber, Alberto, is most likely the next course on the menu.

So, what can I do? How can I stop it? *Can I* stop it? I mean, I went down there before when the bastard was a barely a sack of dusty old bones and he filled my head with hallucinations that drove me half fucking mad. What did John say about it in his notes on communion? It's some kind of evolved defence system that kicks in when he's unconscious and intruders come near. The negative emotions they feel overwhelm them and they freak out.

He remembered the light bulb shattering and the pitch dark that had followed; the sound of the coffin opening; and the certainty that the half-rotten vampire had awoken and was rising. He felt again the terror that had crippled him, groping on his hands and knees, blinded – actually *blinded* – by fear or the power of Underwood's unconscious illusions. 'No,' he said, 'dear God no, I can't go through that again. If he could do that before, what's he capable of now that he's fully restored?'

Another voice, calmer and more rational, spoke up in his mind: *But you're forgetting the resurrection – nothing happened there.*

Yeah, but I wasn't planning on chopping his head off then, was I? I was there to bring him back to life, not send him screaming back to Hell.

So that's what you have to do again. Go down as if you mean him no harm; have no fear, no hate, nothing but love in your heart.

He laughed at the thought. Love? Oh yeah, like I'm going out on a first date – go down with big bunch of flowers with a silver crucifix concealed in the middle. Or a box of chocolates: holy water liqueurs.

You can do it. You can kill him.

I can't! He's too strong. I could never chop his head off now.

Yes, you're right. But fortunately, that's not the only way to kill a vampire.

So what am I supposed to do? Drag his coffin upstairs and out into the fucking sunlight?

His other voice was silent, as if waiting for the inevitable conclusion.

'Oh, no,' said David aloud. 'I can't do that. I ... I couldn't.'

Yes, you can. It's the best way; as old as time. Everybody knows it. Especially you.

Where? Where would I find the stuff?

The garage. There's a work shop in the back, remember?

He nodded slowly. 'Yeah. I remember. Tools, on the walls. Wrenches, spanners, hammers.'

Mallets.

'Yes. Mallets.'

And in the corner, standing upright in an old box, for all the little odd jobs around the house and grounds?

'Timber. Planks and stuff.' David's stomach turned over and he put his hand to his mouth to stop himself from retching. When the moment had passed, he wiped a dew of cold sweat from his brow. 'I can't. I just can't do that.'

You have to, David.

He steadied himself against the wall and took a deep breath. 'Yes. I know. I don't know how I'm going to do it, but somehow, before the sun goes down tonight, I've got to get down to that cellar and hammer a stake through his fucking heart.'

20

THE GARAGE DOORS HUNG OPEN. The padlock and chain still lay in the dust where he had flung them yesterday afternoon. David went inside and moved quickly to the rear of the garage and the door that led to the workshop beyond. The air in the workshop smelled like it hadn't been disturbed for a long time; a warm bouquet of sawdust, creosote, and engine oil. Dust motes rolled lazily in sunlight that seeped through windows opaque with dust and cobwebs. He flicked on the light. Against the back wall was a workbench, and in the corner next to it was a box with numerous pieces of timber sprouting from it. He went over and began to rummage through the contents: it consisted mostly of old planks and off-cuts.

Was there another stash of wood somewhere? He looked around, but couldn't see any more. Where were the fence posts kept? Did they keep them here, or did they get contractors in to do that stuff? He had no idea, and since he wasn't about to go asking Lydia, he pulled a length of wood from the box. It was a short plank of about four feet long. He hit it against the workbench; it seemed solid enough. If he had an axe or a hatchet, he could split it to a pointed end and then he'd have a stake.

On the wall to the left of the window was a rack with various tools mounted on it: hammers, drills, saws, mallets. He went over for a closer look at the mallets. There were three types arranged vertically – one with a rubber head, one with a wooden head and one with a copper head. He took down the wooden one. It was bulky and lacked weight; he'd need something heavier than this. He took down the copper head and felt its heft. Yes, he thought, this was just right – light enough to swing easily and yet heavy enough to smash a stake through breastbone. He set it aside and resumed his search for an axe. Weirdly, there didn't seem to be one, but there *was* a petrol-powered chainsaw. Maybe he could use that? Not to split the plank, but to split Underwood: he wouldn't even have to take the lid off the coffin, he could just tear through it and Underwood's neck in one go. He smiled. No, too risky, too much noise. Even if he didn't wake Underwood, he'd attract the attention of Lydia and her friends. He looked around. There had to be an axe somewhere, it was a farm for God's sake!

At the far end of the workshop, he saw the long wooden handles of more tools rising from behind some old bicycles. He went over and pulled the bikes aside. He realised with a momentary pang of nostalgia that these were the bikes that he and Lydia had owned when they were kids. They seemed so small to him now. His bike had been handed-down to him by way of Martin and then John, but Lydia's had been bought especially for her. He hesitated, remembering her for a moment as the little girl she had once been. She hadn't always been a bitch. Once he had even loved her.

Once?

He came back to the present and put Lydia's bike aside with the others. Then he began separating the tool-handles, tearing thick, crusty cobwebs apart as he pulled the tools out one by one: a shovel, a pick axe, a fork and – ah, here it was – an axe. As he pulled it free, a dusty cricket bat and three stumps fell into view from where they had been pinned behind it. It was the set that they had played with as kids. Or rather, the set Arthur had wanted them to play with, but none of the Flinch boys were ever much into cricket; they'd all been too much into football. Beneath the dust, the bat and stumps looked almost new. He lowered the axe and pulled out one of the stumps. It was about seventy centimetres long and ended in a spike at one end. He thumbed the spike, it wasn't exactly razor sharp, but with that mallet, it wouldn't have to be. He looked back at the planks: he could be here for ages trying to split them into a decent stake. Here, on the other hand, were three, ready-cut and ready to go.

He grinned. 'Howzat?'

A few minutes later he was hurrying around the side of the house with the stumps and mallet wrapped loosely in a small canvas tarpaulin he'd pulled from under the workbench. He was heading for the front door; from there he could swiftly move down the hallway to the library without needing to go anywhere near the kitchen. The last thing he needed was Lydia and her chums asking why he was clutching a mysterious, filthy bundle to his chest.

The front door was open. He went through – and ran straight into Gerald.

'Oh! I say,' Gerald chuckled. 'Beg pardon, David. I didn't see you coming.'

'Oh, no, my fault Gerald,' said David struggling to keep the disturbed contents of the tarpaulin together. The mallet had shifted and he could feel it threatening to spill itself and the stumps onto the floor.

'Here,' said Gerald, 'Let me help you.' He moved to support the bundle but David stepped back sharply.

'No!'

A stump slid out from the tarp and clattered to the floor.

'Hello,' said Gerald, stooping to pick it up. 'Getting ready for a game, are we?'

David tried to sound cheerful. 'Er, no not exactly. I'm, er – I'm taking them to a friend of mine ... in town ... tomorrow. I'm just going to wrap them up. They're a present.'

'Really? You've a friend in town who plays cricket? Anyone I know?'

'Actually, it's for the kids of a friend. They like cricket, but they can't get the necessary kit around here. You know how it is.'

'Oh yes, of course. Football crazy, the Spanish, aren't they? Not that there's anything wrong with that, of course, but it wouldn't be my game, you know. No, I'm much more of a cricket man. What do you make of Flintoff?'

'Eh?'

'Flintoff. You know, Freddie?'

David felt the mallet slip a little against his chest and he shifted the bundle to keep it together. A bead of sweat tricked from his brow and dropped onto the tarpaulin. 'I'm sorry, Gerald. I'm with the Spaniards, I'm afraid: football's more my thing. So, if you wouldn't mind – ?' He nodded to the stump in Gerald's hand.

'Oh, oh yes, of course. Where do you want it?'

'Er ... ?' David shifted the weight of the bundle and managed to reach out with his left hand. 'Just give it to me.'

'Are you sure?' said Gerald, looking for an opening in the tarpaulin into which he could slide the stump. 'I can just pop it – '

'No! Just give it to me,' David's smile strained, as if it were tied to the gently sagging mallet by a length of invisible thread. 'Please, Gerald.'

Gerald raised his eyebrows, a little nonplussed. 'Sorry, old boy. Here you are.' He put the stump into David's hand.

David took it and corrected his grip on the bundle. 'Thanks. Sorry to be abrupt, but I'm, er, desperate to use the loo.'

This put Gerald back on a cheery footing and he laughed. 'Oh gosh, I'm sorry. Here I am blathering on, while your poor old bladder is threatening to burst its banks.' He stepped aside, and David eased gratefully past him into the hall.

David forced a little laugh. 'Not to worry, Gerald.' Then he added, as if as an afterthought, 'Oh, by the way, I'd be grateful if you didn't mention the cricket gear to Lydia. She doesn't know about it, see, and I'm going to, er, surprise her later on.'

'Oh,' Gerald nodded, knowingly. 'Mum's the word, eh?'

'Exactly.'

Gerald gave him a thumbs-up salute. 'Right you are, old chap. I'm just off to the car to get some goodies we bought in town earlier. We're going to have a round of cocktails, but I don't imagine you ... er ... ?'

'No. Not for me, Gerald. I'm firmly back on the wagon.'

'Well, good for you. We have some ginger ale and soda and what not.'

'Oh, very nice.'

'Shall I pour you one?'

'No, no, I, I have to get the old, er, blood transfusion apparatus set up.' He indicated the bundle as if it suddenly contained not cricket gear but blood transfusion equipment. 'I'll join you later, in about twenty minutes or so.'

Gerald smiled and gave him a cheery wave. 'Right you are, then.' He turned and went outside.

David swore under his breath and hurried on down the corridor as quickly as he could without running.

As he turned the corner that led to the library he immediately felt that the air was strangely cooler. He stopped. There was no draught coming from anywhere, yet it was definitely cooler. Gooseflesh rippled the skin of his arms, but not as a result of the sudden chill air.

'No,' he said firmly, closing his eyes. 'I'm not afraid. I'm here as a friend. I'm going down to see my friend and Master. I'm going to commune.' He opened his eyes and walked on towards the library door. The air grew colder still. David stopped and tried to think happy thoughts: childhood summers, ice cream, playing football with Martin and John, songs Dad had used to sing to them when driving round in the Citroën. A snatch of one came to him and he sang aloud in a hushed, faltering voice, '*What shall we do with a drunken ...*' He was standing outside

the library door and could feel the cold emanating from the wood. '...
sailor. What shall we ...'

A hoarse voice drifted from the other side of the door in reply. '*Flog
him.*'

David dropped the bundle and jumped back from the door as if it
were suddenly on fire. 'Wha – what the fuck?'

But he recognised the voice.

'Y-you're dead!' he whispered.

There was a moment's pause, then the voice on the other side of the
door answered. 'Yes.'

David could hardly breathe; his heart was hammering against his chest
so hard it felt like it was going to burst. No, he thought. It's not real. It's
an illusion. The range of Underwood's unconscious, extra-sensory
defence *thing* has extended, because he's now restored to his full power. I,
I just have to push through it. Think happy thoughts! He took hold of the
door handle, ignoring the unnaturally cold metal, and closed his eyes. My
own fears are being used against me. But I, I have no fear. I come as a
friend. He pushed open the door. 'I come as a friend!'

'Of course you do.'

David opened his eyes.

His dead brother John sat on a chair between him and the secret panel
entrance to Underwood's crypt. He looked as he had when he had died:
cadaverous, his body wasted away by cancer. Only now, he didn't just
look like a corpse; he was one. He wore a surgical gown that came down
to just above his knees. His bare feet were planted on the floor, and in his
hand, resting across his knees, was Matthias Flinch's sword.

'You're a friend,' John smiled, his lips were thin and grey. 'I believed
that once, Davey, but now I suspect you may have been fibbing.'

'No. You're dead, John.'

'Yes, we've established that. I'm dead, and you're a liar.'

'No. I come as a friend.'

'*Really?* You dropped your bundle outside, Davey. Tell me, *friend*,
what's in it?'

'Cricket gear.'

'Oh, how nice. Going to play a spot of indoor cricket with His
Lordship, are we?'

David couldn't answer. He sagged against the door frame and closed
his eyes. 'You're not real, John. That's the only truth that matters.'

John chuckled, his throat dry and raspy. 'What is *real*? Surely that which can be perceived is real? And since we're having this little chat, you can, evidently, perceive me. Therefore, I am real.'

David opened his eyes and pointed a trembling finger at his brother. 'No, you're dead, you're a hallucination.'

'Dead, yes; hallucination, no,' John took the sword from his knees and rested the tip on the floor. 'I've been summoned, you see? Brought back from the dead to do my duty.'

'What? What are you talking about? What duty?'

'I am a guardian of Lord Underwood, David. Death doesn't end that. It continues beyond our fleeting mortal existence and on into the hereafter.' He grinned. 'There really is, it seems, no rest for the wicked.'

'I don't ... believe ... in you.'

'No,' said John, getting slowly to his feet. 'But I believed in you.' He raised the sword and pointed its tip at David's face. 'I gave you this to protect our Master with, David. I trusted you! I chose you over Lydia, even when she warned me – *begged me* – not to! I entrusted it all to you: everything our family ever has been, and ever will be.'

'No. You entrusted me with Underwood, a monster that has to be destroyed.'

John shook his head. 'Oh, you fool, David. Underwood *is* our family. If you destroy him, you destroy us all. You have no idea what you're doing. You haven't read any of the diaries. You know nothing of him, or your ancestors – if you did, you would realise that what you want to do here makes *you* the real monster.'

'How do you work that out?'

'Think about it a moment, from a purely scientific point of view: you are about to destroy a creature that goes beyond merely being endangered, he may actually be unique.'

David closed his eyes and put his hands over his ears. 'Shut up! Whatever you are, I don't know whereabouts in my head you're coming from, but I am *not* listening anymore.'

'You *will* listen!' John slashed the sword across the spines of a row of books to his right and sent them tumbling from the shelves. He took a step towards David. 'Look at me, you little bastard! Look at me!'

David opened his eyes.

John drew back the sword and held it poised, trembling with tension and ready to slash David across the throat. 'I won't let you pass, do you hear? So, you can either turn around and resume your duties, or just go. Leave us. Lydia will take on the role of guardian and we'll never trouble you again. Go back to your life, back to your job and your pretty little *fraulien*, Lisa.'

David lowered his hands from his ears. 'I never told you her name, John.'

John suddenly looked confused. 'Yes you did.'

'No, I didn't. Come to think of it, I don't think I even mentioned her at all.'

'Then ... it must have been the detective we had following you. Yes, it was him. He told me her name!'

'I don't think so. I think you know her name because you're an apparition drawn from my own subconscious. You're no more real than that light bulb that shattered down in the crypt was last time.'

'Then what's this!' John turned and slashed the sword at the bookshelves. More books fell torn and broken to the floor. 'Is this real enough for you?'

'Those books are fine, John. They can't have been damaged by the sword because the sword is over the fireplace in the lounge, and you, you're in an urn in a Malaga crematorium.'

'No! I'll cut you down, you traitorous bastard! Run away! Go on! Run while you still can!'

David turned and walked out of the library.

'That's right. Get out and ... ' John's sentence dried to a croak when he saw David pick up the tarpaulin bundle, then turn back and re-enter the library.

'The only place I'm going, John, is down into that crypt to do what I came here to do.' Then without another word, he walked past John and over to the far bookcase and the secret doorway to Underwood's crypt. When neither sword nor further abuse fell open his back, he turned. John had taken his seat again, sitting with his back to him and facing the library door. 'What? Not going to run me through, then?'

Without turning, John quietly replied: 'That won't be necessary. My job is done.'

'Oh? What job's that?'

John chuckled malevolently. 'Look at your hands, David.'

David held one of his hands away from the bundle and saw that it trembled. He clenched it into a fist.

'You're right to be afraid, David. After all, in a few minutes, you're going to die. And when you do, all of us, all the way back to Matthias, will be waiting to welcome you to Hell. Go on, David *Smith*, your death awaits.'

David turned back to the bookcase. It was unlocked and he pulled it open. He reached just inside the doorway and turned on the light.

Nothing happened. A small gasp escaped him, and from behind him he heard John chuckle.

'Anything wrong?'

David's calm, practical, inner voice spoke up in his head. *Ignore him, you're right, he isn't there. And just as he isn't there and the books are fine, so the light in the cellar is on: you just can't see it. Your fear of the darkness is what's creating the darkness. Deny your fear and you will see the light.*

That's easy for you to say, David thought in reply. He closed his eyes and tried to think of something good, something that made him happy. He saw Lisa, and he remembered how she had cared for him when he had drunk himself into a humiliating stupor that last night in Brighton. No one had cared for him for such a long time. He realised, quite out of the blue, that he loved her; loved her and wanted to be with her, either in England or Germany, it didn't matter. Shit, of course she could move in with him. He laughed aloud. He loved her.

He opened his eyes. Light shone dimly from the cellar below. He turned back to John: the chair was empty, and the books were back on the shelves, unharmed.

He smiled and turned back to the stairs. 'All right then, Milord. Let's get this over with.' He stepped through onto the stairs and began to descend. As he did so, he noticed that the light was somehow inconsistent, as if it were flickering ... like candlelight.

His breath stopped in his chest and he looked down into the cellar. Candles burned on the pillars surrounding the stone plinth and in their flickering yellow light, David saw that the coffin was gone.

'Oh, shit.'

Behind him came the sound of the door clicking gently closed. He turned to see Lisa standing on the stairs above him. She wore a robe, similar to the ones worn by the Sect the other night, but hers was white. She wore the hood down, her blonde hair spilling over her shoulders like burnished gold in the candlelight. 'Lisa?'

Without a word, she began to walk slowly down the stairs. He reached out a hand towards her, but she ignored him. She walked past, a trace of her perfume lingered in the air as she brushed by him. She was real ... but she couldn't be. 'Lisa! What is this?'

She stopped and turned back to him, her face sad, yet quietly resigned. 'This is the future, David. This is a result of what you do now.' She continued on her way.

'The *what*?' he said, watching as she went to the plinth and sat down on it. She averted her eyes from his as she raised her legs and lay down on the plinth, her hands resting at her sides.

'No,' David ran down the remaining stairs. 'This is fucking mad!' He was about to run to the plinth when, from the deep shadows at the edges of the room, hooded, black-robed figures began to emerge into the candlelight.

A voice came from close behind him. 'The Sect will have their revenge, David. Surely you must have considered that?'

David turned to see his oldest brother Martin, his face partly shadowed by the hood he wore. He was young, no older than nineteen, the age he had been when he had held David's hand as he led him into the crypt to be baptised into the Sect. 'Martin? What are they going to do?'

Martin smiled and pointed to the group gathering around the plinth. 'Ask Father.'

David looked to where Martin pointed, and he felt his strength suddenly leave him. He fell to his knees, dropping the bundle and spilling the mallet and cricket stumps onto the floor. The figure at the head of the plinth looked down at him with cold eyes. It was Arthur.

'Dad?' David's voice sounded suddenly young, childish in his ears.

'You little shit,' said Arthur. 'Your whore mother must have been fucking someone else when she was fucking me, because there's no way I could breed a treacherous little bastard like you.'

'No, please, leave Lisa alone, Dad.'

'Oh, it's all right for you to murder the one we love, isn't it? But when it's the one you love – typical spoilt brat – you come whining to Daddy. Well, you can cry all you want, this tart's going to Hell!' He raised his hands above his head and candlelight flashed on the blade of a long, curved dagger.

'Oh Jesus, no!' David screamed.

'Oh Jesus, yes!' said Arthur. He plunged the dagger down and into Lisa's chest.

'No!' David stumbled forward but hands seized him, big, powerful, adult hands. He twisted in their grip, looking up at the figures towering above him, their hoods dark and faceless. A terrible crunching sound came from the plinth and he looked back to see Arthur hacking with the dagger at Lisa's chest. Sect members came forward and tore at her robe, ripping its blood-soaked fabric apart.

David was screaming, a child again. His vision was blurry with tears, but he could still see the horrible smile on his father's face as he began to reach into Lisa's chest cavity. 'No, Daddy! No!'

Arthur laughed as he pulled Lisa's still-beating heart from her chest. 'Here, boy,' he said holding the heart out to David. 'You always wanted her heart. Well, now you can have it.' He began to come towards him. David struggled against the hands that held him, but they were too big, too strong to break free of.

Arthur, his figure huge, like something from a fevered dream, loomed above him, the heart in his hands still beating, louder and louder as he brought it closer to David. 'Here, you snivelling brat. You can have the first bite, and then we'll all have a bit.'

David screamed and managed to break the grip on his right arm. He thrust his hand out to ward Arthur away – and as he did so, he saw not the hand of a child, but that of a man. His hand: the grave dirt still under his nails from the night before.

'NO!' he shouted, his voice suddenly his own again. 'You're not real! This is a fucking hallucination! None of you exist! The light bulb is on above me and Underwood lies in a coffin where you want me to see Lisa!' He closed his eyes.

In the silence that followed, the only heartbeat David could hear was his own. He took a deep breath. After a couple of seconds, he released it and opened his eyes. He was on the floor of the cellar. The coffin lay on the plinth beside him, and suspended from a rafter above, the single naked bulb held the shadows at bay. He looked over his shoulder, the stumps and mallet lay where he had dropped them.

He smiled. He had beaten it; whatever this hallucinatory defence thing of Underwood's was, he had beaten it. He felt a sudden feeling of elation. 'My God,' he whispered to the coffin. 'I'm not afraid of you. For the first time in my life, I'm not afraid of you!'

He got to his feet and approached the coffin. He reached over, his hand brushing the smooth surface of the wood. Then he firmly took hold of both sides of the lid, and without a moment's hesitation, lifted it off. It was heavy, but he was able to ease it down to the floor and prop it against the plinth. Then, he looked at the man in the coffin. Underwood was dressed in shoes, black trousers and a clean white shirt. He must have got dressed when he returned last night; most likely after he'd murdered Gavin, as there were no bloodstains on the shirt. But then again, maybe just wasn't a messy eater – after all, he'd had plenty of practice.

David went back to the mallet and stumps. He picked up the mallet and one of the stumps, and returned to the coffin. He rested his forearm on the side of the coffin and carefully aimed the point of the stump a centimetre or two above the vampire's heart. He took a deep breath; drew the mallet back so it was level with his shoulder ...

Underwood opened his eyes. 'Flinch?'

David swung the mallet down with all his might, striking the end of the stump dead-on and smashing it down through flesh, and bone, and into Underwood's heart.

Underwood roared, but his cry of pain and horror was cut off by the blood that erupted into his throat. He grabbed at the stake, but David swung the mallet again and hammered it further down so it skewered Underwood's body to the wood of the coffin.

David staggered back and watched, knowing that at any second Underwood's hands would cease to flail and tear at the stake, and crumble to dust along with the rest of him.

But they didn't.

'Flinch! You bastard!' Underwood screamed through a mouthful of blood.

'What – ?' David struggled to understand what he was seeing. 'What's *wrong* with you? Why don't you fucking die?'

Flame suddenly flashed at the base of the stake. David stared, open-mouthed. 'What the fuck *is* this?' Tentatively, he took a couple of steps closer to the coffin. What he saw sent a wave of numbness through him. At the burning base of the stake, the wound in Underwood's chest hissed and bubbled, and an eerie red mist twisted and twined about the stake like a living thing, scorching the wood and making the blood-saturated shirt sizzle and steam.

'Oh shit!' David cried. 'You – you're healing yourself, aren't you!' Suddenly, he remembered the mallet in his grip and swung it to strike at Underwood's face, but this time Underwood's hand shot up and caught him by the wrist. The sudden, jarring halt caused the mallet to fly from David's hand. It spun over the coffin and skittered across the floor. Then, with his free hand, Underwood wrenched the burning stake from his chest and struck David across the face with it in a shower of cinders.

David screamed, tearing his wrist free from Underwood's grip. He staggering back, clutching at his face, feeling at his eyes for damage. He opened them, blinking, and was relieved to realise he could still see. But the feeling of relief was short-lived, for what he saw was Underwood climbing out of the coffin, the smouldering stake in his fist.

Underwood wiped the blood from his mouth with the back of his hand and thrust the stake accusingly at David. 'A cricket stump!' He shouted. 'You tried to assassinate *me* with a *cricket stump*?'

'It's a fucking stake, isn't it? A stake through the heart, that's what the legends all say! You're supposed to be fucking dead!'

Underwood shook his head, amused. 'Oh, you dolt, Flinch. When are you going to learn that everything you think you know about my kind is nothing more than flapdoodle?' He began to walk towards David, slapping the bloody end of the stake into his palm.

David backed away.

Underwood continued. 'I presume you're a fan of Mr Stoker's much-celebrated novel, eh? Well, the bad news is, Flinch, that whilst *Dracula* is a jolly entertaining yarn, it is, I'm afraid, only that – a yarn, a fantasy. While I,' he grinned. 'I am the reality.'

'No. Nothing can survive a stake through the heart! No living thing can survive that kind of trauma!'

'Oh dear,' said Underwood. 'Then I'm either dead, or – ' he gripped the scorched and bloody hole in his shirt and ripped it apart: the wound in his chest had completely healed. 'Praise the Lord! I must be a miracle!' He chuckled and tossed the cricket stump aside. Then he put up his fists. 'Come on then, Flinch. Let's see what you're made of.'

David frowned, confused. 'What?'

'Come on. Put 'em up. Let's see how you fare against an opponent who isn't fast-asleep.'

David was aghast. 'You – you want a *punch up*?'

'Absolutely! We'll settle this the old-fashioned way. Marquis of Queensbury rules, of course.'

David hesitated for a moment. He quickly looked Underwood up and down, checking his size and weight. Then his eyes darted around the room, taking in those things that might help him or hinder Underwood. Then he nodded. 'Alright.' Then with a smile, he added, 'But as for the Marquis of Queensbury? Fuck that.' He launched himself forwards, dropping down and scissoring Underwood's legs with his own. Underwood toppled hard over backwards, his cry of surprise was cut off as he hit the floor and his head bounced off the flagstones.

David spun, snatching up the copper mallet and rolling to a crouching position. Then he sprang, swinging the mallet in an arc as he came down towards Underwood's head. Underwood saw it coming just in time and rolled, the mallet almost taking the skin from his cheek as it smashed down onto the stone.

In a second, Underwood was back on his feet. 'You *bounder*!' He raised his fists. 'You know, I can almost forgive you for trying to kill me. In a way I almost admire you. I mean it takes guts – and a man in your position needs guts – but really! That trick with the feet: where did you learn to fight like that? China?'

'In the army. I did my time, just as family tradition dictates.'

'Yes, well it also dictates that you fight like a gentleman, which is evidently a lesson I'm going to have to teach you myself.' Underwood came forward fast, two jabs from his left fist striking almost as one before he hit David with a right hook that sent him reeling.

David staggered against a pillar. For a second he clung to it, breathing hard, tasting the blood in his mouth and sensing Underwood's movements behind him. Then he pushed back, spinning around, his right leg lashing out in a karate kick – but Underwood side-stepped, impossibly fast. David's unbroken momentum made him fly off-balance right onto an upper cut from Underwood. He crashed sideways into the coffin lid that stood against the plinth. It rocked and almost fell down, but David held on to it, pinning it with his weight, pressing his face against the cool, smooth surface of the wood and waiting for the two he saw of everything to focus into one.

'Had enough, Flinch?' said Underwood.

David wondered at the potential of the coffin lid as a weapon. It was heavy, no good as a club or even a shield, but ... The flicker of a smile played at the corner of his mouth as an idea occurred to him. He groaned, closed his eyes and staggered backwards, as if he were on the verge of collapse. 'Enough?' he said, woozily.

Underwood kept his fists up and regarded David with a wary eye. 'Yes. Ready to throw in the towel? No shame in losing to a better man.'

'Better man?' David laughed. Even though his back was turned to Underwood, he had fixed his position from the sound of his voice. 'Better man, my arse!' He whirled around and smashed his fist into Underwood's face. Underwood staggered and David followed fast with a karate kick that caught Underwood squarely under the jaw and sent him spinning into a pillar. David ran back to the plinth, seized the coffin lid and came around with it raised like a battering ram. He targeted Underwood's throat, and charged. Underwood saw it coming too late to get clear; he threw his hands up, crossing them over his face in the second before the coffin lid smashed into him, breaking both arms on impact. Underwood screamed. He tried to push back, but his arms were useless.

'Die, you bastard!' David shouted. Bracing the coffin lid against his right thigh, he drove it unrelentingly into the attack. He had heard Underwood's arms break and could see the agony on his face, and maybe something else. Fear.

'That's right, you fucker! Who's the better man now, eh?' David pushed with all his strength, straining so the veins on his neck stood out like cables. 'Who's the fucking dolt now then, you – ' He suddenly shot forward, grunting with the impact as the coffin lid thudded into the empty pillar. He looked to where Underwood had been a moment before and a small cry of fear broke from his lips: all he had pinned now was the collar of a burning shirt.

David glanced down. The rest of Underwood's clothes lay in a blazing heap at the foot of the pillar. 'Oh, shit!' He didn't notice the blood-red mist flowing away from the fire, seething silently around his feet to coil in dark congregation behind him. As soon as he realised what had happened, it was too late. One second he felt himself gripped by hair and the waistband of his shorts, the next he was flying across the cellar towards the wall. He didn't have time to raise his hands – he struck it head-on and dropped to the floor. Conscious, but barely, darkness reached for him. He raised his head, pushing and clawing at the flagstones, knowing that he had to get to his feet or die. From the corner of his eye, he could see Underwood approaching.

'No,' he gasped. 'Keep away, I'll, I'll – '

'You'll do what, Flinch?' said Underwood. His voice was unperturbed, almost cheerful. 'Give me a jolly good hiding?' He took David by the hair and twisted his head back so they were face-to-face.

David looked at Underwood. He was naked, his body completely healed, even his humour seemed restored. David spat a gob of blood onto the floor. 'Yeah. But you'll have to give me a second to get my breath back.'

Underwood chuckled. 'You know, Flinch, for a while there I was seriously entertaining the idea of letting you go and giving the position of guardian to your sister. By her own admission, she's evil, and she certainly knows who's boss. However, after this little scuffle of ours, I've decided I like you. You're a bounder, a cheat, and – very nearly – a murderer. Your father would be proud.' He patted him on the cheek.

'Fuck you, Milord,' said David. 'I'll never serve a murdering bastard like you.'

Underwood's smile twisted into something crueller. His fingers tightened in David's hair. 'Oh yes you will, my boy. As of this moment you can consider yourself hired. You will serve me; you will defend me; and if necessary you will die for me.'

'No – '

Underwood slapped David's face. 'Don't interrupt! Now, as your employer, it behoves me to give you your first verbal warning. This little spat we've just had here: I'll let it go this time, but if you try anything like it again, not only will you fail miserably, but as a punishment, I'll be forced to kill someone dear to you. And should you try to run away, I'll track you down, and again, I'll kill someone dear to you.'

David shook his head as best he could. 'You can't. There *is* no-one dear to me. I've got no friends, my mother's dead, and my only family is my sister – and as far as I'm concerned you can do what you like to her.'

Underwood smiled. 'Oh? No one dear to you? How sad – and yet – how jolly queer. You see, I was having the strangest dream just before I was so rudely awoken. I dreamt about you, and a lovely blonde German girl.' Underwood felt David tense. 'I think her name was Lisa. Yes, Lisa. She was such a succulent creature: young, firm, ripe.' His smile widened to reveal his sharp canine teeth. 'Good enough to eat, in fact.' He chuckled and released David's hair. He stood up and began to walk away. Behind him, he could hear David getting to his feet. He stopped and waited.

David stood shakily. 'You, you fucking bastard!' He ran at Underwood. The vampire turned, and punched him straight back into the wall. David was out cold before his body hit the floor.

Underwood strolled back and smiled down at him. 'Yes, I am, aren't I?'

David opened his eyes. He lay on the cellar floor, his cheek lying against the cold stone in a sticky pool of his own coagulated blood. He moved and winced at the pain. Everything hurt. Slowly, he shifted himself to a sitting position. He saw the cricket stump that he had tried to kill Underwood with a few feet away. The lower half was dark with blood; the centre was still smouldering. He picked it up at the unburnt end and looked at it more closely. Incredibly, Underwood had survived. A stake through the heart – the oldest vampire assassination trick in the book – and he had survived it.

'Which goes to show, everything I know about his kind is just ... flapdoodle.' David threw the stump away and got to his feet.

What now? He asked himself. He looked up the stairs; to what he knew was the rest of his life, whether he liked it or not. Wearily, he took hold of the banister and trudged upstairs. A few moments later he emerged into the hallway and stopped. He could hear a piano. He turned to the direction of the music and listened: he recognised the piece. It was Beethoven's *Moonlight Sonata*. He walked in the direction of the music, following it to its source. He turned a corner and saw a light coming from a room ahead. The lounge. As he came upon the doorway the room slowly revealed itself: first, the gramophone, the music drifting through its gleaming brass horn and the 78 rpm disc revolving on its turntable. Then Lydia, reclining in an armchair, her smiling face turned in the direction of something he couldn't yet see. He continued to approach. On the coffee table was a bowl of water with white rose petals floating in it. The water was pink. Beside it was a discarded white hand-towel, blotted with bloodstains. Under the table, a pair of desert-booted feet lay motionless upon a rug that was raked-up and twisted. David's eyes moved from the feet, up the legs clad in blue denim, to the upper body, slumped on the sofa at an angle that suggested it had been shoved aside. It was Gavin. His skin was as white as freshly fallen snow, stained at the throat by smears of blood that centred around two black puncture wounds. Beside him, dressed in an immaculate black evening suit and tie, Underwood sat listening to the music with his eyes closed. His hair was neatly cut and slicked back, and the smoke from a cigarette unravelled upwards from between his fingers.

'Hello, Flinch. How nice of you to finally join us.'

David looked at Lydia. 'Where was he?'

'Who?' asked Lydia.

'Gavin.'

'Oh, him. He was in the boot of Beltran's car. We parked him about a mile down the road.'

'So, it was you who took him, then.'

'Yes,' Lydia swept a lock of hair over her ear. 'Oh, but don't hate me for it, David. I slept on your idea of releasing him and offering His Lordship no choice other than volunteer blood donors for breakfast. But I came to the conclusion that it was … foolhardy.'

'Foolhardy?'

'Yes.'

'But – what happened to – '

'Oh *do* shut up, Flinch. You're thoroughly spoiling the atmosphere,' Underwood turned to David. 'Yes, Lydia was right to do what she did and you were, par for the course, completely wrong. I mean, can you imagine how I felt when Lydia told me about your little *fait accompli*? Especially after you'd just tried to bally well knock me off with a cricket stump. I was quite livid.'

'So you killed him?'

Underwood drew on his cigarette and raised a questioning eyebrow. 'Why? Someone *dear* to you, Flinch?'

David looked away. The other chairs in the lounge, he realised, were conspicuously empty. 'Where are the Bensons?' he asked. 'The barber?'

'Oh, they're long gone,' said Lydia. 'While the barber was giving His Lordship a trim, Miguel and Gerald went and got your late friend here,' she indicated Gavin. 'They parked the Mercedes outside – with him still in the boot – and then Miguel took my car and ran the Bensons and the barber back into town.'

'Charming couple, the Bensons,' said Underwood.

'Yes, My Lord,' said Lydia.

Underwood looked at David and his expression soured. 'I say, Flinch. Why don't you go and get yourself cleaned up? You can't go out looking like that. You look like you were dragged here behind a team of frightened horses.'

David looked confused. 'What? Go out?'

'But of course,' said Underwood. 'I thought we'd all go into town. I trust you have no objections?'

David looked at the body of Gavin lying beside Underwood on the sofa.

Underwood followed his gaze. 'Oh, don't worry about him; he'll be fine there for the time being. You can take care him of him later on, what?'

'Yes,' said David. His head felt strangely numb. 'Yes, I ... suppose so.'

Underwood shook his head disapprovingly. 'Really, Flinch, I think it's about time we started to observe proper protocol around here. Start as we mean to carry on, hmm? From now on, you shall address me as, "Master", all right?'

David swallowed; his saliva still bore the coppery taste of his own blood. 'Yes ... Master.'

Underwood's blood-stained lips parted in a slow, cruel smile. 'Jolly good, Flinch. Carry on.'

Volume II

Bonded in Blood

1

SERGEI ALEXANDROV STOOD ON THE DANCE FLOOR of his Malaga nightclub, *La Fantasía*, listening with barely concealed incomprehension to a bearded hippy called Stefano. It wasn't Stefano's Spanish Sergei was having difficulty understanding, it was his topic: he was talking about stage lighting. Sergei waved a hand, cutting the hippy off in the middle of a stream of unintelligible babble, and said in Spanish, 'Why don't you just show me?'

Stefano agreed and hurried off to the rear of the dance floor where he ascended to his control booth. Sergei turned to Max, his German club manager, and said in Russian, 'Did you understand any of that?'

Max snorted and scratched his blonde-grey goatee beard. 'More or less. But I cannot say it any more clearly. It is all technical bullshit, Sergei. You were right to ask for a demonstration.' Max was forty-three years-old, overweight, and wore his thinning hair tied back in a pony tail. Originally from Berlin in what had once been Soviet East Germany, Max spoke Russian fluently, and in his youth had done his national service in the Soviet army. He'd spent the intervening years between leaving the military and the fall of the Berlin Wall working in bars and clubs in East Berlin. But he'd really made his money at that time providing club punters with drugs. In 1989, when the Wall came down, he'd been the owner of a small but highly successful bar. It was trendy inasfar as an East Garman bar could be at that time, but after the reunification of Germany, overnight it became shoddy in comparison with what was now available to customers in the Western part of the city. Within six months Max had followed his former customers into the West. He'd tried his hand in West Germany for two years before coming to Spain's Costa del Sol. The process of working his way up in a new territory – and in a new language – had been daunting, but with his knowledge of business, legitimate and illegitimate, it had only been a matter of time before he'd become the owner of his own bar, which he had turned into a fashionable and highly profitable concern on which he had grown fat and been able to indulge his appetite for prostitutes, cocaine and Brazil nuts for many years. Then one day, seven years ago, Sergei had approached him with an offer for the place. Unlike most people who found themselves the object of Sergei's expanding business interests, Max understood his situation and was quick to adapt. His time in the Soviet military had taught him all about the Russian mindset, and had also taught him how to recognise an officer when he met one. Consequently, negotiations between the two men had gone well, with Sergei improving his offer to include a job for Max as manager of *La Fantasía*, which he had then been in the process of acquiring. Max had accepted, and the two had become both associates and friends.

Sergei looked up at the bristling black forest of wire and metal that stretched out above him. Although *La Fantasía* was the jewel in the crown of his business empire, Sergei didn't actually like the place, especially the dreadful music they played here, and he left the running of it as much as possible to Max. However, he liked to know what was going on at every level of the business – legitimate and illegitimate – and so when new fixtures and fittings were required, Sergei liked to know what they were and why they were needed. This included improvements to the sound and lighting systems – things about which Sergei knew nothing and cared less – but it was all part of his overall investment and so when the curious entanglement of metal and wire over his head began to click and move, he paid genuine and close attention.

'Okay,' shouted Stefano from above and behind them. A spot in the darkness over their heads suddenly lit up and a series of coloured beams began to swirl and move about the cavernous room. Stefano shouted out the name of the light and how its companion on the other side of the rig didn't work anymore.

'So we need new light?' Sergei asked Max.

'*Ja.*' Max pointed to an inert shape on the other side of the rig, the deceased partner to the whirling light above them. 'He says it is *kaput.*'

'It can't be repaired? A new bulb, perhaps?'

Max shook his head. 'It is old, Sergei. These things are like anything else: they get old and they die.'

More lights came on, one after the other, whirring and clicking as they flashed, spun and pulsed across the ceiling, all the while Stefano shouting out what the light was called and what he needed to make the effect better. Sergei thought the lights were more than adequate as they were, but he turned to Max. 'What do you think? How much of what he's saying is necessary and how much is just wish list?'

'About fifty-fifty. Stefano has a passion for the lights. He's like a big kid.'

Sergei glanced at his watch: it was just after eight-thirty pm. Staff were beginning to arrive, walking around behind the shuttered bars at the far end of the room. Someone turned on a CD player and the rhythmic thud of reggaeton music began to echo across the dance floor. The sound swelled as a door opened, and Sergei turned to see Anton Marashov and Ivan Trushko entering. He turned back to Max. 'Okay, buy the lights we need and maybe a few extras for our passionate friend. I trust you to make sensible choices, as always.' He clapped Max on the shoulder. 'But now, I need your office for a while to discuss some other business, okay?'

'Of course.' Max gave a wave to Anton and Ivan. '*Hola,* comrades.'

The two unsmiling men each nodded in reply.

Max's smile clung to his face with a crumbling grip. He didn't like these two. He got on well with Sergei's usual minders, but Ivan – the big guy with the flat-top hair do, and Anton, the small, ratty-looking guy with the ugly-looking scar across his nose and left cheek – scared him. Sergei walked over to them and motioned for them to follow him. Once the Russians had exited through the door marked "Private", Max relaxed, just as a sudden whirring and clicking from above caused him to look up. Two sets of rainbow beams sprang out from the shadows overhead and began to swirl about him.

'Hey, Max,' shouted Stefano from far away. 'You are the Dancing Queen, young and sweet, only forty-eight. We have the music and you have the floor to yourself, dance for me.'

Max smiled and raised a finger to the control booth, 'Dance on this, *cabrón.*'

Sergei led Anton and Ivan into Max's office. He crossed the white-tiled floor to the desk and drew out Max's chair. He closed the open laptop computer and noticed just behind it a copy of the Spanish newspaper, *El Pais*. A feature caught his eye and he picked it up, a light dust of Brazil nut shells falling away as he did so. 'Have you been reading the Spanish newspapers?' he asked in Russian, waving Anton and Ivan to sit in the chairs opposite.

Anton looked confused. 'Me? No, Captain.'

Ivan shook his big head. 'Me neither, Captain. My Spanish is shit.'

'This is precisely why you should try to read them, Ivan Trushko. A little every day –*poco y poco*, as they say here – and you will see big improvement. If you had better Spanish,' he held up the newspaper and showed them the picture of Mark Coleman, 'you would be able to read about your exploits.'

Sergei tossed the newspaper to Ivan and sat forward. 'It is yesterday's edition. I have read it. Police are now focusing their investigation on rival drug dealers on Ibiza. You did good job.'

'Thank you, Captain,' said Anton.

Sergei smiled. 'And so, tell me, Anton. What do you have for me on the other English, Keith Mullins and his friends?'

Anton picked up his briefcase, 'We spoke to many people on Ibiza who knew Coleman, but they didn't seem to know anything about the other men. We went through online phone directories for both Portugal and Spain looking for names Mullins, Hodgekiss and Sullivan. Not so many entries for Mullins and Hodgekiss, but many for Sullivan. Too many. So – '

Ivan interrupted. 'So I had brilliant idea. I looked for them on MySpace.'

'Yes,' Anton interjected. 'But Mullins and his friends didn't have pages. So I had brilliant idea of looking for page for Coleman, and bingo! We found him. He had changed his profile name but original email cannot be changed.'

Sergei frowned, confused. 'What does this all mean? What is MySpace? Is children's thing, no?'

'Maybe, yes, but lots of stupid adults use it too. Coleman had many pictures on his page. Mostly irrelevant, but we found some I think you will like.' Anton opened his briefcase and handed Sergei a file containing prints of various colour photographs.

Sergei looked at the top one, it showed Mark Coleman and Damo Sullivan arm-wrestling in a pub with Hodge refereeing between them. Behind them were several drunk-looking spectators, most of whom had flash-induced red-eye. Under the picture, Anton had transcribed the caption, "Mark, Hodge and Damo, John Bull Tavern '05". Sergei smiled.

'You recognise them?' asked Ivan. 'When you bought pub from Mullins?'

Sergei nodded. 'Yes, I recognise them.' He looked at the next picture. It showed a smiling Keith and Michelle behind the bar of the John Bull Tavern. 'And here is our friend Mr Mullins and his good lady wife.'

Anton watched as Sergei browsed through the rest of the pictures. 'We spent a day following different links to Coleman's friends and checking through their pictures. The ones you are looking at now come from other people's pages.'

Sergei examined each of the pictures carefully. He was coming to the end of them when he stopped and took out his reading glasses to look more closely at one picture in particular. He tapped it. 'Did you make note of whose page you took this from?'

'Yes, Captain,' said Anton. 'We took notes of all people with relevant pictures.'

'This one,' said Sergei, laying the picture on the desk so it was facing Anton and Ivan. 'You recognise the place?'

Anton and Ivan leaned in closer to the picture. It showed Damo and a crowd of rosy-cheeked drinkers cheering in a pub. A string of paper shamrocks was strung over the bar in the background. Ivan looked up at Sergei. 'It is the Irish, Sullivan and other people drunk in pub, no?'

'Yes, but I ask if you recognise the place, not the people.'

Anton looked more closely then shrugged. 'Caption says, "Paddy's Day at Paddy McGinty's." So place must be Paddy McGinty's, no?'

'Good,' said Sergei. 'But what about the day, Anton Marashov? What is "Paddy's Day"?'

Anton shook his head. 'I don't know.'

Sergei reached for the bowl of Brazil nuts that was always full on Max's desk. He took the nutcracker and selected a nut. 'It is St Patrick's Day. Very big day in pub trade.'

'So, this is why everyone is drunk in picture?'

'Yes.' Sergei cracked the shell of the nut and dropped the debris into Max's waste paper basket. He popped the nut into his mouth. 'You are right, Anton, this pub is called Paddy McGinty's. It is in Torremolinos. But – ' he pointed at Anton for emphasis, 'this time last year, it was called *The Red Lion*. It was shit-hole English pub. Owner was fat alcoholic. No customers. I bought it, changed it to Irish pub, now it makes lots of money.'

Anton nodded. 'Ahhh.'

'You understand my point?' asked Sergei.

'Er ... no.'

'Why is this "Paddy's Day" important?' asked Ivan.

Sergei smiled. 'Because, St Patrick's Day falls on March 17th. On March 17th last year, this building was shit-hole English pub, *Red Lion*, but on March 17th *this* year, it was Paddy McGinty's, an Irish pub.' He tapped the photo. 'This pub in the picture.'

Anton nodded as realization dawned. 'So this picture was taken *this* year, not last year?'

'To be precise,' said Sergei, 'it was taken five weeks ago. So either Mr Sullivan travelled all the way from Portugal for a night out, or he lives a lot closer than he wants us to believe.'

'So, do you think Sullivan knew he was in your pub?'

'I doubt it. If he did, I don't think he would be smiling.'

Ivan grinned. 'So, you think Sullivan could be in Torremolinos?'

'Maybe,' said Sergei. 'Or maybe he just likes to drop by every now and again to see old friends.

'Take the names of the people whose MySpace pages you got these pictures from, especially the name of the person who took the St Patrick's Day picture. Then go to pub, Paddy McGinty's, and speak with manager. I will call him and let him know you are coming. He should be able to put names to faces and vice versa.' He took another nut from the dish, crushed the shell, and held the nut thoughtfully between thumb and forefinger. 'Then with luck, before too long, we will be able to give the Spanish newspapers some fresh headshots for their front pages.'

David stepped out of the shower. He wiped the condensation from the mirror on the bathroom cabinet and inspected the damage to his face. He looked terrible: his lower lip, right cheekbone and left eyebrow were swollen in vivid shades of purple and black. His head ached, and he touched the bump that had risen where it had struck the wall. Thankfully he had no serious signs of concussion, just the headache, but that was to be expected. He lightly touched his fat lip and winced at the pain. He'd need to ice the swellings as soon as possible.

He opened the cabinet door and took out a box of paracetamol. He popped two pills from the push-out pack and looked at them as they lay in his palm. They would quieten the physical pain and that was all he needed, his mind had been numb since he'd turned away from the lounge, leaving Underwood and Lydia chatting over Gavin's corpse as if he'd been nothing more than an empty wine glass. David had obeyed his master. Like a zombie, he'd walked slowly up the stairs to his room where he'd come straight to the bathroom, taken off his torn and bloody clothes, and got into the shower. He turned the taps to cold and stood beneath the numbing water as it cascaded over the bumps and lesions on his body until he finally began to shiver. Then he'd turned the hot water back on and began to soap away the dried blood from his hair and fingernails. His mind was silent: no anger, no admonishment, no sorrow, no shame. Only one thought now lived in his brain, which was that he had to be clean and well-presented, because the master had said they were going into town and he ... he had to be ... clean.

Now he threw the pills into his mouth and scooped a handful of water from the cold tap to wash them down with. He squeezed some toothpaste onto his toothbrush and began to gingerly brush his teeth, careful to avoid his damaged lip. When he spat into the sink, the toothpaste spit was pink with blood. He looked again into the mirror and his tired, beaten face looked back at him. He picked up his electric razor and began to move it cautiously over his cheeks.

And so, he has won? A voice in his mind spoke up quietly.

David tried to ignore the question, but it hung determinedly in his mind, an obstacle to all further thought. Yes, he thought in reply. So it would seem.

You fear him?

No, I'm past fear.

Then kill him.

He can't be killed. He's immortal.

Then run away.

There's nowhere to run.

So what will you do?

David looked down from the mirror, shutting off the shaver and filling the sink with cold water. He had no wish to continue with this train of thought. Unfortunately, his mind persisted, inferring his answer and responding accordingly.

You're just going to obey him?

Yes.

Why?

Because he's my master. I can't escape that. I can't escape my destiny.

Your destiny? Since when?

Since forever; I just couldn't accept it before.

And now you do?

I have no choice. I'm a Flinch. It's what we do.

Well, then you are truly damned.

David bent to splash cold water into his face. Then he straightened to meet the eyes that looked back at him from the mirror. 'Yes,' he said aloud. 'I know.'

Ten minutes later, David went downstairs dressed in a white t-shirt, black suit and black shoes. He hadn't brought the suit and shoes with him; he'd found them and other formal clothes hanging in his wardrobe. As he descended the stairs he heard some lively nineteen-twenties dance music echoing from the lounge. He listened for a moment before going on to the kitchen. He opened the freezer and took out an ice tray. He found a plastic carrier bag under the sink and popped all the ice cubes into it before wrapping the whole thing in a tea towel and pressing it gently onto his lip. Then he sat down at the kitchen table and listened to the distant sound of Underwood's laughter.

Five minutes passed. David sat smoking a cigarette with the towel dripping onto the kitchen table, watching as the water pooled and soaked into the wood. Eventually, he got up, dropped the wet bundle into the sink and used a hand towel to dry his face and hands. He took a moment to compose himself then headed for the lounge.

The old-fashioned dance music continued to drift down the corridor and as he approached he recognised the tune as *The Charleston*. When he came to the doorway of the room, he stopped, unsure how to proceed. Gavin's legs had been lifted onto the sofa and his body rolled over so its face was to the cushions; the coffee table had been pushed to one side and the hearth rug rolled up and pushed out of the way. In the centre of the room, with his back to David, Underwood was dancing. Lydia stood before him, watching with what seemed to David to be a mixture of astonished delight and mild embarrassment, as Underwood explained each of his moves as he performed them. Evidently David was interrupting a lesson in progress. He cleared his throat. 'Excuse me, My Lord.'

Underwood turned, looking slightly flushed and grinning from ear to ear. 'Ah, Flinch. Do you know the Charleston?'

'Only the tune, sir.'

'So you don't know the steps either?'

'No, sir.'

'You see?' said Lydia. 'It's like I told you, My Lord, no one does that sort of dancing any more, it's just not the fashion.'

'Well, no, of course not. When I lay down back in '58, everybody was doing the Jive.' He chuckled, 'And what a terrific dance that was, eh? I can't imagine what sort of dances you must be doing nowadays.' A thought suddenly occurred to him. 'Hey – ' He lifted the needle from the record and switched off the gramophone. 'Maybe you could show me a few of the modern steps. Do you need a different sort of gramophone? This old machine was on the way out back in the fifties, so I imagine she's quite an antique by now, eh?'

'Er,' Lydia turned to the black glass block that was set into the shelving unit behind her. 'We use this, My Lord.' She picked up a remote control from the coffee table and the stereo lit up with tiny red and green LEDs.

'I say,' said Underwood, impressed. 'Where's the horn?'

'Er, *horn*, My Lord?' enquired Lydia.

'He means speakers,' said David.

'Oh,' Lydia pointed out the speakers. 'That would be those, sir.'

'Interesting,' said Underwood. 'And so where do you put the record?'

'CD, sir,' she picked up a CD from one of the shelves and handed it to him. 'This is the modern record.'

'But they're on the way out now,' said David, walking into the room. 'Now it's more downloads, MP3s, that sort of thing.'

'I'm sorry, Flinch, do forgive me but I've been quite dead these last fifty years. What *are* you talking about?'

Lydia picked up her bag and fished out her mobile phone. 'Here, My Lord,' she handed the phone to Underwood. 'The music David is talking about can be played on this. It's a telephone, but it's also like a portable juke box, amongst other things. I've got hundreds of songs on it.'

Underwood swapped the CD for the phone. He looked at it as if it might have had a genie inside. 'Good Lord. Are you pulling my leg? It doesn't look big enough to hold more than a couple of cigarettes.'

'It's computerised or something,' said Lydia. 'Here, let me show you.' She came close to him so their bodies were touching, and intertwined her arms with his, cradling his hands in her own as she turned the phone on. She accessed the song menu, her touch deft and sure as she selected a song, *You Don't Know Me* by Basement Jaxx. A moment later, tinny music began to pulse from the phone.

Underwood's face lit up. He laughed. 'My word, what a marvelous device.' He looked at the phone in astonishment. 'And, and so, what dance do you do to this music?'

'Well, I ... ' Lydia looked at David and saw he was looking with suspicion at her proximity to Underwood. She withdrew her arms and took a step back, a blush rising to her cheeks. 'David? What dance would you do to this?'

He held her eyes, saying nothing for a moment but sending her a clear message. Then he said coolly, 'Pardon?'

'His Lordship wants to know how you dance to this music.'

David continued to regard her suspiciously. 'I don't.'

'Oh come, come, Flinch,' said Underwood brightly. 'Even a dry old stick like you must go out dancing from time to time?'

David finally turned from Lydia to Underwood. 'Yes, My Lord, but I wouldn't be the best person to ask. My dancing is sort of ... random.'

'*Random?* What about the steps?'

'There are no steps, My Lord.'

'*No steps?*'

'No, My Lord,' said Lydia. 'People nowadays just get up on the dance floor and do what they like.'

Underwood's expression was incredulous. '*Do what they like?*'

Lydia nodded. 'Yes.'

'But ... but that sounds like chaos! Everyone just ... doing what they like. Surely there must be *some* steps?'

'Well, not unless big fish, little fish, cardboard box counts,' said David.

Underwood looked at him, open-mouthed. '*What?*'

David demonstrated to the beat of the music, his hands indicating the length of an imagined big fish before closing the gap between them to indicate a little fish, then switching his palms so they were vertical to each other then back to horizontal, patting an imagined cardboard box. He then repeated in reverse.

'That's it?' said Underwood in disbelief.

'Pretty much,' said David. 'Some people like putting their boxes on shelves and taking them down again, but – '

'That's not dancing, Flinch, that's playing silly buggers.' Underwood handed Lydia her phone back. 'Could you turn this off, please?'

She did so and the phone fell silent.

'What a pity,' said Underwood. 'I was looking forward to expanding my repertoire of moves, but if all people are doing these days is arsing around, putting pretend fish on shelves and whatnot, I don't think I'll bother.'

'Boxes, sir,' said David.

'Come again?'

'You put the boxes on the shelf, the fish don't go anywhere.'

'Don't be impertinent, Flinch.' Underwood looked David up and down. 'I see you've managed to tidy yourself up at least.'

'Yes, sir. I found these clothes in my wardrobe. I don't know where they came from, but they seem to fit.'

'I put them there, David,' said Lydia. 'They were John's.'

'And did John not have shirts and ties?' Underwood asked her.

'He did, My Lord,' said Lydia. 'I put them in David's wardrobe as well.'

'And so why are you not wearing a shirt and tie, Flinch?'

David scratched his head. 'Well, sir, if I may be honest?'

'Please do,' said Underwood. 'Liars and flatterers make good servants for old ladies, but not for me. Out with it!'

'It's too formal, sir. People only get dressed up like you and Lydia are at the moment if they're going to the opera or something. We're going to Almacena, not *Madam Butterfly.*'

Underwood frowned. 'Too formal?' He turned to Lydia. 'Is that so?'

Lydia shrugged. 'Well, yes, I suppose we could dress down a little.'

'How much?'

'Quite a lot, actually.'

'No tie?' Underwood reached for his tie, his fingers finding it with relief and smoothing it gently, as if to comfort it.

'Well, to a restaurant, yes.'

'What about hats?' asked Underwood. 'I didn't see any new hats in my wardrobe.'

'Hats are out, sir,' said David. 'Men haven't worn hats since the sixties.'

'My word,' said Underwood. 'No hats, no steps, dear oh dear, what kind of a brave new world have I awoken to?'

There was silence for a moment then Lydia held up her telephone. 'One with TV and films on telephones – I can show you if you like. It's really quite amazing.'

Underwood smiled as a parent might at a child that offers a bag of boiled sweets at a time of utmost calamity. 'Thank you, Lydia. Not right now.'

Ten minutes later Underwood came downstairs, minus tie – though still sporting his waistcoat and black suit – to find David at the kitchen table smoking a cigarette. On seeing him enter, David got up.

'Please, as you were,' said Underwood. He pulled out the chair opposite and picked up David's cigarettes. 'May I?'

David shrugged. 'Of course.'

'You don't have to, you know?' said Underwood, taking one from the pack and lighting it. 'I won't fire you for withholding your fags.'

David smiled. 'That's a pity.'

Underwood chuckled. He drew on his cigarette and regarded David with interest. 'You know, I sense you've lost a great deal of your initial ... *anxiety* around me. Would I be right in thinking that?'

'If by anxiety you mean fear, then yes, sir, I have.'

'I see, well, that's not altogether a bad thing, is it? A chap like me can't place his well-being in the hands of a quivering jellyfish, now can he? But may ask where this new found spunk of yours has come from?'

'I suppose it was in the cellar when I was coming to kill you.'

'Go on.'

'You've got some ... hallucinatory defence mechanism thing, haven't you?'

Underwood smiled. 'Oh, that. Yes. Handy little trick, though it doesn't seem to have worked on you.'

'Oh no, it worked very well. But I managed to break through it.'

'And so then you were able to have a crack at me.'

'Yes.'

'With a cricket stump.'

'It was the best thing I could find at short notice.'

A look of relief flickered across Underwood's features. 'Just as well.'

David raised his eyebrow. 'Sorry, sir?'

Underwood's smile slipped slightly but was back in a heartbeat. 'I mean, just as well you didn't find something else, like a silver bullet.'

'Are you vulnerable to silver bullets?'

'No.' Underwood drew on his cigarette. 'That's werewolves, Flinch. I'm supposed to be the stake through the heart chap.'

'But you aren't.'

'No. Sadly for you.'

'Could I ask, why not?'

'You mean, why don't I die according to the rules of folklore?'

David nodded. 'Yeah.'

'Because folklore is just wild, unscientific gossip, isn't it? Things half-seen, half dreamed, passed on from one country bumpkin to another as though they were facts.'

'But clearly some of it *is* fact.'

'Well, yes, some bits do have a foundation in truth, and some bits don't. Though you may find the bits that do are the least likely.'

'Like turning into a bat?'

'Yes.'

'Do you have any other tricks like that up your sleeve?'

'Plenty.'

'Like what?'

'That would be telling. Why don't I just surprise you?'

'I don't enjoy surprises, sir.'

'No, especially when they pull stakes from their hearts.'

David ground out his cigarette in the ashtray. 'So, may I ask what you are vulnerable to?'

Underwood laughed. 'Oh, yes. You may well ask, but you'll forgive me if I don't confide in you, my would-be assassin.'

'You can trust me, sir. You see, I've accepted my situation.'

'Have you indeed?'

'Yes, sir. You made it perfectly clear in the cellar what would happen if I didn't.'

'Discipline may result in obedience, Flinch, but in my experience it seldom results in loyalty. Are you telling me that you are now loyal?'

'I'm telling you that you can trust me, sir.'

Underwood stubbed out his cigarette. 'How enormously reassuring.' He sat back and looked intently at David, who met his eyes with unwavering steadiness. Underwood smiled. 'I suppose you're rather miffed about that lad I killed earlier on, aren't you?'

David shrugged. 'Not much I can do about that, now, sir.'

'No, indeed. But you brought it upon yourself, you know?'

'By trying to kill you, I suppose.'

'Exactly.'

'If I hadn't tried to hurt you, you wouldn't have hurt him, right?'

'Yes. And stop anticipating me.'

'Sorry, sir.'

'As I was going to say, if you hadn't hurt me, I wouldn't have hurt him. I was quite happy to go with your transfusion idea, but I'm afraid you rather coal-boxed all that when you tried to bally well murder me.'

'Sorry, sir.'

'Too right, sorry sir.' Underwood snatched up David's cigarettes, took one for himself and offered the pack to David, who declined. Underwood lit up and sat back. 'Damn it, Flinch! Why did you have to go and do that? I thought we had an understanding. I recognise that you have a point when you talk about modern police technology and what have you, and I was, as I say, all set to give it a whirl. I didn't get where I am today by not being able to adapt to circumstances, you know?'

For David, this was unexpected. He'd anticipated a lot of reactions from Underwood to his attempted murder, but not this one. He sat forward. 'Sorry, sir, but are you saying you're still interested in my idea?'

'Of course I am. The world *has* changed, and you, so far at least, have offered the wisest counsel in how best to adapt to it. Your argument that today's constabulary may very likely apprehend me with their latest box of tricks is, I've no doubt, sound as a pound. And it's not like managing my blood lust is a new idea. In times of peace I've always had to be careful, and using donors is nothing new. Oh, I've suckled more than my fair of share over the years, I can tell you – on long sea voyages especially. Most people's luggage consists mainly of bags; mine often consists mainly of willing bleeders, which is what I call them. I usually like to bring a few ripe young ladies along with me – sleeping in different quarters, of course – but, needless to say, I'd have the keys to all the cabins.' He winked.

Lydia came into the kitchen. She had changed into a skirt, a blouse and a light jacket. She stopped before them and smiled uncertainly, unsure as to whether or not she'd interrupted something important. She looked at Underwood and indicated her outfit. 'I hope you approve, My Lord: smart-casual, as we say these days.'

'Charming, Lydia,' said Underwood. He turned to David. 'Well, Flinch, I suppose we should get going, eh? What are we driving? I presume we have a motor car?'

'Yes, sir, we have a choice. We can either take your – what is now *vintage,* Rolls Royce hearse – which isn't exactly inconspicuous; or we can take Arthur's car.'

'Arthur's car?' said Underwood, warily. 'What is "Arthur's car"?'

'It's a Citroën,' said David. 'D.S. Black, late 'fifties model.'

'Oh dear. Not one of those ugly French contraptions that look like a shoe?'

'Yes, that's it,' said Lydia. 'I suppose it does look a bit like a shoe. Although I've always thought it looked more like a boat.'

'Shoe, boat, either way it fails to look like a car. Isn't there anything else?'

'Miguel's got my car,' said Lydia. 'So unless we take Beltran's Mercedes – '

'Oh no, hang on,' said David. 'I thought you said you were gonna get rid of that; as you pointed out, its owner has just made it onto the missing persons list. If we get pulled over by the Civil Guard, we're for it.'

'Well, yes, I know. I told you that. The same applies to Ana's Fiat – not that we'd ever have been seen dead in that thing.'

'So, it rather looks like the Citroën, sir,' said David.

'Oh, fie,' said Underwood. 'I remember your father was enraptured with that hideous car when it first came onto the market. He wanted me to purchase one, but I doused that hope the moment it flickered into being.'

'He bought it as a retirement gift for himself, not long after you were interred, My Lord,' said Lydia.

'Yes, I'll bet he did. Obviously my disapproval did nothing to cool his ardour. You would have thought that I, as his master – and I would like to have thought *mentor* of sorts – would have had some influence on the fellow's taste, wouldn't you?' He sighed. 'But alas, no. He always was his own man. You know, he had the most dreadful propensity, whenever we were in an English eating house, for eel pie and mashed potato. I could never cure him of it, try as I might. Ugh, I shudder at the memory. Oh well, I suppose this Citroën will have to do until we can find ourselves a nice Bentley or something.'

David got up. 'So should I bring it round to the front, My Lord?'

'Yes, do.'

David turned to go, but as he got to the door, Underwood called after him. 'Oh, Flinch?' David stopped and turned back. 'I don't know if your brother mentioned it at all, but I have a watch, an old silver hunter?'

David remembered the old watch he had found in the safe in John's study. He nodded. 'Yes sir, I think I know the one.'

'Good. Would you mind fetching it and bringing it out to the car?'

David nodded. 'Certainly, sir.' He went out and down to the study. He keyed in his code, and entered the room, closing the door behind him. He went directly to the safe, opened it and took out the watch. Should he wind it? What if it broke? He popped open the cover and looked again at its old, scratched face. He read again the worn engraving on the inside of the casing: *To Daniel. Forever yours, Lilly.*

Daniel and Lilly.

Presumably Daniel was Underwood, either that or he'd pinched the watch from a victim of that name. But what would be the point of that? He was rich, he didn't need to steal silver watches. So again, David wondered: who was Lilly? He flipped the case closed and slipped the watch into his jacket pocket.

Ten minutes later, when David drove up to the front of the house, Underwood and Lydia were waiting for him. Underwood smiled and shook his head at the sight of the car, as if he got the joke that Arthur had, perhaps, in some way always intended. David got out and came around to the rear passenger door. He opened it, then reached into his pocket and took out the watch. 'Your watch, My Lord.'

Underwood looked at the watch dangling by its chain from David's fingers. He smiled as he slowly reached out and took it. He held it in the palm of his hand and stroked the face with his thumb.

Lydia took a curious step closer. 'Oh, what a lovely watch.'

'No,' said Underwood. 'Not really, it's very old and unreliable.'

'Then why do you keep it?' David asked, though he was fairly sure he already knew.

Underwood said nothing for a moment, as if he were lost in a reverie, then he looked up at David and said, matter-of-factly, 'That's none of your business, Flinch.' He held the watch to his ear. 'You didn't wind it?'

'I wasn't sure if I should, sir. I mean, it's clearly an antique. If I broke it, I – '

'Oh, don't worry about that, old chap. This watch has been bashed more times than the bells of St Martin's. There's not much you could do to it that couldn't be repaired by a good watchmaker.'

'Though that's something of a dying trade these days, My Lord,' said Lydia.

'Nonsense,' said Underwood. 'I drop this in to Weiss and Sons in Zurich every ten years or so, and they give it back to me after a few days as good as new.'

'What I mean is, these days most watches are electronic – digital. I don't suppose Herr Weiss or his sons get too many watches like that anymore.'

Underwood frowned. 'Digital?'

'David extended his arm and pulled back his cuff to reveal his bottom-of-the-range Casio. He pushed the illuminator button so Underwood would be able to read the numbers.'

'I say! There's no hands? No winder?'

'No sir, a battery.'

'I see. And so, that is the correct time, is it?'

'Precisely, Milord.'

Underwood opened the casing of his watch. David noticed he was reading the inscription on the inside and waited for some sign of emotion or recognition, but the vampire made none; he only gazed in silence for a few moments before looking up abruptly. 'Sorry, Flinch, what did you say was the correct time again?'

David checked. 'It's eight-forty-six, sir.'

Underwood murmured his thanks as he set the hands of his watch. Then he wound the mechanism carefully, indicating to David as he did so. 'You see, Flinch? About seven turns ought to do it. When you feel the slightest pressure on the winder, that's when you stop. I'd say your brother must have been keeping it wound fairly regularly, otherwise it would be considerably less inclined to ... ' He tapped the glass face and the second hand began to move, '... work.' Underwood closed the watch and fixed the chain to his waistcoat. 'And so, from now on, I'll be expecting you to wind it for me every evening before I rise.' He grinned. 'You can bring it to me with my breakfast, whoever they may be.'

David bowed slightly. 'Very good, sir.'

'Right then,' Underwood slipped the watch into his waistcoat pocket and turned to the car. 'Let's go for a spin in Arthur's Revenge, shall we?'

He got into the car and brushed his hand over the back seat. 'I say, it's actually not so bad once you get inside.'

Lydia went to follow Underwood. As she was about to get in, she turned to David, who was still holding the door open. 'Thank you, Flinch.'

David offered her the briefest scowl before closing the door behind her. He went back around to the driver's door and got inside. Then he turned around to Underwood over the back of his seat. 'So, where to, Milord?'

Underwood was still inspecting the upholstery. 'Hmmm? Oh, I don't know. Lydia?'

'Well, we could go to *La Reina de Corazones*, just to meet the Bensons and Miguel for a quick drink. Then we could go on to a restaurant for something to eat.'

'Smashing,' said Underwood. 'But how will they know to meet us there?'

Lydia took out her mobile phone. 'I can call them on this, remember?'

'Ahh, yes, of course. But please, no more of that music of yours. Flinch, is there a wireless in this thing?'

David checked the car stereo. A tape jutted from the player. He pulled it out and inspected it. The label bore his own handwriting: *for Lydia: David's Mix '84.* He remembered how they used to make mixed tapes for each other and swap them during the summer holidays when they were young. Somehow this tape must have fallen into John's hands. What was on it? He couldn't remember for the life of him.

'Yes, Milord. But, would you be interested in hearing some music from the 1980s?'

'Certainly. What is it, one of those CD things?'

'No, sir. It's a tape. Lydia can explain it to you on the way.'

'Oh? What's on it?' asked Lydia.

David pushed the tape into the machine. There was a moment's hiss as the tape wound on, then the jagged opening strings of *Soul Train* by Swansway filled the car.

'Ohhh, my God,' said Lydia. 'Is this one of your old tapes?'

David nodded at her in the rear view mirror. Then he spoke to Underwood. 'Ready when you are, Milord.'

'Jolly good, Flinch, said Underwood, settling back in his seat. 'Drive on.'

2

IT WAS SHORTLY AFTER NINE O'CLOCK when the Bensons entered *La Reina de Corazones*. The pub was busy; nearly all the tables were occupied, and despite the notice on the door that said that smoking was only permitted provided there were no children inside, both cigarettes, and children were being equally indulged within. In Almacena, laws like those pertaining to smoking in public places were only upheld as long as they didn't interfere with people's enjoyment of life. Since socializing was one of life's pleasures, and a healthy social circle included people of all ages from children to the elderly, the smoking ban was largely ignored on the grounds that it was absurd.

As a small boy ran past her in pursuit of its playmate, Cynthia fought her maternal instinct to cuff the little tyke and managed to twist her mouth into a smile of enchantment.

Gerald, who didn't share his wife's disapproval, chuckled with genuine warmth, pointing after the boy as he disappeared behind a table, 'Ho! There he goes.'

'Yes,' said Cynthia through her rictus grin, 'and let's hope he keeps on going.' They'd only just arrived and she needed a drink. Men sat on bar stools the length of the bar making access difficult, but she noticed a break in the line of hunched backs and made for it. Michelle was serving behind the bar and Cynthia waved to her. 'Oh, Michelle?'

Michelle came over to her. She was wearing faded blue jeans and a red Abercrombie and Fitch t-shirt. 'Hello, Cynthia. We don't normally see you in here on a Friday night. What brings you out?'

Cynthia immediately noticed Michelle was wearing more eye make-up than usual, and on closer inspection, she could see why. The whites of her eyes were pink at the edges, and the flesh around them slightly puffy: she had been crying. Cynthia gave no outward sign of noticing. 'Oh, we're meeting Lydia and her brother here for drinks before going on somewhere for dinner.'

'Her brother? What, the one just over from England?'

Cynthia smiled. 'Well it's hardly going to be the one who just died, is it, dear?'

'Oh, shut up,' said Michelle swatting the sarcasm aside. 'You know what I mean.'

'Yes, the one from England. His name's David.'

'Have you met him?'

'Yes.'

'What's he like? Is he nice?'

'Pleasant enough.'

Gerald leaned in. 'Mind you, he's got some pretty queer ideas on the proper use of cricket stumps.' Cynthia kicked his ankle. 'Ow!'

'What are you on about, Gerald?'

Cynthia responded quickly. 'Gerald was talking to David about cricket, you know how dull men can be.'

Michelle's smile faltered slightly. 'Yeah.'

Cynthia noticed it, and asked casually, 'Where's Keith?'

'He's upstairs. Watching football I imagine.'

'Night off, eh?' said Gerald. 'Lucky him.'

'And poor you,' added Cynthia. 'Left down here to run this place on a Friday night.'

'Oh, I'm all right,' said Michelle. 'Damo and Hodge are here. And Luis is coming in at ten for when it gets really busy.' Over the Bensons' shoulders, Michelle suddenly caught sight of her daughter heading for the exit. 'Oi, Mel! Where are you going?'

Melanie stopped and turned. 'Teresa's. I've already told Dad.'

'Well you haven't told me, have you?'

'You're busy, aren't you?'

'Not so busy as I don't want to know where my daughter's going of an evening.'

'I've told Dad. Isn't that enough?'

'No, it's not,' said Michelle, not wanting to have this conversation in full view of the pub's clientele but at the same time unwilling to let the matter slide. 'From now on, you'll tell us both, please.'

'Why's that, because you're not talking to each other?'

At that, anyone at the bar who could speak English suddenly pricked up their ears. Backs stiffened, heads turned. For a moment, Michelle had no answer, she just stared at Melanie. In her peripheral vision she perceived the eyes now upon them, waiting for her response. If this were happening in private, it would escalate. But here, it had to stop. She sighed, gave a silent laugh and shook her head dismissively, 'Go on. But don't be late back.'

Melanie rolled her eyes and continued on her way.

Michelle turned to her audience ranged along the bar and gave a huff of dismay. 'Kids.' To this irrefutable wisdom, everyone could only nod or smile their agreement before turning back to their conversations.

Just as she was coming to the door, Melanie stopped and stepped aside to let Lydia Flinch enter.

'Hello Mel,' said Lydia. 'Off out, are we?'

Melanie smiled politely. 'Yeah.'

Lydia came inside. Then, following behind her, Melanie saw a man she had never seen before. He was tall with slick, dark hair, and he was wearing a black suit. A watch chain glinted against the soft black fabric of his waistcoat. He looked like a cross between a funeral director and a gunfighter. The man smiled down at her, 'Hello.'

For some reason, Melanie found herself at a loss for a reply. The man held her eyes for a moment then continued past her. Melanie watched as he walked up to the bar. Unconsciously, she rubbed her arms. She looked down and noticed they had come out in goose pimples.

'Excuse me,' said a voice from behind her. Melanie turned to see another man, also dressed in black. His face was bruised, like he had recently been beaten up. He smiled and nodded to the other man. 'Don't mind him. We've just been to a funeral.'

It was if he had read her thoughts. Melanie gave a small laugh then immediately put her hand to her mouth. 'Oh, I'm sorry. I didn't mean – '

'That's all right. I know – we look like a couple of penguins, don't we?' He stepped past her into the pub. 'See ya.'

Melanie said nothing; she watched him as he followed the other man and Lydia to the bar. 'Weirdos,' she said under her breath. Then, as she left the pub, she added with a smile, 'And about time too.'

'Speak of the devil,' said Gerald, raising a hand to wave to the new arrivals. 'What can I get you?'

'A gin and tonic for me, please, Gerald,' said Lydia. She turned to Underwood. 'I, er, I don't think they serve your usual tipple, My Lord.'

Underwood grinned. 'By which I assume you mean champagne, Lydia?' Lydia's eyes widened in surprise. Underwood turned to Michelle. 'A bottle of your finest champagne, please.'

'Ohhhh,' said Michelle, slightly taken aback. 'Special occasion, is it?'

'Why yes,' said Underwood. 'I'm alive.'

'Oh? Been sick, have you?'

'One doesn't need to have been sick to appreciate the benefits of being above ground, madam. And to be above ground in such charming company as this certainly merits the popping of a few of your finest corks.'

'Oh, blimey,' said Michelle. 'Well, I hope you stay above ground for a long time, mate, especially if you keep celebrating it in here, eh?' She nodded knowingly to the Bensons, who, like Lydia, appeared dumbstruck, staring at Underwood as if he had just pulled a rabbit from a top hat. Michelle took this as surprise that the new arrival was splashing out on champagne. 'Anyway, if you'd like to take a table, I can bring you over a bottle and some glasses. For five is it?'

'Er, four,' said David. 'I'll have a coke.'

Michelle nodded and turned to get the drinks. Underwood turned back to the group to see them still staring at him in surprise. 'Something wrong?'

'Champagne?' said Lydia.

'Naturally. Why? Don't you like champers?'

'No. I mean, yes. But you? You drink champagne?'

'Well, not as much as I did a few hundred years ago. These days I find it gives me a headache if I have more than three or four glasses.'

'No, I mean, you *can* drink champagne?'

'But of course.'

'But, it isn't ... '

'Blood?'

'Yes.'

'Oh come, come. Surely you didn't imagine I lived by bread alone?'

Lydia looked at David and the Bensons, who all seemed as nonplussed as she was. She looked back at Underwood and nodded. 'Actually, yes.'

Underwood merely chuckled.

'So you drink champagne?' said David.

'When the occasion demands, yes.'

'Anything else?'

'Everything else, but in moderation of course; a gentleman never exceeds his limits. Shall we find a table?' He looked around the pub and pointed out a vacant booth against the far wall. He led the way, and soon they were all seated.

'So what about food?' said Lydia. 'Do you eat things like eggs? Cheese?'

'Cakes? Pies?' added Gerald.

Underwood sighed. 'Ah, sadly, such simple pleasures as the pie are lost to me, Gerald. I'm afraid I can't digest solids. I get all the nourishment I need from my *usual tipple.*'

Michelle came over with a tray laden with four champagne flutes, a coke, and a bottle of champagne nestling in an ice bucket wrapped with a white tea towel. 'Here we are.' She set down the tray on their table. 'So,' she said, addressing Underwood. 'You must be Lydia's brother?'

Underwood smiled. 'No. That would be my friend here,' he nodded to David who was tucked into the corner opposite him and obscured from her view by Gerald.

David leaned forward and held up a hand. 'Hi.'

'Oh. Hello.' Then Michelle winced in sympathy at David's bruised features. 'You look like you've been in a spot of bother, recently. Are you all right?'

'Yeah, thanks. You should see the other bloke.'

'Yes,' said Underwood. 'I daresay he must look a frightful mess.'

Lydia, who sat beside Underwood, held out a hand, loosely indicating David. 'I'm sorry, Michelle. This is my brother, David, and this,' she turned to Underwood, 'is my lor – '

'Daniel,' Underwood interrupted, standing. 'Daniel Underwood, at your service.' He reached over Lydia to take Michelle's hand. She gave it to him, expecting a shake. But instead, Underwood raised it to his lips and kissed it lightly. For a moment, Michelle could only gape in surprise. Then Underwood looked up at her and smiled. 'I take it I have the pleasure of addressing Michelle?'

Michelle laughed. 'Oh my God. Blimey, he's a charmer, in'e Lydia?'

Lydia, who found herself hunched beneath the bridge of their joined hands, tried to smile pleasantly. 'Yes. He's ... er ... a friend of the family.'

'Yes,' said Underwood. 'An old friend.'

'Well, it's a pleasure to meet you, Daniel,' said Michelle.

Unnoticed by all, Underwood breathed in Michelle's personal scent from the back of her hand, savouring it as if it were the bouquet of a fine wine. He looked into her eyes and gave her his most winning smile. 'Oh no, Michelle. The pleasure is all mine.'

A few minutes earlier, at about the same time that Underwood entered the pub, Keith Mullins frowned as he sucked the last dregs of warm beer from his bottle of San Miguel. He sat slouched on the sofa with several other empty beer bottles clustered on the coffee table between him and the TV.

'Bollocks,' he grumbled, leaning forward to put the bottle with the other empties. Suddenly, from the television, an excited change came into the sports commentator's tone. Keith looked up, tensing at the sight of an Arsenal player, the ball at his feet, ploughing down the pitch towards the West Ham goal.

'No!' shouted Keith. 'No!'

The player took a shot at the goal, the ball flying through the air.

'Yes!' shouted the sports commentator. 'Yes! It's a goal!'

'Noooooo!' Keith sank back with his hands over his face to block out the sight of the jubilant Arsenal fans.

Perry, their tiny, mongrel dog, yapped, joining in with the excitement.

'Oh, shut up, you twat!' Keith flung a cushion half-heartedly at the dog, who dodged it, then yapped some more. Perry had been a stray that had hung around *La Reina* all the time when they had first moved in, and Michelle and Mel had decided to adopt him, seeing as he already seemed to have adopted them. The name Perry came from the Spanish word for tiny dog, *perrito*. Keith believed Perry to be the bizarre result of a union between a dachshund and a frog; the frog accounting for how, when he got excited, Perry would bounce up and down until someone managed to calm him down.

'You're supposed to cheer when we score, not them. Who's side are you on?'

Perry looked at him expectantly with his large, bulging eyes.

Keith shook his head and waved a hand dismissively at the dog as Hodge came back from the bathroom. 'What's up, mate? Arsenal scored again, have they?'

'Yeah. Just my fuckin' luck, innit? First me wife says she wants to fucking leave me, then Arsenal go two up on us.'

'Never mind, mate. You need a beer?'

'We're out.'

'Well, at least that one's easily remedied. I'll go down and get some more from the bar.'

Keith grunted and kicked at the coffee table, sending empty beer bottles toppling and rolling in all directions. 'I wish my fucking life could be so easily fucking remedied.'

Hodge sighed and sat down next to his friend. He muted the TV. 'Don't worry, mate. She'll come around. She's just shocked, is all. I mean, it's natural that she's gonna be a bit upset, isn't it?'

'What? On finding out her old man's a murderer? Yeah, just a bit. Who wouldn't be? But, for fuck's sake, H, I did it for her, didn't I? For us – for the family.'

'I know, mate. And so does she. Give her time. She won't leave you. She loves you too much.'

Keith's face contorted with pain and he turned away, taking a breath and getting control of himself. 'Yeah. You say that, mate. But she wants to, all the same. Said she don't want Mel growing up round a fucking murderer, didn't she?' His chest tightened at the thought of Melanie knowing what he had done. He sniffed. 'She said if she had somewhere to go, she'd be out of here like a fucking shot, back to her parents' house or somewhere.'

'But they're dead, aren't they?'

'Yeah. Thank Christ.' He picked up an empty bottle which looked like it had a decent sip left in it. 'I don't mean thank Christ they're dead, you know. I loved 'em an' all, but you know what I mean, it's just as well they *are* dead because otherwise she'd be gone now, wouldn't she?' His voice broke as it rose on the question. He dropped the bottle and screwed up his face against the tears, again, turning from Hodge to hide his pain.

Hodge put an arm over Keith's shoulders. 'I know, mate. I know.'

Keith sniffed and wiped at his eyes. 'But that's – that's all right. They're dead, their house is sold and there's nowhere for her to go, other than her sister's – and she fucking hates her, so that's not gonna happen.'

Hodge patted him on the back and withdrew his arm. 'Well, that's handy then, so the two of you will be able to work it out.'

'Yeah, well, you say that, but she could always buy somewhere, couldn't she? She owns half this place, not just the property but the business an' all. If she wanted to sell, she'll have plenty of money, mate. She could go anywhere she wanted.'

'But you said this morning you didn't think she'd do that, remember?'

'Yeah, but she's thinking about it, H. She's only just found out about the murder. Question is, will she be able to live with it? And me, with it, together like, you know?'

'I think so, yeah. I just can't see her breaking up the family over what's done and in the past.'

Keith stared blankly at the TV. 'Can't you? I can. It's not like the time we was selling a bit of gear is it, not even like I've been shagging another bird. I'm a stupid fucking bastard what's put all our lives in danger. And she's right to wanna leave me. *I'd* wanna leave me! But I just ... ' He turned to Hodge and his face looked frightened. 'I don't want her to, mate. I can't bear the thought of losing her. It makes me feel sick – like really pukin' up sick, you know?'

Hodge nodded. He considered for a moment, then said, 'What if you sold up and moved on together? Maybe went back to England?'

Keith shook his head. 'No. That's the worst thing we could do. You sell up, you put the property on the market – it becomes visible, dunnit? *We* become visible. That's just the sort of thing old Sergei and his boys are gonna be looking for: British pubs and bars suddenly up for sale. It's like setting off a smoke flare, and I said that to Chelle. That's the only reason why I think she's not rushing into selling her half right now.'

Hodge noticed a West Ham player making a run for Arsenal's goal. He picked up the remote and flicked on the sound just in time for the commentator to scream, "He scores!". Hodge turned to Keith. 'Two – one, mate. Things are beginning to look up.'

Keith smiled weakly. 'Yeah.'

Onscreen, the referee blew the half-time whistle. Hodge started to rise. 'I'll go down and get those beers.'

'No,' said Keith, staying him with a hand and getting to his feet. 'I'll go, I should put me face about downstairs. It's a Friday night, after all.'

'But ...' Hodge looked doubtful. 'No offence like, Keith, but, you don't look exactly businesslike: you're unshaven, your eyes are bloodshot, and you stink of alcohol.'

Keith gave an amused snort. 'That's all right, mate. It's Friday night at *La Reina*. I'll fit right in.'

A few moments later, Keith entered the pub to see Michelle's hand being slobbered over by some tall, dark, handsome wanker he'd never seen before. He stopped and stared. Jesus Christ, she looked like the cat getting the cream. He gritted his teeth and tried to relax. He crossed stiffly to the bar, trying to act as casual as possible, nodding to customers and exchanging greetings on the way. He went behind the bar and over to where Damo and Giles were both looking over at Michelle and her new friend.

'All right, Keith? How's it going?' said Damo. 'What's the score?'

'Fucking one-nil to Michelle by the look of things. Who's that wanker in the black?'

'Some friend of Lydia Flinch, apparently. Giles here was sitting nearby when they came in.'

Keith turned to Giles. 'All right, Giles. Who's this wanker sucking my wife's hand?'

'I dunno,' said Giles. 'But Lydia called him "My Lord" and was all airs and graces round him. He came in about five minutes ago with her and another bloke who looks like he just done three rounds with Mike Tyson.'

'My Lord?' said Keith. 'What, like Little Lord Fauntleroy?'

'Yeah. Maybe he's one of the nobility.'

'You mean the no-*ability*. Unless you count quaffing champagne and hunting foxes. Useless bastards.'

'Well, he certainly seems to be getting along with your wife,' said Damo.

Keith said nothing and watched as Michelle rose, laughing, giving the group a little wave as she left them. On seeing Keith, her smile fell. She walked over.

'Friends of Lydia's?' Keith asked.

'Yes,' said Michelle, coming behind the bar and reaching for a champagne flute. 'Her brother and a friend of the family.'

Keith leaned in close to her so no one else could hear. 'Who's the brother? The bloke putting a spit-shine on your knuckles, or the other one?'

Michelle smiled. 'The other one.' She turned to Damo. 'Can you manage on your own for a while, Damo?'

Damo shrugged. 'Sure, no bother.'

'Why?' asked Keith.

Michelle waggled the champagne flute at him. 'Because Daniel has invited me to join them for a drink.' She turned on her heel and walked away to rejoin the Flinch table.

Damo stepped up to Keith, taking him lightly by the elbow and whispering, 'She's only winding you up, mate. Just ignore it.'

Keith nodded and turned back to the bar where Giles and a couple of other customers were watching him. He laughed, 'That's my Chelle. The hostess with the mostest, eh?' The comment was received with smiles and nods of acknowledgement. Keith turned to Damo, the smile on his lips that was at odds with the look in his eyes. 'You're right, mate. Sod her. I came down for some beers and that's what I'm getting.' He opened the beer fridge and took out four San Miguel. 'Stick 'em on the tab, will you? I'm going back upstairs.'

Damo and Giles watched Keith go, his stiff air of nonchalance noticeably stiffer than it had been when he first came over. Once he was well out of earshot, Giles asked, 'Is there some kind of problem with Keith and Michelle? Or is old Keith just really badly constipated?'

'Ahh, don't ask, Giles.' Damo looked over to where Underwood was pouring champagne into the glass Michelle held out to him. 'But either way, if Little Lord Fauntleroy over there keeps that up, there's gonna be a real shitstorm coming.'

3

MIGUEL WAS WALKING THROUGH ALMACENA on his way to
La Reina de Corazones. He checked his appearance every now and again in
the darkened shop windows. He liked what he saw. He'd dressed in black
trousers and a blue short-sleeved shirt, open at the neck to reveal his
unadorned gold chain, bright against the deep tan of his skin. Lydia would
like it, she'd told him "smart-casual" over the phone and she generally
approved of his taste. He smiled, remembering – as he often did – the
aimless confusion that had been his life before he had first met her two
years ago. He'd been a lowly clerk in Malaga department store, living with
his parents who were forever on at him to find a nice girl to marry so they
could have grandchildren.

But Miguel didn't like nice girls.

Unbeknown to his parents, Miguel was possessed of a ravenous sexual
appetite that didn't confine itself to just women. He'd go out on Friday
night and not return until the small hours of Monday morning, spending
the hours in between trawling bars and parties in a restless quest for
sexual fulfillment. He'd fuel these weekend binges with whatever drugs he
could lay his hands on; indeed, the size of a potential lover's drug stash
would often influence the degree of Miguel's attraction to them.

However, despite these meaningless thrills, he would still wake up at
his parents' house on Monday mornings in the single bed he'd slept in
since he was a child, with a sad, hollow feeling within himself. He'd
wondered if it was God that he was missing – which was certainly what
the Catholic teachings of his childhood would have had him believe – but
he knew it wasn't; he'd been an atheist for years and thought all religion
utterly laughable. He'd also wondered if it was the need for a child, if
perhaps he should do as his parents' urged and find a woman to start a
family with, but the thought caused a genuine revulsion in him that he felt
might be what the doctors call a "panic attack". He'd ultimately concluded
that the emptiness in his soul was just a symptom of mortal existence, and
since he'd been unable to fathom that void, he continued to wad and
cram it with his weekend debaucheries, in the hope that one day he'd find
a more permanent solution, which eventually, he did.

He met Lydia.

He couldn't remember how he had come to be at the party. All he could remember of that night were the events that featured Lydia. She had told him later that the party's host was a Satanist that she knew through a particular society that she was a member of (the Sect, he later learned). Many of the guests at the party were naked or in states of partial undress, wandering in out of different rooms in which different pleasures were being indulged. Miguel had introduced himself to Lydia not verbally, but by touch, finding her among a number of anonymous writhing bodies in the semi-darkness of one of those rooms. He'd gone into that room as he had into all the others; with the excitement of not knowing what he'd find and hoping to be surprised.

He was.

The room he'd come into was called the Red Room. He'd assumed at first that was because what little light there was in the room was red. Even when his tongue ran over Lydia's body, tasting something sweet and coppery, he still didn't make a connection. It wasn't until Lydia had guided him to where a man lay blindfolded at the centre of the orgy, that he realised he was in a room devoted to blood-letting. The blindfolded man was bleeding from small cuts all over his body. But he was enjoying it, he had a raging hard-on which one woman was teasing while everyone else was licking and sucking at his wounds.

Miguel's first reaction had been one of horror: he'd tried to move away but Lydia, rising from the man's legs with blood on her lips pulled his mouth to hers and kissed him hard, while at the same time reaching in-between his legs, her fingers slippery with blood. Something had happened to Miguel then – in more ways than one. Looking back, he now knew that it was in that moment that had found his religion, his family, his very meaning in life. He had become complete.

When she released him, he noticed minders step from the shadows behind the blindfolded man. They reached down to him and helped him to his feet, ignoring his weak objections and the hands that reached for his body as they led him away. But he was soon forgotten, as new flesh was led in to replace him. This time it was a woman who was led into the room. She was also blindfolded and already cut and bleeding. As she lay down at the centre of the group, Lydia took Miguel's face in her hands and eased him towards the woman. Miguel made no resistance, allowing Lydia to draw his lips to a small cut on one of the woman's legs. For a moment he hesitated, but the excitement in the bodies that writhed around him was contagious. He licked at an untouched rivulet of blood, his tongue at first cautious, but soon eager. The woman moaned, not only at the touch of his tongue, but at that of all the mouths now upon her. Then Lydia's hand was between his legs again, leading him away to the edge of the group where she guided him into her.

He hadn't lasted long; he'd been too excited. Unsatisfied, Lydia had moved away from him back to the group. But he'd gone after her, anxious to please her, trying to pleasure her as she sought for satisfaction elsewhere. She'd accepted his caresses, though she didn't look at him again, lost as she was to other delights. But he was happy.

He was in love.

Now he felt a tingle in his loins at the memory and forced himself to move on in his thoughts; he didn't want to go into *La Reina* in these loose slacks with a hard-on.

When the Red Room orgy was over, he had approached her. She had been with Beltran, whom she had introduced as her lover. She'd laughed at Miguel's expression of surprise on learning that Beltran had been in the Red Room at the same time as them. Beltran had grinned at him and placed a hand on Lydia's thigh – a gesture Miguel mistook as an invitation; when he reached to lay a hand on her other thigh, Lydia slapped it away. Again, his surprise was greeted with amusement, this time from both of them. Lydia had then whispered something to Beltran who had glanced at Miguel and nodded. Then Lydia had asked Miguel for his phone number; maybe they would call him sometime. He had given it to her. A week later, she called. And that was how it had begun.

He had never minded sharing her with Beltran, nor that they used him merely as an adjunct to their pleasure. Quite the opposite in fact – he loved it. He was her willing slave, and once he had won her trust, she rewarded him with a job as her assistant. He worked whatever hours she dictated and was at her call day and night. She had gradually taken him into her confidence, and he had later learned of the Sect, and how she was devoted to a vampire – not like the sparkly variety in those teenage movies, but a real one.

Miguel's loyalty hadn't flickered for a moment. She had then admitted him into the Sect. She also moved him to a house in Almacena, the town where, in the year leading up to Underwood's resurrection, she had increasingly based her business operation so that she could be near Casa Underwood.

It was only a matter of time before he was asked to join the Black Circle. Lydia had asked him how he would feel about becoming a vampire himself, about the necessity of killing innocents night after night in order to survive.

He had told her, truthfully, that he would enjoy it.

Would he commit murder, then?

He would. For her, he would do anything.

His initiation into the Black Circle required him to cut the throat of a prostitute and to then drink her blood. He'd been afraid, but Lydia had helped him, guiding his shaking hands with her own. Once it was done, she had loved him. And so she always had done ever since whenever they took a victim. But now Underwood was risen; would there be any more victims? And Beltran was dead – which was sad, but perhaps better for Miguel.

He started from his reverie as a shrill electric horn sounded in the street behind him and someone shouted his name. He turned as two young people on a moped drove past, the girl on the back waving to him, her crash helmet in her hand rather on than on her head, probably so everyone could recognise her, as he did now. It was Maria, one of a group of schoolgirls who came into the office to flirt with him whenever Lydia wasn't around. He waved back as the bike, its muffler removed to make it extra noisy, screamed away up the road. He wondered if he could have her; if he could shut her into the shop with him one day and coerce her to drop her devoted Catholic pants for him? He laughed at the pathetic sin of it. How would her god ever forgive her?

He was standing on the pavement outside *La Reina*. He took a last lingering look at Maria's bottom as it receded into the distance through a ribbon of blue exhaust, and turned onto the terrace.

Lydia wore a strained smile as Underwood and Michelle continued their conversation across her. She glanced at David, who was paying attention to the exchange but making no contribution. The Bensons were chipping in here and there, but to Lydia's increasing disbelief, the conversation mainly consisted of Michelle detailing the sparkling facets of her leaden world to Underwood. Underwood himself seemed genuinely interested in the trollop's witterings and listened with fascinated interest to her every word. Miguel's entering the bar came to her as a welcome relief. She caught his eye and indicated to him to stay there. Then she nudged

Cynthia's leg under the table. Cynthia looked at her questioningly. 'Do you fancy a ciggie, Cyn?' said Lydia with a look that said she was insisting rather than asking.

'Er, yes, that would be nice.'

Lydia looked at Gerald. 'Gerald?'

'Hmm? Oh, yes, of course.'

As they got up to go, Michelle said, 'Oh, you don't have to go outside if you don't want to, you can smoke in here, as long as there aren't any kiddies around.'

'Oh, but there *are* kiddies around, Michelle,' said Lydia, indicating the two youngsters who were still dashing to-and-fro around their parents' tables.

'Yeah, but they're not with you, are they?' said Michelle. 'All the bars round here ignore the smoking ban. And if we go and start enforcing it, all our customers'll just go somewhere else, won't they? So ... ' she winked knowingly at Lydia, 'don't worry about it, eh?'

'Oh, but I do worry about it, Michelle,' said Lydia. 'I can't bear to think how my second-hand smoke might be poisoning those sweet, innocent young lungs. We'll go outside.'

'Ahh, isn't she lovely?' said Michelle to David. 'She's so thoughtful, isn't she?'

David watched as Lydia walked away towards the door where he saw Miguel waiting for her. Lydia spoke briefly to him before they and the Bensons went outside. 'Oh yes, she's a real angel.'

The angelic one and her friends found a table on the patio and sat down. 'What the fuck is that old tart playing at?' hissed Lydia.

'Who, Michelle?' said Cynthia.

'Yes, Michelle. She's like a bitch in heat in there.'

'Well it's hardly surprising, His Lordship *is* very handsome, and charming too.'

'So bloody what? She's married, isn't she? I know Keith isn't exactly Brad Pitt, but he's still her husband.' Lydia lit a cigarette and inhaled noisily.

'Oh, don't be so hard on the poor girl, Lydia,' said Gerald. 'She's just being the charming hostess. She's very friendly with all her customers. I've no doubt it's one of the reasons why this place is so popular.'

Lydia ignored the defence. 'How does she know he's not with me? I mean, he might be my boyfriend, mightn't he?'

'Hardly,' said Cynthia.

Lydia shot her an indignant look.

Cynthia, realising her offence, explained, 'I mean, Michelle's used to seeing you with Beltran. She's not to know the poor man's no longer with us, now is she?' Lydia looked away and Cynthia reached over and took her hand. 'I'm sorry, darling, I didn't mean to remind you of that.'

Lydia took her hand back and fiddled momentarily with her hair. 'That's all right, I'm okay. He's gone and, well, we just have to get used to that, don't we?'

'Yes,' said Gerald. 'Of course, this is the first time we've all been together since Belly's death, isn't it? I have to say, that whole thing came as a hell of a shock. I thought – we all thought – including Beltran, that, well ...'

'He'd be coming back?' said Lydia.

'Yes.'

Lydia nodded. 'I know.'

'I'm so sorry, Lydia,' said Cynthia. 'It was an awful way to find out that that wasn't the case.'

Miguel, who was sitting next to Lydia, put an arm around her shoulder, but she shrugged it off. 'Oh, for God's sake, Miguel, stop it. I'm not a little girl.'

'I know, but I thought perhaps you needed consolation.'

'Oh don't worry, luvvie, I have all the consolation I need.'

Miguel seemed surprised. 'You do?'

Lydia drew on her cigarette. 'Oh yes. You know, we may have been amiss in thinking we'd come back just-like-that if we were bitten by a vampire, but we weren't entirely wrong; there were other theories, too, remember?' Everyone around the table looked at Lydia as if she had just emitted a low-level burst of static electricity. She smiled. 'I had His Lordship on my own for a while the other night, while David was off puking his guts up in a toilet somewhere, and we were talking about the whole bite-and-coming-back thing.'

'What did he say?' asked Cynthia.

'Quite simply, he said it doesn't work that way. Vampirism isn't spread like a cold sore. Instead, it's something he *bestows*.'

'Ahhhh,' said Cynthia. 'The Dark Gift, as Anne Rice calls it.'

Lydia nodded again. 'That's my guess, yes. He says he bestows it rarely, because otherwise the world would be overrun with vampires in no time.'

'Well, that makes sense,' said Gerald. 'Every victim would want their nearest and dearest with them, just as we do.' He laid a hand on Cynthia's, and she squeezed it warmly in reply.

'Yes,' said Lydia. 'God, can you imagine it getting loose in the lower classes? All those chavs running around biting each other willy-nilly? They'd want their mums, their dads, their friends. I wouldn't be surprised if they even started biting their sodding muscle dogs as well.'

'Oh my God,' said Cynthia. 'It's too ghastly to contemplate. Such people are only fit for food.'

'Hear hear,' said Lydia. 'And that's exactly what they will be, if I get my way.'

'Hello,' said Gerald. 'Sounds like somebody has a plan, eh?'

'Oh I do, Gerald.' Lydia leaned in closer to the centre of the table and the others moved in to meet her. 'Let's be honest, shall we? We of the Black Circle are devoted to Underwood for one thing and one thing only – the promise of immortality; to become a vampire like him.'

'To walk the night, together, forever – for all eternity,' said Miguel.

'Yes, exactly,' said Lydia. 'Anyway, it seems that he isn't just going to dish that out to us.'

'No,' said Gerald.

'And we knew that that was a possibility, which is why we always had the other plan to fall back on.'

'*You* becoming guardian?' said Cynthia.

'Yes,' said Lydia. 'I should, by becoming his guardian, have been able to seduce Underwood. He would then, quite naturally, have fallen in love with me and wanted to make me a vampire like himself. And then I would have been able to pass the gift on to you.'

'Yes,' said Gerald. 'But that's all rather in the bin, now, isn't it?'

'Thanks to David, yes. But all that really means is that I now have to accelerate things; win Underwood's affections not over time, but right now, before he and David drive off into the moonrise together and leave us behind to wither and die with the rest of the plebs.'

'How are you going to do that?' asked Cynthia. 'I mean, without just throwing yourself at him?'

Lydia exhaled the last of her cigarette and stubbed it out in the ashtray. 'I started putting out signals last night: nothing too obvious, of course, just giving him a taste, so to speak. And he likes me, I know he does. It's just a matter of time before he succumbs to my charms completely.' She sat back, looking at their expressions for confirmation of the fact and not finding it. She frowned. 'I mean, I'm hot, aren't I? He'd have to be gay not to think so.'

'Oh, gosh, yes,' said Gerald.

'Anyone, of any sex, would be unable to resist you if you made yourself available to them, darling,' said Cynthia. 'I know I certainly couldn't.'

'Nor me,' said Miguel. 'You are a goddess, Lydia.'

Lydia basked momentarily. 'Thank you, you're all very sweet.' Then her expression hardened. 'But then *this* happens,' she cocked her thumb in the direction of the pub. 'Fucking Nell Gwynne comes fluttering over, all tinkling laughter and tight jeans. Did you see the way she walked to the bar to get herself a glass? Her arse was positively *winking* at him.'

Gerald smiled at the memory. 'Yes, it was rather, wasn't it?'

Cynthia slapped Gerald's hand before turning back to Lydia. 'Oh, but she doesn't mean anything by it, Lydia. She's married. She has a daughter, for God's sake.'

'That's neither here nor there, Cynthia. I've got just a couple of nights to seduce that man. And if I don't, he'll be gone. Then we'll be left behind to shrivel up like human prunes, watching as one by one we drop off the bloody perch.'

'Well if that's the case, it's all very simple, isn't it?' said Gerald. 'We just drink up here and take him on to some other place where Michelle's arse can't wink at him.'

'Yes,' said Lydia. 'We'll go back inside and tell His Lordship we're hungry and want to go on to the restaurant. He won't argue with that, if there's one thing he understands, it's hunger.'

'Let's just hope *you're* what he's hungry for, eh?' said Gerald.

'Oh he will be, Gerald,' said Lydia, flicking her hair over her shoulder. 'He will be.'

When Lydia and her friends went outside, Underwood asked David to go to the bar and order another bottle of champagne. David did so, and as he waited to catch Damo's eye, he became aware that the man sitting at the bar beside him was watching him. He turned to face him. The man, Giles, acknowledged him with a nod. 'Alright?'

David nodded in reply. 'Yeah. You?'

'Yeah, man.'

'Busy tonight.'

'Always is at weekends, innit? You're Lydia's friends, right?'

'Yeah. I'm her brother. You know Lydia?'

'Yeah. She sold me my house,' Giles extended his hand. 'Giles. Giles Sutton.'

David shook his hand. 'David Flinch.'

Damo came up, drawn by the banknote between David's fingers. 'Howaya. What'll it be?'

David ordered the champagne and, as instructed, asked for an additional glass for Miguel. Damo went off to the far end of the bar to fetch another chilled bottle. Giles leaned closer to David and said in a low voice, 'Word to the wise, Dave: your mate over there? That's the landlady he's getting all pally with, and the landlord's not too happy about it. If your mate knows what's good for him, he'll keep his fingers out of that particular honey pot.'

David glanced back at Underwood and Michelle. They were chatting away amicably enough, but he could see nothing particularly flirtatious in their behaviour. 'Thanks for the tip, Giles. But I wouldn't worry about my friend; he's not that kind of guy.'

'Oh yeah? Gay, is he?'

David raised an eyebrow. 'Well, no. Not that I know of, anyway. What I mean to say is, he's not looking for love.'

'Nor's she, mate. But that's not important, is it? The important thing is what it looks like to the landlord.'

'Well, no disrespect to the man, but if he's gonna get upset about his wife chatting to his customers, he's in the wrong line of work.'

Giles leaned in close again. 'No, it's not like that, man. See, what I reckon is, the landlord and his missus are going through a rough patch right now. Consequently, he's not seeing the world through his usually rose-tinted spectacles. At the moment, they're more like, *green*-tinted, if you know what I'm saying.'

Damo came back with the champagne and glass. David extended the note, but Damo held up a hand. 'Ah no, it's on your bill. Just be sure and pay it before you leave.' Then he turned to serve the next customer.

David picked up the bottle and glass. 'Well, I'll let my friend know what you said, Giles. Thanks.'

'No worries, man. I'd hate to see your mate ending up with a set of bruises like what you've got.'

David smiled. 'Yeah. Sadly, there's not much chance of that.' Then, quickly he added, 'Er, thanks to you. Cheers.'

'Cheers, man. Take it easy.'

As David returned to the table, Underwood was rising. 'Ah, Flinch. Well done. I'm just off to see a man about a dog.'

Michelle got up to let him out. She noticed Lydia and her friends returning and saw that with Miguel's inclusion, there was no longer room for her at the table. Perhaps that was just as well; she'd been away from the bar long enough. 'And I really ought to be getting back to work, as well. Thanks for the drink.'

'Oh dear,' said Underwood. 'Are you sure you can't join us for another?'

'Much as I'd like to, Daniel, I do have other customers. And if they think I'm spending too much time over here with you boys, they'll start getting jealous.' She turned and went back to the bar. Underwood watched her go with an appreciative eye.

Lydia saw this and stepped in to bisect his view. 'I shall have to introduce you to Michelle's husband and child some evening, My Lord.'

Underwood smiled. 'Oh? That would be lovely.' He glanced around, looking for the toilets. 'I say, Lydia, where's the, er ... ?'

Lydia pointed to a far corner. 'Just over there, My Lord.'

'Thanks.'

Underwood left them and Lydia slid into the booth alongside Cynthia. She looked at David who was still standing. 'Aren't you going to join us?'

'Not right now, I'm gonna go out for a fag. I'll see you in a bit.' He turned and headed for the front door.

No one had noticed Keith, who, on his way back to the apartment, had been accosted by a couple of regulars and roped into a conversation. He'd positioned himself so he could keep an eye on Michelle over the shoulder of one of the men he was talking to, and now, as he saw Underwood crossing the floor, he cheerfully disengaged himself from the conversation and followed Underwood into the gents' toilet. As he entered, he saw Underwood was already at the urinals. Keith turned to the sinks opposite and casually began to wash his hands, watching Underwood in the mirror as he did so. When Underwood zipped up and turned around, Keith dropped his eyes. Underwood stepped up to the next sink and began to wash his hands. Keith looked up and spoke to Underwood's reflection in the mirror. 'Nice suit you got there.'

'Thank you,' said Underwood with a smile.

Keith sniffed. 'You, er, visiting town, are you?'

'Well, sort of. I'm staying with the Flinches. Do you know the Flinches ... er ?'

'Keith. Keith Mullins. I'm the landlord here. I think you met my wife earlier.'

'Oh, you're Michelle's husband? How nice to meet you. My name's Underwood.' With an air of contempt, Keith flicked water from his hands, droplets splashing onto Underwood's suit. If Underwood sensed any threat, he gave no indication of it. 'Lovely woman, your wife. You're a lucky man.'

Keith suddenly turned from the mirror to raise a dripping finger at Underwood's ear. 'Yeah? Well, just you keep away from her, do you hear me? I'm all the Lord La-Di-Da she needs, and she don't need any more from the likes of you.'

Underwood turned to him with a look of mild surprise. 'Really, Keith. There's nothing to get excited about. We were only chatting.'

'Well I don't like you fucking chatting, do I. So just leave it out, all right?'

Underwood shook water from his hands and a smile crept onto his face. 'You seem rather tense, Keith.'

'*Tense?* Too right I'm fucking tense. And so will you be if you ain't careful, mate – tense as a fucking ambulance!'

Underwood chuckled. 'Oh dear, well, we wouldn't want that, would we?'

'No, you fucking wouldn't. So just stay away from her, right? She's not been herself lately. She's been under a lot of pressure.'

'Oh? From whom?'

Keith gritted his teeth and reasserted his dripping digit towards Underwood's nose. 'You've been warned, Underwood. If you know what's good for you, you'll take your drinking business elsewhere. Do you understand me?'

'Perfectly.'

'Good.' Keith wiped his hands on his t-shirt and walked out of the bathroom without another word.

Underwood looked around for a towel. There was an automatic hand dryer mounted on the wall and he walked over to it, mystified. He followed the instructions written on the front and held his hands under the dryer. When warm air blasted onto his hands, he laughed. 'Well, well, well. What an interesting development.'

A few moments later Underwood returned to his table. On seeing David outside smoking a cigarette, he decided that he would join him. 'I say,' he said to Lydia and her friends. 'Could anybody lend me a fag?'

Cynthia held up her packet of Moore Menthol. 'Do you mind menthols, My Lord?'

'I don't believe I've ever had the pleasure,' Underwood took a cigarette. 'My, that's a big one, even by today's lengthy standards. Thank you, Cynthia.' He went outside and joined David. 'Hallo Flinch, do you have a light?' David took out his lighter and Underwood bent to the flame. He inhaled then he stood back and inspected the cigarette. 'Mmmm, mentholated cigarettes. How delightfully ... cool.'

David smiled. 'Only with the blue rinse set, My Lord.'

'The what?'

'Old ladies, Milord.'

Underwood raised his eyebrows. 'Really? You mean, you wouldn't choose to smoke one yourself?'

'Not since I was a kid, sir. They were like training fags.'

'Before you moved on to the real thing, eh?' He grinned. 'You were obviously quite the tough nut.'

'Yeah.' David dropped the butt of his cigarette and ground it underfoot. 'Listen, sir. I was talking to a bloke at the bar, and he told me you'd be well advised to keep a distance from Michelle. Apparently she and her husband are having some problems at the moment and he's the jealous type.'

'Oh, I know, I've just been warned off by the man himself. Charming fellow, though a little worse for the beer, I fancy.'

'Oh? What did he say?'

'Oh, the usual.' Underwood wagged his finger at David and mimicked Keith's voice, "You keep away from my wife. Understand?"

'So, what did you say?'

'I said I understood him perfectly.'

David laughed and shook his head. 'What an idiot. As if *you'd* be interested in his wife.'

'Oh, I don't know, said Underwood, inspecting his fingernails. 'She is very pretty. And she has a certain earthy charm, don't you think?'

'Really? You're not serious?

'I beg your pardon?'

'You're not saying you find *Michelle* attractive, are you?'

Underwood frowned. 'Well, why on Earth wouldn't I? Don't you?'

'No! She's ... well, she's married for one thing. And she's got a kid.'

'Oh. Well, that puts a whole new complexion on things, doesn't it?'

'Does it?'

'Oh yes,' said Underwood with mock severity. 'Some things are quite beyond the pale, eh? Finding married mothers attractive? Unthinkable!'

'What? You really think that?'

'Of course not, Flinch. Don't be such an old maid.'

'I'm not being an old maid, sir. I just don't like the idea of *you*, being attracted to *her.*'

Underwood laughed. 'Oh pooh, Flinch. You think I'm going to devour the poor woman, is that it?' Some customers looked over at them and Underwood checked his volume. 'Look here,' he said more quietly. 'I'll make a deal with you, if only to put your mind at ease. From tomorrow onwards, you can consider yourself my personal chef, which is to say that you can prepare my meals your way. I shall restrict my feeding solely to willing donors, just so long as you are able to procure them. How does that sound?'

'Really? You mean that?'

'I do. But remember, one doesn't kill only for food; one also kills in self defence, and for our arrangement to work, you have to allow that as an exception.'

'Sure,' David nodded. 'But with a bit of luck, if we go about getting your food in a humane manner, you won't need to resort to self-defence because no-one's gonna be trying to hurt you.'

'Quite. So, you agree then? You'll serve as my man without any more nonsense, provided I restrict my feeding to willing donors?' He extended his hand.

David considered the hand for a moment, then shook it. 'I do, My Lord.'

'Capital. I knew we could work this out. You're a good man, Flinch, just like your forefathers.'

'Thank you, sir. So, where are you planning on going in the immediate future? I'll need to work out some kind of donor schedule before we start to travel. Actually, come to think of it, I'll need to get a list of Sect members, where they are and how to contact them. I know Lydia has a list, so I'm sure John must have one on his computer somewhere.'

'Oh? A computer, eh? That's very impressive.'

David laughed. 'No, no not really, sir. Computers are pretty common these days.'

'Oh. Well, that's very interesting. Anyway, I wouldn't worry too much about journey arrangements at the moment, Flinch. I thought we might stick around here for a bit.'

David frowned, surprised. 'Eh? Stick around here?'

'Yes.'

'But ... Why?'

'*Why?*' Underwood was amazed. 'My dear chap, surely you're aware that tomorrow night is Eighties Night? Or maybe you were at the bar when Michelle was telling us about that?'

'I must have been.'

Underwood pointed at a poster tacked to the window. 'Well, there you are. Starts at ten. I must say, I'm rather looking forward to it. I quite liked that tape thingy of yours you were playing in the car earlier.'

'But, sir ... it's an eighties disco ... in a pub. It's bound to be crap.'

'Disco? What's a disco?'

'A dance, sir.'

'Ah, just as I thought. So, how then can a dance possibly be *crap* – as you so pleasantly put it?'

'Oh, there are ways, Milord.'

'Nonsense, Flinch. It'll be cracking fun; just the thing to cheer you up, eh?'

'But, what about the landlord?'

'Oh don't worry about him, he'll be fine. I'm sure he's a decent sort underneath. He'll probably wake up tomorrow feeling dreadful about the way he spoke to me earlier.'

'But – '

'No buts, Flinch. Buts are just pesky impediments to progress. Never say but.'

'But – '

'There you go again. Stop it.'

'But – you can't say, "don't say but". Everyone says but sometimes, even you.'

'Ahh yes, Flinch. But my but is different – your but is a lowly servant's but, while my but, my but is assured, confident. My but ... ' he stopped. David was smirking at him in a peculiar manner, like he was suppressing an urge to laugh.

'What is it, Flinch? What's the matter with you?'

David cleared his throat and tried to regain his composure. 'Sorry sir, it's just you were talking about your but. About how your but is different.'

'My but is different.'

David's restrained smile widened. He covered his mouth and looked aside.

Underwood rolled his eyes. 'Oh, I remember now. It's because "butt" is one of the numerous American words for "arse", isn't it?'

David nodded, and when he spoke, a small laugh escaped him. 'Yes, sir. I'm sorry, sir. It's childish of me.'

'Yes, it is rather,' said Underwood. Then he laughed as a thought occurred to him. 'I was going to say something about my but paying the wages around here, though it's probably just as well I stopped when I did.' David laughed aloud, and Underwood found himself laughing along with him.

At that moment, Lydia came out of the pub. She looked from one to the other of them and smiled, confused. 'What are you two laughing at?'

Underwood stopped laughing and turned to Lydia. With a perfectly straight face he said, 'My but, apparently.'

This sent David into a fresh fit of snorts and giggles, and the look of utter bewilderment on Lydia's face only made him worse.

'I don't understand,' she said.

'Schoolboy humour, Lydia,' said Underwood. 'Normally I wouldn't approve, but poor Flinch here has had a rough few days, and laughter is, I'm told, the best medicine.'

'Oh. Well, that's nice, then. We, er, we were going to get something to eat. Is that all right with you two?'

'Of course,' Underwood patted David on the back. 'Come along, Flinch, dinner time. We're going to a restaurant. And er,' he said to Lydia, 'don't worry about the bill, it's on me.'

'Oh, but, My Lord – '

'No, no.' said Underwood. 'I've heard quite enough buts for one night.'

David, who had just managed to regain a straight face, lost it again, sniggering uncontrollably and closing his eyes to Underwood's "who me?" expression. Lydia looked at her brother as if he were insane, for a moment. Then she realised what was supposedly funny. 'Oh, that was some sort of bottom reference, wasn't it?'

Underwood spread his hands innocently.

Lydia gave David a pitying look, shook her head, and went back inside.

4

THE FOLLOWING EVENING, David sat in John's office uploading files to his email account from the data disc John had given him. He wanted a back-up of the information that he would be able to access from anywhere in the world where he might find himself with Underwood in future – although from what Underwood had been saying last night, it was now looking like they were going to be here in Almacena for a while.

David rubbed his eyes and took a sip of coffee. It had grown cold, but he didn't mind. Last night, after the meal at the restaurant, he, Lydia and Underwood had returned home. The mood in the car had been cheerful, even fun, with conversation mainly focusing on world developments over the last fifty years. Then they had come home to the uncomfortable reality of Gavin; his cooling corpse waiting for them on the sofa where they had left him. David looked at Lydia and asked her whether she wanted to lift the hands or the feet. Lydia, who had been more than a little tipsy, immediately insisted she was too tired and that David should take care of the problem by himself since through his trying to kill Underwood he was the cause of it. A blazing row had ensued between them which was settled by Underwood saying that he and David would bury the body and that Lydia should go to bed. It was obvious from the look on Lydia's face that this wasn't the outcome she had hoped for. David suspected that she'd wanted to be alone with Underwood so she could suck up to him somehow, but the vampire had been adamant. Begrudgingly, she had gone to bed. Once she had gone, Underwood had lifted had the corpse as if it weighed no more than a mannequin and taken it outside.

'Right then, Flinch,' he said at the car, the body still in his arms. 'Where do you bury 'em?'

David remembered Gavin as he had been in the cellar: terrified, weak, begging for his life; then the pictures of him in Malaga airport, a photocopy of a family snapshot, smiling, and above it the words DESAPARECIDO / MISSING. Someone had loved him, someone who would never know peace again if his body just got dumped in a hole. 'We can't,' he said. 'His family and the police are looking for him.'

'So?'

'So they – his family – they deserve some sort of closure. They need to be able to grieve.'

Underwood snorted. 'What do you suggest? Should we invite them along? Make a proper funeral of it?'

Ana's Fiat was still parked beneath the trees nearby. David pointed to it. 'We remove all number IDs from and car then wreck it somewhere with Gavin inside. Then burn it to hide any evidence.'

'Gavin? Who's he?'

David indicated the body. 'You're holding him.'

'Oh. Sorry, we weren't introduced, er, at least in the conventional sense.' Underwood looked at the Fiat. 'All right, that's certainly more interesting than just burying him. But how will the police know it's him?'

'Dental records, DNA, that sort of stuff.'

'DNA?'

'I'll explain later, Milord.'

They'd taken a can of gasoline from the garage and set off, Underwood in the Citroën, the corpse in the boot, and David following in the Fiat. Underwood led the way out to a bridge over a ravine he had seen while in the form of a bat the previous night. It was about thirty miles away, deep in the middle of the countryside. It was nearly two in the morning and they met no other cars. When they got there, David pointed out the metal railings that ran along either side of the bridge. 'How are we gonna get it to look like he drove it through the railings?'

'Well, I suppose I could drive it through the railings,' said Underwood.

'But you'd go over the edge with the car. You could never jump out in time, it's impossible.'

'Impossible to jump out before it leaves the bridge, yes. But not after.'

'What?'

Underwood flapped his hands at his sides in imitation of bat wings.

'Oh, yeah. The bat thing. I forgot about that.'

They'd splashed gasoline over the back seat of the Fiat, then Underwood had stripped to his shorts and got in behind the wheel.

'But if you're in the driving seat,' said David, 'how's it going to look like Gavin ever was? You can't arrange him there after the crash.'

'Oh, it's all right, Flinch. I've done this sort of thing before. Bring him over and sit him on my lap.'

'*What?*

'Oh do come along, Flinch. You've seen what I can do. As long as I leave a few windows open, I'll be out of here as soon as we're airborne, leaving our friend here to pilot the car down to Earth.'

With a final look around to confirm they were alone, David dragged Gavin's body over, and then he and Underwood had arranged it awkwardly on Underwood's lap. Then Underwood had driven the car about two hundred yards up the road, turned it around, and driven back at full speed towards the centre of the bridge, before turning off and driving straight towards the railings.

David watched open-mouthed as the car smashed through the steel and flew out into empty space. He ran to the railings to see the car falling down through the darkness. Where was Underwood? Was he still in the car? Had he got stuck? Or was he just enjoying the ride? Then, in eerie silence, the interior of the car flashed into flame and smoke poured out from the windows, obscuring the final stage of the car's plunge to where it impacted in an explosion on the dry river bed far below. A ball of flame soared upwards before burning itself out in the oily black smoke that billowed up towards the bridge. David was about to stand back from it when, from within the smoke, almost as if they were a part of it, huge black wings suddenly unfurled. David stepped back as the hot choking cloud hit him, and as he staggered back, he saw the creature that Underwood had now become flash before him through the smoke. In seconds he lost sight of it against the starry sky, but he waited, unconsciously holding his breath in expectation of its return. But it didn't return. David exhaled; a sigh of relief or disappointment, he couldn't say. He picked up Underwood's clothes, got into the Citroën, and headed home.

As he drove, he reflected on what had just happened: he'd disposed of a body, the body of a murdered innocent, and strangely, shockingly perhaps, he felt nothing. No, that wasn't true, he'd felt something, just not what he'd expected to feel. Instead of feeling guilt, pity or anger, he'd felt exhilarated, alive, and not a little awe-struck. Was this what it was like to really be a Flinch? He suppressed an urge to laugh, putting the sudden surge of happiness that bubbled up through him down to a mixture of tiredness and relief at having disposed of the body successfully. Yes, that was what it was: tiredness and relief. It had been a long night. He turned on the music and his eighties tape resumed with The Stranglers' *No Mercy*. It was queerly apt. 'Nice one.'

When he got home, it was to find Underwood reclining on the sofa in his bathrobe, listening to the crackly recording of some old crooner warbling on the gramophone. 'Oh, hallo, Flinch. I was wondering when you'd get home. I've been trying to turn on the television, but I can't seem to locate the knob.'

David picked up the remote control, showed Underwood the power button, and flicked on the TV. He then showed him how to change the channels. 'Aren't you hungry, Milord?'

'No, no,' said Underwood, concentrating on the images flashing across the screen as he thumbed the remote, 'I had a deer on the way home.'

'Really? How was that?'

'Deer? Oh, it's all right. The best thing about deer is they lead one on a merry chase, so when you land 'em, the heart is pounding like billy-o, mad with fear and exertion. Plenty of oxygen in the soup, you know?'

'So, you can live on animals then?'

'Well, I wouldn't say *live* exactly, but one can subsist for a while.'

'So why don't you?'

Underwood stopped flicking through the channels and turned to him. 'Why? Why dine on scrag mutton when you can have the tenderest cuts of lamb?'

'So it's just a preference thing?'

'No. Human blood is necessary, one grows ... strange ... without it. Don't ask me why, no scientist has ever studied us. But over the years I've swapped notes with others and they all agree; you simply can't beat a drop of homo sapien.'

'Others?' David felt a coldness gathering in the pit of his stomach. 'Other vampires?'

'Yes,' said Underwood, returning his attention to the TV.

'There are *other* vampires?' David took a step around, anxious to get a better look at Underwood's face.

'Yes. Or at least there were fifty years ago.'

'Where?'

'Oh, here and there.'

'How many?'

Underwood suddenly pointed at the TV screen. 'Oh look! It's The Three Stooges. How do I turn the sound up?'

'Sir,' said David, stepping between Underwood and the TV. 'Please, tell me, how many other vampires are there?'

'I don't know, Flinch. We don't advertise ourselves in some kind of personal column. We just come across one another from time to time.'

'So what happens when you do?'

'It depends. Sometimes we get along famously, other times not.'

'And when you don't?'

'We usually agree to avoid each other.'

'Usually? What about the other times?'

'Things get ugly.'

'What, you fight?'

'Yes.' Underwood's tone was casual.

'To the death?'

'Yes.'

'So, you must be very ... successful.'

Underwood chuckled. 'Yes, well, let's just say I'm still standing, shall we? Now would you please mind getting out of the way and turning up the volume?'

David stepped aside, his mind racing with the implications of what Underwood had just told him.

Underwood held up the remote. 'I presume the volume knob is on this device somewhere. Would you mind?'

David took the remote. 'I'm sorry, Milord, I'm just having some trouble digesting this information. How come you – I mean vampires – haven't become the dominant species on Earth? I mean, why don't you just all get together and enslave us like cattle?'

'Now why on Earth would we want to do a thing like that, Flinch?'

David's already furrowed brow, furrowed more deeply. 'Well, because you probably could, couldn't you?'

'Oh, I dare say. But we like the world the way it is, old boy. We like human society and we like to move within it; it's fun, filled with pleasures to glut the soul and senses, from the simple to the exotic, the sublime to the ridiculous. We can – and do – have it all. Rarely do we find ourselves in penury or squalor – though I have known some who revel in that sort of thing like pigs in filth – but then not all vampires are as civilized as I am, some of them are, well, animals. But anyway, for the most part, we live – literally in my case – like lords. We have everything we need: money, luxury, the finest food in teeming abundance, and to top it all, our food supply is also our source of pleasure and entertainment. I mean, just think about it for a moment; if humans were to become an enslaved, uneducated cattle, bred only for nourishment, then all human art, science and innovation would grind to a halt. Not only would there be no future Three Stooges or Mozarts, but wouldn't be any more knob-less television sets or CD players on which to enjoy them.'

'Well, surely a vampire society would do the same thing?'

Underwood laughed. 'Spoken like a true urban human: completely ignorant of the ways of the savage beast. And vampires, I'm afraid, do have a tendency to be rather beastly. Like I said, not all vampires are as civilized as I am.'

David said nothing.

'You look surprised, Flinch. Consider this: humanity has gone through thousands of years of barbaric practices to emerge into a series of highly civilized societies, or at least we like to think so. Now, consider if you will, the sudden rise of a vampire society; the savagery and blood-lust of it all. My God, the world would be plunged into a new dark age of unimaginable horror. All this,' he waved a hand around the room, 'would disappear in no time. And I and my other vampire peers would no longer be special, enjoying our privileged existence and doing whatever we please. No, we'd all be in a fight for survival against all kinds of idiots and ruffians with the same sort of powers as we have. It would be hell on Earth.'

David nodded; the argument was as sound as it was frightening. 'Yes.'

'Perhaps we're just being selfish, I don't know, but under the circumstances, I think you can forgive us.'

'So how does it spread then, your species?'

'We pass it on – rarely, though – by a mixture of our bite, and our blood.'

'Your *blood*? You mean, orally? You feed it to the victim?'

'Yes. The bite transmits a sort of virus to the victim. If you drain the victim to death, the virus dies with the host. But if you *don't* kill them, if you have to abandon the victim in mid-feed for some reason, the virus will develop. The victim becomes weak, shivery, hungry, yearning for something it doesn't understand, and that no conventional nourishment can satisfy. This passes after a few days as the person grows stronger and the immune system drives off the infection. A blood transfusion will accelerate the process. Afterwards, once the victim is recovered, everything returns to normal. This, of course, is what happens if the vampire isn't there to satisfy his victim's strange new hunger.'

330

'That being the hunger for the blood of the vampire that's just bitten him?'

'Yes. A drop or two will suffice to complete the virus, but such a small amount will still leave the victim sick and weakened. If you allow the victim to feed on you, drinking as much as you can let them have without weakening yourself, it restores them completely.'

'But not to what they were.'

Underwood smiled. 'No.'

'I see. But what about the containment of the virus? How do you stop other vampires from spreading it?'

'Well, as I say, Flinch, a vampire world would be an unbearable place, and we explain that to our fledglings, impressing upon them the importance of not passing it on unless they are absolutely sure of whom they are passing it on to, and of course, their reasons for doing so.'

'But there must be some mistakes; chaos dictates that shit *will* happen.'

'Yes. Shit – as you so charmingly put it – does happen. Mistakes do get made. And when they do, it behoves the person who made the mistake to clean it up before it gets any worse.'

'By "any worse", you mean that vampiric dark age?'

'Yes. I know you think I'm a bit of a rotter, Flinch, but believe me, I'm a complete sweetheart compared to some of the vampires I've met on my travels. Not least of all the creature that originally bit me.'

David sat down on the arm of the armchair behind him. 'Really? What, what was it like?'

Underwood chuckled. 'Not tonight, Flinch. Isn't it past your bedtime?'

'No. No, I'm fine.'

'Sorry, Flinch, but I beg to differ. You have business to attend to tomorrow during the hours of daylight – not least of all, procuring my breakfast.'

'But – '

Underwood raised a finger. 'Don't make me tell you about "buts" again, Flinch. Go to bed.'

David sighed. 'Yes, sir.' He got to his feet. 'But you will tell me about what happened to you on some other night, won't you?'

'Yes, yes, at some stage, I'm sure. But before you go, how do I adjust the volume?'

David pointed out the volume buttons on the remote. He took the TV off mute and gave the remote back to Underwood.

'Thank you. Now, run along to bed.' Underwood turned up the volume and the sound of The Three Stooges filled the room.

'Could you turn it down a bit, sir? My room's just above this one and, er, – '

'Oh, I *am* sorry,' said Underwood lowering the volume to little more than a murmur. 'I can adapt my hearing to this reduced level and hear it perfectly well. It's just that I've been tuned in to the level of normal speech.'

'Thank you, sir. I don't really understand, but, you're right, I'm knackered. Goodnight.'

'Goodnight, Flinch. Oh, and do you have any idea who I'll be having for breakfast?'

David turned back at the door. 'I thought we might start with the Bensons, sir. They'll be up for it, I'm sure.'

Underwood grinned. 'Yes, I daresay they will. Jolly good, Flinch. Pleasant dreams.'

Now, it was already eight-thirty on Saturday evening, and from outside came the juddering of a diving board followed by a splash. Underwood had been swimming for the last ten minutes. He'd said he wanted a quick dip before breakfast. David turned off the computer and wondered whether he should check on how "breakfast" was doing. The Bensons had been lying upstairs in one of the spare bedrooms for the last half hour with tubes coming out of their arms. David had converted the room that afternoon into a transfusion suite, which he now thought of as "the breakfast room". It was a simple enough set up: Underwood would sit between the donors and David would bleed them one at a time. Underwood had agreed that a pint from each should be adequate for his needs, but that he might require another pint before he retired – maybe a couple, if he'd been through any exertions. David had spent much of the day worrying about how this extra snack would be accomplished, but a few phone calls to local Sect members had soon allayed his concerns. Everyone he had spoken to was more than willing to come out at any time of night for the privilege of being fed upon by Lord Underwood – or at least they had been once he had assured them that there was no chance of their being sucked dry in the manner of Ana and Beltran.

David left the office and went down the hall to the kitchen. Underwood was waiting there ahead of him, sitting at the table in his bathrobe and inspecting the side of a box of Spanish breakfast cereal. 'Ah, Flinch. What's all this *arroz con chocolate* nonsense?'

'Breakfast cereal, sir. Co-co pops.'

'Chocolate rice? What a revolting idea!'

'You shouldn't knock it if you haven't tried it, sir. Can I get you a bowl?'

Underwood frowned over the top of the box. 'Don't be a smart arse, Flinch. I presume my real breakfast awaits?'

'They do, My Lord. And I imagine they're starting to get quite uncomfortable by now. So, any time you're ready.'

'Oh, I'm ready now, old chap,' said Underwood, rising. 'I could eat a horse – and it wouldn't be the first time either, I can tell you.'

David wrinkled his nose. 'You mean drank the blood?'

'Yes.'

'What's it like?'

'A dashed sight better than chocolate rice, I would imagine.'

David laughed as they left the kitchen and headed for the stairs. 'Somehow I doubt that, sir.'

'Ah, but as you said yourself not a moment ago, don't knock it if you haven't tried it.'

'*Touché*, My Lord. *Touché*.'

Half an hour later, the blood breakfast was over and everyone was back in the kitchen and chatting away like there was nothing remotely strange about what had just taken place. The Bensons were having tea and biscuits, while Underwood was smoking and listening to Cynthia's effusive account of Margaret Thatcher's term as British Prime Minister. David was just pouring himself a cup of tea when Lydia walked in. Everybody stopped talking and stared at her in astonishment. She wore a little black dress with black fishnet tights and high heels, and her hair was back-combed up into a lacquered haze from which glittered two large, hoop earrings.

'I say!' said Gerald. 'Talking of the eighties, who are you supposed to be?'

Lydia batted her heavily painted eyelids. 'Why, isn't it obvious?'

'A French tart?' said David.

Lydia scowled. 'I'm Susanna Hoffs, dimwit.'

'Who's she?' asked Gerald

'A German tart?' suggested Cynthia.

'No, she was the singer in the Bangles,' said Lydia. 'You know, *Walk like an Egyptian?*'

David nodded, amused. Everyone else looked blank. Lydia tutted and turned to call in Miguel who was evidently awaiting his cue outside. 'All right, Miguel, they didn't get me, come on in and let them have a go at you.' Miguel walked in sheepishly. He wore a purple raincoat over a frilly white shirt and black leather trousers, his shoulder length hair had been curled, gelled and coiffed. Lydia looked at everyone expectantly. 'Well?'

'Rolf Harris,' said David.

Lydia ignored him and appealed to the Bensons, who looked as if they were trying to read a Chinese telegram. Lydia put her hands on her hips. 'Oh, come on, it really is too obvious for words!'

'Culture Club!' said Gerald.

'Culture Club were a group, not a person! Oh, for God's sake, he's bloody Prince, isn't he!' she threw up her hands in exasperation. 'God you're all so uncool!' Then she smiled at Underwood, 'With the obvious exception of yourself, My Lord, since you slept through the eighties and so have no idea who these fashion icons are.'

'I fear I must have slept through them too,' said Gerald. 'The only fashion icons I remember from the eighties are Maggie and Diana.'

Lydia rolled her eyes. She came over and joined them at the kitchen table. 'You know, I've spent all day doing us two up for tonight, and none of you have got the vaguest idea who we're supposed to be. God, I hope the people who are going to this disco tonight are a bit hipper to the eighties than you lot, otherwise we might as well go as Steptoe and Son.'

Underwood, who had been admiring Lydia's outfit, said, 'So, this a fancy dress party as well, is it?'

'Not strictly. But you get in for free if you come as someone from the eighties.'

'Well, that sounds like a bargain. Who do you think I could go as?'

Lydia considered a moment then said, 'Well, we are rather limited by the contents of your wardrobe, black suits and white shirts and so on.'

David clicked his fingers. 'I know! He could come as the bloke off the Two Tone label, you know, on the record label itself? He's got the suit, all he'd need is a hat and some sunglasses.'

'Hmm, that doesn't sound very exciting for fancy dress, Flinch,' said Underwood. 'I'm sure I must have something fancier somewhere.' He sprang up and beckoned Lydia to follow him. 'Come on, Lydia. I think I saw an old trunk up in my chambers that I arranged to have shipped before your father and I left Algeria. Let's see if we can't find something in there.'

The subterranean "night club" at *La Reina de Corazones* was a relatively recent development. It had undergone the change from being a mere cellar to becoming Almacena's most swinging hotspot only last year. Keith had been an amateur DJ for many years and had always enjoyed hosting small-scale events at every pub he and Michelle had ever run. *La Reina* didn't have adequate space upstairs, but on their first viewing of the place, Keith had recognised the potential of the cellar to become more than just a place for storing bottles and dry goods. After a Kafkaesque struggle with the local town hall planning department, he had managed to get planning permission for the alterations to the premises and had, along with Damo, Hodge and a few local builders, turned the cellar into the tiny disco that it now was.

It was a relatively small place: a bar in the corner, a few scattered tables around the edges of a rectangular dance floor, and the decks and DJ equipment on a table at the far end along with some basic disco lighting behind it. The bar was closed most of the week because of the cost of staffing it. But on Saturdays it became Keith's night club. Keith, along with his DJ partner, Billy Boy, hosted a sixties night, a seventies night and an eighties night in rotation. The fourth Saturday of the month   which should by rights have been his nineties night – Keith let the room out to a local Spanish DJ, Chulo, who put on a reggaeton night. Keith's events were moderately successful, but Chulo's reggaeton nights were always packed to the rafters. Keith was glad the town hall had made him install state-of-the-art sound insulation because he hated reggaeton almost as much as he hated the fact that Chulo's nights were more popular than his, but he consoled himself with the money he charged Chulo for the room hire, and the bar profits he took at the end of the night.

But tonight was eighties night, and Keith was dressed – as he always was on eighties night – in his "new romantic" outfit, which consisted of a red chiffon headscarf tied around his head in a flowing bandana, heavy black eye-liner, a white puffy shirt, and black leather trousers. It was coming up to ten o'clock, the hour when the doors to the cellar bar were opened and people would start drifting down. Keith and Billy Boy were going through their records and CDs and arguing about who would play what and when. It usually worked with Keith playing a new romantic set, Billy Boy playing the late-decade Stock, Aitkin and Waterman-esque stuff, and both of them sharing everything in between, and it was this that they bickered over constantly. They both wanted to play the ska, electro, pop, rock and new wave hits, though it usually came down to Keith getting his way because it was his club. Billy Boy, a bald, overweight Scot in his early fifties who used to operate a mobile disco in Edinburgh until a drink driving incident cost him his licence, didn't mind. He was happy just to be back behind the decks again.

'Oi,' said Keith, pointing at Billy Boy's record box. 'What's your game?'

'What?' said Billy Boy, pushing Dead or Alive's *You Spin Me Round* back down into the singles box.

'I see what you're doing. You know I always play that one.'

'I was just making a note of where it was in case you're called away upstairs or something and someone asks for it.'

'Yeah, course you were,' said Keith, jabbing an accusing finger. 'More like you were *hoping* I'd go upstairs and then you'd slap it on like a tart.'

'Oh fer fuck's sake.' Billy flicked through his singles and pulled out Cyndi Lauper's *Girls Just Want to Have Fun*. 'You can have yer fucking Dead or Alive, but I'm playing this, or you can stick the whole fucking thing up yer arse.'

'Alright, don't start acting like I'm some kind of hits dictator. All I'm trying to do is make sure the pop is evenly distributed between both our sets.'

'Evenly distributed between both *your* sets you mean.'

'That's not true, Billy Boy. You get loads of hits: you get the whole bleedin' Hit Factory in your second set; you get loads of Michael Jackson, and that awful 5-Star shite you like, you even drew the lucky straw on Wham! tonight, so I've got no idea where you come off whinging.'

'Och, I just wanted to play Dead or Alive for once, is that such a crime?'

Keith sighed. 'Look, not tonight, mate. All right? Next time, maybe, but not tonight; it's just too short notice. I can't – I can't fill the void.'

'You can have *Ghostbusters*.'

'I don't want fucking *Ghostbusters*!' Keith snapped. 'I want Dead or a-fucking-live, it's not so much to ask, is it?'

Billy was taken aback by Keith's sudden anger. 'All right, man, calm down. It's just a record.'

Keith grabbed his cigarettes and lit one. 'I'm sorry, Bill. It's just me and Chelle. Things ain't been so good between us lately and, well, I'm a bit out-of-sorts.' He sat down, avoiding Billy's eyes.

Billy noticed a tremble in Keith's hands as he smoked. 'Is it anything serious? I mean, is it just a passing thing? A tiff?'

Keith shook his head. 'No mate. It's not a tiff. I don't wanna go into it now but it's pretty serious. We might be splitting up.'

'Oh shit, man. I'm sorry.'

Keith, still avoiding Billy's eyes, tried to smile. 'Thanks, mate. But, let's not worry about it now, eh? We've got to turn this place into a rock and pop time machine. Take people back to a time when they were younger and love was,' he faltered as a memory of Michelle as she had been when they first met struck him, 'and ... and love was new.' He forced a laugh as a tear stung his eye and he quickly wiped at it. His hand came away black. 'Oh fuck! I've smudged me fucking eye-liner. And the doors are opening in a minute.'

'Don't worry about it, man. You go and sort out your make-up. I'll take the first set.'

Keith got up and patted Billy's shoulder with his clean hand, not wanting to get wet-eyeliner on Billy's vintage *Frankie Says Relax* T-shirt. 'Cheers, Bill.' He coughed and adjusted his headscarf. 'You, er, you have Dead or Alive tonight, all right? I was just being a dickhead earlier. Sorry about that.'

'Don't be daft, man,' said Billy. 'That's your song. I don't want it. And don't apologise either – you've every reason to be a dickhead.'

Keith laughed and wiped his nose with the back of his hand. 'Cheers, man. I'd better go and sort out me make-up.' He moved past Billy and headed upstairs to the main bar and the flat beyond, where he hoped he could sneak another quick loan of Michelle's eyeliner without her noticing.

Michelle didn't notice. As Keith emerged from the cellar and hurried off upstairs, she was serving someone at the bar. As she handed the man his drink, she saw over his shoulder the entrance of none other than Prince. She did a double take and laughed when she realised it was Miguel. Then Lydia Flinch came in looking like a streetwalker, followed by the man she had been introduced to last night, Daniel Underwood. He wore a billowy shirt with a red tartan shawl thrown over his shoulder, a silk scarlet sash tied at his waist, and black harem pants tucked into riding boots. He saw her and smiled, indicating his clothes.

'Oh, very nice, Daniel. Who are you supposed to be, Sinbad?'

'I've no idea,' said Underwood, coming up to the bar. 'Lydia put it together for me.'

'He's a new romantic, Michelle. I was thinking of early Spandau Ballet.'

'Oh, I know, I'm only kidding. How could I not recognise that look when it's Keith's own favourite? Though I have to say, Daniel, yours is much nicer than his, it looks more ... ' she pouted as she sought for the right word.

'Authentic?' suggested Lydia.

'Yeah, that's it, authentic. Where'd you get it all?'

Underwood leaned on the bar. 'Oh, you know, just picked it up here and there.'

'Anyway, Michelle,' said Lydia, 'who do you think I am?' She indicated her hair and clothes.

Michelle considered a moment. 'It's not Sheena Easton, is it? You and Miguel are Prince and Sheena Easton?'

Lydia rolled her eyes. 'No. I'm Susannah Hoffs!'

'Who?'

'Work like an Egyptian.' said Miguel. He attempted to do the hand movements he had seen cops and construction workers doing in the Bangles' video.

Michelle was baffled by the display. 'Eh?'

'*Walk* like an Egyptian, not *work*, Miguel,' said Lydia. She turned back to Michelle. 'Susannah Hoffs was the lead singer in The Bangles. And don't even think you can try and pretend you're too young to remember.'

'Oh, no I remember them,' said Michelle. 'I see it now, especially those earrings.'

David, who was not in fancy dress, came in with the equally un-fancified Bensons. They spotted an empty table. The Bensons went for it and David came to the bar. 'We've got a table, er, Daniel. Do you, Prince, and Miss Hoffs there want to grab a seat? I'll get the drinks in.'

'Very kind, *David*, but this round's on me. You all go and seat yourselves and I'll be over in a minute.' They gave their orders to Michelle and left. Underwood waited until they were out of earshot, then he turned to Michelle with an easy, yet strangely hypnotic smile. 'So, I see you're working. Does this mean you won't be attending the dance?'

Michelle hadn't intended to go to the disco, preferring to maintain a distance from Keith and not give him the satisfaction of seeing her enjoying herself at an event that he was responsible for. But there was something in Underwood's eyes she found herself almost powerless to resist. The skin on her back prickled. 'Well, I hadn't planned to, but Margarita is coming on at ten-thirty, so I suppose she and Luis could handle the bar up here.'

Underwood's smile widened. 'Of course they could.'

'Yeah. I suppose I could come down for a little while. But I'm not dressing up or nothing.'

Underwood laughed. 'Oh, you've no need to change, Michelle, you look ravishing just the way you are.' A blush bloomed high on Michelle's cheeks and he looked away, releasing her eyes.

She blinked and looked down at her clothes. 'Oh, this? It's just my ordinary stuff: plain old skirt and blouse.'

'There could never be anything plain about you, Michelle, and don't let anyone ever tell you otherwise. But forgive me, I'm sure my compliments are embarrassing you.'

Michelle laughed nervously; her blush had deepened and a growing tingling in her nipples caused her to cross her arms over her breasts. 'Oh, a girl can't complain about getting a compliment, can she? Now why don't you go over and join your mates, you old charmer? I'll bring your drinks over in a minute.'

Underwood inclined his head in a small bow. 'Thank you.' He turned and went to join his friends.

Michelle let out a breath she didn't even know she had been holding and leaned against the bar for support. Jesus Christ, what had just happened? Her heart was pounding and she literally felt weak at the knees. But why? She liked Daniel Underwood. She had enjoyed the harmless flirting that had passed between them the previous night, but that was all.

Wasn't it?

She hadn't thought much about him at all today, though she had to admit he had popped into her mind once or twice. But *this*? How had she come to be in this state? It was like she had gone from a woman with a platonic appreciation of his looks and personality to a love-struck teenager in the wink of one of those deep green eyes of his. As she set the drinks onto a tray, she noticed her hands were trembling slightly. Oh my, God, her mind whispered. This is insane. I'm a married woman. I love my hu – ... She found she couldn't finish the thought, so her mind supplied a substitute: I'm a mother, I have a daughter – a child who depends on me. And yet ...

She glanced over towards his table. He was looking straight at her. When their eyes met, he smiled and raised his hand in salutation. Michelle bit her lip to contain her smile, and went out with the tray of drinks.

Underwood followed her approach through the crowd. He hadn't intended to use his vampiric charm upon her, but for reasons he didn't quite understand, he found he couldn't help himself. Certainly she was a fine-looking woman, and certainly he desired her, but he could normally shrug off such transient attractions without a second thought. But there was something about Michelle that was different. Perhaps it was brought on by the threats and warnings relating to her that he had received last night, for nothing tasted better than forbidden fruit, especially when one hadn't had *any* fruit – forbidden or otherwise – for fifty years. Yet there was something more. As he watched her approach, the memory of her fragrance when he had first kissed her hand came back to him, and something deep inside him stirred. Beneath his lips, his tongue ran over the suddenly descended points of his canines. With a conscious effort, he withdrew them to their normal length and turned his attention back to his friends. Flinch, who had been watching him, asked if he was okay.

'Of course,' said Underwood. 'Never better.'

Now Michelle was coming up to their table. Underwood closed his eyes and scented the subtle change in the air that her nearness brought: the perfume she wore, her soap, her skin cream, and beneath it all, her own unique and delicate fragrance. He savoured it a moment, the bouquet blossoming on his olfactory palate and causing his mouth to water. Yes, he had been too long without a mate. He recalled the moment he had set eyes on her tonight: the way her hair spilled over the curve of her lissome neck, the swell of her bosom, and that saucy smile he felt she reserved only for him; and he felt a yearning. He wondered if it was a result of his long hibernation, a sort of spring time of his rejuvenated spirit. It made sense. But he didn't care about the sense or the cause of it; he only knew he wanted her. And as she set the drinks down on the table and again gave him that wonderfully saucy grin, he knew he meant to have her.

5

DAMO SAT BEHIND A SMALL TABLE next to the door that led down to the cellar bar. He wore a tight black suit; a black and white chequered tie; a pork pie hat and a pair of wrap-around sunglasses. These last he was especially grateful for, as their eye-concealing lenses allowed him to unashamedly admire the way Lydia Flinch had poured herself into her skimpy black dress. However, his ardour was abruptly doused when, beyond Lydia and the Bensons, he saw Michelle approaching with Lord La-Di-Da and his boyfriend. Damo stood up and took off his sunglasses. 'Lydia, I recognise that look. Unless I'm mistaken, you're that bird from the Bangles, aren't you?'

Lydia smiled, delighted. 'Oh bravo, Damien! At last, someone who knows their pop stars.'

'Oh yeah, Jaysus, I used to fancy her something rotten.'

'And who are you? Don't tell me – Alexi Sayle in the Young Ones?'

'I am not!' said Damo, wounded. 'I'm yer man offa the Two Tone label.'

Lydia laughed and prodded his chest. 'Oh, I know, I'm only teasing. We were thinking about that look earlier for my friend, Daniel. But we went somewhat upmarket.' She presented her hand for stamping. 'So, do I get in for free?'

Damo looked her up-and-down appreciatively before taking her hand and pressing the ink stamp to the back of it. 'Course you do, darlin'. In you go.'

The Bensons paid their five euro each, and then Underwood stepped up. 'Three please. Although, I believe I may qualify for free entry. I'm a new romantic.'

'Of course you are. So is this Lydia's upmarket look, then?' He shook his head. 'It's a pity you been to all that bother, coz you're barred.'

'Barred?' said Underwood. 'Surely not.'

Damo looked apologetically at Michelle. 'It's not my idea, Michelle. It's Keith's orders, didn't he tell ya?'

'Keith doesn't give me orders, Damo, it's the other way round.'

'Yeah, but still, I can't ignore what he's told me, can I?'

'Yes, you can.' She took the three five euro notes Underwood was offering to Damo and handed them back to him.

'But, what'll I tell him when he finds out?'

'You can tell him they're with me. And if he's got any problems with that, he knows who to come and talk to.' She held the door open for Underwood and David to pass. 'And I don't think we need to worry about hand stamps for these two. I'm sure you'll remember them just fine.'

'Oh yeah,' said Damo as he closed the door behind them. 'I'll remember them all right.'

As they descended the stairs, the cellar bar was resonating to the sound of Falco's *Rock Me Amadeus*. Underwood looked around at the scene below. It was still fairly early and only a dozen or so people had arrived; most of them were sitting at tables and shouting at each other in order to be heard above the music, but Underwood noticed that others were standing on the dance floor and wriggling lazily on the spot. It took him a few moments to realise that this must be the contemporary step-less dancing that Lydia had told him about. His heart sank.

The Bensons had found a table and they waved to Lydia. She went over. There was one seat beside the Bensons and three opposite. She took the first of the opposite seats, that way she could better ensure that Underwood sat next to her. She waved to him. He saw her and motioned to David and Michelle, the three of them came over. Lydia fixed her eyes on Underwood's and drew out the chair beside her.

Underwood turned to Michelle and extended a hand to the chair. Lydia read his lips as he said, 'Ladies first.'

Michelle said something to him that was lost under the music, and sat down on the seat Lydia offered. Lydia's smile wilted. Then Underwood sat down next to Michelle. Lydia gritted her teeth and tried to rally herself. She noticed how the vampire was studying the lazy contortions of the middle-aged ex-pats on the dance floor and reasoned that it was only a matter of time before he asked Michelle to dance. She decided to take the initiative. She leaned across Michelle and called out, 'So, do you think you could manage these modern steps, Daniel?'

He turned to her. 'Yes, I think I could manage it. It looks as if the general idea is to act as if one is struggling in a large vat of trifle.'

Lydia laughed. 'Yes, My Lord. So, would you care to try it? We can hop into the trifle and see where the music takes us?'

Underwood beamed. 'Thank you, Lydia. I'd be delighted.' He got up and held out a hand. She took it and he led her onto the floor where she immediately began to boogie in earnest. She was a good dancer and she knew it. She moved close to him, undulating her body like a snake dancer.

Underwood watched her sultry gyrations with fascinated interest. As she came in close beside him again, he said, 'I must say, you're very good at this type of dancing, Lydia. You must teach me how to do it properly some time.'

'Oh, it would be my pleasure, My Lord,' said Lydia, writhing momentarily against him and letting her hair tease his face. 'We could go to Malaga one night, that's where I could really show you how it's done.'

'That sounds like fun.'

'Oh, it will be, My Lord,' Lydia tossed her head and spun to face him, 'I guarantee it.'

Meanwhile, Michelle had decided to buy a round of drinks for the table and had gone to the bar. As she waited, she saw Keith coming down the stairs carrying a box of seven-inch singles. He caught her eye and smiled. She ignored him. Keith's expression soured and he looked out onto the dance floor where he noticed Underwood and Lydia dancing. He stopped and stared in disbelief: not only was Underwood here despite Keith's barring him, but he was dressed in a better version of Keith's own outfit. His fingers tightened on the handle of the singles box and he raised it like a fist. He was about to go over when Michelle took a step away from the bar and into his path, her eyes warning him of the consequences if he dared to continue. Keith snorted, turned on his heel, and strode away toward the decks. Michelle turned back to the bar to where Hodge was waiting dressed in a wet-look mullet wig, a suit made of black PVC, a pink shirt and a little red bow tie.

She smiled. 'Still able to squeeze into the Billy Jean gear then, Hodge?'

'Aye, just about, Chelle. Just don't ask me to do the dance routine, there's a love.'

She gave him her order and he was back quickly with the drinks on a tray.

The music cross-faded into *Visage* by Visage, and Michelle knew without looking to the decks that Keith's new romantic set had begun.

She paid Hodge and took the tray back to the table, where a flushed-looking Underwood and Lydia had just returned. Lydia had managed to reposition herself so she was sitting next to Underwood. Michelle noticed this but thought nothing of it. She sat down next to Lydia.

Underwood undraped the tartan shawl from his shoulder and hung it over the back of his seat. Then he leaned across Lydia and said, 'I say, Michelle. May I have the pleasure of this dance?'

Michelle nudged Lydia's arm. 'Oh, hark at Terry Thomas.'

'Yes.' Lydia's smile bore the same strained grace as that of an ambassador who has been served a boiled monkey's bottom at a state dinner and doesn't wish to offend his hosts. She made a noise like girlish laughter and added, 'He is a one, isn't he.'

Underwood extended his hand to Michelle. She glanced over to where Keith was working behind the decks, smiled to herself, then said, 'Oh, all right then, but just one.' She took Underwood's hand and let him lead her on to the floor. It was busier now and they made their way out into the crowd a short way before beginning to dance. Underwood, who was beginning to feel more relaxed with the idea of grooving aimlessly, moved close enough to Michelle so she could hear him talk. 'I must say, you're quite the dancer, Michelle – you stir the trifle delightfully.'

Michelle laughed. 'You're not such a bad stirrer yourself, Daniel.'

'Really? If I'm honest, I feel slightly absurd.'

'Absurd?'

'Yes. You see, this isn't the sort of dancing I usually do.'

'Oh? What sort of dancing do you normally do, then?'

'Oh, anything really – anything with steps, that is.'

'What, like ballroom dancing?'

He chuckled. 'I have danced in ballrooms, yes.'

Michelle was impressed. 'Oh, right. So what dances can you do then?'

'Oh, all sorts. The last dances I learned were the jive dances – the jitterbug, things like that.'

'Really? Did you use to go to Ceroc?'

'Ce – what?'

'Ceroc. It's rock and roll dancing. I used to go every Tuesday night when we lived in England with my friend, Roy. Keith wasn't interested, of course.'

'I see. Were you good?'

'Good? I was bloody brilliant, mate. But that was back in the Nineties. I've probably forgotten it all now.'

'Nonsense, Michelle. It's like riding a horse; once you've learned it, you never forget.'

'I wouldn't know. I've never ridden a horse.'

'Well, we shall have to remedy that. I shall get some horses and you and I can go night riding over the hills. I'll teach you.'

Michelle laughed. 'Course you will, Daniel. Buy some horses indeed. What are you like?'

It was then that Keith, who had been lining up Spandau Ballet's *To Cut a Long Story Short* on the turntable, looked up to see, through a brief parting of the crowd, his wife and Underwood dancing. 'What the fucking *hell?*'

Billy looked out onto the floor. 'What?'

'Him,' Keith pointed to Underwood and Michelle. 'That fucking Lord La-Di-Da. He's dancing with my wife!'

Billy saw Michelle and her partner and nodded. He sighed and put a hand on Keith's shoulder. 'Easy, man. She's just having a dance with the bloke.'

'No, Bill. She's having a dance with the bloke I told to sling his hook last night. I barred him. And now look – here he is, back in my boozer and rubbing his fancy pants up against my woman's arse.'

Billy looked again and shook his head. 'Ahh, he's not rubbing himself anywhere near her, man. But he does have a fine pair of fancy pants, I'll say that.'

'What?'

'His trousers. They're great, aren't they? Better than yours. I wonder where he got them.'

'For fuck's sake, Billy, I couldn't give a toss about his trousers; it's what might be going on inside them that I don't like.'

'Oh, come on, man. It's just an innocent bit o' dancing.'

'There is no such thing as an innocent bit of dancing, Billy. It's all foreplay innit? And if them two think they can foreplay each other right under my nose at me own fucking disco, they've got another think coming.' He snatched Spandau Ballet off the turntable and turned back to his records, skipping over those he'd earmarked for play and riffling through those that rarely, if ever, made it out of the box. Then, finding what he was looking for, he whipped the single out and held it up for Billy to see.

'*Motörhead?*' said Billy. 'That'll clear the floor faster than a turd in a swimming pool.'

'I know, mate. That's the fucking idea, innit? Everybody leaves the floor, and then she comes down here to give me an earful; she's gonna start demanding that the music goes back to what it was.' Keith tapped Billy on the forehead with the single. 'But here's the thing, see – I won't be here.'

'Eh?'

'I will be over there, dragging Lord La-Di-Da out by the ear'ole. And by the time Chelle gets you to turn the Motörhead off and pop the pops back on, I'll have his majesty out back doing a whole different kind of dance with the dustbins.'

'Are you sure that's wise, Keith? If things are nay good between you two, doing that'll only make things worse.'

'Ahh, but will it, Billy Boy? Don't be so sure, my old cocker. Birds love it when blokes assert themselves. It's like a prime ordeal thing, innit – it's like caveman courtship. Oh, she'll bitch about it, yeah, but secretly, she'll love it. Like I said, it's a prime ordeal.'

'You mean primordial?'

'Yeah, that's what I said, innit.'

Billy nodded doubtfully. 'All right, man, if that's the way you wanna play it. So, when Michelle comes down to complain, I stall her, right? I could pretend I cannae hear her.'

'Yeah. Brilliant.' Keith slipped the record onto the turntable and set the needle into the groove, queuing the track up in his headphones just as Visage was beginning to enter its repeat-chorus-to-fade. 'All right mate,' he said, patting Billy on the shoulder, 'it's all yours.' He gave Billy the headphones and moved quickly to the shadowy edge of the room. From here, with the crowd to cover him, he'd be able to move quickly down to Underwood as soon as Michelle came stomping down to the decks. He held his breath and waited as Visage began to fade out. Billy gave him a nod, and a second later, Motörhead's, *Please Don't Touch* erupted from the speakers like a bomb blast. The effect was immediate: everyone stopped dancing and all heads turned to Billy with expressions of dismay and annoyance. Keith chuckled as he saw Michelle turning, her face angry and her lips mouthing his name and something else he was glad he couldn't hear. This, he thought, was going to be as sweet as a nut.

The moment the music changed, Michelle knew it was Keith's petty jealousy at work. She turned, looking for him at the decks, but he wasn't there. He'd obviously ducked down or hidden somewhere. She struck out towards the decks, but before she had taken two paces her hand was suddenly caught and she felt herself pulled back, spinning around and into Underwood's arms. He grinned. 'Now this, I can dance to.'

Michelle could only gawp. 'Eh?'

'It's rock and roll, my dear,' said Underwood. 'A tad friskier than Bill Hayley and his Comets, but still ... shall we?' Before she could say anything, he took her hands in his and stepped back from her, twisting on his toes as he began to lead her in a classic Jitterbug routine. The half-forgotten steps came back to her, her body moving instinctively to his lead: step forward, back, he raised his arm, leading her twirl beneath it, she returned and he twirled her again, all the while their feet twisting and turning to the beat. Michelle laughed, delighted and not a little shocked at the speed and control of Underwood's moves and that of her own responses. They were drawing a crowd, everyone in the club was gathering around them in a circle, cheering, clapping and whooping. Again she laughed, and this time, Underwood laughed with her.

David, who had been listening to Cynthia complaining about how she hadn't had a decent sausage since she'd moved to Spain, became aware of the changed activity on the floor. He turned just in time to see Michelle lifted high above the crowd, and then plunge back down out of sight again like she was on a swing. He stood up to try to see better, but the crowd was too dense. He stepped up onto his seat and looked to the centre of the commotion, and his mouth fell open.

Cynthia, Gerald, Lydia and Miguel climbed up onto their seats too. 'I say!' said Gerald 'Look at him go!'

'And Michelle too,' said Cynthia. 'Isn't she marvelous?'

Lydia's lip curled contemptuously. 'Trollop.'

David continued to stare dumbfounded. But when Underwood suddenly dropped into the splits, spun on his hands and leapt back up again to grab Michelle's hands, he found himself laughing out loud, and he started to clap and cheer along with everyone else.

When Underwood and Michelle started dancing, it threw the proverbial spanner into Keith's mental works. He watched, unable to understand and completely at a loss as to how to proceed. Then the punters surrounded the couple and he couldn't see them anymore. He looked at Billy Boy, but he was as enraptured by the dancing as everyone else appeared to be.

'Fuck!' He started towards the crowd, muttering as he went. 'Fucking la-di-da bastard, I'll teach you how to fucking dance.' He pushed to the front of the crowd to see Michelle spin over Underwood's shoulder; Underwood swung her down, sweeping her across the floor and under his leg; then she was up whirling out to arm's length from him before again spinning in and going back over him the other way. 'You bastard,' said Keith, his voice low and threatening, and so lost beneath the music. 'Get your fucking hands off my wife.'

Underwood saw Keith's boiling red face at the edge of the crowd. As Michelle spun into his arms, he smiled at her, then deftly led her back a few steps in Keith's direction where he slipped his hand behind her back and dipped her low, but not so low as she could see her fuming husband. Then, tossing his head to flick a wayward lock of hair from his eyes, Underwood looked into Keith's eyes and winked at him.

Keith's fists clenched. Underwood was already spinning Michelle back onto her feet and away from him. Keith moved forward. Underwood spun on one foot in a twirl that should have brought him around to connect with Michelle as she came back to him, but he didn't make it – he connected instead with Keith's fist.

It was a terrible blow, given added impetus by Underwood's own momentum. Underwood went down hard, his feet flying out from beneath him and his head cracking on the dance floor so hard that it bounced.

'Keith! You fucking animal!' Michelle screamed. The crowd froze, hands held apart in mid-clap, mouths that had been open and cheering, now merely open.

'Keep out of this, Chelle,' said Keith. 'You started this, but now I'm gonna finish it.'

'Don't be such a fucking arsehole!' she was about to drop to help Underwood, but a hand caught her by the arm and pulled her gently but firmly back. She turned to see Hodge.

He shook his head. 'Leave it, Chelle. Let 'em be.'

She was about to tell him he was fired when a crunching sound followed by a grunt followed by Keith reeling past her and crashing into a table, stopped her. She watched as Keith went down amid a glittering shower of half-full glasses and bottles. Then she turned to see Underwood, one leg still extended from the kick he had evidently just delivered, spin on his haunches and hop up to his feet. Keith swore and got to his feet with considerably less grace. He wiped beer from his eyes, then charged, head down, going straight for Underwood's middle.

Underwood watched him come. Michelle was sure he would step aside like a toreador and watch Keith go barreling past into the crowd, so it was with some surprise that she saw him calmly look over in the direction of David and Lydia's table, as if he were happy to let Keith slam into him – which he did, sending the pair of them flying into the crowd.

Lydia turned to David. 'Did you see that? He was looking right at you.'

David ignored her, watching as Keith and Underwood disentangled themselves from fallen spectators who were now crawling away. Keith grabbed a beer bottle. Michelle screamed Keith's name and tried to break Hodge's grip. David saw her start punching Hodge, but the bouncer held her fast, using his raised arm to shield his face from her blows. Keith swung the bottle, smashing it onto Underwood's head as he was still rising. The gasps from the crowd were audible even above the blaring music.

Lydia leaned close to David's ear and said. 'I think the master needs his guardian.'

David swore and jumped down from his chair. The crowd had fallen back to the sides of the room. Keith was pacing around Underwood in a semi-circle, fists raised. Underwood seemed stunned; slowly he touched his head where the empty bottle had hit him and a look of amusement crossed his features at the sight of the blood that came away on his fingers. He looked up and grinned at Keith as the blood ran down his face. He said something. David couldn't hear what, but whatever it was, it caused Keith to punch Underwood hard in the face.

'All right!' said David, taking Keith by the shoulders. 'That's enough, mate! You've made your – ' He was cut off as an arm closed around his neck. Without a moment's hesitation, David grabbed his assailant's arm and hurled him over his shoulder: it was Damo, and he was flung hard straight onto Keith.

Underwood hopped over them and came up to David with a cheery grin. 'Hallo Flinch. Come to the rescue, have you?' Over David's shoulder he noticed someone coming in fast. 'Oh, look out.' He pushed David aside and Hodge's fist shot through the space where David's head had just been. As Hodge stumbled forward, off-balance, Underwood tripped him and he fell down to where Keith and Damo had been a moment before. 'Hallo,' said Underwood. 'Where did they go?' Keith's fist caught him off guard and he staggered, almost falling; at the same moment, Damo seized David around the neck and pulled him down into a head-lock.

Michelle ran up and slapped Keith hard across the face. Keith pushed her back and raised a finger to her nose. 'Back off, Michelle. I've never hit you before and I don't want to start now, but so help me God – '

'Forget God. Allow me,' said Underwood. He tapped him on the shoulder. Keith turned around and Underwood punched him squarely on the chin. Keith flew backwards, arms flailing. Underwood turned to Michelle. 'Are you all right?' Before she could answer, Hodge's arm was around Underwood's neck and he too felt himself pulled down into a head-lock. The crowd cheered.

A strangled sound to Underwood's left made him twist his face around to see David, similarly head-locked, with his neck held firmly under Damo's arm and his face grimacing. 'Ah, Flinch,' said Underwood, 'fancy seeing you here.'

'I can't – break his grip,' said David.

'Permit me to assist,' said Underwood. He grinned and grabbed Hodge's thighs, clamping them together with terrific force, and lifted his assailant from the floor. Hodge gave a cry of disbelief, he felt himself lifted up into the air as Underwood straightened his back. Underwood spun around, twisting at the waist and whirling Hodge around as a weapon to bear on Damo. Hodge wailed as he saw his feet sweeping towards Damo's head; he closed his eyes, not wanting to see as he kicked Damo full in the face. Damo's grip on David broke and both of them fell down. Underwood continued to spin, ducking forward and sending Hodge flying from his shoulders and into the crowd, scattering them like nine pins.

Then Keith was back. He pulled Underwood around by the shoulder and head-butted him. Underwood staggered. Keith landed a right hook, and Underwood went down. Then, sluggishly, Keith drew back his right foot to kick Underwood in the head; Underwood saw his intention and snatched Keith's left foot from underneath him bringing him down to land on his backside with a howl of surprise.

David and Damo were back on their feet and squaring up to each other. 'Look,' said David. 'We don't want any trouble. We just want to leave, all right?'

'Yeah? Well you shoulda taken my advice when you first came in here, shouldn't ya? I told ya you were barred but you wouldn't fucking listen to me. So now you're gonna have to take a beatin'.'

'Oh come on! You're the ones who are taking a beating!'

Damo grinned. 'Is that so?'

David noticed too late that Damo was looking at something behind his back; he began to turn just as pain exploded across his shoulders and pieces of wood flew all around him. 'Jesus Christ!' he turned to see Billy Boy warding him off with the broken remains of a chair. 'Who the fuck are you?'

Before he could hear Billy Boy's reply, Damo and Hodge fell upon him from opposite directions and he was pummeled by a storm of body punches. He managed to shove Damo back a few feet, but before he could take advantage of the space, Hodge's arms were moving under his and he felt the big man's fingers locking behind his neck. 'Alright, old son. That'll do.'

Damo grinned to see David now helpless and pinned. He drew back his fist. David struggled, but he was held fast. Desperately he tried a new tack: he went completely limp, becoming a dead weight in Hodge's arms. Surprised, Hodge adjusted his stance. David's head was lolling, his chin on his collar bone.

'Oh, don't think you can play dead, you fucking eejit,' said Damo. 'Get his head up, H.'

'I can't, not without getting hold of his hair, and that means – ' Hodge's words were cut off as David snapped his head back hard into Hodge's face. David felt Hodge's nose break with a crunch that resonated through his skull in the moment before Hodge screamed and released him.

Damo saw the blood pouring from his friend's nose and looked at David with fury. 'You fucking bastard!' He charged, but David lashed out with a karate kick that connected squarely with Damo's oncoming jaw, sending him flying backwards and sprawling onto the floor to where he finally lay still.

The music came to an end, the needle scratching over and over in the final groove.

Underwood came up to David and patted him on the shoulder. 'Well done, Flinch. You handled yourself admirably. Thanks for the assistance.'

David smiled and spat a gob of blood. 'Don't mention it, sir.' He nodded to something over Underwood's shoulder. 'But don't let your guard down too soon; looks like it's not over yet.'

Underwood turned to see Keith, Hodge and Billy Boy squaring up for one last joint assault. He sighed and raised his hands in a gesture of appeasement. 'All right, chaps. What say we just shake hands and all have a drink together, eh? I'm buying.'

'Fuck that, you upper-class twat,' said Keith. 'The only way you're leaving here is in an ambulance, you fu – ' his sentence died on his lips as Michelle walked between him and Underwood holding a seven inch single in one hand and a cigarette lighter in the other. 'Whoa! What are you doing with that? That's – '

'Yes, Keith. It's your copy of *Quiet Life* by Japan, as autographed by David Sylvian himself. You always bring it down just to show off with, but you never actually play it, do you?'

Keith raised his hands. 'That's coz it's a museum piece, Chelle. Please – just put it back in the box, or give it to me. You got no idea of the value of that thing.'

'Oh? I'd say it's worth be about a tenner, if that. No big loss to the world if I were to set it on fire.'

'You wouldn't!' Keith's voice trembled. 'You know it means more to me than just money. He signed that to me personally.'

'Oh, I will Keith,' she raised the lighter to the sleeve. 'Unless you stop beating up the clientele.'

'We ain't beating anyone up, Chelle. We're just trying to chuck 'em out is all – which we wouldn't have had to do if you hadn't let 'em in in the first place.'

Michelle sparked the lighter, flashing a flame just long enough to illuminate David Sylvian on the single cover.

'No!' Keith cried. 'All right, they can go.'

'Yeah. Right after you've apologised to them.'

'*Apologised?* To them? What for? They're all right. Look at us! Hodge's got a busted nose and he's ripped the arse on his Billy Jean trousers, and poor old Damo's out for the bleedin' count.'

Underwood stepped forward. 'Really, Keith, there's no need for apologies. Let's just shake on it and we can all move on from this unfortunate misunderstanding.' He offered his hand to Keith. Keith looked at it with contempt. Michelle gave another flash of life to the lighter.

'All right!' said Keith, snatching Underwood's hand and shaking it briefly. 'There.'

Underwood offered his hand to Hodge, who couldn't accept it as his right hand was pinching his nose shut, but with his head tilted back, he offered his left, and Underwood accepted it warmly. He also shook hands with Billy Boy before beckoning David forward to also do the rounds. Once everyone had gone through at least the semblance of reconciliation, Michelle turned to the people who had clustered along the length of the stairs to the pub in order to get a better view of the fight. She pointed to a woman at the top.

'Sharon, go and call an ambulance!' Sharon nodded and hurried up to the pub, and the other punters then began filing out after her. Michelle turned to Underwood and David. 'As for you two gentlemen, I think it would probably be best if you left.'

Underwood nodded. 'Of course. I'm sorry about all of this, Michelle. Please allow me to pay for the damages.'

'No thank you, mate,' said Keith. 'This is *my* mess and *I'll* fucking pay for it.' He walked over to where Damo lay and knelt to help him.

Underwood ignored him, his eyes fixed upon Michelle's. 'Please consider my offer anyway, Michelle. I do hope this unpleasantness won't mar our friendship.'

'No, Daniel ... of course it won't.'

David thought there was something queer in the way Underwood and Michelle were looking at each other. His skin prickled. He put a hand on Underwood's shoulder. 'Er, we should be going, Daniel.'

Underwood smiled. 'Yes, of course.'

Keith was gently shaking Damo's shoulders, bringing him back to consciousness. Damo's eyes opened and Keith said, 'You all right, mate?'

Damo blinked a few times, then replied, 'Yeah, but ... where's that fucker – ?'

'S'all right, mate,' said Keith, inspecting the damage to Damo's face. 'Another time. Believe me.'

As they walked through the pub upstairs, all eyes were on Underwood and David. 'So much for keeping a low profile,' David murmured.

'Yes. Never mind.'

At the door, Lydia and her friends went outside. David was about to follow when Underwood stopped and turned back to Michelle. David was reluctant to leave him alone with her. Recognising this, Underwood said, 'Carry on, Flinch, I shan't be a moment.'

David smiled thinly and continued to where Lydia and the others were waiting on the street.

'Why do you call him, "Flinch"?' asked Michelle. 'It's like he works for you or something.'

'He does,' said Underwood. He glanced around: dozens of eyes were still upon them. 'I'll explain another time.'

'I ... don't think there should be another time, Daniel.'

'Really? Surely not?'

Michelle was about to confirm it, when quite suddenly, she forgot how to. The strange feeling she had felt at the bar earlier flooded her senses again, but this time it was stronger – so strong it stopped her breath in her chest, and everything in the world except Daniel Underwood's eyes seemed to fade away. There were neither words nor pictures in her head, just an overwhelming desire to be close to him. She felt she wanted to reach for him, but when she tried her hands were too heavy, her arms, numb.

Underwood smiled at her, like he somehow understood what she was feeling, that perhaps he shared it. And then she knew it was so – and a joy filled her soul, sweeping away the unhappiness of recent days and causing her to tingle all over. There was no clear thought, just feeling, knowing – knowing that their togetherness *would* come, and soon ... very soon. But first, she understood that she must carry on as normally as possible. Her mouth moved as she tried to speak, tried to tell him she would do as he bade her, but she couldn't. Underwood raised his finger to his lips. 'Shhhh, I know. I shall see you soon, Michelle.'

Lydia called from the street. 'Are you coming, Daniel?'

Underwood released Michelle's eyes and turned back to where his friends waited for him. 'Yes. But just a moment. I think I ought to just pop back in and have a word with Keith. Man-to-man, as it were.' He turned back to Michelle. 'All right?'

Michelle nodded. Her voice was little more than a whisper. 'Yes, My Lord.'

Underwood touched her cheek, then strode back into the pub.

The odour of fresh blood caught Underwood's nose as soon as he went back inside. He followed his nose towards the gents' toilet, the scent increasing as he came across a trail of splattered crimson droplets leading from the cellar bar to the toilet door. He pushed the door open to see Keith and Damo standing outside a toilet cubicle and looking in. As Underwood walked further inside, he saw Hodge sitting on the toilet with his head tilted back and a wad of blood-sodden toilet paper held gingerly to his nose.

'What?' exclaimed Damo. 'What the fuck are you doing here?'

'Geddout Underwood!' said Keith. 'Michelle ain't holding a flame to my vinyl anymore.'

Underwood fixed his eyes on Keith's. 'Forgive my intrusion, gentlemen. I was wondering if I could have a few words with Mr Mullins in private? Just a little chat, man-to-man.'

Keith suddenly felt very relaxed; a fuzzy sensation that calmed his anger like smoke pumping into a beehive.

'What?' Damo started forward, ready to finish what they should have finished downstairs, but Keith stayed him with a hand.

'It's all right, mate,' said Keith. 'I don't mind. Take Hodge outside, the ambulance'll be here in a minute.'

'Are you fucking mental? This is the same bloke we were just talking about, you know?'

'Don't worry about it,' said Keith, his eyes never leaving Underwood's. 'We're just gonna have a little chat. Man-to-man.'

The door opened and Luis stuck his head inside. 'Keith. The *ambulancia* is here.'

'Cub on, bate,' said Hodge, tugging Damo's shoulder. 'Let's just leab 'um to sort it out. I wanna get out to that bloody ambulance to get sumb laughing gas inside me.'

Damo led Hodge to the door that Luis was holding open for them. 'All right, H. We'll get you out there. But if you need me, Keith, I'll be back outside in a minute, all right?'

'It's alright, mate,' said Keith. 'Everything's gonna be fine.'

When they were gone, Underwood walked to the sink and wiped his finger in a splashed droplet of Hodge's blood. Keith continued to stare glassily into the space that Underwood had just vacated. Underwood licked the blood from his finger. He savoured the flavour for a moment, then said, 'You know, Keith, this stupid animosity of yours toward me really won't do. If your wife wants to dance with me, or kiss me, or anything else with me, you should be happy for her. Don't you agree?'

'Y-yes,' said Keith.

'You do want her to be happy, don't you, Keith?'

'Yes. I want her to be happy.'

'Good.' Underwood considered sampling another drop of Hodge's blood but decided it was a pleasure that could wait for another night. 'Very good. You know, I sense a profound guilt in you, Keith. Have you been a naughty boy?'

'Yes.'

'I thought so. And this naughtiness of yours is the source of the problems that seem to exist between you and Michelle, yes?'

'Yes. It's my fault.'

Underwood gave a little laugh. 'Oh dear, dear, dear. Boys will be boys, eh?'

'Yes.'

'Yes, *My Lord*, please, Keith.

'Yes, My Lord.'

'Good. Much better.' Underwood considered his reflection in the mirror. His hair was matted with blood and his forehead smeared with the same. 'Hmmm. You know, Keith, I was thinking of making a suggestion to you. I was going to suggest that your guilt had become quite unbearable. And that as a result of your crushing sense of remorse, later on tonight, you should get into a bathtub with some sort of electrical appliance.' He turned on the cold tap and filled his cupped hands. 'But then I remembered that daughter of yours.'

'Melanie.'

'Is that her name?' Underwood washed his face and swept his wet fingers through his hair. 'Anyway, if Melanie is to lose her mother, she's going to doubly need her father, isn't she?' Keith said nothing. Underwood continued, 'You see, I need Michelle to know her daughter is safe and cared for, even if it is by a slavering oaf such as yourself, otherwise she may have problems letting go of ... well, letting go. Anyway, long story short, I decided that you're more use to me alive, old chap. However, I will need you to clear off for a bit. Make yourself scarce, you know? Can you do that for me?'

Keith said nothing, still staring vacantly ahead.

'Keith, I said *can you do that for me?*'

'I ... I don't know.'

'What do you mean, you don't know? What about this other woman you've been up to naughtiness with? Surely she'll have you, won't she?' Underwood shook pink droplets of water from his hands then went to the hand drier.

'There's no other woman, My Lord.'

'No other woman? Oh. Well, if it's not another woman, what is the nature of your naughtiness?'

Damo banged on the door. 'Keith? Are you all right in there, mate?'

Underwood rolled his eyes. 'Tell him, "yes".'

'Yes, mate!' said Keith, loudly enough for Damo to hear.

Underwood grabbed Keith's hand and looked at his wristwatch. 'Oh blast!' He needed to get going or Flinch would be outside the door as well. 'All right, Keith. I suppose you'll have to stick around until I can decide what's to be done with you.'

Keith said nothing.

Underwood stood considering Keith for a moment. Then slowly, a smile rose to his lips. 'Alright, Keith.' He came around and resumed his position in front of Keith, meeting his eyes immediately as he did so. 'This is what you're going to do ...'

A minute later, Underwood strolled out onto the pub's front terrace. He spotted his friends, walked over, and rubbed his hands together. 'Right then, I imagine you lot must be fairly famished. Let's go and get you all something to eat, shall we? Same place as last night, or somewhere different? Lydia?'

'*El Rincon* is nice, My Lord.'

'Where?' said Gerald.

'The place where they put brandy on your sausage and set it on fire, dear,' said Cynthia. 'Remember?'

'Oh yes, the Blazing Sausage. Smashing place, Your Lordship.'

'Very good then,' said Underwood. 'The Blazing Sausage it is. Shall we go?'

Lydia got up. Miguel and the Bensons followed. Cynthia noticed Underwood wasn't with them and looked back. Underwood gave her a little smile and gestured for her to continue. When they were sufficiently ahead, Underwood turned to David and motioned for him to walk with him. 'How are you feeling, Flinch? Sorry about all that. The last thing I expect you want is a fresh set of lumps on top of the ones you got the other night.'

'I'm fine thanks, sir. Thank you for asking. What about you? All healed up, are you?'

'Yes, thank you.'

'And what about the landlord? You went back in to smooth things over with him. How did that go?'

'Oh yes, he was fine. Obviously a little miffed, but I was able to talk some sense into him. He shan't bother us any further.'

'Are you sure, sir? He was pretty fuming.'

Underwood laughed. 'Yes, he was rather, wasn't he? But don't worry, Flinch. From now on, our friend Keith will be as good as gold.'

6

ANTON AND IVAN stepped into the gloom of McGinty's Irish Pub in Torremolinos, took off their sunglasses, and looked around. It was early afternoon and there was a scattering of people drinking throughout the pub, the majority of whom, going by their varying stages of sunburn, were not Spanish. Anton and Ivan went to the bar. The bar staff didn't seem particularly interested in them; a young man and woman were chatting beneath a television set showing a soccer match. Anton briefly caught the girl's eye, but she pretended she hadn't noticed. Obviously, whatever the young man was talking about was far more important.

'Do you believe this?' he said to Ivan. He rapped his knuckles on the bar. 'Hey!'

Both of the bar staff turned, surprised that anyone would have the temerity to just interrupt them. The girl muttered something to the young man and it was he who then sauntered down to Anton with an easy smile. 'Sorry about that, what can I get you?'

'Your boss. I'm from head office.'

The young man gave a little laugh. 'Look man, I said sorry. We didn't notice you, what with the TV an' all.'

'Then start noticing me now, idiot. We come from head office to see Popov. Where is he?'

The young man shrank back a little. 'Oh, I, I'm sorry. I'll call him.'

'Just tell me, where is his office.'

The young man pointed to a door marked *Privado* on the opposite side of the bar. 'Over there.'

Anton and Ivan turned and walked silently to the door. Without knocking, they entered to find a short, windowless corridor with three doors. The door at the end of the corridor bore the sign, *Manager.* They went straight in.

Boris Popov was eating a banana and reading a Russian newspaper online when the door opened. He looked up and knew immediately that these were the two men Sergei had told him would be coming.

'Boris Popov?' said Anton.

Boris nodded and stood up, hastily swallowing the contents of his mouth and dropping the remains of his banana onto his desk. 'Yes. And you are ... ?'

'You know your bar people lack the passion for customer service?'

Boris frowned. 'Excuse me?'

'They are more interested in each other than in the customers. You should get out and beat them once in a while.'

Boris smiled uneasily. 'They are not mules. Much as I might want to beat them at times, I can't just hit the staff whenever I please.'

Anton and Ivan sat down on the chairs facing Boris's desk. 'Please, Boris Popov, sit. You know who we are?'

'From the way you walk in here criticising my staff and suggesting I beat them, I presume you are from Sergei, no?'

'Yes. And unlike you, we can hit staff.'

Ivan chuckled, deep and menacing. 'We have the permission from head office.'

'Is that what this is about?' asked Boris. 'My staff? Sergei said you were coming to show me some pictures.'

'We are here to do both,' said Anton. He took the file of MySpace photos from his briefcase and tossed it onto Boris's desk. 'There is a connection, I think. Open it.' Boris did so. 'The man in the first picture, his name is Sullivan.' Boris looked at the picture: it showed a number of smiling faces, one of which had been circled in red marker. 'You know this man?'

Boris shook his head. 'No. But I don't mix with the customers, I make a poor McGinty, you understand?'

Ivan's brows knitted. 'What is a McGinty?'

Boris shook his head again. 'Nothing, I mean I cannot pass for Irish man, so I stay in the background. No, I don't know this man, or any of these people.'

'Is no matter,' said Anton. 'But can you tell me, please, who is Denise Kennedy? She works here, yes?'

'Denise? She is a barmaid here. You met her earlier, I think; she is working now, at the moment.'

'The she-mule behind the bar right now? She is Denise Kennedy?'

'Yes. Why?'

'This picture is from her MySpace page. She took it, or at least she posted it to her profile, so we believe she can help us find our friend, Mr Sullivan.'

'Oh.' Boris shifted nervously in his seat. 'So, you want me to call her in?'

Anton turned to Ivan. 'What do you think?'

Ivan looked at his watch. 'What time does she finish her shift?'

'Four o'clock. She works eleven 'til four every weekday, then again on Saturday nights.'

Ivan looked at Ivan and shrugged. 'Perhaps some lunch first?'

Anton nodded. 'I agree.' He took the pictures and the folder back from Boris and dropped them into his case. 'Thank you for your help, Boris Popov. Please forget you ever saw us, yes?' Both he and Ivan rose.

'Yes, of course,' said Boris, also rising. 'Is that all?'

'Just one more thing,' said Anton. 'As this is Sergei's establishment, we don't want any disruption to smooth running of business. Do you have people who come in when staff are sick?'

Boris shrugged. 'Of course.'

'Then you should arrange for someone to cover tomorrow's eleven 'til four bar shift.'

Boris looked confused. 'But why? No one has called in sick.'

'Not yet,' said Anton, 'But there is very high probability that Miss Kennedy is going to.'

David lay on a sun lounger beside the swimming pool at Casa Underwood in the full glare of the afternoon sun. Upon rising, he had taken a leaf out of Underwood's book and gone straight in for a swim. He had swum up and down the length of the pool until he was physically exhausted, then clambered out to flop down on a sun lounger to bake himself dry. He wondered how long he had been lying on his back; he didn't want to get sunburnt. He felt his shorts, they were almost dry. He rolled over, turning his back to the sun, and folded his arms beneath his head like a pillow. He winced and adjusted his face so the bruise on his cheekbone wasn't under any pressure. Then he closed his eyes and resumed his reverie of the events of last night.

They had left the restaurant shortly after two, all of them fully fed – with the exception of Underwood, who had contented himself with a few glasses of red wine while they had been eating. But afterwards, as they were walking down a quiet backstreet away from the restaurant, he announced his earlier exertions had left him feeling somewhat depleted: he was hungry. There and then, he'd asked for a volunteer to donate their blood. Before David could object, Cynthia had stepped forward. 'Oh, take me, My Lord,' she said, flicking her hair back over her shoulder and presenting her neck like a chef whipping the lid off a silver platter. 'I'd be honoured.'

David had thought she sounded a little drunk. He stepped smartly between them, his hands raised. 'Wait a minute, wait a minute. What do you think you're doing? You can't just sink your teeth into her like she's a piece of fruit. Not here on the street!'

'Why on Earth not, Flinch?' said Underwood. 'Should anyone pass by and see us, Cynthia and I would look like two lovers enjoying a canoodle in the shadows. Nothing sinister about that.'

'No,' said Cynthia, stepping around David so she was beside Underwood. 'And I don't mind in the least. In fact, I aspire to be his piece of fruit. I could be his peach.'

'There you are, Flinch,' said Underwood, slipping an arm around Cynthia's waist. 'My peach is willing.'

David turned to Gerald. 'You're not just going to let this happen, are you, Gerald?'

Gerald was looking at Cynthia with a salacious smile on his face. 'Nothing to do with me, old boy. Cynthia is her own mistress ... and mine too, and that's the way we like it.'

'Good boy, Gerald,' said Cynthia.

David shook his head, confused that he alone seemed to understand why this might be a problem. What he was most troubled about was what Underwood had told him about passing on the vampiric infection, but as Underwood had said this to him in private, he didn't want to disclose his concerns in front of the others unless absolutely necessary. 'But what about the mess? All that blood that's gonna go everywhere, all over the street, not to mention all over Cynthia herself.'

'Are you suggesting I'm a messy eater, Flinch?'

'Well, you seemed to make quite a mess out of Beltran, Milord.'

'That was your fault, not mine. Under normal circumstances when dining from willing bleeders, I don't spill a drop.'

'How?' asked David. 'I mean, how can you *not*? When you stop, for example, it must go pumping all over the place.'

Underwood smiled. 'No.'

'How come?'

'I have my means.'

'I wish you'd show me, My Lord,' said Cynthia, proffering her neck. 'Please.'

Lydia rolled her eyes. 'Oh, don't beg, Cynthia, it's not at all becoming in a woman of your age.'

Underwood chuckled. 'Oh, I find it most becoming. Thank you, Cynthia. I promise not to take more than a couple of mouthfuls. It's just to get me over the hump, you understand. And then perhaps when we get home, Miguel, we could get Flinchy here to tease a pint out of you. What do you say?'

Miguel nodded. '*Sí*, My Lord.'

'Good show.' Underwood moved towards Cynthia, but again David intervened.

'What if you can't stop?'

'Don't confuse my drinking habits with yours, Flinch. *I* know when to stop. Trust me.'

'What about pain, then? It'll hurt like hell. What if she instinctively pulls away – you could tear her neck open.'

'I say,' said Gerald. 'Maybe this isn't such a good idea, after all.'

'Relax, Gerald,' said Underwood. 'She'll be fine. She'll enjoy it. Trust me.'

'I trust you, My Lord,' said Cynthia. She hiccupped and put her hand to her mouth. 'Oh, I do apologise.'

Gerald shrugged. 'Well, if you say it's all right, Milord, and Cyn is willing ... '

'Oh, I *am*,' said Cynthia.

'Looks like you're overruled, David,' said Lydia. 'So, why don't you just step aside and let nature take its course?'

'Nature taking its course is precisely what I'm worried about, Lydia.' He turned to Underwood, feeling now that he had no alternative but to risk breaking the vampire's trust. 'What about the vampiric infection, My Lord?'

Cynthia's eyes widened. 'Infection?'

Underwood smiled. 'Oh, don't worry about that, Flinch. It's perfectly all right. It wears off in a day or two ... three at most.'

Lydia's face was suddenly feverish with interest. 'Er, I'm sorry, David, but did you say, *vampiric infection?*'

'Yes,' said David.

'Oh,' Lydia turned to Underwood. 'What's that?'

'It's nothing. Just a sort of queer tingle is all.'

'Forgive me, My Lord,' said David. 'But that queer tingle you're talking about is an infection unknown to medical science. If you're going to sink your teeth into Cynthia, then you should at least tell her what she can expect as a consequence.'

'Oh for Heaven's sake, it's just a tiny infection carried in my saliva. All it means is that the person I bite will feel an attraction to me for a few days afterwards.'

'I say!' said Gerald. 'You mean Cynthia will have the hots for you, sir?'

'Yes,' said Underwood. 'But don't concern yourself, Gerald. I can overcome it completely by entrancing her.' He took Cynthia's hand. 'I promise you, Cynthia, you won't suffer any side-effects, nor will you feel any pain, and any marks that are left on your skin will fade very quickly.'

'Fade very quickly?' said David. 'How do you work that out?'

Underwood smoothed Cynthia's hair over her shoulder and fixed her eyes with his own. 'If I might be permitted to demonstrate?'

'Yes ... ' said Cynthia, surrendering her neck to him as she relaxed into his embrace. 'Yes, master.'

Underwood kissed her throat, tracing his lips along the warm pulsing veins beneath her skin. He opened his mouth, and Lydia saw with a thrill of excitement that his canine teeth had lengthened to bright points. David took a step forwards, but Gerald's hand stayed him.

'It's all right, David. She wants this, and I want it for her.'

David turned at Cynthia's sudden gasp to see Underwood's mouth now pressed hard to her throat. Cynthia's hands ran up to his head, caressing it, running her fingers through his hair and holding him tightly to her.

'By Jove,' said Gerald in a voice hushed with awe.

David ignored him, watching breathlessly as Underwood drank. He looked at Lydia and Miguel; like Gerald, both of them were staring with almost lascivious fascination at the scene before them. At that moment, David had suddenly felt himself to be among strangers. A tiny rivulet of blood ran from the corner of Underwood's mouth and along the line of Cynthia's neck. The sight of it broke David's tolerance. He shook

Gerald's hand from his arm. 'That's enough, My Lord! You said you were only going to take a drop.'

Underwood looked up at him from under his brow then broke off his bite, lifting his mouth away from Cynthia's neck, and for a second David saw the two bleeding holes in her flesh. Cynthia's hands resisted, urging the vampire to return. Underwood, his fangs still descended and glistening with blood, smiled at David and said, 'So I did, Flinch. Just one moment.' He lowered his face to Cynthia's bleeding wounds again, and for a moment David wondered if he were about to resume feeding. The vampire tensed slightly and to everyone's horror, retched up a small amount of viscous, bloody liquid onto Cynthia's neck.

David's face contorted with disgust. 'What the *fuck*?'

'Oh my God,' said Lydia, 'he's vomiting on her!'

Underwood looked up at her. 'Not vomiting exactly, Lydia. I'm just giving her a little something to help her blood coagulate. Does anyone have a handkerchief?'

Lydia opened her bag and took out a packet of tissues. She tossed it to him and he took one out and used it to gently wipe the viscous liquid away from around Cynthia's wounds. David stepped closer and saw to his utter astonishment that the wounds had stopped bleeding.

'That – that's *impossible*.'

'Not impossible, Flinch, just ... unknown.'

'They look older – like they were inflicted hours ago, not seconds.'

'Yes,' said Underwood. 'It's a neat trick, isn't it?' Cynthia moaned and her hands clutched at his face, pulling his attention back to her neck. 'Sorry, Flinch. Excuse me a second, would you?' Underwood gently eased Cynthia's hands away from him and took her face in his hands. 'Look at me, Cynthia.'

Cynthia opened her eyes. She was about to say something when Underwood lay his finger against her lips and gazed deeply into her eyes. 'Shhh, listen to me, my dear. You feel peaceful and happy. You will retain a memory of what has happened between us here, but you will do so without any emotion or sense of need whatsoever. You will feel nothing more than the cheerful contentment of a friend who has just helped another out of a small inconvenience. The details will quickly fade, and by morning, be all but gone. Blame the wine, my dear; you really shouldn't have had that last glass, should you?' He smiled and released her.

Cynthia blinked. 'No, no I really shouldn't have had that last glass at all. I thought so at the time, but I was having such fun that I – ' She noticed everyone staring at her with a variety of expressions. 'What?' Then she remembered: Underwood had been hungry, she had gone to him to give blood, he had put his arm around her, and Gerald – obviously turned on – saying he didn't mind, and then ... nothing, like a warm, dark space in her memory. She touched her neck and felt a stickiness. Her fingers came away dappled with blood. 'Oh my.' She looked at Underwood. 'So you ... ?'

'Yes,' said Underwood. He held up the tissue he was dabbing his lips with and she saw it was spotted with crimson. He winked at her.

David could only stare at Cynthia's neck. 'My God. You know, the medical possibilities are staggering.'

Underwood chuckled. 'Less of that talk, if you please, Flinch. I'm not offering myself up to medical science just yet.'

'Can I see, Cynthia?' Cynthia turned her head so Lydia could see her neck better. 'Ooh, yes. How interesting. Do you always do this, My Lord?'

'Only when I want to be sure the victim will live.'

Cynthia staggered slightly and David caught her, easing her back to sit on the bonnet of a car parked beside them. She held out a hand to Gerald. 'Gerald, darling.'

Gerald came over and took Cynthia gently in his arms. 'Are you all right, Cyn?'

'Yes, I'm fine. A little light-headed, that's all.'

Gerald tightened his hold on his wife and helped her to her feet. 'Come on, old girl. Let's get you home, shall we?'

'Yes. Yes, I do feel awfully tired.'

'Will you be able to manage?' said Underwood.

'Oh yes,' said Cynthia, standing straight and adjusting her hair. 'Gerald's no burden at all, are you Gerry?'

'No, dear,' said Gerald. 'Let's go home, eh?' And with his arm around her, he began to lead her away.

After everyone had bidden the Bensons goodnight, Lydia suggested going on to a late bar that she knew, but David declined, and since he was the driver, they agreed they would go home. Underwood had been cheerful at the prospect.

'I've got an lot of reading to catch up on,' he said. 'Not to mention all the films and newsreels which one can now seemingly pull down out of thin air on that satellite television of yours.'

'Yes, My Lord,' said Lydia. 'And of course, there's the internet.'

'Beg pardon?' said Underwood.

Lydia turned to David, surprised. 'You mean, you haven't introduced His Lordship to the internet yet?'

'Not yet, no. I've been busy burying corpses up until now.'

'Oh well,' Lydia said to Underwood. 'If you think satellite telly is good, just wait until you see the internet.'

'Internet?' said Underwood. 'Do you have one?'

'We do, sir,' said David. 'I'll show it to you later.'

Underwood beamed. 'Capital.'

And so David had done. Lydia had volunteered to stay up to be the vampire's computer tutor, but David hadn't wanted to leave her alone with him in John's study while he went to bed. So over two cups of coffee, David had taken Underwood through the basics of computer education, from how to turn the thing on, to surfing the net and opening an email account. Underwood had become so engrossed in the new technology that he had almost forgotten to have his supper. But at four a.m. he'd walked back into the lounge where David had fallen asleep on the couch and demanded to be fed. David had gone upstairs to wake Miguel, and then they'd gone through into the specially laid out bedroom to transfuse a pint of Miguel's blood.

'You know,' Underwood had said, sucking cheerfully on the blood feeder tube, 'this really is quite an amazing age you people are living in. To think that just fifty years ago, the whole world was trembling on the brink of self-destruction. And now look at you: satellite televisions, internets, mobile telephones with internets *and* little televisions inside them. You know, I really must get one of those. Could you pop into town tomorrow and get me one, Flinch?'

'Yes, sir,' said David yawning. 'First thing, sir.'

Which now, some eleven hours later, he remembered. David picked up his watch from beneath the sun lounger. It was nearly three. He had better get going if he was going to get Underwood a phone and be back here in time to get the evening's blood donors prepped and ready for breakfast. He pushed up from the sun lounger and got to his feet. The paving stones were hot and he trotted quickly into the shadow of the house. He'd just have time for some toast and coffee, then he could be in town just as the shops were re-opening after the siesta. Actually, now that he came to think of it, did they even have a phone shop in town? Of course they must, he assured himself. Everywhere had a phone shop, these days, and Almacena – backwater though it was, was surely no exception.

Lydia, Miguel and the Bensons were sitting on the terrace at Manolo's Bar and Restaurant, lunching over a large paella shared between them.

'I have to say,' said Gerald, dropping a shrimp's head onto the side of his plate. 'Much as I like and admire His Lordship, he's not at all what I was expecting.'

'No,' said Lydia. 'Me neither.'

Gerald looked around to make sure no one was close enough to overhear him. All the red plastic tables around them were all occupied, but the diners were all Spaniards and far too absorbed in their own conversations to pay the group of *ingléses* any mind. He turned back to Lydia and said in a lower voice, 'Call me a lemon, but I was expecting something more sinister. You know? Evil, like Christopher Lee used to be in the old films.'

'Someone cruel, vicious, diabolical even?' suggested Lydia.

'Yes.'

'Hmmm, me too.'

'I mean, don't get me wrong – I'm not complaining. As a matter of fact, I feel rather relieved. I know we'd all been gearing ourselves up for the rebirth of some hell-spawned monster as a result of all the ... well, you know, doing the Satanic rituals we were doing, and so for Underwood to be the way he is, is ... nice. But, as I say, *nice* isn't what I was expecting. I can't help but wonder sometimes if maybe all that black mass stuff was rather, well – ' he left the sentence unfinished.

Lydia, who had finished her meal, lit a cigarette. 'Well what, Gerald?'

'Well, I, I'm starting to wonder if, perhaps it was all somewhat unnecessary.'

'You always seemed to enjoy it at the time.'

'Yes, well, that's as maybe, but what I'm saying is, they haven't actually achieved anything in terms of real pay-off for us, have they?'

'Pay-off?'

'Yes. I mean, we've not been rewarded for our unholy doings, have we? Oh, I know we got our vampire back from the grave, but that was on the cards anyway. No, it seems to me our sacrifices have gone rather unnoticed.'

'I see. And what exactly makes you say that?'

'Well, let's take your position in all this, Lydia: you were supposed to have a pivotal, if not absolutely commanding role in this whole business, but as it turns out, you seem to have been completely sidelined. In the eleventh hour, David turns up and ousts you from your position. It's almost like ... ' He looked up the statue of Christ that stood with arms outstretched at the top of a high hill above the cafe. 'Well, one could almost wonder if we might have perhaps been backing the wrong horse.'

'Oh, I see,' Lydia smiled. 'You think Christ has intervened, do you?'

'Well, you know, David coming along when he did – '

'Oh, get a grip, Gerald.' Lydia sat forward, lowering her volume but unable to keep the anger from her voice. 'David came because *John* sent for him, not Jesus. And as for Satan, if you were expecting him to just pop out of a smoking hole in the ground and start handing out thank you notes and reward tokens, then you're clearly losing the plot. I killed those people at sacrifice because I wanted to, and you joined in for exactly the same reason. Why? Because none of us thought we would be human for much longer; we were preparing for our transformations into vampires, that's why.' She sat back and snatched a drag of her cigarette. 'But of course, that's just not how things turned out, is it? It was nothing to do with God or Satan, Gerald, it was just bad luck. However, I feel our luck might be about to change.' She turned to Cynthia. 'How's that bite on your neck?'

Cynthia touched the light chiffon scarf she wore around her neck to cover the bite marks of the night before. 'Oh, fine. It's faded quite a bit, but it's still there.'

'What about other symptoms. Underwood spoke about a queer tingle and an attraction you'd feel towards him for a few days. Are you tingling in any unusual places when you think of him?'

Cynthia smiled. 'Just the usual places, darling. No more, no less. I'm horribly disappointed.'

Lydia turned to Gerald. 'You haven't noticed anything unusual, have you, Gerald? She didn't get up in the middle of the night and go sleepwalking to the bedroom windows or anything like that?'

'Sleepwalking?' said Gerald. 'Why no, not that I'm aware of. Mind you, I slept like a top last night; she could have sleepwalked straight through the bloody windows and I wouldn't have noticed.'

'I didn't sleepwalk anywhere, Lydia,' said Cynthia. 'That entrancement thing he did must have doused all such urges. I feel completely normal.'

'Nevertheless, there was something there that he had to douse,' said Lydia. 'David called it a vampiric infection, he spoke of it like it was a virus.'

'But the only symptom of that seems to be fancying Underwood,' said Gerald.

'You miss the point, Gerald,' said Lydia. 'The point is that there is at least some element of a virus – a communicable infection.'

'But this infection does not make a vampire,' said Miguel. 'He said it wears off in a few days, vampirism is forever.'

'Yes, but it's obviously the first bit, isn't it?' said Lydia. 'You've seen it in loads of films: the vampire bites the victim, and then he bites his wrist and gets the victim to drink from him, and then hey presto! The victim becomes a vampire.'

'I say,' said Gerald. 'So what you're saying is that, at the moment and for the next few days, Cynthia is half-way to becoming an actual vampire?'

'I believe so, yes.'

'Oh my,' said Cynthia. 'Can you imagine what this queer tingle must feel like? It's such a pity that His Lordship put the dampers on it for me.'

'But the virus is still there,' said Lydia, 'It's like having a toothache and taking painkillers, you still have the toothache, you just can't feel it.'

Gerald wiped a piece of bread around his plate to soak up the last of his paella. 'Hmmm, but tell me, Lydia, how exactly does this change our luck? Cynthia being half-way to undead doesn't really seem much of a shift in our fortunes.' He took a bite of the bread and looked at Lydia expectantly.

'No,' said Cynthia, 'not unless Underwood opens one of his veins for me and offers me a drink of himself, which, regrettably, seems highly unlikely.'

Lydia smiled. 'Yes. But what if you, or any victim for that matter, were to open one of his veins by force and take a drink from him?'

Gerald gasped and almost inhaled the bread he was chewing. He coughed it clear. 'Jesus Christ!' he spluttered. 'That's ... that's ... '

'Brilliant,' said Miguel. He took Lydia's hand and kissed it. 'You are a genius, Lydia!'

'Er, I'm sorry,' said Cynthia. 'But we *are* talking hypotheticals here, aren't we? I mean, you don't actually expect me to take a knife and a cup to Lord Underwood, do you?'

Lydia laughed and took her hand back from Miguel with an affectionate squeeze. 'No dear, of course not, that would be far too dangerous.'

'But you're obviously thinking that one of us should.'

'Yes.'

'Who?' said Gerald.

'Why me, of course. Who else?'

'But how are you going to do that?' said Cynthia. 'I mean, I don't want to rub salt into the wounds, darling, but you tried to turn his head last night, but it was Michelle who was ultimately in his arms on the dance floor.'

Lydia's expression soured. 'I know, God only knows why. But I'm not going to let that put me off. I'll just try a different approach.'

'You mean other than dressing up like a tart and wrapping yourself around him on the dance floor?' said Gerald. 'Sorry, don't get me wrong, it would work for me ten times over, but he didn't seem particularly moved by it, did he? As Cyn says, he only seems to have eyes for Michelle.'

'I don't understand this attraction of Underwood to Michelle,' said Miguel. 'She is not as beautiful as Lydia; she is not as sexy; she is not as intelligent. She is just normal.'

'Beauty is in the eye of the beholder, Miguel,' said Cynthia. 'Perhaps *normal* is what he values.'

Lydia nodded slowly. 'Yes, that's good. I can do normal.'

'Perhaps we're on to something,' said Cynthia. 'What is it that she has that might appeal to Underwood?'

'Keith?' said Gerald.

'Don't be stupid, darling. Let's think about it neutrally, Lydia. She's a lovely person: bright, charming, chatty.'

'Lovely bum,' said Gerald.

'Oh, shut up, Gerald,' said Cynthia. 'But, yes, it's true, she does have a lovely bum. However, I think he's drawn to her warmth, her vivacity.'

'I'm vivacious!' said Lydia.

'Yes, dear, but you're not the warmest of people, are you? Weren't you saying that you told him you were evil?'

'Well, yes, but he asked, and at the time I thought it was an appropriate answer. He was talking about me being guardian.'

'What one looks for in a minder and what one looks for in a soul mate are two completely different things, darling.'

Lydia stubbed out her cigarette and waved to the waiter. She ordered a round of gin and tonics without asking anyone if they wanted one. Cynthia leaned forward and laid her hand over Lydia's. 'So, I say if you still want him to get his teeth into you, darling, perhaps you should try a more sensitive approach. Show him your tenderness, your frailty, your human side.'

'Show him your *backside*, more like,' said Gerald.

'Shut up, Gerald!' said Cynthia.

The waiter returned with a tray of drinks. They were silent until he had gone, then Lydia picked up her drink. 'Of course, you're both right. Somehow or other, I'll get him alone with me tonight before we go out, and I'll show him my human side *and* my sexuality. One of them is bound to work, and if they don't ... ' she smiled at something she saw in her mind's eye.

'What?' said Gerald.

'Let's just say I've got a back-up plan, Gerald. And that tonight, while I may not get myself into his heart exactly, one way or another, I'll get his teeth into my neck, and his infection into my blood.' She raised her glass. 'Chin-chin.'

7

DAVID RETURNED FROM TOWN with some groceries and a top-of-the-range mobile phone for Underwood shortly before seven o'clock. He'd had to go to Ronda to find a place where he could buy a phone; evidently the ubiquity of phone shops didn't yet extend to Almacena. The young salesman had tried to enlighten him on the various wonders of the phone he'd picked out, but neither David's Spanish vocabulary, nor his interest, extended sufficiently to the topic. He'd apologetically stated his English nationality – a by-word for linguistic hopelessness – and he and the salesman had shrugged in agreement at the pointlessness of continuing the conversation.

David's own phone was a seven-year old Nokia. It made and received calls: that was all he'd ever wanted it to do, and he was blithely indifferent to the new generation of phones that bristled with additional functions he had no interest in. For a long time, his only interest had been in alcohol; then in recovery, it had been in abstaining from alcohol; and now, in Almacena, it was in managing an altogether different monster – and if that monster wanted a high-tech phone, David was happy to buy it for him, but he'd have to get someone else to show him how to turn it on.

No sooner had David got the shopping unpacked than the evening's breakfast announced itself by ringing the front door bell. David opened the door. As expected, and right on time, Ildefonso Hernandez, the Flinches' Spanish lawyer, stood on the doorstep along with his wife. They were wearing formal evening wear: he in a black tuxedo and Eugenia in a midnight blue evening gown.

'Hola, David,' said Ildefonso. 'You remember my wife, Eugenia?'

'Of course,' said David, exchanging kisses with Eugenia. 'How are you Eugenia?'

'*Muy bien*, David. And how are you and the Lord Underwood?'

'Oh, we're fine now, after a ... difficult start. Please, come in.'

'Thank you,' said Ildefonso. He looked at David's jeans and faded t-shirt and his brow creased with doubt. 'I, er, I hope we are not overdressed.'

'Oh no, you look great. I'm going to change into something a bit smarter myself in a short while, just as soon as I've made you both comfortable. But tell me, Ildefonso, how is your father after his heart attack? Lydia told me he's out of danger.'

'Yes, he is fine, thank you, David. I think Lord Underwood's return gives him the will to live.'

'Yes, but Lord Underwood's return was very nearly the death of him, wasn't it?'

'Ahh, he is an old man, but strong.'

David took the Hernandezes through to the lounge. He furnished them with drinks and asked them to excuse him while he went to get changed. Once upstairs, he knocked on Lydia's door.

'Hang on,' she called from within. A moment later, she opened the door; she was fiddling with an earring. 'What is it?'

David couldn't help but notice her dress, a white evening gown with a plunging 'v' neckline that left little to the imagination. 'Er, nice dress.'

'Thank you, you like it?'

'Yes, it's, er, very nice.'

Lydia opened the door wider so he could get a better look. The dress fell all the way to the floor, hugging her waist and hips and split to the thigh. 'I know. It cost a packet, I can tell you, but I think it's gorgeous. Sexy and stylish, don't you agree?'

David nodded. 'Yes, well, as I say, it's very nice.' He looked up and met her eyes. She had been waiting for them.

'Does it stir happy memories?'

'*What?*' David was horrified, not so much by the question as by her actually asking it. 'Oh, for God's sake, Lydia, leave it out. That was a long time ago.'

'Perhaps, but doesn't this dress just bring it all back?'

David turned away, uncertain as to where to look. He shook his head, annoyed, then turned back to meet her cool smile. 'Look, the Hernandezes have just arrived and I need to get showered and changed before the sun goes down. So could you go down and keep them entertained for me, please?'

Lydia stepped behind the door, partly closing it as if to conceal herself from him. 'Of course. I'd love to.'

'Thank you.' He was about to go when he noticed her hand holding the door: she was wearing a gold solitaire ring on the third finger, but the stone was missing, the four tiny claws that had held it now grasping at vacancy. He pointed it out. 'Hey, you've lost your diamond.'

'Hmm?' she checked the ring. 'Oh dear. It was there a minute ago. Thank you.'

'You ought to be careful with that.'

'Yes. I will be.'

'You might snag that new frock of yours and we wouldn't want what's left of it unravelling, now would we?'

Lydia smiled. 'No, I'm sure you wouldn't.' She shut the door in his face.

After shaving and showering, David dressed in a fresh white shirt, black trousers and shoes. Then he put on a white doctor's coat which Conchita had been able to supply him with. It was perhaps a conceit on his part, but he told himself it would make the donors feel as though they were in safe hands. The sound of a splash from the pool outside drew his attention to the window. Darkness had fallen and reflected light from the swimming pool rippled through the glass and onto the ceiling. Underwood must be up and taking his early evening swim.

'Right then,' David said to his reflection in the shaving mirror. 'I'd better go and get that breakfast ready.'

Fifteen minutes later, the Hernandezes each lay on a single bed. Between them was a dining chair. Each of them had an I.V. tube running from their arms to a stand behind the chair. Ildefonso was propped up on a pillow and drinking a Martini. 'You're sure the drink is not going to be a problem, David?'

'Not at all,' said David as he fixed Eugenia's I.V. line to the apparatus. 'If anything, His Lordship likes it. Says it gives him a little lift.' From the stairs at the end of the corridor there came the sound of approaching whistling. Eugenia tensed. David gave her a reassuring smile. 'Speak of the Devil.'

The whistling drew nearer until finally the whistler, Underwood, strolled in with a folded copy of yesterday's Times newspaper under his arm. He wore a white toweling bathrobe and espadrilles and his damp hair was combed back from his forehead. He saw the Hernandezes and grinned. 'Hallo. You must be, er ... ?'

'Señor and señora Hernandez, My Lord,' said David. 'Señor Hernandez is your lawyer here in Almacena. You and my father originally contracted señor Hernandez's father back in the fifties.'

'Of course,' said Underwood. He took Ildefonso's hand and shook it warmly. 'Very pleased to meet you, sir. No, don't try and get up, old chap – you're rather pinned down there, aren't you?'

Ildefonso relaxed against the pillows. 'The pleasure is all mine, My Lord. May I introduce my wife, Eugenia?'

Underwood walked around the beds to take Eugenia's hand and lifted it to his lips. 'Eugenia, what a charming name. I think we've met before, no?'

Eugenia blushed. 'Well, not formally, My Lord. We were at your resurrection ceremony.'

'Ahh,' Underwood nodded and sat down on the dining chair. 'Yes, that was it. Terrible mess. Blame old Flinchy here. Rather a bad case of first night nerves, eh Flinch?'

'Yes, sir,' said David. 'Sorry sir.'

Underwood turned to Ildefonso. 'Your father had a heart attack, if I remember rightly. Is he all right?'

'He is recovering, My Lord. Thank you. He sends you his deepest respect and says he hopes to come and see you when he is well enough.'

'Excellent,' said Underwood. 'But hopefully not in the same capacity as yourself, eh?' He chuckled. Ildefonso did likewise. 'No, señor Hernandez, I shall go and see him as soon as he is well enough. I feel it's the least I can do for a senior and highly esteemed member of the Sect, not to mention an old friend of sorts.'

'You honour us, My Lord.'

'Oh not at all,' said Underwood, taking the end of Ildefonso's I.V. tube from the stand and putting it in his mouth. 'My pleasure, old bean.' He nodded to David. 'Right ho, Flinch, dish up.'

'Yes, sir.' David opened the canula in Ildefonso's arm and blood began to flow into the tube.

'Mmmm,' said Underwood when the blood entered his mouth. 'Someone's been at the drinks cabinet, eh?' Ildefonso suddenly looked nervous. Underwood reassured him with a grin. 'Bottoms up, sir.'

When both Ildefonso and Eugenia had been bled to the tune of a pint each, David was about to escort them downstairs for something to eat when Underwood stopped him. 'I say, Flinch, would you mind accompanying me to my rooms for a moment? I'm sure our guests here won't mind making their own way back to the lounge.' He raised his eyebrows at Ildefonso and Eugenia, both of whom confirmed that this wasn't a problem.

'Something the matter, sir?' asked David a few moments later as they were walking along the corridor to Underwood's rooms.

'No, no, nothing's the matter.' They went into the suite of rooms set aside for Underwood's private use, which consisted of a bedroom with a large double bed, a bathroom and a dressing room. First off the hallway was the bedroom; David stayed there while Underwood went on into the dressing room. David had earlier laid out a black suit and waistcoat, underwear, socks, and a shirt and tie. Underwood gave the clothes a cursory glance, a look of incredulity flickering across his features when he saw the tie. 'I, er, just wanted your opinion on something, that's all.'

'My opinion?' David was surprised.

'Yes,' Underwood began to dress, calling back into the bedroom as he did so. 'It's about Michelle. You know, the young woman who owns the pub?'

'Yes, sir. But she's hardly young.'

'Compared to me, Flinch, the Sphinx is young.'

'*Really?*'

Underwood laughed. 'No, good heavens. I'm old, but I'm not *that* old.'

'If I may, Milord, how old are you then?'

Underwood looked around the door. 'How old do you think?'

David shook his head. 'I've absolutely no idea. You look about my age, maybe a bit older.'

'I see. And how old are you?'

'Thirty-seven.'

Underwood chuckled and went back to dressing. 'Ahhh, a mere babe.'

'Well, I'd say Michelle must be more or less the same age, give or take a year.'

'Yes. So a similar age – at least in appearance – to me. She and I would make a fine couple, don't you think?'

David stared at the doorway into the dressing room where he could hear Underwood moving about. Was he serious? Surely not. He gave a little laugh. 'Yeah, but you're not a similar age, are you, Milord? To say you're old enough to be her great grandfather is, I imagine, something of an understatement?'

'Oh, indeed it is, Flinch.'

'So, what then? Great grandfather? Greater?'

'Oh, considerably. I was – I don't know – in my late twenties, early thirties, when I became what I am.'

'Really? No offence, but you look older.'

'Oh, life was harder then, Flinch. Bad diet, and hardships I doubt you could even imagine. That and of course, one continues to age – microscopically, at least.'

'So when did you become what you are?'

Underwood walked back into the bedroom fastening his cuffs. 'Well, let's just say that George the First was on the throne.'

'Oh right,' David nodded, none the wiser. 'Which one was he?'

'Which what? King?'

'Yeah. Sorry but I get all those Georges, Henrys, and Edwards mixed up.'

'He was the first of the Hanoverians, Flinch. The German line, you know? Bit of a dimwit, by all accounts.'

'So this was after Cromwell, then?'

'Oh, yes, about fifty years or so.' Underwood returned to the dressing room, carrying on the conversation through the open double-doors. 'But anyway, Flinch, what do you think?'

'About what?'

'About Michelle and me.'

This again? David followed Underwood into the dressing room. 'I'm not sure if I understand, sir. What exactly are you asking me?'

Underwood looked back at David from the full length mirror and smiled. 'I'm asking if you think she'd make a good Lady Underwood?'

David's head swam slightly. 'But ... but sir, I ... we ... we agreed, you wouldn't ... '

Underwood looked at him expectantly. 'Wouldn't what?'

'Wouldn't kill any more people; wouldn't feed from unwilling victims.'

'Yes, we did agree to that, though I fail to see why that has any bearing here. I'm not planning to dine on Michelle; I'm planning to woo her.'

David stared at Underwood's reflection for some sign that he might be joking, but there was none. David's mouth was suddenly dry. He licked his lips, and again, with a smile, tried to proceed amiably, as if Underwood was only speculating. 'But ... she's already married. She's got a kid.'

Underwood shrugged. 'So?'

'*So?*' David took a step further into the room, his smile fading. 'You can't be serious. I mean, really, on so many levels. She's married for one. Two, she's a mother, and three, she's *alive.*'

'Well thank heaven the last one, anyway. She's no good to anybody dead.'

'You're dead.'

Underwood threw his head back and laughed.

'What? Why's that funny? I drove a stake through your heart, Milord. No living thing could have survived that.'

'Oh, I see. Got it all figured out, have you, Flinch?'

'No. I don't have it figured out at all.'

'No, indeed you don't, old boy. How did you come to this gruesome conclusion about me?'

'Well, when we were preparing you for the resurrection, Beltran listened to your chest for a heartbeat, but there wasn't one. Then there was the stake through the heart, and that didn't kill you. So you must be dead, or *undead*, whatever the hell that is.'

Underwood turned to him. 'I see. Well, that's news to me, Flinch. As far as I'm concerned, I am as alive as you are.'

'Well, would you mind explaining that, sir?'

'I've got a better idea. Let's see if we can reach a conclusion together. Tell me, when you hammered your cricket stump into my heart, Flinch, did it bleed?'

'Yes.'

Underwood smiled. 'Forgive me, but you say you've had some medical training?'

'That's right.'

'So, tell me, doctor or nurse Flinch, what is it that the heart does, exactly? Something about pumping blood?'

'Yes.'

Underwood shrugged. 'So, you see the flaw in your logic then, Flinch? If my heart isn't beating then what is pumping my blood and making me bleed all over your cricket stump?'

'I ... I don't know, but I know I drove a stake right through your heart, and if it had been alive, it would have died.'

'And yet it didn't – *I* didn't. I'm not dead, Flinch. I mean, do you really think you're having a conversation with a corpse?'

'I don't know what to think, to be honest.'

'Alright, well here's another question, doctor or nurse, or orderly even, Flinch: why do I need to feed if I'm dead?'

'I don't know, sir. Why *do* you need to feed?'

'For nourishment, of course. And why do I need nourishment?'

'Because you're alive?'

'Precisely.'

David was looking at Underwood wide-eyed; what the vampire was saying was uncanny in the extreme, but it made sense – much more sense than his being dead, which David had never been able to get his head around. 'Your heartbeat before resurrection – I speculated it was just massively reduced, a fraction of the amount of beats that, say, my heart is performing. Is that right?'

'Well done, Flinch. Not quite the class dunce after all.'

'And the stake, your body seemed to be healing your heart as I was attacking it.'

'Which of course it couldn't have done if I was, in fact, dead.'

'But, *how*? I drove a stake through it – '

'No, Flinch,' Underwood interrupted. 'You drove a *stick* through my heart. There's a big difference between a cricket stump and a stake, old boy.'

David felt as if he had been slapped around the face. He reached for a chair near the door and sat down heavily. 'You mean, you didn't die because my stake wasn't ... '

'Your stake wasn't a stake, Flinch. Simple as that. To slay a vampire you have to destroy the heart, not just damage it. The vampire's body will heal itself when harmed; you've seen that much with your own eyes.'

'Well, well yeah, I have now. But I hadn't at the time – I'd seen you do something funky with your fingernails, but your *heart*.'

Underwood chuckled. 'And that surprised you?'

'Yes. You could say that. Almost as much as this is. Why are you telling me this? I tried to kill you. How do you know I won't try it again – especially now you've told me how to do it?'

Underwood walked up to where David sat and hunkered down so they were face to face. 'Because I trust you not to, Flinch. Our relationship has to be built on trust, and in giving you the means to kill me, I seal that trust. My life is in your hands, David Flinch. You are now, beyond any doubt, my guardian ... or my destroyer.' He patted David on the shoulder and stood up again. 'I leave that decision up to you.'

For a moment, David was silent. Then he said, 'Is, is there anything else I should know?'

'About what?'

'About your ... vulnerabilities?'

Underwood smiled. 'Actually, I daresay you know a few of them from folklore and fiction. It's just a question of doing the job correctly.'

'So, what? Sunlight?'

'Yes, my skin is rather sensitive to direct sunlight. I burn easily, and vigorously.'

'Decapitation?'

'Well, one can't very well regenerate one's body without one's head, Flinch. The brain holds the body's blueprints. Consciously or unconsciously it's the old grey matter that performs the regeneration.'

'What about silver?'

'Silver, schmilver. It's just metal.'

'Crucifixes?'

'Stars of David? Crescent Moons? They're all just symbols, invested with meaning by some, and utterly meaningless to others. I count myself amongst the others.'

'Fire?'

'My flesh will burn, as I mentioned in relation to sunlight. But I heal too – and very quickly. So it depends on the amount, and the intensity of the fire, or sunlight.'

'But you started that fire in the car the other night, how come you didn't get burned then?'

'I said my flesh burns, Flinch, but when I destabilize in metamorphosis, I *am* the heat; moving fast and formless away from the fires I sometimes unavoidably create. However, should you trap my destabilised, formless self in a furnace from which there is no escape, then, again, all that I am will be reduced to ash.'

David nodded. 'So the same as anything else then? But what about the other folklorey things? Holy water?'

Underwood laughed. 'More religious twaddle. Same with those silly Catholic wafers that are forever turning up in my coffin.'

'Garlic?'

'I like garlic. Wasn't keen at first, but one acquires the taste. Of course, one has to if one wants to eat anywhere south of Dover.'

'Or north of Dover these days. Everyone in England eats garlic.'

'Do they?'

'Oh yeah. Indian cuisine, Italian. Curry and pizza are probably the most popular foods in the country.'

'Oh, how interesting.'

'So, is there anything else?'

'What?'

'Harmful to you?'

'Oh, the usual stuff that flesh is vulnerable to: being torn apart by sharks or crocodiles, being blown up, basically anything that can damage me faster than I can heal myself.'

'So *a* bullet wouldn't have any effect, but a hail of bullets would?'

Underwood chuckled. 'Well, I always try to avoid machine gun fire whenever possible. It hurts like hell.'

'So you've survived that?'

'Since I stand here before you, yes, obviously.'

'Because there weren't enough guns?'

'More because the guns weren't targeting the right bits of me.'

David nodded. 'I see.'

'And so,' said Underwood. 'You and I are now on a more equal footing. You have my Achilles' heels, so to speak.'

'Yes. But, I can't believe you trust me with all this information; I tried to kill you.'

Underwood waved the idea away. 'Oh, that was different. You didn't know me then, and we didn't have our little deal about what my eating arrangements were.'

'But – but that's what we've just been talking about: our deal about your eating arrangements. You're talking about breaking that deal and killing Michelle.'

'No, Flinch, I'm not talking about killing anyone. I thought we'd just established that I, and consequently vampires in general, are alive.'

'Well whatever you call it, you're still talking about turning her into a vampire, right?'

'Yes. It's a beautiful metamorphosis. I'd let you watch, but I fear you'd make a nuisance of yourself.'

'You fear correctly, sir. I'm sorry, but I don't think I can allow you to do this.'

'I beg your pardon?'

'I said, I can't allow it.'

'Excuse me, Flinch. I merely wanted to know what you thought of her, not whether you approve of the relationship or not. Who on Earth do you think you are?'

'I'm my brother's keeper, sir ... and my sister's.'

'Oh pish! Michelle is neither to you. She's a woman trapped in an unhappy marriage, most likely for the sake of that daughter of theirs, and she's certainly old enough to go out and make a living for herself.'

'How? By cleaning chimneys? She's just a kid. A twenty-first century kid, mind you, not something out of a Victorian poorhouse. And whatever's wrong between Michelle and her husband is temporary. They've had a row or something stupid like that – all couples do. It's gonna blow over.'

'No, Flinch,' said Underwood. He got up and picked up David's choice of tie, regarding it with disapproval. 'It's more serious than that. I'm not sure what the problem is exactly, but she definitely wants to leave him.'

'How do you know? Did she tell you?'

Underwood dropped the tie and went to the wardrobe to select another. 'Not in so many words.'

'So ... what? You read her mind? Are you psychic too?'

'No, not psychic as such; let's just say, I'm *sensitive*.'

'So you probably know how I feel about you, right now.'

Underwood laughed. 'Oh yes. But it wouldn't take any special talents to do that.' He selected a tie to his liking and turned back to face David. 'As always, Flinch, I admire your motivations, but again, as always, I feel them to be somewhat ... irrelevant.'

'Oh, thank you.'

'Sorry, Flinch. I didn't mean that to come out quite that way. What I mean is, however morally well-positioned you may be, you are nevertheless wrong.'

'Well begging your pardon, Milord, but I disagree. How can you possibly justify transforming a human being into something else, just for your ... what? Romantic amusement?'

'Amusement, Flinch? Amusement? *You* may seek amusement with your German lady friend, but I seek something a tad more meaningful than that.'

'What? Marriage?'

'Don't be an ass.'

'Well what would you call it?'

'I'd call it something beyond your paltry human comprehension, actually. There's no point in trying to explain to you; your experience of love is bound to the flesh and your five woefully limited senses.'

'I've got no complaints about my five woefully limited senses, or my experience of love, actually.'

'Pah! What experience? With that little *fräulein* that you left back in England? You've all but forgotten her already, haven't you?'

'That's not fair – if it weren't for you, I'd still be with her.'

'Oh, what a rotter I am. How you must pine for her. How long has it been now, a week at most? Oh the loss you must feel.'

'What?'

'A week? A month? A year?' Underwood shook his head. 'These are but moments to me. I've been alone for more than your lifetime, Flinch. You think yourself able to judge my need for companionship when you can't even comprehend what love, loss, and loneliness are to an immortal being such as I? You humans talk about loving each other forever without having the vaguest notion of what forever is. What could you possibly understand of these things, you and your German *bird*? Nothing, that's what.'

A look of pain crossed David's face. He looked down. 'Yeah, my relationship with Lisa is young, but if you think that ... ' His sentence trailed off.

Underwood raised his eyebrows. 'But what?'

'Nothing.'

There was something in David's voice that Underwood recognised. He softened his tone. 'There was another?'

David nodded. 'Yes. She died.'

'Oh. I *am* sorry, Flinch.'

'I'd, I'd rather not talk about it, if you don't mind.'

'Of course. Forgive me, I just wanted to impress upon you that I'm ... well, I'm so alone, you know?'

David shrugged slightly. 'Well, it's not like you're really alone, is it? What about us, the Flinches? We've always been there, haven't we?'

'Yes, but surely I don't need to explain why my relationship with my servants isn't the same as an intimate relationship with a woman, Flinch? I seek more than someone to lay out my suits and help me procure my evening meals; I seek a lover, a partner, a mate. I seek a Lady Underwood, and I believe that I have found her.'

'Alright, but you said you'd been alone for more than my lifetime, sir, does that mean that you've had other ... mates?'

Underwood turned back to the mirror and began tying his tie. David waited. When Underwood had finished, he turned and said, 'Yes. I have.'

'And so, where are they now? I mean, you made them into vampires, right?'

'Yes.'

'Well then, I presume they have the same immortal life expectancy as you do?'

Underwood opened his cigarette case and took out a cigarette. He lit it and, without looking at David, he nodded.

'So what happened to them, then? Obviously you didn't divorce them.'

'Don't be facetious, Flinch. This isn't a joking matter.'

'I don't mean to be facetious, Milord. But you're talking about changing a woman from one form of life to another. You asked for my opinion; how can I give it if I don't know what's involved? I mean, you say you've had others, but they're conspicuously not part of your life any more. I'm concerned for Michelle, that's all. I want to know what might await her as Lady Underwood, not just in the near future, but ... eventually.'

Underwood sighed. 'Eventually. What awaits all romance eventually?'

'It ends?'

'Precisely.'

'And so, not wanting to sound insistent, but what happens to your lovers when *eventually* comes around?'

Underwood said nothing.

'Do they die?'

Underwood nodded, 'Sometimes.'

'You kill them?'

'I have done. But other times we agree to part amicably. It depends on the circumstances.'

David held his hand to his head as if to steady it. 'And so, what would become of Michelle in a few years' time? Would you just chuck her out in the sunshine when you got tired of her? Forgive me, sir, I'm not being funny or anything, but you two don't seem to be cut from quite the same cloth. How long do you think forever is gonna be for her?'

Underwood glowered at David. 'Don't assume to know me, Flinch. You know nothing of my cloth.'

'That doesn't answer my question, sir. If I may speak frankly, I think you're being just a bit impulsive with this need for a mate of yours.'

'*Impulsive?*'

'Yes, sir, think about it: you've been asleep for fifty years and you've woken up all full of the joys of spring, so to speak, rejuvenated. And Michelle's the first woman you've set eyes on. Oh, you've had a laugh together, a dance or two, and now you think you're in love. But surely a man of your years and wisdom can see that this is just a whim?'

'Oh shut up, Flinch. You sound like a maiden aunt.'

'I'm sorry, but you asked me what I think and I'm going to tell you. You don't know her – not properly, not like a man and woman should if they're going to ... ' he shook his head, 'I was going to say make a commitment to each other, but I doubt whether her commitment is required, is it?'

'Oh it's required, Flinch, and it is given. And to address your other argument: in the short time since I made her acquaintance, I think I can say I've come to know Michelle far better than that husband of hers has in all their years of marriage together.'

'How?'

Underwood chuckled. 'You wouldn't understand, old boy. Let's just call it empathy. Our souls have touched ... and they like what they feel.'

It was at this moment that Lydia entered.

Lydia had grown tired of answering the Hernandezes' questions about Underwood and had politely excused herself, saying that she was going to find out what was keeping His Lordship from joining them – though more precisely, what she wanted to do was find out where the hell David was. She had planned that as soon as he came down, she'd slip away to Underwood's rooms to catch him while he was still dressing. However, neither of them had come down, and she had been starting to fear that when they did, it would be together. If that happened, she would be unlikely to get another opportunity to be alone with Underwood that evening. Underwood would want to go to *La Reina* – as bloody usual – and he would probably spend the evening slobbering over Michelle. But Lydia had other plans, and it was with a mind to initiating those plans that she had come upon the door to Underwood's rooms and overheard the conversation going on within. Her breath had stopped in her chest when she realised that Underwood was telling David how he was vulnerable to fire and sunlight. She cursed herself for not getting there sooner and, hugging the wall, stood as close to the open door as she could without making herself visible.

She listened, transfixed as she heard Underwood say he was looking for a partner, but with a growing sense of horror on hearing that the partner in question was to be Michelle. Jesus Christ, was he serious? Lady Underwood? The woman was a bloody chav! She wasn't fit to be a scullery maid in the Underwood household. Lydia's mind reeled at the thought of Michelle actually becoming a vampire, giving orders and demanding to be called, "my lady".

No! Never! Lydia waited for as long as she could, then she adjusted her dress – making sure everything it promised was being suitably offered, flicked her hair back, and knocked lightly on the open door. 'Er, excuse me.' She went in and crossed to the dressing room. 'The door was open; I hope you don't mind me disturbing you, but I suspect the Hernandezes might be getting a little bored with just my company. It's not every day they find themselves in the home of a fabled prince of Hell, and well, I fear I rather pale in comparison.'

Underwood gave a little laugh. 'Prince of Hell, eh? That's a good one. Still, if the shoe fits.'

David got up and came to the door. 'I was just coming down anyway, Lydia. Are they in the lounge?'

'Yes. Will you take over for a bit, David? I need to freshen up before we go out.'

'Sure,' David went out, leaving Lydia and Underwood alone.

'I say,' said Underwood. 'You're looking smashing this evening, Lydia. Any special occasion?'

Lydia's face lit up. 'Oh, no, only the Hernandezes, My Lord. As I'm sure David's already told you, señor Hernandez is your local lawyer – as was his father before him. I felt sure you'd want to take them somewhere special and get to know them better, so I've booked a table for five at a lovely restaurant in Ronda.'

'Ronda?'

'Yes, it's a bit further than Alamacena, but it's a lovely night for a drive and you must be itching to go somewhere other than boring old *La Reina de Corazones*, especially after last night's little brou-ha-ha.'

'*Au-contraire*, Lydia,' said Underwood, stubbing out his cigarette. 'I'm rather fond of boring old *La Reina de Corazones*. And last night's little brouha-ha was nothing other than a few chaps letting off steam. I sorted things out with Keith before I left and now we're the best of friends.'

Lydia frowned. 'But, when you offered to shake hands and buy him a drink he told you to – forgive me, My Lord – but he told you to fuck off. He threatened to send you home in an ambulance. What did you do to change his mind?'

Underwood smiled. 'What did I do to change his mind? Well, I, uh, changed his mind.'

'Sorry?'

'Never mind, it's as I said, I sorted things out with him, and now we're as thick as thieves. So, shall we go downstairs to join our guests?'

'No,' Lydia stepped smartly between him and the door. 'I wanted to talk to you – alone.'

'Oh?'

She hesitated a moment then took an awkward step closer to him. 'I don't quite know how to say this, My Lord, but ... I couldn't help overhearing your conversation with David before I came in.'

Underwood frowned. 'You were earwigging?'

'No, sir, not earwigging, just, well ... I didn't want to come in at an inappropriate moment, so I was waiting, and, I just ... overheard you talking about yourself and Michelle.'

'Really? Well, since you know all about it, what do you have to say on the matter? I'd be interested in hearing a woman's perspective.'

Lydia parted her lips slightly and looked into his eyes. 'I, I'm sorry My Lord, I don't often agree with David, but in this matter, I find that I do – not on the issue of whether or not you should take a lover, that I fully understand, but on your particular choice of lover. Michelle's a nice enough woman, but she's married and she has a daughter.'

'Yes, well if you overheard my earlier conversation you'll know my answer to that already; the child's old enough to deal with a mother walking out – it happens every day, probably every minute, or every second, going by the amount of people that seem to be crawling on the Earth these days.'

'Yes, but it's more than just the family aspect, My Lord. What if the daughter simply couldn't accept her mother's leaving? What if she and her father came after Michelle? After both of you? Or what if they went to the police?'

Underwood was nonchalant as he selected a different waistcoat from the wardrobe. 'They won't. Honestly, your brother has no eye for ties and waistcoats, does he?'

'But you can't be certain of that, My Lord. And what if other people talk? The bouncers, the bar staff, the customers? Everyone saw you two together on the dance floor; you're probably already the talk of the town. Michelle's running off with you would really set tongues wagging. It'd draw attention to you.'

Underwood smiled patiently. 'Oh, really, Lydia. So what if they do?' He lay down his chosen waistcoat and took her lightly by the shoulders. 'What does it matter if tongues wag? What does it matter even if the police come after us? We've done nothing wrong, and Michelle will be able to tell them so herself.'

'But she'll be a vampire, won't she? The police tend to make their enquiries by day, My Lord. They'd come out here and the pair of you would be downstairs in your coffins. Unless ... you can go out in daylight?' Though she now knew the answer to this, she wanted to see if he would confide in her as he had done to David.

'There won't be any police, Lydia. Trust me. As long as Michelle is seen from time to time, alive, happy, and in rude health – and I can assure you she will be – then there'll be no problem.' Underwood picked up his waistcoat and slipped it on.

'No!' Lydia stepped closer and her hands went to Underwood's chest. 'There's an easier way still.'

'There is?'

As her mind tried to frame her next sentence, Lydia became aware of a quickening in her heartbeat, it produced a strange, aching sensation she was unaccustomed to. She found she couldn't speak, her throat felt suddenly contracted, as if it were trying to prevent her from saying words that might haunt her for the rest of her life. She withdrew her hands and turned away. 'Nothing,' she said, her voice suddenly embarrassingly unsteady. 'I'm sorry, it's nothing.'

Underwood walked to her back and laid his hands upon her shoulders. 'Lydia – ' he began, but was cut off as she wheeled around to face him.

'Me!' she blurted suddenly, surprising even herself. And then everything she wanted to say came tumbling out of her in a rush. 'You can take me, My Lord. I would never tell the police, and I wouldn't be any kind of complication. I've waited for you my whole life, and now ... and now I finally realise that you are my whole life.' She hesitated, then said aloud the words she had planned to say for effect if necessary, only now to find that she actually meant them. 'I – I love you. I always have, ever since I was a little girl. And I will love you forever and always.'

Underwood was stunned. 'Lydia, I – '

'Please,' she moved into his arms and clung to him. 'I'll do anything you want – you can use me as you like, you can do anything with me, anything. I'll serve you in ways no guardian ever could – but I can be that too: guardian, lover, whatever you want me to be, My Lord, but please, just take *me*.'

Underwood stared, aghast. 'Oh my God, I, I don't know what to say.'

Lydia looked up at him, her eyes bright with love and tears. 'Say yes, My Lord. Say yes and I will give you my life, my blood, every beat of my heart from now until you silence it.'

'Lydia,' Underwood eased her gently away from him. 'You must know, surely, that what you propose, however attractive it may be, is quite impossible.'

'Impossible?' she whispered. 'Why impossible, my love?'

'Lydia, I made a vow to your ancestor and my friend, Matthias Flinch, that none of his line would ever bleed for me. It is a vow I have upheld for nearly three hundred years; it's the one indisputable code that I live by, and one I can never violate.'

Lydia's hands tightened on the front of his waistcoat, grasping at the fabric. 'But that vow isn't relevant to us. I am *offering* myself to you. The only thing you'll be violating is me, and I *want* that, more than anything in the world, because I love you!'

'Lydia, please,' Underwood gently but firmly eased her hands from him. 'We cannot.'

'Why?' she cried. 'What's that cockney tart got that I haven't? Is it dancing? Is that it? Well I can dance too, but you don't know that because you didn't ask me, did you? But I can.'

'Lydia – '

'Why don't you ask me now? We don't need music, we can just dance, the two of us, here – ' she reached for him but he caught her hands.

'No, Lydia. I don't know what's come over you, but you must stop this now. Please.'

'*Why won't you dance with me?*' she cried, tears spilling from her eyes. '*Why?*'

'Because no Flinch shall bleed, Lydia. Don't be offended, I'm not blind to your charms. You are a beautiful woman, and were I to come upon you as a stranger in the night, then you would have cause to fear. But that can never be, because you aren't a stranger to me, my dear, far from it, you're family, or the closest thing I have to – '

'Don't!' she pulled herself from his grip and turned away. 'You don't need to say any more. I get the message.'

'Do you, Lydia?'

She nodded. 'Oh yes, but if you think no Flinch shall bleed, My Lord, you're mistaken. Because I can't live knowing you're with a woman who doesn't care for you – who could *never* care for you as I do.' She turned back to face him and raised the back of her right hand to her neck, feeling the sharp and twisted prongs of her ring bite against her skin. She had removed the diamond herself; it was to be a last-ditch gamble in the event that Underwood refused her. At that time it had been a cool, calculated decision, nothing more than a tactical ploy. But now, she gasped with something akin to relief as the prongs pierced her flesh.

'Goodbye, my love.' With a single, savage movement, she slashed the ring across her throat. There was no pain, but the blood that glistened on the back of her hand told her she had been successful. Her legs felt weak, and as she fell, from far away she heard Underwood call her name. He caught her, whether he was astonishingly fast or time had slowed she neither knew nor cared, all she knew was his mouth was at her throat, and she was in an ecstasy of death. She reached up, her fingers running over his collar and pushing into his hair, and she held him to her. 'Drink, my love, let me serve you in death as I could never in life.' Then from farther away, she heard another voice.

'*What the fuck!*'

David and the Hernandezes had tacitly refrained from acknowledging the distant sound of Lydia's increasingly loud cries from upstairs. Though the words were indistinct, the emotion in her voice was clear. Eventually David had had to politely excuse himself so he could investigate. He exited the lounge and closed the door, then he'd heard Lydia cry out, 'Don't!' He moved quickly to the stairs, as he reached them, he heard Underwood call Lydia's name in what sounded like alarm. He'd started running, racing up the stairs and along the corridor, to come to a staggering halt in the doorway of Underwood's rooms. The sight that met his eyes had a paralyzing effect. His first impression was only one of blood, a spreading crimson pool across the white tiled floor; then, at the centre of it, Underwood on his knees cradling Lydia's limp body in his arms, his face at her neck.

'What the fuck!'

Underwood snapped his head round, his mouth and chin dark with blood. David's paralysis broke and he launched himself in a dive at the vampire, but Underwood lashed out, swatting him across the room and sending him crashing into a wardrobe.

'Get a grip on yourself, Flinch! It's not what you think.'

David rolled to see Lydia trying to pull Underwood's face back to her neck. 'What do you mean it's not what I think? Are you trying to tell me she nicked herself shaving and you're trying to stick a Band-Aid on with your teeth?'

'Closer than you think, actually.' Underwood gently laid Lydia gently down onto the floor. She writhed in protest as he took her hand and removed the ring from her blood-slick finger. He held it up for David to see. 'She used this.'

David stared at the ring, its tiny gold claws clotted with skin and blood. 'She *what?*'

'She slashed her throat with it,' he tossed the ring to David, 'but fortunately I managed to close the wound before she lost too much blood. I'm somewhat more effective than a Band-Aid.'

'Oh my God,' David looked at Lydia, who now seemed to have lost consciousness, then at the blood that pooled across the tiles. 'But you've got her blood all over your mouth.'

'Yes, she was pumping it out quite badly. I needed to get in close to project some bile onto the wound. It was a nasty gash, but it looks like it's closed up all right now.'

'So, you stopped her bleeding?'

'Yes.'

'Jesus. How much blood did she lose?'

'Well,' said Underwood, looking around at the blood on the floor, 'it's not as bad as it looks, I doubt she's lost much more than our guests downstairs.' He moved to pick Lydia up.

David got to his feet. 'Here, let me help you with her.'

'No, no,' said Underwood as he gathered Lydia into his arms. 'I can manage quite well, thank you. She's just had a fright, that's all.'

'Well, let me check her. I'm a paramedic, remember?' David went to her and tilted her head, smoothing blood-soaked hair away from her throat so he could inspect the wound. There was a bubbling dark slash at the centre of the glistening sheen of blood and bile, but it wasn't bleeding. David turned to Underwood. 'It's like Cynthia last night?'

Underwood nodded. 'Yes.'

His hand still at Lydia's throat, David took her pulse. It was surprisingly strong, under the circumstances. 'She, she seems alright.'

'Yes. And so, if you're quite finished?'

'I, uh,' David stepped aside and Underwood carried Lydia through into the bedroom and laid her on the bed. 'But, I don't understand,' said David. 'Why? Why would she do such a thing? I mean, if she wanted to kill herself, why not just take an overdose or use a gun from the armoury? Why this? And why here?'

Underwood didn't feel it was quite proper to share what Lydia had told him with David. He rolled up his sleeves and shrugged. 'She's upset, Flinch. She's been through a lot these past few nights: the death of her brother, the death of her two friends at my resurrection – I understand that Beltran fellow was her boyfriend, is that right?'

'Well yeah, but she never showed any signs of being overly upset by any of it, let alone any suicidal tendencies. She didn't seem to care much about anything, other than you being back in the world of the living.'

'Well, perhaps everything just caught up with her all at once. That happens sometimes.'

'Maybe. So what were you two talking about?'

'I *beg* your pardon?'

'What were you talking about? You know, when she did it?'

'Are you interrogating me, Flinch?'

'No. I, I just want to know what happened. I'm concerned – I mean, she is my sister.'

'Well, your concern is duly noted, but as you can see, she's fine.'

'But – '

'I said, she's fine.' Underwood's tone brooked no argument.

'Yes, sir.'

'Now, tell me. Is there a nurse or doctor from the Sect living nearby?'

'Why do we need a doctor or a nurse? We've got me. I can look after her.'

'Well, you can't very well do that if we're going out with the Henandezes, now can you?'

'*What?* We're still going out?'

'Of course. What else would we do? Stay in and play gin rummy?'

'But, under the circumstances, surely we should – '

'Should what? Keep a tearful vigil at her bedside? A touching thought, Flinch, but hardly necessary, she's just lost a bit of blood, that's all.'

'But what if she tries again?'

Underwood shook his head. 'Don't worry, she won't try anything silly; I'm fairly certain of that. But just to be on the safe side, we should get someone in to keep an eye on her. So, who can we call upon?'

'Well, there's Conchita. She was John's nurse. She was there at your resurrection.'

'Perfect. Call her and get her over. Then go down and extend my apologies to the Hernandezes for keeping them waiting; tell them I'll be down in a short while.'

'But – '

'Flinch, you really are going to have to accept the fact that I know best. Now do as I say.'

David fought a moment to control his emotions, before yielding to Underwood's implacable superiority. 'Yes, sir.'

'Good. Then, once you've spoken to them, fetch a mop and bucket and get this mess cleaned up, would you? While you're doing that, I'll take a shower.'

'Yes, sir.'

'Capital. Then we can all head off to Ronda. Apparently Lydia's made a reservation at a restaurant there.'

'Yeah, yeah that's right. I've got the details downstairs.'

'Excellent. All right then, Flinch, chop-chop. Give that Conchita woman a call and I'll hop in the shower. Oh, and Flinch, talking of giving people a call, did you pick up one of those portable telephone devices for me?'

'Yes, I, uh, I got the same type as Lydia's, as you requested.'

'Jolly good. Bring it along this evening and you can show me how to turn it on.'

Resisting the urge to roll his eyes, David left. Underwood closed the door behind him and began to remove his tie. Lydia's blood oozed from it and through his fingers. He grimaced, ripping it from his neck and dropping it to the floor as if it were a dead thing. He looked at Lydia where she lay sleeping and felt a wave of pity for her; Arthur's little girl, confused and desperate. He was just about to go to sit beside her when it occurred to him that she might wake up. He decided she'd be better left to sleep. He turned and, pulling his bloody shirt from his body, went into the bathroom, and turned on the shower.

Lydia lay motionless on the bed until she heard the water flow of the shower change from a steady hiss to a staccato cascade, indicating Underwood was standing beneath it. Then she opened her eyes. She got to her feet, standing up too fast and feeling a wave of light-headedness that almost caused her to fall back down again. She caught hold of the nightstand, steadied herself, then she went to the door and moved as quickly as she could down the corridor to her room. Once inside, she closed the door, locked it, and went to the dressing table to snatch up her telephone. She quickly selected Cynthia's number.

Cynthia picked up her phone after a couple of rings and, seeing Lydia's name as the caller, she answered: 'Lydia –'

'Cynthia,' Lydia interrupted, her voice sounding shaky in her own ears. 'I need to see you two and Miguel. Meet me at *El Rincon* in one hour.'

'Lydia, darling. You sound upset. Aren't you supposed to be going to Ronda with Lord Underwood and the Hernandezes? I thought you were going to try to steer things to a more intimate arrangement.'

'Intimate? Oh, I've been intimate with him.' She wiped a tear from her eye. 'Just not as I fucking hoped to be.'

'Oh. I see. Does this mean you're not ... ?'

'Making the beast with two backs with His Lordship? No, I'm not, and nor will I be, going by the way things have gone tonight.'

'Oh no,' said Cynthia, sympathetically. 'Oh, I *am* sorry, darling. Of course we'll meet you. One hour, *El Rincon.*'

Lydia hung up. 'Yes, darling. I'm sorry too.' She sat down at the dressing table and looked at her reflection in the mirror; she was deathly pale, and her mascara-stained tears spilled glistening black rivulets down her cheeks. 'But not as sorry as Lord Underwood and his fucking chosen one are going to be.' She smoothed her blood-soaked hair from her neck and saw where the gash had healed. She smiled bitterly. 'Not as sorry by half.'

8

DAVID RETURNED TO Underwood's rooms to find the vampire with a towel wrapped around his waist and a toothbrush jutting from his mouth. He was humming a tune David didn't recognise and browsing the contents of his wardrobe. David set down his bucket and mop and asked where Lydia was. Underwood shrugged and suggested she had probably gone back to her room. David turned to go and check, but Underwood stopped him, saying it was better if they left her alone. David considered a moment before agreeing. He wrung out his mop and a cloud of disinfectant-scented steam rose from it as he slopped it down into the congealing pools of his sister's blood.

'You called the nurse?' asked Underwood.

'Yes, she'll be here soon. The Hernandezes are watching TV downstairs.'

'Jolly good,' said Underwood distractedly. From a selection of short-sleeved shirts, he pulled out a red one, inspected it briefly, then held it up for David to see. 'What do you think of this?'

David looked up from wringing crimson water into the bucket. 'It's a bit bright, isn't it? I thought you were more of a white shirt and black tie type of guy.'

Underwood chuckled. 'Oh, you did, did you? There you go again with those prematurely formed opinions of yours. You really should reserve all judgments about me until you've known me for at least one lifetime. But seriously, you think it's too bright?'

David shrugged. 'I think if you had a tan, it might suit you, but since you look like death warmed-up, I'd give it a miss.'

Underwood laughed. 'Yes, of course you're right, but I think it has a rather jolly air about it, and the evening could do with a spot of jollity.'

'You mean after Lydia's opening up her neck all over the floor here?'

'Yes.'

David sensed that Underwood didn't want to talk about it; but David did, so he asked, 'So, what do you make of that, then?'

Underwood selected the red shirt and a pair of black trousers. 'Well, like I said earlier, she's been through a lot lately, she's troubled.'

'If by "troubled" you mean she's mentally unstable, then yes, I agree.'

'Mentally unstable?' Underwood arched his eyebrows. 'You mean you think she's potty?'

'I mean I think she needs professional help. Though how we'd go about arranging that, I've no idea. She can't exactly talk to a shrink about what's been going on in her life, can she?'

'You really think she's that bad?' said Underwood, taking his clothes into the bedroom.

David planted his mop in the bucket and leaned on it. 'Yes, I think she's that bad. To be perfectly honest, I think she's certifiably insane. Think about it, not just this spectacularly desperate suicide attempt, but all the other stuff she's been up to: her willingness to kill for you, her kidnapping that young guy and holding him prisoner for weeks, and then her readiness – no – *enthusiasm* to cut his throat without even the slightest trace of compassion. Seriously, Milord, she's a psychopath.'

Underwood walked back into the doorway and smiled. 'Oh no, old man; she's a Flinch.'

David had realised the futility of arguing further. He continued to mop up the blood, listening to Underwood witter on about a guardian's need for ruthlessness and his wardrobe's need for variety – as if they were things of equal gravitas – until the floor was cleaned. Then he dismissed himself and went along the corridor to Lydia's room. He knocked; when there was no reply he tried the door handle. It opened and he looked inside. There was a used towel on the bed and the scent of shampoo and perfume hung in the air. He called her name; there was no reply. He entered the room and saw that the bathroom light was on. He called her name again and when no reply came, he pushed the bathroom door open. The floor tiles were wet and condensation clung to the window. Her blood-soaked dress lay crumpled in the corner.

Then the front doorbell rang. He left the room and went downstairs to answer it. It was Conchi. He apologised, telling her that Lydia had gone out without telling him and so it looked like her trip had been for nothing. Then Underwood had come trotting down the stairs, all smiles and salutations. He insisted that Conchi join them for dinner; the reservation was for five persons and he wanted to get to know as many people from the Sect as he could. Conchi was thrilled and David was relieved. To him, Conchi seemed reasonably normal, and she was the closest thing he had to a friend in the weird and sinister world in which he now found himself.

And so, they had all driven out to Ronda, Conchi in the Citroën with David and Underwood, and the Hernandezes following in their own car. While David drove, Underwood monopolized Conchi's attention in the back seat. Being a devoted member of the Sect, she was completely in awe of him, and David, who had hoped they might all chat about something other than Underwood, resigned himself to the position of chauffer, listening in on their conversation as best he could over a Beatles tape of John's that Underwood had taken a liking to.

The meal was a great success. Everyone agreed that Lydia had made an excellent choice of restaurant and that it was a great pity that she couldn't be there. Underwood, ever the charming host, was as interested in his guests as they were in him. David was happy to just sit back and listen to the others, speaking only when he was spoken to and generally playing the role of the dutiful servant. As the evening wore on and the group's conversation became an indistinct background murmur to him, David's thoughts returned to Underwood's desire to have Michelle as a mate. That they had come here to Ronda tonight was hopefully a sign that Underwood was reconsidering; because, it being a Sunday, by the time they were finished here, *La Reina* – if it was open at all on Sundays – would certainly be closed for the night. Maybe Underwood had realised that David was right about keeping a distance from Michelle, or, which was perhaps more likely, the vampire was simply in no hurry to make his move.

David's musings ended when Underwood, having been instructed by Conchi in the use of his phone, started playing with the camera function. At first, David's responses to the command, "say cheese", had been forced, but it was impossible not to be both charmed and amused by Underwood's child-like delight in the results of his phone photography, and David's smiles, and indeed his laughter, soon became genuine. So when the time came to leave, everyone, including David, was in high spirits.

Outside by the cars, David opened the back door of the Citroën, expecting Underwood to get in – but he didn't. Instead, he cleared his throat and turned to address them all, clapping his hands and rubbing them briskly together. 'Well, everyone, I don't know about you, but I've had a delightful evening. However, I really must pop off now and take care of some personal business.'

David grew suddenly tense. 'Personal business?'

'Yes, Flinch,' said Underwood with a wry grin. 'Nothing for you to concern yourself about; it is, as I say, personal business. So why don't you take our guests here on to some other nightspot? If that's what they'd like to do.' He raised his eyebrows questioningly at Ildefonso.

Ildefonso laughed and shook his head. 'No, really Lord Underwood. Thank you for a lovely evening, but I must work tomorrow and I think Eugenia and I are both ready for bed, no?' He turned to Eugenia, who nodded her agreement.

'As you wish,' said Underwood. 'Well, farewell to you both, and thanks for being such charming company.' He shook Ildefonso's hand, then took Eugenia's and raised it to his lips. '*Hasta luego*, Eugenia.' As Eugenia blushed, Underwood fished out his watch, phone, money clip, cigarette case, and lighter and gave them to David. 'Hang on to those for me, will you, Flinch?'

Confused, David took the items. He looked down at them in his hands, his mind suddenly racing. *Why's he giving me these? They're his valuables. What's he going to do that means he doesn't want them with him? Something dangerous? Or ...* David felt the skin on his back prickle.

He's going to fly away.

His clothes are going to burn and he's going to fly off, and he doesn't want this stuff being left in the ashes. That's why he wore the red shirt; because he knew he was going to be burning it later. And that's why he wanted to come here: distance. The distance between here and La Reina that a giant bat can fly in a fraction of the time it would take a car to drive. The sly bastard! David's jaw set tight as his heartbeat began to quicken.

Underwood saw the look on his face and smiled. 'I say, cheer up, Flinch, this means you can take the rest of the night off if you like.'

'Thank you, My Lord. But, if it's all the same to you, I'd prefer to accompany you on this personal matter of yours.'

'Oh no, no, no,' said Underwood with a distinct twinkle in his eye. 'I'm afraid that would be quite impossible.' He started walking backwards, away from them in the direction of the Plaza del Espana. 'Farewell, all. We really must do this again sometime – and soon,' he said, pointing to the Hernandezes. 'I found you both to be quite delicious ... company.' Then with a parting wave, he turned the corner and was gone.

Without a word to the others, David broke into a run and hurried after him. At the corner of the street he looked in the direction Underwood had gone. There were still a lot of people about, but no-one in a bright red shirt. At the end of the street was the bridge, the Puente Nuevo that stood 390 feet over the Tajo gorge. He couldn't have dived off that, someone would have seen him.

Wouldn't they?

David ran back to the cars and the perplexed expressions of Conchi and the Hernandezes. 'Sorry about that,' he panted. 'Just meant to ask him what time he'd be home for his supper.' He gave a little laugh and threw open the front passenger door for Conchi. She got in, watching him with concern. 'Lovely to see you both again,' he said to the Hernandezes as he hurried around to the driver's side, 'But we have to fly too. I mean, get going. So, I'll see you again, soon. And we'll do ... we'll do blood, yeah?' He gave a brief wave and jumped into the Citroën, slamming the door and jamming the keys into the ignition.

As the Hernandezes waved their slightly perplexed farewells, Conchi turned to David and asked, 'David? What is the big hurry? It's still early. It's not even midnight yet. Perhaps we could go for a drink or – '

'No, we can't. We have to get back to Almacena.'

'Why?'

'Because that's where he's going.'

'Lord Underwood? Well, so what if he is? It is his private business, no?'

David glanced at her as he drove down to the street corner. She was Sect, he had to remember that; it wouldn't do to tell her what was going on, or how he felt about it. He nodded, his face a mask of cheeriness. 'Yes, of course. But, you know, I'd like to meet him afterwards and give him a lift home.'

Conchi seemed to accept this, she said: 'You are sure you know where he's going?'

'Oh yes,' David turned the car right, heading in the direction of the exit that would take them to Almacena. 'Dead sure.'

They drove in silence until they were out of town, then David said, 'You seemed to get on pretty well with His Lordship tonight.'

Conchi nodded. 'Yes. He's a fascinating man, and so friendly. I expected him to be more ... I don't know ... evil?'

'Oh, don't worry, he's evil. He just happens to be charming and amiable into the bargain. He's like one of those jolly, seemingly well-adjusted serial killers that, when they get caught, nobody can believe they could've done the terrible things they're accused of.'

'You sound like you disapprove.'

'I do, which is why I'm trying to get him onto a diet of volunteered blood instead of blood drained from unwilling victims. So far at least, things seem to have been going quite well – most of the time anyway.'

'You mean, he drinks from blood donors?'

'Yeah. Sect people. Which reminds me, I've been meaning to ask you if you'd like to donate a pint sometime.'

She smiled. 'Of course. I would give the last drop of my blood for the Lord Underwood.'

David chuckled at the familiar reply, it was the same given by all the donors he had asked so far. He glanced at her. The glow from dashboard highlighted the soft curve of her face and her elegant features. She was a beautiful woman. 'You know, you shouldn't get too close to His Lordship. He has an eye for the ladies.'

Conchi laughed and sat back. 'I'm afraid that, in that, I would not be able to please him.'

'Oh? Why's that? You don't go for undead guys?'

'I don't go for guys, period.'

David turned to her. 'Oh. You mean ... you're gay?'

'Yes.'

David turned back to the road with a smile. 'I see. Although, I don't think your sexual orientation would matter much if he were to take a shine to you.'

'Of course not. If he were to feel that way about me – or any of us – what could we do? He is our master, and we are his servants.'

'Well, I don't know about the "any of us" bit. I think I'm fairly safe in that department.'

Conchi looked at him. 'Are you? What makes you so sure?'

'Apparently, no Flinch shall bleed. It's in my contract, so to speak. Mind you, that only applies to our being bled for the purpose of food. I'm not so sure if it also covers his not shooting, stabbing, or bodily dismembering us if the mood should take him.'

'Oh my God, you don't think he would do this to you?'

David stroked the bump on his head where Underwood had thrown him against the cellar wall. 'Well, let's just say I wouldn't put it past him.'

'But why? Why would he hurt you? You are his guardian.'

'That doesn't mean he wouldn't kill me if I crossed him.'

'But you would never cross him, would you?'

David smiled. 'Oh, of course not, I'm just ... speculating, you know.'

'Well, I don't think you need to worry about him hurting you. I am a good judge of people, David, and I can tell that he likes you.'

David laughed. 'He does?'

'*Sí, claro*, you don't feel this?'

'No, not particularly.'

'Well, I do. So you must trust me, it is true. Why are you so full of doubts, David? He needs you – you are his guardian, guiding him into the twenty-first century. But more than that, I think you are his friend too.'

'If you say so, Conchi. But whatever his feelings are towards me, I think either of my brothers would have made a far better guardian than me.'

'But they are not here, and you are. *Fortuna* has chosen you, David. You are Underwood's destiny, just as he is yours.'

As the road ahead straightened out into a long line, David looked up to the dark hills on the horizon to where the distant yet unmistakable forms of the church and castle of Almacena stood in stark silhouette against the low yellow moon. 'Yes,' he said, easing his foot down on the accelerator. 'Thanks for reminding me.'

El Rincon was Lydia's favourite restaurant in Almacena. She always took clients there when showing them houses in the town to give them a sample of some genuine Andalucian cuisine. Juan, the owner, was a skilled chef; unlike the owners of some of the other restaurants in town whose speciality dishes were a subtle blend of the contents of pickle jars, cans, and anything that could be thrown into a deep fat fryer. As she entered the restaurant, she saw Juan behind the counter at the far end of the restaurant playing with his small granddaughter. Juan's wife, daughter, and his son were all with him watching a chat show on the wall-mounted TV. On seeing Lydia, Juan took the little girl's hand and waved it at her. From behind dark glasses, Lydia forced a smile and returned the wave. She saw the Bensons and Miguel at a table in the corner and went over.

On seeing her, Cynthia rose. 'Lydia, darling, how are you? Here, sit down and tell us all about it.' She turned to wave to the staff, but Juan's son was already strolling over, notebook in hand.

'*Gin y tonica, y grande por favor,*' said Lydia. The young man nodded and went back to the bar.

'Sunglasses at this hour?' said Gerald. 'Not experiencing sensitivity to electric light are you, Lydia?'

'No Gerald, I'm experiencing a sensitivity to stupid questions. My puffy eyes aren't something I care to share with the world this evening.' She thanked the waiter as he returned with her drink. Alcohol measures were usually quite generous at *El Rincon*, as in most places, and Lydia's large gin and tonic was large indeed. She took a long sip of the contents.

'I say, that's a big one,' said Gerald. 'Not driving home, I hope.'

'Fuck home. I won't be going back there again until that bastard's gone. So for tonight at least I'll stay at my place in town'

'Bastard?' said Miguel. 'You mean David?'

'No, I mean Lord fucking Underwood,' Lydia drained her glass and set it down hard on the table. 'But yes, David's a bastard too. Jesus, he'd have to be, he's no son of the father I knew.'

Gerald puffed in surprise. 'I say, this is a pretty shocking turnaround. What on Earth happened up there?'

Lydia waved to the waiter for another drink and proceeded to tell her friends about the evening's events. She left out the bit where she told Underwood she loved him, but otherwise recounted it pretty much as it had happened. When she finished speaking, they were all staring at her, dumbstruck. Lydia picked up her drink, knocked back the last of it in a swallow, and raised her hand for another.

'So, are you ... infected, do you think?' asked Cynthia. 'Any queer tingling when you think of His Lordship?'

Lydia laughed, the alcohol beginning to take effect. 'The only time I get a tingle thinking of him is when I imagine myself dragging his coffin out into the sunlight and flipping the lid off.'

'Oh,' said Gerald. 'Well that sounds like a "no", then.'

'Yes, it's a "no",' said Lydia. 'A bloody big "no" too. The only thing he did to my bleeding neck was to kiss it better; I presume in the same way as he did with you, Cynthia.'

'Ahhh, yes,' said Cynthia, 'his healing secretion. Gerald explained it to me.'

'That's not what I said,' said Gerald. 'I said he spat some red goo on you.'

Cynthia smiled patiently. 'Gerald, dear, he didn't *spit goo* – you make it sound like he was losing his lunch on me. It was something special, a healing balm unknown to our science.'

'Yes, a healing balm of red goo which he spat up on you.'

Lydia tapped her glass on the table. 'Oh do shut up the pair of you. I've had a rough night: I've cut my own throat, lost a load of blood, and finally had the ignominious good fortune to have been spat on with red goo – as you so charmingly put it, Gerald. Let's just move on to the present, shall we? I'm healed, and whatever it was that did the healing, I don't think it carried the vampiric infection.' The waiter brought her drink and she took a sip.

Cynthia closed her hand over Lydia's. 'Oh Lydia, I'm sorry.'

Lydia shrugged. 'What can I say? He doesn't want me. It's as simple as that.'

Miguel shook his head, 'I can't believe that he would choose Michelle Mullins over you. It is crazy!'

'Fair is not fair, but that which pleases,' said Gerald.

Miguel's brow furrowed. '*Que?*'

'Just ignore him, Miguel,' said Cynthia. 'I'm sure if Lord Underwood didn't have his code about no Flinch bleeding, he'd choose Lydia over Michelle any day.'

'Yes, maybe,' said Lydia. 'But he does have it, and there's nothing I or anybody else can do about it.'

Gerald sighed and said, 'Oh well, I suppose that rather puts the kibosh on us then, what?'

Lydia took a drink and let an ice cube flow into her mouth, which she sucked for a moment before crunching it up. 'Unless anybody has any other plans they'd like to air?'

Miguel looked around to ensure they were not overheard: they were not – the only other people in the restaurant were a large Spanish family on the other side of the room. But Miguel felt that what he had to say merited caution, so he leaned in and said in a lowered voice, 'What if Michelle were to ... have an accident?'

Cynthia and Gerald gasped simultaneously, each of them looking at Miguel as if he had just said he was leaving for the priesthood. Lydia simply smiled. 'Oh, don't think I haven't thought about that, Miguel. I thought about nothing else all the way here. But as much as I enjoyed playing out all those delicious scenarios in my mind, sadly I can't think of a way of arranging such an *accident* in a way convincing enough that wouldn't arouse Underwood's suspicions.'

Miguel shrugged. 'So what do you care if he suspects? You said you wanted to throw his coffin open to the sunlight. I say, if he isn't going to give you what you want, then why not throw it open?'

'Now hang on a minute,' said Gerald. 'One minute we're "all hailing" the fellow for all we're worth, and the next we're talking about *murdering* him? Goodness gracious, Miguel, you're letting your Latin passions run away with you, old boy. Let's just take a step back and calm down, shall we? We've got to think about this coolly and objectively.'

'For once, Gerald, I agree with you,' said Cynthia. 'I fail to see how Michelle having a fatal accident will endear Underwood to you, Lydia. And as for killing Underwood, well that's just clottish. When was killing the goose that lays the golden eggs a smart move? If he's alive, we can still find a way to get what we want from him. But if you were to destroy him, well, that really would put the kibosh on us, wouldn't it? We can't very well infect ourselves from the dust of his remains, now can we?'

Lydia's lip curled with contempt. 'Right now, Cynthia, I couldn't care less about Underwood's golden eggs. I'd just like to see him and Michelle die the most unpleasant and messy way possible.'

'Decapitate them,' said Miguel, dragging his thumb sharply across his throat, 'and put their heads on a bench, like the *giri* in the newspapers.'

Lydia smiled. 'Oh, very fitting, Miguel. I don't know what you're on about with the *giri*, but it sounds like a fitting demise all the same.'

'What?' said Gerald. 'You haven't heard about the head on the bench chap?'

'No Gerald, believe it or not I haven't had much time to sit around reading the papers just lately. What happened?'

'Oh, blimey,' said Gerald. 'It's jolly gruesome stuff, I can tell you. Some young British thug got his noggin chopped off and left on a bench on the Ibiza seafront.' Gerald's eyes suddenly lit up. 'Hey, come to think of it, we were talking to Michelle about it just the other day; she seemed to take quite a queer turn when she saw this chap's face on the front of the paper, didn't she, Cyn? And you know, what was really odd was that she said she didn't know him, but as soon as she was gone, young Melanie came along and recognised him immediately – well, not the decapitated chappie, but the other fellow, you know, the Russian.'

Lydia frowned. 'No, I don't know. What Russian?'

'Oh, sorry, beg pardon. You see, the decapitated chap was suspected of being involved in the murder of this Russian fellow's nephew, and young Mel said this same Russian was the chap who bought Keith and Michelle's pub in Benidorm a few years back. Bit of an entrepreneur apparently; owns a string of pubs and bars down there.'

Lydia sat forward. 'What was his name, this Russian?'

'Oh gosh,' said Gerald. 'I don't know. Alandrovich, Alandropov, something like that.'

'Alexandrov?'

'Yes, that's it! I say, you've got an office down in Benidorm, haven't you? Do you know him?'

Lydia smiled. She picked up her drink and sat back. 'Segei Alexandrov?' She gave a little laugh, 'Oh yes, I know him alright; I sold him his house ... amongst other things.'

At half-past midnight on a Sunday night, the streets of Almacena were quiet. Underwood stopped at a house a few doors down from *La Reina de Corazones* to enjoy the fragrance of a lemon tree that grew in its garden. He looked up at the dark windows of the pub. He wore the white shirt, black trousers and shoes that David had packed into a sports bag on the night of his resurrection. On that night, as a bat, he had caught the bag as David flung it up to him and flown directly to Almacena to seek a nest of sorts. He had soared over the streets at a height beyond the reach of street lights, looking for a suitable spot. What he needed was a place to leave the bag: a place where he could land unseen and where the bag would not be found, but also a place reasonably close to the town centre. He had settled, somewhat brazenly, on a cave in the rock outcrop that was the seat of the town's ancient castle. The front of the castle overlooked the town that had grown up in its shadow, but to its rear, there were only a few houses and a cemetery, beyond that, the open countryside. Underwood had flown in over the cemetery, landed in the cave, and left the bag there.

Tonight, after flying back from Ronda, he had returned to it. David had been right about Underwood's plan to give him the slip and fly to Almacena. Once he had transformed back into his human self, he had taken the clothes from the bag and dressed. Then on emerging from the cave, he took a brief look around to ensure he was unobserved. The drop to the ground was about forty feet. He jumped, and landed on a foot-worn path that sent a cloud of dust up around him. He dusted himself off, and strolled around the castle walls and into town.

Now, still unobserved, for there was no one around to observe him, Underwood walked up to the gate of *La Reina de Corazones*. The patio had been cleared of its tables and chairs, and a roll-down steel shutter had been pulled down over the front doors. Shut tight, he thought. Then he noticed another door to the left of the shutters, a private entrance. He walked onto the patio and looked up at the front windows. He closed his eyes, and began to concentrate.

Keith was used to sleeping in the spare bed; any time he drank too much, Michelle would banish him from their bedroom to rid herself of his snoring. However, since their bust-up his banishment had been permanent. This didn't seem particularly out of the ordinary to Melanie because every night since their bust-up, Keith had been drunk. Now, the slumbering Keith was sucking in a particularly turbulent snore when, quite suddenly, he stopped. His eyes opened and his sticky mouth croaked one word, 'Master.'

Underwood was waiting outside the door when it opened. Keith stood naked just inside the doorway with his hand on the doorknob; behind him a flight of stairs led up to the dark apartment. Underwood grinned. 'Hello, Keith.'

'Hello, My Lord.'

'How nice it is to see you again. Ah, but I confess, I'm here to see your wife.'

'She's in bed ... asleep.'

'Perfect. May I come in?'

Keith opened the door wide and stepped aside.

'Sorry, but is that a "yes", Keith? Are you inviting me into your home?'

'Yes, master.'

'Thank you. I just wanted to be sure. Not that it makes a blind bit of difference, you understand, but I'm a stickler for tradition. Now, would you be so kind as to lead the way to your bedroom?'

9

UNDERWOOD FOLLOWED KEITH UP THE STAIRS and into the apartment. As they approached, he heard a low growling from the lounge ahead. He was about to comment when, in a yapping frenzy, Perry, the tiny mongrel, came skittering from the lounge, his eyes bulging in their sockets like large black marbles threatening to pop from his skull. Underwood looked down at the dog with a quizzical expression. Perry fell silent. Underwood waved him aside, and Perry, cringing somewhat, obeyed.

Despite the rear window being open, the room smelled sour. Keith had B.O. and the room smelled mainly of him, but there was also the rankness rising from the coffee table with its fetid nest of beer bottles; a large, empty bag of cheese and ham potato chips, and an ashtray brimming with butts. Underwood was amused. 'I see you're already in training for eligible bachelorhood, Keith.'

Keith stopped and turned, his features slack. 'Sorry, Master?'

'This place is quite a tip. I presume it's all *your* mess?'

'Yes, Master. My wife won't clean up after me, and I, I'm making a statement.'

'What statement is that? "I want to die?"'

'Well, yes, I ... suppose it is.'

'Well, you're certainly off to a good start, old chap. I dread to think what your blood must taste like.'

'Should I ... change my ways, Master?'

'Yes, try and eat a more healthy diet; cut out the beer and drink a lot more water. Oh, and have a wash now and again, will you?'

'I shall, Master. Thank you.'

'Oh, don't thank me, Keith, my motives are purely selfish. I need a few sources of clean, wholesome blood and you've just made it onto the menu. But not tonight.' He sniffed the air, there was a trace of Michelle, as though she had passed through briefly but not lingered. 'No, tonight I have an altogether different meal in mind. Lead on to the bedroom, if you'd be so kind.'

Keith did as he was told, his bare feet moving soundlessly over the tiles and up the stairs to the next floor. At the top, a short corridor opened out on either side of the staircase. Keith turned to the right but Underwood stopped him. 'That's all right, Keith. I can manage from here.' To Underwood's vampire senses, Michelle's fragrance was as a clear path to the door at the end of the corridor. 'But I'll need you close by in case your daughter wakes up; I can't have her bungling in on me, can I? Stay here, please. And if you hear anything unusual coming from your bedroom, don't be alarmed ... be happy.'

'Yes, Master,' said Keith, and his eyes became glazed, as if the dim light within him had just been switched off.

'Good man.' Underwood walked past him and down to the bedroom door. He turned the handle and stepped inside. The white curtains were drawn against the open window, and they stirred with the movement of the door's opening; a flicker of pale moonlight fell across the bed and was gone, but darkness wasn't a problem for Underwood; to his night predator's eyes, everything was clear as day. Michelle lay sleeping under a single white sheet and her hair spilled out across the pillow as she lay with her back to him.

Through the sound of crickets chirruping outside, Underwood could hear her breathing. He narrowed his senses to focus on her alone, and after a few seconds her heartbeat became audible: the slow, even beat of the sleeper. He closed the door behind him, his eyes never leaving her. Her fragrance filled the air and he breathed it in, his own blood quickening, causing his skin to tingle and his canine teeth to extend to sharp points.

She stirred slightly, the sheet whispered with the small movement of her legs; to Underwood it sounded like a whispered invitation. He walked around the base of the bed to stand between her and the window. What grey light filtered through the curtains caused his shadow to fall across her face. There was a small change in her breathing then her eyes flickered open. She saw his silhouette framed against the window, and smiled. 'Daniel? Is that you?'

'Yes, it is I, Michelle.'

She lay back and reached out a hand to him. 'I knew you'd come.'

Underwood took her hand and allowed her to draw him to the bed. He sat down and raised her fingers to his lips. 'I tried to stay away, but I couldn't.'

'How did you get in?'

'Keith invited me.'

'Keith?' There was a note of anxiety in her voice. 'Is he – ?'

'He sleeps.' He smoothed her hair from her brow, and with it, any lines of concern for her husband's presence.

'I ... have no fear ... My Lord.'

Underwood smiled. 'Nor shall you, ever again.' His fingers traced the line of her face. She closed her eyes, breathless as his slow caress moved downward to her neck. His touch lingered there, feeling the coursing heat of her blood beneath the skin, her pulse strong and excited. A shiver of excitement ran through him but he resisted the urge to fall upon her and feed immediately; there were other delights to savour first. A glance along the lines of her body beneath the sheet told him she was naked. His caress continued downwards to where it met the sheet, which he brushed down over the swell of her breasts. She closed her eyes and gasped, arching her back and rising to meet his touch. He smiled and lowered himself to her, kissing her breasts and savouring her warm flesh beneath his lips and tongue. His hand moved the sheet lower over her tummy, brushing the fabric still lower as his lazy caress moved over her hip and down to her thigh. How long had it been? Fifty years – yes, of course – but *before* then? How long had it been since he had felt desire such as he did now? His own clothes suddenly felt unbearable and he sat up to slip his jacket off. As he did so, she reached up and began to unbutton his shirt from the middle. In the darkness, she was working mostly by touch, and he could sense her frustration with the hard-to-see buttons.

'There is a faster way,' he said.

She needed no further encouragement. She sat up beside him and ripped the shirt open across his chest – the buttons flew, skittering in all directions across the tiled floor. She pushed the shirt over his shoulders, relishing the curve of his well-toned muscles. Her body was against his now, and as she bent to tug the shirt from him, he lowered his face to drink in the scent of her hair. It was intoxicating, and as soon as his arms were freed he embraced her, holding her to him and moving his face through her hair to the curve of her neck. He parted his lips and kissed her, brushing his lips over the pulse of her carotid artery, again resisting the temptation – *the instinct* – to bite, and instead, tracing the heat of the artery with his tongue, downward, kissing her as he went, her fingers in his hair as his mouth lingered at her breasts, her heart so close now it sounded like a drum in his ears. He moved on, his kisses following the aorta downward to her tummy. He was about to go lower when his foot made contact with the bed frame and the sound of shoe leather reminded him that he was still half-dressed. He pushed up from the bed and grinned.

'Oh dear, I'm still betrousered. That won't do, will it?' He rolled over and sat on the edge of the bed. He quickly removed his shoes and socks, and then stood to face her while he unbuckled his belt.

She looked up at him and said, earnestly. 'I love you, My Lord.'

'Yes,' he unfastened his trousers and pushed them and his silk boxers down simultaneously, freeing himself in the process, 'and it would appear that I love you too.' He lowered himself down onto her and her mouth rose to meet his. He kissed her and she returned the kiss, at first tenderly but with increasing hunger, then suddenly she gasped and broke off.

'What is it, darling?' said Underwood.

Michelle touched a finger to her tongue. Before he saw the spot of dark liquid on her fingertip, Underwood's heightened senses knew what it was, for the smell was suddenly everywhere around him. Her tongue had encountered one of his fangs; always a problem for new lovers, until they got used to them.

'So *sharp*, My Lord,' said Michelle, and her expression of surprise became one of amused chastisement. 'We shall have to be more careful.'

'The Devil we shall!' He took her in his arms and kissed her, the taste of blood in her mouth spurring him on to still greater excitement. Michelle brought a leg over his lap, straddling him and reaching a hand down to guide him into her, but Underwood lunged forward, forcing her back onto the bed. For a moment he lingered above her, as if savouring her in her last moments of human life, then he fell to her neck. She gasped as his teeth sank into her jugular vein, but the moment of pain was brief before a feeling of euphoria spread out from the area of the bite. She moaned, her fingers softening and entwining in his hair. Ripples of pleasure trembled through her wherever her body was in contact with his. She parted her legs beneath him and his weight moved against her. She cried out as a wave of ecstasy unlike anything she had ever known surged through her.

Underwood lifted his face from the wound, her blood pumping out onto the bed before he drew a small quantity of bitter, viscous saliva into his mouth and licked it over the wound. The bleeding immediately slowed and then stopped completely. Underwood lifted his hips and reached down between his legs, ready to enter her. Michelle looked up into his face, his lips and chin dark with her blood. 'Will it always be like this, My Lord?'

'Yes, Michelle. Every night, from now until the end of – '

The sound of sudden, frenzied barking from downstairs cut Underwood off in mid-sentence. Then came a crash of something falling and an impassioned cry of, 'Get the fuck off me, you mutt!'

Underwood's face darkened. '*Flinch!*'

'My Love?' Michelle's voice was anxious.

'It's my man, Flinch!' said Underwood, rolling off of her and snatching up his boxer shorts. 'The swine has obviously cottoned on to me!'

'I don't understand.'

Melanie called from her room further down the hallway. 'Mum? Dad?'

Michelle turned to the sound. 'Melanie?'

'Oh for heaven's sake,' said Underwood, pulling on his shorts. Downstairs, Perry's barking was becoming more frenzied.

'Mum? Dad?' Melanie's voice held more fear now.

Michelle started to get up.

'No!' said Underwood. 'There's nothing to worry about. She's fine. Stay here. Go back to sleep.'

Without a word, Michelle lay back down, drew the sheet over herself and closed her eyes. She was asleep immediately. Underwood took a dressing gown from the back of the door and went out into the hallway. Keith still stood naked and motionless where he had left him.

'*Keith!*' Underwood spoke in a harsh whisper as he tossed the dressing gown to him. 'Put this on and go and calm your daughter.' The dressing gown landed on Keith's head, covering it. 'And make sure she stays in her room, will you?'

'Yes, Master,' said Keith. He drew the dressing gown from his head and began to put it on.

Underwood hurried downstairs and went into the lounge. The room was still dark, but he saw David immediately; he was holding Perry's violently struggling body at arms' length with a look on his face like a man holding a bomb with a burning fuse. Despite his anger, Underwood laughed. 'You're not a dog person then, Flinch?'

'Get the fucker off me, he's gone completely mental!'

'He's only doing his duty, Flinch; the guardian of the house protecting his masters. You could learn a thing or two from him.'

'Well he's got the wrong fucking man then, hasn't he? He should be attacking you!'

Underwood chuckled. 'I'll tell you what, I'll open the window, and you chuck him out into the street.'

'*What?*' David watched in disbelief as Underwood crossed the room to the window. 'Jesus Christ, I'm not chucking a dog out of a first floor window. Here, Fido, *seize him!*' He lobbed the wriggling dog at Underwood. Underwood stepped smartly aside and watched the yapping hound fly past his face to land on the sofa. Perry was about to spring back at Underwood when the vampire held a hand up to him.

'Sit.'

Perry fell silent and sat down.

Underwood smiled. He turned to David. 'I should tell him to bite you on the arse – what with you coming in here and interrupting me like this. But I shan't; it wouldn't be any fun unless I was going to stick around and watch, and I'm afraid I don't really have time right now.'

'Why's that?' said David. 'Because you're busy murdering his mistress? I see from the blood on your chin that I'm too late.'

'Oh?' Underwood sat down on the sofa next to Perry. 'Too late for what, exactly?' He scratched Perry behind his ears and the little dog closed his eyes contentedly.

'Too late to save Michelle from your kiss of death.'

Underwood laughed. '*Kiss of death.* How melodramatic you are. You should write romantic stories for old women.'

'How can you just sit there and laugh? You've literally got a woman's blood on your hands.'

'Oh, do shut up, Flinch. Anyone would think the poor woman was dead.'

'In human terms, she is, isn't she? Whatever you've done to her up there, she's no longer what she was.'

'Well, yes, it has been said that I'm quite the lover, and a woman's never the same again afterwards. But a gentleman never blows his own trumpet, especially with regard to what goes on in the bedroom.'

A look of deep horror came over David's face. 'What? You mean, you're *shagging* her?'

'Well, I would have been, if you hadn't come crashing in like the Keystone Cops.'

'You mean she's still alive?'

414

'Oh, I should co-co, and once you've cleared off, I shall return to the bedroom and give her the ride of her life.'

'Yeah, and then *end* her life.'

Underwood smiled. 'End it; begin it; *you say to-may-to, and I say to-mah-to.*'

David broke for the door and ran up the stairs. 'Michelle!'

Underwood rolled his eyes and got up.

David got to the top of the stairs. He looked left and right. 'Michelle!' He heard voices from a room to the left. He went down to the door and hesitated. From the corner of his eye he recognised Underwood's shape as the vampire came to the top of the stairs after him. David opened the door. Keith sat on the bed, his arms around a very frightened-looking Melanie. 'Oh,' said David. 'I, I'm sorry. I was looking for Michelle.'

'I do apologise,' said Underwood from the shadows. 'I'm afraid my friend has had a little too much to drink.' He stepped forward and his eyes met Keith's, where they lingered for a few moments before Keith got stiffly to his feet and walked to the door.

'Keith,' said David. 'I don't know what he's said to you, but you need to take me to your wife, right now.'

Behind David, Underwood stepped aside. Then Keith punched David with all his might. David flew back into the corridor, slammed into the opposite wall, and slid down into unconsciousness.

Underwood stepped back into view. 'Again, I am sorry. We've abused your hospitality horribly, Keith. You kindly let us sleep in the pub downstairs rather than us having to walk home, and old Flinchy here, well, he must have started helping himself from the bar while I was asleep.' He shook his head then turned to Melanie. 'Don't worry, young miss. I'll take this drunken sot home with me and leave you all in peace.' He stooped and picked up David's body, draping him over his shoulder in a fireman's lift. Then he straightened up and nodded to Keith. Keith went back into the room and sat down on the bed beside Melanie, who immediately embraced him.

'Night, night,' said Underwood, and closed the door.

Once he was outside, he listened at the door to the tirade of questions that burst from Melanie, but after a few moments, convinced his ruse had worked, he walked down the hall to Michelle's room. He deposited David on the floor outside, stepped over him, and went back into the bedroom.

Approximately an hour later, Underwood was sitting in the back of the Citroën watching the blur of dark landscape slide past the window. Occasionally he would close his eyes, listening to the music that drifted from the stereo, a cassette of Chopin's nocturnes he had found in the glove compartment earlier. However, he was finding it difficult to relax completely and every now and again his eyes would shift to David who was driving the car with a relaxed, easy expression on his face. Finally, Underwood sighed. 'Oh well, much as I might prefer you this way, sadly, you're no good to me unless you're firing on all cylinders.'

'Pardon, Milord?' David replied.

'Pull over just ahead there, Flinch.'

'Yes, Milord.' David flicked the indicator switch before slowing the car and pulling off the road to park onto the dusty verge. They were miles from anywhere, and on both sides of the road fields of sunflowers stretched away towards each black horizon.

Underwood locked the doors to the back of the car. 'Right, on the count of three, you will wake up, and – though I'm sure I'll regret it – you will remember everything. One, two, three.'

David blinked. He saw the road ahead in the spill from the headlights and felt his hands on the wheel. For a second he just stared as things already in focus to his eyes became equally focused to his understanding. Then he jerked in his seat as if he had been jabbed by a cattle prod. He snapped his head around to the back seat to see Underwood regarding him with languid interest. 'You ... you unspeakable bastard! You hypnotised me!'

'Oh, nothing so prosaic as mere hypnosis, Flinch. Believe me, your will was entirely mine; if I had told you to walk off a cliff, you would have done so without hesitation.'

David slammed his hand against the steering wheel. 'How fucking dare you!'

'How dare *you*, sir! It was you who rudely interrupted me, not the other way round.'

'You had no right! No right to do that to me! It's completely out of order!'

'Well, that may be, but at the time, I didn't see that I had any choice. When you started to come round, I could see you were going to make a scene, so it was either that or another blow to the head. You'd already caused quite enough upset in that household for one evening. I couldn't have you waking the place up all over again.'

'*I'd* caused upset? *Me?* God damn you! That's fucking unconscionable! I – You – ! Fuck it!' David threw open the door and got out. 'I'll give you some bloody upset!' He grabbed the handle to Underwood's door and tried in vain to open it. 'Unlock this door, you bastard!'

'No.'

'Come out and face me!'

'I really don't think that would be the for the best, Flinch.'

'It'd be the best for me. Come on!' David kicked the door.

'Oh, really, *do* calm down. You're going to dent your father's car.'

'He wasn't my father! I had no fucking father!'

'Of course you did, everybody has a father, and I've no doubt that Arthur was yours. Granted, you may not bear great resemblance to him, but you're the very spit of some of your Flinch ancestors.'

'Arthur Flinch was just an evil old bastard who fucked my mother. He was nothing to me, and I was nothing to him. I hated him.'

'Of course you didn't, you're just upset.'

'No, I hated him. I hated him and all those evil Sect bastards of his, especially those wankers that he chose to be godparents to me. But most of all I hated you! You killed my mother, Underwood! Oh, you may not have been in the world of the living at the time, but believe me, your evil reach extends well beyond your fucking crypt!' David thumped Underwood's window with the flat of his hand. 'Come out! Come out and let me kill you once and for all! I'll take a rock and smash your head in so fast you won't even have time to regenerate!'

Underwood lit a cigarette. 'Thanks for the offer. Don't think I haven't contemplated letting something like that happen in the past, but these days I find I'm full of the joys of spring. Even your thoroughly insubordinate mischief of earlier on wasn't enough to rile me for more than the briefest time. In fact, as I was leaving I found myself chuckling at the memory of you and that little dog of theirs.' The image of David grappling with Perry surfaced again in Underwood's mind, he laughed. 'Oh, you should have seen your face, Flinch.'

'Well I'm glad I amused you. I hope all that chuckling didn't interfere with your digestion of Michelle's life blood.'

'No, no. Not at all.'

'Oh, so it's done, is it? What is she now? Dead? Transformed into *her ladyship*? What did you do to her?'

'Nothing, thanks to you. As you know, you woke up her daughter, and try as Keith might, he couldn't calm her down again. She wanted her mother, which is understandable I suppose. So I took my leave of Michelle and went to wake you, and as soon as I did you went for me. Tempted as I was to put your head through the wall, I needed to get us out of there and back home as quickly and quietly as possible. Of course, I could have knocked you out again and flown home with you in my claws, but they do tend to lacerate the shoulders terribly. So, hypnotism, as you so inaccurately term it, was the most expedient recourse available to me. I ordered you to take me to the car and drive us home.' He chuckled. 'God, you were so compliant, if only you could always be like that.'

'Yeah, yeah I remember it now ... I remember it all ... dropping Conchi off on the edge of town ... going to *La Reina* ... the door to the flat was open and I went up ... then there was that fucking dog ... then you ... then Keith hitting me ... and then you again. At first I was angry, furious, then suddenly, I, I was calm – no, not calm – numb; no thoughts, no emotions, just ... knowing what to do ... and doing it.'

'Yes,' said Underwood. 'I imagine it must be quite nice in a way.'

David slammed his fist on the roof, but his blow was weaker than before. 'Well you imagine wrong!' He slumped against the car, blocking Underwood's window. 'It was horrible. I was powerless. I presume Keith's in a similar state is he?'

'Yes. I think it rather suits him, don't you?'

'No, much as I dislike the bloke, I prefer him when he's hitting me because *he* wants to rather than because *you* do.'

Underwood laughed. 'Yes, well, I'm sure he wanted to as well, if it makes you feel any better.'

David shook his head and slid to the ground. For a short while neither man spoke, then David asked, 'So what are you going to do? Wait another night and then have another go at Michelle? Obviously it makes no difference what I think.'

Underwood sighed and stubbed out his cigarette. 'No, no, I don't think so.'

David frowned. 'What?'

'I don't think I'll be paying another visit to Michelle. Which is unfortunate for both of us really, as I'll be coursing through her veins like typhoid for the next twenty-four hours or so. She'd melt like butter in my mouth, I can tell you.'

'Wait a minute,' David pushed away from the car and came up on his knees to look though Underwood's window. 'Why? I mean, what's caused you to change your mind?'

'The daughter, Flinch. Her love of that child is ... ' he shrugged. 'Well, it's an obstacle. More so than I thought it would be.'

'I didn't think you gave a shit about the kid.'

'I *didn't*. No one's more surprised than me, Flinch. Damned if I know what's going on.'

David regarded Underwood's bemused expression for a moment or two then his own features lit up with a smile. He turned and sat down again against the door, laughing quietly to himself.

Underwood sat up, and brought his head to the window, trying to look down and see what David was doing. 'Here, are you *laughing* at me, Flinch?'

'You don't know what's going on?' said David, his amusement evident in his voice.

'No.'

'You *care*, obviously! I don't know if it's just for Michelle, or maybe it's for the kid as well. Maybe you even care for Keith! But one way or the other, Milord, you care enough not to kill them.'

Underwood was indignant. 'I *do not*!'

'Oh, yes you do. It's like you said – your full of the joys of spring, and this must be one of them. Obviously during your fifty year nap you've managed to re-grow yourself a conscience, Milord.'

Underwood threw open the other car door and came striding around to point an accusing finger at David. 'Now see here, Flinch. I could've easily killed Keith and his daughter before either of them even knew what was going on.'

'Well, yeah. But the point is you didn't, did you?'

'Because I *chose* not to.'

'Because – you – care.'

For a moment, Underwood could do nothing but stare as the implications of what David was saying swarmed in his head. Then he turned and walked a few slow paces before turning sharply back. 'Well I'm blowed. You know, I think you may be right, Flinch.'

David fished his cigarettes from his trousers and lit one. He then proffered the pack to Underwood. 'You want a fag?'

'Yes. My word,' said Underwood thoughtfully as he bent to take a cigarette. He sat down beside David and accepted a light. 'This is worrying.'

'Why?'

'Because I'm a killer, aren't I? A predator. I can't afford to be burdened with a conscience.'

'I don't think you should think of it as a burden; think of it as an evolutionary step.'

'But I don't want an *evolutionary step*, thank you very much. I like me the way I am, or should that be, the way I *was*? What I mean is, that predatory part of me is necessary: I'm a vampire. I can't function properly without it.'

'Well, I used to think that way about alcohol.'

'Oh shut up, Flinch. There's no comparison.'

'There is, insofar as I thought I couldn't function without it; I thought alcohol was a vital part of me. But I've learned that it's not. I didn't always need it, did I? I didn't need it when I was a kid; any more than you needed to kill when you were a kid.'

'I wasn't a vampire when I was a child, you clod. You changed from non-addict to addict; but I was changed from human to a vampire, and the vampire must hunt, and it must kill. It's in our nature, it defines us absolutely.'

'Well you could say the same about a dog or a cat, couldn't you? They're essentially hunters, but they can be tamed, domesticated. A wild dog will rip the head of a baby as soon as look at it, but a domesticated one'll ... well, it'll let a baby pull its ears and all sorts, won't it?'

'Oh charming. I'm a doggy now, am I? All domesticated and allowing the likes of you to pull my ears.'

'No, of course not. I mean, the dog'll eat the kid for dinner if the kid pushes it too far, but what I'm saying is, it doesn't *need* to eat the kid for food, does it? It's found an easier way of getting its meals. You haven't lost your predatory nature; you're just becoming the master of it.'

'I've *always* been the master of it, Flinch, I'm not a savage, you know. It's not like I'm some sort of newly-made vampire who doesn't know what's happening to him. I became master of my vampiric nature hundreds of years ago.'

'Oh right? Difficult at first, was it?'

Underwood snorted. 'Difficult? By Jupiter, yes. If it hadn't been for Matthias Flinch, I might have become something very different from the dapper chap I am now. He saved me. And himself, of course.'

David waited for Underwood to continue but the vampire had fallen silent, staring into the dark ranks of sunflowers opposite as if his memories were playing out among them. David wondered if perhaps now, Underwood might be ready to share some of his past. 'So, what happened?'

'Hmm?'

'What happened? How did Matthias save you?'

Underwood smiled. 'You'd like to know, would you?'

'Yes, sir. Very much.'

Underwood considered a moment. Then he said, 'I'll tell you what, let's do a deal. I'll tell you something of my past, if you tell me something of yours. Quid pro quo, as it were. I was interested in what you were saying about Arthur earlier; you're obviously angry with him – and me – and, well, I'd like to know why. You said that I killed your mother. Tell me more.'

David shook his head. 'Oh no, don't think you can turn the spotlight around on me like that, Milord. I asked first, after all. I'll tell you about my life a bit later, but first, I'd very much like to hear about yours.'

Underwood laughed. 'Oh dear. To tell you about my life would take considerably longer than the remains of this night, Flinch, or even a week of nights.'

'So just tell me the beginning; about how you were changed from man to vampire, and about how Matthias saved you.'

Underwood flicked his cigarette away and watched it bounce in a spray of sparks on the road. Then he smiled and got to his feet. 'Very well, Flinch. But I'll be damned if I'm going to do it sitting here in the dirt. Drive me home and we'll see if we can find a bottle of brandy and some decent cigars.'

'There's some cigars in John's marijuana garden on the roof.'

'*Marijuana garden?*'

'Yeah. I found it the other day. He was growing a bunch of plants up there. There's all sorts of smoking paraphernalia: pipes, bongs, you name it. I guess he had the cigars for when he fancied a change.'

'Hmm. Do *you* smoke marijuana, Flinch?' asked Underwood as they got into the car.

'No, sir. I'm as clean as the driven snow – as you know.'

Underwood couldn't tell from David's eyes in the rear view mirror if he was smiling, but he fancied he probably was. 'Quite right too, Flinch. Drive on.'

10

JOHN'S "MARIJUANA GARDEN" was situated on a patio roof on the eastern side of Casa Underwood. Once Underwood had found himself a bottle of brandy and a large balloon glass, David led the way through the kitchen to a small pantry room. He pulled aside a curtain and revealed a narrow flight of stairs. He flicked on a light switch.

Underwood smiled. 'Ahh, I know where we're going. I was here with your father that first night we arrived at this house.' They went up the stairs and came out onto the roof patio. The last time Underwood had seen it, it had been simply a flat cement roof with a water tank and a creaky weather vane. Underwood raised his eyebrows; it had changed considerably.

'I say, someone's been busy.' They stood inside a white metal frame, a cube that was bolted to the floor and open to the night on all sides except the back, which was flush with a wall. The top of the cube was slanted at a slight angle and was half covered by a roll-out awning. The floor had been tiled with patio tiles, and all around the "garden" a variety of leafy plants – not all marijuana – grew in large glazed pots and rattan planters. In the centre was a three-piece suite of cushioned rattan furniture which was arranged around a glass-topped coffee table covered with a film of dust. Some floor lights shone up through the plant foliage, and numerous candles clustered here and there, one of which David was now lighting. Underwood's nose wrinkled at a strange, sweet smell.

David caught his expression and explained. 'Mosquito candles, sir. Keeps the biters at bay.'

'Ah, yes,' said Underwood. 'They're not something I have to worry about.' He smiled. 'For some reason, they don't seem to find me all that appetising.'

'Well they love me. I hope you don't mind the smell of the candles.'

'Not at all. But don't go too mad, it'll queer the brandy.'

'No, sir,' said David, lighting another. 'Two ought to do the job.'

'Thank you.' Underwood swept dust from the seat cushion of the armchair and sat down. 'So, your late brother did all this then, did he? It looks fairly new.'

'Yeah, I'd say it's only a few years old at most. The roof and walls can be rolled down in bad weather.'

'Really,' said Underwood, brushing dust from the arm of his chair. 'Going by the dust I'd say that seldom happens.'

Outside the garden-cube stood a small wooden hut that Underwood had presumed was some kind of potting shed. David stepped into the hut and a moment later there came the sound of a fridge opening from within. 'Do you want any mixers with your drink?'

'No, thank you.'

'Now, there are some cigars in here, but I wouldn't know the good from the bad.'

'Are there any Cubans?'

'Hang on,' the sound of rummaging from within the hut. 'Yeah.'

'They'll do fine.'

David emerged with a box of Havana coronas, a pair of cigar scissors, and a small bottle of chilled mineral water. He sat down on the sofa opposite Underwood and passed him the box.

'Thank you. Well, this is certainly very nice. Your brother was handy with a toolbox, was he?'

'Yeah, he liked to fix things up, woodwork, mechanics, that sort of thing.'

'Unlike his father,' said Underwood with a smile. 'Arthur was good with mechanics and whatnot, but he hated getting his hands dirty. I imagine he got some builders in to make the house improvements – unless Mrs Arthur had a knack for such things. By the way, who did he settle down with in the end?'

'He didn't really. There was a woman called Carmella that used to come and stay sometimes. She was nice, or at least she was to us kids. Couldn't speak a word of English mind you, but we understood her well enough.'

'Unlike Arthur, I imagine.'

'Oh, he got to learn the language quite well. He had a tutor, Ana, the housekeeper, you – ' *Murdered her*, his mind suggested. 'Er, anyway, she taught him the basics and I guess Carmella taught him the rest.'

'Ah yes, *the rest* is always the fun part. Sleeping with your dictionary is by far the most enjoyable way to learn a language. I imagine your German was coming along quite nicely, wasn't it?'

David averted his eyes, suddenly uncomfortable. Bringing Lisa into this conversation felt wrong, it was like bringing her closer to Underwood.

Underwood opened the cigar box and selected a cigar. He passed it under his nose to savour the aroma. 'Mmm, very nice. I hope we still have the number of John's tobacconist.' David wasn't paying attention to him. Underwood extended the box. 'Here, have a cigar.' David looked at the open box. Underwood twitched it. 'Go on, if only to keep me company.' David took one. Underwood picked up the scissors and snipped the end off his cigar. 'You haven't told her yet, have you?'

David shook his head.

'May I ask why?'

'I guess I've just been too busy, you know? What with all the corpse disposal, bar fights and saving of pub landladies, I've barely had time to think.'

'Yes, I suppose things have been rather fraught, haven't they? Still, you should call her; let her know you won't be coming back.'

David said nothing. He looked at the cigar in his hands, turning it around slowly. He'd realised that in joining Underwood he'd be forsaking his old life, but so far, he'd managed to push the thought away, to keep it vague and formless. But now, Underwood was making matters definite, and the vague and formless was becoming the faces of people he'd never see again.

'Are you going to smoke that thing or just fiddle about with it?' said Underwood.

David looked up, his face worried. 'Sorry?'

'The cigar, Flinch. Are you going to smoke it? If not, could you give me a light so I can at least smoke mine?'

David fished his lighter from his pocket and handed it to Underwood. 'About my private life, sir.'

Underwood sparked a flame and gently warmed the length of his cigar. 'Yes? What about it?'

'Well, do I get one? Do I get any holidays?'

Underwood chuckled. 'Holidays? Are you serious?'

'Yeah. Why not? Just a few weeks a year. I mean, surely you won't want me around all the time?'

'Oh, by all means, Flinch. Take as long as you need. But don't be surprised if you come back to a cellar full of corpses.'

'Oh come on, Milord. You can control how much blood you take from people. You've already demonstrated that with Cynthia – and Michelle.'

Underwood lit his cigar and began puffing it into life. 'Well, yes, it's true, gorging a victim to death is rarely necessary at one sitting. I prefer to keep 'em in the larder and pop back and forth till they finally drop off the perch after about a week.'

'*The larder?*' David exclaimed in horror. 'You keep victims in a *larder?*'

'Figuratively speaking, yes. The larder isn't an *actual* larder, it's usually the victim's own home, but once I've bitten them, that home becomes my larder.'

For a moment, David just stared. Then he said, 'I see. Well, I was actually thinking more along the lines of someone else could cover for me, you know? Conchi for example, she knows what to do. I could give her a list of Sect people to call on as donors – '

'Yes, yes,' said Underwood with a dismissive wave of the hand. 'As you say, we can work something out. Very well. You can have your holiday.'

'Thank you. And while we're on the subject, Milord, what are the arrangements concerning retirement?'

'Retirement? My, you do think ahead, don't you?' Underwood sat back, puffing gently on his cigar. 'Well, provided you've bred a suitable replacement, you can retire whenever you like.'

'*Bred a replacement?*'

'Yes. Surely that won't be a problem. You do like the ladies, don't you?'

'Yeah, but ... I thought, I thought I'd ... '

'You'd what? Have a family, like a normal man?'

'Well ... yeah.'

'But you are not a normal man – you're a Flinch, the only surviving male heir of a line of guardians stretching back almost three hundred years.'

David tried to smile. 'Yeah. I know. But I guess I keep forgetting the *last surviving heir* bit; that Martin and John are dead, and Lydia,' he looked at Underwood. 'What about Lydia?'

'What about her?'

'Can she have a family? A normal family?'

'Lydia? A *normal* family? I doubt it.'

'But can she? I mean, would you have some claim to her kids as you seem to have had with us?'

Underwood grimaced. 'What a horrible way of putting it, Flinch.'

'But would you?'

'Well, yes, with her consent of course, and provided she was willing to raise them in the tradition, which all your ancestors always have done. Frankly, the whole issue of "to be or not to be" in relation to the position of guardian has never arisen before you and your incessant hand-wringing – which I suspect is about to resume.'

'No, no. I'm committed to this, but, I'm just ... getting used to it, that's all. My duties.'

'And so you understand that those duties including siring children to follow in your footsteps?'

David scratched his head. 'Yeah ... to be honest, Milord, I'm not sure about that bit. I take it you mean shagging volunteer women from the Sect?'

'Yes. It's always proven to be the best way. You get to maintain an emotional distance, and you're also not burdened with the cares and responsibilities of fatherhood.'

'But I, sort of, *want* those cares and responsibilities, Milord.'

Underwood nodded sympathetically. 'Yes. I can understand that. Obviously if your brothers were still alive, the job of seeding the Flinch line wouldn't be solely down to you.' He scratched his chin. 'Still, it's not like you're being asked to scamper barefoot over hot coals is it? Spending the night with a pretty girl – and a game one at that; not exactly an ordeal, is it?'

David said nothing; he was gazing into the night and all the nights that lay beyond: the strange, loveless, bloodstained life of the vampire's guardian.

Underwood leaned forward and poured himself a glass of brandy. 'Still, I see no reason why, once you've given me a few sons, you shouldn't be able to have a few of your own when you retire.'

David looked at him, struck by the phrase, *given me a few sons*. Was that what this was all about? Was that what *he* was to Underwood? It was an odd thought. He picked up the scissors and snipped off the end of his cigar. 'What about you? Did you ever have kids?'

Underwood blew smoke at the moon then said, 'You are all my children, David.'

David's scalp prickled. He averted his eyes from Underwood's, taking the lighter and using it to warm his cigar. Then he said, 'I mean, of your own – physically.'

'As a vampire, I cannot have children. We further the species through other means, as you know.'

'Yeah, but before you were a vampire, when you were human?'

'Ahh, now we get to the matter in hand.' Underwood inhaled the vapours from his brandy. 'I suppose I should begin at the beginning, which I estimate to be around the end of the 1680s.' He took a drink and reclined. 'I was born in London. We lived in a terraced house between the Fleet Ditch and Lud Gate. In total there were thirteen of us living there – my family and two others. My family consisted of me, my brother Billy, my sister Mary, and my parents, though my father was away much of the time; he was a soldier, and we were at war with France. He was killed not long after I was born.'

David was staring at him, wide-eyed with surprise. 'You mean, you weren't born a Lord?'

Underwood laughed. 'Oh, good heavens no. Far from it. I came into this life at quite the other end of the scale. I was neither a lord, nor was I an Underwood. I took that name as I have taken many others over the years, though it's the one that I generally go by since it was the first after my rebirth.'

'So, what's your real name?'

Underwood twirled his glass gently at the stem, watching the liquid swirl. 'I was christened John William Brooks. But that man died a long time ago. Anyway, where was I? Ah yes, the beginning. My mother, God rest her soul, sold oysters, and when my father died she needed further income, so she took to other means. She died of the pox when I was twelve.'

'Smallpox?'

'No, *the* pox – syphilis. An absolute horror of a disease. She hid it from us as best she could, but the sores are such that no quantity of face powder can conceal them indefinitely. After she died, my older brother and sister and I went into an orphanage. My brother and I managed to run away, but my sister, Mary, stayed there and was soon placed into service.'

'Service?' said David, puffing flame into his cigar.

428

'Domestic service. She became a scullery maid and worked her way up. All the way up in fact, but that's another story. She was damned lucky, really, she could easily have ended up like ma, as so many girls did back then.'

'I'm sorry, sir,' said David. 'But what was it that your mother ... I mean, you said she took to other means, you mean ...?'

'She became a prostitute, Flinch.' Underwood smiled at the widening of David's eyes. 'Oh, nothing unusual in that at the time; something like one in five London women were prostitutes back then.'

'*One in five?* Jesus, that's incredible!'

'Incredible now, perhaps, but not then. The enclosure laws had seen the gentry carve up the country for themselves, so the common people were forced from the land and into the cities. There was a vast population of people making do by any means they could, and for a great many of us, those means were not necessarily lawful. My brother Billy and I became pickpockets after father died. Again, nothing uncommon in it, it was easy – and fun, if truth be told.'

'You were a thief?'

'I was. And a good one too.' Underwood grinned at David's dumbfounded expression. 'Anyway, as I was saying, once Billy and I had fled the orphanage, we went back to pickpocketing – living by our wits as it were. We hooked up with some other lads and formed a gang,' he smiled at the memory, 'All of us living together in a rat-infested house down by the docks. Oh, it was squalor on a grand scale, but we were happy enough; we had food, a fire, and whatever we needed that we couldn't steal we had money enough to buy. We were doing fine 'til Billy lifted a handkerchief from a gent who just happened to be a thief-taker as well. Obviously I've looked back on the incident over the years and seen that it was clearly a trap; a fine, red silk handkerchief fluttering just that little bit too flamboyantly from the fellow's pocket? A worm on a hook if ever I saw one. Anyway, my old pal Tom Cobb and I ran into the fellow, making as if we were involved in a game of chase, and Billy swept in, plucked the fogle and was away, quick as an eel. Then, totally unexpectedly, the fellow seizes both Tom and I by the scruffs and calls to some mates of his who were in the crowd, and they were off after Billy before you could say knife.

'Now, Billy was a fast kid, but these lads started a hue and cry that had him caught in no time, and so the three of us found ourselves in the dock.

Tom Cobb and I maintained we were just playing chase, and the jury –
perhaps because we were small and cute – believed us. But not so lucky
was our Billy. He was convicted. He could have gone to Newgate, but
fortunately for him, he was able – as were we all – to recite the first verse
of the 51st Psalm. This he did to the judge and he was able to get Benefit
of Clergy.'

'What does that mean?'

'He got off with a branding.'

'A branding? They branded a kid for stealing a handkerchief?'

'Yes, a "T" for "thief",' Underwood indicated the fleshy part of his
thumb in the palm of his hand. 'Just here.'

'That's barbaric!'

'Yes. But that's the way it was; the penal system at the time couldn't
cope with the amount of people it had to process, the prisons were
desperately overcrowded, so it was branding or whipping for the lesser
crimes, prison for the next up in terms of gravity, and death for
everything else.'

'Death for ... what do you mean, "everything else"?'

'Oh lots of things, everything from stealing a watch to first degree
murder. And of course, repeat offences – once Billy was branded, if he
were caught stealing so much as a pinch of snuff, he could have been
hanged for it.'

'You're kidding?'

Underwood shook his head. 'No Flinch, I'm afraid not. Later in the
18th Century, there were over a hundred and fifty crimes punishable by
death in England, and I knew many – too many folk – who had their
necks stretched. But anyway, getting back to me; fortunately we were all
still young enough to be sent back to an orphanage, from where we were
all, even Billy, soon apprenticed out to different trades: Billy to a
blacksmith, Tom to a butcher, and I to a carpenter. And for the rest of
our childhood years we laboured true and honest as the day is long. But of
course, it didn't last.'

'What happened?'

'Well, in those days, wars with France were almost absurdly frequent.
It seemed like peacetime was merely a chance to raise funds, munitions,
and a fresh crop of young men to be slaughtered, before starting off on
another round. And this round would become known as the War of
Spanish Succession.' Underwood paused for a puff on his cigar and to

look for a sign of recognition in David: none came. 'You've never heard of it, have you?'

'No, sir. Like you say, there were a lot of wars with France.'

'Yes, but this one's famous. I was in it, for Heaven's sake! Not that that should make it famous, but anyway. What do they teach you in school these days, Flinch? This is your country's history, you know?'

David shrugged. 'I wasn't big on history, sir. I was more into science.'

'But they must have taught you *something* about history, surely?'

'Oh yeah, I remember learning about World War One.'

'Is that it?'

'Yeah, pretty much. I opted for sciences in my electives.'

Underwood sniffed. 'Oh well, that's something at least. Anyway, where was I?'

'The War of Spanish Succession.'

'Ah yes. So, by that time we were a trio of fine young fellows, and like most of London, were much excited about this new war with France and Spain. Obviously for you, a bit of background is required: France under Louis the Fourteenth was, as always, looking to expand its territories, and when the king of Spain died without leaving an heir, a civil war broke out over the succession. What was up for grabs here wasn't just Spain, but all its territories, including those now in Italy, the Low Countries and the Americas. One of those in line for the throne of Spain was Philip, who was also grandson of Louis the Fourteenth, and so also in line for the French throne. You see where this might lead?'

'To one big French-Spanish empire?'

'Exactly. Louis the Fourteenth was delighted at the prospect, but our king, unsurprisingly was not. He promptly formed an alliance with Holland and Austria to bung a spanner in the works.' Underwood paused for a puff on his cigar. 'Any questions?'

'Yeah, what did you do next?'

'Well, I joined up, naturally. We were in a tavern one night and there was a bunch of soldiers, all very grand in their red coats, attracting the attentions of the ladies and boasting about the great life they had in the army. Of course, they were a recruiting party, we knew that, but at the same time, we had a mind to be recruited, especially after a few rounds of gin. So we signed up.'

'But you had jobs; you didn't need to go, did you? It wasn't compulsory.'

'No, it wasn't compulsory, but you must understand, Flinch, war wasn't some hideous irregularity in those days, it was something every generation accepted as normal; not a thing to be revered, but equally not a thing to be balked at. As the bard said, *in peace there's nothing so becomes a man as modest stillness and humility, but when the blast of war blows in our ears, then imitate the action of the tiger.* Eh? War was in our blood, Flinch. *Cry God for England, Harry and Saint George!* ... that, and the money was good. And there's no doubt that that uniform used to get the girls going.' He tapped ash from his cigar. 'Anyway, we signed up, me, Billy and Tom.

'Fortunately, thanks to our trades, our request to be in the same regiment was granted; the King's Regiment of Horse needed blacksmiths and carpenters, and the whole army needed butchers – no joke intended.' Underwood smiled, 'Ah, the King's Regiment of Horse. My word, they were something, I can tell you. Obviously I was just a humble chippy in the ranks, but I doubt there was a finer regiment in the army at the time. Anyway, I know from the history books that this would have been 1703 and Queen Anne was now on the throne; and the next year, we were in Germany under Marlborough.' Underwood took a puff on his cigar and eyed David through the smoke.

David took his cue. 'Oh right. Marlborough.'

'Oh, you know to whom I refer?'

David shook his head. 'No. Sorry.'

'Churchill, Flinch! The Duke of Marlborough. I was at The Battle of Blenheim. We saved Austria!'

'That's a famous battle then?'

'Well, I always thought so. Evidently I'm mistaken.'

'Sorry sir, I'll read up on it.'

'Oh, don't do it for me. It makes no difference to me if you're a lackbrained lob when it comes to history. Just so long as you get my breakfast and dinner sorted every night you can be as thick as you please.'

'No, I will. You've inspired me.'

Underwood took a puff on his cigar. 'Well, that's all right then. Good show.'

'So what happened next?'

'I continued my military career. I was doing jolly well before I was shot down at The Battle of Ramillies.'

'You were shot?'

'Yes,' he chuckled, 'the first of a million bullets; musket ball in the thigh. Missed the artery, thank God. Surgeons dug it out of me and I was invalided back to Blighty. Not much good in the infantry if you can't march steadily into a storm of hailing shot, eh? Still, I didn't mind. I'd had enough of it by then. I was damned lucky to have lasted as long as I did without getting my head shot off.'

'What about your mates? Your brother?'

Underwood's smile faded. He swirled his brandy, looking into the liquid as if into the past. 'Billy also fell at Ramillies. Though unlike me, he didn't get up again.'

'Oh. I'm sorry.'

'Thank you. But it's all right. It's ancient history now, even to me.' There was a flicker in the vampire's eyes, a brightness that might have been the start of a tear, but he took a drink and it was gone. 'As for Tom, he got out soon after. He'd done his time and he was having no more of it.

'And so, there we were, back on civvie street. Both of us advanced enough in our respective trades to have easily gone back to our apprenticeships, but at the same time, we'd acquired a whole new raft of skills that we felt broadened our options somewhat.'

David smiled. 'Like what? Shooting guns and dodging bullets?'

Through an exhalation of smoke, Underwood said, 'Precisely.'

David's smile fell. 'Eh?'

'The meagre wages afforded to an apprentice seemed depressingly inadequate to us now, after all, we were men of action! We had stormed the French with flintlock and bayonet; fought hand to hand with sabres over the bodies of the fallen – and we bore the scars to prove it. To some – especially the whores of Covent Garden, we were bloody heroes. Mind you, they would have said that, after all, we *were* paying.'

'So, what did you do?'

'What? With the whores?'

'No, I mean, what did you do next? It sounds like you didn't go back to carpentry.'

Underwood refilled his glass. 'No, I didn't. I went back to an earlier trade, but at a higher level, I suppose you could say. Oh, we could have been content with being mere footpads of course, but besides the fact that I now walked with a limp and couldn't run for toffee, footpadding was, we felt, for the likes of those who lacked the means or the ability to ride.'

He grinned. 'We had the means, and though neither of us had actually ridden as part of the cavalry, you don't get to serve three years in a regiment of horse and not learn how to ride.'

A smile dawned on David's face. 'You mean ... you became a highwayman?'

Underwood was delighted that he had finally struck a note of recognition with his audience. 'Aye, we did indeed. For many years. As fine a pair of highpadsmen as ever terrorised the King's highway.'

'Like Dick Turpin?'

Underwood soured. 'What? That *Rookwood* swine? Don't tell me they're still celebrating him! Let me tell you, he wasn't the gallant rogue he's made out to be, oh no, that's all the work of popular fiction. He was a torturer and a murderer, and when he was hanged it was good riddance to some very bad rubbish.' He sucked on his cigar with an air of annoyance. 'We, on the other hand, were as civil a pair of rogues as ever you were likely to find, which is probably why history has forgotten us. We never killed or harmed any of our victims, and we robbed only when we needed to – for if you were without family to feed, you could live off the takings of a good haul of purses for a fair long time in those days.'

'But the police must have been after you all the same?'

'What police? There were no police. In the cities you'd find constables or men of the nightwatch, but they were nothing to us as we kept out of their jurisdiction. Of course, sometimes you'd encounter a paid guard, but you could spot them a mile away. Our only real adversaries were the thief-takers.'

'What were they?'

'As the name suggests, they were men engaged in the business of taking thieves. Bounty hunters, basically. And of course, a reward was soon placed upon our heads. No one knew who we were personally, and so we became known in the papers and penny dreadfuls as The Butcher Gang. I never cared for the name myself, but it struck fear into the hearts of the public so it worked in our favour.'

'Why were you called that?'

'Oh, that was Tom's fault. On our early jobs we only had one pistol, and that was mine, so he brandished his meat cleaver: very frightening, as you can imagine.'

'Did you say "stand and deliver"?'

'Oh yes, it was the common phrase. I'd stop the coach with my pistol and give the order, *stand and deliver!* Then Tom would get the passengers out of the coach, line 'em up, and relieve them of their valuables. I'd shout instructions to another, fictitious, gang member in the woods to keep a musket trained on the passengers from behind; this gave the illusion of greater numbers.' Underwood drew on his cigar. His eyes shifted from David's to look out into the night, as if he had suddenly lost interest in the story and started thinking of something else.

David gave him a few moments then asked, 'Everything all right, Milord?'

Underwood's reverie broke and turned back to David. 'Sorry Flinch, I was just thinking ... you see, that third fictitious gang member eventually became a reality. Her name was Martha. Martha Hawkins.'

'A highway lady?'

'Yes. She was the daughter of an innkeeper, Samuel Hawkins, an old soldier who I suppose became one of the gang as well. Certainly in the eyes of the law he was. We met for the first time after a job on Hounslow Heath. Sam's inn, The Black Horse, was on the Great Western Road that ran from London to the West Country. I daresay he knew us for what we were the moment we walked in there. His custom consisted mostly of either coaches or the men who robbed them. Martha knew it too, she told me so herself later on; though at the time I could see from the way she looked at me that whatever my game was, she certainly fancied me.' He grinned at David. 'You know how you know when a woman fancies you, Flinch?'

David made vague, non-committal face. 'Sure.'

'My word, she was a ravishing creature. I'd had my fair share of ladies by this time, of course, but this was the first time I'd felt the thunderbolt, you know? That sudden shock you feel on seeing the woman that, on some level, you just know was made for you. You know what I mean?'

David smiled softly. 'Yes, sir.'

'So, anyway, despite the fact that I was walking on the sunny side of the street with her, so to speak, I found I was tongue tied – my usual charm seemed to have fled and I was coming out with all kinds of fiddle-faddle. I must have sounded like an absolute arse. But queer as it might sound, that actually endeared me to her all the more. But anyway, as I mentioned, Sam had clocked me for what I was straight away, and he'd also noticed what was going on between his daughter and I at the bar. So he came over and invited us – Tom and I – to join him in a game of cards. We accepted, and sat down with him. He got to the point fairly quickly. He said that he knew what we were, and while he had no problem with that, he did have a problem with my attentions towards his daughter. I took this soberly, for he had every right to tell me to sling my hook in this regard, but still, I asked him why.

"I don't want my daughter ending a widder 'fore she's twenty-one," says he. And I took his point; men in my profession didn't tend to live very long. Still, I persevered. I could see there was no point in trying to pull the wool over his eyes about what we were, so I told him straight that he was right about our profession, but wrong about our chances of survival.

'Tales of our successes and gentlemanly conduct didn't curry much favour with him, but after a few hands of cards – which I let him win – it emerged that he'd been a soldier and fought against the French in the Nine Years War. Well, as you can imagine, that called for a fresh round of drinks; we told him we'd been with Marlborough at Blenheim and Ramillies, and before long, scars were being produced, along with stories of how they were earned and the fine lads who had fallen alongside us. Anyway, by the end of the night, he was won. He was encouraged by the fact that I had a trade and that I'd every intention of starting up a legitimate business just as soon as I had sufficient funds. He said as long as this was my aim, he'd be honoured to have me as a son-in-law, which I felt was jumping the gun a bit, but still.'

Underwood took a slow draw on his cigar and savoured the smoke. 'Anyway, there was someone else whom I'd won with all this talk of daring-do, and that was Martha herself. Sam had told her to go on up to bed once she'd closed the inn, that this was a private game and we were talking men's talk. And while she seemed to obey, saying goodnight and heading off to bed, she in fact went no further than the other side of the connecting door, at which she listened at until the game broke up.

'Of course, we were too sloshed to ride home that night, so we took rooms at the inn. I passed out as soon as my head hit the pillow. But then, I don't know how much later it was, I was pleasantly awoken when she came into my room.'

'She came to *you?*'

'You sound surprised.'

'Well, I suppose I am a bit.'

Underwood laughed. 'I think you're confusing us with the Victorians, Flinch. The reason the Victorians were such virtuous bores is that *we*, the later Stuarts and the Georgians, were the absolute opposite.'

'I see.'

'I returned a few days later and without Tom. Everything was very civilised, and, with her father's blessing, Martha and I began to walk out together.'

David laughed.

'What?' said Underwood.

'I'm sorry, it's just such a nice phrase, considering you were a notorious criminal at the time.'

'I'll have you know that the only thing criminal about my life was how I made my living, Flinch, in all other areas I was a perfect young gentleman. Anyway, I remember we used to ride into Hounslow, and sometimes into Richmond where I would take her to the music hall and the theatre.'

'So when did you actually tell her what you were? I mean, I know you say she'd listened in and knew already, but did you actually *tell* her?'

Underwood smiled. 'Oh, I remember she asked what I did, and I told her I was a carpenter. I remember there was a twinkling in her eye when I told her that, like she was resisting an urge to laugh. She went along with my lie for a while, but I suppose my dishonesty in this respect finally started to annoy her. We had a row, and it out came that she had known what I was all along. She said she didn't mind me being a highwayman, but she bloody well *did* mind me lying to her about it. I was relieved, as you can imagine; the lie had been festering in me and I knew that soon either it would have to come out, or I'd have to become a lawful tradesman – which I was in no mind to do.

'So, now knowing that I could carry on in my chosen profession and keep the girl of my dreams, I was – for perhaps five minutes – the happiest man in England. Then she hit me with the news that she wanted to join the gang.'

'That was a bad thing?'

'Of course it was. I didn't want her to be in danger, did I? I was completely betwattled by this and turned her down point blank. But she insisted; she said she could ride as well as any man – and she could, for I'd seen the proof of that. But what's more, she said that her father had taught her how to handle his pistols, and she insisted that she could outshoot me as well. Now, at this I had to laugh; girls don't shoot, or at least they didn't back then anyway, and the idea that she could outshoot me just seemed hilarious. So she challenged me to a contest and a wager.

"What are the terms?" I asked her.

"If I win," she said, "I join your gang."

So I asked her, "What if I win?"

And what she said I have never forgotten: "I shall accept your proposal of marriage, and be your honest and dutiful wife".' Underwood smiled at the memory. 'Well Flinch, I swear to you, there was a look in her eyes that set my heart aflutter like never before. I hadn't actually *made* a proposal of marriage, but now that the prospect of having her as my wife was there, well, I couldn't have wanted to win that shooting contest more if had been playing for my immortal soul against old Scratch himself.

'So, in a field at the back of the inn, we lined up some old bottles on a fence, and I'll be damned if she didn't outshoot me just as surely as she could outrun me on a horse.'

'You lost the bet?'

'Oh, I lost the shooting match, yes, and she duly joined our gang. But as to the other half of the wager, well, I don't think either of us wanted to forfeit that.'

'So you got married?'

'Not immediately, no, but I made my proposal, and she accepted it. Of course, Tom wasn't happy about her joining the gang at first, but she quickly proved herself to be an advantage and he relented.'

'What about her dad?'

'Oh, at first we didn't tell him. But then she started bringing home the fruits of her labours and, well, it had to come out. Oh, he was angry of course – and deeply opposed to begin with. But she had joined us because they needed money; another inn had opened further down the Great Western Road and they were losing out as coaches increasingly preferred to stop there. So while Sam didn't like his daughter being a criminal, money is money, and sure enough, he came on board.'

'Was Martha good at it?'

'Oh, duck-to-water, Flinch. She was magnificent. I remember after our first robbery together when we were dividing up the loot, she gave me this as – ' he reached for his waistcoat pocket, but as he wasn't wearing one, his fingers touched the fabric of his shirt. 'Oh.'

'What is it?'

'I was looking for my watch.'

'Hang on,' David reached into his pocket drew out Underwood's watch. 'Here, you gave it to me earlier outside the restaurant in Ronda.'

'Ah yes, for safekeeping.' He took the watch and brushed his thumb over the worn casing. 'She gave me this from her first haul.' He opened the casing and read the inscription on the inside. "To Daniel, Forever Yours, Lilly." I wasn't a brilliant reader at the time but I could read this much, and I remember I said to her that from now on, I would have to call myself Daniel. And she kissed me, and said that she would be my Lilly.' He held the watch by the tip of its chain and let it twist slowly before his eyes. After a few moments, he said quietly, 'And so she was.'

David's cigar had gone out and he put it in the ashtray. He took a drink of water then said, 'I did wonder about that.'

Underwood blinked as though emerging from a trance. 'Hmm? Wondered what?'

'Who Lilly was. I noticed the inscription when I was winding it.'

Underwood smiled. 'Oh, I never met the original Lilly; we took it from a portly old gentleman with two young tarts as his travelling companions – neither of whom seemed to be of the wifely sort. Whoever Lilly was, she was nowhere near that coach that night.'

David nodded thoughtfully. Then he said, 'So what happened next?'

'Oh, for a year or so all went well. Our notoriety grew, as did the bounty on our heads, but we continued to strike seldom and rarely in the same area twice, so we managed to evade capture. Eventually, Martha and I began to think about getting out of it. Sam was getting on in years now and he wanted us to be married and give him some grandchildren. Now the plan was that he would retire and I would take his place as landlord of the Black Horse, and we'd all live happily ever after. But sadly it didn't work out that way.'

David leaned forward, picking up his cigarettes without taking his eyes from Underwood's face. 'What happened?'

Underwood closed the watch and set it on the table. 'I was in Covent Garden one night, Tom was off seeing a whore he was especially fond of and I was playing cards in a tavern. I was losing, badly, and I became convinced that I was being cheated by two of the other men at the table. I think someone may have been lacing my drinks with something stronger than ale, for when I stood to accuse my opponents, the room swam a hell of a lot more than I'd paid for it to. I made a grab for the money they'd taken from me and the next thing I knew, we were fighting, and I wasn't seeing double when I say there were at least four of them setting about me as we tumbled out into the street. Still, I swear I was getting the better of them when the night watch arrived. Oh, there was no denying I'd started the fray, and of course, there was no evidence of their cheating. So, I was done for.

'My second time before a judge, there was nothing small and cute about me. For stealing my own money back and creating a breach of the peace, I was sentenced to a year in Newgate Gaol.'

'*A year?*' said David. 'That seems pretty harsh.'

'Not as harsh as the end of a rope, Flinch, which I thankfully escaped. Mind you, Newgate was no bed of roses, I can tell you. But I was young and strong, so I reasoned that provided I didn't succumb to sickness while on the inside, I should make it. Then when I got out, I'd marry Martha, and settle down once and for all.'

'But something went wrong?'

Underwood nodded. 'Not with me, but on the outside. I mentioned that by this time, the bounty on the Butcher Gang was considerable; well, this had attracted the attention of the so-called Thief-Taker General, Jonathan Wild. Have you heard of him?'

David shook his head.

'Wild was a villain, Flinch, plain and simple, but it took the authorities a while to realise it. They thought he was simply an incredibly efficient catcher of criminals. He ran the so-called Office of Lost and Stolen Property where for a fee, people could apply to have their lost and stolen items found – and most of the time they'd get them too. And why? Perhaps you can guess?'

'Wild nicked the stuff in the first place?'

'Yes. Though not Wild himself, rather, persons of his acquaintance, and he was acquainted with all the villainy of London. But this was merely a sideline. His real business was thief-taking. As I said earlier, there was no official police force at that time. Catching criminals was largely the responsibility of the population. And to motivate them – I'm sure you can appreciate that a little motivation was needed – there was a reward of forty pounds for anyone whose crime-busting actions resulted in a thief behind bars. Forty pounds doesn't sound like a lot now, but believe me, it was a lot of money at that time, much more than the average worker could make in a year. So you can see how, for the more adventurous citizen, the collection of these rewards could be a very lucrative business. These men became known as thief-takers, and Wild turned the business into an industry.

'He had his fingers in just about every racket in London, he knew everything that was going on, and so was able to either take down the real crooks or set up his underworld rivals to take the blame. But we, the Butcher Gang, eluded him. We kept out of London as much as possible and so, despite his knowing of our existence, we were as good as invisible to him. This, as you can imagine, vexed him terribly, and eventually he decided that he was going to get us, by hook or by crook. I was told later by someone in his circle that it had become a matter of pride with him. So he assigned one of his lieutenants the exclusive task of tracking us down, a black-hearted weasel called Edgar Quinnell.' Underwood's lip curled as he spoke the man's name. 'Quinnell hunted high and low but was never able to turn anything up. Nobody could tell him anything, because nobody knew anything. But shortly after I was incarcerated in Newgate, he changed his tactics.'

Underwood blew smoke into his brandy glass. He watched it roll like mist on the surface of the liquid for a moment before inhaling it. 'I wouldn't know all of what happened to my friends until about a year after my release. When I got out, the first thing I did was go to the Black Horse, only to find it had been sold to new owners – not by Sam or Martha, or even by Tom, but by the Crown. I was stunned as you can imagine, and asked the new owner for more details, which he was happy to give as the inn had now achieved some notoriety and he was keen to cash in on it. He told me a version of events that sounded as though it had been lifted straight from the penny dreadfuls, although it gave me the gist. But I'll tell you what happened as I got it from a considerably more reliable source some time later.'

Underwood drained his drink then considered the empty glass. After a few moments he sat forward and poured himself another. 'Quinnell and his men began shadowing coaches – not riding with them, that way they would've been seen – no, but following behind them at a distance of about a quarter or a half mile, depending on the terrain. The idea was simple: should any highwaymen stop the coach they'd have ample time to dismount and begin their thievery. Then the thief-takers would strike, catching them red-handed. And so it was with Tom and Martha.'

He swirled the brandy briefly in the glass, took a long sniff of the vapours then took a drink. 'After I was put away, Tom led the robberies, coming out in front of the coaches and challenging them to stand and deliver, while Martha would come around the rear. Once the passengers were all out she'd cover them while Tom relieved them of their valuables.

'I'm told it all happened very fast. They were robbing a coach one night near Chiswick when suddenly Quinnell and his men came galloping out of the darkness, four of them, pistols drawn. Surprised, Tom turned and fired at them. He was a good shot; he hit one of them in the chest and he fell from his horse, dead most likely before he hit the ground. The problem was that a flintlock pistol only held one shot in it, and Tom only had one pistol. As the passengers scattered, screaming, Quinnell and his men returned fire. Martha fired back, but her hands were shaking and she missed – there's a big difference between hitting a bottle in a field on a summer's day and armed men on horseback shooting at you from the pitch-black country dark. She looked for Tom, expecting to see him running for his horse, but instead he was down on the road clutching his guts. She was about to dismount to help him, but he yelled at her to go. A shot whizzed past her head; it was all the spur she needed. She fled. One of them gave chase but she lost him in woodland. Tom was caught.

'I don't know exactly what happened to him after that, but I do know that he would never have given her up unless they tortured him to the extent that he had no choice. I found out years later from someone who had spoken to him in Tyburn that that's just what they did. He was hanged soon after.'

'I'm sorry,' said David.

Underwood nodded, tight lipped and staring out at the night. Then he took a breath and continued. 'Wild himself led the raid on the Black Horse with about a dozen men including Quinnell. Martha and Sam were caught unawares; it was a working night, they were unarmed, the pub was full of customers. Wild demanded that they surrender in the name of the King. What could they do? They surrendered.' Underwood looked down into his glass and fell silent.

David waited for him to resume, when he didn't, he asked, 'What happened to them?'

'This was the early summer of 1718, Flinch. Had they been caught just a few months earlier, both of them would have hanged as surely as Tom had. But now, a new, third form of punishment had been introduced;

something to take the pressure off the overcrowded prisons, and to offer a more merciful punishment than death for crimes like petty theft and prostitution.'

'Which was?'

'Transportation. I presume you've heard of *that*?'

'Yeah, of course, convicts were sent to Australia.'

Underwood took a puff on his cigar. 'Not yet they weren't.'

'Eh?'

'Colonial America, Flinch. The plantations were crying out for cheap labour, and some bright spark saw the opportunity to both provide it and to empty Britain's overpopulated prisons in one go.'

'I didn't know that.'

'What a surprise.'

'So Martha and Samuel were transported to America?'

'Yes. They were among the first of some 50,000 people who were shipped off to His Majesty's North American Colonies following the passing of the Transportation Act of 1718. And not just petty criminals either, but all sorts, even murderers could have their death sentences commuted on appeal and be packed off to the New World. Oh, this was nothing new, of course, Britain had been transporting its undesirables to the colonies since the reign of Elizabeth the First. But after the 1718 act, things got considerably more industrious.'

'So what were the terms for convicts?'

'Seven to fourteen years, depending on the crime.'

'What did Martha and Samuel get?'

'Fourteen years each.'

'Shit.'

'Yes. On paper it looks so much better than death, but for many convicts it *was* death. The ships were little more than floating dungeons. Men and women, young and old were all chained together below deck for the duration of the voyage. Needless to say, conditions were appalling and many died in transit.'

'How long was the voyage?'

'A couple of months or so.'

'You must have been devastated.'

'Yes. I was. The thought of Martha had been the only thing that kept me going during my time in prison. Now, to find that I had lost not only her, but also Tom – and Samuel, who had become like the father I never knew – well, yes, I was indeed devastated.'

David hesitated, then said, 'Can I ask ... what about your sister? You still had her, didn't you?'

Underwood slowly shook his head. 'No. I hadn't spoken to her in years. I mentioned earlier that she had worked her way up, well, hadn't she indeed – she married the son of the master of the house and now she had a child of her own. Not surprising really, she was a comely wench and I suppose the young master must have had his way with her. No, I didn't want to go to her, any more than she would have wanted me to. Our lives had taken different paths.'

'Oh. I'm sorry.'

'Don't be.' Underwood took a drink. 'Anyway, to get back to my tale, there I was, my best friend dead, and me facing the rest of my life without the woman I loved.' He looked at David. 'Well, what would you have done?'

'Gone after her.'

Underwood laughed, 'Ah, spoken like a true Flinch: loyal to the end.'

'So did you?'

'Oh, by God, yes! I wasn't going to just stand aside and let my intended wife become one of his Majesty's discarded citizenry. Oh no, I was either going to get her back or die trying.'

'But what did you do for money? Surely you must have been skint?'

'Not so, Flinch. You see, for a long time Martha and I been stashing a certain amount of our loot in the trunk of a dead oak tree in some woods about half a mile from the Black Horse. It was untouched, and among the gold coin and jewels was this old beauty.' He lifted the watch by its chain and held it spinning between them. 'It was the only thing from that stash I kept. I fenced all the jewels and went straightaway to the London docks, where, for a small fee, I was able to find out that Martha and her father had been sent to Virginia. So, I bought passage aboard a vessel bound for the same destination. I calculated that I had plenty of money left over to set myself up as a carpenter in Virginia, and to be able to find and buy back Martha and her father from whatever plantation owner had bought them. Then, we would all live happily ever after in the new world.

'But, needless to say, things didn't go quite according to plan.'

11

DAVID TOOK A CIGARETTE from his packet and reached for the lighter. Underwood frowned. 'You're going to have a cigarette when you've a perfectly good cigar on the go?'

David looked at his cigar in the ashtray. 'Oh, well, it keeps going out.'

'It went out once, Flinch, and only because you let it. What's the matter, don't you like cigars?'

'Well, no, not really. I prefer something I can inhale.'

'You can inhale these,' said Underwood, holding up his cigar.

'*You* can maybe, but then you're already dead.' David raised his hand when he saw Underwood was about to protest. 'I know, I know, you're not dead. Let's just say I prefer something lighter.'

Underwood tutted to himself and sat back, settling himself once again into his memories. 'Hmm. Yes. Well, where was I? Ah yes, the *Susannah.* That was the name of the ship I'd bought passage on. I'd been on a ship before, of course, when I was in the army, but even still, I had no sea legs at that time. I used to get seasick looking at ducks on a pond. But anyway, there was no time for concerns about petty maladies; I had to set my mind to the task, and get on board.

'At the dock at Blackfriars, I remember I bent down and touched the ground, perhaps for the last time. My homeland, you know? In my mind I bade farewell to her. I scooped up a loose handful of London dirt and, without thinking, pocketed it. Then I went up the gangplank, praying under my breath as I did so that we'd have smooth passage.

'By the time we pushed off I was feeling as sick as a parrot, and as we sailed down the Thames on the ebb tide I grew steadily worse, until, when we reached the mouth of the river and moved into the open sea, I was finally, magnificently, sick over the side. I hung on there for dear life all the way to our anchorage at Dover. Some of the lady passengers were sympathetic, but every now and again I'd look up and see various members of the crew having a good laugh at me. It was dreadfully embarrassing.

'Anyway, we dropped anchor and waited for a fair wind to carry us across to Chesapeake. We were there for the rest of the day. The sea was fairly calm, and by evening I'd sufficiently recovered to venture back up on deck. To my surprise, I found that I was all right, and I remember making a point of striding about the deck so everyone could see I was now quite the seasoned mariner. I was keen to redeem myself in the eyes of the crew, you see. I didn't like the idea of them thinking me some jelly-legged landlubber. I was the equal of any man on that ship and I wasn't having any of them thinking otherwise.' He puffed on his cigar and looked at David for confirmation of understanding.

David nodded.

'But alas,' Underwood continued with a smile, 'my pride, along with the contents of my stomach, went over the side first thing the next morning. I'd woken to find the ship heaving and hawing like mad, and I staggered up onto deck to see what was going on. Well, all sight of dear old England was gone. Our wind had found us. The sails were full and we were ploughing our way through the grey Atlantic, rising and falling, up and down.' He shook his head at the memory. 'Oh, how I hated it. I went to the side and threw up all I had in me. I remember there were porpoises swimming at the bow of the ship like they were racing us, and I watched them for about half an hour until I felt well enough to crawl back below deck again.' He noticed David grinning behind his hand. 'Oh, you may think it funny, Flinch, but unless you've actually suffered from seasickness, you've no idea how ghastly a feeling it is.'

'I'm sorry, sir, I don't mean to laugh. I've been seasick before and I know exactly what you mean, it's no joke. It's just, I can't imagine you being sick like that.'

'Well, it wasn't the me you know, Flinch; it was the *old* me, the mortal me, the land-lubber me on his first voyage across the Atlantic. But anyway, I found my proper sea legs after a day or so and I was soon up and about on deck, getting to know the other passengers. Most of them thought the conditions were positively dreadful, but I had no complaints. I'd known much worse conditions in my time, and once I was over my initial seasickness, I thought the whole thing really rather jolly. Oh, the food was pretty miserable, yes – especially when, eventually, all the all fresh stuff was gone and we were down to pickled cabbage, salt beef, weevily biscuits and various other nautical delicacies. But again, I'd known worse; I'd been living on Newgate nosh for the last year, and compared to that, this was haute cuisine. But anyway, moving on …

'For the first six weeks we had good weather and a fair wind, and we were making good time to our destination. But then, one afternoon, the weather took a dramatic change for the worse. We found ourselves in a storm that, by evening, was starting to feel more like the end of the world. We passengers were below deck where we prayed hysterically that God would deliver us from the tempest. All of us were trying to hang on to something solid; women and children were crying; others, including me, throwing our guts up. The way the ship was heaving and lurching, we were sure we were all going to go to the bottom of the sea. I kept telling myself it would all be over soon; that we'd be fine, and we'd look back on the whole thing and laugh. But it didn't end; day became night and night became day, and the storm just kept on.

'As the ship took damage, passengers were called upon to help bail out flooded areas and effect repairs. I'd gone beyond my seasickness now, and I stepped forward and made it known to the captain – Peabody was his name – that I was a carpenter. He promptly put me to work as mate to the ship's chippy, a chap called Ned Wallis.' Underwood shook his head. 'Well, I soon wished I'd kept my mouth shut, I can tell you; I soon found myself up on deck with waves the size of houses rising all around me. I don't mind admitting to you, Flinch, I was bloody terrified.' Underwood took a drink of brandy.

David wondered if he were steadying his nerves, as if he were once again on the deck of the *Susannah*. 'Well, that's understandable, sir. I think you'd be mad not to be terrified.'

'Damn right, you would. Especially when you see the man you're working with get washed overboard.'

David's eyes widened. 'Jesus.'

'Oh, there was no Jesus out there, Flinch. Out there we were the playthings of Poseidon. I remember it was night, and Ned and I were working on the quarterdeck. To preserve my sanity, I'd long since stopped looking at the sea, so I didn't see the wave coming. But I remember the look of horror on Ned's face as he saw it rising behind me. Then I felt the ship falling backwards, our bow was rearing up to point at the sky, and for a moment I felt sure we were about to be swallowed by the sea. Then a tremendous weight of water crashed down over us and I was lifted up, completely submerged, surging across the deck as the ship fell back down again. Desperately I stabbed downward with my chisel and it sank into the deck. By a miracle it held, and I clung to it for dear life as the water roared around me. When the deluge had passed, I looked around. There was no sign of Ned. I called his name – screamed it – or maybe I was just screaming, I don't know. But once I knew he was gone for good, I went below deck and I bloody well stayed there, and nothing nor no-one could convince me to go back up on deck again until the storm was past.'

Underwood took a drink. He thought for a moment then said, 'I think we passengers all started to go a little mad then. Fear began to eat our sense of reason. You see, none of us had ever seen weather like it before. On land, storms come and go, usually lasting perhaps no more than a day; it's like they know they shouldn't be on the land, like they've strayed there from their proper domain. But out there in the mid-Atlantic – that *is* their proper domain, and there they rage for as long as they damn well please. Of course, we didn't know that, and no amount of explanation from captain or crew could dissuade us from the slowly-spreading idea that God had damned us, and that the storm wouldn't pass until the ship and all souls on board had been dragged down to the bottom.'

Underwood chuckled. 'And then, on the third day, the storm finally broke, and the despair and sense of divine abandonment we'd felt turned into jubilation and hosannas all round. We felt that we had been tested, yet ultimately delivered by a god who works in strange ways, but whose will is not ours to question.' He took a puff on his cigar. 'Strange ways indeed: it turned out that including Ned, eight men had been swept overboard, and we'd been blown considerably off our course. The ship was battered and in bad need of repair. So Peabody decided to set a course for the West Indies, where we could put in for repairs and take on fresh provisions. He asked me if I wouldn't mind serving as ship's carpenter and obviously I accepted; the better patched up she was the sooner we'd reach port, and I was, by that stage, desperate to set foot on dry land – any dry land, I didn't care where it was.

'So, I got to work. Actually I was quite happy about my new job as it gave me something to do, and for the next few weeks I buried myself in my work, trying not to think of my hungry belly; the first appearances of dreaded scurvy aboard ship; and the distance that still remained between us and a port.'

'There was scurvy aboard?'

'Oh yes, scurvy was rampant in those days, the discovery of any connection with vitamin C was still to be made. We didn't realise it, but the sauerkraut had been staving it off so far, but now that was gone and some among the passengers and crew were showing early signs, fatigue mostly, but some had the red gums. As I say, I just got on with my work and prayed it wouldn't touch me.

'I began to spend more and more time in the company of the crew. I found them reassuring; they were accustomed to the privations of the sea and were less given to the feelings of doom that infected the passengers. Mind you saying that, the crew had their fair share of gripes as well, mostly directed towards Peabody and the company that ran the ship, both of whom they hated.'

'Why?' asked David.

'Oh the usual things: poor wages, harsh conditions and so on. But as you've heard in my tale so far, that wasn't entirely unreasonable of them – their working conditions *were* pretty grim, and they had fair cause to moan. Not like your trade union whingers these days, eh? Oh, by *these days* I mean the 1950s, sorry – but I'm sure it's much the same in your modern factories and whatnot. Anyway, as I was saying, they had a jolly hard time of it, but they were a tough old lot and I liked them by and large.

'So, that was the state of the *Susannah* then: a battered ship with sick and miserable passengers and crew. So you can imagine the elation among us all when the shout came down from the crow's nest, "Land Ho!".' Underwood looked at David and smiled. 'Yes, we'd made it. I remember seeing the dark grey line on the horizon and thanking God, over and over again, for bringing us safely through – for indeed, as all we passengers rejoiced along the deck, we thought we *had* come safely through. So when the lookout shouted, "Ship Ahoy!" we felt no cause for alarm, only more rejoicing – for where there were ships, there were ports; we could fill our bellies and sleep in warm beds once again. God be praised! I remember we even speculated that perhaps the ship had come out to meet us, maybe an advance party of traders keen to sell us meat and vegetables before we made port.

'But the ship didn't come to meet us; it sailed past us at a distance of perhaps a mile. Then, just as I thought it was about to dwindle into a dot and disappear, it slowly came about and began to follow us.'

David shifted in his seat and a long ash tumbled from his cigarette to land silently in his lap.

'And it continued to follow us for hours, never gaining, never falling behind. I was intrigued, and I noticed our new found shadow was causing a tension among the crew. I asked a few of them what the worry was, but they denied any concern, which I suppose they would – after all, I might be a mate, but I was still a passenger, and the last thing they wanted was to set us off on another chorus of *God Preserve Us, We're All Damned*. But it didn't matter, because soon after, I noticed our shadow was gaining on us, and before long we could clearly make out her detail with no need of a spyglass. She was a brig.'

'A brig?'

'A brigantine, it's a type of ship. She was about 80 feet long and square rigged on both masts. A fast and maneuverable ship, unlike us. All eyes were now on her. As she drew closer, I could see the shapes of the men on board working at their tasks. Some of them were watching us in turn. I didn't like it. None of us did. I had a dread suspicion that was gnawing at my nerves like a caged rat. So in some ways it was a relief when finally, from among their number, this tall fellow in a long black coat walks up to their forecastle deck and stands where he could see us and we could see him. His arms hung at his sides, and in each of his hands he held something, but I couldn't see what. And then, as if to satisfy my curiosity, he raised two polished boarding axes.'

'Oh shit,' said David.

Underwood smiled. 'Yes. You've reached the same conclusion as I think we all had by that time. The man turned to the crew and crossed the axes over his head, and a cheer came up from them that carried to us across the water. Then a black flag fluttered to the top of the mast, and I could make out a grinning white skull on it.'

'They were pirates,' said David.

Underwood gave a slow, single nod. 'The Axeman turned back to us and lowered his axes to point in our direction. A cannon fired, smoke shot out from her side, and we heard the cannonball as it flew through the air above us. Fear and panic seized my fellow passengers, but I managed to keep a cool head; I reasoned that these men were just a seafaring equivalent of my own profession, and I watched, curious to see what would happen next. All eyes of the crew looked to Peabody, who took to his cabin with his officers. They were gone for what seemed an interminable amount of time, but in reality must only have been a few minutes. Then they returned and Peabody addressed us all.

"Men of the crew, ladies and gentlemen, the situation we face is apparent to us all and needs no explanation, save to say that in most cases, rogues like these only seek to plunder and be on their way with as little bother as possible. As you know, we are not a warship, and we are

450

certainly in no condition to run. So, one way or another, we are at the mercy of these men. Therefore, my officers and I have decided that it is in the best interests of us all to surrender. And if we give them no trouble, after they have taken what little we have left, they should, by the grace of God, leave us to continue on our way unharmed."

'Obviously that's not verbatim, but that's the sense of what he said, and although none of us liked the idea, I thought he'd made the best choice he could under the circumstances. Everyone was afraid, and naturally there was an especial dread and panic among the women, but Peabody told 'em pirates didn't take women aboard ship because they were a cause of trouble among the men, which was true, generally speaking. Still, Peabody shouted across to the pirates that he'd surrender only if the safety of his passengers could be assured. This was met with laughter from the other ship, but the chap with the axes shouted back that no harm would come to anyone provided there was no resistance. So, it was decided. Peabody took out his white handkerchief and held it aloft. Another cheer went up from the pirate ship, and within a very short while they were coming up alongside us.'

Underwood sneered and shook his head. 'What a bunch of scumbags they were. Perhaps it was just my fancy, but I swear I could smell them even before they came aboard. Many of them were dressed in silks and fancy garments taken from previous plunder, and every one of them was brandishing some kind of weapon, visibly relishing the fear and horror they were stoking in the womenfolk. Then their ropes and grappling hooks were flying on to our ship, and the Axeman made a great show of coming aboard first. He swung over, one axe still in his hand, and landed on our deck with a roar that was the cue to his mates to join him. Then he turned to the assembled passengers and crew. "Ladies and gentlemen," says he, all grand, and yet in his common West Country accent, "Permit me to introduce myself. My name is Henry Verlaine, and these gentlemen," he indicated the rabble now swarming onto the ship like a pack of rabid dogs, "Are my worthy crew."

'Despite the fact that he obviously thought his reputation preceded him, I'd never heard of him, and our crew seemed equally unmoved by the mention of his name. This was a good thing, of course, because it tended to be the more murderous pirates who made a name for themselves.

'Verlaine was now strutting about, enjoying the limelight and tossing his long black curly hair like a tart. As I say, he had on this black frock coat, it was velvet, and I could see now that the lining was of scarlet silk. Beneath that he wore a dirty white shirt, black silk pantaloons and black leather boots. He probably thought he cut quite a dash, but to my mind he was just a thug in fancy dress. Anyway, like all his men he was well armed, with a pistol on one hip and a cutlass on the other, but he seemed to favour that axe as his weapon of choice. He twirled it in such a way as it never left our attention, and he passed the blade in line with our eyes as he told us to hand over all our valuables. Oh yes, and on his flag – for we could see it clearly now that his ship was alongside us – beneath the skull were not two crossed bones or swords, but two axes.' Underwood gave a short derisory snort. 'Of course it was all just a gimmick; he was trying to make a name for himself as the Axe Wielding Pirate of the West Indies. All these chaps were out to make a name for themselves one way or another, which was fair enough, I suppose. I knew from firsthand that notoriety oils the wheels of hasty plunder, and seeing this fellow's pomp and showmanship made me all the more optimistic that we'd soon be released. After all, if we were murdered, how could we pass on word of his villainy to the wider world?

'Anyway, with Verlaine and a few of his grinning curs training their weapons on us, we handed over what we had, which wasn't much: mostly small trinkets of jewellery, handkerchiefs and watches. I had to hand this over.' Underwood held up his watch by its chain.

David looked at it then frowned. 'But you obviously got it back.'

Underwood smiled. 'Obviously, but more of that later. So, the pirates ransacked the ship, taking clothing, supplies – including the remaining food rations and all our money and valuables. Verlaine then asked who among us would like to join him. Well, I was astonished at the question, but not nearly so much as I was when about seven or eight of the ship's crew stepped forward in reply. I knew they had their grievances, but I didn't think things were *that* bad. Anyway, Verlaine now seemed content and I felt that he'd now be on his way and we could continue on ours. However, I was premature in my optimism. He asked his new recruits if any among them was a carpenter. Of course, none of them was, and I remember all the stoical optimism I'd felt through this unpleasant encounter suddenly leave me. I froze. Then one of our defectors,

Fletcher, whom I'd never much cared for, points to me and says, "He's a carpenter, Cap'n."

'Verlaine looks and me with a slightly apologetic demeanour, and says, "Then I regret to inform you, sir, that you are coming with us." Well that put the fire back in my belly, I can tell you. I was damned if I'd go with him, and I said so. But suddenly I was seized from behind and found myself being forced towards the side of the ship. I still wasn't having any of it and I managed to throw them off and land a punch or two before I was sapped on the back of the head and the world went black. When I woke up again, I was in darkness, bound hand and foot, and lying on a bed of coiled rope and rigging. A couple of large black rats were watching me with interest, but they soon scurried away when I started struggling with my bonds. The unfamiliar sounds from above told me I must be in the hold of the pirates' ship.'

'Did they take anybody else?' asked David.

'No, only me. I lay there for a while, wondering what was to become of me. Then a young fellow comes down with food and water. My jailor, I suppose you'd call him. I can see him now as then as he approached through the gloom, his blond hair catching the thin shafts of sunlight that filtered through the deck.' Underwood's eyes narrowed on David as if he were trying to make him at out a distance. 'Yes. It's uncanny, but I see it clearly now; he grew to look just like you. The resemblance is far greater than in any of your kin for generations.'

David sat forward. 'Was he ... ?'

'Yes,' said Underwood with a smile. 'His name was Matthias Flinch.'

12

DAVID'S FACE LIT UP. 'Really?'

'Yes. Not that he introduced himself as such; he told me his name was Jack Tanner. He was a lad of about fourteen at the time. He'd been charged with feeding me and telling me what was what. In other words, he'd been sent to convince me to sign the articles.'

'The articles?'

'Yes, a kind of contract of employment. When you joined a pirate ship, you signed the articles. They stated what was expected of you aboard ship, and what you could expect to gain in return for loyal service. In signing it, you declared yourself to be one of them. But if ever the articles fell into the hands of the authorities, the document was as good as a death warrant for every man on it. Even if you'd fled the ship and weren't aboard when it was captured, it made no difference. It was a damning confession. You may have escaped the pirates, but you wouldn't escape the hangman.'

David lit a fresh cigarette. 'Talk about a binding contract.'

'Yes.'

'And so, Matthias asked you to sign these articles?'

'No, but he told me that things would go better for me if I did. The reason Verlaine had sent him was because he bore a fresh reminder of what I could expect if I didn't sign. Matthias lifted up his shirt and showed me the scars left by a cat o' nine tails on his back.'

David winced.

'Yes. My reaction was the same. Sailors despised the lash, and the flogging of a crew member on a pirate ship was a serious business; it had to be voted on by the whole crew. However, until you signed the articles, you *weren't* one of the crew, and so you were fair game to be flogged, hanged or thrown over the side of the ship as Verlaine saw fit. Matthias told me that as a carpenter, I was a prized asset and would never be released until another was found, and even then there was no guarantee. He'd been in the same situation himself.'

'He was a carpenter?'

'No, a violin player.'

'A *violin player?* That doesn't sound like a very important role.'

'*Au contraire*, Flinch. Musicians were highly coveted by pirates; they made the difference between a happy ship and a miserable one, and it wasn't unusual for them to be kept working day and night.'

David nodded thoughtfully. 'And so Matthias was a musician?'

'On Verlaine's ship, he was, but on his previous ship he'd been a young officer.'

'Officer in what?'

'The Royal Navy.'

'Really? So, what? Did he get captured in battle?'

Underwood laughed. 'Oh dear me, no. I don't imagine Verlaine, good as he was, could have taken on a Royal Navy frigate and won. No, Matthias found his way aboard *The Fortuna* – that was the name of Verlaine's ship – through his own will and folly.'

'How?'

'Well, I suppose you need a little background information. Your family at that time had a long naval history, Flinch. Matthias's father had been a Captain in the Royal Navy, as had his father, and his father before him, and it was naturally taken for granted that Matthias would follow suit. But the taste for the nautical life skipped a generation in Matthias. Just as, I suppose, a taste for the murderous life has skipped a generation in you, eh?' Underwood grinned and tapped ash from his cigar. 'Anyway, Matthias's great love wasn't the sea, but music, and he spent much of his childhood scraping away in his room on a violin. His mother was delighted by this, but his father was less than thrilled. Still, old Captain Flinch knew the value of music in the navy, so he was happy for the lad to learn the instrument – he had a talent for it, and under different circumstances might have gone on to study music at university. But naval tradition came first in the Flinch household and when he turned thirteen, Matthias received his commission into the Royal Navy as a midshipman.'

'Thirteen? That seems very young.'

Underwood puffed his cigar. 'You think so? I've always found young men to be at the height of their savagery in their mid-to-late teens. What better time to bung 'em in the armed forces, eh? Mind you, saying that, when I met him, Matthias was about as savage as a golden retriever – so there you are – for every rule an exception. But no matter, the lad's career was decided the moment the midwife announced he was a boy.

'Oh, he gave the navy life a go, of course. He wanted to try and do well, to please his father as all young lads do, but it was no good, he was a bad fit, and that was that. Once he'd reached that inescapable conclusion, he began thinking of ways he could get out of it. Desertion was the obvious choice, but at the time it was potentially punishable by death. The least you'd get away with was a flogging, so it wasn't something to be undertaken lightly.

'When he finally *did* decide to jump ship, it was in Kingston, Jamaica. As places to desert go, Kingston wasn't without its advantages, but it was equally fraught with perils. A man of more advanced years might have been better able to tell the two apart, but young Matthias, by his own admission, was as green as they came. Anyway, as I say, he deserted. His captain sought for him for a while, but the ship had more pressing matters to attend to, so Matthias was listed with the military police as a fugitive, and his ship left port without him. That was when he started going by the name Jack Tanner – a simple alias to use until he managed to get out of town. Like me, he had a plan to start a new life in America. But before he could do that, he had to find a means of getting there. He couldn't buy his way, so he realised he'd have to work his passage on a ship. He started asking around in the port taverns, and that's how he ran into some of Verlaine's crew. He'd overheard them talking about how they were heading up to Virginia and he asked them if they were looking for crew.

'Now, pirates didn't usually take boys aboard ship for the same reason as they didn't take women, and so initially they were dismissive of him. But Matthias was desperate to get out of Kingston, so he regaled them with a list of ways he could be of service – including playing the violin. Well, that put a different complexion on things, and they promptly took him to meet their captain. On seeing Matthias for the first time, Verlaine's reaction was much the same as his crew members' had been. But, like them, as soon as he learned that the lad was a fiddle player, apparently his eyes lit up and he uncoiled from his seat like a snake, taking Matthias by the hand and warmly welcoming him to the crew.'

'Did Matthias know they were pirates?'

'Oh no. Like I said, he was quite green. Obviously he knew pirates existed, but he'd never actually run into any before. Anyway, his new captain and crewmates proceeded to ply him with rum until he passed out, and the next thing he remembered was waking up at sea aboard the *Fortuna*. He was taken to Verlaine, who presented him with a violin. Matthias took it and played for them sufficiently for Verlaine to then cheerfully present him with the ship's articles. Matthias's happiness at his acceptance to the crew went sour as soon as he read a few lines of the document – that was when he realised he was among pirates. Of course, he refused to sign, saying he'd been misled, but was more than happy to fulfil the terms of their original agreement and serve as a musician for his passage to America.

'Well, once the laughter in the room had abated, he was told he had until the end of the day to reconsider, after which he'd be flogged. Sure enough, he was again presented with the articles and he again declined. Well, it took three lashes of the cat to change his mind. He signed, but, clever cove that he was, he did so under the name of Jack Tanner. So, they may have forced him, but at least they didn't have Matthias Flinch.

'After that, his wounds were salted and he was taken below to recuperate for the night. The next day his career as a pirate musician began. He told me that Verlaine would sometimes have him come to his cabin and play classical pieces for him, but generally speaking, the sort of music Matthias was accustomed to playing wasn't the sort the pirates wanted to hear; he had to learn the various jigs, ballads and shanties that tended to keep the rabble happy. But learn them he did. And that was who, and what, your ancestor was when I first met him.'

'Wow,' said David, nodding thoughtfully. 'So, did *you* sign the articles?'

'Yes. Soon after Matthias left me, I was dragged up to Verlaine's cabin and was presented with them. I'd had time to think it over and saw no point in taking a flogging. Still, at first I tried bluffing it out and refused. Verlaine was in no mood for messing about as his ship was in bad need of repairs. He told his men to take me out and flog me, there and then. I capitulated before they got me to the cabin door.' He looked at David, expecting disapproval, but there was none. 'Perhaps you think I should have stood up to them? Held out?'

David shook his head. 'Not at all, I agree with you. Sounds to me like all you'd have stood to gain was a load of pain before they chucked you overboard.'

'Exactly, Flinch. So I signed – and unfortunately, I had to sign my real name too; unlike Matthias, I couldn't use an alias because Fletcher and the other men from the *Susannah* had told Verlaine exactly who I was. So, swearing allegiance with my right hand on an axe in place of a bible, I put quill to parchment and signed away the name of John William Brooks.'

He gave a little shrug, took a drink, then continued. 'And that was that. I was now a fully fledged crew member of the *Fortuna*. For a while, I settled as best I could into life on board. I certainly had plenty to keep me busy; the previous carpenter had been killed over a month before and the jobs had been piling up ever since, so I was never bored. Then in the evenings we'd put in at some island bay or inlet and play cards, get legless on rum, and sing along to the music of Matthias and the other musicians.

'To be fair, after a week of living that way, part of me began to warm to the life a little, and had I not been determined to rescue Martha and her father from slavery in Virginia, I may well have taken to it. I mean, I was already a thief, so morality didn't come into it. And there was a lot to be said for the way things worked aboard ship. It was certainly the first genuine democratic society I'd ever known. In the articles it was laid down that each man had a vote on the affairs of the moment; had an equal claim to provisions and liquor – unless in times of scarcity; and most importantly, there was the whole issue of who was in charge. Verlaine was captain not because it was his ship and he had recruited the men to work for him – oh no. They were all equal in their ownership of vessel and everything else; a band of criminal brothers, if you like. The captain was elected by the men, and led them only for as long as they agreed he should do so. I didn't *like* Verlaine, but I could see why the men chose him to lead them: he had that certain quality you find in all successful leaders, I'm sure the head-shrinkers have a name for it by now, but I don't know what it is.'

'An alpha?' suggested David.

'I beg your pardon?'

'An alpha, that's what they call them – in this case an alpha male – the leader of the pack.'

'Oh. Right. Well yes, he was certainly that. Anyway, I felt that – good as he was – with a bit of experience of seafaring, I could probably have supplanted him in time. But fortunately for him, I had no such designs. I had to be on my way at the first opportunity, and I wasn't the only one. Matthias, and another forced man he introduced me to, an Irish fellow called Jeremiah Cullen, were as keen to escape as I was. Cullen said he'd been aboard for seven months, and I asked him why he hadn't just jumped ship already. He explained that he was a cooper by trade and that Verlaine kept as watchful an eye on him as he did Matthias and myself.

'We all had our reasons to be out of there, but Matthias especially. One of the pirates, a thick-necked brute named Rudge, had been looking at him in a way that he said made his flesh crawl. I said nothing to the lad, but I decided to have a word with this Rudge to tell him to keep his eyes to himself. I approached him in a friendly enough manner, just to get the measure of him, and as I did so, I noticed on his vest a watch chain that looked very much like mine. I used this as a gambit, and asked him if he had the time. He obliged me, and I was delighted to see it was indeed my watch. Well, I saw no reason why what had been pinched from me as a civilian shouldn't now be returned to me as a brother crew member, and I told him, right there and then, that that was my watch he was handling and I'd be grateful for the return of it. The brute just laughed in my face and pushed me aside.

'Well, I wasn't having any of that, so I went after him, and *insisted* that he return my watch. Other pirates were now gathering around us, no doubt sensing imminent blood, and Rudge squares up to me and with a couple of pokes to my chest told me the spoils of the *Susannah* had been divided up fairly among the crew as it had been at the time, therefore, the watch was now his, and if I wanted it, I'd bloody well have to fight him for it. Fine by me, I thought, and was just getting ready to clock him one when the ship's quartermaster steps in and tells us there'll be no fighting on ship. If we had a matter to settle, then we'd do it on the shore.

'Well, Rudge and I said we did indeed have a matter to settle, and so it was agreed that we'd fight each other when next we made land. Of course, afterwards, Matthias told me that Rudge was a champion fist fighter and that I was most likely going to get the stuffing knocked out of me, but still, I wasn't going to let that thug have Martha's gift to me without so much as a blackened eye for his troubles. But as it turned out, he got considerably more than that.' Underwood smiled at the memory and puffed on his cigar.

'What did you do?'

'Oh, that comes a bit later, Flinch. First there was the attack on the Dutchman.'

'The Dutchman?'

'Yes, a Dutch merchant ship. We sighted her the next day, a three-master. Verlaine went after her immediately. We were lighter and faster than she was, and after only a few hours she was within range of our cannon. All around me, men were preparing for battle: sharpening the blades of their cutlasses; loading muskets, pistols and cannons; filling buckets with water in case the ship caught fire. I have to say, despite everything, it was jolly exciting.

'Verlaine returned to deck dressed in the fancy garb I had first seen him in when he attacked the *Susannah*, the black velvet coat and fancy silk pantaloons, and in each hand he carried one of those polished boarding axes of his. All the men made way for him, and you could see that he loved every minute of it. He went up to the forecastle deck, turned back to us men, and asked us if we would have the Dutchman for our own – and I realised with some pleasure that I was included in the vote. Did *I* want to trade the *Fortuna* for this new ship? Well, I imagined the sleeping arrangements would be more comfortable, so I voted yes. But the vote went the other way; sailors back then were a superstitious lot, and the *Fortuna*'s crew were very attached to her.

'So then, with a rousing *huzzah*, Verlaine raised up his axes and crossed them over his head, and all the men cheered – including me. What can I say? I was caught up in the moment. And as we were cheering, up goes the Jolly Roger. Verlaine then turned to the Dutchman and pointed his axes at her. It was his cue to the gunners to fire a warning shot, and straight away, there was a terrific blast and I felt the ship shake as one of our portside cannon fired.

'Well, I was expecting the Dutchman to just give up as Peabody had done, but either her captain was made of sterner stuff, or he had something worth fighting for, because instead of surrendering, he ran out three of his cannon and fired one of them back at us: an answering shot to ours, of course, just a warning – not intended to hit. Well, at this Verlaine turned and called to us, "What do you say to that, lads?"

'The reply was a unanimous call for blood.

"Drummers!" shouts Verlaine, and four drummers immediately started hammering out a tattoo. All around me, men were running to their battle stations. Some were readying to board, others were climbing up into the rigging shrouds with muskets to get a better shot at men on the other deck. The gun crews had their cannons loaded and trained on target – their job was to go for the masts and cripple her – she'd be no good to anyone at the bottom of the sea. And, as for me, well, Verlaine wanted his skilled tradesmen, including Matthias, to remain on the *Fortuna* and provide covering fire from deck. Until that time I hadn't been given a weapon, but now I was issued a musket, powder, and shot. Verlaine asked me if I could handle it. I told him I could and he pointed to the men with muskets now climbing into the Dutchman's rigging. "Pick of as many of their shooters as you can," says he, "and I'll personally give you a doubloon for every man you kill." That sounded like a good deal to me. I loaded my gun and took aim. Then Verlaine goes to back to the forecastle, turns to us, and yells the order to fire. And by thunder, fire we did. Cannon and musket blasted in a terrible harmony. My first shot got a fellow in the head, I remember seeing his hat fly off him as his head snapped back, and as I reloaded my gun I mentally tallied my first doubloon.'

'You shot an innocent man?'

'Oh shut up, Flinch. It was war. Kill or be killed. If I hadn't shot him, he would have shot me, and make no mistake. Anyway, as I was ramming down my next shot, I tried to pick out another target through the gunsmoke that was billowing all around us. Cannon continued to blast, from our side and theirs, and although my ears were ringing with the sound of the explosions, I could still hear musket balls whizzing through the air around me and thudding into the wood of the ship.

'I ducked down, finished loading, came up, marked a target and fired. Huzzah! Another sniper dropped from their rigging, and another doubloon tallied up in my head. Then there was a god-almighty explosion as the Dutchman's main mast was blown to pieces; one of our cannonballs had found its target. A cheer went up from our ship just as screams of agony came up from theirs.

'Now we were closing in on her, too close for cannon fire, and the men who made up the first wave of the boarding party stood with grappling irons and weapons ready. Then Verlaine throws his grapple and swings over, axe in hand, leading the charge. As he landed on deck, a fellow raised a pistol to him. Verlaine could never have thrown his axe in time, but fortunately for him, he didn't need to: I shot the chap between the shoulder blades. The pirates were swarming aboard now, but Verlaine looked over at me and gave me a small nod. I took that as a sign that I could expect a bonus, and allowed myself to tally two more doubloons. This was turning out to be quite a good day for rebuilding my lost Virginia funds.

'Anyway, now the fighting aboard the Dutchman was hand to hand. God only knew what they had in their cargo hold, but it seemed they were prepared to fight to the death for it. I later learned that this wasn't uncommon with the Dutch, they rarely gave up to pirates without a fight. But still, at the time I was thinking they must have had the Dutch Crown Jewels aboard. Then, as I was reloading, another thought occurred to me:

this was as perfect opportunity to make a run for it. Two thirds of the crew were fighting on the other ship; those who remained were firmly focused on the battle before them, and no more than half a mile off our starboard side was an island thick with jungle. If we could get to it, we could easily find a place to hide and hold up until these bastards got fed up and cleared off.

I looked from the battle to the island: yes, it could be done. Even when the fighting was done with, they'd still be too busy with the hunt for booty to notice that we were gone. I hurried over to where Matthias and Cullen were firing and put it to them.

"God no," said Cullen. "The penalty for deserting ship in battle is death – or worse, marooning." I looked at Matthias. He was tight-lipped, frightened, but I couldn't let his fear stop me. "Listen lads," said I. "I'm going. You can do what you like, but we may never get as good a chance as this again. Follow me if you will. If not, fare you well." And with that I went over to the starboard side, making out as if I was looking for a better vantage point to shoot from. Nobody paid me any attention, so, without a second thought, I climbed up onto the handrail, took a last check that I was still unobserved, then stepped back, off of the ship and into the sea. Then I was swimming for land for all I was worth. When I'd gone some distance I chanced a look back and I saw that two men were swimming after me. For a moment I wondered if they were pirates, but a glance at the ship told me it wasn't so, for if they had been, there would have been shots firing after me as well, and there were none. It had to be Matthias and Cullen. Heartened, I ploughed on, and I think I'd been swimming for about five minutes before the sound of battle behind me ceased. I redoubled my efforts, for now was when we'd be missed; once they'd realised that we weren't among the dead or injured, they'd start looking for us. It was another couple of minutes before the sounds of distant shots started. I was almost to the beach. I turned and saw little puffs of white smoke from the *Fortuna*'s starboard. Thankfully we were out of range, but I knew that wouldn't last.

'Ahead of me was an inlet, and I could see that further inland the jungle rose over a range of hills. I imagined there must be valleys, caves, waterfalls, all sorts of places where we might hide. I staggered from the surf and fell down onto the beach to get my breath and wait for the other two. They emerged a few minutes later. I asked them if by chance they knew the island and they just shook their heads, both of them breathless.

'I looked back nervously into the inlet. It ran into shallow mangrove swamps which to me looked as though they might have fallen from outer space. Obviously being a lad from London Town, I'd never seen terrain such as this. I'd heard stories of it though, tales of monstrous snakes and lizards, big cats, and tribes of savage head hunters. And we were all unarmed. I pushed those thoughts from my mind and we had a hasty discussion about the best course of action. We agreed that we should skirt the edge of the inlet then head up through the mangroves and into the higher ground that rose to the west.

'And when we got to the other side of the island? Who knew? Maybe we'd find civilisation, a town – if not British, then maybe Dutch, Spanish, even French, we didn't care. We looked back to the ships and saw a life boat was being lowered from the Dutchman. Either the pirates were putting the Dutch crew ashore because they'd decided to take their ship after all, or they were coming after us – and we knew it wasn't the former. We started running.'

Underwood drained his glass and set it down on the table with a sigh. 'I say, Flinch, it's no good, I'm hungry. All this talking is giving me an appetite. Send for a donor, would you?'

David was mildly taken aback. 'It's a bit late, Milord, it'll be sunrise in about an hour.'

'Yes, I know, so it's hardly surprising that I'm hungry, is it?' Underwood got up and began to remove his jacket. 'But I take your point. Never mind with the donors, I'll go out and hunt an animal. There's plenty of wildlife around here, maybe I can even find a farm animal: a cow or a sheep.'

'But what about the story? You can't leave it there!'

Underwood began unbuttoning his shirt. 'Sorry Flinch. I'm hungry.'

'Wait!' David stood up, holding out his hand in a stop gesture. 'Hang on. I've got some blood bags in the fridge downstairs. I've taken a few extra pints over the last few days for emergencies.'

Underwood's nose wrinkled. 'Blood from the fridge? Oh dear me, no. Blood shouldn't be served cold, any more than beer should be served hot.'

'Well, I'll pop it in the microwave.'

'The *what?*'

'It's an electric oven. I could warm the blood to body temperature.'

Underwood raised an eyebrow. 'Hmmm. Well, a drop of warm human is always preferable. And I am in full narrative flow.'

'Exactly. So, how do you want me to serve it? In a glass, mug, soup bowl?'

'Blood in a mug?' Underwood frowned. 'Don't be such an oaf, Flinch. A glass, if you please.'

'Right-o, then. I'll be back in a minute.' David moved quickly to the stairs and disappeared into the house.

Underwood put his jacket back on and sat down. He re-lit his cigar and gazed out at the night. It had been a long time since he'd told this story; he hadn't thought about these people in years, though they would forever haunt his dreams. Henry Verlaine: he had been one of a kind – even in those days when such men were unpleasantly common in the Caribbean. Underwood had been aboard the *Fortuna* for a little more than a week, but in that time he had gotten to know Verlaine well enough, both through personal interaction with the man himself and through the various anecdotes of the crew. His initial impression that the man was a dandyprat was unfounded; he was as hard as nails – and a cut-throat too if occasion demanded. Yes, he was flamboyant – a show-off who used to regard the bloody decks of his battles as an actor regards the boards of a stage, but it was all to a particular end: Verlaine wanted to live forever, if not in person, then through legend and folklore – which the man himself had more than a slight tendency to embellish. While aboard the *Fortuna*, Underwood had heard how Verlaine claimed to be descended from French nobility; how his family had come over to England with the exiled Henry Tudor, later Henry VII, and fought to overthrow Richard III at the Battle of Bosworth Field. Under Henry VIII they'd lost their lands and been reduced to poverty. Verlaine had been a Bristol blacksmith until he was press-ganged into the crew of a slaver. He claimed to have been liberated from that life by none other than Blackbeard himself, and to have served aboard *Queen Anne's Revenge* until he left of his own accord to start a crew of his own – though most felt it was more likely that he had jumped ship somewhere and run for his life after getting on the wrong side of the infamous pirate. Either way, he and some other ne'er-do-wells had formed a gang and taken a sloop, which they discarded once they'd taken the *Fortuna*. And from that time to when he had crossed the path of the *Susannah* – about a year, apparently – Verlaine had been sailing the waters from Nova Scotia to the West Indies and making a name for himself as a rogue.

Underwood puffed on his cigar. 'But you were never one of the greats, Henry.' He blew a languid stream of smoke and watched it roll away into nothingness. 'Though, as we both know, there's more than one way to live forever.'

'What's that?' said David emerging from the stairs.

'Oh, just chatting with my ghosts, Flinch.'

'Oh, right,' David handed Underwood a large wine glass filled with blood. 'That feels about the right temperature to me. Try it.'

Underwood sniffed the bouquet and murmured approvingly. 'Mmm, well done, Flinch.' He drank the blood down in three swallows and put the empty glass on the table. 'Perfect. Pardon the gluttony, but I didn't want it to get cold. I may trouble you for another before the sun rises.'

'No problem,' said David, resuming his seat. He took a drink of water. 'So you were on the beach, about to head into an inlet and a swamp and stuff.'

'Ah yes, have you ever been in a tropical swamp?'

'No, sir.'

'Awful places. I remember we got to where the tidal water ended just as the sun was sinking below the hills. That's when the biting insects came out. We were wading through mud, sinking in it up to the knees while the bugs were eating us alive. We slathered ourselves with the mud to try to keep them off. It helped, and it gave us some camouflage too, which was handy.

'We looked back to the sea. The outgoing tide was against the pirates and it had slowed them down, for they were only now entering the inlet. But unfortunately the footprints we were leaving in the mud were like a big arrow announcing, "deserters this way". We had to get out of the mud and into the jungle. Which, it being night, I personally dreaded.' He leaned forward and poured himself another measure of brandy.

'That scared you?'

'Of course it did. And it would have scared you too if your only previous concept of jungle had been Epping Forest.'

'Yeah, I suppose it would.'

'Anyway, darkness – even though I welcomed it like the plague – was our ally, and so into the jungle we went. There was no way we could navigate; we could see neither stars nor moon through the foliage above.

We could only push on and hope for the best. Eventually we found an animal path and that made the going easier. We were soon climbing steadily, and after a while we came out into a clearing. From there, through the trees, we could look down on the inlet below. To our surprise, the pirates pursuing us had tied up their boat and made camp on a strip of beach at the edge of the mangrove swamp. Obviously they felt there was no point trying to track us through jungle in the dark, and there was nowhere we could go that they couldn't find us the next day. Still, we pushed on a little farther until Jer Cullen slipped on some loose shale and gashed his knee. We found a clearing and made camp there, and by the light of the moon we bandaged Cullen's wound using torn strips from our shirts. We didn't have any means of making fire, but that was perhaps just as well because it would have given the pirates below another map marker to finding us. We decided to sleep with one of us keeping watch on rotation. Matthias took first watch then it would be Cullen, and then me.

'I slept like the dead until sometime just after dawn. I'd needed to pee, and on waking I was surprised to see a growing brightness in the sky. Why hadn't Cullen awoken me already to take my watch? I looked around, but there was no sign of him. My first thought was that he too was off watering the plants somewhere, but when I returned a short time later, he was still nowhere to be seen. It was dashed queer. Even if his knee hadn't been injured, he wouldn't have gone on without us. And if the pirates had taken him, why him and not the rest of us?

'I woke Matthias and we searched around for him. When we looked down into the inlet, we saw the pirates moving around far below. There were seven of them and they didn't seem to be in any great hurry. Matthias and I agreed that it was highly unlikely that they would have come up here in the night, found us, taken Cullen without a sound, and then gone back down to camp again. It made no sense. So what then? We looked at each other, each willing the other to say the awful thing that, by now, was lurking in both our minds.'

David sat forward. 'What?'

'Cannibals, Flinch. No animal could have come in and taken him that stealthily, so we agreed it had to have been some native tribe. We examined the camp for tracks so that we might attempt some kind of rescue, but there were none. We were at a loss as to what to do – God help him, poor devil, but there was nothing we *could* do. We said a prayer for him then pushed on.

'We reached the top of the high ground about an hour later and looked back to the inlet. The pirates had gone, so we knew that they were on our trail; that was a spur to hasten us, but at least it was downhill from there. As we descended onto the other side of the island, we were constantly on the lookout for signs of human life – civilised or savage – but saw none. And another growing concern was that we'd found no great hiding places anywhere. We began to speculate about trying to swim over to one of the other islands we could see offshore. The nearest was about two miles away; a long distance for even for the strongest swimmer, and we were weak with hunger by this time. We considered doubling-back and stealing the pirates' rowing boat, but the prospect of paddling out of the inlet only to run straight into the *Fortuna* wasn't one either of us relished. We were trapped by death on all sides: if we turned back, the pirates would get us; if we evaded them and stayed on the island, the people who had taken Cullen would get us; and if we tried to swim for it, we'd probably drown. That made two dead certs and a "probably", so we agreed that the swim was the best of a bad lot. As if to seal the decision, a musket ball came buzzing through the overhead foliage followed by the crack of a shot; the pirates had caught up with us. We ran, abandoning all caution and plunging headlong down through the jungle for all we were worth. They continued to fire into the jungle after us, shouting threats and abuse as they came, taunting us with what they'd do when they caught us. I recognised the voice of Rudge shouting some particularly unpleasant promises to Matthias. It spurred us on all the more. We were leaving a trail even a dog with no nose could follow, but we were past caring about that now, all that mattered was distance.

'And then, suddenly, we were out of the jungle and on a long white beach. Panting, breathless, and desperate, we saw then that if we tried to swim for it, they could easily pick us off from the rise of the beach; and if we ran, our tracks would lead them straight to us. I turned to Matthias and said, "There's nothing else for it, lad, we have to fight them. Quick, find a weapon!" We barely had time to find a good sized stone and a place to hide before they came running out onto the beach. I didn't hesitate: I sprang out and brought my rock down on the head of the last man out. Matthias followed my lead, catching his man over the ear as he turned around on us. I grabbed up the sword from the chap I'd killed and rushed forwards screaming. They hadn't expected this, they had their muskets readied, but their swords were sheathed. I impaled the man directly ahead

of me at a charge and pushed him down, twisting my sword as I did so
and pulling it free. Now they were running backwards away from us, one
of them bringing his gun to bear while the others had discarded theirs and
were drawing swords. Matthias now had his victim's pistol and he fired it
at the man with the gun, hitting him in the chest. Now we were two
against three. I was straight in against Rudge, a fight that had been on the
cards anyway, and Matthias, now with sword, was up and at another of
them. The remaining man, a Portuguese named De Matos, tried to attack
me from the rear, but I spun round and chopped the sword hand off him,
and he dropped to his knees screaming as the blood pumped out of him.
But Rudge was a tougher nut to crack, I have to say; he fought hard, and I
was soon on the back foot and struggling to hold him. Then a shout of
"Enough!" from Dodd, the chap Matthias had been fighting. We stopped,
and I turned, expecting the lad to be dead, but instead Dodd had him
down with a sword point to his throat. "That's enough, Brooks!" shouts
Dodd. "Drop your weapon or I'll fillet him." My grip must have
slackened because Rudge swung and knocked my sword from me.

"Captain wants you alive, Brooks," says Rudge, all smirking and puffed
up like he'd actually beaten me. "Says he wants to make an example of
you so no one else takes a mind to running off all cowardly, like."

"Damn you, Rudge!" says I. "We didn't run out of cowardice, we ran
because we've got loved ones to get to. For pity's sake, can't you just let
us go and tell him we're dead?"

"Now why would I want to do a thing like that," says he, "when I got
a loved one I wanna get to myself?" and he looked at Matthias and licked
his lips. "'Fore you boys get what's coming to you, I'm going to get what's
coming to me."

'Too right, I thought, and I charged him. Catching him off guard, I
managed to get my hands around his throat and send him over
backwards. I came down on top of him and cried, "Fight boy! Better to be
dead than in the hands of these dogs!" Well, I don't remember what
happened after that. The last thing I remember was Rudge's eyes bulging
at me from his empurpled face as I was strangling him, then a crack on
the back of my head put my lights out.'

Underwood put his cigar into his mouth and puffed. It had gone out.
He took the lighter and re-lit it. He puffed it back into life, picked a strand
of tobacco from his lips, and continued. 'When I next awoke, it was to
find myself tied back-to-back with Matthias. It was dark and we were sat

468

in the glow of a campfire. The smoke carried the smell of roasting flesh and burned feathers over to us, and I saw the charred and poorly-plucked corpse of a seabird on an improvised spit-roast above the flames. It was the second course; I could see the picked-over remains of another bird nearby.

'The remaining pirates, Rudge, Dodd and De Matos, were all gnawing at small bones and talking when Rudge saw that I was awake. "Hungry, Brooks?" says he.

'I nodded, "Aye, Rudge. So I am."

"And so you shall stay, yellow-belly. The weaker ye be, the easier ye'll be to get back to the ship."

'De Matos got up and kicked me in the face, saying how he was going to cut my balls off and force-feed them to me before the Captain executed me. He was waving his bandaged stump in my face and saying how they'd had to cauterize it in the fire.' Underwood chuckled. 'He was most ticked off, I can tell you. Anyway, Rudge called him off and I looked around and asked Matthias if he was all right. He said that he was fine. They'd not harmed him. Apparently Matthias had been promised to Rudge as reward when they returned. Of course the lad was terrified, and I tried to assure him that we'd get away somehow before that happened.

'Then the villain in question spoke up again. "Now that you're awake, maybe you'd like to tell us about what happened to your mate, Cullen. Boy here says he was taken by headhunters."

'I nodded and said that was my understanding as well.

"We ain't never heard no tell of cannibals in these parts," says Rudge. "In my understanding, this particular group be uninhabited." I told him that in that case, it must have been an animal, maybe a lion or a tiger. This occasioned much laughter, and Dodd informed me that there were no such animals hereabouts either. "In that case", said I, "he either ran away on an injured knee, or something else took him." This brought the jollity to an abrupt end, and for a short while no more was said. Then they went back to their banter and I, still woozy from the crack I'd had on the noggin, must have dropped off, for the next thing I remember was waking to the sound of voices shouting.

'Rudge and Dodd were up and aiming their muskets into the jungle, shifting their aim constantly. At first I couldn't make out what was going on. They were shouting warnings into the darkness to something, telling it to keep away. "What is it?" I shouted. "What's happening?" Rudge shouted at me to shut up, but Dodd was gibbering with fear.

"They took him!" he says. "Cannibals!"

'I looked around and noticed that De Matos was missing. "Untie us, Rudge, for God's sake! We can't fight tied up like this."

"I'll be damned if I will," says he. "Just you shut your fucking mouth and leave this to us. I ain't giving you two the chance to run."

"Where are we going to run to?" I shouted. "We'd stand no chance stumbling around out there in the dark. Untie us and give us a means of defending ourselves. I give you my word, we'll not run." He looked at me, and I could see him weighing the options in his mind. He was frightened, but he knew I was right. Dodd urged him to do as I asked; he said, quite rightly, that four guns were better than two. So, Rudge relented, we were untied and given muskets. Rudge said if we shot them in the backs and ran, Verlaine would hunt us down and burn us alive. I reminded him he had my word and that he had nothing to fear from us. We loaded the guns and joined them, back to back, aiming out four ways. I told them that whatever took Cullen was as silent as a ghost and asked them if they had seen or heard anything when De Matos was taken.

"I heard a cry of sorts," says Dodd. "No more than a man makes if he's having a nightmare. I opened my eyes, I was sleeping poorly – that bird had given me fierce indigestion – and De Matos … he was gone. But I'd heard him there, a few feet away, just a couple of moments before. And then … and then I heard a scream … but far away – miles away. I couldn't say from what direction, it seemed to come from all around at once."

"It can't have been De Matos," says Rudge. "It must have been Cullen. No one can drag a man through miles of jungle in a few seconds."

"No *man*," says Dodd. "But what if it weren't no man?"

"Nor no beast neither," says Rudge.

'We were silent for a moment then Dodd says, "Well if it warn't man nor beast, then what the fuck was it?"

"I told you," says Rudge, "that was Cullen screaming. Them headhunters must've sapped De Matos over the head and they's right now dragging him through the jungle back to their camp. They've probably got Cullen roasting on a spit there, and that's the scream what you heard."

'Dodd wailed at that, and who could blame him? I would have myself but I was far too busy listening for sounds from the bush. You see, that was the queer thing, Flinch. There were no sounds. It was as if every creature within a mile radius of the camp was holding its breath, listening as we were.

'We stayed that way for I don't know how long, but gradually the jungle began slowly to ebb back to life and I think that caused some of the tension to leave us. We agreed to sit, guns still aiming out from us, talking, trying to reason out what we were up against. Then a thought occurred to me: both of the men who had been taken had been bleeding. De Matos had lost his hand, and Cullen had been bleeding from the wound on his knee. I told the others.

'For a moment they said nothing, then Dodd spoke; he laughed, but in that way men do when they're scared. "So? I've been bleeding. Boy got a cut on me down on that beach."

'But I pointed out that De Matos had been bleeding far worse, his clothes were rich with the smell of blood.

"Don't talk shit," says Rudge. "Cannibals can't smell blood."

'I said nothing to this, but I thought that was all well and good if it was cannibals we were up against, but what if it *were* some kind of animal, something that *could* smell blood. Well, at least I wasn't bleeding. That thought calmed me a little, and soon, despite my fear, I began to doze again.

'I sat there, my head nodding, half-dreaming the kind of nightmarish creatures that could have come into the camp and taken a man as stealthily as those men had been taken. The jungle, as I say, had resumed its strange nocturnal chorus, and that, I think, or the sense of security it gave me, had been responsible for lulling me to sleep. So when it suddenly fell silent again, my eyes snapped wide open.

'In an instant, I was up, alert, my gun raised. The others followed suit, alarmed by my actions, and asked me what was wrong. I told them that the jungle had gone quiet. Rudge called me a stupid wanker, and was just threatening to tie me up again when, suddenly, there was an almighty rush of wind at my back and a sound like a yelp from Dodd. Rudge's threats choked dry in his throat. I turned and looked around. A moment earlier, Dodd had been standing between Rudge and I, but now ... he'd vanished.

'I looked at Rudge; he was staring up at the sky, his musket held loosely in his sagging grip. Then, from far away, came a scream. For a moment I thought it came from all directions at once as Dodd had said

De Matos's had, but then I realised the sound was all around us because it came from exactly the direction that Rudge was staring: straight up.

'I followed his gaze and saw nothing but the canopy of stars. I remember, I stammered out the obvious question, "What happened to Dodd?"

'Rudge looked at me then, his face contorted with terror. "It was the Devil!" he cried. "Swooped down and snatched him away, right before my eyes!" I stared at him as he fell to his knees and began babbling prayers, afraid to believe him and yet knowing, that somehow, what he said was true.

'And then it came again, but from farther away; the scream of a man snatched up into the night and carried off to Hell.'

13

UNDERWOOD PAUSED FOR A PUFF ON HIS CIGAR, then he continued. 'Matthias spoke up. "It wasn't the devil," says he. "It was a bat … or … a kind of bat creature."

'This made more sense to me. I'd considered giant snakes, lions, and tigers; why not a giant bat creature? It was a classic case of mariners stumbling into "here be dragons" territory, and I even suggested that it might have *been* a dragon, but Matthias was adamant.'

'So what did you do?'

'Well, I said we should flee for all we were worth, because whatever this thing was, devil, bat, or dragon, it knew where we were, and it was seemingly intent on coming back to pick us off one by one. Matthias – being a bright lad – agreed. But Rudge – being an idiot – pointed his gun at us and said we were going nowhere; we were still his prisoners. Of course, I remonstrated emphatically with the man, told him the game had changed and that we had to work together if we were to survive. He chewed this over for a moment. Then he gave me a queer look – like an idea had bobbed up into that fat head of his that would serve him well, but which boded ill for me. I should have been more wary, but I thought our shared peril was such that only a complete idiot would have had other ideas about how to survive. But then, I suppose in all that excitement, I'd forgotten whom I was dealing with. Rudge nodded, suddenly Mr Cooperative, and I turned to Matthias. I started saying something to him about direction or something, when I saw his expression change to one of alarm. The next thing, there was a blow to the back of my head, and everything went black.'

'Rudge had clocked you one?'

'Yes, that he had – the blighter. I imagine he would have killed me under different circumstances, but as it happened, it suited his plans better if I was alive. As I say, I passed out. When I awoke, the sun was high in the sky, and I had a splitting headache. I felt the back of my head and found a bump about the size of an egg. I tried to sit up and I felt fresh pain from my torso. I looked down to see my chest and stomach were covered in dried blood – my blood. Rudge had torn open my shirt and slashed me across the torso in three places.' Underwood drew his finger

across his chest and stomach in three diagonal lines to illustrate. 'They
weren't serious cuts; they were intended to make me bleed, not die. This
was obviously Rudge's big idea: had the creature returned to the camp, he
would've found me, marinating in my own juice, as it were, and take me
rather than chasing after them. Though fortunately for me, our flying
friend had evidently had his fill for that night.

'So, anyway, I got to my feet, putting all this together in my head and
looking around to see if Rudge had left anything useful behind in the
campsite. The remains of their dinner lay scattered around and I gathered
up the bones for a breakfast of seagull scraps. I was absolutely ravenous
and ate everything that remained – bar the feathers. I found a canteen,
and washed my breakfast down with all the water that was left in it, and
then, once I was fed and watered, I began to check the other stuff that
had been left behind. And there was plenty of it: besides the canteen,
Rudge had left Dodd and DeMatos's muskets, along with the ramrods; a
cutlass, sheathed in its scabbard; Dodd's hat; and a satchel containing
powder and shot, and some scraps of beef jerky. I took the better of the
muskets and pretty much everything else, then set off after Rudge and
Matthias. It wasn't hard to find their trail; Rudge had left the place with all
the stealth of a bull elephant with a firework up its arse.

'The sun was past the meridian, so they had a pretty good head start
on me, but I felt if I hurried, there was still a chance I could catch up with
them. The pirates had rowed that boat of theirs a fair way into the inlet; if
Rudge had reached it this morning at low tide, there was a possibility that
he'd be left high and dry. Either they'd have to carry the boat down to the
water, or wait for the tide to come and free them.

'I ran on through the jungle. I found a stream and refilled the canteen.
I had my bearings now, and soon I came to the clearing where we'd spied
on the pirates on the evening of our arrival. I looked down to where their
boat had been moored: it was still there, but curiously, the tide was in.
Well, that didn't make sense. Why hadn't they taken it? Could it be a trap?
It didn't matter; I still had to get down there – and fast. I loaded my
musket and ran on.

'When I came to where the jungle met the beach, I approached with
caution. I could see the rowing boat through the foliage, but there was no
one anywhere near it, nor anywhere else that I could detect. I made my
move. I burst out of the jungle, gun raised and ready. But there was no
ambush, no shots fired; just tracks leading to the boat and then away

down the beach towards the mouth of the inlet. I went to the boat and saw, to my astonishment, that it was flooded. It had been *holed*, and through the hole, I could see a bloody great rock that would have taken two men to lift and throw down hard enough to smash through the wood. Could they have done it themselves? Why would they do that? The only thing that made any sense was that our predator had done it to prevent us from leaving. The thought made me sick with fear and I looked up to the sky. The sun was sinking towards the reddening horizon; it wouldn't be long before it was dark.

'I ran on, following the tracks along the beach. As I grew nearer the mouth of the inlet, so the view of the open sea widened. With every step I expected to see the *Fortuna* anchored offshore, but there was no sign of her. Had Verlaine taken them off with another rowing boat, set sail and gone? Was I abandoned? I tried not to think about that possibility. I hurried on out of the inlet and onto the long white beach. The footprints led away to the south and I saw, with a sense of tremendous relief, a thin finger of smoke rising above the trees about a mile further on. I ran on through the gathering dusk, and as I rounded a curve on the shoreline, I saw the distant flickering light of their campfire. I crouched, and made my way nearer, clinging to the tree-line where the jungle met the beach. I was soon able to able to make out the forms of both Matthias and Rudge. At a distance, they appeared to be in an odd cage, but as I grew closer, I could see that they sat in the middle of a copse of long spiked stakes. Essentially, what they had done was fashion about ten or twelve of these stakes – each perhaps six or seven feet in length – driven the bases into the sand, and aimed the pointed ends up at the sky. Obviously a defence against the bat-creature, and in fairness, it was a pretty sound idea.

'Anyway, it was now dark. I saw that Rudge had dampened down the fire and was cooking something over the coals. As I came upon a fallen tree, the tantalising smell of roasting fish reached me. If my next move went well, it'd be me tucking into that fish in a few moments, not Rudge. I crouched down behind the tree trunk and peered over at them. Matthias was tied and had his back to me, while Rudge was paying attention to the fish. I was close enough to get a good clean shot. I ran out my musket and took careful aim; I'd only get one chance. I lined up with Rudge's head, held my breath, and squeezed the trigger. The musket fired, a great boom and flash in the serenity of the evening. I couldn't see through the powder smoke, but I heard Rudge scream. Whether he was mortally injured or just winged, I couldn't tell, either way, I had no option now but to have at him. I drew my sword and leapt up. Rudge was roaring like a lunatic and clutching at the side of his head. I started running at them. He saw me, snatched up his own sword, and broke from the nest of spikes to meet me. I could see dark liquid running from the side of his head as we charged at each other across the sand, the pair of us roaring for blood. There must have been only fifteen feet between us when, quite without warning, *the horror* descended upon us.'

Underwood shook his head in amazement. 'Even now, just thinking of it, I can feel again my initial shock and horror at the sight of it. There was, as I say, no warning: one second Rudge had been running at me, his face all knotted with hate and fury, the next, he's falling forwards like he's tripped over a piece of driftwood. But then, I saw something huge and black following him down, almost like the night itself was riding his back. I stopped fast, tumbling head over heels onto the sand – and as I came up onto my feet, I saw it. It was as Matthias had said – some species of giant bat. It was incredibly fast, like an eagle snatching a fish from a river. The creature knocked Rudge down, its claws in his shoulders, then it threw its wings back. I looked at Rudge. His face was shocked and confused. Then he was curtained behind a flash of blackness as the creature beat its wings. A blast of wind sent sand into my face, momentarily blinding me. I heard Rudge scream as I wiped frantically at my eyes and when I opened them again, he was gone. His sword lay on the beach like a marker to where he had fallen. Then I heard him cry from far away over the jungle. The sound died away. I listened for more. But there was only the crash and sigh of the surf behind me.

'I ran over to Matthias; I fear I may have been a bit hysterical. I cut him loose, babbling about the monster and how we had to make a run for it. All the time he was saying "no" to me, but I wasn't listening. Then he seized one of the stakes and thrust it into my face, shouting, "John! Will you look at this!" I looked. "These things work," says he. "The bat waited until Rudge was out from them before it attacked." That may or may not have been the case, but either way, I still wanted to get away from there. But Matthias persisted. He said that where we were, the stakes afforded us a means of protection, but in the jungle, we'd have none. We didn't know the island at all, but the creature did. Furthermore, we had no means of finding our way in the dark, and again the creature evidently did. Our best bet for survival was to stay where we were and make a stand.

'Well, by now, I'd calmed down a bit. I looked at the stakes and had to admit, he was right, they did offer a solid defence. We also had guns, swords, and fire. And to be honest, the smell of that cooking fish was driving me mad. So I relented and we sat down to eat, and he told me everything that had happened since we were parted.

'Rudge had rifle-butted me and cut me up for the bat-creature, then they'd left immediately. They'd found the holed boat at sunrise, then gone on to the coast to try and find the *Fortuna*, but she'd gone. Rudge figured Verlaine had either gone off after another quarry, or taken flight at the sight of a navy ship. But either way, they'd be back. He'd made the signal fire, then spent the rest of the day fashioning the defensive spikes.

'As night had been drawing in, Matthias had begun to grow worried about what Rudge's plans for their sleeping arrangements might involve. Rudge had been giving him odd looks across the fire as he cooked the fish. Then the next thing, there was the sound of a shot, and his ear disappeared in a spray of blood.' Underwood laughed. 'Oh, we laughed at that. Matthias had been overjoyed, of course. And I was pretty bloody chuffed myself.' Underwood pointed at David with his cigar. 'Don't misunderstand me, Flinch, we were glad to see the back of the Rudge, but we didn't celebrate the nature of his demise – neither of us would have wished that on anyone.'

'Anyway, we chatted on for a while, but eventually, once the fish was eaten and our defensive preparations had been made, there was nothing else to do but to try and sleep in shifts. I took first watch and was happy to find a pipe and tobacco in Rudge's satchel. However, I'd no sooner lit the thing than the jungle fell silent.

'Immediately, I shook the lad awake, and in a moment, we were up and our feet, aiming at the sky through the nest of spikes. We didn't have long to wait before a patch of darkness among the stars began to grow larger, rushing down at us. I fired at it. There was a shriek – I'd hit it! Then Matthias fired too. Immediately, the pall of gunsmoke over us was blown away by a fierce down-rush of wind as the creature shot back up into the night.

'We reloaded, each of us with one eye on the sky in case it came again. But it didn't. We knew we hadn't killed it, but we were pretty damn sure we'd seen it off for the night. We were jubilant, laughing with relief, telling each other how we'd probably hit it in the undercarriage and sent it off with a new set of lead bollocks.' Underwood chuckled and took a puff on his cigar.

David let out a breath he didn't know he'd been holding. 'Blimey … So, was that it for that night?'

Underwood shook his head. 'No. After a while, we settled down again. Matthias lay down to get some sleep and I sat watching the sky. I don't know if you've ever tried to watch the sky for any period of time, Flinch, but it doesn't take long before your neck and eyes get tired from all the looking up. I tried shifting my position various ways, but finally decided to lie down on my back. It was much more comfortable, but obviously unwise. I closed my eyes, just to rest them, you understand, and almost immediately, sleep began to pull me down. I forced myself to move, to open my eyes, and when I did, I noticed the queerest thing.'

'What?'

'A ground mist had settled all around me. This might've not been that uncanny, but for the fact that there was a steady breeze blowing in from the sea. Yet this mist seemed wholly undisturbed by it. It was eerie, unnatural; it clung to the sand, moving like a carpet of vaporous snakes. I sat up, my skin pricking with goose bumps, and my every instinct screaming at me to get up and get the hell away from it.

'Was it my sudden movement, or perhaps the quickening of my pulse? I don't know, but it sensed I was alarmed by it.'

David frowned. 'It – it *what?*'

Underwood smiled. 'It sensed I was alarmed by it. As I tried to rise, faster almost than I could comprehend, *it* rose around me, thickening, flowing up, over and above me, and the higher it got, the hotter it got until it was almost scorching. My eyes were burning and I closed them. I tried to run, but I was suddenly seized, my shoulders crushed in the agonizing grip of solid claws, and I felt myself lifted from the ground. I didn't need to see what was happening to know that somehow I was in the clutches of the bat.

'I opened my eyes. I was rising incredibly, sickeningly fast. Far below my flailing legs I could see camp, the stakes blasted apart and scattered like matchwood. And then we were over the jungle, the tops of the trees rushing beneath me. It was an unimaginable nightmare, made all the worse by the knowledge of the certain death that waited at its end. I screamed.'

Underwood shook his head. 'I suppose to Matthias, it must have sounded like the dwindling screams of all the others; the last terrible cry of the doomed.' He puffed his cigar.

'Bloody hell,' said David. 'So, what did you do?'

'What could I do? I just hung there, begging Jesus to save me, and watching helplessly as we climbed to the highest point of the island. There, the creature began to circle around a clearing in the trees. At the centre of the clearing, the moonlight revealed a tangle of bushes, and at their centre, a sinister slash of blackness that I realised was a hole in the ground. The creature banked and came in again, heading straight for the clearing, and I suddenly felt sure it was going to try to hurl me straight into the hole. I struggled and tried to fight, to somehow put it off its aim, but I had no strength, and every kick I gave tore the flesh of my shoulders. So I just closed my eyes and waited for it, the wind rushing against me, roaring louder in my ears as we dived. And then I was falling. I opened my eyes to see the ground rushing up – not the hole, thank Christ, but the bushes. I barely had time to cover my eyes before I was crashing through them. They broke my fall, but I landed badly; a fresh, white hot agony shot from my ankle: I looked at it, and almost fainted on seeing the horrible angle of my foot. I could hear the wings above me as, swearing and cursing, I scrabbled around in the dark for a weapon. But all I could find were sticks and stones.

'And then I heard the creature come to ground a short distance behind me. I turned and saw it enfold itself in its great black wings. I had a short stick in my fist and I raised it threateningly. It wasn't exactly a dagger, but it'd stab it a lot better than my bare hands would. Amazing how we cling to the hope of survival: at that stage, I still believed I had a chance. But that belief began to crumble then, as I saw the creature's wings beginning to disintegrate before my eyes, like ashes caught in an eddy of wind – and I saw then that it wasn't just the wings, but the whole of the creature's body, coming apart and swirling like black smoke. Instinctively, I began to push myself away from it. I turned to see where I was going and saw that I was moving toward the hole. I stopped and looked back. The creature's form was settling – like a swarm of black flies – into the shape of a man. He was stooped, head hung down, his features gradually becoming clearer as the blackness faded from him.

'He was a native of that part of the world, brown skinned, black haired, perhaps Taino or Carib. He was scrawny of build, not really much to him at all. But his eyes shone in the dark like those of a wolf, and when he turned them on me, I felt my flesh almost trying to crawl away from them. He was stark naked, and he had long, scraggy hair and a thin, wispy beard. The nails of his fingers and toes were long and thick and black with filth – more like claws than nails. When he saw that I'd buggered my ankle, he smiled, and I saw his long yellow fangs. "Jesus Christ", I thought, "what corner of Hell had this devil crawled from?" For now I was beginning to think Rudge had been right: this was nothing made by the hand of God, this was the work of Satan.

'Instinct compelled me to get up – *screamed* at me to get up. I tried to make it using one leg – ignoring the pain from my broken ankle – and I managed to get up, but as soon as I tried to take a step, of course, I came down again; it was impossible. I turned back to the creature. He was advancing slowly, his hands up before him, not in fists, but with the nails forward, like he meant to stick 'em into me. I raised my stick-knife. This did nothing but amuse him. I started shouting at him then, as one might with a wild animal, to try to make it think twice about attacking me, and for a moment, I thought it might even be working; he hesitated, watching me, head on one side, like he was trying to understand. Of course, he wasn't, he was just enjoying the show. That leering smile of his slowly crept back onto his face, and those strange, inhuman eyes seemed to glow even brighter. And then, I remember I couldn't tear my own eyes away from them. Everything else just seemed to fade away: my fear, my predicament, my pain, none of it seemed real any more. My mind went blank. And as the creature closed in on me, I just lay there; I had no will to resist, indeed, I had no sense of why I might even want to. I knew – though I didn't know *how* I knew – that this creature was going to soothe away all the pain and the fear and the horror. All I had to do was yield to him.

'He climbed onto me, sniffing at me as he crawled up the length of my body, till he came to my throat. I didn't like this, but I couldn't lift a finger to stop him, and when he closed his filthy hand over my face to ease it aside, I suddenly remembered I wanted to scream, to shout and kick, but I couldn't move. I felt his hot, fetid breath on my throat, and then the searing pain as his teeth bit into me.'

Underwood had been staring ahead, his expression becoming increasingly distressed as he re-lived the assault, but at the memory of the bite, he turned away.

David waited.

Underwood took a moment to compose himself, then took a breath and turned back with an apologetic smile. 'Sorry about that, Flinch. Haven't been back there for a while. Forgot how bloody awful that blighter was.' He reached for the brandy and poured himself a generous measure.

David nodded. 'Not wanting to be insensitive or anything, sir, but I imagine it must be the same for *your* victims.'

Underwood took a deep swallow of brandy then smacked his lips. 'For some. But not for all. I can make death a pleasure or a torment. Even my hideous experience wasn't all bad.'

David was surprised. '*Really?*'

'Yes. The pain of the bite only lasted a moment. It was as if I'd been injected with some kind of opium; a sense of bliss flooded me. Then the creature faded away, and Martha was there, Martha at my throat, kissing me, I could even smell her hair as I closed my eyes and sank into blackness.

'When I next opened my eyes, it was to an even deeper blackness. The air around me was cold, dank, and there was a thick, awful stench – worse than anything I think I'd ever smelled in my life – and the only sound was the buzzing of flies. The floor beneath me was incredibly uncomfortable, like lying on a heap of shattered cartwheels. I felt my neck where the creature had bitten me. It was sticky with blood, but weirdly, there was no wound, the skin had healed. I tried to sit up and my head swam. The ground beneath me shifted painfully, digging into me. I fell back down and reached around. I picked up the first thing my hand fell upon. It was like a stick. I felt along its length to the knobbly joint at the end, and I realised that it was a bone. I dropped it in horror, crying out and trying to push away from it. Flies erupted from all around me, and the ground shifted again, more bones hundreds of them, cracking and scraping against each other. I put my hand in something soft and wet. I slipped in it and my face came down on something hard and spherical. I felt it. It was a skull, but not human – animal. However, I had no doubt that many of those bones *were* human because as I continued to grope my way through the dark, I could feel fabric, cotton, leather, and then something metal. I closed my fingers around it, and it took a moment for my mind to register the pain. It was the blade of a cutlass. Even though I'd cut my hand on it, I was overjoyed to have found a weapon. I think I must have given some yelp of delight, because a voice then came at me from the blackness ahead.

"*Who's there?*" It was hoarse, weak, but I'd know it anywhere. "Rudge?"

"Brooks? Thank God. You've got to help me. The devil's broke my fucking leg. He's been feeding off me. Drinking my blood."

'I told him I'd experienced the same.

"I heard him come in with you," said he. "Heard him chuck you down over there. I didn't know what it was though. I just played dead and prayed he'd fuck off again. And so he did."

"Where is he?" I asked.

"How the fuck do I know? I can't see a fucking thing. If I tell you he went off that way, does it help?"

"What way?" said I.

"Exactly, you stupid shithead. I'm pointing, but it don't do neither of us no good, does it?"

'Fair point, I thought. I crawled across the rotting dead towards the sound of his voice. When I got to him, I asked him if he had anything on his person we could use in our defence. He said he had a knife, but he'd be damned if he'd give it to me. I asked him if he had the means to make fire, and he said that he did, but I'd be mad if I tried to start a fire in there because it'd attract the devil back to us.

"Look," I told him. "That devil's coming back sooner or later. So we can either lie here and wait for him to devour us, or we can draw him in and make some kind of a fight of it." I told him I had a sword and I tapped it on the ground so he'd hear the metal. Then I told him there were enough bones and items of old clothing around to make torches. "Everything's afraid of fire, Rudge," I reminded him. "And I'll bet that devil's no exception."

'He whined about his leg, begging me to help him out of there, but I told him my ankle was just as crippled, and that the only way we were going to get out of there was if we killed the monster first.

'Well, he didn't like it, he was utterly terrified of the thing, but I told him my plan and he finally conceded it was the best – indeed the only – chance we had.

'So, I began gathering up the bones and clothes I'd need to make torches. The fabric was old and as dry as parchment, so it would catch as soon as it made contact with a flame. Once the torches were made, Rudge took out his flint, steel and tinderbox. I'd torn some thin strips of rotten fabric for kindling and I handed them to him. We offered up a quick prayer, and then I crawled to where I would lie down nearby him, and Rudge began to spark a fire. The sparking of the flint on steel flashed in the darkness, and for split seconds I could glimpse the horror of the charnel pit around me. Then the first torch began to catch, its light growing and revealing the corpses all around, human and animal, desiccated and rotten, but in the case of some, fresh: the bodies of Cullen, DeMatos and Dodd lay nearby, their throats ripped out and black with flies. Poor old Cullen lay facing us, the tail-end of a rat bristling in his mouth as it dined on his tongue. When Rudge saw it all, he started screaming, and it took all the guts I had left not to join him.

'I forced myself to look away. I could see now how the chamber stretched away into the deeper cave. The plan was, on seeing Rudge awake and full of beans, the creature would go for him. As it approached, it'd have to walk past me. The moment it did, I'd lash out with the sword and run it through. And so, I lay there, waiting, playing dead as Rudge wailed on.

'I had one eye open and fixed on the darkness in the deeper cave. For a short time, nothing happened and Rudge's first torch began to die down. Then, as he lit and raised the second torch, I saw those two, eerie nocturnal eyes glowing at us from the dark.

'Look away! My mind yelled at me, and I tried to, believe me. But it was already too late.

'I felt a curious sensation: not fear, but … comfort, and I realised with numb incredulity, that I actually wanted the creature to come to me – to ignore Rudge and to finish what it had started with me earlier on.

'I didn't know it at the time, of course, but that weird attraction was the creature's bite working on me – the first stage of vampiric infection. But still, I had the brains to know it made no sense; that I was looking at certain death, and I fought against it. I remember pressing my face down hard against the rock floor, and the pain brought me back to focus. I clenched my teeth and managed to summon my natural feelings of hatred and fear, and I tightened my grip on my sword, and waited.

'The creature began to move closer. It was still in its human form, and it was staring with curiosity at Rudge's torch. I realised then that it'd seen the first one burn out, and was simply waiting for the second one to do the same.

'I lay as still as a corpse, barely breathing. Rudge shouted at it to come and get him, calling it all manner of names and giving full flow to his unpleasant line in threats. But the creature just watched and waited for the torch to begin to die down. Gradually the flame burned less brightly and Rudge's threats and challenges began to lose some of their conviction.

'As the light began to recede from it, the creature smiled, its teeth glistening in the fading orange glow. It began to move forward, never taking its eyes from the torch. Rudge picked up the third torch and began to touch it to the flickering remains of the second. As the creature grew closer, I looked at the ground, trying to affect a dead man's stare. I listened to its slow steady footfalls as it grew closer, and I felt my skin tingling at its nearness, as if my traitorous blood was calling out to it. Then, I heard the vampire's tread stop.

"Come on!" shouted Rudge as the third torch flared up. "Come and get me! *Me*, damn it! *Me!*"

'An icy feeling of absolute terror seized me: why was Rudge stressing himself as target? Slowly, I turned my head. I looked up to see the vampire standing over me, his eyes bright through the tangle of filthy hair that hung down around his face. I tried to raise my sword, but I couldn't, I was paralyzed. Try as I might, I simply couldn't move. And then I realised, he'd known our game all along. But what did it matter? I thought. I found I didn't care anymore; I didn't want to move, or to escape. I wanted it to take me.

"*ME!*" Rudge shouted. Then I heard the torch roar through the air in the moment before it struck the vampire's head in a shower of sparks. Its hair caught like tinder, and the vampire went berserk, whirling around with its hands flailing at its head. The spell on me was broken. My hand closed tightly on the sword handle and I lunged up, stabbing him in the back and pushing the blade in to the hilt. It screamed again and twisted, pulling the sword from my grip. I watched as it dropped to its knees, blood gurgling in its throat as its hands groped blindly behind its back for the sword handle. They faltered, as if giving up, then ceased altogether. The vampire pitched forward on its face, and the sword was pushed back through its body. It tottered for a moment, then clattered free of the wound.

"We did it!" Rudge shouted. "We got the bastard!"

'Words cannot convey what we felt at that moment. We both cheered and swore and congratulated ourselves on our amazing deed, until we saw the torch was dying. Rudge lit another, and I began to drag myself over to him, telling him that the next thing we needed to do was splint our legs with bones and try to find our way out of there.

'He was just getting the next torch to catch, when we heard a shifting of bones behind us. We turned, and in the slowly flaring light, we saw it. The vampire stood where it had fallen, and I saw with utter disbelief, that the hair that had been burned from its head a few minutes ago, was now completely restored.

'It smiled, and before I could even blink, it had leapt over the space between us and was upon me. Its foot struck my broken ankle and I screamed; the pain, all consuming, blinding me to all other senses. I was barely aware of its weight upon me, barely sensed its hands upon my shoulder and face, pushing my head back and exposing my throat; and when its teeth sank into me, I was grateful – grateful for the opiate bliss that flooded my system from the bite.

'So quickly I felt myself slipping away, the darkness and horror of the cave giving way to the bright blue sky of a spring day, and Martha in my arms again, so happy to see me. I reached up to touch her face … but then she seemed to spasm, her face contorting with pain. I felt distress, I ached to help her. I tried to get up – and the cave returned in all its horror. Rudge was roaring beside me, his hand in the creature's hair, pulling its head back from me. Its teeth and beard were glistening with my blood, and its eyes were wide and unbelieving. And then I saw why. The blade of the cutlass was sawing through its neck from behind. I could hear the flesh, bone and sinew tearing, feel the vibration of the hacking cuts through the creature's body. Then its blood was splattering down onto my face in torrents. I turned my face away just as the blade came hacking through the last remaining tissue and Rudge ripped the head away.

'The headless corpse dropped on top of me, blood still spurting from severed arteries, gushing into my mouth, nose, eyes and ears. I was drowning in it. How much of the vile stuff I swallowed I cannot say, but I remember it went down the throat in a similar fashion to this stuff.' Underwood waggled his brandy glass. 'Like alcohol, it burned my throat and put heat in my belly, then that heat bloomed through my body, and I remember everything went woozy. I remember seeing Rudge propping himself up and holding the severed head aloft by its hair. Oh, he was roaring victorious, but to me, it was like he was underwater. *I'm dying*, I thought. And my head fell to one side, and I watched as the torch that lay sizzling in blood beside me, finally sputtered out.'

Underwood took a puff on his cigar. It had gone out. He considered it for a moment, and then threw it out into the night. He sighed. 'When I awoke, I knew only one sensation: hunger. But it was unlike any hunger I had ever felt before; my stomach was cramping – a terrible pain, it caused me to double up in agony. I felt like I'd been poisoned. Then I remembered I had drunk the creature's blood. Could it have been poisonous? It must have been.

'I looked at Rudge: he appeared to be unconscious, slumped against the wall with the vampire's head still on his lap. Everywhere was the reek of its blood. But far from repelling me, as one might expect from the odour of poison, it seemed to *draw* me. I bent to the headless corpse and sniffed at the stump of neck. My body seemed to yearn for it, as if the hunger I felt were reaching for the source of the odour, and without even knowing what I was doing, I licked at the torn flesh. My craving responded immediately – yes – *this* was what my body wanted. I sucked at the flesh, but it was dead, the blood didn't flow. I lapped at a sticky pool of blood that had coagulated where the neck had bled out, and I felt the waves of pain softening, easing with every drop I swallowed, but it was a pitiful amount, and soon I was lapping at the rock floor. I groaned, angry and frustrated. I hardly noticed Rudge stir. Then he spoke.

"Brooks? That you? I thought you were dead."

'I looked at him; he was staring into space like a blind man, his eyes darting about like they were trying to find me. I realised how I must look, my face bent to a pool of gore on a cave floor. I quickly got to my feet and stepped away from the corpse. "Aye," I replied. "It's me. Not dead yet."

'His eyes darted in the direction of the words I'd uttered, but they still had that frightened, sightless look. Was he blind? I wondered. I looked around me at the bodies of the dead, the walls of the cave, the way the cave opened out in two directions, and how in one there was a dim glow, as if there were light coming in from far away.

'But that didn't make sense, because there *was* light; if there wasn't, how on Earth could I see?

'And then, I realised I was standing ... standing on an ankle that had been horribly broken. I dropped to my haunches and felt at the joint: it was healed, intact, like the bones had knitted from memory rather than from a doctor's setting. I fell back, repelled, as if my own leg were somehow alien to me. I must have cried out because Rudge shouted at me to stop fucking about and come and help him. I looked at him with his frightened face and his hands held out into the air before him.

"Come on, damn it!" he shouted. "We gotta fix our legs and get outta here."

'I walked over to him and took his hand. The warmth of it sent a shiver through me and I closed it in both of mine. I could feel the rush of life of within him, the blood singing in his veins. He looked in my direction, still blind, his face confused. He pulled his hand back from me. "Whatchoo doing?"

'And to tell you the truth, I honestly didn't know. I knelt down by his side and raised my hand close to his face, feeling the warmth that radiated from him. I held out my palm about an inch from the surface of his skin, and moved my hand slowly, caressing his heat, his life-force; I noticed its subtle variations, and how it radiated with tantalising vigour from the arteries on his neck. And again, I felt stirrings of that strange new hunger.

'Suddenly, I noticed a sound. A ticking. Once I'd noticed it, it seemed to become louder, as though it were demanding my attention. My eyes went to the source and I saw my watch chain, still attached to Rudge's vest. Without a second thought, I snatched it from him.

"Hey!" he cried. "You gimme that back."

'I said nothing. I opened the watch case, and in what I now knew was pitch darkness, I read the inscription inside.

"Gimme it back, you fucker, or I'll give you what I gave that fucking cave monster!"

'His hand groped around for the sword. I saw it about a foot from where his hand was. I kicked it away. His face turned to the sound, then became angry. "You double-crossing bastard, Brooks. What's your game? I saved your fucking life!"

"Aye, Rudge, so you did," says I. "But this is *my* watch."

'I watched a hundred emotions flicker across his face as he weighed this unexpected development. He obviously thought I was as blind as he was, and his face betrayed everything he was thinking. I could see his intentions developing as clearly as if he been drawing me pictures. Oh yes, he'd go along with my taking the watch for now, but sure as eggs are eggs, he'd cut my throat the first good chance he got. He grinned before settling his face onto something close to resignation. "All right," says he.

"Fair's fair. You keep it. I didn't much like it anyway. Now, come and give us a hand splinting my leg." He reached out a hand in my direction. I looked at it and considered for a moment; it represented so much. If I took it, what would happen to me, to Matthias? And if I didn't take it, what would happen to Rudge? The man had, after all, saved my life.

'But curiously, this very human dilemma didn't trouble me at all. I walked over to where I had kicked the sword, picked it up, walked back to Rudge, and chopped his hand off. Blood erupted from the wound, and before I even knew what I was doing, I had grabbed his wrist and lifted it to my open mouth. His blood gushed over my tongue, and I drank it ravenously and without thought; just obeying some new instinct that now seemed to be commanding my decisions.

'Rudge must have been in shock, he just sat there with a stupefied look on his face. He tried to pull his arm back, and instinctively, I bit down on it. That broke his stupor, he ripped it from me, and I felt his flesh tear on my teeth. I touched my teeth with my tongue and felt the extended canines, long and sharp – as the teeth of the creature had been.

'Rudge roared and struck out at me with his good hand, but I caught it before it made contact and snapped it down savagely, breaking his wrist.'

David winced.

'I climbed onto Rudge's legs, ignoring his screams as my weight came down on the broken one, and I reached for his bleeding stump. I got a hold on it, but it was slippery, and when he pulled it away, I lost my grip. Anger flashed in me, but only for a moment; there was, after all, another source. I pushed his head back against the wall and bent to his neck at the point where I had felt his life-force was at its strongest, and with no thought whatsoever, I sank my teeth into his throat. His whole body spasmed and he tried to pull away, but he was hopelessly pinned and bleeding to death. All he could do was twitch and jerk until the euphoria began to spread through him. Then he grew calmer, and after a few moments, in a childlike voice not much louder than a whisper, he began to sing to himself.'

Underwood swirled the brandy in his glass then took a sip. 'I drank from him till his heart stopped. Once the pump stops, that's it. But I was glutted, full to bursting. I sat there for a while, my eyes closed and my head resting on his shoulder, just feeling this ... I don't know ... *radiance*. I felt aglow, all my senses *thrumming* in a way I'd never experienced before. Ironically perhaps, I felt more *alive* than ever before.'

Underwood raised his eyebrows at David. 'You see the irony, Flinch? What with you and others always supposing that vampires are dead?'

David nodded. 'Yeah, I get it.'

Underwood chuckled. 'Well, anyway, yes, I sat there, glutted and aglow with Rudge's blood, and, well, I suppose in some ways, now that I had fed and was satiated, I was reluctant to lift my head and see what I'd done to the poor chap. But eventually, I *did* open my eyes ... and what I saw so struck me that I quite forgot everything else.

'It was as bright as day. Well, sort of. There was light, but no colour. It was as it had been after I'd drunk the vampire's blood, but much brighter, much more vivid. I realise now that having fed, I was fully restored, like a battery on full charge, if you like.

'Rudge's freshly spilled blood was almost *vibrant* to look at, and the odour was heady – stronger than anything else in the cave. For then, you see, I noticed there were a million odours in the cave that I hadn't noticed before. When I was human, all I had been able to smell in there was rotting flesh and dankness. But now, I was aware of a million subtle nuances of scent. I could smell not just the dead but the degrees of their decomposition, and beyond that, I could smell both fresh air and something else, a mustier aroma. I'd smelt the same thing on the creature, but what drifted to me now was more concentrated. The human thing to do would have been to go towards the fresh air, but my new instincts compelled me in the other direction. I wanted to know more about the creature that had attacked me, and I felt sure that I'd find some answers at the source of that smell.

'I got up and I picked up the sword – just in case he had a mate or something down there – and began to follow the scent. The charnel cavern didn't continue for very far, but random bones littered the way, sometimes grotesquely arranged. I went on, rats scurrying at the sight of me, and the smell thickening with every step. I was beginning to wonder just how far it went, when suddenly I found it.' Underwood grinned.

'Found what?'

'The vampire's lair. It was a chamber that branched off from the main passage, curtained by a ship's sail. I went inside, and what I saw fairly made my head spin.'

David sat forward. 'What? What was in there?'

'It was the creature's horde; obviously taken from ships, their crews and passengers, over God knows how many years. He had all sorts of junk in there, from fabrics and clothes to ornaments and weapons. The clothes and fabrics lay scattered all over the place: coats, shirts, dresses, and trousers, all filthy and mouldering to various degrees, and I remember there was a great heap of matted silk in one corner of the chamber – that was where the stink was at its strongest. It was obviously the creature's bed. But that was all just so much trash. I was far more interested in the other stuff.'

'The ornaments and weapons?'

'Yes,' Underwood smiled, 'and the rest. My late friend seemed to have a predilection for crafted things, delicate objects, smooth metals, things made of glass or porcelain and so on. It was all laid out around the chamber, some of it heaped, some of it arranged decoratively – as it might be in any home. However, the creature's idea of what constituted *tasteful* was somewhat at odds with anything I'd ever encountered in an English home.'

'Like what?'

'Like a row of children's skulls with polished gemstones set in the eye sockets. That was the centrepiece.'

David started slightly. 'Gemstones?'

'Yes, gemstones: diamonds, emeralds, rubies, sapphires, you know.'

'So ... there was *treasure* in there?'

Underwood smiled. 'Oh, yes. I mentioned the smooth metals, didn't I?'

'You mean ... gold?'

'Gold and silver, brass and steel. But yes, what has your eyebrows raised now is exactly what had my jaw dropped at the time – there was a fortune in gold coins, plate, watches, jewellery casings, and all manner of other pieces. It was like I'd stumbled upon Aladdin's Cave.'

At this point, David's jaw also dropped. 'How much? I mean, what sort of value?'

'Oh God, far more than I could calculate. It was more than I'd ever imagined, more perhaps than any *pirate* had imagined, and certainly more than any pirate had ever possessed. I dropped to my knees and began sifting through it, trying to get a sense of how much was there, and the further I went through it, the older I noticed the dates and heads on the coins got. I began to wonder if perhaps my friend had been the last in a long line of creatures such as himself; for naturally, it never even occurred to me for a moment that he might be immortal.

'Anyway, as I mentioned earlier, in addition to valuables, there were weapons – not any old rubbish – the cutlass I'd found in the charnel cave was old and rusty, but this stuff was all fine polished steel, rapiers, sabres, daggers – some with jewelled handles. There were also pistols – one of which struck me as a very handsome piece. It was a double-barrelled flintlock. I'd heard of such things, but I'd never seen one before. I gave it a closer inspection, and noticed that it was made by Underwood and Sons of Birmingham.'

David grinned. 'Really?'

'Yes. Lovely gun. As I handled it, I wondered at what kind of journey it had undergone en-route to that foul-smelling resting place. I sniffed the barrels; it had been fired, but not for a very long time. Well, I thought, this is far too fine a pistol to end its days here. I went to put it in my belt, and that's when I realised just how smothered I was in gore. I stripped off and rooted among the clothes that lay heaped around the cave until I managed to put together an outfit that both fitted me and didn't stink too unpleasantly. Then I tucked my new pistol into my belt, sheathed a fine Spanish cutlass, and shoved a handful of gold coins into my pocket to show Matthias when I got back to the beach.

'I then made my way back through the tunnels, enjoying the feel of good solid boots on my feet again. I went back through the charnel cave, and then on towards the incoming fresh air, and the glow of daylight that grew stronger the nearer I got to it. My head was still reeling with everything that had happened to me, but the one thought that overrode everything else was the fortune that I had just found, and how life in America for Martha and I was now going to be so wonderful; we would be rich beyond our wildest dreams and never want for anything ever again.'

'But you were a vampire, didn't that bother you?'

'What was a vampire? I didn't know. Nobody had ever *heard* of vampires. All I knew was that I'd been sick, almost killed, and that blood had brought me back to health. I had no reason to believe that it was a permanent change in me. For all I knew, now that I was healed, it was over. The creature's bite had improved me in some ways, it seemed only beneficial. All in all, I was starting to think my encounter with the creature had been a blessing.'

David nodded thoughtfully.

'Anyway, there I was, lost in a thousand swirling thoughts, when at the sound of birdsong ahead, I looked up. The light was strong now, almost painfully so. I put it down to my eyes being overly accustomed to the pitch blackness, and – as one does – I shielded my eyes. I hurried on until I saw the entrance to the cave. It was overhead, and the sunlight came streaming down through it like liquid gold. I could feel the heat as I ran to it, I was so happy to see it again – so relieved – that I ran straight into it, my face turned up, eager to feel its life-giving warmth once again.' Underwood's voice caught on this last word and his lips tightened. He took a drink of brandy.

David could see the memory clearly pained him. 'Are you okay, Milord?'

'Yes,' said Underwood, putting down his glass. 'Yes, I'm fine. It's just been a long time … a very long time since I talked about – or even thought about – that moment. I ran into the sunlight, and it was like running into a cascade of fire. I burst into flames, Flinch – or at least my exposed skin did. Thank God I'd put those clothes on. My eyes were open, shielded by my hand, but it made no difference, they burned as well. My face, my hair, my hands aflame, I fell back into the cave, screaming, beating and pounding at myself. Blinded, I could feel my clothes burning and I dropped, rolling around on the ground until all the flames were extinguished. Even then, I could hear my flesh sizzling, smell the smoke from it thick in my nose.'

Underwood closed his eyes and pressed a hand to his forehead, clearly shaken by the memory. David didn't know what to say. He waited. Underwood said nothing for a few moments then he took a deep breath and continued. 'I lay there, screaming, and not just because of the physical pain. I was screaming because I realised that what had happened to me at the hands of that creature, wasn't a blessing; it wasn't a miracle; and it wasn't over. I was damned, cursed, forsaken by God – for He himself had scorched me, cast me from His holy light and forced me back into that Caliban's cave to lie with the rotting dead.

'The man I had been had died back there in the darkness, and whatever I was now wasn't human anymore. I had become whatever the creature in the cave had been, and now, I had replaced him – *I* was the creature in the cave.

'I staggered blindly back into the caverns, back into the dank and stinking depths of my new home, consumed with grief and sorrow – not just for me, but for Martha, for Samuel, for the life I knew I had lost and the man I could never be again. My new senses led me back to the creature's nest, and there, I crawled onto its grimy bed of silk, and wept.

'I fell asleep eventually. And when I woke again, I was restored. My eyes fluttered open and they could see again, my flesh had healed, my hair had re-grown. This gave me neither delight nor came as a great surprise. I sat up ... and was immediately racked by pain from my stomach. I was hungry again. I doubled up in a foetal position. Would it *always* be this way? Would my every awakening now be to this terrible hunger?

'Oh, it wouldn't, but I didn't know that then. I didn't know that the process of regeneration and healing had used up all my reserves of strength.' Underwood closed his eyes. 'All I knew was the ferocious and overwhelming need for human blood, and that the only source of sustenance on the island flowed within the veins of Matthias Flinch.'

14

'BUT, YOU DON'T have to have human blood,' said David.

'Well, no. I know that now, but I didn't then. At that point in time the only blood I'd had that had done the trick had been human, so my hunger was telling me to get more of the same. Anyway, the clothes that I'd so carefully picked out earlier were now burnt and tattered, so I discarded them in favour of anything that fitted and a rather fancy – if a tad smelly – black frock coat. I took my watch from the burned vest, but that was all I bothered to bring with me. I then went back to the cave entrance. Night had fallen and I looked up at stars through the yawning hole in the cave roof. The only way out was to climb so I looked for handholds in the walls, and that was when I discovered another interesting change in my physical abilities. Upon grasping the rock I discovered, to my amazement, that my hands could adhere to the surface. Well, at first, I thought there was something on the rock – something sticky that I couldn't see. But I quickly realised that the stickiness was in fact coming from me. I could literally stick to walls.'

'Oh, I've seen that in Dracula movies,' said David. 'How do you do it?'

Underwood raised the palm of one hand and stroked it with the fingers of the other. 'Hairs. Millions of tiny adhesive hairs.'

David leaned forward, squinting at Underwood's palm. 'I don't see anything.'

'That's because they're presently uncalled for. But they're there when I need them, which is jolly handy.' He chuckled. 'Oh dear, a joke, unintended but quite apt.'

David's eyes were wide with wonder. 'Can you ... summon them?'

Underwood smiled and extended his hand. 'Certainly. Shake?' David warily took the hand and Underwood's fingers lightly closed on his. 'Now try and take your hand back.'

David tried, but he couldn't. 'Ugh, it's like some kind of Velcro; it prickles. You're not even squeezing my hand but I can't pull it free.' Underwood opened his hand and David was immediately released. David looked at his palm and brushed it with his fingers. 'There's no residue.'

'I should hope not, that would be most embarrassing, wouldn't it?'

David continued to stare at his palm. 'That's amazing.'

'Yes, it is rather, isn't it? Anyway, if I might get back to the story?'

'Sorry,' said David, unconsciously wiping his palm on the leg of his trousers. 'Go on.'

'So, I climbed up the walls; it was, as you say, amazing, but I didn't hang about to marvel at my new ability – I was hungry, and when I'm hungry, my focus narrows to one thing and one thing only – blood. I climbed out of the hole and emerged at the spot where, the night before, the creature had dropped me and broken my ankle. But it was all changed; the jungle, the night, it – it was like stepping into another world or another dimension, everything was different. Of course, it wasn't the world that had changed; it was me and my perceptions. For the first time, I experienced the world with my new senses, my vampire senses … and it was breathtaking. By the light of the moon, I could see *colour*, Flinch. Colour in the darkness! Down in the cave there had been no moon, so my vision was limited to a monochrome, but up above ground, it was like … well, not quite the full colour spectrum that you see in the daytime, but still, colour! But that was only the visual element, add to it the auditory – my hearing was startlingly acute; I could detect precisely the source of a sound, its whereabouts and distance. And smells also – can you imagine what the jungle smelled like to my new nose? The air was teeming with a richness of odours that your human hooter couldn't even dream of – not that noses dream, but you take my meaning. Of course, I'm used to it now. I take it for granted, just as you do your senses.'

'Yeah, you're right, I suppose. I don't even know they're there half the time. I guess I just don't appreciate them.'

'No one does, Flinch. Humans blunder obliviously through the sensual world. It's quite wasted on them.'

David nodded thoughtfully. 'Yeah. I should try and take the time to appreciate them more.'

'Yes, so you should. Start first thing, eh? When I go to bed later, why don't you stay up and savour the sunrise with all your senses? See it, feel it, listen to the world as it awakens around you. God knows I wish I could.'

'Yeah, I'll do that.'

Underwood took a sip of his brandy. 'Mmm, good man. Anyway, where was I? Ah yes, I'd emerged, and the night was vivid, alive with sights and sounds and smells like never before – and amid this sensual riot, my hunger latched onto something that wiped all thoughts of

Matthias's blood from my mind. A smell – rich, warm and pungent.' He looked at David with glittering eyes. 'A pig!'

'A *pig?*'

'Yes, a pig. A porker. Ships used to carry a living larder back in those days: pigs, goats, chickens and so on. I don't know if they still do, but certainly back then, wherever Europeans went, their pigs went with them. Now, maybe this little piggy had been shipwrecked on the island or maybe he'd been born and bred there, I don't know, I didn't ask him. All I cared about was the fact that even though he'd passed through there a good while ago, his trail still glowed where he had treaded through the bush. My canine teeth lengthened, and I was off after him immediately, my senses narrowed upon the trail that grew ever more vivid as I closed upon its source. By the time I caught up with him, I was in a frenzy of excitement. The poor blighter never knew what hit him. I pounced, landing on his back and pulling him off his feet. I had my teeth in his throat before either of us knew what was going on. He squealed, struggling tremendously, but I wouldn't be denied: I held him tight, knowing that his struggles would cease as soon as the bliss from my bite hit his system, and within five or ten seconds, he was lying still. I abandoned myself to the pleasure of killing him, closing my eyes and gorging myself, feeling his life restoring my life, his strength restoring my strength. I drained him to the death, and once I was glutted I lay there for a while, my eyes still closed, my head buzzing with sweet intoxication, and my whole body thrumming like the engine of a new Rolls Royce. I dozed briefly, dreaming strange and blissful dreams.' Underwood grinned. 'And then I awoke to find a dead pig in my arms. Charming, I thought. Misery does indeed acquaint a man with strange bedfellows.

'Anyway, now fully restored to my strength, I shoved the corpse away and set off for Matthias's camp. I ran, retracing the direction of my flight with the creature, and before long I caught the whiff of smoke on the breeze. I followed it, and when I came out on the beach, I saw the distant light of his campfire about a quarter of a mile away. I noticed that he'd reconstructed the nest of stakes. Little did he realise that the monster was now on foot and in the guise of his friend. Well, that gave me pause. What would I say to him? How could I explain what had happened to me when I barely understood it myself? Should I tell him that I'd killed Rudge – moreover, should I tell him why and how? These thoughts were churning in my head as I walked slowly towards the camp, all the time staring intently at the young man at its centre. I didn't give any thought to how I might have appeared. When he saw me, he jumped up with a look of joy and relief on his face. He called to me, waving. I didn't know what to do, I stopped, uncertain of how to approach. Then I saw the happiness drain from his face. He told me later that he saw an unnatural glow in my eyes as I stood there, the moonlit spray from the surf enveloping me like a mist. He said he thought I was a ghost come back from the dead to haunt him. He picked up a flintlock pistol and a branch from the fire, and shouted, "Who are you?"

'The question struck me as bizarre. Didn't he know me? I walked closer, still unsure of myself, but alarmed by his attitude. He was my friend and I wanted to be with him, to share my experiences around the fire … But at the same time, I was aware of another sensation: fear. What if I was again seized by the instinct that had led me to tear out Rudge's throat? Had I not, just a short while earlier, intended to feed on the lad? Oh, I was satiated, yes, but could I be sure I would stay that way? I raised my hand nervously, "It's me," I called, and my own voice sounded strange to me, even though it was unchanged in itself; I later realised it was because I doubted what I was saying: it wasn't *me* anymore, or at least not the *me* that he knew.

'He called upon me to identify myself by name, and I did. I came closer, and as I drew nearer to the light of the fire, I saw him recoil in horror. "Is that *blood?*" he asked pointing to my face. I touched my mouth and chin, and I realised they were still stained with pig's blood – and my shirt and coat were sodden with it. I looked at him, ashamed and confused. "I was hungry," I told him truthfully. "I killed a pig."

"And ate it raw?" he asked.

"Yes."

'He wasn't convinced; the torch and flintlock were still raised against me. He asked me about the bat creature and how come I wasn't dead. I told him I'd killed it and escaped. But he still looked doubtful. Then I remembered my watch and I held it up for him to see. I told him Rudge was dead and that I'd taken it from his body. "What use would a ghost have for a timepiece?" I asked. That seemed to win him over a bit. He lowered the flintlock but kept the torch raised. "What's happened to your eyes?" he asked. "You have the eyes of a wolf'. That reminded me of a childhood story, and I laughed, "All the better to see you with, my dear." But he didn't see the funny side; he raised the gun again.

'Well, something in me shifted then: without warning, the new instinct I'd feared would return, did, stepping from out of the shadows of my soul and seizing control of me. I looked at him and said calmly, "Put down the pistol, Matthias."

'He took a step back, wavered for a moment, then dropped the gun. He looked sick, frightened, but I didn't care. I told him to return the torch to the fire, and again, he did as I instructed; I could see he didn't want to, but he couldn't refuse me. I smiled, and in the light from the fire, he saw my teeth, my fangs extended. A look of revulsion rose on his face. He tried to cry out, his mouth open, but all that came out was a low moan. I … I remember I took pleasure in it. I'm ashamed to say it, Flinch, but I could feel this tremendous power over him, and it thrilled me. He was mine: his life was in my hands. If I had chosen to, I could've played with him as a cat plays with a mouse.' Underwood took a drink of brandy. 'Thank God I had already fed on that pig, otherwise I fear I might have done something I'd have lived to regret.'

'But why?' said David, disturbed. 'He was your friend. Had you lost all sense of that?'

Underwood sighed. 'Well, it's hard to explain, Flinch. Newly turned vampires are confused creatures, often not understanding what they are and operating on two conflicting instincts. You may have heard legends of recently interred vampires returning to their family homes to prey upon loved ones: we go *home* because that's where the human in us longs to be; but the vampire in us also knows it's where we'll be admitted without question and embraced in warm, loving arms.'

'That's awful,' said David, adding hastily, 'for everyone involved.'

'Yes, it is. As I was saying, I think had I not fed, John Brooks would have had no voice in me at all at that moment. But thankfully, I had fed and I was suddenly shaken by a wave of horror at what I was doing. I turned away, breaking the weird spell that I'd put on him – and myself, and fighting the urge to vomit. I ran away, back the way I'd come, falling to my knees in the sand about thirty yards from the camp.

'Eventually the nausea passed, but not so easily the sense of self-disgust and revulsion I felt. I cried out to heaven, a bloody awful scream from the depths of my soul. It's embarrassing to admit to, Flinch, but I suppose I had something of an emotional outpouring: pounding and clawing at the sand, writhing and howling like a madman until eventually I calmed down.' He took a drink.

'So, what did Matthias do in all of this?'

'What could he do? He kept close to the fire. He told me later he didn't know what to make of it. The best case scenario was that I was sick with a tropical disease that had affected me mentally and physically. The worst case – and he admitted at the time this seemed the more likely – was that I was possessed by demons. In hindsight I suppose I was lucky he didn't shoot me.'

'Why didn't he?'

'Because he was made of better stuff than that, Flinch; it was I who had lost my humanity, not Matthias. After what seemed an hour, he began to cook some fish. The smell drifted to me. The night before it had made my mouth water, but now it was nothing to me. And then,' a smile touched the edges of Underwood's mouth. 'And then he did something I'll never forget.'

'What was that?'

'He walked out from the camp, unarmed, and brought me a piece of the cooked fish on a leather satchel. I couldn't bring myself to look at him, nor even turn in his direction. Without a word, he laid the food on the beach beside me, and then went back to the fireside. I remember, it wasn't much, but it was half of what he had. My eyes filled with tears.'

Underwood smoothed back his hair. 'Tentatively, I took a piece of the fish and brought it to my mouth, but before it was even close, I felt my gorge rise at it. I held it for a moment, hoping the nausea would pass, but it didn't. Of course, the last thing I wanted was to do vomit a bellyful of pig's blood up in front of the lad, so I carefully returned the fish to the satchel and made as if I wasn't hungry. Matthias called to me then, he said, "What's happened to you, John?" I didn't know what to say. I told him ... I was changed.'

"To what?" says he, "a demon? Is it that beast that's infected you?"

"Very like, very like," Underwood nodded, his eyes focussed on the past. "But with what I neither know nor understand. I'm sick, but never healthier; mad, but never more aware; changed, but still ... still me." Matthias said nothing for a few moments then he asked if I intended to kill him.'

Underwood helped himself to one of David's cigarettes. 'Well, that was the big question, wasn't it? I told him the closest answer I had to the truth, which was, *no*, I didn't *mean* to. But that despite my best intentions, I couldn't guarantee that I wouldn't.

"In that case," said he, raising his pistol to bear on me, "I think it'd be for the best if you'd leave." Underwood lit his cigarette and looked at David. 'Fair enough, I think you'll agree. What else could I do? I got to my feet and, without another word, I walked away.' Underwood sighed a long stream of blue smoke. 'I walked for hours. The night was alive to me in ways no mortal man had ever seen, yet I took no delight in any of it. I was consumed by turbulent emotions; rage and sorrow over what I had done to my friend, and above all, over the appalling, unnatural injustice of what had been done to me: I'd survived real physical death only then to find myself *as good as dead* – at least as far as human society was concerned. I mean, how was I ever going to be able to walk among men again, when all I wanted to do was cut their throats and feast upon their blood? Like a leper, I would have to make a life for myself there, alone on that island, running around like some kind of savage. For what else could I do? The *evil* feelings I'd had towards Matthias sickened me, and the thought that I might feel that way towards him again or – God forbid – Martha ... ' Underwood's words trailed off and he shook his head. 'I tell you, Flinch, at that moment, I wanted to die. I wanted to finish off what that bloody creature had started. By all rights I *should have been* dead! But thanks to Rudge's damnable intervention, I'd managed to cheat fate. So, I asked myself, why not just end it? To be or not to be, hmmm? That *was* the question.'

'But obviously, you didn't end it.'

'No.'

'Why not?'

Underwood smiled, 'I'm sorry to disappoint you, Flinch.'

'No, seriously, what stopped you?'

'Oh, I don't know. Hope? Love? Selfishness? One or all of the above. For just as I knew I was changed and the world I'd known was seemingly lost to me ... I ...'

'You couldn't let it go.'

Underwood replied in a voice barely more than a whisper, 'No.' He drew on his cigarette. 'I didn't *want* to be alone; I didn't *want* to be the creature in the cave.' He turned his eyes to David. 'I was still in love, Flinch. My life had had purpose and meaning, and those things hadn't died in me. You can understand that, can't you?'

David nodded. 'Yes, of course.'

'I couldn't end my life, nor could I simply accept a self-imposed banishment. Why should I be marooned and condemned to live like a beast? I didn't deserve that, and there were people – people I loved – who *needed* me. There had to be another way: one that meant I could return to civilisation and live as a man as I always had done – oh yes, as a changed man, a strange man, but still as a man.

'And so I began to think. To analyze what had happened to me and my various reactions. I knew that the pig's blood had nourished me and so stopped me from wanting to feed on Matthias. And while, yes, I had been cruel to him, perhaps now that I knew such impulses existed, I would be able to master them. Just as humans had learned to master their savage instincts, why should I not be able to master mine?

'I wandered on and on along the beach, lost in my thoughts for miles and hours, until I started to become aware of a queer tingling sensation. I stopped, curious as to what was now afflicting me. The sensation quickly became almost painfully urgent; every nerve in my body was jangling like some internal alarm had been sounded. Then I looked up, and immediately understood the significance of it all.'

'What was it?'

'The horizon was beginning to glow.'

'Dawn?'

'Yes. The sun was coming. I was immediately terrified, the memory of my solar roasting still fresh in my mind. I turned and ran, reaching the tree line just as the first rays of sunlight broke the horizon. But the jungle was sparse there and I had to run like hell for the denser forest through shafts of sunlight that raked me like whiplashes. My flesh began to smoke, and I screamed, certain now that I was going to be burned alive – for although I was running as fast as I could, the myriad fingers of the rising sun were reaching through the trees around me like a closing fist. All I could think was, *faster! Faster! FASTER!* ... And then it happened, for the first time – and with not even an inkling of forewarning.' Underwood looked at David to see if he was suitably on tenterhooks. He was.

'What? What happened?'

'I changed.'

'Changed?'

'Yes. One moment I was a biped, stumbling along with all the hopeless limitations of a biped in a tangled treescape, and the next ... I was a wolf.'

'*A wolf?*'

'Yes, a large black timber wolf. And by God, did I ever hurtle through the jungle then.'

'You can turn into a wolf?'

'Yes. You sound surprised. I thought you'd read Dracula.'

'I have, but ... Well, what you read on the page is one thing, but,' David struggled for words, all the while trying to ignore the amusement dancing in Underwood's eyes. 'Oh fuck it. Bat, wolf, mist, you're right, why am I surprised?'

Underwood laughed. 'Good fellow. Anyway, there I was – a wolf – lower to the ground, bounding over and under logs, darting through the brush and soon tearing into the darker reaches of the jungle. There, in the gloom, I found a fallen tree, its underside half rotten and the ground beneath it soft and peaty. I dug with great speed and was soon in a hollow underneath it. It was cool and dark, and – now returned to human form – I kicked the dirt behind me to block out what little light could still filter through. When it was done, I lay there, naked, shaken, but by a miracle of the most unnatural proportions, alive.'

'What did you do?'

'Well, the first thing I did was check my body for burns, but to my astonishment, I discovered that the transformation had completely healed me. I was fine! I began to laugh, relieved and not a little hysterical. Christ, what a night: one minute I'd been thinking of ending it all, the next I was lying under a rotting tree laughing like a madman because I'd managed to outrun the rising sun – and I'd done it as another species! I hadn't chosen to do it, I hadn't intended to do it, and yet call me Fido – I'd done it all the same.

'Anyway, eventually I fell asleep. I slept through the day and awoke the next evening. I crawled out from under the tree, dusting bugs from my hair and feeling fairly famished, but not – I was happy to discover – painfully so. I'd undergone a physical transformation and there had been some healing, but I hadn't used up all my strength in doing this, and so I wasn't getting the cramps. But all the same, as I say, I was famished. The jungle was resonating with life, and I set off immediately to hunt something for breakfast. I tried – consciously – to change myself into a wolf again, but I couldn't. It would be some time before I mastered the skill of conscious, deliberate metamorphosis. However, I had plenty of other incredible new abilities, and it wasn't long before I was tucking into my prey for the early evening – a species of large rodent that I'd never

seen before and never seen since. Hunting and killing him was
tremendous fun – exhilarating even – and I remember thinking that the
life of a wild predator *did* have a certain appeal. But I wasn't the creature
my progenitor had been. I was an Englishman: I was no more at home in
the jungle than my maker would have been in Piccadilly; I was of civilised
human society and I wanted to get back to it as soon as possible. More
specifically, despite my changed circumstances, I wanted to get back to
Martha. The night before, I'd begun to turn the problem over in my mind,
and now I'd come to a solution.' He took a sip of brandy.

'What was that?'

Underwood set down his glass. 'Well, when I first found the vampire's
treasure horde, I'd intended to share it with Matthias. But now I saw that
it could be better used in inducing the lad to help me get safely to
America.' He checked David's expression for disapproval, but found
none. 'See, you have to understand, Flinch, I needed him to help me; I
needed someone to watch over and protect me as I slept through the
daytime, otherwise I'd never get anywhere.' David nodded his
understanding and Underwood continued. 'But the problem would be in
winning him to my cause. Obviously, by that time I'd revealed myself as a
threat to him, a monster even. I felt that if I simply handed him a bag of
gold and jewels and asked him to look after me, there was a better than
average chance he'd be off on the first ship that sailed by in the daylight
hours. But if I could hold back the promise of riches until we both
reached America safely, then, I reasoned, he *would* stick by me – monster
or not.

'And so, once I'd fed, I determined to go and speak to him. First, I
needed to get my clothes; I presumed I'd somehow shed them at the
scene of my transformation, and so I returned there. When I did, I was
confused to find my clothes all burnt. The ashes and scorched remains
ran in a roughly straight line in the direction that I'd been running. I
reasoned that the clothes must have caught fire as the sun was burning my
flesh. But of course, I know now that that's not the case; it's all to do with
molecules and energy and whatnot. Anyway, I kicked among the remains
for anything I could actually wear. I found my watch and the remains of
the waistcoat I'd been wearing, the boots were reasonably intact and there
was a belt – for what little good that was – because everything else was
absolutely frazzled. Then I remembered that smelly black coat I'd been
wearing. I'd been walking with it slung over my shoulder just before the

dawn, and I remember I'd dropped it as soon as I started to flee. On searching, I was relieved to find it at the edge of the trees. I put it on and buttoned it up, then, carrying the corpse of the large rodent which I'd brought along for Matthias's dinner, I made my way back to his camp. But upon finding the camp, I was somewhat taken aback to find he wasn't there.

'My first thought was that Verlaine had returned, in which case Matthias was either captured or had fled to hide elsewhere on the island. But my concerns were allayed when the sea breeze momentarily dropped and I caught his scent coming from just inside the edge of the jungle. I saw him lying low and watching me. I waved to him and he started, no doubt wondering how I could see him in the dark. I called out to him to come back to camp so we might start a fire and warm ourselves. He got up warily and returned, his gun cocked, but not pointing directly at me. He looked questioningly at my attire and asked me what the game was. I hoisted the rodent and said that I'd explain everything over dinner. And I that's just what I did; I told him of everything that had happened to me, including the treasure in the vampire's cave – though I didn't tell him quite how much there was, and I certainly didn't tell him *where* it was. He listened to my story with horror and pity and he agreed that after all I'd been through, it was only right that I should have full possession of the treasure. That's when I offered him my deal: I told him that I would pay him handsomely if, in the event of our rescue, he would guard me as I slept until we reached Virginia. Once we arrived, I'd pay him a substantial extra sum that would set him up for life in America, and then he'd be free to do what he liked. Well, he accepted gladly, though of course he had some concerns for his safety. I told him he didn't need to worry on that account as I was now master of my new desires – which was a small exaggeration, but in everybody's best interests, I felt. And to seal the deal, I gave him my word that he would never shed a drop of blood at my hands.

"Ah," says he, "What about the other people on board ship? If we are rescued and then you then start rising in the night and preying upon the crew and passengers, they'll jolly well throw us overboard." And of course, he was right.'

'He sounds a bit like me,' said David.

'Yes, well, he was like you, as I said earlier. And not just in looks, but in manner as well. Do you play the violin by any chance?'

David shook his head.

'Hmm. Anyway, we began to work out a plan of how we could travel without my dietary requirements getting us chucked over the side. I needed to be able to lie below decks by day and then, after sunset, to emerge and be sociable. But of course, I also needed to feed somehow.'

'That sounds like it'd be quite difficult, Milord.'

'Well, yes, that's what we thought. But by the time I got the tingle of the approaching day, we'd concocted our story. We would become new men. Instead of an ex-convict and a naval deserter, we were to be a shipwrecked lord and his faithful valet. I would be Lord Daniel Underwood – I took the name from the inscriptions on my watch and pistol respectively – a tragic fellow who, alas, suffered from a rare skin disease that forced him to hide himself away from the sun during the daylight hours, while Matthias would henceforth be known as Pringle. Apparently, a Tom Pringle had been an elderly servant in the family home when he was a nipper. He'd always liked the old fellow, and the name felt very comfortable to him.'

David frowned. 'But surely, you'd have been a bit ... how can I put it? A bit too *common* to pass yourself off as a lord at the time?'

Underwood laughed. 'Oh my word, yes, I was as common as muck. But Matthias wasn't.'

'So why didn't he play the lord and you play the servant?'

'Why on Earth would a lord be devoted to a servant with a weird skin disease?'

David conceded that he wouldn't and Underwood continued with a smile, 'Exactly. We felt it was necessary for one of us to be an aristocrat because, at the time, we were still at war with France and Spain, and if one of their ships happened by, the best a couple of shipwrecked common Englishmen could hope for was to be clapped in irons and set to work scrubbing the decks day and night. But a member of the aristocracy could always be assured of a civilized welcome. So, we decided that over the coming nights, he would teach me how to speak and carry myself like a lord.' He laughed, 'Oh, that was some rare fun I can tell you. Have you ever seen Shaw's *Pygmalion*?'

'I've seen *My Fair Lady*, the film version.'

'Well, it was a bit like that, but around the campfire on the beach of a desert island.'

'That must have been fun.'

'Yes, it was, though somewhat frustrating at times. Being a lordly type didn't come naturally to me; my only previous dealings with the upper classes had been when I was pointing pistols at them on Hampstead Heath. But Matthias was a good teacher, and I was soon able to carry myself with a certain *hauteur*.' He chuckled. 'Any rough edges on my character we'd put down to my having spent too much time among the rank and file during my military career, which was a subject I could expand upon with gusto if required.

'I suppose really what we were doing was a bit like forgery: trying to pass off the fake as the genuine article. Of course, you can fool your loobies and your mopsqueezers without too much bother, but proper gentlefolk would be a different matter altogether. As a matter of fact, I actually hoped we *would* be found by the French, since they think all Englishmen to be mad, and so would be less inclined to notice any peculiarities. But as it happened, it was a Portuguese ship that eventually came to our rescue, which was far better really, as they were on our side in the war at the time. They landed in daytime, and Matthias explained to them that his master was off in the jungle hunting and would be back later on that evening. They had no problem with that; they rather welcomed the thought of some fresh meat.' He grinned. 'Little did they know they were in danger of becoming fresh meat themselves.'

'You don't mean you killed them?'

Underwood chuckled. 'No. But there were a few cases of anemia on board before too long.'

'So how did you feed?'

Underwood smiled, finished his brandy and set down the glass. 'Not tonight, Flinch. Look,' he pointed to the east where the silhouettes of the hills now stood black against the brightening azure of the pre-dawn sky. 'Time I was in bed. And you too, you must be shattered.'

'I hadn't noticed actually, but yeah, now that you come to mention it, I am.'

Underwood got up and looked to the coming dawn. 'It's a beautiful time of day, isn't it? Sometimes I stay up to the very last moment before the sun breaks the horizon, before I then have to hide myself away.' He fell silent and watched the brightness grow until the edges of the hills began to burn. Then he sighed, 'Well, that's it for me, Flinch. Time for bed.' He turned and went into the house.

David followed him and asked, 'Why do you call that coffin *bed*? Why don't you just do away with it sleep in a proper bed?'

Underwood stopped just inside the doorway and turned back. 'Well, the coffin is the perfect dark space. It's secure, ideal for travelling, and it's comfortable. A proper bed would be nice, but over the years, I've grown to feel vulnerable in anything other than the old wooden box.'

'Well, what if we got the windows of your bedroom bricked up? Would that make you feel more secure?'

Underwood considered a moment then said, 'Well, that sounds like a jolly good idea. And of course – so much more comfortable for the ladies, hmm?' He winked. 'Could you arrange that for me?'

'Certainly, sir. I'll get onto señor Hernandez in morning and see if he can recommend a good brickie.'

'Good show, Flinch. Well thought of.' They went back through the house. At the entrance to the cellar, Underwood stopped. 'Well, thank you for a very pleasant evening, David.'

'Thank *you*, sir for entertaining me with your story. All I did was sit and listen.'

'Ah, but being a good listener is a vital, and often sadly overlooked, element of the art of conversation. And anyway, you'll have your chance to speak tomorrow night, eh? I look forward to hearing your story. We'll go out for dinner and drinks and you can tell me all about yourself.'

'When you say going out for dinner and drinks, you don't mean to Michelle and Keith's, do you? Because – '

'No, no, no. I told you, I'm past all that. We'll head off somewhere farther afield. Somewhere with a bit more life, eh?'

David was relieved, he nodded gratefully. 'Yeah, alright. That sounds like a plan. But don't expect much from my story, compared to what you've told me tonight, my life seems totally uneventful.'

Underwood smiled. 'Somehow, I doubt that. Goodnight, Flinch.' He stepped onto the cellar stairs and was just closing the door when David stopped him.

'Oh, sir, before you go, can I just ask you one thing?'

'What's that?'

'About Martha: did you find her?'

'Another night, Flinch,' said Underwood as he eased the door slowly to a close, 'another night.'

For a moment, David lingered at the door, and he realised he was disappointed that the night had to end. He turned, and was just about to go to bed when he remembered he had one more thing to do before turning in. He looked at his watch, scratched the stubble on his chin, then retraced his route back up to the roof terrace to watch the sun rise.

15

KEITH SAT AT THE KITCHEN TABLE watching a fly crawling on the tomato ketchup bottle. He pushed a fork-load of fried egg and toast into his mouth and chewed mechanically. The kitchen door opened and caused the thin haze of bacon-scented smoke to billow and roll. Melanie entered, grimacing at the smell.

'Dad! Open a window!'

Keith looked up, dazed. 'Eh?'

Melanie rolled her eyes. 'You'll make everything stink,' she crossed the room and opened the door to the patio, fanning her arms to encourage the flow of fresh air. She turned to him. His face was saggy with lack of sleep, his eyes were half-closed and bloodshot, and his cheeks and chin were dark with a two-day beard growth. She shook her head. 'You and those mates of yours really went for it last night, didn't you?'

'What?'

'I said, you and your mates – you got really drunk.'

'Did I?'

Melanie gave a sarcastic laugh as she poured corn flakes into a bowl. 'Er, *yeah* – just a bit. Don't you remember?'

'No.'

She looked at him doubtfully. 'You're kidding.' The blank expression on Keith's face told her he wasn't. 'Jesus, Dad,' she took her carton of soy milk from the fridge. 'You're starting to lose your marbles. Maybe you should give the booze a rest for a while.'

Keith followed her movements around the kitchen, his expression unchanging. He clutched a fork in his hand and a forgotten piece of bacon quivered at its end. Melanie sat down opposite him and poured the soy onto her cornflakes, she glanced up to see him staring at her, confused. 'What? You really don't remember anything?'

Keith shook his head. 'No.'

Melanie sighed. 'You and those two mates of yours were up boozing all night.'

'Damo and Hodge?'

'No, the *new* ones. You know – that bloke that talks all posh and his mate with the bruises?'

Keith considered this for a second, then his face seemed to brighten a little. 'Master,' he whispered.

'What?'

'He is … Lord.'

'He's a lord? Well, that figures. But that doesn't make him your master, does it? What would that make you, a serf?'

'He is Master.'

Melanie shrugged. 'Whatever. So, you don't remember coming to my room then?'

'No.'

'I got scared because I heard Perry barking and some guy shouting. I thought we were being burgled, and then you came up to my room? Remember?'

The lines in Keith's forehead deepened for a moment, then softened. 'Oooh yeah, yeah, I remember. You were afraid, and I was, I was …'

'You were what?'

'I was … drunk.' He noticed the bacon on his fork and ate it without enthusiasm. 'Sorry about that, love. I've been a bit … out of sorts lately.'

Melanie nodded. She'd noticed a lot of odd behaviour in her parents over the last few days. She took the opportunity to probe the matter further. 'So, where's mum?'

'Mum? She's … asleep.'

'I'm not surprised: all the racket you lot were making last night. She still not talking to you?'

'What?' Keith seemed to come into focus. 'What do you mean?'

'Oh come on, Dad. You both try to hide it, but it's totally obvious. She's pissed off with you, isn't she?'

'Oi! Don't swear.'

'Okay, but she *is* cross with you, isn't she?'

Keith looked down at his breakfast. It was beginning to look congealed. He nudged the remains of a sausage with his fork. 'Yeah, she's … cross with me.'

'Why? What have you done this time?'

'Nothing that concerns you, alright. Leave it.'

Anger flashed in Melanie's eyes. 'What are you going on about, "leave it"? 'Course it concerns me, you're my parents!' She stood up. 'What's going on, Dad? You've had rows in the past but this has been going on for a couple of days now. And then there's these strange men stumbling about the house in the middle of the night and you not sleeping in mum's bed!'

'Well, they're just a couple of blokes, love,' said Keith standing and reaching out to her. 'Just a couple of mates.'

'Are they? That's not what I've heard.'

Keith tensed. 'What? What have you heard?'

'People have been talking about them in the pub – not to me, but I've overheard them. They're all talking about the disco the other night, how that posh bloke and Mum were dancing and about how you and him got into a fight over her.'

'That – that was nothing. Just a couple of mates having a friendly spat. It wasn't even about her.'

'So what was it about?'

Keith's fogged brain searched for a lie, groping through the events of discos past and present. 'He … he spilled beer on the record I was playing. Oh, Jesus – I was *livid*.'

'What record?'

'Eh?'

'What record?'

Keith floundered, his mind unable to cope with the questioning. Would she ask him to produce a beer-sticky record to validate his claim? What would he do then? 'I – I can't remember.'

'What do you mean, you don't remember? You got into a bloody fight over it, didn't you?'

Keith raised a warning finger to her. 'Just you watch your mouth, young lady.'

'Or you'll what, Dad? Hit me? Is that what you did to Mum?'

'Jesus Christ, Mel!' Keith put his hands to his head. 'How can you say that?'

A cool voice came from the doorway. 'It was Visage, wasn't it, Keith?' Michelle stood in the shadows of the hall. She wore one of the long t-shirts she liked to sleep in and she was rubbing a hand through her tousled hair.

Keith nodded, relieved. 'Yeah. Visage, that was it.'

'Your dad was drunk, Mel. He completely over-reacted; started a fight with some new customers over a 7-inch single. So yeah, I was angry with him. We had a big row afterwards. But he's admitted he was wrong, and last night he apologised to the gentlemen concerned and now they're thick as thieves. They've forgiven him, but I was still a bit cross with him last night so he took the spare bed.'

'There you go,' said Keith, 'just like I said. It's nothing to worry about, love. Just me being a tit is all.'

Melanie looked from Michelle back to Keith. 'Well, I wish you two would sort it out, then, 'cause you're totally freaking me out.' She snatched up a paper napkin and wiped tears from her eyes; angry, embarrassed, but above all, relieved. 'Look at me! I have to go to school like this – all puffy-eyed and smelling like a greasy spoon café, and it's all your fault!' She scrunched the napkin and threw it at Keith. 'So you'd better make it up to Mum by the time I get home this afternoon, or you'll be well sorry,' she turned to Michelle, 'both of you will.' She sniffed and managed a smile.

Keith came around the table and took her in his arms. 'I'm sorry, love,' he kissed her hair. 'Course we'll make it up.'

'You'd better,' said Melanie, hugging him extra hard for emphasis.

'Go on now, Mel,' said Michelle, 'or you'll be late for school.'

Melanie came to Michelle and hugged her. 'All right. Sorry if I woke you up, Mum.' She kissed her mother on the cheek and went out to get her school bag. 'I'll see you later.'

Keith and Michelle stood in silence, neither of them looking at the other. At the sound of the front door banging shut, Michelle turned to go. Keith held out a hand, reaching for her. ''Chelle?' She stopped and turned back to him, her face had lost all trace of sleepy affability and she looked at him coldly.

'Do, do you want some breakfast?'

'No.'

'I'll make your favourite if you like, eggs Benedict. I can do it, we've got the ingredients here, I – '

'I said no, Keith.'

'But what about Mel? You just said – '

'I only said what I did to stop her being upset. My feelings towards you haven't changed.'

'But what about when she comes back? Are we just gonna pretend?'

'It won't be for long, Keith.'

Keith took a step back as the understanding of what she implied hit him. He sat down hard on his chair. 'So, you really don't love me anymore.'

Michelle walked back and stood in the kitchen doorway. She looked at him as though she were trying to fathom a riddle, like she were seeing him perhaps for the second time ever and was trying to remember his name. 'I … I don't know.'

'You can't say that, 'Chelle. You must know – it's like, it's either there or it's not there, innit?'

Michelle looked away and stroked her neck, feeling the smooth skin that had, the night before, been corrupted by Underwood's bite.

Keith saw this and turned his face away. 'Yeah, I understand. It's him – it's his will.'

She nodded. 'Yes. He will come for me tonight. He told me so.'

'Yes. He spoke to me too, but I can't remember what he said, only the sense of it, you know? It's cloudy. Every time I try and remember, I feel all peaceful and then I just – sort of – forget.'

'And what is the sense of it?'

'It's like, I'm gonna lose you, but … that it's a good thing – that I should be happy, rejoice.'

Michelle came in and sat down beside him. 'And are you happy?'

Keith rubbed his head. 'No. I'm confused. My heart wants you to stay here with me, but my head is telling me to let you go … and rejoice … there's a line that keeps going around in my head every time I think of you: "Rejoice, for she shall be eternal". What kind of bollocks is that? I wouldn't say that, I wouldn't even *think* in them words, and yet, when I hear it, I feel happy … that you're leaving me.' His voice caught on the last part of the sentence and his eyes suddenly glistened with tears. 'But that's mad, coz it's the last thing I want, Chelle, I swear.'

Michelle watched the tears spill onto his cheeks. She knew she should feel pain at the sight, that she should want to take him in her arms and hold him and long for him to put his arms around her, enfold her. But instead she watched the man before her, his face downcast, his tears falling onto his bare thighs … and she found herself thinking of Daniel Underwood. She closed her eyes, feeling a warm flush at the memory of his hands on her flesh, his mouth at her neck, the pain – and the exquisite pleasure that followed. The warm flush spread to her breasts and down between her thighs. Keith sniffed loudly and she opened her eyes. She closed her arms over her breasts and got up. 'I should go.'

Keith looked up and sniffed again. 'Yeah. Of course.'

She went to the door, intending to return to the privacy of the bedroom, but she stopped in the doorway. Without turning back, she said, 'I do love you, Keith … I do … It's just that – I can't feel it any more. He … he wills it.'

Keith nodded. 'I know, girl. I know. He is our master and ... I rejoice.' He smiled at her and fresh tears spilled from his eyes. 'You shall be eternal.'

'We,' she said, uncertainly, 'we'll have to be … like we used to be before, when Mel gets back this afternoon.'

'Yeah. No worries, girl.' He thought for a moment, then said, 'He comes for you tonight?'

'Yes, after the pub's closed; after Mel's in bed.'

He nodded. 'That's … probably for the best.'

'I – ' her voice caught in her throat, and for a moment, she wanted to go to him, rocked by a sudden rush of emotion, she staggered slightly, catching the doorframe. She steadied herself, and then Underwood was once again in her mind, his eyes reassuring her and silencing her thoughts. From behind her came the sound of a chair moving back, Keith was on his feet, about to come to her. She held up a hand to stay him. 'Sit down, Keith,' her voice was again cold, unemotional. 'Eat your breakfast. I'm going back to bed. I need to sleep.'

Keith sat down. She left without another word. His eyes followed her silhouette down the hall until it was lost in the other shadows. After she had gone from view, he continued to stare into the shadows, his thoughts merging with their cool darkness, until they too were lost. Then he blinked and his mind returned to the kitchen. He turned back to the table and saw his unfinished breakfast awaiting him. 'Oh yeah,' he murmured, pleased. 'Breakfast. Nice one.' He forked a piece of sausage and some beans into his mouth and frowned on discovering they were stone cold. He shrugged and carried on chewing. The fly that had flown away when Melanie entered the room earlier, returned to once again settle on the tomato sauce bottle, and Keith's eyes once again settled on the fly. And then both of them resumed their meals in silence.

Lydia checked her make-up in the rear view mirror. Beyond her reflection loomed the shape of Sergei Alexandrov's nightclub, *La Fantasía*. Satisfied with her appearance, she looked outside. Besides her Land Rover, there were four other cars in the car park. One of them a white Mercedes with tinted windows: probably Sergei's latest car. She put on her sunglasses, opened the door, and stepped out of the air conditioned comfort into the furnace of the midday heat. She walked quickly into the shade of the building and then around to the glass panelled front doors. She tried them, but they were locked. She looked up at the dark eye of the security camera. It stared back unmoving. Feeling mildly ridiculous, she waved at it. Still nothing happened. She walked to the intercom and pushed the talk button. 'Hello?' She waited, but no reply came. She tried again. Had he forgotten about her? Maybe that wasn't his car round the back after all. The intercom was silent. 'Shit,' she muttered. She had an appointment for God's sake; she'd called him last night right after Cynthia and Gerald had told her about Michelle's reaction to the newspaper story featuring his picture about the beheaded Brit on Ibiza. She'd known immediately that Sergei was almost certainly behind the murder; his reputation as a leading player on the Costa Del Crime was well known to anyone who strayed into the wrong circles, and for many years now, Lydia had been straying into all kinds of wrong circles; not just for the purposes of exsanguinating prostitutes, vagrants and the occasional businessman, but also into what had been the wild criminal frontier of Costa Del Sol property swindles. She had made a small fortune selling foreigners off-plan apartments in complexes that didn't have planning permission to begin with. She would operate out of numerous bogus shop fronts set up solely to do the deals, and then disappear as soon as the deals were done. And by the time the hapless buyers found out they'd been had, she would be long gone.

She also had no problem handling sales to buyers who lacked the proper paperwork, provided that their lack of correct credentials was compensated for – generously – in her final commission. One such client was Sergei Alexandrov. He had acquired a number of bar and club properties through private arrangements with the owners, but his personal home on Malaga's Marbella seafront was something he'd had to buy through one of the estate agents offering the property. He'd tried, unsuccessfully, to come to a satisfactory arrangement with two of her competitors before coming to her, and from the moment they met, it was obvious to each of them that they'd found a kindred spirit. Since then, she'd helped him with a number of purchases, and he had rewarded her services not only with a generous commission, but also – as they got to know each other better – little tokens of his appreciation in the form of her favourite recreational drugs.

She had been involved in the purchase of this place too, the 1970s-built bingo emporium that was now *La Fantasía*. She'd been here a few times socially since, but she didn't care for the place, it played to the lower end of the market and was usually heaving with drunk youth from all over northern Europe all getting their tits out and screaming their heads off.

Suddenly the intercom crackled into life. '¿Si?'

Lydia looked up at the security camera. 'Lydia Flinch. *Tengo una reunión con señor Alexandrov*. Chop chop!'

The intercom hissed for a moment then a voice with a Russian accent replied, 'Wait, please. Someone comes down to meet you.'

Lydia looked at her watch impatiently then folded her arms to wait. Presently a door opened in the gloomy interior and a huge silhouette stepped through. She recognised it as Ivan. He opened one of the front doors and gave her a broad smile. 'Miss Flinch. Is good to see you again.'

'Is good to see *you* again, Ivan. Is the master of the house at home?'

Ivan's brows knitted. 'What?'

'Is Sergei here?'

Ivan laughed. 'Ah, for a moment I am confused. *Master of House*. Is song from *Les Misérables*, yes? I like this theatre very much. I think you mean bad man who owns pub and am confused.'

'But that's exactly who I am here to see, Ivan,' Lydia took off her sunglasses and smiled. 'Will you lead the way, or shall I see myself up?'

'Lydia!' Sergei rose smiling from his chair as she entered his office. 'What is this? You have an exciting real estate opportunity for me? You were very mysterious on the phone last night.'

'Well, one never knows who might be listening in on your phone, Sergei, you're a popular man.' She extended her hand, palm down.

Sergei chuckled, taking her hand and raising it to his lips. 'Not *so* popular, I hope. But tell me, what is it you have for me today? Bar, pub, maybe golf course?' He laughed at this last suggestion and Ivan, who had followed Lydia in and was now standing by the door, chuckled along with him. Anton, who was standing next to Sergei, didn't register the joke; he was far too absorbed in his appreciation of Lydia's legs.

Lydia was accustomed to such attention and ignored it. 'I didn't know you were interested in golf, Sergei.'

'I am not. I believe the cost of watering the grass these days must swallow all the profits, no?'

'Quite possibly. Who wants to play golf on a dead lawn? Not so much a green, as a brown.' She smiled at her joke, but Sergei looked confused. Lydia explained: 'In English, they call a big lawn *a green*. So if one's green is dead, it'd be a brown, you see?'

'Ha!' Sergei clapped his hands and laughed. 'A brown! Playing golf on the brown. That is very funny, Lydia.' Taking that as a cue, Ivan chuckled. Sergei looked at Anton, who was still leering at Lydia's legs. 'Anton, a brown. The grass is dead.'

Anton looked up at his name. 'Sorry Captain, I was thinking in Russian.'

'I'm sure you were,' said Sergei. He then switched to Russian himself to say, 'but put those thoughts away and act like a gentleman.' Anton corrected his posture, straightening up and inclining his head to Lydia in the smallest of bows. Sergei switched back to English and turned to Lydia, he indicated a seat opposite his desk. 'Please, Lydia, sit. Can we get you a drink?'

'Only if you're having one yourself,' said Lydia, slipping into the seat.

'Of course. What would you like? I have excellent Russian vodka from the distillery that supplies the Kremlin.'

'Really? Well, what's good enough for the Kremlin is good enough for me. Thank you.'

'How do you prefer it?'

'However you're having it.'

Sergei gave an order to Ivan, who then crossed the room to a small bar to fix the drinks while Sergei sat back in his chair. 'And so, to business. What do you have for me today?'

'A pub.'

'Whereabouts?'

'Inland, about seventy kilometers from here.'

'*Inland?*' Sergei laughed and shook his head. 'No, no, no. I have no interest in inland. My business is here on the coast, where the money is.'

Lydia smiled. 'Oh, I think this particular property might be of great interest to you, Sergei. It's run by some old friends of yours.'

'Friends?' Sergei seemed surprised. Ivan handed him a glass of neat vodka. 'I have no friends. Not inland, anyway.'

Lydia also accepted a drink from Ivan. 'Oh, perhaps I'm mistaken. Keith and Michelle Mullins? I'm sure they said it was you who bought their old pub in Malaga from them.'

Sergei's smile fell and he put down his drink. 'Mullins?' He had been starting to lose hope of finding the Englishman. Anton and Ivan's interrogation of the pub staff in Torremolinos had come to nothing – other than all the pub staff quitting; he'd had to close the place for a week as a result. But now this. He regarded Lydia warily.

'Yes,' said Lydia with a sweet smile. 'Lovely couple. Earthy.'

Sergei exchanged glances with Anton and Ivan before turning back to Lydia. 'Where exactly did you say this property is?'

'I didn't. But it doesn't matter if you're not interested – '

Sergei leaned forward, all trace of his cheery demeanour gone, 'Don't play games with me, Lydia. Where is Mullins?'

'Oh, so you do know him? I rather thought you might. To be honest, they didn't actually *say* they knew you, but Mrs Mullins had a bit of a queer turn when she saw your face in a newspaper story about some poor chap losing his head in Ibiza. Your work?'

'What?'

'The decapitation? Oh, I don't mind, by all accounts he was a bit of a scumbag.'

'You are asking me if I murdered a man?'

'Yes. No need to be shy, Sergei. I've killed more than a few myself.'

'*You* have killed men?'

'Oh yes. I'm quite prolific,' she smiled, 'I suppose I'm a bit of a serial killer really.'

'Really? So why are you telling me this information?'

'Because we're friends, darling. It came to my attention that you might be looking for Mullins, and so here I am. You see, I'm not so much selling you the pub, as the landlords.' Sergei picked up his glass and took a drink. Lydia followed suit. 'Mmmm, very nice. You can really taste the grain. It is grain, isn't it?'

Sergei ignored the question. 'So you want money for the location of Mullins, is that it?'

'Oh no, nothing so vulgar, Sergei. I want the same thing as you.'

'And that is?'

'I want Mr and Mrs Mullins dead.'

Sergei sniffed dismissively. 'But if you are big serial killer, Lydia, why don't you kill them yourself?'

'For a couple of reasons: first and foremost, because I believe that's a pleasure that you want to indulge in far more than I do, and so I bring this information to you as a gift.'

'And secondly?'

'Because I want something more. Not money, not Keith, not Michelle. And I believe you have the resources to get it for me.'

'What is this?'

Lydia took a sip of her vodka and smiled. 'Tell me, Sergei, do you believe in vampires?'

16

THE CITROËN'S HEADLIGHTS raked the darkness as David drove Underwood down the driveway away from the house. In his rear view mirror, the lights of the car behind them flashed intermittently. In the moments in between he caught glimpses of Underwood on the back seat gazing out of the window. On his face was the blissed-out expression he sometimes wore after feeding. The donors of tonight's meal were in the car that followed them – a Dutch banker and his wife that had come over for the resurrection ceremony, and had been vacationing in Cadiz in the time since. Up ahead, David could now make out the end of the driveway. He felt a prickle of sweat break out across his brow. Which way should he turn?

Last night, Underwood had said he'd changed his mind about making Michelle his bride, and he'd been game for going somewhere other than *La Reina de* bloody *Corazones*. But Underwood's decisions were as fickle as his moods. Sure, he'd changed his mind last night, but after a day's slumber in the coffin, he could easily have changed it back again. David hadn't had the chance to raise the topic earlier; Underwood had been absorbed in chatting with his guests as he'd breakfasted on their blood through I.V. tubes. The Dutchman had been explaining the single European currency and its current position in the international money market. Underwood had listened with fascination but David had found himself tuning-out, preoccupied as he was with his concerns for their night's social schedule. He'd wondered – cautiously optimistic – if Underwood might invite the banker and his wife out for dinner with them. But once he'd fed, Underwood had thanked them for coming – adding that they must do it again sometime – then asked David to show them out and to prepare the car.

Now, as he brought the car to a stop at the junction with the road, David looked for Underwood in the rear view mirror.

'So, where to, Milord?'

Underwood met his eyes. 'Hmm?'

'Last night you were saying you fancied going somewhere different this evening.'

'Oh … yes. Anywhere you particularly fancy?'

'In Almacena?'

'Oh no, I've had enough of that dull little town. Let's go somewhere with a bit more life, shall we? Where do you recommend?'

'Well, I'm a bit of a stranger here myself, Milord, but I know if we turn right we'll eventually hit the road for Seville.'

'And how long will it take to get to Seville?'

David shrugged. 'I dunno. Two hours?'

'Hmm, bit of a jaunt then. Still, I'm sure we can stop off at a tavern somewhere along the way. Turn right, Flinch – let's see what the night throws at us.'

'Yes, sir.'

The cold fist that had been gripping David's heart relaxed. He flicked on the indicator light and turned the wheel away from Almacena. In the rear view mirror, he saw the Dutch couple's car pull out of the drive and turn in the opposite direction. 'Looks like your breakfast companions are going into town, sir.'

'Yes. Nice chap, wasn't he? Do you know him?'

'No, he was just a name on the Sect database – guests over for your resurrection, you know? I gave him and a few others a ring yesterday, so we're all set up with donors until the end of the week.'

'Oh, good show, always nice to know where one's next meal is coming from.' Underwood closed his eyes and sat back. 'No risk factors any more; quiet, domesticated – some might even say civilised.'

'Well, certainly more civilised than murdering people in dark alleyways, Milord.'

'But one never knows whom one will find in a dark alley, Flinch: a harlot or a lady, a cutthroat or a king? Every night's a lucky dip. I'll miss that.'

David didn't like this. He thought for some compensatory remark. 'Well, yes, but at least you don't have to worry about Scotland Yard or the FBI chasing you down the alley afterwards.'

Underwood laughed. 'Ah, but that's all part of the fun, Flinch; the thrill of the chase – whether one is the hunter or the hunted. It's all good sport, and anyway, the Yard and the Feds are nothing to worry about. Ah, but the SS – that was another story.'

'What? You had the SS after you?'

'Oh yes. I've had just about everything after me at some point or other.'

'I've seen some of Arthur's wartime souvenirs, but I don't know anything about the SS. What happened?'

Underwood shook his head. 'Oh no, Flinch – you're the storyteller this evening, not me. Tonight, it's my turn to hear all about you.'

'Well, there isn't really much to tell, sir.'

'You mean there isn't much you wish to share, Flinch. Anyone raised as a Flinch has a story; the question is, whether or not they are willing to tell it. However, we had a deal – *quid pro quo* – I've told you mine; now you have to tell me yours.'

'Yeah, but your story spans centuries, sir. You've only given me the opening chapter.'

'And that's all you're ever likely to get if you don't honour your side of the bargain.'

David sighed quietly to himself, but Underwood, with his acute sense of hearing, heard him.

'Oh, don't worry, Flinch, you can trust me to keep things in the strictest confidence. Tell you what, have a think about how you want to tell your story, and then as soon as we spy a suitable watering hole we can pull in and you can tell me everything over a coffee or whatever it is that fuels your chatterbox. In the meantime, why not pop on one of those musical tapes of yours? I still have much catching up to do on the popular music front.'

David reached into the glove compartment and fished for a tape. He was getting bored with the tapes they had, and he made a mental note to go into town tomorrow and buy either a CD player or something that could play MP3s. He rummaged deep, hoping to find something different, and pulled out a cassette of Pink Floyd's "Dark Side of the Moon". Satisfied, he flipped the tape from the box and pushed it into the machine.

It was shortly into side two of the tape that they crested a hill and David saw the neon sign winking in the blackness like a rude joke. It was about a quarter of a mile ahead; a red neon outline of a naked woman, breasts like baby bottles, and one of her long legs kicking high above a couple of buildings enclosed by a high wall with a gated entrance. Beyond the sign, the dark farmland rolled on unbroken for miles. How far was it to the next town? Jesus, *was* there a next town? There had to be a motorway turning for Seville soon, didn't there? Had he taken a wrong turn? He drove on past the neon stripper.

'What was that?' said Underwood.

David turned down the volume on the cassette player. 'Sorry?'

'We just went past a place.' Underwood turned, looking out of the back window, but the flashing sign was now obscured by trees.

David didn't slow down. 'Oh, that. That was just some kind of strip club or pole dancing place.'

'Pole dancing?'

'Yeah, naked women swinging themselves around on poles on stage.'

'Gymnastics?'

'Not exactly. I can't imagine you'll find any budding Olga Korbuts in there.'

'I'm sorry Flinch, but this isn't making any sense to me at all. Let's turn back and investigate.'

'Er, no, really Milord, you don't want to go in there, it's gonna be full of sad yokels tossing themselves off under tables.'

'How do you know? Have you ever been there?'

'No, but – '

'No buts, Flinch – that place is the first sign of life we've seen since leaving home. I'm growing impatient to hear your story, and I, for one, would love to see how a woman dances with a pole.'

'But we could take the motorway for Seville, sir. There are bound to be some hotels, diners – nice places where we could eat and – '

'Oh, *hang* the nice places! That club looks like much more fun.'

David continued to drive on. 'It won't be.'

Underwood leaned forward so that his face was behind David's ear. 'I shan't tell you again Flinch, you have your orders.'

David set his jaw and slowed the car to a stop. He did a three-point turn and drove back in the direction they had come. As they passed the line of trees the neon stripper re-emerged in the distance. Underwood shifted to where he could see better and chuckled at the sight.

'I say! She looks like she's having a good time.'

'That's because she's a sign, sir. The other one where she's crying over her pay cheque doesn't attract quite as many wankers.'

Underwood laughed. 'Oh very droll, Flinch, very droll.'

As he signalled to turn in, David noticed that behind the scrub trees, the high walls surrounding the place were topped with iron spikes; along with the big iron gates, it gave the impression of the place being more like a secure compound than a nightclub. Maybe they needed the barrier to keep mobs of protesting locals locked out – not that there *were* any locals this far out. Then another idea occurred to him: what if they needed the wall not to keep people out, but to keep people in? The thought chilled him, and he dismissed it as absurd as he drove through the gates and into the front car park. There were only two other cars. David parked and turned off the engine. Underwood got out and stretched. He smiled up at the sign, then looked around.

'Not exactly busy here, is it?'

'Well, it's only ten, sir,' said David as he got out. 'Still dinner time for a lot of people. I don't imagine it'll be getting busy for another hour or so.'

'Yes. Either that or the girls are ugly, eh?' He gave a short laugh and slapped David on the shoulder. 'Come on, this is on me.'

David didn't follow. He was looking at the other building set further back from the club. Like the club, it was low-set. Light filtered around the closed shutters in some of the windows. He noticed that the windows were all barred. Nothing unusual about that in this part of Spain, but he couldn't shake the feeling of disquiet he got from the high, spike-crested walls.

Underwood stopped and turned back to him. 'Come on, Flinch. What's the matter?'

David pointed in a general sweep to the walls that surrounded them. 'What do you reckon they need these walls for?'

Underwood shrugged. 'Security, I imagine – what else?'

'A spiked wall around a strip club?'

'Why not?'

David rubbed the stubble on his chin thoughtfully. 'You know, there's still a thriving slave trade in Europe.'

Underwood smiled and pointed at the neon stripper. 'And so you think what? That our buxom friend here is a slave? Oh really, Flinch, I hardly think that they would be advertising with such gay abandon if she were.'

'Well, you never know.'

'Oh, I think we do. That wall's at least thirty years old – as is this building – but the sign there is nearly new, I'd say. For all we know, this might have been a warehouse or small factory until recently. The spiked walls are just a leftover from then.'

David looked again at the wall. It *was* old, and even in the dark he could see that the spikes were rusty and broken in places. He shrugged, and wandered over to join Underwood. 'Yeah, you're probably right. It just seemed so odd being around a strip club, you know?'

'Yes, of course. It *is* out of keeping. But I like the fact that you spotted that. It shows you'll make a good guardian; you've obviously a keen nose for things irregular – and that could save both our skins one night.' He gave David another cheery pat on the shoulder as they walked up to the club.

Above the door in red neon cursive script, the name, *El Chupeton* glowed beside a pair of pouting lips. 'The Love Bite', said Underwood, and he turned to David as he pushed open the front door. 'Sounds like my kind of place.'

They stepped into a small anteroom that was ripe with the smell of cigarette smoke and body odour. A fat, bearded man sat behind a counter talking to two other men on stools. These two rose as Underwood and David entered, their eyes running up and down the new arrivals as if weighing them up. Obviously the bouncers, thought David. They were both in their thirties – more fat than muscle, but formidable-looking, nonetheless. One was bald and wore a thick moustache. The other had curly hair, cropped at the sides but long on the top and back. It hung down his neck and shoulders in a magnificent mullet that glistened with hair gel.

The man seated behind the counter grunted. '*Dos?*'

Underwood beamed and replied, '*Si, por favor.*'

He took out his money clip and paid the mumbled entry fee. Then, the two bouncers parted like a fat sea and allowed Underwood and David to push through the doors into the club.

It was a long, dark, low-ceilinged room with a stage at the far end that extended out among the tables in the classic runway style beloved of strip clubs the world over. At the end of the runway a skinny blonde was grinding around a pole to a booming Spanish dance track.

Underwood leaned closer to David. 'Ahh. So, that's the pole, is it?'

David nodded. 'Yeah.'

'A fireman's pole?'

'Yeah.'

'And so, what? She just wraps herself around it?'

'Yeah. And, well, dances ... sort of.'

'Oh. Oh well, I suppose it's an innovation of sorts.' Underwood glanced about the place. 'Anyway, where shall we sit?'

David looked around. The place was almost empty but for two men, each the sole occupant of a table on either side of the dancing girl. Another bouncer sat on a stool in the shadows near the entrance to the stage. All the other tables on the floor – perhaps twenty or more – were all empty.

David pointed to a table at the back of the room near the bar. 'Maybe over there? We stand a better chance of hearing each other.'

Underwood nodded and they went over and sat down. A topless waitress appeared and asked in Spanish what they wanted to drink. Underwood ordered a gin and tonic. David asked if they served coffee. The waitress closed her eyes against the stupidity of the question and gave the barest shake of her head. David ordered a lemonade.

'Hmm, not a local girl,' said Underwood once the waitress had gone.

'What?'

'The waitress – she's not Spanish. Hard to pinpoint the accent, but she sounded East European.' He pointed to the girl on the stage. 'She doesn't look like a native either.'

David nodded. 'Families are pretty tight around here; church-going, supportive communities. I can't imagine too many local girls doing this sort of thing for a living – it'd be too shameful. These ladies were probably brought in from elsewhere.'

'Yes, I'd say you're right there.' Underwood turned to David and tapped the table. 'Anyway, come on, tell me everything.'

David sighed and sat forward. 'Where do you want me to start?'

'At the beginning, of course.'

David took out his cigarettes and lit one. 'Well, I suppose it begins with my mum, back in the early seventies. She and her boyfriend were travelling around Europe in a VW camper. Hippies, you know?'

Underwood shook his head. 'No.'

'Oh, well no, of course not. Well, they were young and just, sort of, bumming around – doing jobs like grape picking and stuff. Just making enough money to buy food and petrol, I suppose; knocking around with similar travellers from all over the world who were doing the same thing – hanging out, getting high, having a laugh, you know?'

'This is "hippies", is it? They sound like tramps.'

'Yeah, well, I suppose they do a bit, but it was all a bit groovier than tramps.'

'*Groovier?*'

David smiled. 'Never mind. Anyway, they were travelling in Andalucia and they wound up olive-picking in the groves of Casa Underwood – that's what we always called your place.'

Underwood nodded.

'Anyway, as I say, they were working there and Arthur noticed my mum and … well, basically, he fancied the arse off her.'

'The dirty old devil. What did he do, kidnap her?'

'No … at least, not literally. He started inviting her and her boyfriend – Jim was his name – up to the house for food, wine and weed. He didn't smoke it himself, but he grew some for social occasions.'

'I see. Did he make a habit of frolicking with the farm hands? What about that Magda woman you said he was with?'

'I don't know if she was around at that time, but if she was, she would have known the score. Arthur wasn't just getting his leg over, he was doing his duty; as you so charmingly put it last night, he was "breeding heirs".'

'And he did so with women outside of the Sect?'

'I don't know, but in this case – in *my* case – yeah, he did. Martin, John and Lydia all had mothers from within the Sect, but I was the only one whose mum was an outsider – something that Lydia always took great pleasure in reminding me of. Not that I cared, mind you. In fact, I was bloody glad of it. If my mum had been hard-core Sect like Lydia's parents, I might have grown up as sick and twisted as she is. But anyway, after a few of these little get-togethers of theirs, Arthur decided he wanted her to be the next Mother Flinch – his phrase, not mine. And for this to happen, she'd have to be inducted into the Sect.'

'What about her boyfriend?'

David looked down to where his hands rested on the table. 'Arthur bought him off. They were skint. Arthur offered them five thousand pounds for her to be a surrogate mother. I don't know if that's what they called it back then, but that's what it amounted to. Part of the deal was that Jim would make himself scarce until after the deed was done. Once Mum was pregnant, he said Jim could come back and he would set them up with a house in Almacena. Between the money and the house, it was a very tempting offer back then.'

'Ah. So they weren't worried about the dark nature of the Sect?'

'No, this was the early seventies – bands like Black Sabbath were in the charts; the Rolling Stones had done the whole *Satanic Majesties* thing; and

Arthur knew that lots of kids thought black magic was cool – so he pitched it to them as a kind of groovy black magic cult. He said that he was high up in the ranks of it, second only to Lord Underwood himself. He also sold them the idea of the Sect as a kind of funky Freemasons – an organisation that could make problems in life disappear, and doors that would otherwise be shut to the likes of them swing wide open.

'Well, Mum and Jim talked it over and, as I say, all in all it was a pretty sweet deal. Neither of them really believed in all that black magic bollocks – they figured it was nothing more than a bunch of old age pensioners dancing naked round a bonfire.'

'And since you were evidently born, I take it they agreed?'

'Yeah. Arthur gave Jim an envelope of cash to fuck off with until after it was all over, and Mum moved into Casa Underwood.'

The waitress came back with their drinks. She put them down and left without a word. Underwood picked up his gin and took a sip. He wrinkled his nose at the taste but put the glass down without comment. 'So, what was her name, your mother?'

'Kathy. Kathleen Smith. Arthur started shagging her right from the first night. He'd go to her room, do it, and then skulk off back to his own bed. She never talked much about that, as you can imagine. Basically, she endured it, keeping her fingers crossed that he'd hit the baby jackpot sooner rather than later, which, it turns out, he did. I was conceived in the first week, apparently, but she couldn't go anywhere until after I was born. She was stuck there.

'Arthur waited until she was five months pregnant before inducting her into the Sect. He wanted her to be, you know, *round-bellied* before he did it – wanted to show me off to the gathered guests. Apparently, that's quite a big deal.'

Underwood nodded. 'Yes, part of the Mother and Child ceremony.'

David stubbed out his cigarette and took a sip of his lemonade. 'Did you come up with all that stuff?'

'Oh, God, no – that was Vanessa.'

'Vanessa?'

'Yes, Lady Vanessa Crichton. She was the original architect of the Sect and all of the ceremony and custom that goes on within it. She was a Satanist. Lovely woman – frightfully pretty. She bore Matthias's first son and heir.'

'Really? So I'm related to her? Was she in love with Matthias?'

528

'No, she was in love with *me*.'

'That must have been weird.'

'Oh, it's all been weird, Flinch – right from day one.' Underwood raised his glass in a toast. 'And long may it continue to be.' He gave David a few seconds to clink his glass; when he didn't, Underwood grinned and took a drink anyway. 'So you were saying – she was inducted? And how did that go?'

'Well, she was sane, so it went badly. All the local Sect were invited, robes were donned, a chicken got its throat cut – I'm sure you know the drill. All this didn't trouble her, she'd expected as much. But then … then the lid came off the coffin, and she was introduced to you. That – that scared her.'

Underwood raised an eyebrow. 'Charming.'

'Well, you can understand why, can't you? I mean – you've never seen yourself lying there, dead but not dead – it's a pretty fucking scary sight, I can tell you. She freaked out, they had to grab her and hold her to stop her from running out of there. She was screaming – saying that she wanted out, clutching her belly and saying that they couldn't have me. That pissed Arthur right off. Up until then, Mum had figured Arthur was just a dirty old man who wanted a baby. But now, that mask dropped and the real Arthur showed himself. He had her dragged back to the coffin, grabbed her by the hair and pulled her so that her face came close up against yours. Then he told her that there was no out – she was Sect now. Told her that she had been honoured above all the other women to bear the vampire's servant, and if ever she tried to run or do anything to harm the child then you, Milord, would come after her and her loved ones, rip out their throats and damn them for all eternity.'

Underwood chuckled and gently clapped his hands. 'Oh, bravo! What a rotter.'

'It's not bloody funny!'

'I know, I know, of course it's not – but you never knew Arthur like I did, he was such a card. Oh dear, really, I *am* sorry – do go on.'

'He was *sick*, Milord – *sick*.'

'Oh, no he wasn't, he was just good at putting the willies up people. I'm sure he was very fond of your mother.'

David couldn't hide his disgust. 'Christ almighty, you …' He shook his head and looked away.

'Oh, come on David, I'm sorry – really. Please, do go on. I presume Arthur's display of temper had the desired effect?'

'Well, if you mean, did it terrify her into absolute submission, then yeah, it did.'

'Yes, I'm sure it did.' Underwood took a drink. 'But when did she tell you all of this? Obviously not when she was bouncing you on her knee as a toddler?'

'No. She kept it all in until shortly before she died. She always gave me the accepted Sect version of events – stuff that would make me happy and proud to be a Flinch: about how great you were, and what a wonderful man Arthur was, and my brothers – especially Martin, who was due to become guardian when you were revived. I was brought up to believe in you as an almost god-like being; and that I was the last of a noble and heroic line of your defenders. Of course she was crap at communicating this with any sense of authority or belief. I could see the fear and dread in her eyes when she said all of this stuff, but she always had my appointed godparents, Uncle Bob and Auntie Iris to help her.'

'Godparents?'

'Yeah. Arthur's idea. Bob and Iris were part of his inner circle – they were *my* guardians. Their job was to make sure that I was safe and well, but also to make sure I believed in the gospel according to Arthur; that I talked about you with the right balance of happiness, reverence and duty. They were like a pair of fanatical Sunday school teachers, only their god was you. Arthur sent them because he knew Mum wasn't versed enough in Sect bollocks to raise me properly in *the tradition.*'

David spoke bitterly and as he did so his eyes fell repeatedly upon Underwood's gin and tonic. He felt an almost overwhelming desire to snatch it from the table and to drink it off at a gulp. He closed his eyes and took a deep breath.

Underwood lit a cigarette and flashed the case to David. 'Hmm. Well, not the perfect Sect upbringing, I have to say. Your mother must have been quite a looker for Arthur to have deviated so far from the normal breeding protocols. Here, have a fag.'

David took a cigarette and bent to Underwood's offered light. 'Yeah, she was, at least before she met Arthur. After that I suppose you could say that she went downhill. She became a drinker – a serious drinker. She had problems with anorexia and all kinds of other anxiety disorders because she was living in fear – not just for herself, but for me as well.'

Underwood sipped his drink, watching David thoughtfully. Then he said, 'Hmm ... we've moved ahead in time somewhat, haven't we? Let's go back. What happened after the initiation. She ... settled in?'

'*Settled in?*'

'For lack of a better word.'

David's cigarette trembled slightly as he drew on it. 'Yeah she ... *settled in*. She knew she had to survive in that place for nine months or more, and if she and I were going to get through it alive, she'd have to start going along with it. But after the initiation ceremony, that wasn't so difficult; she let herself become indoctrinated. She came to believe that she was indeed chosen and that you were a powerful demon, a prince of Hell, and that there really was no escaping you either in this world of the next.'

'Yes, that is a standard intimidation tactic, we've been using it since we started out.'

'"*We*"? Who's "we"?'

'Why, the firm, of course – Underwood and Flinch. Who else?'

David took a drink of lemonade, hating it for not being vodka, and returned the smile sarcastically. 'Of course – who else?'

'So – you were born. Did she move into the house with whatsisname?'

'Jim. No.'

'Oh? What happened there, then? Run off, did he?'

'Not exactly, no. Once Arthur was sure Mum was properly indoctrinated, Jim was allowed to come and visit her, but only under supervision. Bob and Iris – before they got the job of being my godparents – got that job. So, with them watching, Mum made an act of telling Jim how happy she was, what a great place Casa Underwood was, and so on. Mum knew from the look on Jim's face that he didn't believe her. He went away that day, but came back the next; he ignored the minders, took her by the hands and pleaded with her to leave with him. "Forget the money", he said, "let's go, let's just get out of here now."'

David paused to take a drag on his cigarette. 'Well, it got ... emotional, shall we say. Bob stepped in to pull him away while Iris went to fetch Arthur. Jim started shouting, fighting with Bob, then some of Arthur's boys turned up and dragged him away. Mum never saw him again. Arthur told her he'd paid him a lot of money to disappear, but she never bought that. She always thought Arthur did away with him.'

Underwood nodded. 'Hmm.'

'What? You think that's true?'

'Well, yes. This Jim fellow had become a problem for Arthur, and under the circumstances, murder *would* have been his first choice. I'm sorry.'

David nodded, his jaw set tight. 'Like I say, that was what she always thought anyway.' He drew on his cigarette and the coal at the tip glowed fiercely. 'Anyway, into this world of love and happiness, I was born. Arthur was happy that I was a boy after the disappointment of Lydia being a girl – not that he didn't love her, of course, but being born a Flinch without nuts does kind of write you off, doesn't it?'

Underwood said nothing.

David continued. 'But anyway, shortly after I was born he threw a party for me. My brothers and sister – along with their parents – were summoned, and for the first time Mum got talking with the mums of my siblings. They were all very well-to-do, Sect born and bred, with big houses in places like Oxford and Windsor. Arthur didn't give them any of these things, he didn't need to – they were all Old Money. But Mum couldn't see why her kid should have anything less, so when the party was over she told Arthur that she wanted a house too – not in Alamcena, but in England. And to her complete surprise, he agreed – not so much because he felt she'd been indoctrinated to the point she could be trusted, but more to do with the fact that he was sick and tired of me screaming the house down at all hours.'

Underwood chuckled. 'And who could blame him, eh?'

'The only condition was that she accepted Bob and Iris as my guardian godparents.'

'And, of course, she did?'

'Well, what choice did she have? It was either that or stay in Almacena with that nutcase.'

'Indeed.'

'So, he did what she wanted; he set her up with a house and an allowance.'

'Where was the house?'

'Brighton. Well, no – Hove, actually. But he also saw to it that Bob and Iris had a nice little place nearby so they wouldn't have too far to walk when they came around for their visits.'

Underwood smiled. 'You clearly dislike Bob and Iris now, but how did you feel about them as a child?'

'Well, I was a toddler, I was easy to please. They used to come round and bring me toys and sweets, and tell me stories about my family, and you … so yeah, when I was very young I liked them well enough. But I could always sense a change in Mum when they came round. She would get tense, nervous.'

'So you grew to dislike them?'

'Yes. I grew to feel tense and nervous around them as well, but unlike Mum I didn't understand why, you know?'

A female voice broke in. 'English? You wanna dance?' A topless woman in her late twenties sidled up to Underwood and pushed her fingers through his hair. Underwood grinned and started to rise, but the woman pushed him down into his seat. He laughed.

'Well, how am I to dance if you won't let me stand up?'

'She means a lap dance,' said David.

'What? You mean she wants to dance on my lap? In *those* heels? No, thank you.'

The woman, who was only wearing high heels and a red satin bikini bottom, brushed herself against Underwood's arm like a cat that wants to be fed.

'No, she dances for you, giving you an up-close eyeful but, er, you can't touch her.'

'Not touch her? That's an interesting development.' Underwood reached out and touched the woman on the arm, but she swatted his hand away.

'No touch! Touch is extra. See him.' She indicated a man propped up against the bar. It was the bearded man who had earlier been taking admissions; he smiled and nodded a greeting.

Underwood seemed amused. 'Oh, I see – a taster, is it? Well, thank you, missy, but not tonight. Maybe some other time.'

The woman uncoiled from Underwood's side of the table and moved to David, who held up a hand in refusal. 'Same here, love. *No gracias.*'

Rejected, she dropped the sex kitten act, adjusted her panties, and walked away in the direction of one of the single drinkers near the stage.

'Funny, that,' said Underwood. 'You know, I think you may be right.'

'Right? About what?'

Underwood was delicately passing the hand he'd touched the woman's arm with under his nose. 'Fear.'

'Fear? What – you can smell that from her arm?'

'I can smell it from her everything, Flinch – the girl positively reeks of it. And the accent; again – foreign.'

'No. She's Spanish.'

Underwood shook his head. 'South American. Hard to say where, exactly, I haven't been down that way for a good while.' Underwood turned to the big man at the bar. He was looking to where the woman was now dancing for one of the lone drinkers. 'And while I'm no Sherlock Holmes, I'll bet our bearded friend there is the cause of her fear.'

'Him and his mates on the door, eh?'

'And over there,' Underwood pointed to the bouncer to the left of the stage, then to an area of pitch darkness on its right, 'and there.'

David squinted at the darkness trying to get a glimpse of whatever Underwood could see. 'I can't see in the dark, sir. How many are there?'

'One on either side of the stage. So, with Beardy here and the chaps on the door, that makes five. Possibly some others backstage as well, or in that other building.'

'We should drink up and go. I'll contact the police tomorrow.'

'Police?' Underwood laughed. 'What do you expect them to do?'

'I don't know, check it out?'

'Oh, I have no doubt that they check it out quite regularly, Flinch. Perhaps that's even one of them over there right now with that woman's bottom wiggling in his face.'

'Alright, whatever – but we should go anyway, on principle if nothing else.'

'No, no, there's no need for that. Their only offence as far as I'm concerned is their gin.'

'Yeah – very funny.' David stubbed out his cigarette and rose. 'Come on, let's get out of here.'

Underwood grabbed him by the wrist. 'Sit down, Flinch – I think you forget yourself. *I* decide when and where we go, and I like it here.'

David tried to pull his wrist free. Underwood's grip didn't even tremble.

'Well, I *don't*. There's a bad vibe here, a very bad vibe.'

'A bad vibe? Is that what you call it these days?' He sniffed the air. 'Yes, so much more here than the smell of cigarettes, sweat, and sour beer, isn't there? A subtle bouquet of misery and desperation ... and something else.' He sniffed again. 'Ah yes ... evil.'

'Then why are we staying?'

'As I said, I like it here; I'm a vampire who has spent the last fifty years lying down in a closed box. To me, the heady aroma of human suffering is like a breath of fresh air.'

David shook his head, appalled. 'How can you *like* it?'

'Perhaps because it so often marks my feeding grounds.' Underwood's smile fell and his face darkened. 'Now, sit down. I shan't tell you again.'

David looked at where Underwood gripped his wrist then lifted his eyes to the vampire's. 'Do I have a choice?'

Underwood released him. 'Always.'

David sat down. 'Alright, but if I'm going to stay here and go on with this story …' His eyes went to Underwood's drink where the beads of condensation had settled into a wet pool at the base.

Underwood smiled. 'Ah yes, I understand.' He held up a hand to the waitress. '*Señorita, dos gin y tonicas, por favor?*' He turned back to David. 'Now then, where were we?'

17

'I DON'T remember.'

'I do. You were telling me about your Uncle Bob and Auntie Iris; about how you liked them, but grew to feel uncomfortable when they came to call.'

'Yeah. Well that about covers it. They used to talk, them and Mum; I'd be playing or watching TV or whatever, and their eyes would always, sort of, flit over in my direction. Bob and Iris always cool, Mum always nervous, fearful. She told me that they were the ones who always arranged our Spanish holidays when we'd go out to see Daddy.'

'How often did you visit?'

'Once or twice a year. Me, Mum, Bob and Iris, all off on our jolly holidays.'

'Is that more sarcasm? Or were they really jolly?'

'Actually, for me, they *were* jolly. I forgot any sense of Mum's anxiety, there. Spain was hot, sunny, alien – in a good way, and Dad's house – your house – was vast; to me, it was like a labyrinth. And it had a pool, too, where I first learned to swim. And of course, I met my siblings. Our visits were often scheduled to coincide with theirs. Martin and John were older and tended to hang out together, but Lydia and I … we hit it off right from the start.'

The waitress returned with their drinks. She set them down and left. David drew one of the glasses towards him and looked down into the sparkling liquid.

'Chin chin.' Underwood raised his glass in a toast. 'Here's to the firm, eh? New blood, old blood, Underwood and Flinch.'

David clinked his drink with Underwood's. 'Cheers.' He brought it to his lips, hesitating as he scented the aroma of gin. In his mind the arguments against taking a drink clamoured to be heard, but he chose not to hear them. In a very short time, he knew, they would fade like ghosts in the morning air. He took a sip. He held the liquid in his mouth for a moment, savouring the bittersweet chill. Then he swallowed.

'Anyway,' said Underwood brightly. 'You were saying about yourself and Lydia.'

'Yeah, we became best friends. We were always together, running around that big old house and grounds; making camps among gnarly old olive trees and in the sheds and outbuildings. Arthur would take us out in the Citroën with him when he went into Almacena, or sometimes for days out to the lake at Zahara. I remember he used to hold our hands when we walked together. He used to wear this white Panama hat – he used to put it on *my* head, and we'd all laugh because it was so big.' David smiled. 'He could be funny, you know? And he loved us, I knew that … and … we loved him too.' He took another long sip of the gin.

'He took me down to your coffin right from the start, back before I can even remember. Sometimes he'd take both of us, me and Lyddie together. I guess he wanted us to get a sense of you, to understand that there was nothing to be afraid of. And we *weren't* afraid. I had a toy coffin at home – courtesy of Bob and Iris – and I'd come to think of it, not as a symbol of death, but of you – you the powerful, you the magnificent. If anything, I felt a sense of awe around it. I got a lot of that from Arthur, of course, he was always a bit melodramatic down there, talking about you and gesturing to the coffin like it was a person. He'd tell us how lucky we were, because one day, long after he was gone, you would rise again, and we'd be able to serve you just as he'd done.'

'Did he ever open my coffin?'

David shook his head. 'No. Not until my official baptism into the Sect.'

Underwood smiled. 'And how did that go? Better than for your mother, I hope.'

'No. I'd say it was about the same.'

Underwood laughed. 'Oh dear, was I that frightful?'

'I don't know. I kind of … lost it before I even saw you. I mean, I was a little kid for fuck's sake; it was dark, smoky, torch-lit, loads of hooded Sect nutters looming over me chanting all sorts of bollocks. Arthur was hooded too, with blood all over his hands – sure, it was just chicken blood, but blood's blood when you're a child, you know? And then, well then I just lost it.' He took a drink.

'Oh dear, I am sorry. Under normal circumstances I would have known the young Flinch all his life. I'd be standing there in person, an old avuncular friend and idol. But it sounds like your negative emotions down there must've triggered my unconscious defences, turning your fear against you and playing tricks on your mind.'

'Oh yeah, they did that, alright. I believed you were rising! And there was nothing glorious about it, believe me; your fingers curling around the lid of the coffin, the nails long and spider-like.' He shook his head. 'They had to hold me, Martin and others – I was screaming, struggling to get away. Arthur must've known it was the hallucinations, but he pressed on anyway. They held me still while he daubed my forehead with blood. Mum trying to soothe me, calm me down. Then they took the lid off for real. Arthur telling me it was all right, and there was nothing to fear. "Look upon the face of the master," he was saying. "Behold the Lord Underwood!" He turned my face to look at you, but oh, I wasn't having any of it. I wouldn't open my eyes again. I guess he decided the best thing to do was just carry on as if I had. He said a load of stuff in a language I didn't understand, then he let Mum and my brothers take me out.'

'That must have been quite traumatising for you.'

'Yeah, just a bit! After we went home, Bob and Iris tried to set me straight on the matter, telling me I'd been seeing things because I'd let fear control me. Which made absolutely no sense, but I knew Mum wanted me to go along with it, and so I did. But after the ceremony, I was more like her; the two of us pretending to them and each other that we accepted it all. But we didn't. I was changed. I didn't revere you anymore; I feared you.'

'Oh, dear. Well, that explains a lot, doesn't it? Did you overcome it, or just bluff it out?'

'I bluffed it. I got real good at hiding my dread and loathing and playing the dutiful Flinch boy.' He took a drink. 'Mum and me continued to go to Spain every summer. She'd spend most of the time pissed in the bars around town. She didn't fit in with the mums and stepdads of my siblings, and she didn't want to either. Then, when I was thirteen I was allowed to travel alone. She hated me leaving her, but at the same time, she was glad she didn't have to come any more, so she didn't complain. And I was happy too, to be honest. Not just because she was getting out of it, but also because – and I'm ashamed to admit it – her being around always made it harder for me, you know? When I was very young it didn't matter, but as I got older ... well, it did. It was like she was pissed all the time. She hated everyone and everyone hated her. They didn't say that, of course, but Lydia told me so.'

Underwood smiled. 'How nice of her. So you two were still pals, were you?'

'Oh yeah. Thick as thieves. In the years after our parents stopped coming, we spent almost all our time together.' David sat with his back to the stage, his features deep in shadow, but Underwood noted with interest a sudden flush of heat at his collar.

'You were obviously very fond of each other.'

David smiled thinly. 'Yeah. Once upon a time.'

'What went wrong?'

'Nothing, we – we just grew apart over the years, we're very different; and that – that became more obvious as time went by. We fell out when were in our teens.'

Underwood watched the blush rise up David's neck. 'I see.' He lit a cigarette. 'You loved her?'

David sat up sharply. '*What?*'

'I asked you if you loved her; surely not an uncommon emotion between brother and sister.'

'Oh, well, yeah. Yeah, I suppose I did.' David lifted his glass and took a large gulp.

Underwood's nostrils flared minutely. He smiled. 'But nothing more?'

'*More?* More than what?'

'Oh come, come, Flinch. We're both men of the world. She's only your half-sister after all. It's perfectly natural – '

'*What?* What are you suggesting?'

Underwood calmly finished his sentence, ' – to want to sleep with someone you love.'

'Jesus! I didn't love her like *that!*' David grabbed his cigarettes and fumbled one from the pack.

'Oh, such bristling indignation, Flinch. But I'm afraid your sweat betrays you. Either you slept with her, or you tried to and she turned you down. Which is it? Come on, you can tell me, we're pals after all.' He watched with amusement as David's unlit cigarette fell from between his fingers. 'Butterfingers.' Underwood opened his cigarette case and extended it. 'Here, take one of mine.'

David looked at the offered cigarettes for a full five seconds before taking one. Underwood clicked a flame from his lighter. David bent to accept it, all the time avoiding the vampire's eyes. 'You're very … perceptive, sir.'

'Yes, I am. Oh, I've had my suspicions for a while, of course. There's a definite *frisson* between the two of you, a kind of static. And, of course, there's the way you look at each other sometimes.'

'*Look at each other?* You mean, I look at her like *that?*'

Underwood laughed. 'No, no, no. It's not lust I see in your eyes – or hers. But there's definitely something there. Will you tell me what happened?'

David drained his glass and sighed. 'She was seventeen, I was fifteen. We'd … kissed the year before. Fooled around a bit, you know. We knew it was wrong and we weren't supposed to, but I think that made it all the more … I dunno.'

'Exciting?'

'Please,' David held up a hand. 'I can manage without the prompts. But yes … exciting.'

'Were you in love with her?'

'I thought so at the time, yeah, but, I was just a stupid kid. Of course, now I know it was just raging hormones on both our parts. She wanted me, I wanted her.'

'Interesting, you said *she* wanted *you,* first. Do you mean she started it?'

'Yeah, she did. But it was me who finished it.'

Underwood chuckled. 'Why am I not surprised? What happened? Guilt get the better of you, did it?'

David slammed the table with his flat of his hand. 'Yes! Damn you! You say that as if feeling guilt – not fucking my sister – was wrong!'

'Half-sister,' Underwood corrected.

'It's still fucking wrong, isn't it?'

Underwood shrugged. 'Well, that depends, doesn't it? It's not as if you were planning on starting a family together, were you? It was just a little hanky-panky. And you did love each other, after all.'

'No. I didn't say we loved each other. I loved her, yeah, but she … she was just having a bit of fun.'

'Well, good for her. There's nothing wrong with that. You're so Victorian, Flinch. Really, you should have just let the thing follow its own course. I'm sure it would have died a natural death soon enough, and who knows, maybe you two would be getting along a lot better now if it had.'

'Oh, pardon me, but do put a sock in it, Milord. You're talking out of your arse. It was *incest*, for God's sake.'

'Oh *piffle*, brothers and sisters have been doing it together since time immemorial.'

'What? That's no argument. Just because it's a primitive urge doesn't make it right. You could say the same about murder.'

'I often do.'

David shook his head and looked away, disgusted. 'Oh, what's the point in talking to you about it, you're completely fucking immoral.'

Underwood smiled. 'Perhaps. But at least I'm not judgmental,' he tapped David's glass. 'Another?'

'I can't, I'm driving.'

'We can call a cab.'

'You wanna get me pissed, do you?'

'I want to hear your story, and if it takes a drink or two to loosen your tongue, then so be it.' He gestured to the waitress to bring David another drink then turned back to him. 'Do go on. You were saying you finished it with Lydia. Was she upset?'

David snorted with contempt. 'No. Not at all. If anything she was amused. I told her that what were doing was wrong, and that we had to stop before our feelings got too deep.'

'What did she say?'

'She laughed in my face.'

Underwood laughed. 'Ouch! That must've smarted.'

'Yeah, it did.'

The waitress returned with David's drink. She put it down and took away his empty glass. David picked up the drink and took a mouthful. He swallowed it and crunched on an ice cube. 'I left Casa Underwood the next day. Never went back.'

Underwood's eyebrows arched. 'Really? You mean you didn't sort things out?'

'What was there to sort out? She laughed in my face, called me a stupid kid.'

'Well, you've just admitted that that much was true.'

'No, I was talking about me being stupid for doing it in the first place, not for finishing it. Finishing it was the only smart thing I did all summer. And anyway, if she was hurt, why did she laugh at me?'

'Self-defence? Some people hide their pain behind a mask of indifference, or even hostility.'

'Lydia? Bollocks.'

'As you like.' Underwood took a sip of his drink. 'But how did Arthur take your disappearance?'

'He was dead by then. John was the head of the family by that time.'

'Then how did John take it?'

David shrugged. 'No big deal. I was at school, final years, exams, you know? He used to check up on me, both directly by mail, and indirectly through Bob and Iris. But I just fed him the sort of reasonable excuses I knew he wanted to hear: first school commitments, then university, and then eventually the army. He had no argument with any of it, especially the army. Bob and Iris had been *reminding* me and mum for years that a spell in the army was expected of me. So, it was to everyone's relief when I joined up.'

'Including your own?'

'At that time I didn't really give a shit. All I knew was it made Mum happy; me doing my *duty*. After all, when you're a Flinch, you've gotta understand discipline, haven't you? Gotta be able to stand to attention; say "sir"; take a gun to bits and put it back together again.'

'Well, it certainly helps. I've had guardian Flinches with and without military experience and I've always found former serviceman to be considerably more effective. Did you see any action?'

'Yeah – and before you ask, no, I didn't kill anyone. I trained as a medic. '

'Ahh, yes, the ambulance man. May I ask, why?'

'I guess I prefer healing wounds to making them, Milord.'

'I see. You're quite the family rebel, aren't you?'

'I'll take that as a compliment.'

Underwood chuckled. 'Yes. So, where did you drive your military ambulance?'

'Bosnia.'

'Really? What happened there?'

'Well, we weren't there as combatants. We were UN, blue helmets, there to escort Bosnian Muslims to designated safe havens.'

'Why?'

'Because Bosnian Serbs were killing them. It was a genocide. There were thousands of them, refugees in their own country; it was unbelievable.'

'Mmmm. I see. And did *you* ever come under fire?'

'Yeah, artillery bombardment. We weren't the targets, supposedly, but we were in the target zone. It was an "accident".' David framed the word *accident* in air quotes.

'Oh, how unfortunate. And what was it like? How did you find it?'

'How do you think I bloody found it? It was terrifying.'

'Hmmm.' Underwood regarded him thoughtfully for a moment. 'Tell me,' he leaned in confidentially, 'did you ever think that perhaps your number was up?'

David moved back, drawing his drink with him. He looked down into it, bobbing and stirring the ice before muttering, 'Yeah.'

'And, who did you think of, at that darkest moment? Whose face came to mind?'

David looked up. 'Why are you asking me that?'

'I'm nosey. Tell me.'

'Well it wasn't yours, and that's for sure.' David waited for a reply, but Underwood gave none; he simply sat, watching David thoughtfully before giving a little smile and sitting back in his seat. David wondered if the vampire had somehow read his mind. 'What?'

'Nothing. That's all. Let's move on.'

'Move on?'

'Yes. Oh, we can discuss your military career on another occasion, but right now, I'm keen to move on in your life. What did you do next?'

'Well, when I got out of the army, I decided to become a paramedic.'

'And this was where? Hove?'

David took a drink and nodded. 'Yeah, home sweet Hove.'

'Your mother must have been happy to have you home safely.'

'Of course, yeah, but she was in a bad way by then. Bob and Iris had retired back to Spain once I'd joined the army. They were no longer needed, but Mum was sure she was still being watched by secret Sect operatives. She was paranoid, drunk, losing her grip. She ... she took her own life in 2000. Sleeping pills. She didn't feel any pain.'

'Oh no. I ... I am sorry to hear that.' Underwood's tone was sincere.

'Thanks. It was a merciful release really. She'd been ill for some time.'

'You said last night that it was I who killed her.'

'I was thinking in terms of cause and effect, Milord. You were the reason she started drinking, and the reason she continued; you and the organisation that's dedicated to your welfare.'

Underwood ground out his cigarette. 'Yes, well, it's most unfortunate. Certainly, she would have had nothing to fear from me; she sounds like she was a fine woman, David, and I'm sincerely sorry for all that happened to her.'

David said nothing. At a smattering of applause and a change of music, he turned to see a new dancer emerge onto the stage.

'And so, what then?' asked Underwood. 'You continued your ambulancing career in Hove?'

'No. Once Mum died I felt … I dunno … like the things that had held me … didn't hold me anymore. John and I wrote to each other; he offered to let me stay in Mum's house, but that – to be living in Flinch property – was the last thing I wanted. I told him to sell it. I wanted to sever the connection completely.'

'What did you do?'

'I trained as a TEFL teacher and went to work in Rome.'

'TEFL teacher? What on Earth is that?'

'Teaching English as a Foreign Language – I taught English to Italians.'

'Oh? And how did you like Rome?'

'I loved it. I loved the job, too. I was good at it. It was while I was there that I met Sarah.'

'Ah. A new love interest?'

David traced a line with his finger through the condensation on the side of his glass. He nodded. 'Yeah, but ... I don't want to talk about her.'

'Why ever not?'

'Because it's private, Milord. Isn't that enough?'

'Oh come on. I don't want to know your intimate secrets, Flinch. Just the basics. I need to get a better sense of who you are. I did no less for you last night.' He tapped the table. '*Quid pro quo.*'

David looked at the expectant face opposite him. What choice did he have? As much as he didn't like the thought of Sarah's name on those cruel lips, it was unavoidable; sooner or later, Underwood would get what he wanted. He shrugged and took a drink. 'She was a teacher, like me. She was already working at the language school when I joined it. She had a lot more experience than I did, so I had a good excuse to talk to her. But, obviously, getting classroom tips wasn't the only wasn't the only reason I wanted to talk to her; she was beautiful … but, she didn't care about it, you know? She didn't wear makeup or fancy clothes; she wore things that she liked regardless of fashion: simple, inexpensive things, but on her, always so ... well, beautiful. She always shopped in second hand stores and those little out of the way places where you find hidden treasures. She had a nose for them.'

'She sounds like your mother.'

David smiled. 'I suppose she was, yeah; my mother before she had the misfortune to stumble onto Casa Underwood. But anyway, we started seeing each other and ... well, we fell in love. We rented a flat together in Rome and stayed there for a year. It was a good time. The best. Of course, after a while, we started talking about kids; if that was gonna happen, she said she'd wanna be near her family, you know, for support. That and, of course, we'd need more money. So we moved back to England. She was from Bristol. We rented a flat there, about ten minutes from her mum and dad's house. She got a job with a local language school, but since I was gonna be the main family provider, I went back into the ambulance service.'

'Did you tell John any of this?'

'No. I'd managed to disappear from their radar and I wanted it to stay that way. The last thing I wanted was "the firm" as you call it getting wind of Sarah. I mean, what if we'd had a kid – a son?' He shook his head. 'No fucking way I wanted John hearing about a new branch on the Flinch family tree. I was using my mother's name by now – Smith. Good luck trying to find that, John, I thought. Well, it turns out he had done, of course; he had a private dick from the Sect keeping tabs on me.'

'Resourceful chap. But he never tried to contact you?'

'No.'

'Any idea why?'

'Well, I like to think he knew what I wanted, and that what I wanted wasn't them. He was a nice guy, John – normal, you know? He was Guardian; he had everything under control; there was no need to bother me. I guess he only wanted to know where I was just in case anything went wrong. Which of course, it eventually did, which is why I'm sitting here now and not him.'

'Or Lydia.'

'Or Lydia, yeah.'

'She was telling me that John passed her over for the job of Guardian because he thought she was *evil*?'

'Yeah. When he told me that on his deathbed it struck me as bizarre, but since then I've had more than enough opportunities to cop on to what he meant. She's a psychopath, Milord. Her only true loyalty is to herself. John saw that, and I guess he felt you'd be safer in my hands.'

'A psychopath? Well, I've had plenty of guardians that the headshrinkers would have called "psychopaths", I can tell you. And while I admit that they can sometimes be a handful, by and large, they've always served me very well.'

'Well if you'd prefer Lydia to be your guardian, Milord, I shall gladly step aside. But don't come crying to me when she gets up to whatever mischief she's got brewing in that nutty head of hers.'

Underwood smiled. 'Actually, I think you've rather misread the Lydia situation. Your sister doesn't mean me any harm. Quite the opposite, in fact.'

'What?'

'I don't want to go into any detail, Flinch, a gentleman doesn't discuss such things, but suffice it to say, her only "agenda" is … me.'

'You?'

'Yes. She, er, made her feelings plain last night before she cut herself with that ring.'

'What do you mean? Are you saying she *loves* you?'

'It's a tender subject.'

David laughed. 'You *are* joking?'

'Why would I joke about such a thing?'

'No, of course not. But fuck me!' David scratched his head as he tried to re-examine recent events in the light of what Underwood was saying. Then his expression changed to one of dawning belief. 'You know, it *is* plausible.'

'I'm glad you think so.'

'And you turned her down?'

'Well she didn't cut her throat because I said yes.'

'So she's in love with you, and you turned her down?'

'Please, Flinch. Let's drop it, shall we? You were telling me about Sarah and your time in Bristol.'

'Yeah, but, we can't just drop this. It's too big.'

'It's not big at all. Your sister is upset. The next time I see her, I'll take her pain away and everything will be fine again.'

'How? You mean with that mesmerism thing you do?'

'Yes, with that *mesmerism thing*. Now,' he tapped the table. 'Bristol, if you please.'

'Actually, while you're poking around in Lydia's head, is there any chance you could reshuffle her deck and make her a nice person?'

'Flinch. Enough.'

'Sorry, sir. Yeah. So, what do you wanna know?'

'What happened to Sarah?'

'She died. Next question.'

Underwood paused in raising his glass. He lowered it back to the table. 'I'm sorry to hear that.'

'Thank you, though her death was nothing to do with you, which makes a change, doesn't it?'

'Would you like to tell me how it happened?'

'No, but I guess *no* isn't really an option, is it?'

'It is, if it pains you, David.'

'Oh no, no,' said David, his manner was all insincere cheeriness. 'No more than anything else we've had to rake over tonight, Milord. *Quid pro quo*, eh?'

Underwood said nothing, but watched David patiently.

'Fine. So, let me think. It was a Tuesday. I was at the ambulance station watching a repeat of *Changing Rooms* on TV when we got the call. Car collision. A pissed-up boy racer had ploughed into another car at a set of traffic lights. Multiple casualties. When we got to the scene and I saw the car they'd smashed into was a green Fiat Punto, my first thought was, thank God it wasn't Sarah's. She had one the same, see. A green Fiat Punto. But it couldn't be hers, because she was safe, at home, waiting for me to finish my shift. But then I saw the registration number.' His jaw tightened, his mask of cheeriness slipping. He took a drink. 'I ran to the car. It was … all wrapped around the one that had gone into it, the wanker had been travelling so fast he'd caused her whole driver's side to crumple like – ' his words caught in his throat and he pressed a clenched fist to his lips.

'I'm sorry, David. There's no need to continue.'

'No,' David took a sharp breath. 'No, it's okay. She was dead, of course. Killed immediately. So were the two fuckers in the other car. I took some comfort from that. After that, my life, just … fell apart. I'd always had a fondness for alcohol. They say it goes in with the mother's milk, don't they? But after Sarah died, I … I couldn't cope. I mean, we were gonna get married, you know? Have kids, do all the things normal people do. No Sect, no you, none of that shit that had done my mum in. I was free of it, see? I'd escaped. We were gonna be happy.' He drained the glass and set it down. 'You know, for a while, I wondered if maybe *they'd* arranged it somehow, you know? John, Lydia, The Sect. But that was insane and I knew it. What happened to her was, was just ... shit happens, you know?' He looked up, and his eyes were wet with tears. He lifted his empty glass. 'Tide's out, Milord. My round. Same again, is it?'

'I think perhaps it's best if we don't have any more tonight, David.'

'Why? I thought you wanted me to get pissed?'

'Let's be on our way, shall we? Will you be okay to drive or should we call a cab?'

'But I don't wanna go now, I'm just warming up. This place isn't so bad when you've got the beer goggles on, is it? Even the girls look alright.'

Underwood stood up and reached out a hand. 'Come along. I'll drive.'

'No!' David brushed the hand aside. 'Really, I'm alright. Sit down, I'll tell you the rest. You wanna hear the rest don't you?'

'Not if it's going to upset you any further.'

'It's not. Really. It won't take long. I stayed pissed. That's all there is really. I lost my job, of course. Can't be a piss head and a paramedic, can you?' He laughed. 'So I drank. I signed on with the dole office and they sent me for job interviews for jobs I didn't want, but when you're a drunk, interviews are a pushover to fuck up. They stopped my dole, but I – *we*, she and I – had some money put away. I lived off that, I guess for the best part of a year, till finally, I started to pull myself together again. I knew I needed to change my life, all of it, so I moved out of the flat in Bristol and went back to Brighton. My drinking was under control now, sort of, and I got a job teaching English. The hours suited me – or rather they suited my hangovers. I was drinking a lot less, stopping for days at a time, even the odd week. But I'd always backslide. It was after a particularly bad backslide that I realised I couldn't do it alone. So I started going to Alcoholics Anonymous. And that was the turning point. Slowly, I got my shit back together again. And I was doing fine. Just fine. Until you needed your wake up alarm call.'

David reached across the table and pointed at Underwood's drink. 'Are you gonna finish that?' Underwood shook his head. David picked up the drink and drained it at a swallow. 'And that, as they say, is that.' He wiped his mouth with the back of his hand. 'See? I told you my life was uneventful compared to yours.'

'I'm sorry, Flinch.'

'That's alright,' said David, glancing around. 'Where's the waitress?'

'What happened to you and your mother as a result of poor planning on Arthur's part is deeply to be regretted. But, well, we're here now, aren't we? Making the best of it, the pair of us. And you have your girlfriend too, Lisa, isn't that her name?'

'*Had* a girlfriend, you mean? I don't see her anywhere, do you? Not like she's gonna be meeting us here in half hour and we're all going out for pizza, is it?'

'You can still have a girlfriend, Flinch. I'm not a monster. It's just that you won't get to see her quite as often as you might like to. And of course, there's the breeding issue; you'll need to breed with women from within the Sect, lest – God forbid – your poor offspring should have to go through the kind of hardships you've had to endure. Probably best not to tell Lisa about it, though; keep it all hush-hush.'

'*What?*'

'Well, unless you think she wouldn't mind.'

'Are you … ?' David was aghast. 'You can't still be on about that, can you? After all I've just said? I told you, last night: I'm not doing that.'

'You said you'd consider it.'

'Well I have fucking considered it and the answer's no.'

'David, you're upset. And what's worse, you're drunk. Your tolerance for alcohol isn't what it was, you know.'

'That's got nothing to do with it, your lordliness. My answer's still no. If you think I'm going to shag witches from the fucking Sect so you can get your next generation of Flinches, you're seriously fucking mistaken. *No way* any kid of mine is going to be brought up to be like Lydia. No fucking way!'

'Flinch. That's enough. You're making a show of yourself.' Underwood stood up and took David by the arm.

David tore his arm free. 'No. That's not enough. I've told you. I don't mind protecting you, but I'm not gonna breed for you.' He raised his hand and gestured to the waitress. 'Two more gins, *por favor.*' He turned to Underwood. 'And what'll you have?'

Underwood looked around. The bouncers had noticed them and were eyeing them warily. 'You're trying my patience, Flinch. Come on, damn you.'

'No, sir. I've decided this is my night off. I deserve a night off after the week I've had and this is it. You're welcome to stay with me, but if you do, you'll have to take that surly look off your face, and we'll have no more crap about breeding heirs. Alright?'

Underwood grabbed David by the shirt front and hauled him from his chair. David was caught off guard, he swung for him, but only managed to land his forearm on the side of Underwood's head. Underwood slapped him across the face. 'You bloody fool!' He turned and strode through the tables towards the door, dragging David behind him.

'Let fucking go of me!' David grabbed at tables as he passed and managed to snatch a glass ashtray from one of them. Without thinking, he swung it the back of Underwood's head. The ashtray struck Underwood at the base of his skull. The realisation of what he had just done shocked David into instant sobriety. He dropped the ashtray as if it were on fire. 'Oh, shit, I – ' Underwood turned, his face a mask of fury, his eyes – David took a step back at the sight of them – his eyes were inhuman. They were yellow, the eyes of an animal – the eyes of a wolf. 'Oh shit, I'm sorry, that was well out of order.'

Over Underwood's shoulder, David saw the mullet-haired bouncer approaching from the front door, his friend not far behind him. He glanced towards the stage. The dancer was still gyrating to the music, but she was watching as the bouncers from either side of the stage now emerged from the shadows. 'We should go.'

'How *dare* you strike me!' said Underwood, his voice simmering with barely controlled rage. 'You despicable wretch.'

'Milord, really,' said David, trying to prise Underwood's fingers from where they still gripped his shirt front. 'I think we should leave.'

'*We* should leave?' Underwood's lips drew back to reveal his canine teeth now long and sharp. 'Oh no, Flinch. The only one leaving is you. You're fired! Now get out of my sight before I rip your miserable throat out!' He flung David away from him, sending him flying backwards, scattering chairs and tables like skittles before he crashed to the floor.

'No!' David shouted, struggling to right himself and pointing to where the bouncer with the mullet was now almost upon Underwood. 'Behind y – ' The words stopped in David's throat as he saw Underwood turn and thrust his hand at the bouncer's throat. The bouncer stopped suddenly, his eyes wide with shock. Underwood must have had him by the neck, but the bouncer was doing nothing to try and free himself. David got to his feet and saw why. Underwood didn't have him by the throat; he had his fingers *in* his throat. Blood now bubbled to the bouncers lips.

Underwood turned back to David. 'Here, Flinch. Catch this. Something to remember me by.' He snapped his arm upwards; the bouncer's body began to leave the ground before his head tore free of his neck and was sent flying through the air. David watched as it spun between him and the stage lights, the mullet hairdo fanning wide and blood splattering in an arc before it dropped to the floor and rolled away under the tables. David looked back to Underwood in time to see the headless corpse crumple to the floor behind him. The other bouncers stood frozen, terrified, unsure how to proceed.

The dancer had abandoned her pole and was fleeing to the far end of the stage, the waitresses were screaming and running for the door, and the two solitary punters, who had evidently had their eyes elsewhere, sat open-mouthed, wondering what the hell was going on. David got to his feet and held up his hands appeasingly. 'We can still get out of this, Milord. It's not too late.'

'It is for you, Flinch. Didn't you hear me? You're fired.'

'But ... you *can't* fire me. I'm your Guardian!'

'*Were* my Guardian. I've someone else in mind for the position now. Someone eminently more suited to the task.'

'Lydia? Are you mad?'

The paralysis broke on the other bouncer who had been rushing Underwood from the front door. He ran to the bar. Underwood didn't pay any attention to him, his eyes remained fixed on David. 'I was mad; mad to think I could work with the likes of you. But now, thankfully, my dalliance with lunacy is over.' A pistol fired from the bar. Underwood winced as the bullet struck him in the shoulder. He turned in the direction of the shot and saw the bouncer aiming from between the glistening beer taps. The gun roared again and a mirror on the far side of the room exploded in a shower of glittering fragments. 'Get out, Flinch!'

'No. I won't leave you like this!'

Underwood turned to him, the flesh of his face beginning to smoke as if acid had been thrown in it. When he spoke his voice was deep, an animal growl. 'Get. Out. Because if they don't kill you ... I might.'

'Y-you wouldn't – ' David broke off suddenly as Underwood's clothes flashed into flames. 'Oh shit!' A black shape leapt from where the burning rags fell, too fast to follow as it vanished beneath the tables. The bouncer with the gun stared stupefied at the burning debris, where moments before a man had been. Then from nowhere, a huge black timber wolf leapt up onto the bar and seized him by the throat. It started shaking its head violently from side to side, ripping the man's flesh. The bouncer managed to fire a shot into the wolf's ribcage before his legs buckled and he dropped down behind the bar. The wolf, unwilling to release its prey, followed. Another shot fired and a bottle shattered in a shower of glass and whisky. David stood frozen. The music stopped.

The dancer who had just left the stage ran for the door; chairs dragged back as the two punters got to their feet. David's feet began to move, carrying him to the door as all the while he looked to the bar where the gargled screams had now stopped and the only sound was that of an animal feeding.

The two remaining bouncers began to shout commands to each other. David couldn't follow their words exactly, but they were talking strategy. The fools really thought they had a chance. He ran. He reached the door in time to follow the other two punters out through the foyer and into the car park. The waitresses and dancer were huddling together near the exit to the road; two other women had joined them. David recognised the first stripper who had been on when they entered. They must have come from a back door.

The punters ran to their cars. Seeing this, the women ran after them, screaming in more than one language for help. Then more screams, male screams echoed from within the club. David clutched at his head. 'Oh Jesus. Oh Jesus fucking Christ! This is my fault! Shit! Shit! Shit!'

The two cars fired into life and screeched in the direction of the exit. One man had taken some of the girls with him, but the other was leaving alone, chased by the screamed curses of the two women he'd left behind. As the cars drove out onto the dark road – headlights raking wildly left to right as the drivers fought to keep control of their speeding cars – the remaining girls ran to David and clutched at his arms, both pointing to the Citroën and babbling Spanish he recognised as meaning "take me". A gun fired inside the club and the women screamed, their fingers pinching deep into the flesh of his arm. David shook his arms free. 'Get off me, for fuck's sake! I need to think!'

Then he heard a strange noise. He couldn't place it. A ringing. His mind focused on it. He became aware of a vibrating sensation in his pocket. His phone. Who the hell would be calling him at a time like this, he wondered, as if the caller had no sense of decorum. He pulled out the phone. Lydia's name glowed on the caller screen. David accepted the call and held the phone to his ear. 'Lydia?'

'David? Oh thank God, please hurry,' she was whispering, her mouth close to the phone. She sounded scared. In the background there was some kind of commotion. 'You've got to tell Underwood.'

'What? Tell Underwood? What are you – ?'

'I can't explain. I'm outside *La Reina*. There are men. I *know* them. They've got guns – ' she broke off in a gasp so loud it hurt David's ear. 'Oh, my God!'

'What? What is it?'

'Oh, Jesus. No! I have to hide. Call Miguel, Cynthia,' she was muttering instructions to herself, almost as if she had forgotten David was there.'

'*Lydia?*'

Through the phone came the sound of rush and clatter. Then Lydia, her voice tight with rising terror, 'Get Underwood! Oh my God, they're burning – ' There was another mysterious clattering. Then the line went dead.

'Lydia? Lydia?' David looked at the phone. 'Oh Christ. What the fuck is …' He called back, but a recorded Spanish voice told him the phone was either switched off or unreachable. The women were pulling at his arms again and he shrugged them away. 'Look just fuck off, will you! Wait a minute, okay? I, I need to … ' He looked back to the club. 'I have to go back in there.' He started for the door. The women tried to stop him; one of them knew the English for *car* and was saying it over and over. 'It's okay. I'll be back. I'll take you in car. Okay?' He prised their hands from him and went back into the club.

Inside, the lights continued to flash on an empty stage. The hazy layer of cigarette and gun smoke rippled as David pushed through the doors. Tables were toppled and chairs scattered. David picked a cautious path between them, listening. His feet kicked something. He looked down and saw the contents of Underwood's pockets among some scorched scraps of clothing. His watch and silver cigarette case were intact, but his mobile phone lay burnt and smouldering. David bent down to pick up the salvageable items. Then he froze at a sudden sound. It was like the snap of branch in a forest. He listened. a wet crunch came from near the stage. Something was eating. He pocketed the watch and moved towards where the sound had come from. As he grew nearer, his eyes caught a flash of reflected light from the floor. He looked and saw a pool of dark liquid. Then, severed and lying in the middle of it, he recognised a human arm. He closed his eyes and steadied himself against a table. He tried to speak, but his throat was too dry. He mustered spit enough to swallow and tried again. 'Lord Underwood?'

No reply other than a wet snuffling sound. David didn't want to turn the corner and see what he knew was making it. 'Lord Underwood, it's me, Flinch. I gotta talk to you.'

The sound stopped.

'Milord, it's Lydia. She just called me.'

Suddenly, from between the tables near the stage, the huge black timber wolf sprang up onto the stage. David gasped and stumbled back against a chair that screeched on the floor. 'Jesus!'

The wolf padded closer to the end of the runway, blood dripping from its muzzle and the fur of it chest.

David regained a semblance of composure and managed to continue. 'I, I think she's in danger.'

The wolf lowered its head slightly, its eyes narrowing.

'Did you hear me? I think – ' He didn't notice the tension building in the wolf's haunches; when it sprang towards him, he screamed, 'No!' He threw his hands up and leapt backwards, his legs crashing into a tangle of chairs and tables that sent him tumbling over backwards. He landed on his side and immediately began scrabbling to find his feet before the wolf was upon him. Then he saw a pair of human feet standing in the pool of blood.

'Of course I understand you, you idiot.' Underwood held out a hand to him. He was completely naked, but not a drop of blood was upon him. 'What are you talking about? What do you mean she's in danger?'

David looked doubtfully at the hand for a second before accepting it and feeling himself hauled to his feet. 'I – she – she phoned me. She was terrified. Said she was at *La Reina*. There were men with guns, and to get you.'

'What? Men with guns at La Reina?'

'Yeah. She said they were burning.'

'What was?'

'She didn't say. She was cut off.'

Underwood took a moment to digest David's words then started for the door. 'Right. Come on. You take the car and meet me at *La Reina* as quickly as you can.'

David shook off his inertia and hurried after him. 'But, but what about this place? What about these men?'

'What about them?'

'What about them? *They're dead!*'

'So? Isn't that what you wanted?'

'What? No, I … I …'

Underwood seized David's face beneath the jaw and pulled him close. 'I've had about enough, of your insipid conscience, Flinch! I could see the hatred in your eyes earlier when you were looking at them. You've met men of their ilk before, haven't you? In Bosnia, perhaps?'

'I … that's – that's nothing to do with it.'

'Isn't it? You wanted them dead; I wanted to kill them. I don't expect a pat on the back, but at least spare me the violins.'

'You promised me you wouldn't kill.'

'I fired you first.'

'So what are you doing giving me orders?'

'Don't be a dolt, man! Lydia is in danger, your sister, Arthur's daughter, she's family, damn it!' he released David and resumed his course for the door. 'You may not understand that, but I do.'

David stumbled after him, massaging his jaw. 'But, but how are we going to explain it to the police?'

'We're not. These men were obviously attacked by a wolf.'

'But, do they even have wolves in Spain?'

Underwood waved a hand at the carnage behind them. 'Evidently, yes.' He exited to the car park. At the sight of the women clustering around the Citroën, he turned back to David. 'I suppose you'll be rescuing these ladies, will you?'

'I thought I should.'

'Good, we don't want them hanging around for the police. Dump them at the edge of town.'

'Dump them? You don't mean *kill* them, do you?'

'Of course not, you idiot. Drive to the edge of town, chuck 'em out of the car – *alive* – and get going. Give 'em some money if you like, but don't hang around. Drive straight to *La Reina*.'

'But … they've seen you do the wolf thing.'

'Yes, they have. And now they're going to see me do the bat thing as well. Stand back, will you?'

David took a few hurried steps back. 'But what if they tell people?'

Underwood grinned, and his canines glinted in the light from the red neon sign. 'Who on Earth would ever believe them?' He threw his arms upward and David watched – still in utter astonishment, despite having seen it before – as the vampire dissolved before his eyes into a stream of swirling red molecules that vanished into the night like smoke from a bonfire. There were a few moments of breathless silence. Then the women started screaming. They began crossing themselves and crying about *El Diablo*.

'It's all right,' said David, starting towards the car, 'it's not *El Diablo*.' From above came the sound of beating wings moving in the direction of Almacena. David glanced up at the sound and added, 'But it's not far off.'

At his approach, the women ran away from the car and toward the gates of the club.

'Oh, for Heaven's sake,' he muttered. He watched them go. How could he reason with them after what they had just seen? He shook his head and hurried to the car. A few seconds later, he drove out through the gates and turned towards town. The headlights picked out the women running down the road, still screaming. He wound down the window and drove slowly alongside them. '*Por favor*? Did you want a lift?'

The women both looked at him, their eyes almost bulging in fear.

David smiled. '*Coche*?'

The women screamed in unison and ran, off of the road and into the dark scrubland beyond.

David sighed and put his foot down on the accelerator. 'Oh, please yourselves. I guess this counts as the edge town … ish.' He began to scrape his fingernails gently around an area of the interior door panelling. His nails found a concealed slit. He pulled it and a flap came down to reveal a small compartment. Arthur's luger was fixed snugly in its fastenings, exactly as it had been when the old man had showed it to him when he'd been a kid. He slapped the flap closed again and smoothed it into place. 'Welcome to the firm, Davey boy,' he muttered, glancing in the rear view mirror. 'Welcome to the world of Underwood and Flinch.'

18

MICHELLE SAT AT THE KITCHEN TABLE LISTENING to the night through the open door to the patio. Sounds from the pub below drifted up. It had just closed for the night and she could hear Keith, Damo and Hodge going through the motions of tidying things up: their voices, the clatter of terrace tables being stacked, the occasional laugh. Music came on, it was quiet, but she recognised AC/DC – a popular choice after the bar closed; nice to work to and nice to sit back with once the work was done. But there would be no more nights tidying up after the close of *La Reina* for her; no more sitting around with the staff at the end of the shift with a few cold beers, laughing about the events of the evening and life in general. Nothing quite so good as that first sip of cold beer after a long night of dishing it out to everybody other than you and your own friends. It was their time, after time.

But no more. Tonight her life was going to change forever. Tonight, Daniel was coming for her. She had told him to wait until the pub had been closed for an hour; give the staff time to get away, give Keith time to … well, do whatever he wanted to do. As it turned out, she and he had decided it would be best if he weren't there at all. Keith had spoken to Damo earlier in the evening and they'd agreed to have a few beers after work around at his place for a change. So soon, they'd be away and she'd be left alone. Of course there was Melanie, but she was sound asleep in her room.

The thought of Melanie sent a ripple of disquiet through her sense of tranquility, as if someone locked in a dungeon in the depths of her soul were banging on the door, demanding to be heard; but as soon as she tried to focus on that feeling, it faded away, leaving her again in a state of blissful anticipation of Underwood's arrival. She sipped her cup of tea and looked around at the kitchen that had been at the heart of their family home. Her eyes rested on a photo, curling slightly at the edges and held to the fridge door with a Homer Simpson magnet: she, Keith, and Melanie, smiling at the camera from the door of John Bull's Tavern in Benidorm, shortly after they'd first moved to Spain. So much hope and happiness for their new beginning back then. Mel had seemed so small, she'd grown so much – even in the time that they'd been here in Almacena. She frowned as that feeling of unease stirred in her again, deep down, distant. She put down her cup of tea, and the movement was like someone had turned a page in her mind. Daniel Underwood returned, and with him, the feeling of joyful expectation. She looked up at the clock on the wall. It was half-past midnight. Damn it, Keith, hurry up and get out! Daniel could be downstairs right now, watching and waiting, as impatient for her as she was for him. She got up and went to the sink, dumping her tea and rinsing the cup out under the tap. She put the cup on the draining board and looked up at the moon through the window. It was low in the sky, large and almost full. Her hand strayed absently to her neck where Daniel had kissed her last night. At the touch, her impatience melted away as a wave of sensual pleasure swept through her. She leaned against the sink and closed her eyes, biting her lower lip as she imagined his mouth against her neck again.

Then she heard a sound from outside. Her eyes opened. It was a footstep. Then she heard another, ascending the stairs that led up from the garden. She turned to face the door to the patio. It must be him. Like her, he couldn't bear the wait. He must have been sitting in his car across the street, waiting for Keith and his mates to go, but tonight, thirty minutes felt like thirty years. She turned back to the window and checked her reflection, fussing momentarily with her hair. Then as the footsteps approached the door, she turned and smiled, 'I'm ready, My Lord.'

'No, it's like I said, I don't *mind* going round to mine,' said Damo, 'I just don't understand why we can't stay here.' He and Hodge were gathering glasses and wiping down tables as Keith counted up the takings behind the bar. 'We always stay here. You've got the music, the beers. Why do we need to go anywhere else?'

'I think it's fair enough,' said Hodge. 'Keith has people coming round to his place day and night all week long. He wants a change of scenery, don't you mate?'

'Thank you, H,' said Keith, not looking up from counting bank notes at the till. 'Exactly.'

Damo exchanged a look with Hodge and mouthed the word, *Chelle*. Hodge nodded. Damo brought a tray of glasses and half-nibbled bowls of complimentary nuts up to the bar. He came behind the bar and began emptying the glass washing machine. He looked at Keith. He was acting weird tonight; something was definitely going on between him and

Michelle. He considered just coming out and asking him about it, but Keith had a look of intense concentration on his face as he slowly thumbed through the notes, like he was having trouble counting them. Maybe later, Damo thought as he bent to load dirty glasses into the glass washer. Get a few beers in him first, and then ask him.

Keith was sweating. He wiped his brow and carried on counting. They were almost done. All the furniture had been brought in from the front terrace, the chairs and tables stood stacked near the front door, and the outer shutters had been brought down. From the corner of his eye Keith could see Damo watching him. He lost count again. He closed his eyes and took a deep breath. What was the point? What was the point of any of it? To count the cash; to tidy up; to go on as though nothing had happened; to wake up tomorrow morning to Mel getting ready for school and asking the inevitable question: where's Mum? And then what? Tell her Mum had gone to live with another man? Had just taken off in the night without saying goodbye because it was easier for *her* that way? Easier for him to ...' Keith felt a sudden ache in his head that caused his thoughts to stumble and fall silent. The bank notes slipped from his fingers, spilling onto the till drawer, and he massaged his temples.

It is his will. I am to go on. The child will come to understand. He murmured this last phrase aloud in a brief silence between changing tracks on the AC/DC album.

'You what?' asked Damo as he switched on the glass washer.

Keith opened his eyes, 'What?'

'Were you talking to me?'

'When?'

'Just then. You said something about the child understanding.'

'Yeah, the child will ...' he frowned, confused. 'The child will come to understand.'

'What do you mean?'

'I,' Keith pinched the bridge of his nose and squeezed his eyes shut, 'I don't ... I don't know. Mel. Mel will come to understand.'

'Understand what, mate?' said Hodge, his face concerned as he joined them at the bar.

Keith slammed the till drawer back into the machine sending notes fluttering all around. Then he punched his head with the heels of his hands. 'Mel! Mel, damn it! Mel will come to understand. She ... she'll be alright.' His expression became calm again and he opened his eyes. 'Sorry about that, lads,' he said with a smile. 'Anyone for a beer?'

Damo and Hodge stared at him, dumbstruck. Then Damo said, 'Are you all right, Keith?'

'Yeah. Course. I was just blowing off a bit of steam. It's been a difficult couple of days, you know? Me and Chelle – we haven't been seeing eye-to-eye lately, see? And … well, Mel's been a bit upset about it. But, you know, like I say, she'll come to understand.'

'Understand?' said Hodge. 'Understand what, Keith?'

Keith's brow furrowed, he looked as if he didn't know the answer himself. 'You know, *understand*.'

'No, not really,' said Hodge. 'Listen, is there anything you want to talk about, Keith?'

'Talk about? Naah, everything's peachy, mate. Just a spot of marital turbulence, you know? It's his will.'

'Whose will?' asked Damo.

'Eh?' said Keith.

'You just said it's his will. Who's "he"? Don't tell me you've found God, Keith.'

'Did I say that? Oh, well, yeah, that's what I meant – God. It's God's will, innit? Fate.' He turned and opened one of the beer fridges. 'Now then, who's for a beer? I say we drink 'em on the way to Damo's. Fuck all this mess, we've done enough for tonight. I can finish it off in the morning.' He took out three bottles of San Miguel, uncapped them, and handed them around.

Damo took one, looking doubtfully at the banknotes scattered all over the floor behind the bar. 'Sure, if you say so. But, I have to say, Keith – you're not like yourself at all lately.'

'Aren't I?' Keith seemed surprised.

'No, you're not, and it's not just me who sees it either. You're like, away with the fairies, you know?'

Keith shrugged. 'Oh, well, that's stress for you, innit, mate?'

Hodge took a sip of his beer. 'And you look ill, too.'

'Well, same thing, innit? Stress.'

There was a knock on the shutters outside.

'We're closed!' shouted Hodge. '*Cerrado!*'

Keith looked at the front door and the grey shutters beyond. 'Not now,' he murmured. 'It's too early.'

'You what?' said Damo.

'It's too early.' Keith hurried around the bar and over to the door marked *Private* that led to the side entrance hallway. 'I need time, time to get away. I don't wanna be here.' He disappeared through the door.

Damo looked at Hodge. 'Ah sure, he's gone completely fucking mental.'

'Aye, he bloody has, mate,' said Hodge.

In the hall, Keith went to the door, muttering under his breath. 'Please, My Lord, just give me some time – just five minutes and I'll be gone. Just five minutes.' At the door he hesitated, took a deep breath, then opened it. 'I'm sorry my – ' he began, but the face that greeted him outside caused the sentence to die on his lips.

'*Dobrii vecher,* Keith Mullins,' said Sergei. Ivan stood behind him. Sergei levelled a silenced pistol at Keith's stomach. 'Are we too late for the last orders?'

Keith was too stunned for words – all he could manage was, 'You?'

'Yes. I wasn't serious about the drinks, but we *do* come in; either with you, or over your dead body.' He jabbed the barrel of the gun into Keith's stomach. 'I think together is better, yes?'

Damo and Hodge were talking about Keith's strange demeanour when he walked in looking even stranger than he had when he'd gone out. Then over his shoulder, they saw the reason following him in through the door. Damo put down his beer. 'Sergei? What the fuck are you doing here?'

'Ahh, Mr Sullivan and Mr Hodgekiss. Now we have our three eggs in the one basket. You know, you are hard men to find.'

'What's this all about, Sergei?' asked Keith. 'You wanna buy this place? Is that it? Coz if you do, then you're in luck – I might be selling.'

'Really, Keith Mullins? And what is price you are asking?'

'Make me an offer.'

'An offer? No, no, no. I am not here to make offers, Keith Mullins. I am here to collect debt. So, why don't we start with Mr Hodgekiss?' Sergei aimed the silenced pistol at Hodge's chest. The gun coughed once.

Hodge blinked, surprised. His beer bottle slipped from his fingers. He looked at Keith, opening his mouth to speak, but no words passed his lips. He crumpled to the floor.

'*Hodge!*' Damo leapt over the bar and was at his friend's side in an instant. He rolled Hodge over. The floor beneath him was wet with blood. Damo felt his neck for a pulse, but there was none. He turned to Keith. 'He's ... he's fucking dead!'

'As is my nephew, Mr Sullivan. Tell me you had nothing to do with that, and I will gladly pay for your friend's funeral expenses.'

'You fucking bastard!' Damo started to rise, his fists clenched. Ivan stepped between him and Sergei; he held a baseball bat, raised and ready to swing at Damo's head. Damo stopped.

'That is better,' said Sergei. 'Now, why don't you and Keith Mullins take a seat over there?' He motioned to a booth against the far wall beneath a black and white portrait of a laughing Sid James.

'Look, Sergei, let me explain,' Keith began. He glanced at his watch – Underwood should be there any minute – if he could keep them talking long enough, the Master would surely save them. 'We didn't mean to kill your nephew. It was an accident.'

'Ah, an accident? Like the accident I just had with Mr Hodgekiss?'

'The only accident was that we got your nephew and not yourself,' said Damo.

'Ahh, yes, I suspected that might be the case.'

'Well, what did you expect?' said Keith. 'You murdered Pete!'

'That was not me – that was Ivan, here.'

'Oh, we know that, and meant to kill him too,' said Damo as he and Keith sat down in the booth. 'The pair of youse had a lucky escape.'

'Yes. We are very lucky – just as you, it seems, are not.'

Ivan went behind the bar and located the CD player. He turned up the volume just as, from upstairs, Michelle screamed. The end of her cry was lost beneath the music.

'Michelle!' Keith went to rise, but Sergei halted him with a shot that tore a hole in the seat beside him.

'Don't hurt her!' said Keith, 'she had nothing to do with what we did. She only found out about it the other day – and she's fucking leaving me because of it. Please, Sergei – Mr Alexandrov, don't hurt her.'

'It is a pity,' said Sergei, speaking louder now to be heard over the increased volume. 'Your wife and my nephew, they are innocents in this unpleasant business that is between us. Why did you ever have to bring them into it?'

Despite the music, Keith heard Melanie scream upstairs. 'Oh, Jesus, no! No! Mel!'

'For fuck's sake, Sergei,' said Damo. 'Not the girl. She's just a kid.'

'*Please*,' Keith clasped his hands together and came out of the booth to fall on his knees. 'I'm begging you. Kill me! Kill me a thousand times over, but don't kill my girls.'

'Much as I would like to, Keith Mullins, I cannot kill you a thousand times. It is a pity, no? But still, as a favour to you for the old times' sake, I will not kill your girls. I have for them, other plans.'

To Keith's left, the door that connected the pub to the apartment opened and Anton entered. He held a silenced pistol, and on seeing Hodge's body, his face cracked into a smile. He said something to Sergei in Russian and stepped aside for Michelle and Melanie to follow him in. Their eyes were tear-soaked and terrified, their mouths sealed with duct tape. Keith saw that their hands were secured behind their backs with plastic zip ties, and behind them came another of Sergei's men.

At the sight of Keith on his knees, both Michelle and Melanie cried out helplessly against their gags. Anton laughed and said something in Russian that got a chuckle from Ivan.

'Michelle!' Keith called. 'Oh, baby, no, no. Mel!' He turned to Sergei. 'I'll do anything, anything, you say. But please let 'em go. They had nothing to do with it, I swear!'

'It is terrible business, I know, Keith Mullins. But you and I both know what will happen if I let them go. They will tell police everything, and that will make life very difficult for all of us.' He waved his gun vaguely to indicate his men. 'So you see, I have no choice but to take them.'

'No! No! Don't kill them!'

'I told you, Keith Mullins. I am not going to kill them. No one will buy them if they are dead.'

A wave of numbness went through Keith's body. 'What? What do you mean, *buy* them?'

'I have a Serbian friend who has brothels in Barcelona,' Sergei walked slowly to Michelle and Melanie, appraising them with a buyer's eye. 'Brothels are not my business. I find them depressing places – so full of pain and misery. But my friend, he likes this, and it makes him a lot of money. I've no doubt he will want to sample the goods first, of course, but I don't think he will be disappointed.' He smoothed Melanie's fringe away from her eyes, where it had become wet with her tears. 'Do you?'

Keith roared, struggling to his feet and charging at Sergei. Anton's gun coughed twice and brought him crashing down onto his face, screaming and clutching at his legs where blood now soaked through his jeans. The first bullet had grazed the thigh of his right leg, but the second had shattered the knee of his left. Damo moved quickly to Keith's side. Melanie and Michelle both screamed against their gags, and Sergei and Anton had to restrain them from running to Keith.

'Enough of this noise!' said Sergei. He spoke in Russian to the third gunman, whom he addressed as Nicolai, telling him to take the women out into the entrance hall and to keep them quiet. Nicolai nodded and pushed Melanie and Michelle away, as instructed.

Sergei walked over to Keith and looked down at him. 'That was very stupid of you, Keith Mullins. Now, you might bleed to death all over pub floor – and this is not what I had in mind for you at all.' He nodded to Ivan, who went behind the bar.

'You fucking bastard, Sergei,' Keith hissed through gritted teeth. 'You think we're fucked, but you're wrong – it's *you* who's fucked.'

'Oh? And how is that? You are going to bite me on the toes?'

Ivan was lining up bottles of spirits along the bar. Anton took two of them and came to Sergei's side. Ivan then swung the baseball bat at the bottles fixed in the optics behind the bar, shattering them in a shower of glass and alcohol.

'*My Lord!*' Keith shouted. 'Help us! For fuck's sake, help us!'

'I see,' said Sergei, 'this is your secret weapon, yes? *Jesus?*' He laughed. 'Well I'm afraid Jesus doesn't help murderers like us, Keith Mullins, he leaves us to the fires of Hell.' He spoke in Russian to Anton and Ivan: '*Spread it all around, but not on them. I want them to see it coming.*'

Anton flung the two bottles he held into each of the booths adjacent to where Keith and Damo had sat. Ivan came up behind Anton and threw another two bottles of spirits so they shattered across the floor on either side of Keith.

'My Lord!' Keith cried. 'Please! Kill the bastards!'

Sergei chuckled. 'What happened to "forgive them, they know not what they do"?'

Anton and Ivan went to the bar and began throwing the contents of the remaining bottles of spirits around the pub, soaking fixtures and furnishings everywhere.

'You stupid Ruskie fuck! He's gonna be here any minute, and when he sees what you've done, he's gonna tear you apart.'

'Is he now?' Sergei accepted a bottle handed to him by Anton. It was half drained and a handkerchief protruded from its end. 'Well, then perhaps it would be best if we take our leave.' He turned and walked towards the exit.

'Sergei!' Keith roared. 'You hear me? You might kill me, but he's gonna come for you!'

At the door, Sergei stopped and turned back. 'Who will? Your Lord Jesus? I told you – '

'No. Not My Lord Jesus, you fuck! My Lord Underwood!'

Sergei's smile fell.

Keith pointed at Sergei. 'Ah – you, you know him. You know him, dontcha!'

Sergei drew a lighter from his pocket and lit the Molatov cocktail. The rising flame cast a flickering glow over his features. 'I know only one thing, Keith Mullins: that you are going to burn alive, knowing that your wife and child will spend the rest of their lives being raped. *Dasvidanya*, asshole.' He threw the Molatov behind the bar and watched the immediate conflagration. He smiled to see Damo dragging Keith back towards the booth. Then flames swept across the pools of alcohol that separated them from him, distorting the men behind a haze of fire and heat. He went out through the door and closed it behind him.

Outside, Lydia and Miguel stood in the shadows at the side of the front door. Lydia was talking into her phone in a voice constricted with fear, 'I can't explain. I'm outside *La Reina*. There're men. I *know* them. They've got guns! Oh my, God! Oh, Jesus. No! I have to hide. Call Miguel, Cynthia!' She broke off as Michelle and Melanie were dragged out of the pub, closing her hand over the phone until they had passed. Then, as an orange glow flooded the corridor from which they'd emerged, she concluded her call: 'Get Underwood! Oh my God. They're burning – !' She swung her phone and slapped it against her thigh then she turned it off.

'Okay?' asked Miguel.

Lydia slipped her phone into her bag. 'Yes, of course it was. One thing you can always depend on with David is his gullibility.'

Miguel looked anxiously to where the Mullins women were being bundled into the back of a black-windowed BMW. 'It's a dangerous plan, Lydia. If we fail, Lord Underwood will kill us all.'

'Don't be afraid, Miguel,' she touched his cheek. 'We won't fail.'

He caught her hand and held it to his face. 'I'm not afraid.'

Sergei stepped out of the door and pulled it closed behind him. 'Not afraid of what?'

'Of anything,' said Miguel.

Sergei dusted his hands together. 'I am relieved to hear it. Lydia's plan depends on you, Miguel. You are the only one who knows what has happened here and the terrible thing that has happened to poor Lydia.' He smiled at Lydia and extended a hand to his car.

'Don't worry about me,' said Miguel. 'I know what to do.'

'Good,' said Lydia as they stepped onto the street. 'Now, you'd better get out of sight until Underwood and David arrive. Then the three of you can come racing to my rescue.'

'But, Sergei,' said Miguel. 'When we get to the club, how will your men know not to shoot me?'

Sergei opened the rear door of his car. 'You have nothing to fear, Miguel. My men know who you are and will not shoot at you – provided, of course, that you don't shoot at them first.'

Lydia got into the car. 'Oh, and do be sure to tell Underwood that Sergei has Melanie and Michelle as well. That'll really piss him off.'

'I will,' said Miguel. He watched as Sergei followed Lydia into the car and pulled the door closed behind him. Miguel wrung his hands and looked down the road. Then he bent to the car window for a final reassuring glimpse of Lydia, but all he saw was his own worried reflection looking back at him from the black glass. The car pulled away, following behind the one carrying Melanie and Michelle. He stood, hand raised in a wave, watching them go, and wondering if this might be the last time he would ever see her. He lowered his hand and suppressed an instinctual impulse to cross himself. Then, as the cars turned off the road, he whispered, '*Buena suerte, mi amor.*' He turned at the sound of exploding windows behind the shutters of *La Reina de Corazones*. Smoke began to pour through the shutters and rise up into the night.

Miguel looked left and right. The street was still deserted. But it wouldn't be for long. He crossed the street and ducked into an alley. There, he pinned himself to the shadows, and waited for the commotion to begin.

19

DAMO SHIELDED HIS EYES FROM THE HEAT as the heavy curtain of fire swept all around them. Sergei hadn't sent them to this booth at random; he'd chosen it because it was situated half-way down the length of the pub; equally distant from both exits, and now hopelessly cut off from both. He looked to where Hodge had fallen – and wished he hadn't; his body was already being consumed by fire. The sight was too awful to bear and he turned his face away to see Keith dragging himself under the table. No, he thought, that wasn't going to work. Already the air in the room was becoming unbreathable, the fire was devouring the oxygen and the smoke rolling across the ceiling was thickening fast. He looked around desperately for a way out; anywhere that wasn't burning and could offer them some kind of a chance. The alcohol hadn't touched everything, and there were still areas where the fire was sparse. If he ran with Keith over his shoulders, he might be able to get to the door where Sergei had exited.

Damo tried to stand, but it was like rising head-first into a fan oven. He dropped back down to his haunches but fell down onto his side. Then, coughing, clawing his way closer to Keith, he spotted a stretch of floor that was clear of flames. It ended in fire, but just beyond the fire was a door marked "*Señoras*" – the ladies' loo! Jesus! They could do it. If they could manage to get in there, they'd be able to get out of the window. 'Keith!' he shouted. He turned and thrust his head under the table to see that Keith had pushed himself as far back against the wall as he could. 'Keith!'

Keith lowered his arms from his face, 'I'm sorry, Damo. Get out if you can. Save yourself!'

'Come on, man! We gotta get outta here!'

'No, mate. I can't, I'm fucked. You go. Leave me.'

'Shut the fuck up, man! We're both going. There's a way.'

'Not for me, there ain't. I've been shot in the fucking knee, you plonker! Now go on –' Keith was cut off by his own scream as the agony from his wounded knee exploded afresh. He looked down to see Damo had him by the belt and was dragging him out from under the table. 'What the fuck are you doing?'

'Saving your fucking life, you asshole! Now come on!' Damo ignored Keith's screams and hauled him out. Then he took him under the armpits and tried to lift him to his feet. 'Come on! Get up on your good foot and hang on to me!'

'I don't have a bloody good foot!' Keith could feel himself blacking out as his mind tried to shut itself down to escape the waves of agony that hammered through him. 'I can't!' he screamed. 'For fuck's sake! I'm crippled! Just leave me willya!'

Damo looked over his shoulder; the fire was starting to thicken between them and the ladies' bathroom. It was now or never. 'Fine! You stay down, but I'm not leaving you. So unless you happened to have put on a pair of asbestos underpants this morning, hang on to your bollocks – coz we're leaving!' He encircled his arms under Keith's and clasped his hands across his chest, then he began dragging him towards the ladies' bathroom and the fire that lay between.

'No! Damo, forget m – ' Keith's plea was cut short by a paroxysm of coughing. He surrendered, allowing himself to be dragged and watching as the booth receded into smoke behind them, his blood-soaked trousers trailing a red slick in their wake. He was about to pass out when fresh pain assaulted him, this time from his hand. He snatched it back and realised with horror that Damo was dragging him *into* the fire. 'Jesus Christ! What are you fucking doing?'

'Would you shut up and just push with your good leg!'

As the flames closed around him, Keith put his hands over his face and pedalled and kicked as best he could.

Then suddenly, they were through. Damo pushed the door handle down with his elbow and the door swung open. He dragged Keith through and they both collapsed onto the cool tiles, beating at the flames that had taken hold on their clothes. Damo kicked the door closed, then got to his feet and started towards the window, but he stopped at the sight of the bars. 'Shit!'

'What?' said Keith.

'The fucking window's got bars on the outside!'

'Yeah. All the downstairs windows are barred. That's the same everywhere, innit.'

'For fuck's sake! Why? *Why?* It's not like there's fucking Vikings around, is it?' Damo went to the window. It was about two feet wide, three feet high, and consisted of two panes of glass in aluminium frames.

To open it, one pane slid sideways to cover the other. Both could easily be removed by pushing them up and lifting them out of their runners. Damo quickly got them out and gripped the black steel bars that were fixed to the outside wall. He shook them but they were solid – not even a wobble. 'Shit!' He put his face to the bars and shouted into the night. 'Help! *Socorro! Incendio!*'

'You saved my life,' said Keith. 'I didn't deserve it.'

Damo turned back to him and saw the smoke pouring in at the bottom of the door. 'I ain't saved your life yet, Keith.' He ran to the two sinks and turned on all the taps, thankful that they'd never got around to getting in those fancy ones that turn off when you stop pressing down on them. He jammed the stoppers in both of the sinks and started scooping water out and splashing it all over himself. As the sinks filled, water began to flow into the overflow vents. He looked around for something to block them with. Then he ran into each of the two toilet cubicles, emerging from each with a toilet roll. He returned to the sinks and began unravelling the paper.

'What are doing?' asked Keith.

'I'm having a big shit. What do you think I'm doing?' He doused handfuls of paper in the water and jammed the sopping wads into the overflow vents, blocking them. Then he ran to the door and dropped the remainder of the wet paper at its base, but it wasn't enough; smoke continued to pour in. He ran back to the sinks, pulling off his shirt and plunging it into the water. 'Gimme your shirt, Keith!'

Keith tried to pull his t-shirt over his head but fell over sideways, unconscious.

'Shit!' Damo dropped his wet shirt at the base of the door and kicked it up against the seeping smoke. He ran back and pulled Keith's shirt off of him. 'Keith! Wake up!' The floor was now awash with water splattering down from the blocked sinks. With one hand, Damo swirled Keith's shirt in the water, with the other, he checked his pulse. It was weak, his blood was blooming into the water like a crimson flower; he needed a tourniquet. Damo drew his belt from his waist and tied it around Keith's thigh. He twisted it as tightly as he could then slapped Keith's face. 'Keith! Wake up, you fucker!'

Keith came around, numbly mouthing incoherent questions.

Damo thrust the twisted belt into Keith's hand. 'Here! Hold this, and hold it fucking tight! It's a tourniquet, okay? Hold it tight or you're a fucking goner. You hear me?'

'Yeah, yeah, I hear you.' Keith took the belt in both hands, focussing all his attention on it. 'Cheers. I got it, mate.'

'And would you call for help, or something? That'll help keep you awake.'

'Help!' shouted Keith.

'No, no, I mean shout "*socorro*" – that's the Spanish word. If you shout "help" we're fucked – unless someone happens to be passing by with a phrase book.'

Keith nodded and began to call, '*Socorro! Socorro!*'

'Good man.' Damo ran to the door and flung Keith's wet shirt against the bottom of it – for all the good it would do; smoke was now seeping into the room from all around the door. He touched the surface and pulled his fingers back at the heat. 'Shit! It must be catching on the other side. We don't have long.'

He looked around through the thickening smoke haze for something else – *anything* that might help them survive until help arrived. In one of the toilet cubicles, he spotted the tall cylindrical toilet brush holder. He ran over, grabbed it, and returned to the sinks. He held it under the overflowing water until it was full, then walked over to Keith and upended the water over him.

Keith's cries for help were cut off by the sudden deluge. He spat water and looked at the toilet brush container. 'Oh thank you. That's fucking lovely, that is.'

Damo was already refilling the container. 'Yeah, you're fucking welcome. Now have you got a snot rag?'

'Eh?'

'A snot rag, a fucking hanky!' Damo tipped the contents of the toilet brush holder over himself.

'Yeah.'

'Well, give it a soak then breathe through it.' Damo refilled the container, hurried back to the door and flung the water at it. It began to evaporate immediately, and even through the smoke, Damo could see the wood surface steaming.

Keith began to pull one-handedly at his jeans pocket to pull out his handkerchief. It came free with a flourish into the air. He soaked it then pressed it to over his nose and mouth. '*Socorro!*' he shouted through the wet mask. Damo dragged him over to the window where he propped him up against the wall, then turned his own face to the bars and shouted, '*Incendio! Socorro!* For fuck's sake, *socorro!*'

High over Almacena, too high to be seen from the ground, a huge bat flew towards the column of smoke rising from *La Reina de Corazones*. It briefly circled the burning pub before swooping down into the smoke. A moment later, through that same smoke, Underwood entered the kitchen where a short time before Michelle had sat waiting for him. 'Michelle!' he shouted. 'Keith! Where are you?'

His only reply was a frantic barking from deeper inside the flat. He ran through the billowing smoke and opened the door to the lounge. Perry shot out between his ankles, then stopped once clear of the room to turn back and bark at him. Underwood ignored the dog, he ran through the lounge and up to the bedrooms. 'Michelle! Keith! Melanie!' As he opened door after door, there was no reply. Then he heard a cry from far below.

'*Socorro!*'

It was the barman, the Irish chap he'd been in the scrap with the other night. The voice was outside, coming from the back of the pub. Underwood ran back through the apartment. Perry was waiting for him outside the kitchen, barking and bouncing up and down like a mad thing. Underwood snatched him from mid-air as he passed and ran down the stairs to the garden.

'*Socorro!*' Damo's voice was weakening, his cries interrupted by fits of coughing. '*Incendio!*'

At the foot of the stairs, Underwood lobbed Perry into the dirt garden as he headed for the window to the ladies' toilets. The dog landed on its paws and scampered after him.

Damo's eyes were streaming, so much so that when he saw the naked man running towards him from the garden, he thought he'd begun to hallucinate. Then he recognised Underwood. 'You? Lord La-Di-Da – ' his sentence broke into coughing.

'Master?' Keith looked up from the floor. 'I knew you'd come. But you're too late.'

'Too late?' Underwood gripped the bars. 'Too late for what? Don't tell me you've eaten all the marshmallows, Keith.' He pulled on the bars but found them solidly fixed to the wall. He put a foot up onto the wall and pulled again, harder. This time the bars tore away from the wall with such force that bricks and window frame came tumbling out after them. Underwood stepped deftly aside as bars, bricks and broken glass crashed to the ground.

'They took Michelle,' cried Keith. 'And Mel. They killed Hodge.'

Damo stared in disbelief as Underwood thrust a hand out to him. 'Wha – ? How the fuck did you do that?'

'No time to explain, come on!'

Damo took Underwood's hand and felt himself hauled out through the hole where the window had been. Then he was lying outside, coughing and gasping for breath. He looked back to the window and saw Underwood had gone inside. Through the smoke there was a sudden flare of orange light. The door must have gone. 'Keith!' He tried to get up but his head swam.

Inside, Underwood knelt beside Keith, unfazed as the door flared into flame. He made a lightning assessment of Keith's wounds then eased Keith's head back so their eyes met. 'Keith, what happened here?'

Keith gripped Underwood's arm. 'Russians. Sergei. He took Michelle and Mel. He's gonna – ' His grip tightened, then went slack. Underwood gathered him into his arms and lifted him up. With the flat of his foot he kicked the remainder of the wall beneath the window away, showering it out in a cloud of bricks and dust. Then, he stepped through the hole, taking care not to hit Keith's lolling head as he did so.

'Keith!' called Damo. 'Is he alright?'

'He's alive.' Underwood carried Keith clear of the building, trying not to step on Perry as he barked anxiously up at his master. He lay Keith down and the little dog immediately began to lap at his master's face. Damo came over and fell down beside them. 'He told you about the Russians?'

'He started, but he didn't manage to finish.' said Underwood as the sound of approaching sirens began to echo from the street. 'Would you care to fill me in?'

'His name's Sergei Alexandrov. We've had a couple of run-ins with him over the years. He's a murdering bastard. He killed our mate, Pete. He killed Hodge. Jesus Christ, he took Michelle and Melanie – ' he broke into coughing as his voice rose with emotion.

'*Why?* What on Earth did you do to make him want to do something like that?'

Keith pushed Perry away from his face. 'We killed his nephew. Accident. Meant to kill Sergei. The cu – ' He grimaced as Perry's tongue lapped his mouth. 'Fuck off, Perry!'

'I see. So it's a vendetta, is it?' Underwood picked up the little dog and held him at arm's length away from Keith. 'All right, where can I find him?'

'Malaga,' said Keith, his voice woozy from blood loss. 'His, his club.'

Damo nodded. 'Yeah, that's what I reckon. It's called *La Fantasía*. Fucking great big nightclub down there on the coast.'

'Is it a distinctive building? Easy to spot from the air?'

'From the air? Janey, don't tell me you've got a fucking helicopter!'

'No, I haven't, but that's neither here nor there. Is it easy to spot from the air?'

'I dunno. Why? Why do you wanna know about the view from the air?'

'Because I haven't been to Malaga for some fifty years; I'm rather unfamiliar with the modern landscape.'

'*Fifty years?* Fuck off!'

Keith smiled. 'Fifty years is nothing to you, is it Milord?' He coughed, and lowered his head again.

'Eh?' said Damo. 'What is he going on about? Who the fuck are you? And – and while I'm at it, where are your clothes? And how the fuck did you pull them bars out? Where did you even *come from*?'

Underwood smiled and handed the wriggling terrier to Damo. 'I'm Lord Daniel Underwood, pleased to make your acquaintance.' He stood up. 'Now, pay attention, would you? My man, Flinch, will be here presently – you know him, you gave him a smack in the chops the other night – anyway, I need you to tell him exactly what you've just told me. Also, you're to tell him to fully prepare the Rolls and drive to this *La Fantasía* place as quickly as possible. I'll leave further instructions for him there when I know the lay of the land.' He started to walk away, then stopped. 'Oh, and do stress to him that he should *fully* prepare the Rolls, all right?'

'No, that's not all right. When you say "rolls", you're not talking about a packed lunch, are you? You mean a Rolls Royce, right?'

'Yes.'

'Well, what good is a fucking posh car gonna do you?'

'It's not *just* a posh car, old boy – it's a hearse. I'm afraid I don't have time to explain. I need to get going.' Underwood backed a few steps away. 'Now, shut your eyes, will you?'

Damo frowned, wondering what on Earth this naked man was suddenly feeling bashful about. He decided he didn't want to know. He closed his eyes and felt a sudden flash of heat against his face. Perry bolted from his hands. Damo opened his eyes to find Underwood had disappeared. Perry was cringing and whimpering by the garden wall, his ears pressed close to his head. 'What the ...' he looked about. 'Underwood? Where? ... Where'd you go?'

Urgent Spanish voices were approaching from around the side of the building. He heard the side gate splintering beneath the blows of an axe, then a moment later, and there were firemen all around him, they were speaking to him in Spanish – too fast for him to follow. They were joined by paramedics; more words flying at him – a meaningless clatter of vowels and consonants. Damo shook his head, looking around for Underwood. 'Underwood? Where are ya?' He watched as the paramedics surrounded Keith. One of them turned to Damo and placed an oxygen mask over his nose and mouth. He inhaled: the rush of oxygen into his lungs was beautiful, but it distracted him only momentarily from his more pressing concern. 'Where did he go?' he said to the paramedic who held him. 'Underwood? Where the fuck did he go?'

20

AS UNDERWOOD WAS MAKING HIS EXIT from the Mullins' back yard, on a high road about fifteen kilometres from Alamacena, the Citroën DS shot out of a mountain tunnel and David caught sight of the town in the distance. The landmark buildings – the hilltop castle and church – were floodlit as ever, but behind them glowed another radiance: an orange stain that seeped up into the night. David put his foot down on the accelerator, and ten minutes later, he was speeding up the deserted streets towards *La Reina de Corazones*. His window was open and the smell of smoke tinged the night air as he grew closer. Now there were people on the pavements around him moving towards where the emergency lights of fire trucks, ambulances, and police cars pulsed at the centre of a crowd of gathered onlookers.

David parked the Citroën and hurried to join the people that had come out to watch the pub burn. Many of them were in night clothes – dressing gowns and slippers, all of them talking excitedly and trying to get a closer look beyond where policemen were holding them back from the scene.

David pushed through the crowd to the front. Two fire engines were tackling the blaze, their spotlights aimed at where hoses drove thick torrents of water into the blackened building. It looked as if the fire was under control. The metal shutters at the front of the pub had been opened to reveal the interior; it was gutted, a black cave, drenched and steaming. Where was Underwood? He pushed forwards, but a police baton touched his chest. David faced the cop at the other end of it, and said in Spanish, 'They're friends of mine.'

'You can't help them or anyone else,' said the policeman. 'Just stay back and leave it to the firemen.'

David knew there was no point in arguing. He scanned the crowd for Underwood or Michelle. Then a hand fell on his shoulder.

'David?'

David turned to see Miguel. He looked shaken. 'Miguel? Are you alright? Is Lydia with you?'

'I'm okay, but Lydia, no, she isn't with me. I have to talk to you, away from here,' he glanced meaningfully at the policeman.

David nodded. As he followed Miguel to the outer edge of the crowd he asked, 'What about Underwood, have you seen him anywhere?'

'Lord Underwood? He is with you, no?'

'No. He came here ahead of me.' David glanced around at the rooftops for a sign of the vampire. 'He should've arrived here by now.'

Miguel started slightly. 'But – ' He was about to question David, but he checked himself. 'No, no I haven't seen him. But listen to me – I have to tell you something. I spoke to Lydia on the phone before this happened.'

'Oh? How long before?'

'I don't know exactly. She called me; she was coming home from a restaurant and she saw some cars arrive at *La Reina de Corazones* and men get out. She recognised one of them, a businessman she knows – she also knows he is a criminal, but business is business, you know?'

David nodded. 'Go on.'

'So, she told me who he was, a guy from Malaga – some say he is a gangster, but she has sold him property, so she wasn't afraid. When she saw him, she was going to say hello, but then she saw one of the other men had a gun. That stopped her. She watched them go up to *La Reina*; it was closed, but they knocked, and Keith Mullins – he opened the door. Lydia told me that she can see from Keith Mullins's face that he recognises the man, and he is very afraid of him, but still, he let him in.'

'Well, you know Lydia – she is very good friends with Keith Mullins. She was worried about him. So, she waited until they had gone inside, and then she went over to see if she could find out what was going on. They didn't close the front door after them, and she was able to hear some of the talk from inside. She couldn't hear much, but when she heard a voice say that a man is dead, she came away fast and she called me. She told me what had happened, and for me to come down here and meet her immediately. Well, I was in bed, but I got dressed and came here as quickly as I could. When I got here,' he gestured to the burning pub, 'there was only this.'

'You said she recognised one of the men; can you remember his name?'

'Si. His name is Sergei Alexandrov. He is Russian. I met him once with Lydia. *El es un hombre muy malo.*'

'Shit,' David again glanced around for Underwood. 'She called me too, must've been shortly after she called you. She told me to get Underwood and get here as fast as I could. Then ... there was something – I dunno – sounded like ...'

'Like what?'

'I dunno. But she rang off fast. I tried to call her back, but she wasn't answering.'

'Oh my God. Sergei Alexandrov, he must have her.'

'Well, *maybe*, yeah. That's one possibility.'

'No maybe – I *know* it. He has her and he has taken her with him; she knows too much. We should tell the police, tell them immediately.' Miguel started to make for the flashing blue lights, but David caught him by the arm.

'Whoa, hold on, Miguel. You don't want to get the police involved – not yet, anyway. We need to wait for Underwood. He came here ahead of me and told me to meet him here. He travels fast – so for all we know, Lydia could be with *him*.'

'*What?* You mean, you believe Lord Underwood ... he has been here already for some time?'

'I don't know, he might have been. Like I said, he travels fast. But if he *is* here and he *does* have her, we'd best wait for him to make the next move, don't you think? We don't want to involve the police in Underwood's business, do we?'

'No, no, of course not,' Miguel looked around uneasily. He'd known David wouldn't let him speak to the police – his trying to speak to them had just been an act. However, the disquiet he was now feeling was no act: when David said Underwood had come ahead of him, he hadn't thought for a moment that he could already have arrived; he'd been watching the street constantly and there'd been no sign of him. This was unexpected. 'Well then,' he said, 'if he is here, where is he? Why doesn't he come to us?'

'I don't know. But let's just give him a few minutes, okay? Tell me more about this Alexandrov guy. What do you know about him?'

'I met him only once. I was with Lydia in Malaga. She had a bar that she was selling to him and we went to his night club with the papers. It is a huge place, he does all his business there – it is his head office, you know? I didn't like it at all – I was fucking scared, if I tell you the truth.' He spat into the gutter and took out his cigarettes. 'If he has taken Lydia, that is where he will have taken her; it is like his castle, you know?'

David accepted a cigarette. 'I see. So, you'd know how to get there? I mean, if we needed to?'

Miguel lit their cigarettes and nodded. 'Si, but I wouldn't go there without Underwood. They have guns, David.'

'Yeah, well, they're not the only ones, are they? But hopefully it won't come to that.' David took out his phone. 'Let me try Lydia again. If she's with Underwood, she'll be able to answer.'

As David called Lydia's mobile, Miguel scanned the crowd for a sign of Underwood. Maybe he wasn't as fast as David seemed to think he was. Obviously they'd have to wait for him to arrive, as there was no point going without him – but the night was slipping away. He felt panic prickling at his scalp and took a long drag on his cigarette to calm it. He wished he could just call Lydia and tell her what was happening. She wasn't going to answer David, but she'd answer him. Only he couldn't speak to her in front of David; no, he'd have to get away from him, maybe pretend to see a friend in the crowd and ... His train of thought was suddenly derailed as David grabbed his arm.

'Miguel, look!' David was pointing to where firemen and paramedics were emerging from the black cave of *La Reina* – but they weren't alone. Someone was being carried out on a stretcher, while another man, his face obscured by an oxygen mask, was walking unaided. David turned to Miguel. 'That's Keith Mullins on the stretcher, and the other one's that Irish guy – his bouncer mate, you know? Whatsisname?'

Miguel's throat was suddenly dry, but not from the smoke. 'Damo,' he whispered, then more loudly, 'his name is Damo.'

David turned back to the emerging survivors and shouted, 'Damo!'

Damo looked up to see someone waving at him from the crowd. It was Underwood's pal, Flinch, the guy Underwood had told him would be here. He looked at Keith where he lay unconscious on the stretcher. The paramedics had said he'd be out for a while, but was stable. Flinch continued to wave at him. Damo took off his oxygen mask and handed it back to the paramedics. He thanked them and told them he'd be okay without it. Then, before they or anyone else could say anything, he slipped into the crowd and made his way quickly to David. He gave him a brief nod. 'You're Flinch, right?'

'Yeah. What the fuck happened here?'

'Russians. That's what fucking happened. Bastards caught us off guard. They murdered Hodge. Shot him down in cold blood. Poor bastard never even saw it coming.'

'Jesus Christ,' said David. 'You mean, your mate? The other bouncer?' Damo nodded.

David turned to Miguel. 'That must have been what Lydia overheard – you know, when she heard someone was dead?'

'Si,' said Miguel. 'And now he has Lydia, I know it.'

Damo looked at Miguel. 'Wait a fucking minute. You *know* Sergei?'

'No, I don't *know* him, but I was with Lydia once when she did some business with him. And tonight, Lydia, she recognised him – she saw him go into the pub. She called me. And now ... and now she is gone.'

'Jesus,' said Damo. 'Well she's not the only one; he took Michelle and Melanie an' all.'

'He *what*?' said David.

'He fuckin' kidnapped them. He shot Hodge. Then he shot Keith in the legs and doused the place in booze before setting it alight. We were all supposed to be burned to death in there, and we would have been too if it wasn't for your mate Underwood.'

'Underwood?' said David.

'Yeah, he got us out of there.'

'So, where is he now?'

'That's what I'd like to know, mate. He's fucking disappeared. Said he was going to Sergei's place in Malaga.'

'The club?'

'Yeah, *La Fantasía*. You know it?'

'No, but Miguel was just telling me all about it. He said he reckons that's where Sergei'll have taken Lydia.'

'That'd be my guess, too. But listen, there's more. Come here to me now,' Damo beckoned David to come closer then steered him a short distance from Miguel. 'Your Lord La-Di-Da said that you was to prepare the Rolls – I mean the hearse, yeah? And he emphasised you should *fully* prepare it. Now, does that make any sense to you? Because aside from the possibility that he's arranging his own funeral, it makes fuck-all sense to me.'

'Prepare the Rolls?' David remembered the guns, suit of clothes and passports in the secret drawer in the back of the hearse. He nodded.

'Yeah, I think I know what he means. Where does he want me to drive it?'

'The club, *La Fantasía*. He said he'd leave further instructions for you there.'

'Where?'

'He didn't say.'

David flicked away his cigarette. 'Right, well. Thanks for passing on the message.' He nodded to where Keith was being loaded into the back of an ambulance. 'How's Keith?'

'He's lost a lot of blood, but he'll be grand, he's a tough old bird.'

'So you'll be going to the hospital with him, will you?'

Damo's face twisted with disbelief. 'The fuck I will! I'll be going to Malaga with you.'

'What?'

'I said, I'm coming with you. If youse is gonna have a scrap with them Russian bastards, then I'm in, pal.'

'Well, hang on a minute – '

'Fuck hang on, man. Those fuckers killed two of my mates, crippled another, and then kidnapped his fucking wife and kid. If anyone's gonna be dishing out the payback, it's gonna be me.'

Miguel had been listening in on the conversation, all the while trying to figure out what to do next. Damo was telling David all the things that *he* – Miguel, was supposed to be telling him, and what was worse, now Damo was trying to get in on the rescue mission. This wasn't supposed to happen – it was supposed to be David and Underwood, with *him* – Miguel, leading the two of them into Lydia's trap. But now it turned out that Underwood not only knew where to go, but had gone on ahead of them. Shit! He should call Lydia now while the other two were busy. He was just fishing his phone out when he saw Damo start to lead David away towards the Citroën. Miguel put the phone back and called out, 'Hey! Where are you going?'

'Nowhere,' said David.

'Don't even think about going anywhere without me!'

'What's he going on about?' said Damo. 'Is he coming an' all?'

'No, and ... ' David took Damo's hand from his shoulder, 'as far as I'm concerned, neither of you are coming. It's too dangerous.'

'Of course I am coming,' said Miguel. 'If Sergei has taken Lydia, I am going to kill him. You cannot stop me.'

'Alright, Miguel!' said Damo, approvingly. 'Same here, David; either I'm in, or I'm going to the cops. You choose.'

'Jesus, you two,' said David, 'this isn't going to be a standard punch-up, you know?'

'Yeah, I know. They've got guns. But that's alright; I've got a gun at my place. We can stop off there on the way and get it.'

'No, that's not what I mean. What I mean is, Underwood, he's not like ...' David stopped, unsure if he should tell Damo just what Underwood was.

Miguel made the decision for him. 'Lord Underwood is a vampire.'

'Oh yeah,' said Damo, 'Well that would explain his taste in clothes – whenever he actually wears any. But anyway,' he pointed to the Citroën. 'That's your car, right? Come on, let's get going.'

'He's not joking,' said David. 'Underwood *is* a vampire.'

Damo saw that David's expression was deadly serious. He thought back to Underwood ripping the bars from the wall; Keith saying fifty years was nothing to him; Underwood talking about the view of Malaga from the air, and then his sudden, absolute disappearance from Keith's back yard. A vampire? It was bizarre, but in its bizarreness, it made a kind of sense. He frowned at David. 'You wouldn't be shitting me now, would you?'

Both David and Miguel shook their heads.

Damo shrugged. 'Well then, I won't say if I believe you or otherwise, but I'll give you the benefit of the doubt. His being a vampire makes about as much sense as any other explanation I can come up with for what I've seen that fella do tonight. Come on, let's get going.' He continued to the car, checking his watch as he went. 'Now, it's just coming up on half-two. We've gotta get to my place and get the gun, then we gotta get the hearse from yours. So by the time we get to Malaga it's gonna be about, what? Four, half-four?'

'Maybe less,' said David. 'We don't need to go to your place for a gun.'

'Course we do,' said Damo. 'Even if we do have Dracula on your side, we're still gonna need a fucking gun. That is, unless you've got Frankenstein and the werewolf working for you as well?'

'Sadly no. But we do have guns.'

Damo raised an eyebrow. 'Guns *plural?*'

'Oh, yes.'

Fifteen minutes later, in the garage at Casa Underwood, David, Damo and Miguel stood staring down into the concealed drawer in the back of the hearse with its two Thompson submachine guns.

Damo lifted one and held it up to admire. 'Fucking hell. Where did you get these?'

'Same place as I got this,' said David, lifting his shirt and drawing the Luger from his belt. 'They were my old man's. World War Two ordnance. Perfectly maintained, fully loaded, and ready for use. You can take one and I'll take the other.'

'Hey!' said Miguel. 'What about me?'

'Oh, don't worry, Miguel. There's plenty more where these came from. Follow me.' David led the way into the house. As they crossed the lounge, he pointed to a bookcase set in an alcove on the far wall. 'I only found this place recently. Lydia told me there was an armoury, but I had to search John's notes to find out exactly where it is.'

Damo looked doubtful. 'That's a bookcase, David. Are you sure you're thinking of armoury and not library?'

David ran his finger along a row of books, stopping on an aged volume of the complete works of Lord Byron. He eased the book out and set it aside then reached into the space it had vacated and pushed a button. There was a click. He smiled and pushed gently against the bookcase, so that it, and the wall behind, swung on creaking hinges into a small room beyond.

'Whoa!' said Damo. 'That is *so* cool. A secret room.'

'Yeah, one of many,' said David. 'And now I'll show you why it's a secret.' He flicked on the light switch.

Damo's mouth fell open, 'Fuck … me.' The walls to the left and right of him were lined with vintage weapons. As a boy, Damo had had an interest in World War Two, and he recognised guns from both the Allies and the Axis powers mounted together. 'You could start a bloody war with this lot.'

David nodded. 'Yeah, I know. Scary isn't it?'

'Scary?' Miguel went to over to a German MP40 submachine gun and ran his fingers along the length of it. 'David, this is awesome. We can annihilate them.'

'Yeah, well, hopefully it won't come to that, eh? With a bit of luck, if we can show the Russians we mean business, Underwood'll be able to convince them to just give us our friends back without a shot being fired.'

Damo laughed. 'Yeah, fat fuckin' chance of that, mate. Those bastards ain't letting anyone go without a fight. Underwood knows that, so when he says prepare the Rolls, he means lock and fucking load.' He turned to the wall opposite the door. Here, there were no guns, just an old desk, and above it, fixed to the wall, a number of framed black and white photographs. Damo stepped closer to inspect them, and the smile on his face melted. He turned back to David. 'These are Photoshopped, right?'

'What? Oh, no,' David shook his head. 'I haven't had a close look at them, but they're all genuine, I can assure you. Why?'

'They're ... ' Damo turned back to the pictures, 'they're all of Underwood, but they're like, *old* – I mean, fucking *ancient*.' He bent closer to the pictures. Many of them were of a yellowy tinge – some because they were sepia tone, but there was also the yellowing that comes with genuine age. All the pictures showed Underwood with different men and women in a variety of locations. Fashions varied from picture to picture, but Underwood's features were the only unchanging constant. Damo turned to David. 'So, you weren't shitting me, were you? He really *is* a vampire.'

David nodded. 'Yeah. He's been around since the turn of the 18th Century.'

Damo breathed an exclamation and looked again at the pictures. In one of them, Underwood was posing with a group of men in what looked like India. They all wore handlebar moustaches, stiffly waxed at the tips, but Underwood's was by far the most impressive. Damo tapped on the glass. 'Hey, have you seen this one? He looks like Kitchener in the old recruitment posters.'

'No,' said David, glancing over from where he was showing Miguel the open-bolt firing action of the MP40. 'I haven't looked at any of them yet. When I found this place, as you can imagine, I was more interested in the guns.' He put a hand on Miguel's shoulder, 'So you'll be alright with this, Miguel? If you'd prefer a pistol or something – '

'No, no, this is perfect,' Miguel had the gun strapped over his shoulder and was aiming it at the wall. 'I feel like it was made for me.'

'Hey! Have you seen this?' said Damo excitedly. He was pointing to someone in one of the pictures. 'It's fucking W.B. Yeats!'

'That doesn't surprise me,' said David, coming over to take a look. 'Underwood told me he's had a lot of friends in the arts.'

'Yeah, but look – here,' Damo pointed to another man in the picture. 'That's Aleistair Crowley. See? It says so at the bottom.' He pointed to some faded script on the picture mounting. "Underwood, W.B, Sidney, Aleistair Crowley, Henry Verlaine. 1900." I dunno who Sidney and Verlaine are, but who cares? An original picture with Yeats and Crowley together must be worth a fucking fortune, eh?' He turned to see David staring at the photo with a look of stunned disbelief. 'David?'

David took the picture from the wall and held it closer to his face. 'It *can't* be.'

'Oh, it is,' said Damo. 'Definitely. I can't say for sure about Crowley, but that's definitely – '

'Henry Verlaine.'

' – W.B. Yeats. Eh? Who?'

'Verlaine. It can't be! Nineteen-Hundred? Why, he'd have been dead for the better part of two hundred years.'

'What are you going on about? Who's Henry Verlaine?'

Miguel came over. 'Who? Who are you talking about?'

'That fella,' said Damo, pointing to Verlaine. 'Do you recognise him?'

Miguel shrugged. 'I don't know any of them, except Underwood. He looks cool there, no?'

David slowly sat down on the desk, his eyes never leaving the picture in his hands. In the photo, the men were standing stiffly posed around a fireplace. Henry Verlaine? The pirate captain from Underwood's story? It wasn't possible! It had to be a descendant, a great grandchild or something. The man in the picture was perhaps thirty years old, his face lean and handsome, but it also had a rugged quality that stood out in contrast to the soft, aristocratic features of Yeats and Crowley. David tried to read his expression: was that the ghost of a smile tugging at the corner of his mouth? And on his left cheek, an imperfection on the print? Or the shadow of a scar? David was visibly pale as he put the picture down on the desk. 'We ... we have to go.'

Damo caught his arm. 'Whoa, hang on, what about these shooters? I'm gonna need another one, aren't I?'

'What?'

'Another gun. I mean, you've got that Luger, haven't you?'

David, still stunned, waved vaguely at the weapons. 'Er, yeah. Sure, sure, but be quick, we have to get going. I'll ... get some extra ammo sorted out.'

'Oh, and do you have a shirt I can borrow as well? As you can see, I lost mine in the fire.'

'Yeah, yeah, whatever.'

Miguel walked back towards the lounge, stopping in the doorway. He stood with his feet apart and planted firmly on the floor, the MP40 poised in his grip as if he were about to open fire on the room at any moment. Then a thought occurred to him: why didn't he? He spun slowly on his heel to face David and Damo. He could do it now: so easy – just pull the trigger. They both had their backs to him; David was bending to an ammo box, taking extra magazines and putting them into a satchel, and Damo was feeling the weight of a pistol. They hadn't the vaguest suspicion of him. His finger caressed the trigger, tightening ever so slightly against the cold steel. He held his breath. Oh yes – Lydia would be so ... so what? His finger relaxed. No, that wasn't the plan. David and Underwood were to go to *La Fantasía*, and he was to go with them. That was what he had been told to do, and that was what he was going to do. The fates of Underwood and Flinch were for Lydia to decide. He let out his breath and gave a little laugh of relief.

Damo glanced over at him. 'And what are you laughing about?'

'Nothing,' said Miguel. He waved a hand at the photos on the wall. 'I was just looking at Underwood's moustache in that photo. I shouldn't laugh, but it is so funny, no?'

'Yeah, it's a real beauty. He should grow it back again. Hey, can you imagine? Dave? Can you imagine?'

David stood up and slung the ammo satchel over his shoulder. 'Imagine what?'

'If Underwood grew that moustache back. Sure he'd be fighting the birds off, wouldn't he?'

David looked at the picture of Underwood in India. 'Yeah, to stop them from nesting in it. Now, are you ready?'

'Yeah, I wanna take this.' Damo held up the Colt semi-automatic pistol he'd been weighing up. 'My Action Man had one of these when I was a kid. I never thought I'd get me hands on a real one.' He nodded to Miguel's MP40. 'He had one of them an' all. Sure, he was well fucking hard.' Then a thought struck him. '*Hey!* Have you got any of them German stick grenades?'

'What? Don't be stupid. We aren't gonna need stick-grenades.'

'No, but it wouldn't hurt to have a couple just in case, now would it? There – ' he pointed to an ammo box. 'That one's got "grenades" written on it.'

'No,' David steered them both from the room and turned out the light. 'No grenades. Come on, we have to get going.'

As soon as they stepped into the lounge, Miguel's eyes fell upon the swords crossed above the fireplace. He thrust a finger to point at them. 'David. I want a sword.'

'You *what?*'

'A sword. You two both have pistols; I want a sword.'

'Oh, don't be mental, Miguel,' said David. 'You're not gonna get into a bloody swordfight.'

Miguel ignored him, shouldering the MP40 and going over to the fireplace. He didn't intend to be getting into *any* kind of fight. The thought of the sword had occurred to him earlier, when they'd first come into the lounge: when all this was over and David and Underwood were dead, a new order would rise with Lydia as Master and he as her faithful servant. The sword of the master would go to her, and so the sword of the servant should then logically pass to him – or at least it was logical as far as he was concerned.

He reached out and touched the sabre. 'This one; I want to carry the sword of Matthias Flinch.' He looked at David and raised his eyebrows. 'Unless you are you going to use it.'

'Of course I'm not gonna use it, you don't bring a sword to a gunfight – not if you want to survive it, anyway.' Distracted by Miguel's seeming idiocy, David didn't notice Damo slip back into the armoury.

Miguel took down Matthias's sabre and wielded it at an invisible foe. 'I will use it to vanquish the enemies of the Lord Underwood.'

'You'll use it to chop your bloody leg off more like. Put it back.'

'No, David. Please. If I am to die fighting for you and Lord Underwood, it is the least you can do for me, no?'

David shrugged. Miguel had a point. 'Alright, alright.' He pointed out where the scabbard rested by the fireside. 'But don't forget to sheathe it, at least that way you'll get there with all your limbs intact.'

Damo returned quietly from the armoury and resumed his position behind David. He coughed, and as he did so, deftly slipped something into David's satchel. Then he said, 'Hey, come on, we should get going, lads. The night's getting away from us, you know?'

'I know,' said David. 'Don't tell me, tell Zorro over there.' He shook his head and led the way back to the cars.

A few minutes later, David turned the key in the Rolls and the engine fired into life. Damo was sitting beside him wearing a t-shirt of David's they'd pulled from the washing line on their way. David flicked on the headlights and drove the hearse slowly out of the garage and around to the front of the house where Miguel was waiting behind the wheel of the Citroën. He drove up alongside the Citroën and wound down the window. 'Okay, we'll lead, you follow us down. But if for some reason we get separated, you know where *La Fantasía* is anyway, right?'

Miguel nodded. 'Don't worry, David. I don't think you will lose me in *that* thing.'

'Oh, don't be so sure. John upgraded her engine a few years ago. She may look like a banger, but she goes like a bomb.' He gave Miguel a small salute before winding up the window and setting off down the drive. When he reached the turning onto the road he stopped and waited for the lights of the Citroën to catch up. Then he turned to Damo. 'Right then, quick check list: one coffin; one suit of Underwood's clothes; two passports; and various guns and ammunition. I'd say that makes for a fully prepared hearse, wouldn't you?'

'Oh yeah,' said Damo. He gently patted the ammo satchel where he held it on his lap. 'We've got everything, Dave. Everything we could possibly need.'

21

UNDERWOOD HAD APPROACHED Malaga from the dark hills to the north-east following the path of a motorway towards the steadily increasing glow on the horizon. Now, as the city spread out below him, he headed towards the coastline and the port. He had been here many times over the years, and though the city had grown exponentially since the last time he was here, certain sights of the old town were still familiar: the port and lighthouse, the dark circle of the bullring, and below him now, the Plaza del Obispo and the cathedral. Underwood began to circle high beyond the reach of the floodlights that illuminated the majestic building.

Below, the plaza and streets were still dotted with people. He swept lower, still keeping above the sodium glow of the streets but coming low enough to get a better sense of potential prey; he had expended a great deal of energy and needed to feed.

He noticed a group of young men and women remonstrating with the doorman of a bar. He heard them telling him they weren't drunk but the doorman was having none of it. As the pointless argument continued, one of their number slunk off into an alley, fumbling at the front of his Bermuda shorts. Underwood swooped down to land on one of the rooftops whose walls ran down into the shadows of the alley. He changed back to human form and looked over the edge to where the man was now urinating. He crouched down and reached over the edge of the building, the hundreds of tiny hairs on his hands and feet pricking as he grasped the sheer surface of the wall and began to descend.

Gary Cox was on holiday with his mates. They'd been out partying all night and had been wending their merry way back to the hotel when Terry had suggested they go for a nightcap. Gary had been up for it, if only to use the toilet. But since it had been looking unlikely that they'd get in, he'd decided to slip into the alley to empty his bladder anyway. He grinned to himself as he thought about how he'd managed to pull that blonde from Manchester. He wasn't the best-looking guy in the world, and back home he doubted if she'd have given him the time of day. But sun, sea and sangria could always be counted on to lower a girl's standards. Phil had had his eye on her, but like a total knob, he'd told her

she was pretty fit for a fat bird, and that had fucked his chances right up.
Gary laughed and weaved the flow of his urine left and right. 'You fucking
plonker, mate. You fucking plonk – ' Gary's pee stream cut off sharply as
he heard something hit the ground behind him. He turned to see a naked
man approaching him.

'Good evening.'

'Whoa, now,' said Gary, thrusting his penis back into his shorts and
throwing his hands up in defence. 'I'm not like that – I mean gay! I've got
a bird, see? She – ' The man raised his hand and Gary's mouth stopped
working. The man's eyes seemed to glow strangely, sapping Gary of any
desire to do anything but be still and silent.

'Now listen, old boy. In a moment you're going to give me all of your
clothes and a couple of pints of blood. But first, I need to give you a
message, okay?'

Gary managed to nod.

'Good show. Now, tell me, do you know a club around here called *La
Fantasia?*'

Gary nodded.

'Then listen very carefully.'

Four minutes later, Underwood emerged from the alley wearing Gary's
clothes: a white England football t-shirt, Bermuda shorts and a pair of
canvas plimsolls. Outside the bar, the bouncer was chatting amiably with
some Spanish girls; evidently Gary's friends had given up trying to get into
the bar and had wandered off without him. Gary would wake up soon,
naked but for his boxer shorts, to find his mobile phone and wallet lying
on his belly with all its contents intact – minus twenty Euros. Underwood
now raised the twenty euro note at a passing taxi, and it slowed to pull in
just ahead of him. Underwood got in the back and smiled. '*Hola, señor.
Club La Fantasia, por favor.*'

It was a short ride. Underwood paid the driver and tipped him, leaving
him with ten Euros to get into the club. The street was busy with people
coming and going from the club in high spirits. Underwood went in
through the front door and stepped up to the box office. '*Uno, por favor,*'
he said brightly.

The girl behind the glass wore a bored expression. 'Twelve.'

'Twelve? Oh dear.'

The girl's reply was to blow and burst a bubble with her gum.

Underwood took his ten euro note and slid it to her across the counter. The girl looked at it, then at him. He smiled. 'Twenty. Keep the change.' The girl hesitated, transfixed by his eyes. 'Where can I find Mr Alexandrov?'

'I don't know if he's here,' said the girl in Spanish. 'I haven't seen him.'

'If he were here,' Underwood replied in Spanish, 'where would he be?'

'Upstairs in his office.'

'And how do I get there?'

'Turn left, go along the corridor, through the door marked private, upstairs, along – '

Underwood held up a hand and she stopped talking. He looked to where she indicated. There were three black-jacketed security men with wires in their ears in the corridor. It was too public. He looked at the girl. 'Another way?'

'Through the club. Backstage area. Go up from there. Or there's the fire escape at the back.'

'Gracias.' Underwood released the note. The girl took it and pressed a rubber ink stamp onto the back of his hand. Underwood smiled his thanks then went through the doors into the nightclub. The room was vast, and heady with the scent of human pheromones; he could scent pleasure, attraction, arousal; alcohol was heavy in the humid air, but so were newer, stranger aromas. The music was loud, booming, almost tribal, and crazy moving lights flashed and sent beams over the heads of the hundreds of people wriggling together in a seething dark mass. 'Interesting,' he muttered to himself. 'Fred and Ginger, your day is well and truly done.'

He saw the stage area on the other side of the room. Crowds of people were shuffling around on it, some waving their arms as though they were sending signals to the rest of the room. He checked left and right, but no one was returning the signals. He braced himself, then set off on his journey across the floor. 'Excuse me,' he said as he pushed through the crowd. 'I do beg your pardon. Oops, careful there.' He was being nudged, bumped, and jostled. He found the easiest way to move through the crowd was to move with it; he began to wriggle and bob with the rest of them.

A pretty girl in a bikini top began moving in time with him. Underwood smiled appreciatively, wondering as he did so, *Are we dancing?*

The girl moved her body against his. *It appears so.* He moved with her, admiring her openly as she was him. *Well,* he thought, *perhaps this modern dancing isn't so bad after all.* 'Forgive me, miss,' he said, 'But I have to run. I'm meeting a friend.'

The girl rested her arms over his shoulders. Underwood was about to apologise again when – quite without warning – she started kissing him. Underwood was completely taken aback. As her arms slid around his neck, he found himself returning her kiss. He put his arms around her, moving his hands up her back as he drew her close to him. He could hear her heart beating almost in time with the music. Then she broke off and resumed dancing with him. Underwood laughed. 'I, er, I really do have to go, but if you're around later?' The girl gave him a smile and melted away into the crowd.

'Well, well,' he said to himself. 'This is obviously the place to be.' He was now almost on the other side of the floor. To the left of the stage area and behind one of the huge speaker stacks, he noticed a glowing exit sign. He pressed on through the crowd, putting his fingers in his ears as he grew nearer the speaker stacks. As he came around the speakers, he saw another black-jacketed security guard barring the exit door. Underwood went up to him, feigning drunkenness. 'Alright, mate? Is that the kaazie?'

The guard regarded him with disinterest and said nothing.

'I said, is that kaazie? The bog?'

'Is private,' said the guard. He was about to tell the stupid Englishman to get lost when he suddenly found himself arrested by the man's eyes.

'I've an appointment to see Mr Alexandrov,' said Underwood in Spanish. 'It's very important. Where do I find him?'

'Through here,' the guard cocked a thumb back at the door. 'Go along the corridor to the stairs. Go up to the second floor. Turn right, then left –'

'Yes, yes, so it's on the second floor, is it?'

'*Si.*'

'*Gracias.* Now, step aside and open the door for me.' The guard did as he was told. 'When I go through, you're to close the door behind me. Then the moment it closes, you will forget me and everything about this conversation. You understand?'

The guard nodded.

Underwood smiled. 'Good.' He stepped through the door and the guard closed it after him. He then walked quickly down the corridor till he came to the stairwell. He pushed through the doors and trotted up the stairs to the second floor. As he neared the landing, he heard voices in the corridor above speaking in Russian. The security men downstairs had been Spanish. Evidently it was a two-level set up; domestic security downstairs, and mob security upstairs. Underwood got to the landing and listened at the door: two men, very near, they sounded quite heavy-set. No matter. He again affected a slightly drunken gait before pushing through the doors into the corridor. 'Alright, lads,' he said, dropping back into his cockney accent. 'Where's the kaazie?'

The guards turned, each of them reaching without hesitation for the guns that Underwood now noticed on their belts. As the pistols were drawn, Underwood threw up his hands, 'Whoa! Hang on now. I'm just looking for the bog. You know? El boggo? La Lavvy?' Despite his placating hand gesture, Underwood walked steadily towards them.

One of the guards was raising a walkie-talkie to his mouth when Underwood suddenly seized his gun by the barrel, ripping it from his fingers before swinging it back to land a savage blow on the man's temple. He fell down, out cold to land in a heap against the wall. The other guard was completely taken by surprise. One moment he'd been ready to roll a drunkard, now he found himself staring down the barrel of his partner's gun. 'Easy there, comrade,' said Underwood. Then he switched to Russian. 'You want to live?'

The guard nodded.

'Then drop your gun and radio and take me to see Mr Alexandrov, can you do that for me?'

The guard nodded, bending to drop his gun and radio and then turning, hands raised, to lead the way down the corridor. As they went through a pair of fire doors, Underwood picked up Michelle's scent. It grew stronger with every step as they proceeded down the corridor. Then the guard stopped outside a door. Before he could turn, Underwood struck him on the back of the head and he collapsed, unconscious. He then tapped on the door with the barrel of the gun. A Russian voice on the other side commanded him to enter. He did, with his hands raised and the pistol barrel held between finger and thumb. He immediately assessed the four armed guards and the two men – one seated, one standing – behind the desk, before his eyes went to Michelle and Melanie. They were sitting on a sofa on the right side of the room, their wrists secured with zip ties and their mouths silenced by duct tape. At the sight of him, Michelle sat up. He smiled at her and turned to the men behind the desk. When he'd entered, they had been admiring some glass-fronted black boxes that hung from a shoulder high metal truss behind them. The seated man was middle-aged and wore an expensive shirt with his tie loosened about his neck. The man standing behind him was a chubby, balding Spaniard in jeans and a t-shirt who wore his remaining hair tied back in a ponytail. This man was holding a black box about the size of a cigarette packet that he'd evidently been explaining to the other man, who now took it and put it on his desk next to some sort of machine pistol.

'Good evening,' said Underwood.

'Good evening,' said Sergei. Anton and Ivan, who flanked him, drew pistols to bear on Underwood. Sergei held up a hand to stay them. He smiled. 'I'd say you were lost, but for the fact that you are carrying a pistol.'

'Yes,' said Underwood. 'One of yours, I'm afraid. I took it off one of your men.' He smiled at the look of alarm this caused. 'Oh, don't worry, he's relatively unharmed. I come in peace.'

Sergei had realised as soon as he'd seen the gun that this must be one of the men Lydia was expecting. But which one? Either way, he was early. Sergei's smile didn't reveal a hint of his disquiet. 'I see, and you are?'

'My name's Underwood.' Underwood offered his gun, handgrip first, to the nearest guard. 'I'm a friend of your guests on the sofa here. And I have to say, Mr Alexandrov – I presume I have the pleasure of addressing Mr Alexandrov – you really don't know how to treat a lady.' He looked at Michelle. 'Are you all right?' Michelle nodded.

'You make an interesting first impression, Mr Underwood. Your clothes announce you as a fool; your actions, as a man who is tired of living. Perhaps you are both, no?'

'Oh, I've been those and many things besides, but not tonight, I'm afraid.'

Sergei laughed. 'Very good. Yes, yes, I am Alexandrov. Captain Sergei Alexandrov, retired. Please, lower your hands.'

'Thank you, but it's *Lord* Underwood, actually. My fault, I should have said so.' He gestured to a chair opposite Sergei's desk. 'May I sit down?'

'Please.'

'Thank you.' Underwood took the seat and sat back. 'Well, you've had a busy night tonight, haven't you, Captain?'

'Have I?'

'Yes. What with kidnapping these ladies and Miss Flinch, murdering Mr Mullins and his friends, and – ' A cry of stifled anguish came from Melanie. Underwood ignored her; Sergei thought Keith and his friends were dead and he didn't want to disabuse him of that belief, he continued: '– and burning that charming pub of theirs to the ground, I'd say you must be fairly pooped.' He nodded sideways to Melanie and Michelle. 'Why have you brought them here?'

'That is not your concern.'

'I'm sorry, but it is. They are my friends; as is Miss Flinch – wherever she may be; as were the late Mr Mullins and his associates. So you see, your busy night has had a seriously detrimental effect on my social life. And that, if nothing else, makes it very much my concern.'

'You keep mentioning a Miss Flinch. I know nothing of this woman.'

'Oh come along, Captain,' said Underwood with a smile. 'We're both gentlemen, aren't we? Let's not get our relationship off to a sour start by telling fibs. I know she's here somewhere. She was in this very room not half an hour ago.'

Sergei raised an eyebrow. 'Really? I didn't see her. Did you see her, Ivan? Anton?'

They both shook their heads. 'No, Captain.'

'Well perhaps she didn't introduce herself, but she was the woman you were beating, Ivan. You still have her blood on your knuckles.'

Ivan looked at his knuckles. There were some traces of Lydia's blood, but just in the creases of skin. Not so much as you could see from where Underwood was standing. He frowned and spoke to Sergei in Russian. 'Captain, I don't like this man. You want us to kill him?'

Underwood replied in Russian. 'I'd prefer it if you didn't. Just let me take the women, including Miss Flinch, and we'll put all this unpleasantness behind us.'

Sergei smiled, 'You speak Russian like Moskvich, Lord Underwood. I'm impressed. But I'm afraid I cannot let you take them anywhere. You see, they are not mine to give; I have already sold them.'

'Sold them?'

'Yes. I'm sorry, but this is revenge. Ah, I see from your expression this surprises you. You see, Mr Mullins and his friends murdered my nephew and two of my men.' Sergei rose to his feet, anger now in his eyes. 'They murdered my flesh and blood, Lord Underwood! Gunned down and hit with car!' Sergei slammed the desktop with his hands. 'For years that English pig was like thorn in my mind. Now, he burns in Hell where he belongs. And whenever he looks up from where he squirms in Satan's asshole, he will see his women suffering for the rest of their lives. They go to a Serbian brothel. It is unfortunate, but vengeance is always so, I'm sure you understand.'

Underwood fought to contain his fury. 'Dear God, man. I understand your need for revenge, especially since you've lost a member of your family. But you go too far. You lost three men, and now you've killed the three men who did it. That's justice. So I entreat you, let these women go. They have no place in your revenge.'

'I decide who has place in my revenge. And I say they do – along with your precious Miss Flinch; she interfered while I was doing my revenge on Mullins. She tried to call police.' He shook his head. 'No. She has seen too much and wants to share it. Like you, now. You think you can just walk in here – a football hooligan telling me what I can and can't do? Who do you think you are? You are police? FBI? Where is your fucking army?'

'Mr Alexandrov – '

Sergei picked up the Uzi machine pistol on his desk and fired a burst at Underwood's chest. 'Shut your fucking mouth!' Underwood was sprayed with bullets, toppling him sideways from his seat. Michelle and Melanie screamed against their gags as Sergei rose from his seat. 'What, you were going to make me an offer I couldn't refuse?' He fired the Uzi again, raking Underwood's body with another burst. 'Fuck you and your fucking offers. Look at you now.' He dropped the gun to the desk and turned to Anton and Ivan. 'So much for this footballing Count Dracula, eh?' He laughed. 'The Flinch woman is mad. But we honour our part of the deal.' Then he noticed Ivan's smile fall, his eyes on Underwood's body. From behind him, the other guard said, 'Captain?' Sergei heard the sound of movement where Underwood had fallen.

'As I was saying, Mr Alexandrov,' said Underwood.

Sergei turned around to see Underwood, his head down, getting unsteadily to his feet. As he rose, bullets fell from him like crimson raindrops into the pool of blood at his feet. 'Either you let me and these ladies leave here quietly,' He looked up; the bullet holes in his face were smoking, 'or I'll tear every last one of you to pieces.' Underwood put his fingers through the torn and bloody holes in his shirt and tore it apart to reveal his torso had completely healed. He dropped the shirt to the floor and smiled. Sergei gasped to see that his canine teeth were long and sharp.

'Oh my God,' Sergei whispered as he fell into his seat. 'It's true. You are wampyre!' He picked up the wired device on his desk he'd been fiddling with when Underwood had entered.

Underwood's yellow eyes never left Sergei's. 'Please, don't bother shooting me anymore, comrade. All it does is cheese me off.'

'You,' Sergei's tone was one of hushed astonishment. 'You are incredible.'

'Thank you, but don't think flattery's going to save you.' Underwood extended an inviting hand to Michelle and Melanie. They looked nervously at the man guarding them, who in turn looked to Sergei for instruction.

Sergei didn't notice, he was watching Underwood in awe. 'I didn't believe it when she told me, but who would? It was like fairy story.'

'She being Miss Flinch, I presume,' said Underwood.

'Yes.'

'Bring her here. And pray to God that your meat-headed friend over there hasn't hurt her too badly. Like I said, she and these ladies have no part in your revenge.'

'Ahh, no, Lord Underwood; it is as *I* said – they do.'

Underwood frowned. 'I beg your pardon?'

'I sell them ...' Sergei raised the device in his hand and smiled, '... and I kill you.' He pressed a switch and the black boxes behind him burst into dazzling violet brilliance.

Underwood threw his hands up against the sudden wave of searing heat. His exposed flesh began to burn and he screamed, falling to the ground and trying to roll to cover, but there was no cover; the violet light was everywhere. And then, as suddenly as it had started, it stopped. The light was gone.

Sergei stood up and patted the pony-tailed Spaniard on the shoulder. 'Bravo, Stefano. This is the best light show you've ever designed.'

'Despite the fact that he looked as if he were about to start screaming, Stefano managed a brave smile. 'Thank you, señor Alexandrov. Can I ... can I go now? My mother, she – '

Sergei shook his head, all the while looking at Underwood. 'Soon.' He motioned to Ivan and the guard at the door. 'Get the flashlights.' Ivan and the guard went to the small bar area and each picked up one of a number of hand-held UV lights. Sergei addressed Underwood, who lay smouldering in a foetal position on the floor. 'Oh dear, my Lord, you seem to have a touch of the sunburn. Perhaps we have calamine lotion somewhere.' He laughed and his men joined in.

Underwood uncoiled, his burned flesh breaking and bleeding as he did. 'What ... what are those ... things?'

'What, these?' Sergei gestured to the lights behind him. 'An innovation you're obviously unfamiliar with. Ultra-violet lights. Stefano here brought the big ones up from the club downstairs, but the little ones we had to go shopping for. I don't like them, myself; I think they make my teeth look weird. But you obviously have a far greater reason for disliking them, no?'

'So ... you were ... expecting me,' Underwood said, shakily trying to find his feet.

'Yes. We had some time to prepare. Miss Flinch told us you would be coming to save her. She told us what you were, and with a little persuasion from Ivan here, how to hurt you.'

Underwood had slowly been getting to his feet and now he looked at Sergei with murder in his eyes, 'You unutterable swine.'

Sergei nodded for Ivan to switch on his UV flashlight. He did, and a beam of concentrated violet light raked across Underwood's flesh like a heat ray. Underwood cried out as his already scorched flesh ignited, he fell back to the floor, hands raised to protect his eyes as the other guard approached. This man had a device with a single UV tube; to Underwood, it glowed in his hand like a small sun.

'Don't get any ideas about changing your form, Lord Underwood,' Sergei said with a smile. 'These lights will destroy you no matter what form you take.'

'Stop it!' cried Underwood.

'Can I trust you to behave?'

Underwood pedalled his feet against the floor, sliding through the slick of his own smoking blood and pushing himself away from the approaching lights. 'Yes! Damn you! Just turn those bloody things off!'

'Good.' Sergei nodded to Ivan and the other guard and they switched off their lights, though they continued to hold them ready and aimed at Underwood. 'And so. Now you will accompany my men to your precious

Miss Flinch. I am expecting my Serbian guests any minute and I don't want you making the place stink like barbeque.' He laughed and all his men joined in. 'Take him away, and for God's sake,' he waved his hand in front of his nose, 'somebody open a window.'

Underwood was bundled down the corridor by three guards; two of them carried UV flashlights, switched on and aimed at the floor, but ready to flick up onto Underwood if he made a move to escape. Ivan led the group, he carried a UV light about the size of a cereal box with a plug trailing along the floor behind him. He came to a door which he unlocked then stepped aside from.

'You see this?' he said, holding up the light. 'I plug this in out here and aim it at door. It is like Rottweiler waiting outside for you, yes? Alexi here will be also with gun and flashlight. If you or bitch try to escape, he will kill you, understand?'

Underwood nodded. He could barely walk. Every step was agony and he was exhausted. His body was struggling to maintain his vital functions, unable to regenerate his burned flesh. He cursed himself for not killing the lad in the alley earlier and drinking all his blood. After the night's flights and transformations; the shooting, blood loss and burning he'd taken, he was on the brink of collapse. He staggered to the door and one of the guards pushed him into the room. He fell to the floor and the door slammed behind him.

'My Lord!' cried Lydia. 'Oh my Lord, my Lord, what have they done to you?' She came to him, kneeling at his side and easing him over to face her. She gasped at the sight of his face, the skin burnt raw in patches, his eyebrows and much of his hair singed away. 'Oh my God.'

He smiled. 'Hello, Lydia.' He reached up to touch her face, his fingers lightly brushing the bruises and swollen cuts inflicted on her in his name. 'I'm sorry.'

'*You're sorry?* Oh my Lord, no, no, I'm sorry. This is all *my* fault; it's my fault you came here, my fault they did this to you, and -' she put a hand over her mouth to stifle a sudden sob, 'It's my fault they knew how to hurt you. I'm sorry, I should never have told them what you were, but they beat it out of me, they beat it out of me.' She broke down in tears.

'There, there. Don't blame yourself. You were … very brave,' his voice was slipping away, his eyes closed and his hand fell.

'My Lord! Lord Underwood? Oh Jesus, please don't die! Don't die on me now! I need you! Michelle and Melanie need you too!'

Underwood opened his eyes. 'Sleep Lydia ... I ... Must sleep. Can't fight like this. Need, need to regenerate tissue.'

'But you can't! There's no time. The Serbs will be here any minute and that bastard Sergei will sell us. He's going to sell me as a fucking whore! You can't leave me! You can't!'

'No other way, Lydia. Only sleep ... or blood.'

'Blood? Well then drink from me. Quickly,' she leaned forward so her throat was close to his lips. He did nothing. She shoved him. '*Come on*, bite me!'

'No,' he whispered, 'No Flinch ... shall bleed.'

'Fuck that shit! No Flinch shall be fucked senseless for the rest of her life is what's worrying me.' She sank her nails into a cut on her cheekbone and tore at the wound. Blood flowed onto her fingers. She wiped it on her throat above the jugular and pressed it to his lips. For a few seconds, nothing happened. Then she felt his tongue against her skin. She held her breath as she felt the twin points of his teeth growing against her. As he moved his mouth, his breath sent shivers down her spine. Then she felt his hand at the back of her head. He hesitated for a moment, then pulled her head forwards, his fangs breaking the skin and sinking into her neck. She gasped and fought to resist the natural instinct to pull away from the source of pain, like she was holding her hand over the flame of a candle. And then, suddenly there was no pain, a wave of warmth flowed through her and she felt his arms close around her body. 'Oh, my Lord. At last, I'm yours. Drink! Drink from me and be strong!'

She caressed him, running her fingers over his face and into his hair. She could feel the singed areas growing back under her palms. He was returning to her. She was bringing him back to life. She was so intoxicated by the moment that she didn't notice the door opening behind her.

'Well, well, well,' said Sergei. 'It looks like I'm arriving at the inopportune moment.'

Underwood pulled away, closing the wound at Lydia's neck in a second and raising his face to Sergei, his fangs bared in a bloody snarl. The tiny sun in Sergei's hand flashed on and Underwood fell back, hands over his eyes. 'Stop! Stop it!'

Sergei chuckled. 'You are not accustomed to being beaten like this, are you, Lord Underwood? When was the last time you were reduced to begging for mercy?' The UV light in the hall was switched on, and to Underwood, it was like Sergei was suddenly surrounded by a halo of fire. 'Miss Flinch needs to be cleaned up and made ready to meet her *new* masters. They will be here soon and ... they might want to try before they buy, you understand.'

'No!' Underwood tried to move towards Sergei, but it was like advancing into an inferno. He curled back into a foetal position as his flesh began to burn. 'Nooo! Damn you!'

Anton came in and seized Lydia by the wrist. She screamed as he dragged her past Sergei and out of the room. 'Daniel! My Lord! Help me!'

'No time for goodbyes, Lord Underwood. She goes, and you,' Sergei beckoned to someone in the corridor, 'you die.' He turned and walked out.

Through his burning fingers, Underwood watched as Sergei's silhouette melted into the fire. But the door didn't close after him as he'd expected, and the light began to come closer. 'No!' he screamed. 'No!'

'Da, vampire,' said Ivan holding the large UV light before him as he advanced. 'Now we see how brightly you burn.'

22

ONCE THEY WERE FAR ENOUGH down the corridor to hear themselves over Underwood's screams, Lydia and Anton stopped. He offered her a cigarette and she accepted it. They looked back to the room from which Sergei now exited, smoke trailing behind him through an eerie violet luminescence. He came down to join them with a satisfied smile on his face. 'Well, that went very smoothly, no?'

'That's easy for you to say,' said Lydia. 'You didn't have to get a battering in order to earn his trust.' They started walking towards the office.

'You think Ivan was too rough with you?'

She shook her head, 'No. If he hadn't been rough, Underwood would never have fallen for it.'

'So, he did fall for it? I wasn't sure if he was co-operating with your plan or killing you.'

'Oh, yes,' she stroked her neck where Underwood had bitten her. 'He was co-operating wonderfully.'

'And so, how do you feel now?'

'In a word, horny. I want to run back into that room and fight like a banshee just so he can get his teeth back into me again.'

'That seems, I don't know … '

'Crazy?' suggested Anton.

'Yes,' said Sergei. 'Exactly this. Crazy.'

'Oh, it's alright. My lust's just a symptom of his bite. It'll pass.'

'If it doesn't,' Anton said with a leer, 'My place isn't far from here.'

Lydia blew smoke at him. 'Why Anton, I never knew you cared. Maybe once I've had something to drink, I'll take you up on that.' She turned to Sergei. 'Did you get it?'

A look of mild disgust flickered over Sergei's features. 'Oh yes. Please come.' He led the way into his office. Michelle and Melanie looked up from where they sat on the sofa, their eyes wide with fear. Sergei gestured to the bloodstained floor tiles in front of his desk and the wall that was pock-marked with bullet holes. 'Your Lord Underwood made quite a mess, as you can see. Viktor here managed to mop up a fair amount from the floor.'

'Where is it?' asked Lydia with a note of barely concealed desperation in her voice.

'Ahh, but that is not all. His Lordship was kind enough to give us his shirt too.' Sergei used a pen to lift Underwood's ripped and blood-soaked England football shirt from the sink behind the bar. It dripped slow, thick droplets of blood. Sergei grimaced and dropped it back into the sink. 'Viktor Dubrovsky! What is this? Still there is blood in this thing? I thought you squeezed it all out into the glass.'

Lydia fought to restrain herself from lunging for the bloody shirt. From the moment she'd entered the office, her heart had begun to pound at the smell of blood in the air. 'Where?' she asked, trying to keep the composure in her voice. 'Where is the glass?'

Sergei nodded to one of the men guarding Michelle and Melanie. 'Viktor, give Miss Flinch her ... beverage.'

Viktor, a lean man in this late twenties with his hair tied back in a pony tail, came over and went behind the bar. He gingerly lifted a pint glass filled almost to the brim with cold, dark blood. He held it at the rim; the sides were slick and dripping from where the shirt had been messily strained over it. With a look of open revulsion on his face, he handed the glass over the bar to Lydia. 'Cheers.'

She reached out trembling hands to take it. She hadn't known how much blood Sergei would be able to extract from Underwood, but as she saw the glass before her, she knew she had more than enough for the transformation to work. Finally, she was to fulfill her destiny.

'Be careful,' said Viktor. 'The sides are slippery. You want me to wipe?'

'No. Give it to me.' She closed her hands around it and brought it close to her face, breathing in the odour as it as if it were the bouquet of a fine wine.

'Are you okay?' said Sergei. 'You look ... strange.'

'Do I?' Lydia giggled. 'Yes. I *feel* strange.' She brought the glass to her lips. 'And in a few moments, I dare say I'll feel a whole lot stranger.'

'Maybe this is a bad idea, Lydia,' Sergei began, but he stopped speaking as she suddenly began to drink the blood. His lips curled disdainfully as she drank faster, gulping at it so the liquid spilled from the corners of her mouth and ran down her cheeks. 'Oh, Jesus. Lydia, you will be sick.'

Lydia drank until the glass was drained, tilting her head back to allow the last dregs to run into her mouth before finally letting the glass fall from her fingers to the floor where it shattered on the tiles. She stared at him, her eyes wide as blood dripped from her chin onto her blouse. Then she smiled a lunatic grin. 'Be sick? Oh no, Sergei, I ... I'm never going to be sick again. I'm ... immortal ... I ...' Her smile faded and a look of doubt clouded her expression. She took an unsteady step back, then another to one side. She looked at Sergei, and her eyes were suddenly afraid. She clutched her stomach. 'No! It's not supposed to hurt.'

'You should sit, Lydia. Maybe throw up? Anton, get her chair! Viktor, a bucket from behind the bar.'

'Oh Jesus, no,' Lydia's faced was pained as she clutched more tightly at her stomach. 'It must've been too old. The blood ... it was cold, thick, too old.' Anton brought over a chair a moment too late as she collapsed to the floor. Viktor came around with a bucket and bent to her. She looked up at him, her eyes confused, 'I'm dying. Oh, Jesus. I'm dying.'

Anton looked to Sergei. 'What should we do, Captain?'

Sergei shrugged and replied in Russian. 'Leave her. The silly bitch has drunk a pint of blood. She'll puke it up when she's ready.'

Lydia suddenly spasmed violently, then heaved in a breath. Her lungs sounded tortured, as if her air canals were closing up. She grabbed at Viktor, her bloody hands scrabbling for purchase on his jacket sleeve. He eased her down and held her to the floor, more to protect his jacket than for her benefit. She convulsed, her whole body tensing and her eyes rolling back in her head. Then suddenly, she went slack and lay still.

Viktor felt around her neck for a pulse but couldn't find one. He looked at Sergei. 'I ... I think she is dead.'

Sergei shrugged. 'Oh well. At least, this will make things easier for us when her brother and Miguel arrive.'

'Why?' asked Anton.

'Why? Because Miguel just lost his protection.' Sergei lightly kicked the sole of Lydia's shoe and smiled. 'Now we can kill them both.'

David drove the hearse slowly down the road towards the entrance of *La Fantasía*. There were a number of people milling around outside, most of them smoking, others leaving in high spirits. 'Well, it looks like it's still open all right.'

'I told you so,' said Damo. 'This place stays open till about seven o' clock in the morning.'

'No sign of Underwood, though. Do you see him?'

'No. Hey, check out that guy. Looks like someone's had a mad night.' He pointed to a man who stood a short distance from the front doors clad only in his boxer shorts. The man was clutching something in his hands and staring straight ahead like a zombie.

'Oh yeah. Bet he's feeling chilly.'

As they drove across the path of the man's gaze, he started, as if suddenly awoken from a dream.

'Hello,' said Damo. 'Looks like your man's taken a fancy to this hearse of yours.'

David checked the rear view mirror and saw that the man was now running along the pavement after them. 'Oh great, that's all we need, a naked vintage car enthusiast on our tail. If I live past lunchtime today, the first thing I'm going to do is get us a nice, inconspicuous camper van.' He eased his foot down on the accelerator, and gradually the man fell behind and dwindled away. 'Thank fuck for that. The sooner we get out of this stupid car the better.' David took out his phone and checked for messages or missed calls from Lydia or Underwood. There were none. He swore and slipped it back in his pocket.

'Still no word?'

'No.'

'Well then, I guess we assume the worst: he's either been captured or killed.'

'Yeah. I guess so. Incredible though it seems.' David checked his mirror; Miguel was right behind them in the Citroën. David flicked on the indicator to signal his intention to pull over.

'I don't know why it's so incredible to you; he's not Superman, you know. They could've staked him through the heart.'

David gave a short, humourless laugh. 'Oh, take it from me; that's not as easy as you might think.' He parked at the side of the road and Miguel rolled in ahead of them.

'Well he's either banjaxed somehow, or he's fucked off and left us. Which do you think is the more likely?'

'He'd never leave us.'

'Sure then, he must have fucked up somehow. He's only human ... sort of.'

Miguel got out of the Citroën and walked back to join them. He leaned in at Damo's window, 'So what's going on?'

'Dracula's fucked up,' said Damo. 'Looks like it's gonna be Plan B.'

Miguel frowned. 'What is Plan B?'

'We are. Meet the 7th Cavalry: you, me, and Dangerous Dave here.'

David managed a smile. 'Yeah well, I dunno about the 7th Cavalry. We need to work out a proper plan. We don't wanna just go in, guns blazing, now do we?'

'Well, yeah, obviously. But guns are gonna have to blaze at some stage.'

'I don't know if it's a good idea to start shooting,' said Miguel. 'Someone will hear and call the police.'

'Sure, they won't hear nothing,' said Damo. 'That place has got industrial grade soundproofing. They have to have it if they're gonna be banging out the club anthems all night. A plane could crash land right through the neighbours' front door, and the clubbers wouldn't be any the wiser.'

Miguel noticed something to his side. He straightened up, suddenly wary. 'Hey, better change the subject, here comes a first-class *giri*.'

David and Damo looked back to see the boxer shorts man come panting along the pavement behind them. David sighed. 'Oh joy. It's the Hearse Appreciation Society.'

The man in the boxer shorts stopped and leaned against the roof of the hearse, panting hard, too breathless to speak. He held up a hand in a gesture for them to wait until he had his breath back. In his other hand he clutched his wallet and mobile phone.

'Are you alright, pal?' asked Damo.

'Fucked ... ' said the man in between gasps. '... Knackered ... Why ... Why didn't you stop for me?'

'Have you had a look at yourself lately?'

'I've ... I've a message for you ... From Lord Underwood.'

'What?' David threw open his door and got out. 'What did he say?'

'He said you'd give me a hundred euros to cover the cost of my clothes and the money he took from me.' He rubbed his neck where Underwood had bitten him earlier. 'Nice guy.'

'Is that all?'

The man – Gary Cox – held up a hand, still trying to get his breath. 'No, he said he was going in. He's going to convince Sergei of the error of his ways.' Damo got out of the hearse and handed Gary a bottle of water. Gary took it and drank. Once he'd slaked his thirst, he went on. 'He said that if he hasn't got in touch by the time you get here, things have gone skew-whiff. You're not to worry about him, but the ladies must be rescued.'

'Did he say any more?' asked Damo.

Gary nodded as he took another drink.

'Well? What was it?'

Gary wiped his hand across his mouth. 'Tally-ho.'

'Shit!' said David.

'Yeah, well,' said Gary, 'shit happens, man. Can I have my money now? I suddenly feel very tired. He said I'd feel very tired.'

David took out his wallet and handed Gary two fifty Euro notes. 'There you go, mate. Drink plenty of liquids and you'll be all right in the morning. Do you remember the name of your hotel?'

Gary nodded. 'Yeah. I ... I hope Phil hasn't copped off with that bird from Manchester. She was mine.'

David hailed a passing taxi. It slowed and it swung in beside them. 'Don't worry. I'm sure she still is.' The driver gave Gary a wary look, but David told him in Spanish that Gary was a generous tipper. Gary got in and they drove away.

'Jesus,' said Damo. 'He stood out there all that time, and then came running after us like a mad man just to pass on a message? How'd Underwood talk him into that?'

'Underwood can talk anybody into anything,' said David as he got back into the hearse.

'Can he now? I'd say he'd be a handy man to have around when you're out on the pull, eh? He'd save you a fortune in buying drinks for the *chicas*.'

'So, what now?' asked Miguel. 'Is Plan B?'

'Yeah,' said David starting the engine. 'Now is Plan B.'

They drove back in the direction of *La Fantasía*, turning off a few blocks before it into the back streets. Pressing in on the narrow streets were sleeping apartment blocks bristling with TV antennae and satellite dishes. Cars and motor scooters were parked everywhere, but they managed to find some spaces just down from the back of a small bakery. The bakery door was open, and as they got of the cars they could hear tinny flamenco music drifting from a radio.

Damo sniffed. 'Mmmm, fresh bread. Couldn't you just murder a bacon and egg bocadillo right now?'

David went around to the back of the hearse and opened the door. He looked down to the rear of the baker shop, its open door a yellow rectangle of light in the otherwise dark building. He could hear distant voices but couldn't see anyone. 'Be careful of that doorway. Someone could pop out for a fag or something.' He opened the concealed drawer and they each took their weapons. Miguel took off his belt and attached the sword scabbard to it; he then fastened it over his shoulder. Over the other shoulder he slung the MP40.

'You're seriously taking that feckin' sword with you?' said Damo.

'Si. I am like *Blade*, no?'

'*Blade?*' Damo snorted in amusement. 'Not in any film that I've seen.'

David checked the sword on Miguel's back. It seemed secure enough, and Miguel had arranged it so he could draw it easily. He nodded. 'All right, but if trouble kicks off, your priority is the gun. Damo's got the ammo, so if you need any more, tell him, alright?'

Miguel nodded. '*Si.*'

Before they had left Casa Underwood, David had packed Underwood's suit and shoes into a small backpack which he now pulled onto his shoulders.

'Are you sure he's gonna need that stuff?' asked Damo.

David secured the shoulder straps and shrugged. 'If you were running around in a gunfight, would you wanna be in bare feet with your bollocks swinging in the wind?'

'Ahhhh, no. Fair enough.'

'Right then. Let's go.'

The back of *La Fantasía* was a dark, two-storey block against the street glow beyond. Enclosing the car park was a six foot wall with two metal gates open into the grounds. David peered around the corner to look inside. There were four cars, two of which – though David had no way of knowing it – were the ones that had brought Lydia and the Mullins women from *La Reina*, earlier. A fire escape zig-zagged the back façade of the building; although its stairs ran down to the car park, an enclosed gate at the junction with the first floor level prevented access to the fire escape from the ground.

Beneath the fire escape were two closed loading doors, but around the corner, at the side of the building, light spilled from an open single door.

A bouncer stood outside it smoking a cigarette and fiddling with his mobile phone.

David turned back to the others. 'One guard. He's busy with his phone. We might be able to sneak around and jump him.'

Damo peaked around the wall. 'Ah, no. I got this. Follow my lead.' He handed David his guns, cracked his knuckles, then started walking woozily into the car park. He went around to the other side of the wall. He scuffed his heel and staggered a little, swearing and catching the wall to stop himself from pitching forward. Then he began fumbling with his fly.

The guard looked up at the sound and saw him. He pocketed his phone. 'Hey!'

Damo turned, saw the guard and waved him away. 'Shi – I'm pissing. Fuck off will ya.'

The guard started to come over. 'You can't do that there. Go on! Get out of here.'

Damo pretended to be focused on the quest for his penis. He thrust two fingers in the guard's general direction. 'Fuck off!'

The guard strode over, angry now. He went to grab Damo by the shoulder, but as soon as his hand made contact, Damo seized him by the wrist and threw him over his side in a judo throw. The guard struck the wall head-first, and fell down, out cold.

David and Miguel came over and David handed Damo his guns. 'Nicely done, sir.'

'Thanks.'

David bent to check the guard. 'He's alive, but he won't be bothering us again this evening.' He frisked him and found a walkie-talkie and a pistol. He held up the gun. 'Either they get a very rough crowd in here, or we're expected.'

'I'd say the latter,' said Damo.

David walked to a nearby drain and dropped the gun into it. 'Yeah, so would I.' The walkie-talkie crackled and a voice spoke in Russian. David looked at the others. 'Anybody understand that?' They shook their heads. 'Then it's no good to us.' He dropped it into the drain. 'All right. Miguel, where's Sergei's office?'

Miguel pointed to a strip of lighted windows on the second floor. 'That's it, I think.'

'You *think*?'

'Well, it was a long time ago. But, no, no, no – I'm sure, that's it.'

'It'll be obvious when we get there, David,' said Damo. 'Sure, it'll be the one with the guards outside.'

'Yeah. But that'll be the same with wherever they're holding Lydia and the others.'

'So, every one's a winner, eh?'

Despite the tension, David smiled. 'Yeah, let's hope so. Okay, let's go.'

They sprinted across the car park to the open door and peeked inside. The muted thudding of dance music echoed through the corridor, but there were no other sounds. David crept in and peeked around the corner into a corridor: it was clear. He looked back to Damo and Miguel and gave them the thumbs up. Then he started down the corridor. Damo and Miguel followed, all of them staying close to the wall as they advanced. At the end of the corridor, David peered around the corner: about twenty feet away in the next corridor, two guards were talking outside the double doors to a stairwell. David drew back and whispered, 'Two guards.'

Damo lifted his Thompson and raised his eyebrows in a silent question.

David shook his head. 'Not until we have to. If we start shooting, it'll bring them all down on us. No, we'll have to rush 'em. If we're fast enough, we can take 'em down before they raise the alarm.'

Damo nodded his understanding.

'Ready. On three. One. Two. Three!' They broke from cover and charged. The guards turned at the sound of running footsteps, only to each take a rifle-butt to the forehead before they could so much as shout.

Miguel looked around the corner and sighed with relief to see David and Damo silently congratulating each other. 'Shit! You did it. Thank God.'

David pushed open one of the doors to the stairwell. 'Come on, let's get these two under the stairs in case someone comes along.' He took one of the guards by the shoulders and began to drag him inside. Damo took the other guard and followed suit. Once they were ready, they went quickly and quietly up to the second floor. As he neared the top of the stairs, David crouched, then crawled onto the landing to peer under the doors. The shadows of two sets of feet broke the thin strip of light. David crept back and whispered. 'Another two.'

Damo made a quick assessment of the doors: they opened into the stairwell, so there was no chance of just crashing through them to the other side and knocking the guards flying. He turned to David. 'Two of us can pull the doors open, and the other one can take them down.'

David shook his head. 'No. One couldn't get them both in time. You and me both need to pull a door, and then attack straight after.'

Damo winced. 'It'll be tight.'

'I know.'

'What if Miguel backs us up with the sword?'

Miguel couldn't believe his ears. '*What?*'

'It's the only silent weapon we have,' whispered Damo.

David quickly considered: if they fumbled this, one of the guards could easily call for back up or even get a gun on them. He looked at Miguel. 'You think you can handle it?'

'*Handle it?*' Miguel hissed. 'Jesus Christ! Are you *serious?*'

'I thought you wanted to vanquish the enemies of the Lord Underwood,' whispered Damo. 'Don't tell us you've changed your mind.'

'No … but … it is crazy!'

'Not as crazy as getting shot if we don't have to,' hissed David. He reached behind Miguel and drew the sword from its scabbard. 'It probably won't be necessary, but here, take it, and stand over there against that wall, just in case. We'll pull the doors open and rush the guards, but if one of them gets the better of us, you run in and take care of him.'

Miguel took the sword. '*Madre de dios.* Can't I use the gun?'

'No.'

'But, you said the gun was priority. '

'Forget what I said earlier. The plan's changed.'

Damo put a hand on Miguel's shoulder and led him to the wall opposite the doors. 'Don't worry, Miguel. It's just a precaution.'

Miguel held out the sword, the blade trembling from base to tip. 'Jesus Christ. I don't like this.' Which was true. It wasn't that he had a problem with killing people – he enjoyed killing people – it was that Sergei's warning not to attack any of his men was still very fresh in his mind; neither Sergei nor Lydia would be impressed if he were caught – literally red-handed – thrusting a sword into one of Sergei's guards.

David and Damo took up positions behind the doors, each of them taking a door handle in one hand, and raising their Tommy guns to strike with the other. David looked first to Damo then to Miguel and mouthed, "*Ready?*" They both nodded. David fixed Damo's eyes and whispered, 'Alright, again, on three. One, two, three.' On three, they wrenched the doors open and lunged with their weapons. David's guard had his back to the door and took the Tommy gun stock square to the base of his skull, but Damo's man had taken a few steps away from the door and had been facing his partner when the doors opened: he saw it coming – and ducked. Damo's lunge missed, but his momentum carried him forward so the guard was able to get his shoulder into Damo's solar plexus. The Tommy gun flew from his hands as the guard pushed back against him, the two of them now tumbling back towards Miguel. Miguel didn't have time to think; he jumped aside, raised the sword and brought the hilt down hard into the centre of the guard's back as he piled Damo into the wall. Winded, Damo dropped to the floor, but the guard turned, enraged and reaching for his gun. Miguel dropped the sword and grabbed the MP40.

'No!' cried David.

Too late. Miguel pulled the trigger and the guard staggered back as bullets tore into his body. In the concrete shaft of the stairwell, the sound of the gun-burst was deafening: it must have been heard everywhere on this side of the nightclub.

'Shit!' David turned his Tommy gun around so it was ready for firing. 'So much for fucking stealth. How's Damo?'

Miguel dropped to help Damo, who was trying to push the body of the dead guard from his lap. 'He's okay.'

They rolled the corpse aside and Damo got to his feet. 'Me gun! Give us me fucking gun!'

David ran into the corridor and snatched it up just as Ivan and another guard came running around the far end of the corridor. David fired a burst of shots in their direction and threw Damo his gun as he ran back to the cover of the stairwell. He glanced around the door to see Ivan and the other guard had taken cover around the corners, and the barrel of an Uzi aiming straight at him. He pulled his head back just as a spray of bullets hammered into the door. 'We're pinned!'

From below, the sound of Russian voices growing louder, followed by the crash of a door at the bottom of the stairwell.

Damo aimed his gun over the handrail and fired a short, deafening burst. Shouts from below, then a volley of shots was fired back at them; the bullets thudding into the ceiling and raining down a shower of dust and debris. 'Fuck! No retreat, neither!'

David fired blind around the door then chanced a look down to the opposite end of the corridor. It ended in a fire exit. It was their only chance. 'There's a fire exit! If we all go together, shooting back at them, we can get out!'

'And go where?' shouted Damo. 'Home? Fuck that. I came here to kill Sergei, and I say we fucking take it to 'em.'

'No, they'd cut us down before we got anywhere near them, but the fire escape runs round the building – it leads to Sergei's office. We can shoot him through the windows.'

'Well now that sounds like a plan!' said Damo as another burst of gunfire from below rained plaster dust down around him. He shook the debris from his hair and joined David at the doors. 'How many of 'em?'

'There was two a minute ago. Could be more by now.'

Damo glanced into the corridor. Three men were advancing towards them, all with weapons trained on the stairwell doors. He barely had time to blink before all three weapons opened fire. He snapped his head back as bullets sprayed the corridor. Damo aimed the barrel of his gun around the door and fired blindly at the advance. There was a cry of agony followed by shouting, before more shots fired back at them.

'They're coming up!' shouted Miguel, looking down into the stairwell.

'So fucking shoot them!' shouted David. He ran to the handrail and fired down at the ascending guards, killing one and causing the rest to fall back under cover.

Miguel took a furtive glance over the hand rail; assured that there were no guards in sight, he fired a few shots down into the shaft to make David believe he was on the right team. 'Okay, I've got it.'

David joined Damo at the doors. 'Any ideas? Coz as soon as that ammo runs out, they're gonna have us.'

Damo grinned. 'What we need is a decisive weapon.'

'Yeah, like what? Unfortunately that sword ain't Excalibur!'

Damo took off the ammo satchel and threw it over to David. 'Take a look in there,' he said before blind-firing a burst of shots into the corridor.

David opened the satchel and rummaged for a moment. Then he drew out the hand grenade. He looked at Damo in amazement. 'You brought a hand grenade?'

'I told you it'd come in handy.' From below there came an electronic crackle and the tinny sound of an urgent voice over a walkie-talkie. Then from the corridor, the shouting intensified. Guns opened fire. 'This is it, Dave, they're making a push.'

Miguel jumped away from the handrail as bullets whizzed up the shaft and raked the ceiling. 'Why don't we just give up?'

'Because they'd kill us!' David looked at Damo. 'Cover me?'

Damo nodded.

David moved to the doors and gently squeezed the lever of the grenade to its body. He put his finger through the ring of the safety pin. 'Okay. You fire, I chuck it. When it blows, we run down to the other end of the corridor and out the fire exit.'

'Nice one.'

'Right.' Holding the lever tightly to the grenade, David pulled the pin. Damo aimed into the corridor and opened fire, fanning the Thompson from side to side as David ran out from behind him into the corridor.

As David drew back his arm and released the grenade lever, he saw the scene before him in bright and vivid detail, as if time had stopped to allow him a last look at the world: the corridor was empty but for the body of a dead guard on the floor; gun smoke swirled in the air; the walls were pock-marked with bullet holes and blood splatter from the fallen man. At one corner at the end of the corridor he saw a flash of a man's shoulder. Then on the opposite corner, the side of a man's head, his eye looking straight at David. And then the grenade was flying away from him. He saw the man's eye widen at the sight of it. David dived back into the landing, grabbing his gun as Miguel fired a burst over the handrail. He would remember later that he and Miguel had locked eyes then; each of them frozen in fear as their heart beats ticked away the seconds.

Ivan could barely believe his eyes when he saw the grenade flying down the corridor towards them. His first instinct was to get as far from it as possible; he broke from cover and was about to start running, when then the grenade struck the ground, bounced and spun to a standstill at the base of the wall. How long did he have? He didn't think; he acted. He dived for the grenade, snatching it up and hurling it back down the corridor before throwing himself back behind the shelter of the corner.

David heard a thud in the corridor. Something thrown that had struck the floor outside. His mind pictured it before it could find the words: the grenade had come back – and it was near. 'Shit! Get down!' He flattened himself to the floor and put his hands over his head. The last thing he heard before the explosion was Miguel asking, 'It's not that powerful, is it?'

Ivan and his men walked down the corridor with their guns trained on the stairwell. Shattered fluorescent light fittings dangled from the ruin of the suspended ceiling, with flashes of raining sparks lighting up the smoke as the men advanced. The walls were blackened, and all around was studded and scarred with shrapnel. With his gun raised before him, Ivan pushed open the remains of the blasted stairwell doors. The three intruders all lay still. He kicked the heel of the guy who had thrown the grenade. He didn't move. Ivan smiled and spoke into his walkie-talkie. 'Stand down everybody. We have them.'

23

DAVID DRIFTED IN AND OUT of consciousness. He was moving, but not on his own two feet; he realised that he was being dragged, one arm held over the shoulder of one of the guards and his feet trailing beneath him. He tried to walk but his feet refused to obey him. Up ahead he could see Damo draped over the shoulders of the big Russian. He looked either dead or out cold, and David remembered that he'd been right behind the door when the grenade had exploded. Jesus, the grenade. David glanced down the length of his body for signs of damage and was relieved to see that he was still in one piece. His ears were still ringing from the explosion, but he kept catching snatches of babbling Spanish behind him. Then he recognised Miguel's voice. Thank God – at least he was okay. David listened as best as he could to what Miguel was saying, but it didn't make any sense: over and over he was saying, "*Soy Miguel*" – I'm Miguel. Why would he be introducing himself? This thought followed him, echoing like a voice down a well, as he slipped back into unconsciousness.

A slap across the face brought him back again. He tried to focus. He was sitting in a chair. A man sat behind a desk about five feet in front of him. On the right hand side of the room, Michelle and Melanie sat on a sofa. Their mouths were taped shut, their wrists bound. They were looking at him with frightened eyes. David saw the white floor tiles beneath him were stained with dried blood; someone had attempted to mop it up, but in doing so had only made it worse. He noticed used rounds – not casings but spent bullet heads – lying sticky in the gore. The big Russian who had slapped him now moved to Damo, who was sitting slumped in the seat next to David. Ivan lifted Damo's head by the hair and slapped him, once, twice.

Damo jerked into consciousness. 'Wha – ? Fuck.' He looked around and realised where he was. 'Oh shit.' He turned to David. 'So much for decisive weapons.'

'Welcome gentlemen,' said Sergei. He was sitting at his desk and admiring Matthias's sword, turning it this way and that beneath the light. David saw that his back pack, the ammo satchel, and all their weapons were also piled the desk. 'Mr Sullivan and Miguel I recognise, but you,' he pointed the sword at David, 'You must be Mr David Flinch, yes?'

David nodded. 'And you must be Mr Sergei Alexandrov.'

'I'm told you've made quite a mess of my corridor. I heard the hand grenade from here. But unfortunately for you, no one else will have. Even if the zombies in the club had heard it through the sound-proofing, they probably will think it was part of the music.'

'Well, I'm sorry about the damage,' said David. 'But you did kidnap my friends and my sister.'

'Yeah,' said Damo, 'And you shot Hodge, and set me and Keith on fire.'

Sergei laughed. 'And I applaud your escape, Mr Sullivan. Too bad you got out of the fire only to now find yourself now in the frying pan. I hope I have the right idiom.'

'Please, Mr Alexandrov,' said Miguel. 'Can I speak with Miss Flinch? She is here, no?'

'Oh, she is here, Miguel. We put her over there, out of the way.' He pointed the sword to where Lydia's legs and feet protruded from between a filing cabinet and a pot plant in the corner.

Miguel gasped and stood up, only to be shoved back down again by one of the guards.

David turned to Sergei, fury in his eyes. 'You murdered her!'

'She murdered herself, Mr Flinch. I'm afraid she drank something that *severely* disagreed with her.'

'What?'

'The blood of your friend, Lord Underwood. She seemed to think it would do wonders for her, but as you see, she was mistaken. Evidently the blood of the vampire is not for human consumption.'

'So, you know about Underwood. Is he here?'

'Why yes. You may have noticed the smell when you came in. No? You are lucky. I can still smell it – it's like it's stuck in my nose.'

'You mean ... you've hurt him?'

'Oh yes,' Sergei chuckled. 'We've hurt him. See the mess on the floor here? That was just the beginning.'

David sagged in his chair. 'Oh, Jesus.'

'Yes. It has been a terrible night for all of us. Still,' he gestured to the weapons on his desk, 'Once I sell these, I should at least make enough money to pay for the damages to the corridor. Especially this,' he waved the sword. 'What is it, 18th Century?'

'Let me see her,' said David.

'Who?'

'My sister.'

'What for? She is dead. Ahh, perhaps you want to kiss her goodbye?'

'Something like that. I just ... I want to be sure.'

'Very well,' Sergei nodded to Ivan to allow David to rise. Then, with a smile to his men, he tipped out the contents of David's backpack onto the desk. 'Oh, Mr Flinch, what are these?' He held up a pair of silken boxer shorts. 'You are going to a party?' All the guards laughed as Sergei flounced the underwear up and down.

David ignored them as he went over to where Lydia sat slumped against the wall with her head sagging forward so her chin rested on her collar bone. He knelt and gently lifted her face to his. Her lips and chin were still sticky with blood. David smoothed her hair away from her forehead. 'Oh Lydia. What the fuck were you doing?' He felt for a pulse on her neck and found none. Then he eased his arm around her shoulders and brought her close to him, her head against his breast and her hair, soft against his lips. 'I'm sorry we didn't get here sooner, Lyddie, I'm – '

Lydia moved.

He froze.

Lydia moved again; a small shudder, like a nervous twitch through her upper body.

David eased her back against the wall and felt again for a pulse at her neck, and to his utter disbelief, he found one. He took her hand in his and patted it gently. 'Lydia? Lydia?'

'That's enough, Flinch,' said Sergei. 'You've said your goodbyes, now it's time for you and your friends to go and join your Lord Underwood.' He turned to Anton and Ivan and said in Russian, 'Take them down and kill them quickly and quietly. I don't want any more blood on the floor in here; it's like a fucking slaughterhouse as it is.'

They nodded and Anton gestured to Viktor and another guard to get Damo and Miguel up on their feet. Ivan walked over to David. 'Come. Let's go.'

'She's not dead,' said David.

'What?' said Sergei.

'She's not dead. She's alive. She has a pulse – she's breathing.'

Sergei looked at Viktor. 'You said she was dead.'

'She was,' said Viktor. 'I made no mistake. You saw her yourself.'

Lydia opened her eyes. David was holding her hand. He was warm, almost radiant with life. 'David?'

David squeezed her hand. 'Yeah, yeah it's me. Jesus, Lydia, we thought you were dead.'

Lydia smiled and her teeth were long and sharp. 'I was.'

'Oh my – ' David let go of her hand and fell back on his haunches. Lydia reached for him. 'Kiss me, David. Kiss me like you used to.'

'Lydia, you – you're – '

'What I've always dreamed of being. Oh, please, come to me.'

David found he couldn't take his eyes from Lydia's. They were irresistibly beautiful. 'He – he did this to you, Underwood.'

'Not exactly, it would be fairer to say that *I* did it to him.'

'What ... Lydia, what do you mean?'

'I can't say in front of the others, come closer and I'll whisper it to you.'

Sergei sat up in surprise as Lydia began to crawl out from behind the filing cabinet towards her brother. Something was wrong with the way they were looking at each other; as Lydia advanced, her brother sat, tremulous, yet unmoving. It was like watching a mouse mesmerized by a cobra. He reached for the controller of the UV lights behind him. Once it was safely in his grip, he sat forward to watch the scene unfold, waving to his men to stand back and let it happen.

'Lydia!' cried Miguel. He attempted to go to her but Anton pushed him back.

Lydia ignored him as she continued to creep across the floor towards David. 'I know you want me, David. You never stopped wanting me, did you?'

'Lydia, please ... You're sick.'

'Oh, I'm far worse than sick, David. I passed sick *years* ago.'

'No,' David shook his head, but his eyes never left Lydia's.

'Yes, Davey. Lie down and let me kiss you.'

David found his arms weakening and he lowered himself down before her as she closed the few remaining feet between them.

Damo turned to Sergei. 'Are you gonna let this happen?'

'Of course I am. It is incredible.'

'If she is what I think she is, she's gonna kill him.'

'So what? I was going to kill him. The end result is the same.'

'The end result is not the fucking same! If you'da killed him, he'da stayed dead. But would you look at her? Do you want another one of her up and running around?'

Sergei *was* looking at her. He couldn't help but look at her. He watched as she slowly climbed the length of David's body. He felt the switch that would flood the room with UV light and felt assured of his safety. But Sullivan had a point: he should stop it; he didn't want things to get out of hand and to then have to burn Lydia. He found instead that he wanted to make love to her – an idea he'd often entertained in the past, but never acted upon. Looking at her now, crawling on her hands and knees with blood all over her, he knew his desire was insane – and yet, nevertheless, it persisted. He forced himself to close his eyes, rubbing his face and shaking off the weird inertia that had settled on his mind like a fog. 'Lydia!' he shouted. 'Leave your brother alone and come and join us.'

'No. I'm hungry. Hungrier than I've ever been before. And David wants to feed me, don't you, baby brother?'

Damo noticed that all the guards had swapped their guns for small hand-held lights that they now trained on Lydia. He saw that Sergei had a controller in his hand and realised for the first time that the bank of lights behind him were UVs. Of course – that must be how they'd defeated Underwood. Everyone in the room now had their eyes on Lydia, including Michelle and Melanie. The guard beside him seemed to be almost turned on by the scene. Damo looked over and saw that Lydia was now lowering herself to David's neck. *Jesus Christ,* he thought. *She is gonna bite him. It's all real. She's a fucking vampire.* 'Well, fuck this!' He leapt to his feet, and snatched the UV light from the hand of the guard beside him then head-butted him. The other guards turned on him but had nothing in their hands but flashlights. Damo spun to aim his UV at Lydia and switched it on.

Lydia was just about to sink her teeth into David's neck when the side of her face burst into flame. She screamed and rolled off of David, using his body as a shield against the light.

'In the name of the Father, the Son, and the Holy Ghost,' Damo advanced towards her with the flashlight. 'I command you to get the fuck offa him and burn in – '

The guard Damo had attacked now seized him around the neck. Damo jammed an elbow back into the guard's stomach, but the man hung on as the other guards in the room came to his aid. Viktor smacked the UV light from Damo's hand; Ivan punched him across the jaw; and Anton came up alongside him and pressed a pump-action shotgun to his temple.

'Well, well,' said Sergei. 'It seems we have found our Van Helsing. I can't believe you'd want to destroy this beautiful butterfly now she is only just freed from her chrysalis, Mr Sullivan.'

'She's no butterfly,' said Damo. 'She's a fuckin' bat.'

'Ahh, butterfly, bat, whatever. Take him away and kill him.'

'No!' Lydia slowly got to her feet, the burned skin of her face smoking as if it were coated with acid. 'He's mine.'

'I thought you wanted your brother,' said Sergei.

'All in good time.'

'Lydia, no,' said David, starting to rise. Viktor came over to him, drawing his pistol and pointing it at his face. David stopped and turned to Lydia. 'Lydia, we can fight this. Underwood must know a way to change you back.'

'I don't want to change back, you idiot. Don't you understand that?' She approached Damo. Anton still held the shotgun to his head and Ivan had his arms locked behind his back.

'What do we do, Captain?' asked Anton.

'Let her have him,' said Sergei. 'I want to see what happens.'

'Lydia, no!' David tried to get up but Viktor struck him on the forehead with the butt of his pistol, and he fell back down.

Damo twisted and fought to be free, but he was held firmly. 'Fuck you, Lydia! You fucking whore!'

'Oh no, Damien,' said Lydia, taking Damo by the sides of his head and forcing him to look at her. 'This is where *I* fuck *you*.' She smiled, baring her teeth, and pushed his head aside to expose his throat.

'Oh Jesus, no,' Damo cried. Then Lydia's teeth were in his neck. He screamed and strained at where Ivan held him, but there was no breaking his grip. 'No, Holy Mother, no – n – ' His cries softened and his muscles relaxed. 'Oh, Janey. What … what are you doing, girl?' He shuddered, his eyes rolling back as a small moan of pleasure escaped him.

On the sofa, Michelle cried out against her gag.

'I know,' said Sergei, 'It is fascinating, isn't it?'

Now both Michelle and Melanie were howling, their gags made it hard for them to breathe and Sergei became aware that his merchandise was in trouble. 'Anton, take the tape off the women's mouths for a minute, let them breathe.'

Anton lowered the gun from Damo and went over to rip the tape first from Melanie, then Michelle, who promptly screamed Damo's name. Damo made no reply. Ivan released him into Lydia's embrace and she sank with him to the floor.

'Lydia!' Michelle screamed. 'Stop it! Get off him!'

Lydia raised her face from Damo's neck and blood spurted from the wound. She put her hand over it to staunch the flow and turned to look over her shoulder at Michelle. 'Oh shut up, you trollop. You've been in the same situation with Underwood; I can smell it off you. I bet you didn't want it to stop then, did you?' Damo's hands reached for her. Seeing the pain this caused Michelle, Lydia smiled and lifted Damo's face to her blood-soaked neck and the open throat of her blouse. Like a man in a dream, and even as his own blood was still ebbing from the wound in his neck, Damo kissed Lydia, licking at the blood, tentatively at first, but with growing excitement. Michelle looked away, her eyes filled with tears. Lydia laughed and allowed Damo to kiss her for a moment longer before forcing him down and resuming her feeding.

Melanie started screaming.

Sergei rolled his eyes and indicated Anton to re-tape their mouths. Anton gladly obliged.

A guard entered from the hallway and said in Russian, 'Captain, the Serbs are here.'

'Oh shit,' said Sergei. 'Now they come! Delay them. Tell them I'm concluding a meeting. Take them to VIP lounge – drinks, girls, whatever they want. Just keep them amused for ten minutes.'

The guard nodded and left. Sergei snapped his fingers at Viktor and Ivan, then pointed at David and Miguel. 'Get them out of here.'

In Russian, Ivan replied, 'You still want us to kill them?'

Before Sergei could reply, Miguel cried out, 'Lydia! Lydia, *por favor!*'

Lydia looked up from Damo's neck, glanced to where Miguel reached out a hand to her, then turned to Sergei. 'What are you doing? We had a deal – they're mine.'

'Don't worry, Lydia,' said Sergei. 'We still have deal. I'm just trying to make this place a little tidier for my Serbian guests.' He shook his head at Ivan and switched to Russian. 'Not yet. Just put them in with their dead vampire friend. We decide what to do with them later.' He smiled at Lydia. 'So, have you, er, finished your meal?'

'Not yet,' she nodded at Miguel. 'It's alright. Go with them.'

Ivan took Miguel by the arm and started pulling him towards the door. Miguel resisted, 'Lydia, please! Let me stay with you!' But Lydia sank back to Damo, ignoring him.

Viktor kicked David's legs. 'Come on. Up!'

David, who was still stunned from the blow to his head, rolled onto his side and got slowly to his feet. 'What do you mean, "We had a deal"? Lydia, you fucking bitch. What are you talking about?'

Sergei chuckled, 'Why don't you ask Miguel, Mr Flinch? I'm sure he'll be happy to fill you in.'

David was pushed past Lydia and Damo. Damo was beneath her, his arms holding her in a loose but loving embrace as she fed from him.

Viktor's gun jabbed David in the spine. 'Move it.'

David looked at Miguel, who was suddenly looking very nervous as he was bundled out into the corridor. 'Miguel! What does she mean?' Viktor shoved him hard in the back, pushing him after Ivan and Miguel.

'David, I don't know,' said Miguel. 'Believe me. Lydia is mad with the vampire curse. We have to save her.'

Ivan laughed as he and Viktor now led them down the corridor. 'You believe this asshole?' he said to David. 'He is full of shit. He brought you here because that is what she wanted. You and the vampire were led into trap.'

'No! That's a lie,' said Miguel. 'He wants to turn us against each other, David. You can't believe a criminal like him.'

Farther down the corridor was a door with a UV lamp outside, it was switched off with the flex looped and casually thrown over it. David suddenly became aware of a smell of burned meat that was growing stronger the nearer they got to the door. It wasn't like anything you smelled at a barbeque, but it was unpleasantly familiar. To Ivan he said, 'So, where is he, then? Where is the vampire now?'

Ivan smiled as they stopped outside the room and he opened the door. The smell inside was overwhelming, and David immediately remembered where he knew it from. He'd come upon it in both Bosnia and in his role as a paramedic: it was the smell of burned human flesh. Still smiling, Ivan pushed Miguel into the room and stood aside for Viktor to shove David in after him.

The room was almost bare save for an over-turned plastic chair in one corner, and a black, misshapen thing in the other. It was a corpse, the walls around it blackened and burned by the flames that had, no doubt, come from the body. David put his hand over his nose and mouth. The door slammed shut behind them, and a key turned in the lock.

'Oh my God,' said Miguel. 'Is it … ?'

David said nothing. The body was burned black from head to foot and curled tightly into the corner. The face was turned to the wall and the hands were rigid where they had been raised to try and shield the head. Ashes and fragments of burned clothing lay scattered all around; streaks of blood clotted with ash where the burning man's body had made contact with the walls and floor tiles. David moved closer and was better able to see the horrific extent of the burns to the flesh. The skin over all of the body had been almost entirely scorched away, but there were some areas – especially around the shoulders, back and buttocks – where the heat had burned right down into the underlying muscle. The flesh of the hands had been seared to the bone in places, making the fingers appear like charred black spider legs. David turned away. 'Jesus Christ, how could they? How could anyone do this to another living creature? I used to think Underwood was a monster, but … ' he shook his head.

Staring at the corpse, Miguel sank to his haunches and hugged his knees close to his body. 'Oh my God. It is him, no?'

There was no way of telling from this angle. David would have to turn the body around. Among the remains of clothing on the floor were two twisted and blackened sandals. David picked them up by the soles and, using them to cover his hands, carefully eased the corpse away from the wall and turned it slowly around.

Miguel screamed and put his hands over his eyes. 'No! Noooo! Nooooooo!'

David stumbled away from the sight that now confronted him. In disturbing the corpse, he released a fresh wave of stench, and smoke that had gathered beneath it. Miguel fell to one side and vomited, clutching the overturned chair for support. David ignored him, as the medically trained part of his mind took in the damage to the corpse. Like the rest of the body, the face was covered in third and fourth degree burns: the cheeks were raw black meat; the nose, little more than a burned stub of bone and gristle; the eyelids were burned away, and what remained of the eyes smoked from within the two black sockets; but it was the mouth that almost made David fall to his knees in despair. It was wide open and the lips had been burned away to reveal the teeth: the canines, long and sharp, could leave no doubt as to whose corpse they were looking at. 'It's him. It's Underwood.'

Miguel wiped his mouth on the back of his hand. 'Oh, my God. They killed him. They can kill vampires. Shit, we're all gonna die!' He got to his feet and ran to the door. 'Let me out! Let me out!'

'Shut up, Miguel! For fuck's sake. They're not gonna let you out, you fucking idiot. We're prisoners! Don't you get that?'

'No! Not me! *You* are the prisoner. I have to get out of here!' He turned his face to the door and screamed, 'You hear me? I'm with Lydia! Let me out of here!'

David got slowly to his feet as the meaning of Miguel's words sank in. Ivan had told the truth: Lydia – his own sister – and this, this *bastard* – had led him, Damo and Underwood into a death trap. Fury consumed him. He leapt upon Miguel, seizing him by the collar and throwing him against the wall. Miguel opened his mouth to say something, but David's fist smashed him in the face, knocking his head against the wall and causing him to collapse to the floor. 'Get up, you fucker!' David grabbed Miguel by the lapels and hauled him back to his feet. He slammed him up against the wall. 'You did this, didn't you! You and Lydia!'

'No, I am a servant of the Lord Underwood. But … I love Lydia. I can't resist her.'

'Oh, you're a servant of the Lord Underwood, are you? Have you seen him lately? Have you seen what your *service* has done to him?' He spun Miguel around to face Underwood's body. 'Look at him! You did that! You!'

'No!' Miguel cried.

'Yes, Miguel. You and Lydia. You murdered Underwood, murdered me, Damo, and Hodge. And now it looks like you've even gone and murdered yourself!'

Miguel tore free of David's grasp and pushed him away. 'No. You are dead, but not me, not Lydia!' He pointed angrily at Underwood. 'You say this is my fault?' He shook his head. 'No! It is *your* fault! You should never have come here. Lydia was supposed to be guardian to Lord Underwood, not you! She would have seduced him, won his love; and then he would have made *her* a vampire, and she would have made *us* vampires. We would have left Underwood then, and he would never have had to die.

But you! You fucked all that up with your interfering and your stupid ideas!'

David frowned, "Made *us* vampires"? Who's "us"? Who else is involved in this?'

'The Black Circle. Me, Lydia, Beltran – ' he threw up an accusing finger. '*You* killed Beltran, not Underwood. His death blood is on your hands! Lydia loved him. And soon, she will revenge him with a thousand nights of torture on your ass, you *hijo de puta!*'

David punched him again and Miguel fell back against the wall. Miguel touched the back of his hand to his mouth and it came away crimson. He spat blood to one side; it landed on Underwood. 'You can hit me all you want, David. You can beat me to death if you like, but you will never stop Lydia. She … ' His voice trailed off as a look of terrible doubt came onto his face. He turned to Underwood. 'No. No, please,' he shook his head vehemently. 'It is not my fault, My Lord! She, she made me do it.' He threw himself at the door again and resumed his pounding and cries for release.

David looked from Miguel to Underwood's corpse and back again, puzzled. What was that about? Why did Miguel just beg forgiveness like that? Like Underwood could actually hear him. And why did he now keep glancing over his shoulder at the body as he hammered on the door? His hammering and hollering were getting more and more hysterical, his eyes increasingly mad with fear as he looked back. It was as if he thought the burned corpse were coming for him, crawling across the floor in some nightmarish hallucination.

An eerie shiver ran up David's spine. Memories of the cellar at Casa Underwood, and the terror he'd felt on approaching the coffin with the intention of killing the vampire. And then it dawned on him. 'The fear,' he whispered. 'You've got the fear. The harm you intend to Underwood – to me … ' And so … what? Underwood's unconscious defences had kicked in? But that would mean … David turned back to the corpse. *Or was it a corpse?* In that burned shell, was Underwood's vampire heart still beating? At Underwood's resurrection, his body had had no pulse, no sign of life – and yet, when Beltran's blood had run into his mouth … 'He came back.'

'Please! Lydia! Help me! Let me out!' Miguel continued to pound and scream at the door.

David calmly but firmly grabbed Miguel's right arm and twisted it behind his back. Miguel cried out in shock and pain. David put his other arm around Miguel's neck and pulled him around to face Underwood. 'What is it, Miguel?' he hissed. 'You seem frightened.' David pushed him forwards.

'No, please, My Lord, forgive me!'

All anger had left David as he pushed Miguel closer to the body. There was a coldness in his heart and mind that he'd never felt before. But he liked it; it made everything so much easier. 'You want him to forgive you, do you? Well you'd better get down on your knees and beg.' David pushed Miguel down to his knees, still keeping one arm pinned behind his back, but now seizing him by the pony tail and pulling his head back to expose his throat. 'Beg, Miguel. Beg the master's forgiveness.'

'Please!' Miguel sobbed, 'Please, My Lord!'

'I don't think he can hear you,' said David. 'He's lost his ears, you see? Maybe you need to get up close.' He pushed Miguel's head closer to where Underwood's bared fangs rose from the blackened hole of his mouth. 'Real close.'

'No!'

'Closer.'

'Please, Jesus!'

'Wrong saviour, Miguel,' David pushed Miguel's head forward steadily until Underwood's fangs pressed against the skin of his neck.

'Please David,' Miguel gasped, 'you're a good man, don't do this to me.'

'I'm sorry, Miguel,' said David as he took the back of Underwood's head and eased it forwards. 'But I'm the guardian of Lord Underwood; a job for which *good* men need not apply.' Miguel began to scream as he felt the fangs break his skin and sink into his neck. David held him fast, pushing Underwood's mouth to his neck and easing Miguel into a position where his spurting blood poured down into Underwood's throat.

Sergei handed one of the Tommy guns to Anton. 'Take this and the rest of these guns out to my car and put them in the boot.' Anton beckoned another guard to help him and they began to gather up the guns. Anton reached for the sword but Sergei stopped him. 'No. Not this.' He nodded to Lydia who now lay with her head resting on Damo's chest with her eyes closed. 'This may come in handy,' he made a head-severing gesture, slashing his finger across his throat. Anton nodded and he and the other guard started for the door. 'No,' said Sergei. 'Not that way, you might run into the Serbs.' He cocked a thumb to the fire exit door. 'Take the fire escape down to the car park, then come straight back up.' Anton and the other guard left, and Sergei, sword in hand, got up and went around to the other side of the desk.

'You look like the post-coital woman, Lydia. Tell me, was it good for you?'

'Shhhh,' said Lydia. 'I'm listening to his heartbeat. It's fluttering like a tiny bird trapped in his chest.'

'You mean, he is still alive? After all your drinking of him?'

'I didn't drink enough to kill him,' Lydia opened her eyes and sat up. 'I never bolted my meals in life, and I see no reason to start in death.'

Sergei chuckled. 'But clearly, you are not dead.'

'I am *undead*,' said Lydia, with a touch of the dramatic as she rose to her feet. 'The Queen of the Night.'

'Really? There is a – how do you call it? – a *drag act* at one of my English pubs who calls himself the very same thing. You may have to have the cat fight to see who wins the title.'

Despite the tape across her mouth, Michelle laughed. Lydia shot her a look. Then smiled, 'Yes, you laugh, Michelle. Laugh as much as you can, because after tonight, luvvie, you'll never laugh again.'

Michelle fell silent.

'And so,' said Sergei, walking with the sword to where Damo lay. 'What do we do with this mess now? I need it off the floor before my guests arrive. At this stage I'm happy to just throw it over the fire escape and into the car park and we can put it in car boot – '

'No,' said Lydia. 'He's mine. I'm enjoying him.'

'You can't have everybody, Lydia. You have your brother – feed on him. Sullivan is my enemy, and mine to kill.' Anton and the other guard returned. Sergei waved a hand at Damo. 'Take him to car boot.'

'But we just put guns in car boot,' said Anton.

'Well, put him in *other* car boot! Jesus, is it that hard to figure out?'

Michelle and Melanie cried out against their gags as Anton and the other guard took Damo by his hands and feet and began dragging him to the fire exit leaving a slick of blood in his wake.

'Ah! Will you two ever shut up?' said Sergei. He looked down at the floor then threw his hands up in disgust. 'Jesus Christ. Look at this mess. Where has that mop gone? Where are my men?'

'The mop's over there,' said Lydia, pointing to where the mop handle rose from behind the bar.

'Well get it then, woman! Clean this shit up! I can't keep Serbs waiting any longer.'

Lydia laughed. 'Oh, I'm sorry Sergei, but I've only just recently had my nails done.' She smiled, baring her fangs. 'I'm afraid you're going to have to do it yourself.'

Sergei was about to threaten her, then thought better of it. He put the sword on his desk and strode angrily behind the bar to return a moment later carrying the mop and bucket. 'Fine,' he said, his back to her as he wrung pink water from the mop and slopped it down into Damo's blood. 'But when Serbs are gone,' he glanced aside at the bank of UV lights, 'You and I are going to have the little talk.'

David watched, fascinated by the eerie red vapour that rose from the flesh of Underwood's mouth as Miguel's blood flowed down into it. Miguel continued to struggle, but David held him fast, ignoring his screams and pleas for mercy, as he fought to hold the flow of blood on target. Then, despite Miguel's cries, David heard a noise. Miguel must have heard it too, because he stopped screaming. Then the sound came again, clearly now. It was a gastric rumbling from within Underwood's body.

Suddenly, the heel of Miguel's hand smashed into David's face, knocking him back and causing him to lose his grip. Miguel lashed out with his foot, striking David on the side of the head and sending him tumbling back to the wall. Miguel fell away from Underwood. He pressed his hand to the wound on his throat as he struggled to find his feet. 'No, no,' he cried, 'I don't want to die!' The blood poured through his fingers, soaking into his shirt and splattering down to the floor. 'I'm supposed to live – to live forever!'

David turned back to see the tottering Miguel slip in his own blood and fall back down to the floor. Beyond him, Underwood's whole body now appeared to be steaming, enveloped by a thin veil of seething red mist. David smiled. It was working: Miguel's life blood was restoring life to Underwood. But now, that precious fluid was spilling all over the floor, with Miguel slipping and writhing in it as he tried hopelessly to get up again. David held out a hand to him. 'Here Miguel, let me help you.'

Miguel reached out the hand that wasn't trying to staunch the blood pulsing from his neck. 'Get Lydia, David. She can still save me, she ... she has the power to ... '

'It's all right, Miguel,' David hauled him to his feet and held him. 'Forget Lydia. If you give yourself to the Master, *he* will save you.' He turned Miguel around and started to ease him back to Underwood.

'No!' Miguel tried to pull away, but he had lost too much blood. His head sagged and his limbs were practically numb. 'No ... he will kill me, like Beltran.'

'No he won't, Miguel. Look, see how you've healed him? He wants to thank you.'

Miguel raised his head to see the burnt corpse on the floor was no longer black, but raw meat red. It moved, the face turning to him; the eye sockets – two smoking holes in the skull – fixing on him; and the hands – with the bones of the fingers still protruding from the flesh – rising to reach for him, dripping with blood and ichor. With all the strength Miguel had left, he screamed.

Viktor stood outside listening outside to the sounds of violence within the room. He'd found the initial sounds of fighting amusing, but things had been starting to sound weird: off and on – one minute fighting, then screaming, then silence, then screaming again. He'd radioed Sergei when Miguel had started his hysterical hammering and screaming at the door, and the Captain had told him to ignore it and let them fight it out between themselves. But did that extend to letting them kill each other? His thoughts were shattered by another terrible scream from inside the room. Fuck it, this was crazy: he'd have to intervene, if only to get a bit of peace and quiet. He drew his gun and unlocked the door.

At the sound of the key turning in the lock, David jumped behind the door. It opened, and he heard Viktor's shocked exclamation before his gun rose into David's view. David threw himself against the door. It slammed it into Viktor, knocking the gun from his hand and sending him crashing into the corner. David dropped and snatched it up, but Viktor, unfazed, dived at David and brought him down. Then both of them were grappling for the gun – each punching and clawing at the other with one hand, while desperately reaching for the gun with the other. Their fingers swiped and snatched at it, spinning it on the bloody tiles. Then, suddenly and with force, a red hand came down upon it, stopping it from spinning before sweeping it aside. Viktor looked up to see the living cadaver that was Underwood fall upon him.

David rolled clear of Viktor's thrashing legs and got to his feet. He leaned against the wall, watching as Underwood, having torn a hole in Viktor's neck, now drank from the gushing wound. Miguel lay discarded, one hand weakly reaching for Underwood as if beckoning him back to finish him off. David considered doing the honours by bashing his head in with the pistol grip, but Underwood and Viktor were between him and the gun, and he didn't fancy trying to step over them. So he waited, watching as Underwood's body restored itself beneath the red mist that clung to his flesh. Slowly the mist faded in places to reveal healthy new skin beneath. Any sense of fear or horror David had ever had of Underwood had now completely left him. Now, all he knew was a sense of awe, and for the first time, he finally understood why his ancestors had always remained the vampire's loyal guardians. And as Underwood, satiated and restored, rolled off of Viktor and wiped his mouth with the back of his hand, David reached out his hand. 'Welcome back, Master.'

Underwood looked up and smiled. He took David's hand and got to his feet. 'Thank you, Flinch. I don't mind telling you, I thought it was curtains for me earlier. That bastard Sergei's got some kind of electric sunlight. He roasted me like a pig on a spit.'

'It's called UV light, sir – ultra-violet.'

'Yes, so I gather,' Underwood bent and picked up the gun. 'And that's why our first order of business once we're out of this room is to shoot the dickens out of it. And then, we'll see how Comrade Alexandrov likes to burn.' He noticed Miguel. 'Ah, my restorative. Thank you Miguel. We'll, er, get you an ambulance just as soon as we've taken care of Sergei.'

'Don't bother, sir,' said David. 'He betrayed you. He and Lydia set this whole thing up.'

'*What?*' Underwood was stunned. '*Lydia?*'

'Yes, sir. I'm afraid so. She's ... she's a vampire, Milord. I don't know how she did it, but there's no doubt about it. I've seen her attack. Jesus, she nearly had me.'

For a moment, Underwood could do nothing but stare in disbelief, as if David were playing some grotesque joke on him, but then he recalled the events just prior to his burning at the hands of the Russians. He had drunk from Lydia. She'd insisted, tricked him; and from somewhere –

most likely the blood he'd lost in Sergei's office – she'd managed to drink from him. He closed his eyes. 'Oh dear God. How could I? How could I have been such a fool?'

'I'm sorry, sir. There was no way we could have known what she was up to.'

'No, Flinch, there was every way; I was just too vain and blind to see.' Underwood took a couple of deep breaths, then said, 'We have to put this right.'

'Yeah, and fast. There are some Serbian guys here – gangsters. They're gonna take Melanie and Michelle.'

'I know,' Underwood checked the gun for bullets. 'You say they're here now?'

'Yeah.'

'Then we'd better get going. There's not a moment to lose.' He handed David the gun. 'Here, you'll need this.'

'But, what about you? You're not gonna fight them like that, are you?'

'Like what?' Underwood stepped into the corridor. He picked up the UV light and inspected it.

'Well, like – *naked*. I brought your clothes. But Sergei's got 'em. Still – ' he glanced around at Miguel and Viktor. 'Maybe you could grab some trousers from one of these two?'

'Trousers?' Underwood grinned and hurled the UV to shatter against the wall. 'This is no time for trousers, Flinch. Let's go!'

24

DARKO PETROVIC, A STOCKY, FULL-BEARDED MAN in his early fifties, followed Sergei's guard out of the service elevator and immediately caught the whiff of cordite. He looked aside to his bodyguard, Milos, and wrinkled his nose. Milos nodded. So this was the "meeting" Sergei had been having that had kept them waiting in *La Fantasia's* VIP lounge for the last twenty minutes. They rounded a corner and came into the corridor where David and Damo had battled Sergei's men.

The guard turned and spoke over his shoulder in Russian. 'We had some trouble earlier, but it's all been taken care of.'

'Trouble?' said Darko. 'It looks like you had a war.'

'It was problematic. But we overpowered them.'

'You killed them?'

'We killed the one who mattered. The rest, Captain Alexandrov will deal with later.' The guard stopped outside Sergei's office and knocked smartly. At the call to enter, he opened the door and stepped aside to allow Darko and Milos to pass.

'Welcome, Darko!' said Sergei in Russian. He rose from his desk with arms spread. 'Come in, come in. I am sorry to keep you waiting.'

Darko looked down at where Sergei had tried, and failed, to adequately mop up the blood. 'From what I hear about your *meeting*, Sergei, I am glad you did.'

Sergei laughed. 'Ahhh, yes. I see you've noticed the floor. It looks like we had a pig-sticking party in here, I know. Again, I apologise, we haven't had time to make the place presentable. Please,' he gestured to the bar as he came around his desk. 'You will join me for a drink before business?'

Darko looked around and saw Michelle and Melanie on the sofa. He smiled, and was about to agree to the offered drink, when Lydia stepped in from the fire exit, a cigarette smouldering between her fingers.

'Hello,' said Lydia. 'You must be Sergei's Serbian friends.'

Sergei, who had gone behind the bar and was pouring himself a vodka, sighed and switched his language to English. 'Ahh, yes. Miss Flinch, this is Darko Petrovic. Darko ... ' he took a much-needed swallow from his glass. 'This is Miss Flinch.'

For a few moments, Darko could only stare the woman who now sauntered over to sit on the edge of Sergei's desk. Her mouth, her hair, her hands and dress were all stained with blood. 'Are you ... Are you injured, Miss Flinch?'

Lydia glanced down at herself. 'Oh, no. Just a little soiled.'

Darko turned to Sergei and said in Russian. 'We agreed two women, yes? Is this a third? She looks mad, but give her a bath and, er ... ?'

Sergei handed Darko a drink. 'No. Much as I might like to include her, it's the two on the couch. Mother and daughter.'

Darko went over to where Michelle and Melanie now shrank away from him. 'How old is the girl? Fourteen, fifteen?' He reached for Melanie's hair. Michelle shouted against her gag and lashed out with her foot, kicking Darko on the thigh, which was all she could effectively hit from that angle. Darko responded immediately with a vicious back-handed slap across Michelle's face. Sergei nodded to his man now standing guard over the women – a shaven-headed weightlifter named Dimitri, who then immediately caught Michelle under the armpit and pulled her away. She kicked out again, missing Darko's face by only a few inches. Dimitri pulled her, kicking and thrashing, from the couch onto the floor. Under normal circumstances, he would just punch her into submission; but as she was sale goods and in the presence of her buyer, he refrained from doing so and so had to struggle to contain her fury.

Darko laughed. 'Oh she is a fighter, Sergei. I will enjoy breaking this one in.'

Sergei turned to Ivan. 'Help Dimitri. Tape her ankles together.'

Lydia, who only knew the few stock phrases of Russian she'd learned for her estate agency business – none of which were being used here – was beginning to feel excluded from the conversation. 'What are you talking about, Sergei? You know, it's terribly rude to speak in a language when some of your guests can't understand it.'

Sergei switched to English. 'It is nothing; just business.'

'Well since I provided the "business", could you please speak English? Or at least Spanish. The ladies and I – and your lighting engineer friend over there – have no idea what's going on.'

Sergei turned to see Stefano, the lighting engineer, whose slow retreat from events in the room had resulted in his now standing in the far corner next to the flight cases he'd used to bring up the UV lights. The lighting man warily raised a hand. 'I don't mind not knowing, really. But, please, señor Alexandrov, if there is nothing else – '

A gag-stifled scream from the couch drew everyone's attention. Darko was pawing at Melanie's chest and trying to open her shirt; her screams meant nothing to him, if anything, they encouraged his ardour. Ivan and Dimitri restrained Michelle from attacking him. Milos started chatting to Anton. Sergei poured himself another drink.

And then, quite suddenly, the sound of gunfire erupted from somewhere in the corridors outside. Everyone stopped what they were doing and looked to the door.

'What is that?' said Darko.

Lydia brightened. 'Oh, that's a bit of Russian I actually do know, and I know the answer too.' She turned her ear in the direction of the door then smiled at Sergei. 'Unless I'm very much mistaken, it's David.'

Underwood stepped over the broken glass of the UV light and set off down the corridor towards Sergei's office. David took a last look at Miguel – who had now either passed out or died – before hurrying out into the corridor after the vampire. '*Pssst!*' he whispered urgently. 'Wait for me.'

Underwood stopped, listening to the sounds ahead as David caught up with him. 'What's the plan?' David asked.

'Plan? I've no plan, Flinch – other than to cry havoc and let slip the dogs of war. I trust you've no objections?'

'No, absolutely. But what about Lydia?'

Underwood shook his head. 'I don't know.'

'Well, what do you normally do in this sort of situation?'

'*Normally* do? Good God, Flinch, there's nothing *normal* about this mess; a Flinch tricking me into making them a vampire? The situation's quite without precedent.'

'Well, what would you do if she wasn't a Flinch?'

'What do you think?'

'Kill her?'

'*Kill her* is an understatement.'

'But you're not going to kill Lydia, are you? I mean, you can't.'

'Why ever not?'

'Well, because she's a Flinch, and no Flinch shall bleed – you said so yourself.'

'Well, I'm afraid she's rather forsaken that right. She *was* a Flinch; now she's something altogether different: she's a vampire, and a dangerous rogue at that.'

'A rogue?'

'Yes. She wasn't chosen; she wasn't made in the way I would have made Michelle, for example. She's untutored, undisciplined, and untrustworthy – and that last is the understatement of the century; she stole my blood and left me to burn to death.'

'I know, but ... maybe, maybe *you* could tutor her?'

Underwood turned on him. '*What?*'

'You could tutor her, show her the ropes, or whatever it is you do. And then together we could make sure she ... ' he faltered, doubting his own words, 'she does things right.'

'Well well, haven't you come full circle, Mr Hammer and Cricket Stump? One minute you're out to slay the vampires, now here you are offering to start up a bloody finishing school for them. I – ' Underwood stopped talking as he heard voices approaching from the corridors behind them. He pushed David against the wall just as two guards rounded the corner, but he was too late: on seeing Underwood and Flinch, the guards drew their guns.

Underwood dived for the floor, his transformation from man to wolf so fast that neither David nor the guards even saw it happen. For the guards, in one second there had been a man in their sights, in the next, a huge black wolf was racing down the corridor towards them. Despite his incomprehension, the lead guard managed to shift his aim to the animal, but his finger went slack on the trigger as a bullet from David's gun entered his head just above the right eye. The second guard fired at the wolf, but it was too fast to hit, then he felt a white hot pain rip at his shoulder; he staggered back, knowing he'd been shot. He looked up just as the wolf leap at him. He screamed, raising his hands in time to feel the weight of the animal crash against him.

David's gun was empty. He threw it aside and ran down to where the wolf was now standing on the second guard's body, shaking its head from side to side and tearing out the man's throat as he twitched and shuddered in his death throes. David picked up the pistol of the first guard, then turned back at the sound of running footsteps. Ivan, Anton and Dimitri appeared at the other end of the corridor, no doubt come from Sergei's office.

'More of them, Milord!' he shouted. 'Take cover.' Underwood had returned to human form and was getting to his feet. David stepped between him and the Russians and started firing. The Russians scattered, ducking behind the corners then immediately leaning around to return fire.

'After you, Flinch,' said Underwood as he snatched up the other guard's pistol. He started firing and David flung himself around the corner.

Pressing himself to the wall, David checked the magazine of his pistol: there were four bullets left. 'Shit!'

Underwood joined him, bullets whizzing behind him and tearing holes in the plaster of the walls. 'Problem?'

'Ammo, sir. I'm down to four.'

'Yes,' Underwood tossed his pistol aside. 'And I'm out altogether.'

'How do you want to play it? You can't do that wolf thing again, the distance is too far against three guns, and one of them's a shotgun.'

'Yes. And did you see that big fellow? He's the one that roasted me with the sun ray lamp. He's going to be sorry, I can tell you.'

'What? How? What are you gonna do?'

'I'm going to go down there and give him a sound thrashing, that's what. Cover me.'

'Cover you? Did you hear what I just said? One of them's got a pump action shotgun. They'll blow your brains right out your furry wolf arse!' David peered cautiously around the corner.

'Who said anything about a wolf, Flinch? Just keep them pinned and try not to spend all your shots at once.'

David felt a sudden heat at his back. He turned to find Underwood had vanished. He looked in all directions, but there was no sign of him. 'Wha – ? Where did you – ?' A bullet smashed into corner just behind his ear and ricocheted away in a plume of debris. 'Shit!' Another shot, then another. Now they were pinning him; possibly advancing. He reached around the corner and fired a single shot. Then he saw him – or rather, the *it* that Underwood had become. Lit by sporadic electrical flashes from the grenade-shattered ceiling, a pale pink mist clung to the base of the wall and was slowly creeping towards the Russians.

The shotgun boomed at the end of the corridor and David pulled back. 'Fuck!' He'd seen Underwood change to mist before, so he was able to recognise it. But would the Russians? Surely not. But they might get spooked if they saw it, and that would cost Underwood the element of surprise that he was obviously counting on. Another shot smacked into the corner, sending a chunk of plaster flying. David dropped to his knee and fired a shot blindly before risking another peek. The Russians were all still taking cover around the corners at the far end of the corridor, but their guns were all aimed at David's position. He glanced up along the corridor to see that the mist was now almost upon them. David pulled himself back in time to dodge more shots. 'Come on, Milord,' he whispered under his breath, 'Get the bastards.' Then, almost as if in reply, a man cried out at the end of the corridor. David grinned. He got up, took a breath, and stepped out.

'Go! Kill them all!' shouted Sergei as Anton, Ivan and Dimitri ran out.
'No!' said Lydia. 'We had a deal!'
'Fuck the deal! Stefano, turn on the lights!'
Stefano scurried over to Sergei's desk, 'Really, Mr Alexandrov, please, after this, can I – ' He froze. Lydia was pointing Sergei's Uzi at his face. In her other hand she held the UV light controller. She smiled. 'Yes, Stefano. You can go now.'
'No!' shouted Sergei. 'Stefano! Turn them on!'
From the corridor, the sound of gunfire resumed.
'I'm sorry *señor*,' said Stefano. 'But my mother, you know? She worries.' He ran across the room and out through the fire exit.
Lydia turned and casually aimed the Uzi at Sergei. He raised his hands before him, 'Wait, Lydia. I forgot that you – that the lights would hurt you. But I – I don't think your brother is alone. Underwood – he is dead, I know. But then … so were you.'
'Oh, I see. And so turning on the lights was just a precaution?'
'Exactly.'
'We almost had a nasty accident there, didn't we?'
'Yes. An accident, yes.'
'Well, I think we should make sure such a nasty accident can't *almost* happen again.' She turned and fired a burst of bullets along the length of the UVs, exploding the lights in a streaming shower of glass. She gave a little scream and laughed. 'Ooh, what a super gun! Can I keep it?'
'Damn it, Lydia!' Sergei snatched up the last UV flashlight remaining on the bar.

'Put it down, Sergei,' she swung the Uzi to bear on him again. 'I *will* kill you.'

'Lydia, for God's sake! I won't use it against *you*. I just need it to protect myself against Underwood.'

'I could try and shoot it out of your hand, but this gun of yours sends out such a scatter of bullets, I'm afraid I might miss – several times. So just put it down, will you?'

Darko had been watching all of this with a mixture of bafflement and growing impatience. He looked at Milos, standing easy, yet poised to go for his gun if given the order. Darko gave it to him: he nodded and cocked his head at Lydia.

Sergei put down the flashlight, and Lydia smiled. 'That's it, Sergei. Now we can all – ' She was cut off abruptly as three bullets slammed into her and sent her toppling back over the desk.

'Yes!' shouted Sergei. 'Milos, you are the best! When all this is over, you must come and work for me.' He laughed at the look of anger on Darko's face. 'It is a joke, Darko, joke. You Serbs have no sense of humour. Come on, get the women and let's get out of here before this *thing* gets up again.'

Darko and Milos began to pull Michelle and Melanie to their feet. Milos put Michelle over his shoulder and Darko laughed as Melanie struggled ineffectually against him. 'Get up again? I don't think so, Sergei.'

'Really?' said Sergei. He held a finger to his lips. 'Shhh!'

Darko frowned. 'What?'

Everyone, including the Mullins women, fell silent. From behind the desk, the sound of broken glass began to scrape and crunch. Sergei raised his eyebrows at Darko. 'You see? She gets up. Bullets can't kill her.'

'But … that is not possible!'

From behind the desk, Lydia called in a slurred voice, 'Sergei?'

Sergei nodded. 'Oh, it is possible.' He started for the fire exit, ushering them to follow. 'This way, come on. Hurry!'

Lydia stirred amid the broken glass of the shattered UVs. She could feel three points of radiant heat on her torso where the bullets had hit her. She looked down to see a thin red mist smouldering over the bullet holes in her clothes. Her fingers cautiously explored the wounds. The holes were sticky and bubbling. She gingerly probed at one, ignoring the pain, to find it almost healed. On each wound, there were loose, solid lumps. She picked one up and held it before her eyes. It was a bullet head. It had risen, expelled from her body by the healing flesh. She rolled the gory slug between finger and thumb, and smiled. 'I'm immortal,' she whispered. 'They can't kill me.'

She could hear men speaking in Russian, the gagged screams of the Mullins women. She moved but the glass cut her. 'Shit,' she muttered. Then she noticed all the voices had fallen silent. 'Sergei?' she said, dazedly. 'Sergei? Come here.' She saw the Uzi where it had fallen just beyond her grasp and she reached for it. She could hear Sergei and the others now moving out onto the fire escape. 'Wait. Sergei. I've got something for you.' She got a hold of the gun and sat up, looking across the top of the desk to the fire exit where Darko was the last to leave, pushing Melanie out before him.

Lydia fired. The bullets sprayed the doorway for a second before the gun clicked empty. She didn't hit Darko, but she could hear him cursing outside, obviously shaken. Lydia laughed and tossed the gun aside. 'Wanker!' she screamed after him.

Darko stepped back into the doorway, a small automatic in his hand aimed straight at her. She dropped onto her back as he fired two shots that whizzed over her and smacked into the wall.

'Missed me!' She laughed as her new improved hearing picked up the sound of his scurrying retreat down the fire escape. She considered chasing after them, but why bother? They were of no consequence now. She could always drop in on Sergei one night in the future to finish him off.

The sound of sporadic shooting and shouting continued in the corridor. She touched her flesh where she had been shot to find she was now completely healed. 'Right then,' she said, getting to her feet. 'Let's go and see how baby brother is getting along.'

Ivan and Dimitri were completely unaware of the thin red mist that had drifted around their shoes to gather and pool behind them. Ivan was firing shots around the corner at David while Dimitri was reloading his pistol. With their backs turned, neither of them noticed as the amorphous red shadow rose behind them to cohere once again into the form of Underwood. As soon as Dimitri snapped the new magazine home into his gun, Underwood seized him around the neck with one arm while grabbing his gun hand with the other and raising it to the back of Ivan's head. Dimitri had barely a moment to cry out before Underwood's teeth were sinking into his neck. Ivan turned to see Dimitri's gun aimed right between his eyes. Without breaking off from his meal, Underwood squeezed Dimitri's finger on the trigger.

Anton, who was wielding the shotgun from the opposite corner, turned at Dimitri's cry just as Underwood's shot blew the back of Ivan's head off. For a moment, Anton could only stare in shock as pieces of his friend splattered on and all around him: then, as Ivan fell, he saw Dimitri's gun aiming at him – still in Dimitri's hand – but aimed by the naked man with his teeth in Dimitri's neck. The vampire! Somehow, incredibly, he had got past them. Anton found he couldn't move, the shotgun was suddenly heavy in his hands and a warm wetness was flowing down his legs.

Underwood noticed, and winked at him.

'*Mudak!* Son of bitch!' Anton raised the shotgun and fired, blasting both Dimitri and the vampire off their feet. He pumped the gun again, chambering another cartridge, before advancing through the gun smoke. 'Come on, pig!' Anton stepped over Ivan's body and aimed the gun at the tangle of limbs on the floor. 'Let's see you try to bite thi – ' A shot fired in the corridor to his right, and as agony exploded in his arm, he realised he'd walked out into the other Englishman's line of fire. He turned to see David now advancing down the corridor, gun raised and aiming straight at him. He managed to raise the shotgun, but David fired again before he could pump another cartridge; this time the shot whizzed past Anton's head so close that it could have left a parting through his hair. Anton cursed and threw himself back behind the corner.

'Looks like you've had it, old bean.'

Anton turned to see the vampire standing over Dimitri's body. He was removing the batteries from a UV flashlight Dimitri had brought but not had an opportunity to use. Underwood smiled as he let the batteries fall to the floor and roll away. 'Check mate, I think you'll find.'

'No!' Anton stumbled back. 'You can't be ... Ivan burned you!'

'Yes, he did. But as you see,' he gestured to his wholly unscathed body, 'here I am, in the rudest of health. I put it down to a high iron diet.'

'No! Leave me alone!' Anton turned and ran. 'Leave me alone!'

Underwood chuckled to himself as David came up to join him. 'I love it when they run screaming. It always makes the kill so much more satisfying.'

'Yes, sir.' David dropped his gun and picked up Dimitri's pistol. He checked it for bullets. Satisfied with the count, he slapped the magazine back into the gun. 'Are you ready?'

Underwood raised an eyebrow. 'You *did* hear me, didn't you? I'm going to hunt him down and kill him in cold blood – him and his friends.'

'Yes, sir. I heard you.'

'You've no objection?'

'None whatsoever, Milord. If you don't do it, I certainly will.'

Underwood raised an eyebrow. 'I see. Well, you really have changed, haven't you?'

'Just doing my job, Milord – like, perhaps, I should have done from the start. I'm a Flinch, after all.'

'Yes,' said Underwood thoughtfully. 'Aren't you just.'

'So, shall we go then?'

'Yes, of course, Flinch. Carry on.'

Anton ran down the corridor to Sergei's office, intent on switching on the UV lights. As he neared the end of the corridor, he pumped the shotgun, gritting his teeth against the agony in his arm. Then it occurred to him that if Sergei and the others were still there, they could have guns trained on the door. He shouted in Russian, 'Don't shoot! It's me, Anton!' He could see a silhouette coming into the doorway. 'He's behind me! Get the UVs on!' Then he stopped as the shadowy figure emerged into the light of the corridor.

'Hello,' said Lydia, barring his entrance. She saw the wound in his shoulder and sniffed appreciatively. 'Mmm, you smell nice. Shame about the pee in your pants.'

Anton raised the gun to her. 'Where is Captain Alexandrov?'

'He's gone. He and his whore-mongering chums all ran away.'

Anton saw over Lydia's shoulder that the UVs were all shot to hell. He looked at her furiously. 'Get out of my way.'

'Why? Oh, don't tell me you're leaving too.' She fixed his eyes with hers. 'I thought you liked me, Anton.'

Anton shut his eyes and pulled the trigger, blasting Lydia off her feet and backwards into the room. He opened his eyes to see her lying motionless on her back. The almost point-blank shot had left a terrible hole in her chest, and from the blood that was seeping out from her back, he knew that the exit wound was even worse. He gave a little laugh of triumph. 'Sorry, bitch, but you're not my type.' He noticed the last UV flashlight on the bar. He stuffed it into his pocket and pumped another cartridge into the shotgun. 'If you see your friend, Underwood, tell him if he comes after me, he'll get the same as you.' He froze at the sound of running feet in the corridor. 'Shit!' He ran to the fire exit and stumbled out into the grey twilight of dawn.

David saw her immediately. 'Lydia?' He entered cautiously, gun raised, checking the corners and other likely hiding places for shooters. 'Lydia!'

'What is it?' said Underwood from the corridor. 'Are the UVs taken care of?'

'Yeah, yeah, they're all shot out.' Satisfied that the Russians were all now outside, David knelt beside Lydia. At the sight of the wound in her chest, he put his hand to his mouth. 'Oh Christ!'

Underwood came in. He looked down at Lydia. 'She'll live.'

David turned to him, stunned. '*What?*'

'She'll live. Shotgun wound – nasty, but not fatal. If he'd hit her a few inches to the left, he'd have done for her, but her heart's only partly damaged. As I told you before: you have to destroy the heart, not merely damage it. That's a bad wound, it'll take a few hours to heal, but it *will* heal.'

David took her pulse. 'I don't feel a pulse.'

Underwood's eyes followed the bright trail of Anton's blood to the fire exit and the coming dawn. 'Trust me, she's alive. Be wary of her – being wounded, she'll have a heightened need for blood.' From outside came the sound of slamming car doors and voices shouting in Russian. Underwood picked up the pistol that David had dropped, and then went to the fire exit to look east. His skin tingled unpleasantly in the twilight, and he squinted; to his eyes, the silhouettes of the buildings were aglow with the rising fire that was soon to break over them. How long did he have? No more than perhaps five minutes. But he had that. He turned to David. 'Stay with her. I have to finish this, and I have to be bloody quick about it too.'

'But – ' David started, but Underwood was already out the fire exit door. He turned back to Lydia and took her hand in his. 'Oh you stupid, stupid cow. We should leave you, you know that? You betrayed us. I can't believe you'd – '

Lydia opened her eyes. 'David?' Her voice was weak, but she smiled at the sight of him. 'David, you've come to rescue me. I knew you would.'

'Oh yeah, you bloody well counted on it, didn't you? Miguel told me everything.'

'Miguel? Where is he?'

'He's dead.'

She frowned. 'Dead? *Miguelito*? No, no he's supposed to be with me.'

'Yeah, he told me. But it hasn't worked out that way, has it – Underwood's had him for breakfast.'

'Underwood? He is alive, then.'

'Yeah. No thanks to you.' Outside, the shooting had started, and David's head turned at a sudden, terrific crash of metal.

Seeing his distraction, Lydia squeezed his hand and brought him back to her.

'You hear that?' said David. 'I wouldn't want to be in your shoes when he's done with them.' He looked around the room. 'Hey, where's Damo? What did you do with him?'

'Sergei took – ' she coughed and blood spotted her lips. 'Oh no, oh Jesus, I'm dying. That bastard's killed me.'

'No, such luck. Underwood said you'll make it.'

'He's wrong David, I can feel myself slipping … slipping away. I'm cold … so cold.' She closed her eyes and her voice grew faint. 'Hold me, David ... please, forgive me. Don't … don't let me die un … unloved.'

'Oh come on, you'll be alright,' David touched her forehead. She was cold – really cold. It was obvious from the pool of her blood that he knelt in that she'd lost a very dangerous amount. Could that be fatal to vampires? Surely. He felt a tingle of fear. 'Lyddie, it's okay. Underwood said you'd be alright. Really.'

'Goodbye, David,' she whispered. 'I … I always … loved you.'

'No!' David cried, shocked by the feelings that suddenly rushed up inside of him. He clasped her hand in both of his. 'No, Lydia! Don't go!'

Lydia opened her eyes, and in a voice that was little more than a breath, she whispered to him, 'Kiss me, David.'

David stared into her eyes. They were soft, strange, and intensely beautiful. He was drawn to them, just as they were drawing everything else into them: all suffering, pain, and loss, everything was melting into the soft oblivion of Lydia's eyes. Underwood's scream ... that too would be forgotten. As she rose to kiss him, he closed his eyes, and a shiver of expectation ran up his spine.

Underwood's scream again.

Outside.

Underwood ... Underwood shouldn't be screaming.

David jerked awake, tearing himself from Lydia to see her teeth – *her fangs* – poised to bite him. 'You fucking bitch! You did it again! You were gonna fucking kill me!' He got to his feet, staggering away from her. 'I should kick your fucking head off of your shoulders. And I would too if it ... ' Again, from outside, the sound of Underwood screaming in agony. He looked out of the window; the sun was sending its first shafts of light through the trees and in between the buildings. 'I have to go and help him.'

'You can't,' Lydia reached out a hand to him. 'David, you can't leave me.'

David ignored her. He saw that Underwood had taken his pistol and he looked around for another. He ran to Sergei's desk where their guns and ammo had been heaped earlier.

'David, don't let me die,' Lydia moaned.

'Oh, shut up! I am *not* falling for that shit again.' On the desk there was nothing other than Underwood's clothes and his various small possessions that Sergei had tipped out of the satchel. David rummaged through everything, in vain. 'Fuck it! Why isn't there a fucking gun here? What kind of mobster's gaff is this?' He turned to Lydia. 'Did you see where he put our guns?'

Lydia moved her arm slowly to point to the shattered glass behind Sergei's desk. David followed her finger and saw what she was pointing at. 'Oh, no. For fuck's sake. Is that it?'

Lydia managed a low chuckle. 'Good luck, guardian.'

At the same moment Underwood ran into Sergei's office, Milos had just managed to bundle Michelle into the back of Sergei's BMW, and Darko was pushing Melanie in after her – which wasn't easy because the brat kept kicking him. Darko caught her foot in his hand. 'Kick me again and I'll slam the door on your legs. My customers don't care if you can't walk.' Melanie stopped fighting and drew her legs close to her body. Darko slammed the door and dusted his hands as Sergei opened the driver's door and got inside. Darko leaned in at his window. 'Okay, Sergei. You follow us to my place and we close deal there – away from your fucking vampire woman.'

Sergei nodded. 'I apologise for this mess, Darko. It is a regrettable business; one that I underestimated the complexities of. But I will make it up to you.'

'Yes? Perhaps you will start by waiving the price on the mother, eh?'

'Hey!' shouted a voice from the fire escape. 'Wait for me!'

Sergei looked up and saw Anton clutching at his bleeding arm as he came hurrying down after them. 'What? You are shot? Where is Ivan?'

'Dead. The fucking vampire killed him, and that other bastard shot me.'

'Vampire? Please tell me you mean Lydia?'

'No,' Anton panted as he came down the last few stairs to the car park. 'Underwood.'

'Shit,' Sergei muttered. 'Darko, go now, get in your car and go.' He checked the sky and was relieved to see the glow of the sunrise soaking into the east. Darko quickly hurried over to his car and got in to the passenger seat beside Milos, who had already started the engine. Anton came around Sergei's car to the passenger side. Sergei leaned over and gestured to the third car. 'No, take the other car and follow us.'

'Please, Captain, I'm shot. I can't drive.'

Sergei looked with distaste at the blood seeping between Anton's fingers and down the sleeve of his shirt. 'Okay. Get in. But try not to bleed all over the upholstery.'

Anton got in. 'What about Underwood?'

Sergei waved at the sky. 'What do you worry about? The day is come. Underwood will have to hide in a closet till sundown. We can come back with more men later and finish him – '

'Sergei!' called a voice from above.

Sergei looked up to the fire escape to see Underwood, completely naked, aiming a pistol at him.

'Let the ladies go, Captain. Then I'll let you and your friends leave here alive.'

'That is very magnanimous of you, Lord Underwood. But unless you cover yourself in factor one-thousand sunblock,' he glanced up at the sky before offering Underwood a conciliatory smile, 'I'm happy to take my chances.' He started the engine just as Darko's car screeched into motion and started for the rear gates.

Underwood turned his gun to fire at Darko's car, but knew immediately that the chances of killing the driver were zero. He had to stop the lead car if he was ever to stop the second. He threw the pistol aside and looked to the east where the fire of day was rising. His skin's warning tingle was turning to a painful prickling, like he was being bitten all over by red ants. Darko's car was almost at the gates. He had to do it; there was no other choice.

Underwood dived over the handrail, taking the form of a bat and swooping down toward the car park before soaring upward, climbing high over the cars. As he touched the sun's rays, his body ignited, bursting into flame, but he held his trajectory until he was directly above and just ahead of Darko's car. Then, with all the force he could muster, he plummeted downward, a streaking ball of fire that smashed down onto the roof of the Mercedes, crushing the roof and blowing all the windows out in a multi-directional explosion of shattered glass. The car crashed into one of the gate posts, blocking the exit; there was no sign of life from within.

Underwood dematerialised immediately after impact and, as mist, poured into the shadow of the wall and its overhanging trees. There he took human form, but he was terribly burned; the damage caused by the sun was far greater than his bodily reserves could immediately repair. He was bald, his skin raw and smoking. The pain was excruciating, but he couldn't show it. He straightened up, and turned to face his enemies.

Sergei's car had stopped, and now the passenger door flew open and Anton got out, shotgun raised. He fired, hitting Underwood and sending him staggering back to the wall. Anton pumped the shotgun again, but there were no more cartridges. He dropped the gun and hurried around to the boot of the car.

Sergei got out and folded his arms over the door. 'A very impressive move, Underwood. But if you'll pardon me for saying so, it seems to have hurt you almost as much as it has poor Darko.' Anton stepped up alongside him, he held the MP40 in his hands. Sergei took the gun and walked around the front of the car to where he had a clear shot at Underwood. Anton followed him, fishing the UV flashlight from his pocket and clicking it on. He raised it at Underwood, who screamed as the beam hit his flesh.

Sergei laughed. 'Look at you. You thought you would beat me, didn't you? Thought you would stop me and save these bitches. Well, you have failed, My Lord. They may not become whores, but they will become dead. But not before you. And this time, I don't leave it to others; this time, I kill you myself.' He pulled the trigger and a burst of bullets ripped across Underwood's body. Underwood cried out, clutching at his stomach before rolling onto his front and starting to crawl for the space under the wrecked Mercedes. Anton pursued him, training the UV on Underwood's back and enjoying the way it caused flames to spit and blaze from his flesh on contact. Underwood screamed through gritted teeth, clawing forward even as the edges of his vision began to grow dark. Then Sergei fired another burst from the MP40, raking the backs of Underwood's legs.

Sergei chuckled. 'Ahh, if only we could drag you out of the shade and wait until the sun is high enough to fry you. But I'm afraid time is the unaffordable luxury; I've no doubt someone has heard our shots and called police by now. So, sadly, our sport must end here.' He raised the gun.

Underwood closed his eyes, bracing himself for what he knew would be a continuous onslaught of bullets … but it didn't come.

'Drop it, Sergei,' said David.

Underwood turned to see David. He stood behind Sergei, one hand holding him by the hair, the other holding the blade of Matthias's sword against his throat. Sergei dropped the gun. Anton wheeled around, the UV flashlight before him and shining into David's eyes.

'Sorry, mate,' said David. 'You'll have to do better than that.'

Anton was about to go for the guns in the boot when a hand seized his ankle and yanked his leg out from underneath him. He fell down flat on his face. For a moment, he was too stunned to realise what had happened, then he howled in pain as his face started to drag against the asphalt. The hands that were pulling him were moving higher up his legs as they drew him in. He twisted around in time to see Underwood grab him by the belt. 'No!' he screamed. He had just a moment to see the bared fangs before they were buried in his throat. Anton beat and flailed at Underwood's head and back, screaming as he felt a chunk of his flesh tearing away and blood erupting from the wound. Underwood spat the flesh aside and closed his mouth over the severed carotid artery, drinking ravenously as Anton began to twitch and jerk in his arms.

Sergei held up his hands and spoke fast, his voice unsteady, 'Listen to me, David Flinch. I give you the women, and as much money as you can take with you, yes? And you, you can let me go. It is okay, your boss, he said so just a moment ago. I give you the women, and we all go home, yes? You can be rich man. Yes? Yes?'

For a moment, nothing happened. Then slowly, Sergei felt the blade lift from his throat. He breathed a sigh of relief. 'Good. Good man. You are wise indeed. I have money in the boot of my car, just let me go, and I'll fetch it for you.'

'That's alright, Sergei, you keep your money,' said David, still holding Sergei firmly by the hair. From where he had brought the sword around to Sergei's back – the tip of the blade now just below the rib cage – he suddenly thrust it upwards. 'You can have this as a parting gift from Underwood and Flinch.' Sergei stiffened, his scream choked as the three hundred year old blade drove steadily up through his body, skewering his heart before finally emerging just above his collar bone.

Underwood got to his feet, now fully restored, and wiped the blood from his mouth with the back of his hand. 'I say, well done, Flinch.'

David released Sergei's lifeless body, withdrawing the sword from the corpse as it slid down the blade. 'Thank you, sir. Are you all right?'

'Yes – thanks to a skinful of claret from our late friend here.' He kicked Anton's body.

David looked around at the shortening shadows in the car park. 'We should go, Milord. This shade isn't going to last much longer – and as Sergei said, someone's bound to have called the police.'

'Yes, I know.' Underwood went over to Sergei's car and leaned to look in at the back seat. Melanie shrank away from him, her eyes filled with terror. But her mother sat up; her eyes held only love for him. Underwood lowered his gaze, ashamed to look at her, ashamed to look at either of them.

'We have to go, sir,' said David, gently. 'And there's still Lydia, remember?'

Underwood nodded. 'Yes, Flinch. I remember.' He took a deep breath and raised his face again to Michelle. The effects of his bite – the partial infection that filled the victim with yearning – would be fading now; all he had to do was to free her mind. He gazed deeply into her eyes.

Michelle came back to herself with a start. She fell back in her seat, dizzy, but rapidly clear-headed. She looked at Underwood, and she remembered everything – knew everything that had happened to her, but the eerie fog of devotion she had felt towards this man for days had lifted. She looked at him, his mouth and chin dark with blood. He was a vampire, a monster, and he had seduced her. Part of her recoiled, shocked and furious at his violation of her mind and body, but she was confused to find that the feeling wasn't absolute; an inexplicable affection for him still lingered in her.

'I'm sorry, Michelle,' said Underwood. 'You may still feel some attachment to me. But it will pass.' She glared at him, her mouth still taped shut. 'Oh, here, let me take that off.' He reached out and tore the tape off in a quick movement.

'What did you do to me?' said Michelle.

'It'll fade. My – ,' he'd been going to say "bite", but he noticed Melanie's eyes burning upon him. There was no need for the child to know the truth of what had happened to her mother. 'My ... behaviour was appalling. I drugged you; beguiled you into having feelings for me. There may be some residual effects, but they will fade. I know you can't forgive me, and that's alright – I don't deserve your forgiveness. But I want you – both of you – to know that Keith isn't dead; he's going to be okay.' He took some comfort in seeing some of the fear and hatred leave Melanie's eyes at the news that her father was alive. 'I helped in that, so, I'm not all bad.' He tried a smile, but Michelle's expression doused it. 'Er, anyway, as I say, I'm very sorry. And neither you, nor your daughter, nor Keith will ever see or hear from me again.'

'Untie us,' said Michelle.

'I can't, I'm afraid. I have to go and finish something upstairs. Flinch will release you in a moment. But before I go, there is just one thing.'

They both looked at him, and he at them: his eyes, deep and penetrating. 'Never speak of me, or David, or Lydia to anyone. For your own sakes, we will start to fade from your memory as soon as we're gone from here. Of these recent events, you know only that you were kidnapped from your home; your abductors words were foreign; your eyes were blindfolded. There was an argument, shooting, and you know nothing more. Nothing more.' He released their gaze.

'Milord,' said David. 'Lydia.'

'Yes, I know, Flinch. Untie these ladies then go and get the car.'

'We could take this car,' said David as he began to unpick the tape on Michelle's wrists, 'the tinted windows'll protect both you and Lydia, and – '

'*You have your orders, Flinch!*' snapped Underwood. 'Get the car. *My* car. The Rolls.'

'But, sir. There won't be room for Lydia. She can't ride in the passenger seat now, she'll burn.'

'Just take the bloody sword and get out of here! Come on, step lively, man.' He started for the stairs of the fire escape.

'What're you gonna do?' David shouted after him.

Underwood stopped and looked back. 'What has to be done.' There was no time to explain further; the sky was an ever brighter blue, and he could feel his skin starting to burn, even though he was still in the shade of the building. 'Now go!' He ran on.

David turned back to Michelle. She had finished freeing herself and was now untying Melanie. 'Are you ... are you alright?'

'*Alright*?' she turned on him. 'Course I'm not alright.' She went back to unpicking Melanie's bonds. 'But I'm alive. We both are. I'm thankful for that.'

David hesitated, he wanted to say something more, to apologise, but Michelle turned sharply. 'Are you still here?'

'Eh?'

'You heard what he said, didn't you? Get the bloody car!'

'Yeah,' David retreated a few steps. 'Yeah, of course.' He started running for the hearse.

Underwood entered Sergei's office to find Lydia lying more or less as he had left her, though now he saw a fine red mist clung to the wound in her chest. He crossed to her and knelt by her side. Her eyes were closed. She was sleeping, healing. He stood up, and saw his clothes on Sergei's desk. He smiled to think David had actually taken the trouble to bring them. He went over to the desk and found his watch, lighter, and cigarette case. He picked up his watch. 'You and me, eh? Funny how, when all is said and done, we always seem to find each other.' He popped open the case. The watch told him it was five-past two. He shook his head and tapped the face; the second hand began to move. 'God knows why I bother with you. You don't even keep good time.'

At the sound of his voice, Lydia stirred. 'My Lord?' She reached out a hand to him. 'Thank God, you're alive.'

'Yes. Thank God, but no thanks to you.'

'I'm sorry ... they ... they made me do it. I said you'd come and rescue us and, when I told them what you were, they said they'd trap you, sell you.'

'Did they indeed?' He lifted the shirt by the shoulders and shook out the creases.

The sound of distant sirens drifted through the open door.

'My Lord. The police. They're coming.'

'I know, Lydia. Relax, they're a few minutes away yet. We've plenty of time.'

'No, we've no time,' she tried to rise, but her head swam. 'We have to get out of here. If they catch us, they'll experiment on us, like David said – he was right about that.'

'He was right about a lot of things, Lydia.' Underwood slipped on the shirt and began fastening the buttons. 'Just you relax. I'll be with you presently.'

At the sight of Underwood's leisurely dressing, Lydia felt a sudden and terrible dread. 'You … you won't leave me, will you, My Lord?'

'No, my dear,' he smiled at her, as a father to a child. 'You and I are leaving together.'

David got to the hearse, out of breath and sweating. He opened the back and pulled open the concealed drawer. As he put the sword inside, he made a mental note to get their guns from the boot of Sergei's car. Not because he thought the police could trace them, but because he wanted them; they belonged to the family, to the firm. He shut the drawer and swung the back door closed. Then he saw a group of men staring at him from the open door at the back of the bakers. Had they seen the sword? Probably. He waved as he got into the driver's seat. '*Hola!*' As David started the engine, some of the men raised their hands in uncertain reply. 'Take it easy, Davey Boy,' he murmured under his breath. 'Just act natural, drive like you've got all the time in the world.' He put the car in reverse and backed into two mopeds parked closely behind, knocking them over. 'Shit!'

The bakers, evidently now discussing him, moved out from the door to get a better view of his bad driving.

'Oh, fuck it!' David put his foot down and reversed over the mopeds, scraping and crushing them as they went under his wheels. 'Can't stand the noisy fucking things anyway.' As he drove out of the tight space and into the service road that lead to *La Fantasía*, he waved a hand to the bakers. '*Buenas!*'

The bakers returned his wave, watching as the hearse drove into the service road with a moped's side mirror wedged under its rear bumper and trailing sparks. One of them turned to the rest and said, '*Ingles.*' The others nodded and replied in unison. '*Si.*'

Underwood, now fully dressed in black suit and shoes, walked over to Lydia. He adjusted his watch so it matched the time of a clock behind Sergei's bar and slipped it into his waistcoat pocket. Outside, the sirens were very close. He knelt beside Lydia and began to ease his hands beneath her. 'Come on, Lydia. Time to go.'

'Yes, yes,' she slipped her hands gratefully around his neck, gasping at the pain in her chest as he lifted her. 'Oh, Christ, that hurts. Why hasn't it healed yet?'

'You need blood, Lydia. But don't worry. We haven't far to go.'

Lydia held him close, with her face against his chest she was finally feeling safe; safe enough perhaps to brave a small confession. 'Daniel, do you forgive me?' She looked up at him. 'I only did what I did because … I love you.'

'Of course you do, Lydia. And I love you too.' He began to walk towards the office door and the corridor beyond.

Lydia, confused at his choice of direction, tightened her grip. 'But – but, this is the wrong way. We need to get *out* – the fire escape. The police will be at the front, people – they'll see us – see me like this.'

'No one will see us, my dear. You've nothing to fear.' He walked down the corridor and stopped at the doors to the stairwell. He pushed them open.

'Oh, oh of course,' said Lydia, relieved. 'The sun must be on the fire escape, is it? We can go down and out the back door.'

Underwood stopped on the landing. 'You know, I think I can tell you something now; something I haven't really spoken to anyone about in perhaps two hundred years or more.'

'Really, My Lord? What is it?'

Underwood began to walk up the stairs. 'Matthias, your ancestor – he never agreed to sire a line of servants for me. We made him do it.'

'You?' Lydia looked around, alarmed at their direction. 'You did what?'

'And once it was done, we took the child away from him. A little boy called Samuel.'

Lydia was frightened now. 'Why are you telling me this? Where are we going? Daniel, the police – we have to get out, or, or at least *hide*.'

'And that was the end of us. Matthias was horrified at the man I had become, and even more horrified at what he thought I might do to his child. He was afraid I'd taken the boy as a kind of surrogate son, and that I'd make him a vampire like myself. But I told him he needn't fear; no Flinch would ever bleed. And I've always kept that promise. Until now, until you … I suppose that makes you last of my many betrayals of him.'

As Underwood rounded to the final flight of stairs, Lydia looked to the top to see a fire door directly opposite the steps. On the door were the words, *Cubierta de acceso* – roof access. 'Oh my, God! Daniel, no! You can't! I've only just begun to live! Daniel! My Lord, you can't! Please!'

'I'm sorry, Lydia. But there's no other way for us. I can't let you live – you're far too evil, and if I were to let you fall into the hands of the police, then they would, as you say, hand you over to the government. They'd keep you in a lab and perform all manner of ghastly experiments on you. I could never let that happen to Arthur's little girl.' He began to ascend the final flight of stairs.

'No! Oh Jesus, please. *Help!*' Lydia's shout brought blood to her throat, she choked on it and spat it aside. 'David! Help me! David!'

'He can't hear you, Lydia, I sent him away. You know, once, I would have taken delight in how he's finally come to accept his family calling, but not anymore. Thankfully it's not too late for him. But it is for you, my dear. Far, far, too late.'

'But he could still be guardian – *our* guardian – he could serve us.'

'No Lydia. You still don't understand. Now David's going to be able to live his own life, just as I should have let Matthias live his life all those hundreds of years ago, as I should have let you all live your lives in the sunshine. Your lives are not mine; you're not my family – you're not even my friends. Matthias told me that, but I was far too evil by that stage to listen, or even to care. And gradually, I forgot, forgot it all … until David – so much like Matthias – reminded me of what I was – of *who* I was – so long ago'. He stepped onto the final landing.

'Oh Jesus,' Lydia writhed futilely in his arms. She tried to push herself away from him but her ravaged heart wracked her body with agony and she screamed, 'Help me! Somebody! Help me!'

Underwood held her close to him, kissed her on the forehead and raised his foot to the crash bar. 'Close your eyes, Angel.'

The wreck of Darko's car blocked driving access to *La Fantasía*, so David abandoned the hearse near the car park entrance and ran back to where Michelle and Melanie were now kneeling at the open boot of a car. As he got nearer, he saw Melanie was holding someone's hand, someone in the boot. It was Damo. His clothes were soaked in blood and he was unconscious. Melanie's massaging of his hand didn't seem to be registering any effect on him. David knelt beside her. 'Is he alive?'

'I don't know,' said Melanie, tearfully. 'He won't wake up.'

David felt for a pulse. He couldn't find one at the wrist so he tried the neck. He noticed that Damo's skin there was unbroken; Lydia had closed the wound. He pressed hard, and after a moment, he felt something, a fast, but very faint beat. 'He's alive. Cover him up, keep him warm, maybe there's – '

Suddenly, from above, came a woman's scream. It was loud enough to be heard over the sound of the approaching sirens, and it went on, continuous and intensifying as David and the women looked up to see smoke rising from somewhere on the roof.

'Oh Jesus.' David started running.

'What is it?' Michelle called after him as he started up the stairs of the fire escape. He ignored her – but she knew. She turned Melanie to face her. 'Stay with Damo, Mel. Keep him warm.'

'What? What do you mean? You can't go after him, it's dangerous. We need you here!'

'I have to, love. I have to know what's happened.'

'*Why?*'

Michelle tried to reply, but she found she couldn't; there were no words that could ever explain what she felt, or why she felt it, she only knew that she had no choice. She kissed her daughter, and went after David.

David entered the office to find a pool of blood on the floor where Lydia had been, but no sign of Lydia, and no sign Underwood. He ran out into the corridor. 'Underwood!' No reply, but on the floor, a trail of fresh blood droplets. He followed it to the stairwell. He pushed through the doors and saw the blood trail led upstairs. 'Oh no, please, no.' He ran up the stairs taking them two or three at a time, rounding the final landing to see the open doorway at the top of the stairs filled with sunlight and slowly rolling smoke. He ran up the stairs, stumbling as he neared the top and catching the doorframe to steady himself as his eyes took in the scene.

Outside, a scattered trail of ash and black debris stretched out onto the roof. David walked out slowly, following the trail of scorched and twisted remains. Much of the debris was unrecognisable, just scraps and fragments of smouldering clothing. He saw a burning woman's shoe, and then its pair nearby burned to little more than a heel. He looked around for more, for Underwood's remains. For a moment, he felt a surge of hope that perhaps Underwood had escaped. Then the breeze stirred the ashes and a piece of smouldering black cloth tumbled to his left. He followed it, and saw a man's shoe smoking a few feet away, and beyond that something bright caught his eye as it glinted in the sunshine. He walked over, knowing before he got there what it would be. Underwood's watch lay on a piece of smouldering cloth. David fell to his knees.

'Oh no. No, not like this.' He looked around, as if perhaps Underwood were hiding in the shadows, playing a trick on him. But there was no one. 'Why? We could have got away. We could have … ' He put his hands to his head. 'Shit!'

In the car park below he could hear the excited voices of Spanish police as they ran around shouting at each other. They'd be up here soon. Carefully, David lifted the watch, letting it twist and cool in the breeze before taking it in his palm and wiping the soot from the case with his thumb. It was partly open. He flicked it all the way. Soot covered the face and most of the inscription. He wiped the glass and saw the second hand ticking.

From behind him came the sound of footsteps in the stairwell. He turned back to see Michelle emerge, looking down at the trail of debris. She looked up at him. 'Where … where is he?'

David wiped the soot from the inscription on the watch case. 'He's gone.'

'Gone? What, you mean … dead?'

David looked back to where the breeze whispered over the scattered black remains. So little ash, he thought, for two people. So little ash.

'Dead?' He closed the watch and slipped it into his pocket. 'No. I mean, he's gone. That's all.' He smiled to himself. 'Somehow, I don't think death is really Underwood's style.' He got to his feet and walked to the edge of the roof. Below, the car park was swarming with police and he saw Damo being stretchered away by paramedics. David took out his cigarettes and lit one. Then he sat down on the edge to watch the sun rise.

Thank you for reading Underwood and Flinch: Resurrection (Volume I) and Bonded in Blood (Volume II).

The Chronicles of Underwood and Flinch will continue in Volume III: Blood and Smoke.

To sign up to my mailing list and get all the U&F news as soon as it's hot, please visit my website, www.MikeBennettAuthor.com. There you can also find more ebooks and free podcasts by me, including my novel, One Among the Sleepless, and the story collection, Hall of Mirrors: Tales of Horror and The Grotesque.

Download Underwood and Flinch Volumes I1 & II as free audiobook podcasts (read by me, Mike Bennett) at Podiobooks.com.